SHEET MUSIC:
A PORTLAND SYMPHONY COLLECTION
BOOKS 1-4

I0747311

Copyright © 2025 by London Price

All rights reserved.

No part of this publication may be reproduced, distributed, or transmitted in any form or by any means, including photocopying, recording, or other electronic or mechanical methods, without the prior written permission of the publisher, except as permitted by U.S. copyright law. No part of this publication may be used for training AI, including large language models, predictive models, or neural nets. For permission requests, contact The Sun Will Come Out Publishing at londonpriceauthor@gmail.com

The story, all names, characters, and incidents portrayed in this production are fictitious. No identification with actual persons (living or deceased), places, buildings, and products is intended or should be inferred.

Book Cover by London Price

HERE COMES TREBLE

CHAPTER ONE

RAIN IS MY FAVORITE thing. I love the muted patter of it hitting leaves and the dull thud of it against concrete. I love the tinny ping of it on mailboxes and street signs. I love the *swoosh* of cars crawling through puddles and the rush of it into storm drains, like a secret waterfall under my feet while it carries leaves and trash along like it can't stand to see Portland dirty. I like the squeak of windshield wipers for those stuck in traffic, the rain cutting through the beam of their headlights.

I soak it all in as I cross the street to Hillary's new apartment building. The contemplative feeling gifted to me by the symphonic rain lasts exactly as long as it takes to ride the elevator up to the fourteenth floor.

"Baby brother!" She smashes into me with the exuberance of a much younger person, squeezing me before I even have a chance to get my arms open. "You're here—good! I need you to make a salad."

"I see you're not taking advice from Miss Manners about not putting guests to work." I smirk as I wash my hands. Her betta fish Francis is doing laps in his bowl on the kitchen counter.

"You're not a guest, weirdo. Now get slicing. There's carrots and lettuce in the veggie drawer. Feel free to improvise." It is well-known in our family that I hate boring salads. I only discovered this when I started working at Marble, a farm-to-table restaurant downtown. Before that, my only salad experience had been of the iceberg/

carrot/cucumber variety. I have since learned the error of my ways.

I pull out broccoli and red onion. "Do you have any bacon?"

"Um, maybe? Check the freezer."

I open the upper compartment and step back. "Wow. I see you haven't had time to work your special chaos method on this yet." Everything is stacked neatly in rows by category, and someone (definitely not Hil) used a *label maker* to organize things. I find the bacon easily.

"Hush," Hillary chides in a hissed whisper. "He doesn't know about my special chaos methods yet. And I'm trying to keep it that way."

I chuckle. Yeah, she'll be busted on that before she pays her second month's rent.

I set the bacon on a low heat, crammed onto a back burner, since she's using the front two. "How'd you find this guy, anyway?"

"We knew each other in undergrad. He mentioned he was looking for a roommate and *voila*."

I pull out a knife to chop my veggies. "I'm a little surprised you picked a guy."

She shrugs. "I'm branching out a bit. I know it makes them happy to know I'm not living by myself downtown." By *them*, I know she means our parents. Though Hillary hasn't quite forgiven Mom and Dad for moving overseas with the State Department, I'm personally looking forward to spending a holiday on a white sand beach.

"I don't mind it myself. Downtown can be a dangerous place."

She snorts. "Who got their wallet stolen last week? Not me."

"Hey." I point the knife at her playfully, nowhere near close enough to hurt her. "That was an outlier."

"Maybe *you* should carry mace and a fake wallet you can throw and run in the other direction. The only reason that gets recommended to *me* instead is that you have a penis."

"Please don't say *penis*. Do you have any mayo?"

She steals a broccoli floret and munches it. "I think I have Miracle Whip."

"Oh, that is..." I sigh. "That is not at all the same, but fine."

As I whip up the dressing using her subpar ingredients, we talk. She tells me about her classes—she's a women's studies major at Rose City University, not far off from graduating—and I tell her about a new group I'm working with at Mead College, that bastion of liberal thought. I find some dried cranberries and sunflower seeds, and my salad is almost ready.

Just as I go to take the bacon off the heat, a flash of red out of the corner of my eye draws my attention. I look up just in time to see someone with short hair wearing a red sweatshirt land jeans disappearing into the other bedroom. The door closes.

"That your roommate?"

"Yeah."

"He didn't want to meet me?"

"Don't take it personally; he's just really shy." She hands me a woven basket covered with a thin towel. "Can you get out plates?"

It is such a blatant attempt to distract me, I almost laugh. But she knows my weakness for homemade carbs, and I have to admit that the rosemary-and-olive scent wafting from the crusty bread is making my mouth water.

"Sure. Should we invite him to join us?"

Hillary turns from the stove where she's stirring her sauce. "No," she says, annoyed. "I just said he's very shy. Besides, you're here to have dinner with *me,* not hit on my roommate."

"How do you know I'd hit on him?" I ask, probably too loudly. That's slightly insulting, after all. I have self-control. Some, anyway.

Hillary snorts.

"Your pasta timer is done," the black cylinder on the counter intones without inflection, and she silences it with the press of a button as she goes to drain the boiling water into the sink.

"You're giving it information about you again. Now it knows you like pasta."

"Everyone likes pasta, Col."

"I bet even shy people like pasta," I wheedle, but her hard look says to drop it. "Fine. You're right. I just want to know if the guy living with my big sister is trustworthy. So sue me."

"No, you're just a nosy flirt when it comes to men." Hillary hands me a steaming pot of pasta. "And you've already met him."

"I have?" *Impossible. I would have remembered that ass.*

She nods, her light brown hair bobbing. "Remember the friend I brought home for Thanksgiving my sophomore year?"

I think back, scanning the Rolodex of my brain for a hot dude who'd stayed at our house. "No?"

She smirks. "Think harder. It was your junior year. He didn't look quite the same as he does now."

"He—oh. *Oh.*" Recognition finally dawns. Yes, she had brought a friend home...but he does not look like the same roommate. I have a vague image in my mind of a quiet person with dark blonde hair. I don't think I'd looked him in the eye long enough to see what color his eyes were. I hadn't been that interested; I'd been trying out my newfound interest in guys at the time and I didn't come back around to girls for quite a while.

"Huh."

"Can we eat now?" Hillary gripes, sitting down at the table.

"Who's stopping you?" I ask, shamelessly helping myself to two pieces of bread. The conversation shifts to plans for her birthday (did someone say 'house party'?), the new sculpture outside her building (what was it even supposed to be?), and why social media was so addictive (so many reels. So little time). I scored her a ticket to my gig tonight, so we clean up and she hits the bathroom before we head out.

I'm playing on my phone while I wait when I hear another door open, and out of the corner of my eye, I see her roommate come out of his room and start to creep quietly toward the kitchen. *I'll show her. I don't have to flirt; I can just be polite.*

"Hey, man. I'm Colby." I stick out my hand. He eyes me suspiciously but reaches out and shakes it firmly, adjusting his thin, black-rimmed glasses.

"Chance."

"Great to meet you."

"Yeah, you too. You..." He falters. "You work with the symphony?"

"Yeah, I'm a sound guy. I work with all kinds of music groups." I pocket my phone. "What do you do?"

"I'm a research assistant at Rose City U." He's edging away from me toward the fridge, so I figure he's either really hungry (it's 7 o'clock, after all) or just ready to be left alone.

"Oh, so just down the road, nice. Cool. Well, just wanted to say hi. Hillary and I hang out a lot, so I'll be around."

"Okay." He finds a takeout container and makes a beeline back to his room. "See you around."

"Yup."

He's just closing his door again when Hillary comes down the hall, her expression thunderous.

"Colby, what did I say?"

"I didn't do anything!"

She rolls her eyes and huffs like I just told her I was going on NASA's next mission, and I am not an astronaut. Closer to a space cadet.

"What?" I ask. "Seriously, I'm not supposed to say hi when someone walks through the room?"

"Colby, this is the best place I've ever lived, and he's the best roommate I've ever had. He's neat, does the dishes, hates loud parties, and doesn't invite unsafe sex partners over. It's close to my job so I don't need a car. I love being on the park blocks; I love being near Saturday Market and the library and the museums. But every time you date my friends, it ends badly, and then it's awkward and I have to move or distance myself from them, and I hate that."

She isn't wrong; it had never been my intention, of course. We just have the same taste in people, and I didn't mean for my breakups to affect her like that. But there's real hurt in her eyes, and I immediately feel ashamed.

"I'm sorry. You're right. I will respect your wishes." I snag her around the neck and give her a kiss on the forehead. "You ready to go?"

CHAPTER TWO

THE NEXT TUESDAY, I get a text from Hillary inviting me over to watch TV on Wednesday. I'm lucky; such invitations usually come same day. Fortunately, Wednesday is usually a slow day for me unless I get called to help with a church concert. What is it with Christians and Wednesday night? I never realized it was such a thing before I started doing sound.

Hillary being Hillary, she gave me a key (hopefully with her roommate's permission) in case she locks herself out so I can come rescue her. I swear, she forgets that I'm the younger brother. But as such, I let myself in.

"Hey."

She's finishing up washing her dinner dishes. She must really want to impress Chance.

"Hey. What'd you bring?"

I hand her the paper bag. "Always the grabby hands with you. No, 'Hi Colby, how was your day? How were your gigs? Have you talked to Mom and Dad lately? Are you seeing anyone new?'"

She glances up at me momentarily as she rummages for the ice cream scooper. "*Are* you seeing anyone new?"

"No, and thank you for bringing up *that* hurtful subject."

"I didn't bring it up. *You* brought it up. You didn't get vanilla. We like vanilla better than chocolate."

"*We* like, the Cook family? Who are we talking about here?"

"*We* like the inhabitants of this apartment."

My body perks up, but I quickly squash my interest. I'm not supposed to be interested in the guy.

"I saved you. I saved you from a terrible ice cream experience. Also, there's more." I pull out the vanilla from the bag I'm still holding. "You got girlfriends coming over?"

She gives me the side-eye. "No, just us. You, me, and Chance."

Delight tingles through me.

"Do you have chocolate sauce?"

"You need chocolate sauce *and* chocolate ice cream?"

"I have taste. What are we watching?"

"*Westworld*." At the sound of another voice, I spin. Chance is slipping behind me, getting himself a bowl.

"Oh, hey," I say, trying too hard to sound relaxed. Then my brain trips over what he actually said. "Is that that old movie about the people who live on the boat? The dystopian thing?"

Hillary chokes on her ice cream, then laughs. "That's *Waterworld*. This is a western futuristic-type show. Came out not long ago."

I let my shoulders relax. "Oh, okay, that's fine. As long as it doesn't have..." My gaze falls to her roommate again, and I clam up.

"Robots?" Hillary taunts. She turns to Chance and lowers her voice confidentially. "He's afraid of robots."

"I'm disowning you," I deadpan, and Hillary cackles as she moves to the couch, where she plops herself in the middle.

"In fact," she says, her voice far too singsong-y for me to feel comfortable, "Colby likes..." *Oh no. She's seriously going to tell him. She's going to make me a queer cliché with one word and knock out any chance with this guy.* I'm too far away to stop her, to slap a hand over her mouth before she can spill my secret.

"Musicals." She croons the word like it's her most favorite thing to ever come out of her mouth, and all I can do is cringe as I top my bowl with sprinkles.

"What's your favorite?"

Voice level. Pitch low. A cautious glance confirms that he isn't teasing me. He's down on the far end of the couch, leaving the close seat for me, and I just stare for a second, baffled, before I stutter out, "Uh, *Chicago.*"

He nods. "I'm partial to *Annie*, but *Chicago*'s good, too. It's got *Cabaret* vibes."

"But you can't beat Bernadette Peters and Carol Burnett. We watched that so much when we were kids."

"*You* watched it," Hillary interjects grumpily, pointing at me with her spoon for extra emphasis. "And I forgot that there's no point in making fun of you for this pastime when I'm talking to another queer person."

Out of the corner of my eye, I see Chance smirk as he digs into his bowl, and I steal a long look at him while she cues up the show. *He likes musicals. It'll be nice to have someone on my side for once when we pick a movie.*

I'm still distracted as the show starts playing...and then they start taking one of the people apart.

"Oh, what the fuck? I said no robots!"

"You actually didn't." Hillary laughs. "Should I hold your hand?"

"Fuck you. And they look like people—oh God, that's even worse."

I curl myself into the corner of the couch with my knees to my chest. Some people are afraid of clowns. Some people can't do spiders or snakes. For me, it's robots. They are the creepiest thing ever invented, and I do not care if they bring drinks to sick people or look like cute dogs—it is a mask they will use to seduce and enslave us someday. Mark my words.

Curling up like that reminds me that my bladder is kind of full from the pop I drank earlier, and I get up to use the toilet.

"We can put on something else," Chance says as I go by. "I think *Dreamgirls* is streaming now."

I stop next to his chair. "Oh, I'm not leaving. I just need to pee." I give him a winning smile. "Thanks, though."

He gives me a nod and quickly shifts his gaze back to the screen. It's hard to tell in the dark, but I could swear he's blushing a little. I'd just shut the bathroom door when my phone dings.

Hillary: See, isn't he nice?
Colby: Yeah. Unlike you.
Hillary: Don't screw this up for me.

Colby: I'm not going to! Sheesh.
Hillary: Sheesh? Who says sheesh? You are such an old.

I roll my eyes. She seems determined to get me to talk like she does. Not going to fall for it. I happen to enjoy being taken seriously.

Colby: Sticks and stones, whippersnapper.

When I get back to the couch, I find Hillary in my spot, so I sit in hers. It's harder to glance at her roommate that way, so it's probably for the best. It gives me more mental space to watch the creepy robots get controlled by the creepy humans.

I'm serious. It's just a matter of time.

CHAPTER THREE

ON SATURDAY MORNING, I head down to the basement to do my laundry. It's dark and musty down there, which is why most houses in Portland don't even have basements; the water gets in. Since this is technically my parents' house, I try to pay extra attention to stuff like that. I flip on the light at the top of the stairs, but when I get to the bottom, I see Evan asleep on the couch with a woman on his chest. Even more surprisingly, it's the same woman I saw him with the previous weekend.

He blinks at the light I turned on, looking around, confused.

"Sorry," I whisper, lifting my laundry basket in explanation. Evan waves at me like it's no big deal, then rubs his eyes in a pinching motion, like his head hurts.

"What time is it?"

"7:30."

"What the hell, Col?"

The woman stirs, her dark hair spilling over the edge of the couch.

I roll my eyes. "You have a bedroom. This is nowhere near it. This is a *common area*," I chide, still in a whisper. I open the washer lid quietly and start pre-treating.

"It's too fucking early. And you're doing whites?" He groans softly and throws his left arm over his face.

"What are you even doing down here?"

"We fell asleep talking." He strokes the woman's long hair, and she settles deeper into his chest with a content sigh.

"About what?"

"About music, actually." Evan plays percussion for the Portland Symphony and a few other groups. That's how we met. But he usually keeps his dates light; music is too close to the center of him to talk about...usually.

"Must be someone special. What's her name?"

"Leah." He says it softly, still stroking her hair even though she's asleep. It's strange how that one word suddenly makes me feel like I'm intruding. We tell each other about the people we're seeing, so it isn't like either of us is particularly private, but...I don't know. I can't explain it.

I sift quickly through the rest of the basket's contents, then dump them all in the machine and start it just to leave this space that's now been claimed by the way he said her name.

"You guys want breakfast? I'm making pancakes."

"Sure. We'll be up in a minute."

"Light on or off?"

"On."

I shut the door quietly behind me and turn to find Tony sipping coffee, leaning against the counter like it's the only reason he's still upright.

"Hey."

He grunts in response, the sound echoing into the half-full mug.

"Pancakes?"

He nods.

"Do you have any guests?"

"Guests?"

"Someone who'd want to eat with us? Just trying to get a head count."

"Just me," he mutters. Antonio is unfairly handsome, but he only uses it for good. I pat him on the shoulder as I squeeze by him to get to the mix. "But I think Darren had two people here last night..."

That gives me pause. I don't like to judge, but I do like juicy gossip. I'm only human.

"Two?"

"Not a sex situation...I don't think. It was too quiet for that." Darren and Tony share a wall, and they had some logistics to iron out when they first arrived. He sips his coffee again. "Not that their talking didn't keep me up..."

"Basement was taken," I say, buttering the griddle. "Sorry."

"Not your fault, Col."

"You working today?"

Tony nods. "You want catering work? We're doing some university party in a couple of weeks."

I shake my head as I pour the first eight pancakes. "I'm all booked up, actually."

"That's good. The guys at Marble miss you, though. Trevor and them are always asking how you're doing."

"And what do you tell them?"

"That you're still a terrible basketball player who'd rather play with electronics than deliver seventy-five-dollar steaks."

I laugh. "You're just mad we lost last week. I'm going to step up my game. I've been practicing three-pointers."

"Man, the day you make a three-pointer is the day I start going to Mass again."

"What happened with that production you tried out for? The Ibsen thing?"

He gestures toward his phone. "Still waiting to hear." He's one of my scholarship housemates. His family broke ties with him when he came out, so we're all he's got now. My mom always gives him extra hugs when she comes home. I wish there was more I could do for him.

Evan and Leah appear at the top of the basement stairs, and there's introductions all around. I watch as he gets her a plate and pours her a glass of orange juice. Tony and I share an amused glance. He's not usually so...gentlemanly? His last guest stood around in the kitchen until I finally couldn't take the awkwardness and poured her a cup of coffee. Yeah, there's definitely something between them, at least on his end.

We all chat about weekend plans and soccer (Leah's a Timbers fan) and things we're watching on TV. Darren shows up, sweating from his ten-mile run, and grabs a plate to take upstairs. Patrick's probably still asleep, so we try to keep the conversation down to a dull roar. They all thank me for cooking, and Evan and Leah start the dishes before I can say anything.

As I jog down the musty steps again to put my laundry in the dryer, gratitude grabs me. These guys make life a little easier with most of my family so far away. I'm lucky to have these kinds of friends around me. At least, that's what I'm thinking until I discover that I've turned my whites pink. A red pair of underwear got left in the bottom of the drum.

Gotta be Evan's.

CHAPTER FOUR

THAT AFTERNOON, I HAVE a gig at Lola's for PDXtrings, a string quartet that's just getting started. They play jazzed-up versions of old standards, and they've started adapting classical pieces to sound more modern. Being not-yet famous, they're easy to work with and trust my judgment to mix them correctly and get tracks for their YouTube channel. I wish more people came to their shows; it's depressing to see such talented people play to a half-empty room. They're still working on their sound, but there's so much potential there, I feel like I'm rediscovering them every time I hear them play. But working at 1:00 means I'm done by 3:00 and don't feel like going home before my gig at Keller Auditorium at 6:00. Plus, Hillary has free food in her fridge, so that's a decision made.

What I am not anticipating is her socializing with other women. No, not just socializing. It's a party. A *baby shower*, complete with pink, blue, and white streamers twisting from the central light fixture to eight different points around the room. I recognize about half of her friends, and the ones who recognize me smile back. Her friend Raina is sitting in the seat of honor, opening some kind of gender-neutral swaddle wrap. The soft green reminds me of pistachio ice cream, which reminds me why I'm here.

I stick my head in the fridge to find a beer, and by the time I emerge again, Hillary is standing next to me, arms crossed. "What are you doing here? You can't have that." She plucks the bottle from my hand and puts it back in the fridge.

"I'm killing time until my next gig."

"And it didn't occur to you that we're busy here? What are you going to do, join the shower?"

"I could run down to the corner and get diapers or something," I joke, but Hillary is not amused.

"You can hang out in my room. I don't want you messing up the party." If memory serves, Raina is one of her more particular friends when it comes to...well, everything. Hillary turns me by my shoulders and marches me through the living room. I grin and wave at the ladies, most of whom smile back. Except for Raina, who shoots me a glare like I've already proclaimed her baby ugly. (I mean, I usually wait until the child is born, just in case...)

I sit down in Hillary's room at her desk. It's messy and stacked, but there's room for my laptop in the middle. But I don't want to be in here by myself. I'm an extrovert. Shoving me into an empty room when there's a party happening out there is just cruel. I consider going to the library before an even better idea comes to me.

Peeking into the hallway, I make sure there's no one coming, then slip down the hall toward the living room to Chance's room. I knock softly on the door frame. I mean, the door is open a little bit. If he didn't want visitors, he should close it. His blond head is bent studiously over his computer, but I can't see what he's doing. Seems like he's always reading something, and I can't say I hate what a smartypants he is. He's got that Saturday vibe in stonewashed jeans and a heather gray hoodie. If he doesn't hear me, I'll just go back to Hillary's room. I'm not going to bother him. But then he notices me and slides one earphone up, which skews his glasses off kilter. *Oh, my heart.* He fixes them before he answers.

"Hey."

"Hey. Can I ask a favor?"

He starts spinning a little in his chair, back and forth, moving the seat with his bare toes. "You can ask…"

I smirk. "It's kind of loud out there with all the ladies doing their thing. I've got some work to do for my class…"

He looks almost disappointed. "Of course. Come on in."

"You sure? I don't want to bother you. I'll be quiet, I swear."

"No, it's fine. Come in. And can you shut the door?" My foolish heart preens that he's letting me in while he shuts the others out. *It's just to keep the noise out, not for privacy.*

Sliding down to the floor by the door, I open my laptop and stare at my essay for a long time. Chance is watching a video with headphones, but I can't see if it's work or play. Then he taps the spacebar and turns to me.

"So you're taking a class? Did you do Rose City's sonic arts program?"

I shake my head. "I studied at a community college in Eugene," I mumble. "It's just an associate's degree." It shouldn't bother me that my academic-type friends are all getting their graduate degrees while I never even got a bachelor's, but it does. I'm not unintelligent; I know that. There's nothing wrong with community college, and their program is excellent. I'm doing exactly what I want to be doing, and I'm *good* at what I do. I just wish it looked more impressive sometimes.

Like now.

"Nothing wrong with that if it gets the job done," he says, shoving his hands deep into the kangaroo pocket of his sweatshirt.

"I'm taking a film music class this semester at RCU," I say quickly.

He's spinning again, toeing at the ground. "Oh yeah? Is it good?"

"Yeah, it's really good. It's really interesting to think about the interplay of the lyrics with the other elements, how they can augment or emphasize different parts, even change the meaning or cast doubt on the speaker's point of view." That's right, I used the word *augment*, which I have never used before *in my life*, in order to impress the guy I am absolutely not allowed to flirt with.

FML.

Chance rubs at his chin. "That is interesting. My AI doesn't write music with lyrics yet. I don't think it could get the contradiction in that without a lot of modeling...I don't suppose you could share a list of the music you've been using for that?"

"I'm sorry...your AI does what now?"

Chance has his phone out before I register his grin. "Do you want to hear some of its compositions?"

"Your artificial intelligence...writes music?"

He waves a hand. "My main focus is medical AI that can help us diagnose people better, so this is peripheral to my actual research, but yeah, this one does. I know I have some saved here. Let me see..." He shoves it toward me like a dad showing off pictures of his kids, and I get up to see it better. "I'd love to know your thoughts on it."

We stand close together in his bedroom so I can hear, him holding up the phone between us. I can't help but notice his light cologne and his veiny hands; both are very attractive. His square glasses frame his pretty blue eyes. He has a little acne along his jawline, but his beard hides it well. It isn't clear whether he meant to grow the beard or not. But the music...

It sounds like something out of a movie soundtrack, something heroic where the main character has to rescue his love or battle the dragon or throw jewelry into a volcano. It isn't the most creative composition I've ever heard, but it has nice phrasing, and it has a good balance between parts. I get so lost listening to it, I don't notice Chance staring at me as carefully as I'd been watching him just a few minutes earlier. Only he looks like he just put his kid on the bus to kindergarten.

"It's good," I say, and his face lights.

"Really?"

"Yeah, I like it. It gives me movie vibes."

He plays me three more, which is probably more than I need to hear, but I listen politely. Then he launches into an explanation of how he trained the AI ethically, how he obtained the licenses, detailing which ones he'd used. I write down for him the ones we're using in class, and he reads the list voraciously. I'm pretty sure it's only good manners keeping him from ditching me and going to look up these pieces immediately to see if his university license covers them, too.

"But let's be clear," I say, plopping down on the floor next to his bed. "Your AI is still the enemy."

He sits back down in his desk chair but doesn't put his headphones back on.

"My AI is a wonderful gift to the world. I'm sorry you don't think so."

"Isn't it putting artists out of a job?"

His face crinkles. "My main research wouldn't, but I guess this could. But it's just for fun; I'm not selling what it produces or anything." I seem to have made him feel bad, so I try to shift the conversation, even as I shift myself on the floor to get more comfortable.

"Is there any way I could make friends with it? Like, cozy up to it now so I get better treatment later on?"

"Well," he says slowly, picking up a stress ball and tossing it to himself, "I would think that being friends with its creator would bode well for you."

I nod somberly. "That makes perfect sense. I'll have to develop our friendship. For the sake of my continued survival, mind you. No reason other than that."

"I'm game," he says, his mouth hitching up on one side. "And if you're really nice to me, I'll create a subroutine to teach it you're on our side."

"It will be a complete lie, but thank you in advance," I say, re-opening my computer to finish my essay. I wish

I didn't have to; there's not much I wouldn't have given to just sit and talk with Chance instead. But I also don't want him to think I'm here under false pretenses. So I type, and he puts his headphones back on and continues watching what appears to be a TedTalk. I manage to complete the assignment after I stop staring at the back of his head.

When I pack up to go, Hillary is still cleaning, so I give her a hand.

"Sorry if I crashed your party." I stuff a pile of wrapping paper into a white trash bag.

"No, Col, I'm sorry. I shouldn't have snapped at you. I'm glad you're here; you're welcome any time. For real." She looks exhausted, and I give her a big hug, the kind where I rock her from side to side until she laughs.

"Come on, let's get dinner on my way to work."

Hillary grins, but her smile falters. "What about the dishes?" Believe it or not, it's personal growth that she even remembered.

"I can finish up," Chance calls from his bedroom. "I don't mind."

"Thank you," Hillary sings back, and I chuckle as she hurries to grab her stuff.

CHAPTER FIVE

I WORK THE REST OF the weekend and take Monday to do chores and remind my roommates their rent is due. In response, they throw an impromptu party Tuesday night (Landlord Appreciation Day? Really?) and buy me beer since they don't have it. I tell them I'd rather have the money in part than drinks, but as usual, they ignore me. They'll all have it by Friday, which is what I really need, so that's all that matters.

Living with my best friends is worth the noise and hassle...mostly. I wonder if they know they don't all pay the same amount...

Around midnight, I go out to the small guest house behind the main house where my parents stay when they visit and crash. But I'm still tired on Wednesday when I head over to Hillary's. We haven't been playing the scary robot show for twenty minutes when my eyelids start to betray me, fluttering shut. I'm actually startled when her phone rings.

"Um. Hang on. Pause for me. I'll be right back." Not taking her eyes off the screen, she tears out of the living room. I hear her door shut down the hall. Chance pauses it because he's more polite than I am.

We are both on the couch today, a fact I hadn't noticed until the moment we're sitting in awkward silence together. Knowing Hillary, "right back" could mean anything from a few minutes to an hour.

After a few minutes, Chance clears his throat. "Did you know that when it comes to customer service AI, there's a strong gender role bias?"

Um. What? What am I supposed to say to that? I don't know if I'm smart enough to make small talk in this apartment...

"I did not," I say honestly. "What does that mean?"

He takes off his glasses and cleans them on his shirt. "Just that if you call up a department store, you'll get a female AI, because we think of women as being good at service jobs. But if you call up the company that makes your lawn mower, you'll get a male AI, because we think of men as being good at fixing tools. Isn't that interesting?"

I nod slowly. It is interesting; it's probably the most interesting thing anyone has told me all day. But I'm not exactly sure why he's telling me this. Still, I can't be mad that he's talking to me, even if it is about robots.

Chance shifts his weight. "Sorry. When I get nervous, I talk about my research. It's kind of my...fall back."

Well, that's adorably honest.

"If you want, I can talk about speaker brands. Then we'll be even."

"No, that's okay." He gives me a shy smile. "I mean, unless you want to..."

"No," I say, grinning at him. "I don't want to. I mean, I do feel strongly about how overhyped Bose speakers are, but you probably don't want to hear about that."

"I could give it a chance," he says, folding his hands like he's really getting ready to listen.

"Is that meant to be a pun? Because it's pretty great."

Chance chuckles, and I reach for the remote just to have something to play with. Because I am really curious what he's going to say next. When he goes quiet again, I fill the silence.

"Are you really nervous around me?"

He shrugs, keeping his gaze on the remote. I'm pretty sure he wants me to restart the show. But I don't.

"Why?" I ask.

"You're important to Hillary," he says. "You're here a lot. I just..." His gaze wanders then, traveling to the corners of the room. "Want you to like me, I guess."

"I do like you," I say, and I mean it. "So you can relax. Seriously."

"You say that like it's easy."

"Isn't it?"

"*No.*" He's staring at my hands again as if willing me to restart the show with Jedi mind tricks. "For people like you, maybe. Not for people like me."

"What's that supposed to mean?" I laugh. "What's so special about me?"

"I heard the women talking at the baby shower. You're one of those *people* people who makes a new best friend on a bus ride or flirts with waiters like it's nothing or gets invited to New Year's Eve at the governor's mansion because you met his dentist once and made quite an impression, or..." His voice trails off. "It just seems so easy for you."

"Well, I think that's a fucking unfair characterization," I say cheerfully. "I'll have you know that I work damn hard to act this casual all the time."

Chance snorts, shaking his head. But he isn't staring at the remote anymore. He's staring at me now, his piercing blue gaze focused on my face and unabashedly curious. "Are you serious?"

"Of course I'm serious!" I throw out my arms emphatically. "You think it's easy to look this effortless? No. If there's one thing I've learned from the women in my life, it's that everything that looks easy is the exact opposite. And that's true for me, too. I was really shy in middle school; I think one of my teachers put on my report card that it was such a shame that I was mute."

"That's not true." He frowns, leaning forward to put his elbows on his knees.

"No, it's not. But it could have been. I never said a word unless someone asked me a question."

"So what changed?"

"Well, in high school, I tried out for a theatre production, but I bombed my audition. The teacher had one of the older students teach me how to do sound; I think he felt bad for me. And it just kind of snowballed from there." I nab some chips out of the bowl on the coffee table. At least Hillary abandoned us with snacks. "I think it helped to watch the actors. Even when someone was giving them the words, they didn't always know what they were doing. It helped to remember that. And then, since it was a theatre group, I met some guys who were out, and a few I was pretty sure were closeted, and

I realized that I was like them. Somewhat, anyway. And knowing you're part of a group helps."

"That sounds really nice. I wish I'd gone to your high school." His face is wistful, and I wish I hadn't said all that. I didn't mean to make him sad.

I put down the remote between us, in case he is truly uncomfortable and wants to restart the show.

"I'm afraid to ask what it was like at yours," I say. I know plenty of people—especially trans people—with horror stories from their teenage days.

"Oh, no one was cruel," he says quietly. "I just didn't have any kind of community. I slipped into whatever social group would have me, and because I was reasonably pretty, there were several that were happy to have me around. But that was far as it went. No one knew who I really was."

"A guy?" I don't know much about his life before his transition.

He snickers softly. "Not just that, but yeah, that too. A computer nerd. A bookworm. I pretended to like shopping and doing my hair and makeup and all sorts of other crap. I actually wrote an app to help me keep track of all the useless information they expected me to know."

I chuckle. "Couldn't you just make a spreadsheet like a normal guy? Sheesh."

"I'm not a normal guy." Chance is eyeing me, then he lunges for the remote and snatches it up like he's worried about what I'll say next.

"I'm not so sure about that," I say with a mouth full of Doritos, "but if it is true, I like you anyway."

Chance smiles, but says nothing as he hits play and turns his attention back to the screen.

CHAPTER SIX

A FEW WEEKS LATER, we've only got about half of Hillary's guests in the house, and already, it's loud. Not 'call the cops' loud, but still. I turn down the stereo again on my way by and remind a particularly raucous group that we do have neighbors (which earns me several eye rolls). And then I see Chance.

He's nursing something in a red Solo cup in the corner, which surprises me because I would've thought he was a wine drinker, since he's all smart and shit. I guess that's on me for stereotyping. But there's another thing: he looks miserable. Like someone just put his dog down, he lost his winning lottery ticket, and he spilled coffee on his computer all on the same day.

"Hey, man." My feet have carried me to him, which only proves they are in league with my traitorous cock to try to get me things I know I can't have.

"Hey. Good party."

"Thanks. You wanna dance?" It's a fast song. It's not unreasonable. My sister doesn't have to know that I asked him; maybe he asked me.

Yeah, right.

"Oh," he says, attempting to back even further into the corner, "that's okay. I'm not a dancer. I mean, I don't really..."

"Come on." I lead him out of the living room and up the stairs toward my bedroom. He trails after me, looking a little bit bewildered and a lot relieved. Is it the noise? The strangers? I don't know. When I open my bedroom door, there's a man and a woman I don't know making out on my bed.

"Goodbye," I say, holding the door open for them, and they quickly hurry out, giggling. I think about whether I need to change the sheets now and decide that yes, that will happen.

"You can practice here," I say to Chance.

"It's not a matter of practice," he says, in a tone that reminds me of Maggie Smith in Downtown Abbey. "I just don't dance well. My body doesn't move like it should."

"Show me."

"What?" Chance snaps. He is holding that Solo cup real tight, and for a second, I think he's going to walk out.

I wiggle my hips suggestively. "Show me your moves, come on. I can't fix what I can't see."

"I don't need fixing," he says, but it's wholly unconvincing. His body is so stiff, if I pick him up and put him over my shoulder, he'll stick out straight like a board.

Not that I should be thinking about picking him up, or touching him, at all.

I know I'm a goof, so I don't feel self-conscious when I shimmy toward him with a smile. I rock my shoulders side to side suggestively, and his glower softens a little. I make a circle around him, hitching my knee up like a cowboy, one hand on my belt, making a circle over my head like a lasso.

"That's not really dancing," Chance grumbles, but I just grin as I come back around to his front.

"Sure it is."

"I'll look ridiculous doing that."

"And I don't?"

"No." His voice is as low as I've ever heard it. "You look…"

I bow out my knees and shift my hips from side to side, putting my hands behind my head.

"Goofy? Cheesy?" I turn around and shake my ass at him. "Come on, you have to try."

Chance shakes his head. When he puts down his cup, I think maybe I've won him over, but it turns out, he just needed his hands free to lock his arms in place over his chest in a show of defiance. *Damn.*

"I'll just drink in the corner. It's what I do."

"All right," I say, holding out both hands to him. "If that's what'll be fun for you. But maybe you just need a friend. Someone to play off of. Half of good dancing is just responding to your partner."

He leaves me hanging, so I tip my head back and pretend I'm limboing under an invisible bamboo stick, shuffling my feet toward him. I'm almost out of goofy ploys when I stand up, closer to him than I realized. I'm so close, I can smell the caramel sweetness of rum and Coke on his breath. He's looking at my lips like maybe he can smell my margarita, too.

My brain suggests another reason he might be looking at my lips, while we're standing close together in my bedroom, the noise of the revelers muffled by the closed door so that our breathing sounds louder than it should. Then Chance puts his hands on my arms and lifts them to his shoulders. His own hands fall to my hips, and he begins to sway us. He meets my curious gaze briefly before he pulls me so close, there's no way I can look into his eyes. I let the weight of my arms rest on his narrow shoulders and rub my stubbly cheek against his, and I feel his shoulders drop. His shaky breath skirts my ear, and I smile.

"This the kind of dancing you like?"

When he nods, his fingers tighten on my hips, and my breath catches as he starts to slide them lower over the pockets of my thin pants.

"Colby!" My roommate's voice startles both of us, and Chance jumps back. Evan knocks firmly on my door. "You in there?"

"Yeah," I call back, but my voice cracks. "I'll be right there."

"We're outta ice," Evan says.

"I said I'll be right there."

"Who've you got in there? Adrian? Saoirse?"

"Fuck off, Evan," I say. "I'm coming!" I turn back to Chance, unsure how to put him at ease again...or possibly for the first time. "You can hang out in here as long as you want. I've gotta go—"

"Yeah. No problem." He's staring at my meager collection of famous composer figurines on my desk, and I wish I had a few minutes to talk about what just happened, but I know my roommates. The longer I stay here, the more questions they're going to ask. Questions who

I snuck away with despite the fact that I was hosting a party. I put my hand on the doorknob.

"See you on the dance floor?" I ask hopefully, and he just chuckles and shakes his head, still not looking at me.

I have the door open and closed in a flash, so Evan's neck-craning to try to see around me is for nothing.

"Who've you got in there?" he asks again as I start down the hall to the kitchen.

"Fuck off. There's such a thing as privacy."

Evan snorts. "In this house? Are you sure?"

I open the door to the garage and point toward the freezer. "There's three more bags of ice in there."

"Sweet. I'm doing daiquiris for the birthday girl. You want?"

"Yeah, I'll take one."

I'm halfway done with it, sitting on the couch with Hillary's friend Giada on my lap, before Chance resumes his place in the corner. I give him a smile and shimmy my shoulders. He laughs and shakes his head before he sips his drink and looks away.

CHAPTER SEVEN

WEDNESDAY MORNING, I text my sister.

Colby: We still on for tonight?
Hillary: yes?
Colby: Why did you use a question mark?
Hillary: the question is why we wouldn't be?
Colby: You have a tendency to forget.
Hillary: that is ridiculous.
Hillary: honestly
Hillary: what kind of sister would I be if I forgot?

So Wednesday night when I let myself into her apartment and she's not here, it really isn't any kind of surprise. She probably got wrapped up in a group project or a discussion, I tell myself. She'll be here any minute.

Any minute now.

After twenty 'any minutes' later, I get out my laptop and start to work on my film music class. There's all this mandatory forum commenting that I'm supposed to do, giving other people feedback on their work...but everyone pretty much says the same thing.

Still, I'm engrossed in my 'good work, nice thoughts' BS when Chance comes out of the bathroom wearing jeans with holes at the knees and a ratty pink sweatshirt, still wiping his hands on a towel. He freezes when we make eye contact.

"Hey," I say, trying to sound casual.

"Hey. I didn't, uh, know you were here." Given what he's wearing, I'm not surprised to hear that. I've never seen him wear anything remotely ratty before.

"Yeah, sorry. It's Wednesday. *Westworld.*"

"Oh, right. Hillary texted and said she'd be late coming home, so I assumed that was canceled." Of course she did. At least she let one of us know. He starts toward his room, then pivots back. "I had a really bad day."

"Sorry to hear that." I keep my voice sincere, but it doesn't wipe the distressed look from his face. If anything, it makes it worse. "You want to talk about it?"

"No."

"Anything I can do to help?"

"No."

I shrug. "Okay." I go back to my computer, trying to ignore the fact that he's still standing there. But it's hard to focus on my bullshittery with him staring at me.

"This sweatshirt has sentimental meaning to me. It fits me just right."

I slide my laptop to the coffee table and prompt him to come nearer with one finger. He shuffles over, bare feet dragging against the rug. I pull him down onto the couch next to me, and his eyes widen when I give his hand a squeeze. I don't think I've touched him since that night in my bedroom when we danced. But that broke the barrier.

"Dude. I don't care if you wear a pink sweatshirt. This is your house. Wear whatever you want. Especially if you had a crap day."

"It makes me feel better and worse at the same time."

"Why?"

He shrugs but he leans over and nestles his head on my shoulder. "Pink's a girl color, and I'm not a girl. But my grandpa gave me this sweatshirt, and he's gone now, so..."

I let my fingers drift up and down his arm over the soft fabric. "I get that. I mean, mine's a knife, but..."

He snorts. We just sit there quietly like that for a while, him literally leaning on me, me enjoying the feeling of it.

"I thought of a way you could help," he says quietly.

"Oh yeah?" I hope he doesn't want a foot rub; I'm crap at those. Maybe I could go get us comfort food or something. Voodoo Donuts isn't that far away.

When his lips meet my neck, I suck in a harsh breath.

"Oh." It has clearly been too long since I had a guy's lips on my neck, because my cock is already sitting up and taking notice. *Or maybe it hasn't been too long. Maybe it's just him.* Let's face it, I've been enamored with the guy from the minute I saw his ass. I'm not proud of it, but there it is. And there is much more I like about him now.

"This okay?" he asks between kisses.

"Yeah. Wait, no," I say, my voice cracking a little. "Hillary...she said—"

"She told you not to flirt with me, right?" He takes a big lick of my neck, and I can't help imagining him doing the same thing to my cock. "Heard her through the door."

"Right."

"But you didn't. I'm flirting with *you*."

"If this is flirting, I'd like to see you come on to me."

Chance chuckles. "That can be arranged. Are you willing to be a distraction?"

God. The challenge in his gaze. How he's gone from defeat to seduction, I don't know. But if he needs this kind of help, I can do that.

He isn't wrong; I didn't pursue him. Not like I usually would, anyway. It's a loophole, maybe, but it is valid. I give him a wary nod.

Then the man falls on me like I'm a desert oasis, like he's afraid I'll disappear if he doesn't dive in immediately. He moves to straddle me, and all my doubts fall out of the back of my head like *I'm* a creepy robot in *Westworld* and someone just wiped my circuits. I let my hands wander over his perfectly round ass, and he moans a little into my eager mouth. The weight of him and heat of his mouth and his hands and the way he smells like chocolate has my head spinning a little. I'm trying desperately to keep up with him, trying to show him without words that I'm all in, totally available for this "distraction."

Then he slides off my lap and onto the floor. When he parts my knees, my eyes go wide.

"But Hillary—"

"Won't be back for hours. Never has to know." He pulls down my zipper and mouths my cock through my boxers. "It's distraction, not dating."

Okay, so a 'friends with benefits' thing? I've never been someone else's dirty secret before, but I can't say I dislike it. I put my hands in his hair as he teases the head of my cock through the slit in my boxers, and the sweetness of his tongue on me has me caving.

"Okay," I breathe. "Just this once. Only because you had a crap day."

He wastes no time in pulling me out and wetting my cock with long, sloppy licks, and I let my head fall back against the couch. He hums his pleasure, and as he wraps his strong fingers around me, bringing his hand up to meet his mouth, I jerk my hips forward. Before I can apologize, his other hand comes up to my hip to hold me down.

"Holy shit, Chance."

"Yeah. Do that," he murmurs, pulling off momentarily.

"Do what?" I pant.

"Talk. Tell me I'm good. Tell me this isn't charity."

"Hell no, it's not charity. You have a fucking gift." I pull him back by his hair to look into his eyes, gently enough that I won't hurt him. "You're hot. And you're very good at this."

He meets my gaze, his own a little hazy, and then drops it quickly back to my cock as he licks his lips and strains to get at me again. I let go of his hair and he takes me deep, his head bobbing in the perfect rhythm to have this over quickly.

"If you slow down, I'll last longer," I whisper, and he pulls back.

"I don't want you to last," he mumbles, still kissing and mouthing me up and down my too-hard cock. "I want you to break for me."

Holy hell. Where is the guy I was watching cling to the corner at Hillary's birthday like it was his only chance at survival? Chance the quiet academic is dominant AF in the sex department, and I am still processing this when he pauses and catches my gaze.

"That okay?" His lifted eyebrow. The quirk of his lips. It all makes me sit up and pay attention.

"Yes. I can...I can do that." I can tell my mouth has a lot more babbling in store, so I shut it and try to smile at him. His answering grin tells me I'm not fooling him at all. He goes at me a little slower then, stroking my thighs with his free hand, pushing my shirt up to caress my abs and my chest.

"Oh, fuck." I am going to die. Chance is trying to tease me right into an early grave. That has to be it, because I've rarely felt so much tension inside during sex before. I feel swollen and heavy, like I'm somehow now permanently part of the couch. I spread my legs wider, but it doesn't inspire hurry in the man.

And when he snakes a hand into his own pants, I moan.

"That's fucking hot." I try to thrust up into his mouth, but he holds me down again, taking my cock in long, leisurely sucks. "Chance, please," I plead. Even as the words come out, disbelief rocks me. I never beg in bed.

"I thought you wanted to last," he taunts, his voice thick.

"Now I want to come," I say in a rush. "Break me. Please."

He lifts his head, his lips red and glossy, his glasses slightly crooked on his face, and he still looks perfect to me. He takes me in hand and begins pumping me at the perfect speed. But the look in his eyes says he's about to come, too; why isn't he thinking about himself? I lean forward and take his mouth in a deep kiss, trying to give him everything he needs but hasn't asked for, trying to propel him over the edge. My own orgasm is edging closer, but his hand falters and loses its rhythm as he gasps into my mouth. I whimper, trying to hold off, too aware of the fact that this is not my couch. But after a moment, his focus comes back to me, and before I can ask, he bends and sucks me into his mouth with a scorching, soft lap of his tongue, and I arch and come and come as he swallows me.

Chance leans over and lays his head on my leg, and I rest a hand on his crown. We fight over the available air in the room, both of our chests heaving, and it takes me a few minutes to find words again.

The words I find are not very appropriate. "Holy shit."

Cut me some slack here; it's the best blow job I've ever had, and my brain is still catching up.

Chance chuckles, then sits up. "That good?"

"Uh, yeah," I say, tucking myself back into my pants, aware that my sister could actually be home any moment. "Really good. Really amazing."

"Good."

And it was good. But staring at him, I don't have a fucking clue what to do now. If I leave, it'll seem like I think this was a mistake. But if I stay, will he expect snuggling? Handholding? He's been clear that this is not a dating situation but...surely he wants some kind of closure?

Chance takes off his glasses and cleans them on the edge of his shirt. "Let's watch *Westworld*."

I smile a little at his suggestion, grateful that he's trying to help me out of my dilemma but unwilling to face my sister's wrath if we watch without her, even if she did ditch us.

"No. Let's watch *Dreamgirls*."

"Good idea. No robots." He grins, plopping himself on the couch next to me, shoulder to shoulder.

"No robots," I confirm as I reach for the remote.

CHAPTER EIGHT

HILLARY COMES HOME, all apologies, about thirty minutes into *Dreamgirls,* so I'm spared any awkward conversations with Chance about what we've done. A few days go by, and I find myself wanting to text him. With the way we left things, it seems like our fun was a one-time deal. But that doesn't mean I can't try to be friends with the guy, right? It would be a lie to say I'm not hoping for a repeat at some point, but I swear, all I have in mind is friendship. My roommates and I have a weekly pickup basketball game in Grant Park on Thursdays, so I invite him to join us. He texts back that he's not sure if he can make it but that he'll try. As far as I can tell, he doesn't have much of a social life, so I know that's probably an excuse. I try not to take it personally. Try and fail. But I know he's shy, so it isn't fair to be disappointed that he isn't willing to lay out emotional energy just to meet my friends.

I keep telling myself that all day as I do my laundry and make a radicchio salad with radishes, chickpeas, blueberries, and sunflower seeds. I change into an old shirt, because last week, Darren kept yanking on one of my favorites and stretching it out, that fucker. If he can't guard me without ruining my clothes, he shouldn't be playing. He and Evan are going down. I'm on Patrick's team this week, along with Tony.

I'm still walking to the park when Chance's car passes me. I wave, but he doesn't see me because he's so busy looking at his phone, probably trying to figure out where the place is. I still have a block to go, so I kick it into gear, intending to be there when he arrives. Something tells me if I'm not, he might just keep on driving and go home. I'm out of breath when I get there, but Chance is just getting out of the car.

"Who's that?" Evan asks, his gaze interested.

"Hillary's roommate. His name is Off Limits, and his sign is Forget It."

"Off limits to *you*, maybe. Hillary likes me. She won't mind." My best friend looks like he wants to devour Chance whole, and I certainly understand the feeling.

"What about Leah?"

"We're not exclusive..."

"Colby never brings the guys he likes to basketball, anyway," Patrick says. "He doesn't want them to see him lose."

They're mostly done teasing me by the time Chance comes up to the group, looking somewhat relaxed. But something is different about him, and I can't quite put my finger on it.

"Hey, you made it!" I smile, hoping I don't look as happy as I feel. I've never been good at playing things cool. "Any trouble finding it?"

"No, it was pretty straightforward."

Liar. It just makes my grin grow.

I make introductions like a good host. "This is Darren; he's a fucking cheater. You'll be on his team."

"Gee, thanks for that glowing review, Col." Darren laughs as he shakes Chance's hand.

"This is Tony, he's on my team, and so is Patrick." They both give him a nod.

"And this is Evan. He's handsy and has no social skills. Should we get started?"

Evan shoves me, and I stumble to the side laughing.

"I want skins this week," Evan says, and Chance's gaze flies to me. *If Chance has to take off his shirt...his scars. Chance won't want to take off his shirt.*

Without thinking, I whip my shirt off and flex my abs. "And deny you all this view? I don't think so." I do a few bodybuilder poses as the others laugh, and Chance's shoulders drop when he realizes I've gotten my way. "Besides, Darren stretched out my 'Shut Your FACE' shirt last week." The shirt spells out F-A-C-E in notes climbing up the staff, so it's extra funny. These dummies just don't appreciate good humor.

We get the ball first, and Tony gets up under the hoop and puts up two points right away. We're pretty evenly matched now that they have Chance. He's a good player, not real aggressive, but he doesn't get intimidated when the others get in his face, and he catches on pretty quick that he's allowed to throw elbows to get them to back off.

As Patrick starts to get tired, I switch to point guard and find myself face-to-face with Chance's electric blue eyes, sparking with intensity as he stares me down. *Glasses. He's not wearing his glasses. That's what's different!*

"You're going down, man."

"You think so?" He smirks, and when I reach out to slap the ball away from him, he just smoothly switches to dribble with the other hand. I lunge again, and he moves around my back toward the hoop and puts it in the hole. But I'm not mad that he's making me look bad in front of my friends. Seeing Chance here, laughing, getting his back slapped and his cute butt patted, actually feels pretty good. I don't pretend to know what other people need, but I've definitely noticed a lack of guy friends in his life, and my guys are the best. I don't mind sharing.

Hillary's probably right; something will probably go wrong at some point with our fuck buddy system, and they'll pick him over me, and I'll have to find a new place to live or something. I mean, really—why wouldn't they? He's fucking magnificent.

He says something funny then, probably at my expense, and Patrick laughs so hard, I think he's going to give himself a hernia.

I bump up against him every chance I get, especially when I can get him between my legs, putting my hands on his back and his backside, pressing my sweaty chest against him. He never once complains about the fouls. In fact, as he checks me the ball, I think I see a hint of challenge there.

"Distracted?" I ask quietly, smirking.

"Nope," he returns, popping his lips on the 'p.' "You?"

"Who, me? No, I'm not distracted." He holds my gaze as he dribbles forward, then turns and passes to Evan. I reach out my hand, but it's too late; they've caught it and drilled to the hoop while I was, in fact, distracted. *Damn it.*

We lose 55 to 69, and I'm fairly sure it's mostly my fault. There are sweaty handshakes and hugs all around as the game ends, and all of them ask Chance to come again next time. As predicted, he says he'll think about it.

"I hope you don't," I mutter as they start back to the house. "You think too much."

Chance glares at me, probably trying to look intimidating, but I just laugh.

"Come on. You know it's true. Sometimes you need to quit deliberating and just do. I know you're an academic so it doesn't come naturally, but yeah." I put my shirt back on. "You think too much."

That's too much for him, apparently. Chance grabs my wrist and starts dragging me across the grass toward where he parked.

"What are we doing?"

"Not thinking," he says, resolutely facing where we're headed, and I feel my eyebrows try to jump off my face when he pivots to the bathrooms instead. He still has a death grip on my arm, but I don't pull back; I kinda want to see just how badly the truth pisses him off and where he's going with this. And my heart rate, which had mostly returned to normal, is now back up to athletic levels, new sweat soaking the back of my shirt.

It's one of those single-stall bathrooms with one toilet and a sink, and when he pulls me inside and locks the door, I hold up my hands.

"Look, I'm sorry. I probably could've said it more nicely. But I—"

The clash of his mouth against mine shuts me up momentarily, and the rough feeling of the concrete against my back through my shirt perfectly contrasts the soft touch of his fingertips against my abs. I let him kiss me for a long minute, stroking my tongue against his as he growls, then I push him gently back.

"Chance, I—"

He puts a finger to my lips, panting lightly. "No talking," he whispers. "Talking leads to thinking and thinking leads to wondering and doubting and hesitating and stopping, and I don't want to stop." He rubs his free hand over my clothed cock, and I bite back a groan, not wanting it to echo in the concrete structure. "I want to do what I've been thinking about since you shamelessly rubbed this against me in front of all those guys."

Yes, please. I don't let the words out even though I want to. Even though I desperately want to know what he's been thinking about.

"Don't get on your knees," I whisper back. "It's filthy in here. God only knows what people do in here."

"You're one to talk." He chuckles as he comes back in for another kiss, less desperate this time, apparently content that I'm not going to stop him. I stroke along his jawline, enjoying the feel of it under my fingers, trying to gentle him a little.

"Let's go to my house." Even though I'm whispering, the sound echoes off the concrete at an uncomfortable volume. *I really don't want us to get caught.*

"There's at least four other people there."

"They won't come upstairs." I rub the bulge in his shorts, too, and he curses.

"I just want to be *alone*," he mutters, lowering his head to suck on my neck where my tattoo starts to slip down under my collar. I let my head fall back. "With you. You have no idea all the things I want to do to you."

Really?

"Dirty things?"

"Yeah, Colby. Dirty things." The edge in his voice says he's starting to lose patience with me.

"What kind of things?"

"Take your shorts off and I'll tell you one."

I put my hand on my waistband, but don't lower them. "There's going with the flow, and then there's getting in trouble for public indecency."

"Aww, are you shy?" he taunts, and I scowl at him.

"No, I'm not *shy*. I just don't want either of us getting arrested, but especially not you."

Before he can protest, I flip the lock and throw open the door, dragging him out behind me the same way he'd dragged me in. We almost run into a mom with two little kids in swimsuits, and she looks annoyed AF that we kept her waiting.

"My house is two blocks. Let's just—"

He pulls his wrist out of my grip; he's stronger than I thought. "Why *especially not me?*"

I glance around at all the people in the park; they appear to be minding their own business, but I'd rather be moving for this conversation, just in case.

"Come walk with me. You don't have to come in."

He balls his fists at his sides but follows me down Thompson Street.

"*Especially not you* because trans people are seven times more likely to experience violence at the hands of police, that's why. And getting me off isn't worth that, not when I have a perfectly good bedroom where no one will ask any questions only two blocks away." I gesture over my shoulder. "You think that Karen would mind calling the cops on us if we prevented her sweet offspring from using the toilet? No. She wouldn't."

He's quiet for a minute as we walk, and I'm afraid to look at him.

"How do you know that? About the violence?"

"There was a fact sheet. Found it online. I'll send it to you if you want." Academics. They always want your sources cited, even when you're arguing about sex. After that first hookup, I made it my business to know a little more in case we happened to meet again. And our pants happened to come off. "But the point is that we've gotta be careful. I want to be spontaneous, too, but not over-thinking can't mean not thinking at all."

"I don't think that's the point," Chance says slowly, and I feel his hand slip into mine. "I think the point is that you're researching safety for trans people, and I ap-preciate that." He squeezes it, then lets go. I drag a hand through my sweaty hair and immediately regret it; I wipe my wet hand on my shirt.

"There's a lot I don't know yet, but—"

"No, it's okay. You're right. I hadn't thought about that; I was just thinking about...you." His gaze falls to the flowers poking between the wooden slats of a short white fence. He's quiet the rest of the way to my house, and I drop his hand and slow my steps as we reach the front walk.

"So...do you want to come in?" When he hesitates, I lean closer. "You can safely ignore any comments my roommates make. I have the power to evict them."

He pulls back, and his head snaps toward the house. "*You* own this house?"

I shake my head. "My parents. But they live overseas. They stay in the guest house when they come home. They'd rather have it lived in than sitting empty."

"Oh, right. I think Hillary mentioned that." I can see him appreciating the little Romeo and Juliet balcony off my room, the Japanese maple by the big front window, the low hedges, the blue paint the color of clouds over the ocean.

"My room's that one, right in front. You've been in there before, remember? What's different this time?"

That seems to entice him just a little bit more.

"And no one's going to know?"

I push his shoulder a little. "You were the one egging me on in public! It is conceivable that I'm just having you over as a *friend*, you know." I can see Chance mentally gathering up his courage. He's almost there; I can feel his *yes* coming...and then those assholes have to go and ruin it.

Out of the corner of my eye, I can see them crowding around the big bay window, staring at us. Behind my back, I try to subtly signal them to *go the hell away*, but it's too late. His gaze bounces anxiously between mine and the window.

"Another day."

I'm disappointed, but I get it. "Okay, man. See you Wednesday?"

"Wednesday?" If he gets any more disoriented, I'll have walk him back to his car just to make sure he gets there in one piece; that's how flustered they have him. Ridiculous.

"Yeah, you know. Scary robot show. Wednesday. Snacks. Hillary. Us waiting for Hillary."

That seems to snap him out of it. "Wednesday. Right. Yes, I'll be there."

"Sounds good." Any physical contact between us would undoubtedly be blown completely out of proportion by my housemates, so I just give him a nod and start up the walk. I must be glaring, because all four of them scatter like I threw a brick in their direction.

"Hey, Colby?"

I spin back around. "Yeah?"

His face is adorably flushed. "Thanks for inviting me to play. I had fun."

I give him a grin as I back toward the front door. "Me too. Come again next week. Don't overthink."

He returns my smile with a wave as he starts back toward the park.

CHAPTER NINE

I'M COILING A MICROPHONE cord at the Howitz on Friday when my phone dings.

> **Chance:** I wish I'd come in on Thursday.
> **Colby:** Oh?
> **Chance:** Yeah. Can't stop thinking about it.
> **Chance:** Can I have a do-over?

I grin, and I'm poised to answer when someone clears their throat in front of me. I only look up halfway: red pumps, toe tapping discontentedly, red pencil skirt. That's enough to identify her. *Sigh.*

"Mrs. Parker," I greet my boss, lifting my gaze to her face. "What can I do for you?"

"You can put your phone away, for one thing."

With a grimace, I tuck it into my back pocket, then go to grab the microphone stand that's sitting near center stage.

"Arnie said you weren't available for all the high school graduations." Arnie is Mrs. Parker's nephew or something. Nepotism. I'm showing him the ropes, because he's got some aptitude and a pretty good ear, but still. Annoying.

"Right." PDXtrings is starting to take off, and they asked me to run sound for them at all their shows. She crosses her arms over her blazer. If she's waiting for an explanation, she'll be waiting a long-ass time. I'm a contractor. She doesn't own me.

"What's the conflict?"

I disconnect the microphone from the stand and tuck it under my arm as I continue to coil the cord. "There's no conflict, I'm just not available. I'm pretty booked up. You waited kind of a long time to send out the schedule." My phone buzzes in my pocket, and my irritation skyrockets. Chance is probably already freaking out that I haven't said anything when he put it on the line asking for a second chance.

"You have the reputation that you do because of the work you've done here. Let's not forget that."

No, I have the reputation I do because I'm fucking great at what I do.

I give her a flat smile. "Sure. Sorry I'm unavailable." I don't mean it. Not a word.

"I'd like you to reconsider your availability."

"I can't do that. Those groups are depending on me."

"We're depending on you *here*. The staff at the Helene Howitzer Concert Hall is a team, and right now, you're letting us down."

Is she...threatening me? Mild panic has sweat beading on my forehead, but I try not to let it show.

"I'm very sorry you feel that way. Please excuse me; I need to finish cleaning up. I have another engagement tonight." My only other engagement tonight is with a video game controller and a beer; the stage crew is capable of putting this stuff away. I just don't like to see the cords all bunched and tangled. She doesn't say another word as I pass her, and I wait until I get to the bathrooms before I pull out my phone again.

Chance: Never mind. Dumb idea.
Chance: Forget I said anything.

I sigh, then hit the call button.

"Hello?"

"Hey, it's Colby. Sorry, I got caught in a conversation with my boss at just the wrong time."

"Oh." The word is light, like he's reconsidering all the dire things that had been playing through his head. And I hope he is.

"So...a do-over how?" I ask.

"Well..." There's a long pause, and I silently grin. I'm starting to think the boldness I saw that first time we were together was a total fluke.

Chance clears his throat. "I'd like to fuck you in my bed with a big black dildo I've got picked out until you come so hard you scream my name. If you have time."

Okay. So, not a fluke. The blood rushes to my cock, and my knees go a little bit wobbly while my body tries to sort out what's happening. *This is a bad idea*, my brain puts in, and the rest of my body throws shit at it until it shuts up, shouted down again by my baser desires.

"Y-yeah, I've got time." Did I just *stutter*? What the fuck is this man doing to me?

"Now?"

"Yeah. Yes. I can come now." I'm already moving, in fact, to the sound booth where I stashed my bag under the desk. If I see my boss while I'm negotiating sex with my sister's roommate, I'll just pretend I didn't. "Is Hillary home?"

"No, she went out. Probably for the evening."

"I'm on my way."

"Good. See you soon." He hangs up without saying goodbye.

I feel like I should have second thoughts about this, but I just don't. It isn't complicated; he's coming to me, not the other way around. Technically, I haven't broken my promise not to flirt with him...he's merely whistling, and I'm running to him like a happy Labrador.

And speaking of running, that's how I catch the bus outside the Howitz, which is good, because I don't want him changing his mind again. I've thought about the blow job he gave me...a lot. And now, I'm getting a chance to live the whole experience. *Did he have another bad day? Is this just stress release again? Do I care?*

The gray evening turns into rain just as the bus lets me off in front of Hillary and Chance's building. I hustle for the front doors but still get pretty wet. My trench coat is a classic style, but without a hood, it doesn't always do me much good.

I ruffle the water out of my hair as I wait for the elevator, and an older lady scowls at me. When the doors slide open, I motion for her to go first, and that seems to earn me back some good will. Not that it matters; the person whose favor matters is upstairs waiting for me.

Unsure whether it's kosher to use my key, I knock, and I don't have to wait long before he answers.

"Hey." I don't know what I expected, but Chance opening the door in workout clothes, his white shirt sweaty, took me completely by surprise. "Sorry. You made better time than I thought. I'll just hop in the shower." He waves me inside, and I obey, shedding my wet coat.

"Yeah, we both know I can make myself comfortable here."

"Yes, you excel at that." Chance grins, and I can't help but think I haven't seen him smile all that much. Then he steps forward and kisses me, just a brief peck against my lips. When I freeze in surprise, he steps closer still, glancing up at me as if for permission. I lean down and close the gap between us, giving him more than a brush, letting my tongue lap a little at his bottom lip.

I start to pull back, and his hand comes up behind my neck to keep me firmly in place against him. Then both our mouths are open, his other hand stroking restlessly up and down my side. Chance kisses with a determination and focus I've rarely encountered, and before I know it, I'm walking us toward his bedroom. The couch is closer, but too public without knowing Hillary's exact schedule.

"Wait," he pants at the door, planting his hands on the frame, as if to bar our entry. "I've gotta shower."

"Shower after," I say, kissing him again. "You smell great." I mean it, too. It's possible I already snooped in their shower, and he has some kind of body wash that smells like juniper and sage. It's far superior to my cheap Irish soap.

He grunts, then pushes me back again. "I'm serious. I can't...I need..." His troubled gaze concerns me, and I snag his hand and squeeze it, anxious to get close to him again.

"What's up?"

"I haven't done this before."

Oh. I let my gaze fall to the floor. "So you're...a virgin?" That's the surprise of the century, given his blowjob confidence and the way he laid out what he wanted on the phone.

Scowling, he tips my chin up and takes my lips—and my breath—with a kiss I can only describe as *devastating.* His fingers trap my chin, tilting my head the way he wants it, scraping against the stubble on my jawline.

"Does that feel like you were just kissed by a virgin?"

It takes me a moment to reclaim my senses...then I shake my head slowly.

"Okay, so *not* a virgin...but you haven't done this since you transitioned—is that what you're saying?"

There's a flash of vulnerability in his glacial eyes, and I realize I'm fucking this up.

"Hey." I capture his face in my hands. "I want this; I want you. I'm in. But I want it to be good for you, so I'm just trying to figure out how to make that happen. If you want to shower, go shower. I'll be here."

"Okay." Some of his trepidation seems to fade, and his shoulders drop a little. "I'll shower after."

"You sure? Because I want you to be happy. You feel me?"

He bumps his hips meaningfully against my hard cock with a smile. "Yeah, I feel you."

"Smartass," I mutter as I walk him backwards toward the neatly made bed, and he laughs. Fuck, he has the best laugh. It's better than Mahler, more nuanced than Mozart.

I can't keep my hands off his body. Pushing him down onto the bed, I intend to go slow, but that challenging look he gives me, the one that says, *you think you can make me come?* makes my self-control harder to locate than clean dishes at my house. I.e., impossible.

He takes off his glasses and sets them carefully on the nightstand, and I know things are about to get real.

"Are you a bonus hole guy? Where can I touch you?" I'm frantic to make him feel good, as good as I feel with a flood of hormones raging through my veins, but I've done enough reading to know that not every trans guy wants all his parts played with, so I want to tread lightly.

"*Not* a bonus hole guy," he grunts. "Touch me anywhere else."

"Anywhere?" I let my hand slide down his chest, and he shudders.

"Anywhere," he whispers. I grin. *This is going to be good.*

"What do we call this guy?" I unzip him slowly and pull off his pants, leaving him in his boxers.

Chance's cheeks pink a little before he answers. "Clitasaurus Rex."

"Fucking fantastic," I say, dead serious. Then I bend and tug his boxers down far enough to give him a kiss. "Nice to meet you, Rex." I feel his hand thread into my hair, gently keeping me there, so I spend some time lavishing Rex with some attention. He's tense at first, sitting straight up on the bed, so I try to slow down a little and give him time to relax. I glance up just in time to see his eyes flutter shut, his head falling forward, and he lets out a big sigh that makes me smile. His hand on my head is gentle, scratching his fingers through my short hair mindlessly, and when he finally lies down, I start to go at him a little harder. I'm rewarded with a long, quiet moan, and his hips start to bounce in time with my tongue. I keep it up until Chance lifts my head.

"Hang on." He sits up and works his shirt over each arm before he pulls it over his head. "Still can't get my arms too high since my surgery." The intimacy of that detail makes me want to pull him closer. We aren't in love, obviously, but I'm surprised he'd confess anything that draws attention to the fact that he is trans. I'd be insecure as hell if I was banging someone for the first time as a guy, but Chance doesn't seem shy about showing me his body. And I know for a fact it's nothing I'm doing to put him at ease. I'm pretty sure the best thing I can do is let him lead. So that's what I do. I'm careful in how I touch him, though. He said anywhere, and I believe him, but he might still have sore spots. I don't know enough about top surgery to be sure, and that has me keeping my touch light on his chest. Just in case.

We make out on his bed until he eases me onto my back.

"Fuck, I can't believe you're here," he whispers. "I liked you from the moment I met you."

His hands are up my shirt now and his lips are still on my neck as I process that comment. "Really? You seemed skeptical."

"No, not at all. Even though you were younger than me."

Are we talking about the same instance? That first night I came over, Hillary barely let me converse with him at all.

"We didn't talk about my age when we met, did we?"

"Yeah." He licks my earlobe. "You said you were a junior. I asked about your classes."

"Wait, you're talking about Thanksgiving? When you came to my parents' house with Hillary?"

"Right." He's unzipping my pants and getting rid of them now, totally in control while I reel. "That's when we met."

I don't mention that I barely remember the moment.

"What'd you like about me?" I ask.

"Same things I like now." He grabs a bottle of lube and makes himself comfortable between my legs. "Confidence. Kindness. Your crooked smile."

"Huh." It could be a thinking sound, and it is, but it is also a direct response to the feeling of his fingers on my cock, swiping the slick liquid around the head.

"Feel good?" he whispers, and I nod jerkily. But I want his body heat back, so I reach up behind his neck and pull him toward my lips, surprised when he resists.

"Can I assume you're clean?"

I blink. "Oh. Yeah. I get tested, and I always use protection. That's a hard limit."

He hums his agreement. "Me too. Any other limits I should know about?"

"Um." It's hard to think with his hand on my cock. "Not that come to mind."

"Well, you can always say stop with me. I'll listen. I promise." His gentle gaze and reassuring words are in such contrast to the firm treatment he's giving my cock, my mind struggles to keep up. I force out some words.

"Yes. Good. Me too. Thank you." *Thank you? Smooth, Colby. Way to be polite.*

Chance laughs. "You're hilarious. I like that, too." His hand slips away from my cock and down to my hole as his lips fall to my nipple. *Fuck.* He's playing me like an instrument, fine-tuning his actions. He has me vibrating like the ringing harmonics the violins sometimes produce that just go on and on, filling up the hall with their brightness. He slips a fingertip inside me experimentally, and I breathe out hard, wrapping my arms around him, rubbing at his soft skin.

"Sorry to go fast," he whispers, bringing his kisses back up to my neck. "I don't know how much time we have."

That has me pushing him back by the shoulders to see his face. *Damn, he has nice shoulders.* They're more defined than mine, anyway.

"I thought you said she'd be out all evening."

"I said *probably* all evening. You know how she is." Unease means my cock starts to fall, and my stomach twists uncomfortably.

"Should I text her and ask?"

"Under what pretense, exactly?" He lowers his voice in what I assume is a poor imitation of me. "Hillary, your roommate is giving me the boning of a lifetime. Will you be back soon?"

"I sound nothing like that." I sniff, and Chance just laughs into my neck.

"Well, the good news is that my door is closed, and she always knocks, so you can relax. She's very good about privacy." Chance lowers his body fully to mine again, and the feel of his hot skin against mine distracts me momentarily. I tangle our arms and legs, weaving us together, and Chance grunts with satisfaction as I kiss him hard on the lips. He pulls away momentarily and grabs something out of the drawer. The next thing I know, he's adding more lube and something rubbery is at my hole.

"It's new," he says breathlessly. "Keeps my hands free."

Wow, he has really put a lot more into this moment than I have, and I don't mind being the recipient of all that thoughtfulness whatsoever.

I push out a little and it glides partway in, stretching me with a light burning sensation. He plays with it, in and out, a little farther each time, until the plug is fully seated inside me...and the thing is fucking huge.

"Yes, please," I mumble, and he smiles.

"So beautifully polite." Chance descends like a storm, stopping any more words I might've had. He drops kisses on me as my hole throbs. His fingers in my hair are the wind. He rubs himself against my leg, spreading his wetness over me, marking me with rivulets. His low moans are the thunder, and the lighting? It's inside me, playing up and down my spine as he works my cock tenderly. Before I know it, I'm shaking, close to coming.

"Chance..."

"I know," he says between kisses. "Turn over." He's got me warm and loose and feeling so good, I'm slow to react. He gets off the bed while I'm getting into place, and I hear the hook and loop of the harness.

"You really do like your hands free," I mumble, and Chance chuckles as he slides a towel under me. *Again, so prepared.* Firm hands rub my ass when I finally get it in the air. The stinging bite he places on it as he pulls the plug out distracts me from the weird feeling, and then his hard silicone cock is there, pressing inside. The plug was big; this is bigger. He runs a hand through my hair, ruffling it and tugging at the ends.

"It's...I don't know if I can..."

"I'll go slow," he promises, still massaging my ass, digging his short nails into my tender flesh. It takes a few minutes, but he uses the same process he did with the plug, working it in and out with care, and I relax, dropping to my elbows. He reaches one hand forward to wrap it around my flagging cock, which is distracted by Chance lighting up my prostate. The dual sensations are even better, and I let out a wanton moan. He struggles with the timing at first, and I'm reminded that this is his first time doing this. *How can this be his first time doing this?* Maybe he had a boyfriend who liked to be pegged...

My wandering brain is brought back when he gets the timing right: pushing into me as his hand comes down, bringing it up as he pulls back. I pound a fist against the bed and whimper, at a loss for words.

"Good?"

"So good. More. Faster. Please."

Chance complies, and then we're panting in time, and I hear him coming behind me, his cursing high and tight like he forgot to modulate his voice down. Thinking we're done with this part, I start to sit up, but he pushes me back down.

"My cock doesn't go soft. You're not done." His voice is authoritative, and it sends shivers down my spine. I almost throw out a *yes, sir*, but I'm afraid he'll think I'm making fun of him. I'm not. I wouldn't. Instead, I thrust back and fuck myself on his cock while he languidly plays with me, pinching my nipples, tugging at my hair, still working my cock but slower. I relax into the motion, losing myself in the feel of him behind me, when I hear him start to peak again. He thrusts harder, and it pushes me over the edge into a claiming climax as I shoot onto the towel he laid down. I wait for him to pull out, but before I can roll away from the towel, he's pulling it between my legs to clean off the lube, and I just...

He's amazing. The consideration. The care. It's fucking hot.

I collapse down onto the bed, spent and sweaty, and after a moment, I hear him slide off the harness and slip into bed next to me. When I open my eyes, he's watching me expectantly.

"So? Analysis?"

My chuckle sounds deeper than usual because my throat is dry. I roll him over so I can spoon him and press a kiss to his neck.

"Seriously? No feedback?" Chance sounds both confused and disappointed, and I can't help but laugh again.

"Still catching my breath, bud."

"Oh, okay." He's patient while I let my breathing return to normal, and I feel him relax into my hold.

"Ten out of ten, would fuck again. Gold star."

I can't see him smile, but I can hear it in his voice when he says, "Good." He seems to have forgotten all about that shower he wanted so bad when he falls asleep in my arms.

CHAPTER TEN

BY SOME MIRACLE, I do manage to sneak out of the apartment before Hillary gets home. I let Chance sleep rather than wake him to say goodbye, but I leave him a note on his nightstand. The next morning, I do my duty as a good son.

"Hey, Mom."

"Hi, Col!" she says. She doesn't look as tan as I thought she would. It's been a while since we video-chatted. "Happy first day of hurricane season!"

"They call them monsoons here," my father calls from somewhere off-camera.

"Oh right," my mother says, touching her forehead like she's upset the fact got out of there. "Monsoon season. But at least there's mangos."

"What do you make with mangos?" I ask, thinking about how I could work them into a salad with sliced almonds and a peach vinaigrette, green onions...

She grins. "Cocktails and boozy popsicles, but my neighbor said she has a very nice mango-rum sorbet recipe that a missionary taught her in Haiti while she was posted there."

"I didn't think missionaries drank," I say, tossing another handful of trail mix into my mouth.

"Apparently, this one did. Or maybe it doesn't count if it's frozen?"

I chuckle. "Don't know."

"You must have a lot of gigs lately," my mother says, pouring on the guilt the way some mothers pour syrup onto their children's pancakes. "We haven't heard from you in weeks."

"Only two weeks," I emphasize, "and..."

And here I hesitate. Because they're not going to tell Hillary. She's barely speaking to them. And they don't really talk to my housemates, but...if it did get back to Hil, the consequences could be disastrous.

Still, they're my parents. I've never been good at lying to them, and frankly, having them thousands of miles away makes it hard to find stuff to bond over. No more 'did you see that interception Wilson threw?' or 'did you hear the wind last night?' or 'the dogwoods are spectacular this time of year.' That last one is fake, I'd never talk about dogwoods, but you get what I'm saying. Those little points of connection just come easier when you're in the same geographical place.

My mom tried to start a family book club at one point, but that flopped hard (No, I don't want to read *Eat, Pray, Love,* and I don't care if it changed your life.). So, with my conscience still twisting uncomfortably over being honest with them and not with Hillary, I tell them.

"I'm kind of seeing someone."

The only immediate reaction I get is from my mother, who appears to be biting the inside of her cheek to keep from breaking out into a giant grin.

From the back, I hear my father yell, "A boy someone or a girl someone?"

"That doesn't matter," my mother chides, but the grin is now out and proud, just like my sexuality. She leans closer to the screen. "That's exciting, Colby. Tell me about them."

"It's pretty new," I hedge, "and it's kind of a casual thing, but I like him. He's got kind of a nerdy, academic thing going."

She sips her flavored water. "How did you meet?"

"At work," I lie. "He's a composer." I mean, it's not entirely untrue. He's got that AI writing music, and it came from his brain, so that counts, right?

"An artist," my mother coos, and I can almost hear my dad rolling his eyes. He'd really like it if I married someone who did something lucrative, I'm fairly sure. Doctoring. Lawyering. Bankering. Something more like what he does than what I do.

"What's his name?" Mom asks.

"Yeah, I'll be withholding that information for now." If he was named John? Sure, I'd tell them. But Chance is just unusual enough that they're going to put two and two together and come up with Hillary's roommate immediately. Not that I wish his name was more common—it actually fits him perfectly, in my opinion. I have a few trans friends and some of them are better at picking names than others...

"Stan!" my father yells. "Ford! Cohen! Dennis!"

"Darling, if you want to participate in the call, please come over here. Otherwise, stop shouting." She turns back to me and smiles. "What kind of dates do you have with your mystery man?"

"Mostly movies. He likes musicals." Another half-truth, but my mother beams, and I can tell she's now very invested in this working out.

"Take him somewhere nice!" my dad yells. "I'll send you some money! Guys like to be wined and dined, too."

"I don't need any money," I call back. "And I'll take care of him my own way, thank you very much."

Guilt stabs at me. I really haven't taken Chance anywhere. I haven't even bought him a gift. It's a casual thing...do I need to buy him stuff?

"Colby knows how to treat a partner, Chris," my mother parries. "We raised him to be a gentleman no matter who he's with."

If she only knew what I did with Chance last night. I smirk at the memory, but successfully wipe it off my face by the time she turns back to me.

"What's new in Thailand?" I ask, and that finally brings my father over to the screen. We talk politics for a few minutes before they say they need to get to bed; I forgot it was almost eleven there.

I wish them sweet dreams, and they wish me a good Saturday, and then they're gone. I stared at my screen for a minute. The app is asking me to rate my call. I click out—the app developers don't need any more information on me than they already have. But it was five stars. It's always five stars.

CHAPTER ELEVEN

A MONTH FLIES BY, AND I find myself lying on Chance and Hillary's couch on a Friday, watching some rom com. We've been spending lots of casual time together over the last few weeks, both at my house and his apartment. He's playing basketball with us regularly, and if we sit shoulder to shoulder on the couch instead of at opposite ends, Hillary doesn't seem to think anything of it. Chance and I have been squeezing in quickies where we can, but we never really get time to be together...and now, we haven't had any time alone for ten days.

With all the music groups trying to squeeze in one more concert before summer, I've been booked almost every night. And when I'm not, he has to meet with his team or run a long experiment. *Sigh*. I don't know how I fucked up my karma so bad, but I can't stop staring at Chance across the room.

He gives me a stern *knock it off* look behind Hillary's back when she goes to refill the chip bowl, and I just run a hand up the inside of my leg suggestively from where I lie on the couch. His eyes go wide with disbelief.

"Oh!"

My heart stops. *Did she see me?* But when I look, Hillary's staring at her phone. "Blake's in town!" *Good, go out with Blake and let me kiss and cuddle your roommate in peace.*

"Who's Blake?" Chance asks, rolling his empty root beer bottle between his fingers.

Wait, kiss and cuddle? Is that really what I want?

"Our cousin," I answer.

"Col, he wants to meet us at Ground Kontrol."

Oh, fuck.

I adjust my hat as I stall to figure out what to say. "I'm too tired to go all the way out there."

Hillary marches over to me and puts a hand to my forehead.

"Stop that," I say, pushing her hand away and fixing my hat again.

"You must be sick. It's the only explanation for why you would pass up the chance to spend time at your favorite place with your favorite people."

On any other day, she'd be right. Ground Kontrol has all these classic video games and pinball machines and good food. It's the best kind of vibe. Problem is, tonight, my favorite place is *Wherever I Can be Alone with Chance,* and my favorite person is *Chance.* End of list.

"It's kind of a long way..."

"Are you serious?" When she sees that I am, she turns to Chance. "You should come meet him. Blake's so great. And he's an engineer, so there'll be lots of good sci-ence-y talk."

"I'm not into crowds, as you well know," Chance mumbles, avoiding her gaze. We're both terrible liars, and I have no idea how she isn't seeing through this. It's as transparent as Saran wrap.

"I don't believe you two! It's not even 9:00! And it's the weekend! Come on, you've both done nothing but work lately. You need this. Also, I don't want to go alone."

No, what I need is Chance. I don't analyze the thought.

"You should take Janey," I offer. "She'd love Blake."

Hillary taps her chin in thought. "He'd love her, too. They're both 4's." When we both stare at her blankly, she clarifies, "Enneagram." She sighs when we keep staring blankly. "Fine, spoilsports. I'm not going to let you bring me down. I'm going to text Janey."

"Good." I switch over to the football game I recorded yesterday.

The next twenty minutes are longer than waiting for the dentist to come back in the middle of a filling when he "just has to step out for a minute." I pretend to watch the game; Chance doesn't. He's like a panther, poised to strike, his muscles taut and still. And his stare...seriously. How am I supposed to *not* respond to that smolder?

As Hillary looks for her shoes and her wallet and gives her teeth a quick brush, I let one hand wander over my chest, drawing circles around all the places I want his mouth. The other hand I leave resting on my pants zipper. His gaze bounces between them; both seem to be driving him wild, and I grin.

"Okay, I'm off," Hillary sings. "You boys have a nice, boring night."

"You too," Chance replies, obviously not listening at all. The moment the door closes, he's up out of his chair, but I hold up a staying hand.

"Wait," I whisper. I know she'll be back in five, four, three, two...

The front door flies open. "Forgot my phone!" She laughs. "How the heck was I going to get a ride without it? LOL."

If she notices that Chance is standing like a statue in the middle of the living room, she doesn't mention it. The door slams again as she leaves, and Chance looks at me for confirmation that he can move.

I give her another ten seconds to remember something else, but there's no sign of her. So I open my arms to him and find myself delightfully smothered with kisses by the hot, happy man I've been wanting.

Getting a word out between kisses proves tricky.

"Can we unplug the..." I gesture toward the black speaker on the counter.

He quirks an eyebrow. "Why?"

"You know I don't like them."

Chance laughs. "Why?"

"They're always..." I squirm uncomfortably. "*Listening.*"

"Well, yeah. That's kind of the idea."

"But I don't *like* that, especially when I'm..." I lower my chin and stare at him meaningfully. He makes a circle with his left hand and starts poking his pointer finger through it, and I slap them away. "I'm serious! I can't focus, I can't..."

He puts a finger to my lips and clears his throat. "Computer..." He glances at me. "Reduce lights to 20%." She pings in response, which sends a shudder down my spine, but the lights dim pleasantly. "Computer, play Sweet Talk by Saint Motel."

"Playing Sweet Talk by Saint Motel." From the speaker pours a pseudo-retro pop tune, heavy on the piano, up-tempo but not cloyingly peppy.

"Computer, do not disturb."

"I'm not saying it's not fancy and useful, I'm saying it's listening to me. It's recording everything I say. It heard me watching the Masters, and Hillary started getting ads for golf clubs. It's *creepy*."

Chance rolls his eyes and gets up off the couch. He walks over to the kitchen and pulls the plug abruptly from the wall, killing the music as well. "There. Can we get down to business now?"

I lean back with my hands behind my head and tilt my hips (and growing erection) forward meaningfully. "You're going to give me the business, huh?"

"Only if you shut up about the robot already." Chance smiles down at me.

"Thank you for indulging me."

Chance flops down next to me. He puts his head on my chest. My chest is great, don't get me wrong, but my most fun parts are either higher or lower, and I thought we were heading in those directions, so I'm a bit confused.

"AI can create its own language. Did you know that?" *He's reverting to research talk. Is he nervous? What would he be nervous about?*

I wrap my arms around him and squeeze a little. "No, I didn't."

He nods, his fingers wandering aimlessly over my pecs, my abs, my side. "They told them to negotiate, these two AI, and they started creating their own shorthand. The researchers didn't know what they were saying."

"And then they pissed themselves, re-examined the life choices that had brought them to that critical juncture in history, and shut it down?"

Chance chuckles into my chest, his warm breath tickling me even through my shirt. "It makes sense to me, though. When you find someone who's like you, it's easier to say things. Even if no one else understands." He goes quiet, and I just hold him, waiting to hear what he'll say next. "I feel that way with you sometimes."

"I feel that, too," I say, kissing the top of his head. "Talking with you is so easy. There's this..." I couldn't think of the word. The feeling reminded me of Debussy, the easy way the notes in *Claire de Lune* just come, tortured and light and free all the same time. "It's like a resonance. It's like when I'm in a room with great acoustics; the things that should be amplified are, and the rest falls away. I don't know. It's just a feeling I get when I'm with you. Everything just...works."

"Yeah." He presses a kiss to my chest as his fingers find the skin under my thin T-shirt. "That's it." And then I fall into the feeling as Chance kisses every other thought out of my head.

CHAPTER TWELVE

SATURDAY NIGHT I HAVE to work again, but I figure it can't hurt to stop by Chance's in case Hillary's out and we can get two nights in a row. A foolish hope. I show up just in time to see Chance putting on a tie.

"What's this? Hot date?"

Hillary glares at me. "Chance is a very desirable person, and it's not unlikely that he *does* have a hot date, Colby Christopher Cook."

I shoot him an apologetic look. I guess that joke only makes sense if you know he's banging *me*.

"So who's the lucky guy?"

"His name is Garrett."

Wait, what? I feel my face flush with irritation, and I'm suddenly gripping my coat like I'm trying to strangle it. Hillary turns toward the kitchen, and Chance lifts an eyebrow at me behind her back.

"He's one of the major donors for my program at the university, so they're having a wine and cheese thing tonight." I take a good look at him: he's got product in his hair, and he's wearing a black dress shirt with a maroon tie...and no glasses.

"Here," I say, taking him by the arm and dragging him toward the hallway, "I don't think that tie's quite right. I'll pick you a better one."

"What's wrong with my tie?" he asks, sounding adorably and genuinely confused as I close his door behind us.

"Where are your glasses?" I ask, much hotter under the collar than I have any right to be.

His eyebrows dance. "Um, in the bathroom, I think?"

"You're putting in your contacts for *them*? You hate your contacts!"

"Hillary says my eyes are one of my best features. So did you, actually." He crosses his arms, and my traitorous dick jumps when his muscles flex like that, even under his shirt. "And I'm still waiting to hear what's wrong with my tie." I reach out and touch the silky fabric, then slowly draw him toward me by it.

"The problem is that you're wearing it for someone else," I grump. Chance just stares at me for a moment until he grins.

"Jealous much?"

"I'm not jealous. I just don't want you dressing up for someone else."

"One: that is the very definition of jealousy, and two...we never said we were exclusive."

My hands twitch to pull that fancy shirt out of his pants, get on my knees, and remind him who's been driving him wild in bed, but I don't want to make him late. Well, I do want to, but I shouldn't. Because he's right. Instead, I stomp over to his closet and rifle through it until I find a pale blue tie with a diamond pattern.

"Here," I say, thrusting it toward him. "This one will bring out your eyes." I've already got my hand on the doorknob when he catches me.

"Colby. Talk to me. Why are you upset?"

I open my mouth to say I'm not, but I can't deny it. "I don't know."

It's all very confusing. We're just messing around. I don't have rights here. But then he engulfs me in a hug from behind, resting his cheek between my shoulder blades, and it isn't confusing at all. Because if I knew he was mine, I wouldn't care who he went out with.

"I want to be exclusive," I blurt out. Chance laughs as he turns me to face him.

"You *know* this isn't a date, right? It's a work function."

"I know," I mutter, staring at my shoes, "but it has brought some feelings to light that I didn't realize I had."

It isn't fair. The realization has me hanging my head; it isn't fair to ask him to hide our relationship. He should be mad, wondering if I'm ashamed of him. But when I glance up, he's giving me this warm smile.

"I'm proud of you for sharing your feelings."

"Oh, shut up." I laugh, pushing him away, but he holds me by my shoulders.

"Kiss me," he demands softly.

"Is that a yes? You're okay with this?"

He nods, and I give in, taking his lips, moving my hands to his waist and drawing him flush against me.

"If anyone compliments my tie tonight," he murmurs, "I'll just tell them my boyfriend picked it out." The thought fills me with silly pride.

"Good. I could also write 'taken' on your back if that would help."

He grins. "No need."

"But your ass is magnificent," I say, moving my hands lower to massage it. I know he feels dysphoric about it—I've seen him scowling at it in the mirror—but I really do love it.

"Nah, I'm good."

"All right." I let him go even though I'd rather move this affectionate touching to the bed and make him super late. He must notice the disappointment in my gaze, because he smiles as he puts on the blue tie.

"You gonna come by after your gig?"

I raise an eyebrow at him. "It'll be late."

"I'll be up."

CHAPTER THIRTEEN

CHANCE WASN'T EXAGGERATING; it's nearly one in the morning before he gets back. I let myself in quietly with my key after my gig running sound for a local production of Othello. It's an emergency key, so I feel slightly bad that the only emergency is that I desperately want to be with Chance. I lie down on his bed for just a minute to rest my eyes and find myself being awoken by warm, slightly sloppy lips against my neck.

That should be my first clue that something is not right. Chance is many things, I have discovered. An academic. A budding gym rat. Not amused by how long it takes me to make a salad. But he is never sloppy. Not in his room, not in his appearance, nothing. So those too-wet lips scraping my skin with his unintentional beard should've been a dead giveaway. But I must still be half asleep, because they don't register as anything but sexy.

"I love the way you look sleeping in my bed."

"You're home," I say, rolling onto my back to give him better access, and he nods, letting his nose drift over my cheek.

"How was it?"

"Funds were raised. Cheese was consumed. A rousing success."

"Mmm." His weight feels good, like a heavy blanket after a long day, pressing me into the mattress like I belong here. *I want to belong here.*

I bat away the too-serious thought and go after his shirt, unbuttoning him quickly as he continues to attack my neck, lavishing it with little bites and licks. He doesn't usually do that, but that doesn't register either. Strike two.

It isn't like he's never aggressive with me...but this is different. He's coming at me with a desperation that feels deeper than getting off. I feel Chance's need in my bones.

He quickly opens up my pants.

"I want you inside me," he grinds out.

I stop. "Inside you...here?" I tap his bonus hole, but he shakes his head and moves me farther back. Ah, the rear entrance. This does register as strange; Chance always tops. Always.

"No condom," he says, stroking my cock. "Nothing between us. Just rail me there, right there."

"Wait, hang on," I say, pushing him onto his back, but he's started opening himself up with his fingers, slick with his own wetness, and I momentarily get distracted watching him. "I'm not taking you without a condom," I whisper.

I'm not a fool. I've been reading. Trans men are far more likely to get diseases than other segments of the population, not to mention...

"You've tested. I've tested. What's the problem?"

"The problem," I growl, "is that diseases aren't the only reason to use condoms. There's a lot at stake for you." I know I'm not being completely rational, but neither is he. I know that testosterone does not guarantee that he won't get pregnant, but I don't think it wise to bring up the *p word* during sex. Even though it's not the right hole, things happen. And more than that, it's not abiding by the limits we discussed.

Although based on the stunned look on his face, we aren't having sex. Not anymore, anyway.

"What's your problem?" he says too loudly, and I want to shush him, but I don't want to piss him off more—not with my sister asleep in the next room.

I get off the bed. "My problem? Don't have one. But I know my limits and that's outside them. Now, do you want me to put my mouth between your legs and make you feel incredible, or are we done?"

Now the hurt is compounded by anger. Chance whips off his shirt and kicks off his pants. But it isn't until he pointedly rolls away from me, facing the wall, that I figure I have my answer.

My cock is weeping–not literally, we hadn't gotten that far yet–and I give it a little apology rub as I tuck it away.

Maybe he isn't drunk, but he's at least tipsy. That alone is enough of a reason to tread lightly. But when he starts demanding things we've never discussed? That's a no go. He means more to me than that. And as fun as that sounds, it isn't worth sacrificing our...whatever this is.

Yeah. I try explaining that to my cock the whole ride home.

CHAPTER FOURTEEN

I SLEEP IN THE NEXT morning. I'm a little depressed, wondering if I messed things up with Chance. But when I reach for my phone, I have an email.

Dear Colby,

I didn't want to take the chance that I'd wake you up, but I needed to apologize immediately for last night.

Obviously, I was not in a great brainspace last night. Public events like that sometimes mess with my head, and I came home feeling a little drunk and a lot needy. But that doesn't give me the right to renegotiate our agreements on the fly. It was very wrong of me, and I'm sorry I pushed you like that. Thank you for being level-headed enough to say no; it would've been a really boneheaded thing to do.

I don't expect you'll want to see me, so I'll just sign off by saying thanks for looking out for both of us.

Sincerely,

Chance

I roll my eyes as I text him, lying on my back.

Colby: Are you alone?
Chance: Yeah.
Colby: Why wouldn't I want to see you exactly?
Chance: I'm so sorry.
Colby: Yes, so you said. But that doesn't answer my question.

There's a long silence, and I'm not sure Chance is going to answer me at all. What kind of messed up relationships has he been in? People are allowed to make mistakes. If they're not, it certainly disqualifies me from participation.

Chance: Aren't you mad at me?
Colby: You think I've never done anything stupid when I was drunk?
Chance: That doesn't answer my question.
Colby: Okay, fine. Was I annoyed last night? Yeah. But I'm over it now.

When there's another long pause, I break the silence.

Colby: If you're really consumed with guilt, I know a way you can make it up to me.

And then I send him a picture of my morning wood. Is it mature? No. But I figure nothing says "I forgive you" like a dick pic.

My phone rings immediately, but his face says he isn't sure about this.

"Hi."

"Hey. You hung over?"

"Kinda." He rubs his face like his head hurts, mussing his hair adorably.

"I was kidding about the video sex. Just trying to make you laugh, overthinker."

"Just being impulsive, underthinker."

"Probably." I grin. "Do you need caring for? Should I bring you breakfast or something?"

He groans. "You shouldn't bring me breakfast when I screwed up so bad last night."

"You're too hard on yourself. Forget it. Seriously."

"I'll try." He flops back onto the bed and licks his lips, staring into the camera. "Do you have plans today?"

"Just laundry and cleaning and stuff." I sometimes still did that stuff on weekends, a holdover from the days when I worked a normal schedule.

"You're not doing anything fun?"

Is he offering something? I can't tell. Maybe he's had enough time to think about my other idea...

I shrug. "Might play video games or something. My roommates are usually up for trouble."

"I'm up for trouble," he says, his voice cracking a little.

"Are you?" I ask, straight-faced. "My overthinker's up for trouble? That doesn't sound right." Without thinking about it, I reach down and stroke myself, and when Chance's eyes light, I know he noticed. He must set the phone down on the bed, because I get a very nice view of his ceiling for a minute, and then he isn't wearing a shirt.

"Oh, all right," I say, grinning. "Let's go then, troublemaker."

Chance smiles shyly at me, then he starts touching himself with his free hand, caressing his neck. He runs a hand over the top of his head, showing off that lovely bicep, and I give myself a little tug, pulling a groan from my chest.

"What do you want to see?" I ask, keeping my voice quiet. "My face or my cock?"

"Show me your cock," he murmurs, tweaking one of his taut nipples. "I want to see how hard I make you."

Is it possible for your brain to do a keyboard smash?

"What do you want to see?" he asks.

"Anything you want to show me," I say, my hand speeding up. I flip the camera view so I can still see him. "Just talk to me. Tell me."

"Tell you what?"

"What you'd do if you were here."

"Well," he hedges, licking his first two fingers, and I groan again as his fingers go south. "First I'd kiss your perfect mouth until you start squirming, rubbing against me in that way that I like."

"Too late," I say, bucking my hips into my hand. "Then what? Tell me, babe." Bud. I'd meant to call him *bud,* which isn't really right either. The pet name just slips out, and I watch to see his reaction, but if he notices, it doesn't bother him.

"I work my way down your chest, slow."

"No, fast."

"No," he says, his voice pitched low and serious. "*Slow.*"

How is he dominating me when he's not even here? I don't have the brain cells to figure it out, I'm already so close to coming.

"Stop. Take your hand off your cock and turn the camera so I can see your face."

"Really?" I whine.

"Colby. You asked what I'd do. This is what I'd do. I'd pin down your arms so you could only take what I give you, so you have to go my speed." His glare allows no argument, and I slowly remove my hand, sinking into that place he's put me between pain and pleasure. I reach back to grab onto the smooth wood of my headboard, wishing it was my smooth skin instead, my cock still throbbing in protest, then turn the camera so he can see. His answering smile is gold.

"Good boy."

"Ugh, no good boy." I say, crinkling my nose. "I don't do daddy kink."

"Fine. Good work, then."

"Better. Then what?"

"I'd press my skin against yours, wetting it with my mouth, making you slide against me. Rev you up until you're sweating and flushed." I buck my hips into the air, but there's no relief. I fucking love messy sex, and he knows it; I can almost feel the hot stripe of his tongue against my stomach.

"More. Please, babe. Don't leave anything out." I'm struggling to keep my grip on the wood, my muscles shaking.

"Then I turn and straddle you, lowering Rex to your lips."

"Fuck, fuck, fuck," I chant, bucking wildly now, even though it's not doing me an ounce of good. "Chance, let me touch myself. Let me pretend you're here, giving me what I need. You're so fucking good at it."

"Not yet."

My desperation is not made better by the fact that I know he's still touching himself, the cords of his arm straining as he moves his hand faster.

"Show me Rex. Show me what my mouth would get. I'd treat you right, I swear I would."

"Col..."

He's so close, I can tell, but he doesn't want to let go until we can come together. He flips his camera, and there it is, standing proudly between his fingers as he rubs and rolls it, glistening from his own wetness.

"I'd take you in my mouth and suck you hard. I'd keep lapping and sucking and licking you until you come so hard, you can't remember your own name."

That does it. Something in Chance's gaze breaks, and he gasps out, "Do it. Finish." My hand flies to my cock so fast, I'm amazed I manage to do it without hurting myself. I hold his gaze through the phone as I come, and his mouth drops open in a silent gasp of pleasure.

I love this guy's post-orgasm face. He just always looks so fucking pleased with himself, and it makes my heart sing. Not just because he wanted to be with me, but because I want to give him every good thing that he wants. I want to gently stroke the hair along his sweaty temple and watch his face go slack in all the little lines around his eyes as he relishes my touch. I want to kiss him and melt into him, sharing each other's heat, burying ourselves in the bed until we're both too hungry to stay there.

He beams. "That was fun."

I laugh; I can't help it. "I'm so glad you approve. I'm gonna go get cleaned up now. Will you be around this afternoon if I come by?"

He nods vigorously. "I sure will."

I DON'T WAIT UNTIL the afternoon. I'd rather hang out with him all day if I can. When I get there, Hillary's just pulling cinnamon rolls out of the oven.

"Oooh," I say, but she slaps my hand before I can snag a taste.

"Those are for the ladies."

"What ladies?" I ask, sneaking some of the fruit salad on the counter. "Is that ginger? I've taught you well."

"It's a *recipe*. I'm having some ladies over for brunch. If you ever *called first*..."

"Whatever. I'm here to see Chance, anyway."

"You are?"

"Yeah," I say, rolling my shoulders back defiantly. "We're going to the art museum."

"You are." Her tone is flat and skeptical, and I resent it all. I happen to know my nerd loves the art museum. It's completely plausible.

"Yes!" I say, throwing out my hands. "What, you think I'm just making all this up?"

"Kinda," she says, smirking as she licks a bit of frosting off the side of her hand.

"That would be ridiculous, and I'm not you," I say, skating across the floor to Chance's room. "Ready to go to the art museum?" I ask loudly as I arrive at his open door.

Chance looks up at me, clearly perplexed, then down at his t-shirt and sweatpants. They're a little crummy from the toaster pastry still in his hand, and he wipes them off.

"Um. Yeah. Let me just change."

I stand in the doorway with my hands in my pockets until I notice he's looking at me weird.

"Could you..." He motions with two fingers to the side.

"Oh." I step inside and start to close the door, but his eyes widen.

"No," he whispers, "you have to step out, remember?"

Right. Privacy. Because only someone who's already seen him naked would step *inside* when he says he needs to change...

"I'll just be out here, eating cinnamon rolls," I announce. "Take your time."

"You're not getting a cinnamon roll," Hillary says again as I wander back into the kitchen.

"You should put blueberries in this salad."

"I don't have any blueberries."

I don't mention that there are frozen ones in the freezer that she could defrost since I only know they're there because I kind of elbowed Chance in the chest the other day while we were banging and he needed ice. And I can't exactly admit that.

"Who's coming over?"

"Some gals from my program. Raina, Posey, Giada. And Janey."

"Huh."

She's fanning her baked goods with a large cookie sheet like they do on those baking shows I don't watch.

"What time are they coming?"

"Um. Ten minutes?"

I look around; it's clean, but she doesn't look ready. "You want me to get out plates or something?"

"Oh, would you? You're a lifesaver, Col."

I smile as I wash my hands and get out the plates and silverware. I even find fancy napkins tucked away in the back of a cupboard that coincidentally also has candles. I hope she doesn't ask how I know that, either.

After a suspiciously long time, Chance opens his door wearing jeans and a T-shirt with a miniature, scale model of the solar system on it in a vertical line. It's the same shirt he was wearing earlier.

"Have a nice brunch," he says to Hillary as he grabs his coat. "Say hi to everybody for me."

"Will do! Have fun looking at art!"

I let him go first, because I'm a gentleman, then quietly close the door behind us. I don't start to tease him until we get into the elevator.

"This is how you dress for a date?"

"See," he grumbles, dragging a hand through his hair, "this is exactly what I knew would happen. If I dressed up, she'd wonder why, but if I didn't, you'd feel unimportant. It was a lose-lose situation!"

I laugh and give him a kiss on the cheek. "I don't feel unimportant. Sorry I threw you a curve ball; you handled it beautifully. Out of curiosity, though...how many times did you change your clothes before you decided on this?"

"Four," he grumbles, and I laugh again. It's not raining when we step outside, so we just walk. I don't usually go out with Chance anywhere other than basketball, so it feels strange to just walk next to him, disconnected. Maybe we look like we're dating, but I doubt it. Chance is talking a lot, because he's excited. I'm listening a little but mostly still taking in the music of the city, even if Chance is the melody. I'm wired to listen to the whole.

He lets me pay since it was my idea, and it makes me feel kind of gooey inside to get to take care of Chance for once. We start in a room full of portraits, and he goes quiet for a while, looking at all the oil paintings. They just look like a bunch of faces to me.

"I like the self-portraits best. It's so interesting to me the way people draw themselves. I always wish I had a photograph of the person to compare it with."

"You could probably find one on the internet," I whisper, because, I don't know, art museums remind me a little of church.

"But I'd want them side by side," he says, holding up his hands. "So I can really look at the differences. Nobody sees themselves as they really are, I don't think."

I stare at him. "No, that's why people need friends."

"You think?"

"Yeah," I say, still keeping my voice soft. "To tell you when you're painting in too many wrinkles. To lie and tell you your forehead isn't too big and your ears don't stick out that much."

"Maybe his did," Chance says, still staring at the portrait. "Maybe people teased him."

"You should make your AI paint a self-portrait."

As usual, where his work is concerned, he does not have a sense of humor. "Oh, I don't think I could. That would require a lot of robotics; plus, I'd have to show it a lot of data in order to help it understand the concept of..." His voice trails off as he takes in my smiling face. "You were joking, weren't you?"

"Duh," I say. After a quick glance around, I kiss him. He leans forward against me, pressing his hips into mine, and I don't want to look at any more dusty old paintings of people with big ears. I don't want to think about my self-portrait, littered with lies. I want to bang him in the bathroom.

"Let's go upstairs," Chance says, pulling out his map. "I think that's where Isaka Shamsud-Din's collection is."

"Sounds great. Lead the way."

At least I can watch his ass as he goes up the stairs.

CHAPTER SIXTEEN

"YOU GET TO DRIVE ALL the time. I think I should be in charge tonight."

Chance moans softly as I pull down his zipper. It's late on a Tuesday night. Super late. Hillary's in bed. Hopefully asleep. Because we are not stealthy.

"Hush." I laugh into his neck, taking off my hat. "Rex isn't going to get any action if you get us caught." I can feel the muscles in his neck straining under my gentle kisses as he tries to hold back his sounds, and it just amps me up even more. "Are you going to be good, or should I stop?"

His high, strangled moan makes my scalp tingle, and I move my kisses back to his mouth to swallow his sounds.

"So you just want Hillary to hate me. I get it," I whisper. "Fine, have it your way." He laughs then gasps as I wet my fingers and shove them into his open pants.

"Yes. You feel amazing. This is the best."

I grin against his lips. "You think this is the best?" I hold his gaze as I drop to my knees, and I legitimately worry he's going to fall as his eyes glaze over.

"Oh, god. I don't know if I can..." He bites his lip, and I wait, hands on his hips.

"We don't have to," I whisper, even though I'm pretty sure I'll die if we stop things now. He digs his fingers into my scalp as I breathe warm air over his very needy boy bits.

"I want to—I want to so bad. I just don't know if I can keep quiet."

"How about this..." I caress his inner thigh. "I'll go slow. And if you want me to stop, just say 'red.'"

"You're assuming I'll still be able to form words," he grumbles. "You do things to my head, asshole." But when his fingers draw my head closer, I know I have a green light.

I lap at him languidly, and his head falls back against the wall with a satisfying thud. Closing my eyes, I let my lips play around the sides, sliding the tip of my tongue up and down, nuzzling him with my nose. He smells like Chance, like clean linen. I feel his hips start to move, and I reach up to intertwine our fingers. He's whimpering a little loud for comfort.

"Be good," I whisper sternly again, and he claps a hand over his mouth like he can't help the sounds coming out of it.

"I can't," he pants in a whisper. "I can't, I can't, I'm going to give us away. Red."

I pull back immediately. "What if I keep you quiet?" I stand up, wobbling a little as the blood comes back to my legs, and he clings to me, piercing me with his desperate crystal blue gaze.

"How?" he whispers, and I just smile devilishly.

"Hands on the wall." Looking wary, he complies, and I carefully work his shirt off to put his skin on display. I'm fascinated with his back; I'd noticed the other day that he has all these beautiful little muscles, all these moles and freckles and a birthmark that looks like the state of Michigan. It's so fucking sweet. I've never even been to Michigan, and I still love it.

"It reduces plausible deniability if I'm half naked," he hisses over his shoulder, and I capture his frown with a kiss.

"Just wait," I say, snaking my hand into his pants, and he groans softly. That reminds me why we're positioned like this, and I reach up and cover his mouth with my free hand. His breath comes fast against my fingers, and I nuzzle against his neck. Wetting my fingers again, I dive back into his pants until I find Rex. And I am somewhat devastated, because in the interim between when I was on my knees and now, Rex has gotten excited. Very ex-cited. Placing myself behind him, I grind my still-clothed cock against Chance's ass, encouraging him to move, and he takes the hint. Hands still on the wall, he rocks into my hand like this is his last chance on Earth to come. His high panting has me all wound up, but there's no way in hell I'm unzipping my pants with Hillary in the next room.

Chance taps my wrist, and I remove my hand from his mouth.

"I want you inside me," he grunts, still thrusting.

"What about plausible deniability?" I whisper.

"Fuck plausible deniability," he whispers back harsh-ly. "I need you, Col. Now." Even when I'm driving, this guy manages to take control from the back seat.

Fuck. I want to give that to him, I really do, but I'm already crossing the line between what's smart and what's selfish.

"Not this time," I say, swallowing his complaint with a deep kiss as my hand speeds up, and then he's coming, shaking in my arms, and I'm kissing him like he's precious and perfect because he is, pulling him against me so he doesn't collapse. Panting, I turn him, cradling his face in my hands in a totally platonic way. You know, like fuck buddies do. And he stares back at me looking debauched and content, and I can't do anything but smile.

Then he's dropping to his knees, and I…I don't have the willpower to stop him. "Wait," I say, pulling a pillow off the bed. Instead of waiting for me to come back, he follows me, pushing me down to sit on the edge, then flops the pillow onto the floor at my feet.

His hands are gentle as he takes me out, and I can't help digging my fingers into his bedding, soaking in the warmth and wetness of his mouth. *There's no way I'd be able to talk my way out of this one.* Then immediately after, I think, *But why on earth would I want to?* The slick slide of his mouth feels like heaven on my dick, and I let out a soft groan.

"Shh," he chides, teasingly. "You're going to get us caught…" And for a moment, I almost think he doesn't care, that he *wants* to get caught. But I don't have time to think about it before he sucks my head hard and I'm coming, coming, coming, my mouth open but silent, using every bit of willpower I have not to just shout my pleasure to the rooftop. We're on the fourteenth floor, after all; it wouldn't be that far to go.

I flop back onto his bed and put one hand over my eyes. My head is still light, and I swear he sucked so hard,

I've got no blood left in my brain. After a minute, I tuck my cock back into my pants and give him a kiss; I probably have beard rash.

For a split second, I think maybe Chance has the right idea. Maybe we should just tell her. The problem is that I know my sister. She saw our parents' move as a betrayal even though it wasn't. She sees all sorts of things as personal affronts that just fucking aren't. But this? No, she'd be right about this. Because I haven't just given her request that I stay away from Chance the middle finger, I've fucked it up against the wall while she was in the next room. Guilt bites at me, but I don't want Chance to think I regret anything, so I kiss him again.

"I should go."

"Oh, I see. It's hump, thump, thank you grump, is that it?"

I laugh and push at his shoulder. "I'll snuggle you extra next time," I say, and to my own surprise, I actually mean it. This guy loves to be held, and I like holding him. "You are kind of a grump, though."

He throws out his hands and his whisper-yell is adorable. "Only when men don't snuggle me! It should make you grumpy, too!" His complaint is just another reminder of how unfair this is to him, and the guilt that was nipping at me clamps its jaws around me in full.

I avoid his gaze as I retrieve my hat. "I'll see you on Wednesday?"

"See if I hold your hand during the robot parts," he snarks, and I grin as I close his door behind me.

CHAPTER SEVENTEEN

THE WEEK GOES BY AS expected; a children's the-atre during the day is a nice change of pace, but most of my gigs are at night. It's late Sunday night when I get home. Evan's sitting at the kitchen table with a bowl of mint chocolate chip, and I do a double take. Leah isn't with him.

"Everything okay?"

He shrugs, digging deeper into the bowl.

"Something happen with Leah?"

He lifts his head, and the pain in his gaze is unmis-takable. "No."

I pull out a chair and sit down slowly. "I see. So, it's come to this. We're lying to each other now. Some best friend you are."

One corner of his mouth lifts, but I can see his mus-cles resisting. "Sorry, Col. Just not ready to talk about it. And you've been so busy...you haven't been around much."

I adjust my hat as the guilty feelings pour in. He isn't wrong.

"I'm sorry, man. I didn't realize you needed me. I'm here now."

"Can't really talk about it. But I appreciate that." He takes another spoonful of ice cream and eats it slowly. I sit there with him, unwilling to just walk away when my friend is in pain.

"How's Chance?" he asks, glancing at me sidelong.

I adjust my hat again. Yeah, I have a tell, okay? It's why I don't play professional poker.

"Fine, I assume. Why do you ask?"

Evan laughs softly. "You know why."

Now I'm sweating. If Evan knows, maybe other people do, too. "No, I don't."

He sets his spoon in the bowl. "Are you seriously trying to bullshit me? Come on, Col. I know you're banging him. You two are about as subtle as a herd of elephants."

"Okay, fine," I hiss, leaning forward, "but don't tell Hillary. She'll be mega pissed with me. Like, *no forgiveness ever* pissed."

"Did you really think we didn't know?" He chuckles. "All those trips up to your room after you two spend the whole basketball game feeling each other up?" His voice takes on a high falsetto. "Oh, I just wanted to show Chance this book I'm reading." His voice returns to normal. "Like you read. You're the worst liar in the world."

"Hey, I read!"

"Graphic novels don't count."

I point at him, truly offended now. "Graphic novels *definitely* count. You're elitist, is what you are."

"*Elitist?* Now you even sound like Chance."

The fear I've been fighting starts to gain ground. "No, I don't!"

Evan shushes me. "Dude, people are sleeping. What's so bad about that?"

"Nothing. I just..." I look around for a way out of this conversation. I just criticized him for lying to me, and now I'm considering the same thing. "I think I might be falling for Chance."

"Obvious. Old news. What else?"

"*Old news?*" Not for me. Not until this very minute did I realize how deep in I am. And I'm so freaked out, I can't even name what I'm deep *in*.

"Yes," he says, nodding as if to punctuate how strongly he believes it. "Old news. Now what are you going to do about it?"

I squirm in my seat. "There's nothing I can do."

"Why?"

"I told you, Hillary—"

He blows a raspberry. "Come on, Colby. That's an excuse."

He might as well have flipped my anger switch. "It's not, actually. I told her I wouldn't flirt with Chance or go after him."

"But you did. So now what? You either man up and go after what you want, or end it before someone gets hurt."

I take off my hat and sit back in the hard wooden chair. "It's not that simple."

"Bullshit. Does he love you?"

"I don't know." His glare says he doesn't believe me. "I really don't. I mean..." My brain pulls up the memory of us snuggling after Hillary went to Ground Kontrol, and I falter. That resonance, that perfect, frightening feeling of being in the middle of something big and all-consuming. He felt it, too. But he hasn't ever said the words. Hasn't ever talked about a future between us.

"Ask him."

I let out a wry laugh. "Yes, it's just that easy. Just go up to my sister's roommate who I've been screwing around with and say, 'Hi, yes, quick question, are you in love with me?'"

Evan shrugs. "It's worth a shot. It's the only way to know for sure."

"I guess." He isn't wrong. The problem is that Chance's 'yes' scares me a hell of a lot more than his 'no.' If he says no, I can pretend this is temporary. But if it isn't…then I am in deep, deep trouble with my sister. And maybe with Chance.

"You really can't talk about your Leah problem?"

"Don't change the subject, asshole."

"Geez. Touchy." I move to get up, but stop when I feel his hand on my arm.

"Sorry. I…" He sighs. "No, I can't. But you should talk to Chance. Find out what he's thinking."

I grab my hat and go upstairs, too tired to do anything except take off my clothes and fall into bed. And once there, too awake to do anything but stare at the ceiling.

CHAPTER EIGHTEEN

I DON'T GET ANY ALONE time with Chance for the next week, and in that time, I can feel my heart getting more invested with every passing moment. The starstruck way he looks at me is not helping, nor is hearing more of his AI compositions—classical this time—or quick kisses when Hillary goes to the bathroom or into her room to take a call. *Shit.* This is not going to work. And it's going to be messy.

On my way over to their place on Wednesday, I get a text.

> **Hillary:** Chance said you helped him move his new dresser up. Thanks for being nice to him. I seriously love living with him. Thanks for keeping your word.

I'm so torn up, I can't even respond with a lie. I have to break it off. End it now before it gets any worse...for me, anyway. I still don't know for sure what he's thinking.

The longer I have to put it off, the more stressed I get about it. On Sunday, Hillary invites me over for dinner.

"You want some bread?"

"No, I'm good."

"Are you sick?" Hillary asks as I pick at my plate of pasta. Chance looks similarly concerned but says nothing.

"No. Just not hungry."

"That's not normal." She frowns, and I shrug. I need to get away before she starts asking too many questions.

"I should probably get going to work."

"I thought it didn't start until 7:30?"

I mumble something about setting up, which is total bullshit, and scrape my food into the trash.

"Okay, well, I'm heading out, too," she says. "I'll go with you."

No.

"I think I'd rather go alone."

She presses her palm to my forehead as her frown deepens. "Now I know you're sick. Seriously, what's wrong?"

"Nothing," I lie, not even having the energy to push away her touch. Chance looks like he's fighting a mighty scowl, staring down at his food in an attempt to be neutral about my weird mood.

"Okay, well, I'm off. See you tomorrow?"

"Yeah, probably."

She squeezes me tight and gives me an air kiss on the temple.

"Hope you feel better, Col," she calls over her shoulder as she grabs her purse and heads out the front door.

"I feel fine," I call after her, even though the door is now shut.

Chance is by my side the moment she's gone, and he squeezes my hand. "Seriously, though. Are you okay?"

"Chance, I can't do this anymore. I'm so sorry."

I watch the moment his heart shatters. I watch it happen. The door flies back open, and I think I'm having a heart attack. Chance recovers quicker than I do and removes his hand from mine before Hillary pops back into the kitchen.

"Forgot my phone. I swear, if my head wasn't attached..." she mumbles, grabbing it off the counter. We both hold perfectly still until the door slams once more.

I try to take his hand again, but he pulls away, and I feel my heart snag and pull with him. "Things between us are getting..."

"Serious."

I swallow. "Yeah. And I like it, I really do. But I promised Hillary I wouldn't mess up her housing situation, and I feel like maybe I'm going to do that."

"You won't."

"But if we get too close and then it goes sideways..."

"It won't." He pulls me into a tender kiss, hands on my face, holding me close. "And if it does, I won't take it out on Hillary."

"I promised her, man. I promised I wouldn't get involved with you. And this is feeling more and more involved all the time."

His face hardens, and he pulls back again. "Don't fucking make excuses, Colby. If this scares you, either get your shit together and face it, or just say that you don't trust me."

"I do trust you!" I burst out, and I wish he could see the way my heart is breaking, wish desperately that he'd believe me. "Seriously. Look at my phone."

I scroll to her latest message, the one that pushed me over the edge, and turn it so he can see.

Thanks for being nice to him for me. I seriously love living with him. Thanks for keeping your word.

He scratches at his beard. He glares at me, then the screen again, then me.

"Don't be mad," I whisper. "I'm really sorry. Can we please still be friends?" The words sound so pathetic, such a pale shade of what I really want. Even as they come out of my mouth, I know they're wrong.

"I don't know."

Fuck. I really hurt him. This has been a bad idea from beginning to end; someone was bound to get hurt. Too bad it wasn't just me catching feelings. Watching him pinch the bridge of his nose like he's staving off tears, the snag in my heart begins to pull faster and faster, the fabric of me unraveling.

"I'm sorry, I'm so sorry." I bury my face in his shoulder, seeking comfort even though I have no right to. I don't know what else to do. I'm not far from tears myself, and I don't want him to see, even though it would probably help my case. I want him to comb his fingers through my hair, to sigh and tell me it's okay, that he understands. That he loves me anyway, the way I love him.

Instead, his voice is scratchy and high. "Could you go?"

Yeah, that makes more sense.

I wipe my annoying tears as I straighten. "Yeah. I'm sorry."

"Yeah, you said that," he snaps. "Just get out, Colby. And do me a favor and stay away for a while. You're such a fucking coward, I can't stand to look at you."

Anger flares hot for a heartbeat, then snuffs out. This is my fault. He has a right to be angry. I don't. I should've pushed him away when he got on his knees in that pink sweatshirt instead of giving in. If I had, we wouldn't be in this mess. Or if I'd just told Hillary...but I can't do that.

I get up and find my bag, shutting the front door quietly behind me. I run down the stairs so fast, I think I might trip and tumble the rest of the way head over heels. It would feel good, in a way. Congruous, to hurt on the outside as much as I do on the inside. He taught me that fucking word.

She's my family; he's not. I *have* to side with her, don't I? Living with the lies is killing me, even if the sneaking around was kind of hot. I slam my fist into the side exit and step out into the bright sun. *Fuck off, Sun. I'm heartbroken.*

· · · ·

THE NEXT DAY, I GET a text.

Hillary: Hey, you left your coat here.

Colby: Oh, thanks. I was wondering.

Hillary: I gave it to Chance. He'd said he'd give it to you if you want to come by tonight.

He may have said that, but there's no way he meant it.

Colby: I'll just use an umbrella. Thanks though.

Hillary: LOL. What?

Colby: What?

Hillary: I have never seen you use an umbrella. I didn't know you even owned one.

Colby: I have one.

It's weird and raggedy because it got turned inside out once on a really windy day and it fucked up those little metal supportive pieces. But I do have one.
I can't keep lying to her.

Hillary: Whatever, weirdo.

Colby: Thanks though.

Colby: also, I'll be really busy next week, so you might not see me for a while.

Hillary: You're going to miss Westworld? I thought you didn't usually work on Wednesdays.

Colby: Date.

Okay, maybe I can keep lying to her, just a little. But this is different; this is *protective* lying. There is a long pause, and I think I'm caught for sure.

Hillary: Oh, that's great! Anybody I know?
Colby: No, someone new.

Great. Now I'm going to have to produce a date at some point even though my heart is still being a big whiny baby and screeching about losing Chance every time I think about him, which is basically all the time. I can't stop second-guessing myself; I have no idea if I've done the right thing. The first time I go over there, it's going to be hell.

Hillary: Wig! When do I get to meet this person?
Colby: It's only our first date. It's casual.

I shove my phone into my back pocket. I can't keep doing this. I broke up with Chance so I could try to salvage my integrity, and here I am, still lying to her. I screwed up the best relationship of my adult life for this; if I can't do better, maybe I should just come clean and beg him to take me back. Not that I think he would; he was pretty clear that I disgusted him. But maybe if I really sell it, get on my knees...

No. That isn't fair. I made the decision. It's over.

Hillary: Well, I can still hope it's true love. You know me.

Colby: Yeah, I know you.

CHAPTER NINETEEN

TWO WEEKS LATER, I'VE sort of dragged myself out of mope mode, burying myself in work until I just can't feel anything anymore. I'm in the middle of another high school graduation when I get a text from my sister.

> **Hillary:** HALP
> **Colby:** What's wrong?
> **Hillary:** Come over RN! HALP HALP HALP

That's like SOS in Hillary-speak (is she really older than me?). Frowning, I dial her number. No answer. I hang up before the voicemail kicks in.

> **Colby:** What's going on?
> **Colby:** Hil??

I call again three times, but no answer and no text messages. I still have half an hour of work before I can go check on her. I'm twitchy, my leg shaking under the counter. Maybe Chance would answer...I grimace. I know he wants space, but if it's an emergency, he'll want to know about it. It might be about the apartment. *Yeah, now I'm even lying to myself.*

Colby: Sorry to bother you. Do you know what Hillary's freaking out about? I can't get a hold of her.

Chance: No. I'm out.

Is that 'I'm out' like, 'I don't want to be part of this' or 'I'm out' like 'I'm not home right now'? Should I bug him and ask? Either way, it doesn't sound like he can get involved right now. Then my phone buzzes again.

Chance: But she texted me. 'Come home RN'

Apparently, my sister does not spell out 'right now' for anyone.

I turn to Arnie with a grimace. "I have to go. Family emergency," I mutter. "Don't touch anything. Turn on this mic"—I point—"when he's ready to give his spiel and make sure to turn it off again when he's done. Think you can handle that?"

Arnie nods vigorously, beaming like he's just been called up to a major league team from the farm league.

"Seriously, don't touch anything. Except that." I point again. "I'll come back and shut it all down later. Here's my number if something goes wrong." I scribble it out on a green Post-It note, and he salutes me as he accepts it.

I grab my bag and quietly head out of the booth. Mrs. Parker is scowling at me, but I ignore her. I'm good at what I do; she's not going to fire me. And if some-thing's wrong with Hillary, I have to find out.

The bus won't be here for another 20 minutes, so I get a car. It isn't hard this close to downtown. The guy driving is cute, and he keeps trying to chat with me about politics, weather, anything, glancing at me with these big brown eyes in the rearview mirror. One-word answers fall out of my mouth by some miracle. I can't give him any more than that; not with my brain on fire with all the things that could be wrong with Hil. I can't even pre-tend to be interested in an attractive guy who's clearly hitting on me. *What's wrong with me?*

Chance. That's what. He's out tonight; I won't have to see him. Won't have to break my heart all over again, staring at his cheekbones and his kissable face and his light beard that screams he isn't trying to be stylish, just a forgetful academic who has such deep thoughts he can't remember to shave. But I'll still have to be in his space, inhaling his scent, sitting on the couch where we were together for the first time, seeing his posters on the walls...a painful trek down Memory Lane. And maybe the reason he's not there is that he's out with someone else, maybe someone who has their shit together.

I love Chance. I didn't mean to, but there it is.

The driver finally leaves me alone, and driving in the dark, crawling along the park blocks, I know I'll never find anyone else like Chance: his sharp-yet-distractible brain, his shy smiles, his delightful taste in movies, his teasing way in bed and out. I don't know if that means I can't love anyone else again, but I know it means something.

When I finally push through the lobby doors, the elevator is still on the twentieth floor. Cursing, I rush for the stairs and pant my way up fourteen fucking flights. Her apartment had better be flooding or on fire.

I let myself in, still out of breath from the stairs.

"Hil? You here?"

She jumps up from the couch, her face flushed and her eyes red. "There you are! What took you so long?"

"I was working. What's wrong?"

She launches herself into my arms. "Francis died."

I let a long breath out slowly and put my arms around her. "You called me away from work because of a dead fish?"

Still holding her, I feel my gaze drawn to the rest of the room. There he is, sitting on the couch, frozen mid-slurp over a bowl of noodles. He blew off whatever he was doing to help, too.

"Hi," I mouth, but before he can answer, Hillary pulls away, her face tear-stained and swollen.

"Francis was not just a fish!" She whacks my chest, and it actually really hurts. "I've had him for so long, he was practically a member of the family!" Hillary wipes her tears. "Do you know how many betta fish live for five years? Almost *none*. He's been with me since high school."

Ah, okay. So this isn't really about Francis; this is about Mom and Dad.

"I'm sorry," I say. "You're right. Francis was important to me, too. I'm sorry he's gone."

She releases a shaky sigh and squeezes me around my middle. "I forgive you. It must have been quite a shock for you."

"Yes, it was," I say as somberly as I can manage. "Had he been sick?"

"No," she moans. "It was completely out of the blue." Then her gaze sharpens. "You haven't been over in a long time, or you'd know he wasn't sick."

"Right," I say quickly, shoving my hands into the pockets of my jeans. "I've been busy."

She wipes her nose on her sleeve. "Was the date good?"

Chance's head snaps up, his gaze wounded, and I quickly shake my head just a little, a tiny signal meant just for him.

"I didn't go." I chew on my lip for a second, then admit, "I never had one planned, actually." He has to know that. I can't let Chance think I've moved on so quickly, that I just went about my life as if nothing had happened. Even if he's seeing someone new, he has to know I'm wrecked without him. It's not like we're getting back together, but I still want him to know what he means to me.

"You lied to me?" Hillary's voice is still thick with tears. "Why?"

"I was protecting someone."

"Who?" Behind her, Chance abandons his bowl on the coffee table as he moves almost silently toward his room...but Hillary hears him. "Freeze, you!"

Chance complies, then slowly turns back to her.

"Both of you sit down." She points to the couch insistently. I glance at Chance and shrug, then move to obey her. He moves toward the couch more slowly, sitting as far on the opposite end as he can.

"You have both been acting weird and avoiding me, and I want to know why." Hillary flips her hair over her shoulder and crosses her arms tight across her stomach. Her sniffle is so pathetic and hurt, I open my mouth out of sheer sympathy before realizing I don't know what to say exactly.

"I'm not avoiding you," I say gently, leaning forward to rest my elbows on my knees.

"You never picked up your coat," she accuses. "It's still in Chance's room. I saw it there yesterday when I went to borrow a stapler. On his *bed* of all places."

Oh Lord. I don't look at Chance, but I'm sure his face is bright red.

She whirls to face him. "And you. I hear you crying in the shower—these walls are ridiculously thin. What's going on?"

He clears his throat. "Nothing. I'm fine."

Hillary pivots back to me, fire in her gaze. "And you—being so weird all through that dinner and then ghosting us immediately after. Are you going to lie to me, too? Are you *fine*?" She snarls the word, and I flinch. I wish I could tell Chance there's more going on here than it seems, but I don't want to embarrass her.

"No. I'm not fine. But I've just been busy. It's not about you. Not at all."

Chance snorts, and I finally give in and turn toward him.

"It's a little about her," he mutters. "Or a lot."

"Somebody start talking!" Hillary screeches, and I wince at her volume.

"Look, Hil," I cajole, "can we talk about this later? When you're not so upset about Francis?"

"No! I can't even get you two in the same room lately." She pushes back her shoulders. "I want answers. You two seemed like you were getting along so well, and now...this. What is going on, and how is it about me?"

"It's not," I start to protest again...but then I sigh. "Okay. So." I hesitate, wiping a hand down my face, desperately trying to figure out a way out of this without lying.

"Colby." It's a warning. My big sister's patience is expiring.

"Okay, okay. So I didn't keep my word."

"About what?"

"About staying away from Chance." I let my hands drop and hold them out, a gesture of helplessness. "But I made it right. I broke up with him. I'm sorry I didn't talk to you about it earlier; I was going to, but I just...didn't want you to know that I'd broken your rule." I hold my breath as I watch her take in this news. But she just stares hard at me.

"To be fair, I started it," Chance mutters, but she holds up a flat 'stop' hand and ignores him. My heart pangs that he's trying to help me even after all I've put him through.

"Go on," she prompts me sternly. "How long were you together?"

Now is not the time to split hairs about what *together* means, so I figure I'll just count from the pink sweatshirt day.

"About three months."

Her eyes go to the ceiling like she's trying to do math in her head. "So...March."

"Yeah. But to be honest, I wanted him way before that. I held out as long as I could, Hil. I really tried."

She holds up that firm hand again, indicating she wants silence.

"So what I'm hearing is that these past few months, when I've noticed the two of you were happier than you've ever been, it was because you were sneaking around together behind my back?"

"Yeah," I croak, glancing at Chance to see how he's taking this. He's shamefaced, but he nods his agreement. I catch his gaze, and for some reason, he doesn't look away. I want to touch him so bad, to reassure him. Conversations like this are not good for his anxiety.

"Hil..."

She holds up her hand again. "Shut up, Colby." She turns back to Chance. "That's why you had his coat in your bed. And that's why you've been crying and barely eaten and ditched work. Because he broke your heart."

Now that I look at him, I can tell he's lost weight. That's not good. I feel horrible all over again.

"Yes," Chance whispers, looking at his bowl on the coffee table.

"And that's why you didn't come by. Because you didn't want to see him."

"I did want to see him," I say softly. "I...love him." I pause, as if to see if the words feel right. And they do. "Yes, I'm in love with him. But he didn't want to see me."

Her face is still hard, but the way she looks at me, I can tell she's softening a little. Maybe I'm not completely fucked.

"And you?" she says to Chance. "Were you in love with him, too?"

His gaze meets mine, and it's like all that resonance, all that understanding is still there, waiting for us. He nods slowly, and I can't help my half smile.

"And you both thought," Hillary goes on, "that it would be better to try to lie to me than to just come clean and tell me you were in love. That I wouldn't care about you enough to realize that this is something special, something worth breaking my rule for."

I don't know what to say. Chance talks a lot in his work about 'expected outcomes,' and this isn't a scenario I planned for. Pissed because I lied to her? Yeah. But pissed because I didn't think she'd understand? Nope.

"You are both fools, and I am officially mad at you." Hillary storms over to the coat rack and snatches her purse off it so hard, the whole thing tips over with a crash. "I am leaving now so you two can talk things over and make up. I do not want details when I come back." She opens the front door. "I could've been squeeing over your love all this time. How dare you? One of you *will* ask me to be the best bitch at your wedding. I hate you both." Hillary slams the door. The silence in the room feels oppressive.

"I can't believe you told her," Chance says. He still hasn't moved.

"Yeah, well. I was tired of lying." I fiddle with a loose thread on my jeans. "Were you really that upset?"

"Of course I was. Weren't you?"

I nod, and my chin is doing that wonky thing I hate right before I cry. "Miserable. Absolutely miserable." I hazard a glance at him and see the tears pooling in his eyes. "Oh, baby. C'mere." I open my arms, but Chance shakes his head.

"You don't get to just stroll back in here and pretend like all is forgiven."

I rub the back of my neck; shame and regret burn inside me, looking for a way out. "I know that. I do. I just want to help if you're hurting. I hate seeing you cry. Especially because of me."

"You chose her. You chose her over me." His hands are balled, his voice tight. But I have no pride left. I get to my knees in front of him, putting my hands tentatively on his thighs to see if he'll push me away...but he doesn't.

"I did. You're right. But you have to understand, she told me when she first moved in to stay away from you. She's all I have here for family." Now my eyes are welling. *Damn it.* "It was important that I respect her. But I fell in love with you, and I got scared that I'd lose you both, and I ended up hurting you, and I'm sorry for that. I'm so fucking sorry, Chance."

I should get out of here. I should leave him alone.

I already have one foot on the floor, about to press up and away, ready to flee this awkward, painful situation, when I feel his hand on mine.

"You did hurt me. And I tried to stop loving you. But..."

My heart lurches forward in my chest, like it's trying to get to him on its own.

"But you failed?" My knee is starting to hurt, but I'll stay here all damn night if he wants me to.

"Yes, I fucking failed. Because of all the reasons you could give to abandon me, I did actually understand that one." He takes my scruffy chin in one hand possessively, and I feel my face flush. "Do I still think you should've put on your big boy pants and told her from the start? Yeah, I do. But I also know Hillary, and I know that wouldn't have gone over well. We would've been over before we started."

"I told myself I had to know we were worth fighting for first," I murmur, trying to get closer to him. "But then I still didn't. I should've. I will now, if you let me." I rub the muscles of his thighs in a way I hope is sexy.

His hand drops away, and his gaze narrows, and I suddenly feel very out of my depth. "All right."

"All right?" My heart is pounding in my ears. Am I hearing him correctly?

"Yes," he says, nodding slowly. "I'll let you fight for me."

Relief courses through me, and my blood feels more like light than liquid. "Thank you." I pick up his hand and kiss the back of it. "You won't regret this."

Chance smirks a little, shaking his head. "No, but you might."

I might?

"How long do you think she'll be gone?" I ask.

He raises an eyebrow. "You want the first thing she sees when she walks back in is us boning on her couch? I don't think so."

I shrug with a smile. "Technically, it's your couch..."

Chance puts a finger over my lips. "You're not getting in my pants until I see some serious groveling. Get planning."

I blink. "Seriously?"

He leans closer. "Do I look like I'm joking?" He does not. His blue eyes are steely and serious, his cheeks smooth. His lips aren't even twitching with a smile.

"Okay," I say, sitting back on my heels. "Thank you, Chance." I look around the living room. Groveling. I can grovel. I know all his favorite stuff. I can do this. I'll be back in his good graces in no time. "What if I just get you off?"

He laughs. This is a good start. No, this is a good restart. He's gifted me a bonus life, and I'm not going to screw it up this time.

CHAPTER TWENTY

WHEN CHANCE GOES TO bed, too exhausted to stay up, I call Arnie and ask him to clean up and settle in to wait. I wait as long as I can at the apartment, but Hillary doesn't come home. Finally, around 11:30, I text her.

> **Colby:** Can we talk?
> **Hillary:** not ready
> **Colby:** I'm really sorry I lied to you.
> **Hillary:** ok
> **Hillary:** you two get back together?

I hesitate for a minute. Because it seems like she was mad she didn't get to participate, not that I actually lied to her. Maybe it's both and she just hasn't articulated that; she left in a bit of a huff. But I was determined not to lie to her anymore.

> **Colby:** Yes. Please don't be mad.
> **Hillary:** Mad you're together? No. Mad you lied to me? HELLS YES.

Hmm. That isn't great. But maybe if I give her a few days to cool off...

> **Hillary:** I hope you sit on a tack, Colby Christopher Cook. And I hope it hits you right in the nuts. That's how mad I am.

Or maybe not.

Colby: I'm sorry, Hil.

Hillary: I hope you're walking down Couch and one of those dogwalkers trips you with a million dog leashes.

Hillary: I hope you get five hundred papercuts. I hope you hit your funny bone on every door jamb from now till Christmas. I hope you rub your eyes after you've been cutting up a jalapeño.

Colby: That's intense.

Hillary: Now you're getting it. Fuck off, Colby.

So. Time to cool off is probably the wisest choice...but I've never been a patient person. I track her down a few days later.

"Chance thought I'd find you here." I stop next to Hillary's study carrel in the RCU library.

"And the betrayal continues," she mutters, not looking up from her reference material. She scribbles something unintelligible into her notes, continuing to ignore me.

"Hey, Chance didn't betray you. Don't blame him for this."

"I think I will," she says, pushing away from the desk. "After all, according to him, he's the one that started it."

I grimace. "He shouldn't have said that. It's not his fault. I mean, I could've said no. I'm capable of that. And I'm the one who promised you, not him."

Hillary glares up at me. "You're not defending yourself."

I put my hands in my pockets. "Nope. There's no excuse for lying to you."

She leans back in the padded chair, still shooting daggers.

"Brought you a peace offering." I pull the piece of paper out of my back pocket and hand it to her. She's somehow still glaring at me as she opens it.

"Ground Kontrol gift certificate?"

I nod. "And I convinced Blake to come back to town. We'll all go together. I'm sorry I blew you off last time."

"I knew it!" she whisper-yells. "I knew there had to be another reason you'd bag on Ground Kontrol." Her expression turns sour. "You didn't do it on the couch, did you?"

No lying. No lying. *Fuck.*

"Yes. But I promise no bodily fluids were spilled."

Hillary whacks me in the stomach, and I angle away from her blows.

"Gross. Disgusting. Repulsive."

"Just the first time. After that, only in his room. Ow!" *And that one time in the shower.*

"You're gonna buy me a new couch."

"It's technically Chance's couch..." The death glare is back, and I hold up my hands. "Okay. Whatever you want. If that's the penance you require, that's fine."

"Penance?" she asks, and I can see a smile trying hard to break through. "Chance uses that word."

"Yes. Sadly, he's teaching me the meaning of it."

Hillary betrays herself with a tiny smile then. "Good. He deserves to have someone at his beck and call."

"I know he does. I spend a lot of time with him." I swallow, embarrassed for some reason. "And I really am in love with him."

"I know." She fiddles with the paper in her hand, rolling the edges. "And I'm happy for you. I just wish you'd been honest with me."

I glance around the quiet room, wishing there was a way out of this question, but I need to ask it.

"Would you have listened?"

"Probably not," she admits with a sigh. "But I wish you had anyway."

"Fair enough." I pull out my phone. "So this 'new' couch can be used, right? Because that's all the budget I've got..."

"Save your money for dates with Chance," she mutters, turning back to the desk. "You've got a lot of lost time to make up for."

"Groveling is expensive," I agree. "Hug before I go?"

"Next time," she says, pulling her books toward her. "Love you, Col."

"Love you, too," I say, slowly turning to leave. I'm only ten steps away when she catches up with me, bear hugging me from behind.

CHAPTER TWENTY-ONE

"HOW DOES THAT FEEL?"

He grunts contentedly. I've gotten really good at backrubs over the last two weeks, and he's been lifting heavy, so he wants them basically every day. Is dragging my hands over his bare skin a unique form of torture? Yes. And he seems to like it that way. I even got massage oil, which as it turns out, is great for jacking off when the massage is done. Because he's certainly had no mercy on me. Sadist.

Even now, straddling his ass on his bed, I wish I could just lean over and kiss his strong neck. But he shut me down quick when I tried that the first time I gave him a massage. Kicked me out of his room and sent me home with my proverbial tail between my legs...though honestly, my cock had been nowhere near my legs, if you get my drift. So even though I feel like I'm going to die from lack of boning, I've kept my lips to myself since then with the exception of some chaste goodbye kisses when I leave. Hillary always grins so big when we do that.

I press my elbow carefully along the inside of his shoulder blade. "How's that? More pressure?" I learned that move on YouTube, and it's a winner.

"No, it's good," he mutters, his eyes still closed. I dig my thumbs into the top of his shoulders, dragging them outward.

"That one knot just doesn't want to move," I complain, focusing on that shoulder blade again. In fact, I'm so focused on it that I'm confused when he flips over.

"Go close the door."

I stare at him, not daring to hope I'm interpreting him correctly. "On which side of it?"

Chance's face immediately falls. "I think I've been too hard on you." He pulls me down to his chest and I lay there, laughing a little.

"I'm just trying to be considerate," I say, trying to sit up, but he doesn't let go.

"But you've cooked all my dinners and given me massages and taken out the trash. You even did my laundry."

"I did do your laundry, and it was far less disgusting than mine." I pry myself away from him, but he still looks guilty. "If I close the door, will you show me how much you appreciate my groveling?"

Chance nods. "We have to be quiet, though."

I peek out into the living room. Hillary has her headphones on. I swear she somehow knows what we're up to, because she hardly ever wears them.

"It'll be fine." I close the door quietly nonetheless.

I can't even play it cool. I dive onto the bed and land on him with a thud, and Chance exhales hard.

"Horny much?"

"So horny," I whisper, gleefully abandoning all pride. "Need you so fucking much."

Chance gives me that cocky grin, the one I love, the one that tells me he knows how important he is to me. "I missed this—missed us."

I kiss him hard. The molten heat of his mouth has me squeezing my own erection, trying to calm it down. I break the kiss and look down at it.

"Are you seriously going to embarrass me like this?"

"Colby, are you talking to your cock?" Chance sounds like he's holding back laughter.

I ignore him. "Yes, I know he's handsome and amazing and sweet...even if he has been enjoying denying us a little too much." Something soft whacks the side of my head—his pillow, I assume—but I'm not going to be distracted. This is important, damn it. "You're acting like no one's touched us in a year, not a month."

Chance shoves me backwards, pinning me on my back. "So you go off early *and* you can only come once? Hate to say it, but being cisgender sounds like a scam."

I laugh sarcastically, but he shuts me up when he starts sucking on my neck with the perfect amount of pressure, lowering his warm body to mine. But I recover quickly.

"Fuck yes. Give it to me, babe. Do whatever you want."

"I was planning on it," he murmurs, "but it's nice to know I have your full consent." And that smug amusement in his voice hits me right in the chest. *I did that. I put a smile on my favorite face.*

I push against his hands on my wrists, but it has no effect. He just tsks at me, teasing, his blue eyes sparkling.

He really is getting ripped, but I know he wouldn't hurt me. He'd scramble off the minute I asked.

His face loses some of the teasing but not the warmth, and as he lowers his face to mine, I feel my breath catch. I've stared into his eyes plenty of times, but there's something different about them now. I see the future when I look at him: I see us shoulder to shoulder, back to back, supporting each other through life, crying over Hillary's babies together. Maybe our own babies. Fixing shit around the house. Arguing over how our society is inevitably going to decay and the right way to grill a steak. Unplugging the robot regularly.

"Move in with me. Please."

He lifts his head, and his lips are shiny and red, his eyes hazy. "What about Hillary?"

"She's not invited."

"You know what I mean."

He's right. I'm probably getting carried away. As usual, I'm ten steps ahead of myself. "Fuck me now, and we'll talk about it later. Deal?"

He nods. "Later." But he releases my wrists to cradle my head as he kisses me deeply, like he's drinking me in, savoring me. I try to catch my brain long enough to stop its spinning, but every kiss, every touch, amps me up more until he has me writhing under him, holding him as close as I can, rocking my hips desperately, and I haven't even taken off my pants yet.

"Please, Chance. I need you."

"Glad you haven't forgotten your manners while we've been apart."

"Fuck you."

"Spoke too soon…" He's reaching for the lube, but I can't stop kissing him. I can't stop trying to show him how much I missed him and love him and want him. That I know I screwed up and will make it up to him however he wants.

"Here," I say. "I can do it." His narrowed eyes tell me I've made a mistake, and I hurry to take off my pants.

"Why?"

I swallow and shrug one shoulder. *Because I'm sorry. Because I don't want to risk pissing you off again. Because I can't lose you.*

"Colby." His stern tone is turning me on and stressing me out at the same time. My cock doesn't know what to do, and my heart is flailing around in my chest, going vivace, vivacissimo, allegrissimo, faster and faster.

"Never mind."

"No. Look at me." He gentles his tone, but he sits still until I obey, slowly raising my eyes to meet his hard gaze. "I like caressing you; I like stroking you. I like pushing my fingers inside of you until you're ready to take my cock. I like every part of having sex with you, because I love you. So you're not going to act like it's a burden. Got it?"

"Got it," I mutter, but I want to turn my face away again. He doesn't let me. Chance kisses me so tenderly, so sweetly that my heart finally stops doing its trapped butterfly impression and settles down to a regular tempo. Then the cold lube touches my ass and I gasp a little into his mouth. Chance chuckles.

"Serves you right."

"Does not."

"Does too," he whispers, running one finger around my rim. "I'm not going to make you warm yourself up, underthinker. You know me better than that."

"Yeah," I breathe, finally letting myself relax. "I do." And when he picks out the biggest dildo in the drawer, I totally saw it coming.

CHAPTER TWENTY-TWO

IT'S THE EIGHT-MONTH anniversary of us getting back together after I fucked everything up, and I paid all my roommates to get lost so we could actually celebrate however we want to. Well, I offered to pay them, but they like Chance, so they did it for free. They like him better than me, I know it.

After some very satisfying making out on the couch, I lay on his bare chest, watching TV, his fingers playing in my hair.

"This is nice," I murmur, half-asleep, and Chance grunts his agreement. "We don't get enough *just us* time."

"Yeah." Chance presses a kiss to the top of my head. "I'll second that motion."

"You'll what?"

"Never mind. I agree. Perfect way to spend an anniversary. Which reminds me, I got you something."

I sit up. "You did?" I fucking love presents. It says so much about him that he knows that. It's about the size of a pizza box, but it's heavier than I expected, and I shake it a little. "Jewelry?" I snark.

"Better." He has a devilish look on his face, and it has me a little scared. This smacks of a trap.

I pull out my knife and delicately cut down the tape of the cardboard box. "Not good enough to wrap, though."

"You don't need wrap. You don't appreciate wrap."

I grin as I pop the ends of the box and pull out the contents. I'm holding a large black disc with a power button in the middle. I recoil when I realize what it is.

"Oh, no."

"Listen," he says, putting a hand on my arm as if to calm me down. Which is not fucking necessary, because there's no way in hell I'm letting this fucking robot into my goddamn house. "It doesn't listen. It doesn't make product recommendations. It just uses its beautiful algorithm to clean under your couch. And if I'm moving in, you're going to have to work on that aspect of your housekeeping routine."

"I don't have a routine," I mutter as I open the instruction manual. "I just clean whatever's dirty."

"As I said. We'll work on it."

His words finally register past my anxiety.

"Wait...you'll do it? You'll move in?"

"We have to get Hillary squared away first. I'm not leaving her in the lurch."

I've mostly stopped listening and am pulling him toward the stairs up to my room. "We'll find her a new roommate. Maybe even a better roommate."

He snorts. "Not possible. I'm an amazing roommate."

"You're an even more amazing boyfriend. Even if you are allied with my future oppressors." I pause. The more I think about it, the more this seems like Chance is losing out. "You're really okay to live here with all these guys?"

Chance shrugs one shoulder. "It's where you live. I want to be where you are. And I can't imagine Hillary's going to be comfortable listening to us bone through the wall all the time."

My brain's still spinning, forming a plan...Chance's genius brain requires quiet and space and order. This house is anything but.

I pull out my phone. 7:00 in Portland means... *Yeah, I can call them now.* "I might have a solution. Can you hang out for a minute?"

He sits back down on the couch. "Sure."

I call my mom. She'll be the most understanding. Probably.

"Colby!" She answers with a smile. "This is a nice surprise."

"Oh. Yeah, hi. Hey, I need a favor. A kind of big one."

"Oh? What kind of favor?"

"A housing favor."

My dad appears next to her. "We're already letting you and your friends live in our house for the cost of the mortgage and upkeep. What more do you need, exactly?"

"Um." That's the moment when I realize I really should've written out a speech or an outline or something. "I want to live with Chance. In private. So could we live in your guest house? And when you come to visit, we could like, take the master in the house or something? Or I could pay for a hotel room?"

My mother's smile was warm. "I think we can work that out."

"You're giving away my guest house?" my father grumbles, and my mother shushes him.

"I have one condition, though," my mom goes on. "Will you and Chance come visit us? We'd love more time with both of you."

I glance at him over the top of the screen, and he's nervously chewing on his thumbnail, his arms tucked tight into his body. *My sweet, dominant, anxious love.*

"We can probably do that, yes. That'll be good. Let me talk to him and find a time that works." Watching the relief wash through him when he realizes I'm not going to put him on the spot makes me smile.

"Wonderful. We'll talk to you soon, darling."

"Sandy," my father starts to complain, but the video ends. Chance and I look at each other and burst out laughing.

"Is this okay?" I ask, gathering him into my arms. "I thought it was a good solution."

"Yes." He kisses me. "I think it's an excellent solution. And when it feels too claustrophobic for you, you can go be social in the big house."

"And when the big house is too much, you can go be in the guest house."

"It's perfect. Just like you."

I snort-laugh. "Not perfect. Not by a long shot."

"Well, perfect for me, anyway," he says, stroking my cheek. "My resonance. My matching wave."

I lean into his touch and sigh. "Yeah, mine too, nerd. Mine too."

HIGH STRUNG

CHAPTER ONE

"Failed?"

I stare at the screen. I blink. I hit refresh. *This is impossible.*

"What?" Janey looks up from her phone as we stand in my kitchen. We celebrated being done with this semester by taking a brisk walk around the city. The urge to check my grades hit me just now, I don't know why.

"I...failed. I failed our pottery class."

"Oh, honey." She wraps her arms around my shoulders. "I'm so sorry."

"But...but...how?" I splutter, still staring at the screen. "It was a basic pottery class! It wasn't even three-hundred level!" I let my head rest against hers. "Did you pass it?"

"Yeah," she says a bit sheepishly. "I got a B."

"Damn it." I want to cry. I have not cried about school since I was in third grade and I forgot my diorama of the St. Johns Bridge at home on the day it was due. Do you remember dioramas? Weren't they great? I wish I could diorama my way out of this situation, but it doesn't seem likely.

"Could you reach out to Mx. Rasmussen?"

"Maybe." I hadn't paid them all that much attention, to be honest. Tall. Beard. Liked to wear skirts. That's pretty much all I can tell you about them. I give Janey's arms a squeeze, and she takes the hint and lets me go so I can pace.

"Whatever. I'm going to go talk to them. Maybe I can do a summer thing. I might be able to redo something.

Janey scrunches her nose. "Are they going to be there?"

I'm already putting my shoes back on and looking for my keys. "Teachers don't finish until the 21st."

"It's the 23rd."

"Is it?" I look at my phone. She's right. *Damn it.* "All right, well, I'll email them."

"Calling would be faster. I think their number was on the syllabus."

"Their home number?" It doesn't really matter; I never really looked at the syllabus and didn't know where to find it now. This class was supposed to be easy; get in, get my required arts credit for my liberal studies degree, and get out. I've still got a French minor and a women's studies certificate to finish.

"You know what? I bet my brother has it. I think they know each other from the symphony. Is that invasive? Never mind, don't answer that—plausible deniability. This is a crisis." I text my brother.

Hillary: Yo baby bro.
Colby: Not a baby. What's up?
Hillary: Got myself into kind of a sitch.
Need your friend Glenn's number.
Colby: What kind of...sitch? Can I help?

I snicker because I know he hated using that word. He hates the way I talk. Which is partly why I talk that way, but not entirely. I'm not a monster.

Hillary: I think they were my professor at RCU for my pottery class. Gonna need to re-take that thing.

Colby: You should go through official chan-nels if it's a school complaint.

Hillary: PLLEEEAASSSSEEE? It was Janey's idea!

Colby: Don't see why that matters...

Hillary: PLEASE, I will owe you a million beers. NO, you have already STOLEN a mil-lion beers from my fridge. YOU OWE ME for the million beers I paid for that you drank!

I'm on edge waiting for his response. I have other ways to accomplish this, so I probably shouldn't have in-volved him. But my brother usually comes to my rescue in situations like this, and I'd like to think I can depend on him.

Colby: No.
Hillary: Why do you make my life difficult

It's a joke. Colby is my hero, and not only because he's one of the few people I know who'll drop everything to help me. He even left work a few months ago when my fish died. Best brother ever.

> **Colby:** From where I sit, you're doing a fine
> job of that yourself...
> **Hillary:** THE WORST.

I don't know if that last line is regarding him or me, but I let it stand. I don't have time to correct misapprehensions. This is an academic emergency. I open my computer up.

"I take it he wouldn't give it to you?" Janey has helped herself to a glass of ice water while I was distracted and is making herself comfortable on my couch, as she should. I don't want her to go downstairs to her apartment yet, anyway; she'd just be able to hear me freaking out through the floor.

"No." I sigh. The initial shock is giving way to something else, a deeper fear I don't want to name. I carry my laptop over to sit next to her and pull up my school email. "Help me craft something to get myself out of this mess, will you?" After a few minutes, we have what I'd consider a decent draft.

Dear Mx. Rasmussen,

I am contacting you to find out if there is any possibility of retaking Ceramics 250. (Not even a three-hundred level. Sob. How did I let this happen?) *I need a passing grade in order to graduate next year, and it would be wonderful if I could get this out of the way over the summer. I would be very interested in any extra credit opportunities as well if my current grade is not final.*

Thank you,

Hillary Cook

I make both of us a strawberry smoothie, because we passed a lady on the street with one during our walk and it looked so amazing, I can't stop thinking about it despite my Crisis Brain™. Before I'm even done, my computer dings with a reply.

Dear Ms. Cook,

I have looked at your assignment record for this class, and it seems you had several assignments that were not completed. This has negatively affected your overall score. (You think? Geez, I'm not a total noob.) *Unfortunately, the grade you earned is final and has been recorded by the university. If you had come to me earlier, there's more I could've done for you. But as it is, this grade is unalterable.* (Snort. Who talks like that? Unalterable? You are.)

There is one seat left in my summer course, but it's Ceramics 321, and if you struggled with the 250 level, I can't see you being successful in a higher class. (Oh? Watch me, punk. I've got nothing better to do.) *There's considerably more history material, as well as advanced throwing techniques and hand building.* (Blah blah blah, send me the link, buster. I've got this.) *Therefore, I don't think it's a reasonable solution. Your best option is to retake the 250 class with Ms. Ketchum in the fall.*

Sincerely,

Glenn Rasmussen

No. Oh, no. Our conversation is NOT over.

Dear Mx. Rasmussen,

I understand it will be a challenge, but I will put in whatever effort it takes to get this done. Since I am taking a lighter load over the summer, I'll have more energy and brainpower available to tackle the curriculum with complete focus. I would ask you to please reconsider allowing me to take part in the summer class.

Sincerely,

Hillary Cook

There is a longer delay this time, during which I chew on my stubby thumbnail, shake the couch with my bouncing leg, and try to watch an old 30Rock episode. The one where Tracy goes to hide in Kenneth's hometown is one of my favorites. Do you know it? Great, right? Of course it is. When the response finally comes, my heart sinks.

Dear Ms. Cook,
I'm sorry, but my decision stands.
Mx. Rasmussen

Well. That's non-optimal. Very non-optimal. Over the summer, I would've had more time. Now I'm going to have to cram retaking it into an already-full schedule. At least it sounds like I'll have a different instructor...this one is kind of a jerk. I mean, could they be any more condescending? Yes, I could've put more effort into their class, *obviously*, but that doesn't mean I couldn't have passed the higher class. I know I could've. I did honors in high school, and I've got most of a college degree in several subjects, for heaven's sake.

"They said no, huh?" Janey's gaze is sympathetic. When I just nod, she leans over and gives me an enormous hug. That's the last straw.

"How could I have failed?" I blubber. "I mean, I'm no Picasso, but I can do simple art. I'm a creative person."

"Picasso was painting."

"Whatever!" I say, trying to flail my arms emphatically, even though she's holding me. "It's fucking liberal studies. I only needed it for my fine arts credit; I need to know what art is, not how to make it! And I'm sure I totally learned all the history. I nailed every test!"

Janey rubs my back soothingly, and I tip over onto her shoulder. I give a shaky sigh. "This sucks. They suck. Glenn Rasmussen better not come down with anything I can cure—that's all I can say."

"You're not a doctor, sweetie."

"I could be. Maybe I'll get my doctorate next."

Her big blue eyes widen comically behind her glasses. "You really want more school after six years of this?"

"I don't think medical school is for me, anyway. I'd probably lose my keys in somebody's chest cavity."

"Oh, yeah. Let's not, then." She gives me a big squeeze, then kisses the top of my head, which actually makes me cry a little harder. "Ice cream?"

"No, I think I'm just going to veg out and try to forget this day happened."

"Fair enough. I'll text you tonight and check on you, okay?" Janey quietly heads out, and I go back to the show, but my mind is elsewhere.

Three months. I'll fix this in three months when the fall quarter starts. I can hang on until then.

CHAPTER TWO

THREE MONTHS LATER

Someone is already going over the syllabus when I slip into the ceramics studio. It smells earthy and sweet in the room, and I sneak toward a long table in the back.

"You will need to purchase your textbooks as soon as poss...ible." That little pause. It happens at the same moment that I turn and see who my instructor is. Not Ms. Ketchum, *as they promised me.* Instead, it's none other than the person at the top of my shit list: Glenn Rasmussen. They're wearing a long mustard yellow cardigan over a gray T-shirt that says 'clay rocks' and a knee-length, black A-line skirt with tall black boots. I like those boots. I almost got them when I saw them at the trendy thrift store near my house, but they were too big for me. *Do they live in my neighborhood?*

I sit down quickly and get out my computer so I can record the class. Someone passes me a syllabus, and I give them a tight smile. Maybe they're filling in for Ms. Ketchum. Maybe she's sick today, and they're being a nice person. Maybe...but all the maybe's I'm clinging to with so much hope fall apart when I see the top of the page: *Mx. Rasmussen, Instructor.*

Great. It's not fair to say that I've been harboring a grudge against this person. Harboring sounds passive, whereas I have taken an active dislike to this individual. I have nursed this grudge, fertilized and cared for it, nurturing it from a tiny sprig poking out of the soil of my soul into the now-proud shrub which I water daily. I pour into it my hopes of graduating on time. If they had let me take this class over the summer, I'd be done by now. But instead, I had to delay my internship—the internship I worked for months to angle my way into—until the spring quarter, when I am already taking a full course load.

I won't say Glenn Rasmussen ruined my life—that's not true. I have lots of other things going for me. But they are definitely the last person I want to see right now, and based on the flat look they give me, they forgot I would be here and aren't any happier about it than I am.

I hit record, but I am already not looking forward to listening to this person's voice in my ears. Their voice is kind of raspy, low and rumbly. They're so quiet, I can hardly hear them from the back, and I wonder if the microphone is even picking this up.

"You will have three primary projects: a handbuild, a thrown vase, and a set of tiles that you decorate to demonstrate your skill with slips and glazes." That's not news to me; since I failed, I kept my projects from last quarter. I should hardly have to be here at all except for tests and quizzes. Which is nice because then I won't have to look at their pleasant, beardy face, gray hairs springing up like weeds in a field of mousy brown. How old are they, anyway?

Never mind. Doesn't matter. Irrelevant.

I check my email, flesh out some notes from my first class, and check the schedule to make sure I'm in the right place and that Ms. Ketchum doesn't have another section I could try. She doesn't. She's on my shit list now, too. At the end of class, as everyone is packing up, I hear their heavy boots coming up the aisle between the paint-spattered tables.

"May I speak with you for a moment?"

I glance up at them hesitantly. "Sure. But I have another class after this."

They nod, tugging at one sleeve of their cardigan. "I wanted to apologize; I gave you the impression that Ms. Ketchum would teach this class. But it turns out she required more maternity leave than previously anticipated. So I'll be your instructor again."

So maybe putting her on my shit list was a bit hasty; sometimes, I jump to conclusions like hopscotch, bouncing right past whatever logic has been tossed out in front of me and whatever reservations most people have in their brains against judging others. My temper goes zero to sixty, and I hate it.

"That's fine."

They don't leave. I stare up at them.

"Was there something else?"

They purse their lips. "No, Ms. Cook. That's all." They've turned to go when I come up with something to say.

"At least I can still use the same projects as last time."

Glenn pauses ominously. I do not like it. I want them to keep walking. I want them to walk right back up to the front of the classroom and talk to the students lined up there, waiting for them. But they do not.

Mx. Rasmussen turns back to me slowly. "You have to create new projects."

"Why?"

Their eyebrows snap together. This was apparently not the reaction they were expecting. "Because this is a new quarter. I expect fresh work. Better work than you gave me last year."

Now I'm the one scowling. "What was wrong with my work last quarter? I got passing grades on everything I turned in."

"You must do fresh work," they repeat insistently. "I will not grade anything you haven't done this quarter. And if you think I won't remember, you're wrong."

Anger rises inside me, looking for a way out. I want to tell them that's the most asinine thing I've ever heard. I'm the same student, doing the same assignments. Why the hell would I do them over again? But I clamp my lips shut and force a bland smile. After a moment, I'm collected enough to form civil words.

"Good to know. Have a nice day, professor." I turn my attention back to gathering my things. Of all the idiotic, patronizing...I have it in mind to go to the department head, but she'd probably be on their side. Academics tend to stick together. I'm fuming, muttering, shoving my stuff into my bag when I notice they're still there. *Oh, fuck. Did I make them mad? Did I say that out loud?*

"I'm available to help throughout most of the day when I'm not in classes. Please feel free to come into the studio if you need extra time to work on things." Their voice is metered, careful. Almost like they're the one worried that *I'm* upset. Which is weird because hardly anyone ever cares if I'm upset. It happens too often for that.

"Okay." I rise, slinging my bag across my body. "See you tomorrow."

"Thursday."

"Right, Thursday."

"Wait."

They charge back up the aisle, and I have this itchy feeling inside that just makes me want to leave. They snag a white index card off their desk and scribble something onto it. The scribbles are taking a while, and it makes me feel worse because I have no idea what this is about. Is this some kind of extra homework? Are they assigning me a tutor? Writing a recipe for browned butter banana bread? (Actually, I have one of those, and it's amazing.)

Then they hurry back to me, holding it out. The next class is filing in, and I need to get to mine, too, so I just take it with a forced smile and shove it into my bag.

"Thanks. Thursday."

"Thursday," they agree with a nod, then they turn to attend to the next class.

It's not until I get home that I remember the card and dig around in the front pocket of my bag until I find it, along with several pens with no cap, some change, a hair tie, and a box of matches for a restaurant called Jimmy's, which I don't remember going to. At the top, it says "BEFORE THURSDAY" in big box letters. Then there is a short list:

[ ] obtain keycard from art department for after-hours access to the studio

[ ] purchase textbook if not retained from previous class

[ ] read syllabus

"Bold of them to assume that I'm organized enough to get rid of old textbooks," I mutter, putting the card on my fridge. Or rather, I put it there once I take down an expired pizza coupon, a reminder to call my brother from ten days ago, and a bill I was supposed to mail three days ago that is now overdue. I would be offended that they don't think I can make this list myself, except it would've taken me longer than I care to admit to suss out all this information from the syllabus. Even though I took this class last quarter, I don't think I ever went and got that badge, and it would've been helpful.

The question is why they're trying to be helpful.

I stare at the jumble of papers on the fridge, and there's never been a better representation of the inside of my head: random facts and dates and information held together loosely by physical laws of attraction.

I really need to get my shit together.

CHAPTER THREE

I MANAGE TO GET TWO out of my three notecard assignments done before Thursday, and I feel pretty good about that. Maybe this time will be different from last semester...although I don't really know what went wrong there. No, I didn't turn in all my assignments, but I tried. Mx. Rasmussen's words ring in my head about better work, so I take a notepad up with me when they demo a simple plate technique on the wheel. But do I remember a pencil? A pen? Any kind of writing implement? No. So I just stand there and hug the useless thing to my chest as I watch.

"This is B-Mix Cone 5/6 clay," they say as they slam the lump firmly in the center of the wheel, their gaze lowered as we all crowd around. "It's a good one to try for this kind of project, because it's got a nice smooth texture. The color is neutral, so it's fun to try different finishes on it." They have no trouble getting it centered, and the clay looks almost fluid under their touch. It's frankly mesmerizing, and I'm remembering why I failed this class before. They raise it into a cone, still talking, getting more slip, rubbing a thumb over the spinning lump almost affectionately.

"Ceramics isn't about perfection, it's about practice. You do it over and over, and your body learns the pressure it needs to apply." They're still not looking at any of us, and I wonder for a fleeting moment if they're actually shy. Because if memory serves, my nemesis never looks up while they're demonstrating things.

Whatever. Being relatable isn't being likeable. I needed into that class. I hate this kind of pressure. In my fidgeting to see better, I bump into the woman next to me and whisper an apology.

"It's okay," she whispers back, touching her hijab. I recognize her as my tablemate from Tuesday.

"Sorry, did I...?"

"No, no. It's fine."

"Ms. Cook has some experience with clay," our instructor says, as if they're just making conversation. "So feel free to call upon her if you're struggling. She did some lovely work last semester."

Ugh, what? Didn't they basically imply that my work last semester was crap *when they said it had to improve?* I give the students look at me a flat smile to hide my dual dismay at their unwanted praise and the insinuation that I am some sort of expert, ready to help.

While I wasn't paying attention, Mx. Rasmussen flattened the plate, and I missed how they did it. *Of course.* At least I already know this isn't one of our projects. Their muscles stand out as they press their thumb into the clay, shaping it into a gentle lip along the edge of the plate while preserving a slight spiral in the center.

"Compression is important here, or you'll get cracking. You really want to get all the air out of the clay. Otherwise, that air will expand in the kiln and damage your piece." They let it stop spinning. "Voilà." I could pile the crap out of some sugar cookies on that beautiful thing, and they made it in like sixty seconds. So unfair.

Glenn finally looks up, and their crystal blue eyes catch on me. "Everybody grab a hunk of clay from the front table. We just have a few minutes, but see what you can do in that time." They're still staring when I turn to get my clay. I get to the table before my tablemate, so I get her one, too.

"Thanks!" she chirps. "I'm Fatima. I know nothing about this, so I'm glad I'm sitting by you."

"Our professor is overselling my skills a bit," I say, kneading the clay like dough, and with annoyance, I notice other students copying me.

"Oh, I don't think so." Mx. Rasmussen's voice makes me jump.

"So my failing grade was just for funsies, huh?" I stare at them as I roll my clay into a long, lumpy snake. Maybe it'll come to life and bite their smug face.

"The failing grade was due to lack of work, not the quality of what you produced. Would you like to see a better way to do that?"

"You're the teacher, teach." I shove the clay toward them, but they take up a position across from me and place their hands on top of mine.

"If you keep the pressure consistent and adjust the position of your hands across the clay, you'll get a more even coil." Their hands are surprisingly warm, and their touch on the backs of my hands is gentle but firm as they help me roll it.

"It's a snake, actually."

That gets a smile out of them (not that I was trying) and I notice their subtle lip stain for the first time. "Call it whatever you like."

"I call it a snake."

"Does your snake have a name?"

"Christopher." As with most of my jokes, this is only funny to me, because that's Colby's middle name and I'm mad at him because he brought *kettle corn*, objectively the worst snack in the universe, when he came over to watch a movie with Chance and me over the weekend. Unbelievable. Just because his boyfriend likes it doesn't mean I should have to suffer. But Mx. Rasmussen seems amused despite my inside joke, and now I'm wondering if it's funny from some angle I haven't considered.

"I would've thought Lucifer."

"Not a religious studies major, sorry."

Mx. Rasmussen and Fatima both chuckle at that, and they slowly straighten, brushing off their hands. I wish I could do the same; their warmth has seeped into my skin, and it's very hard to dislike someone who's just helped you make a clay snake named after your brother, but I try.

"Do you remember how to make your coil into a pot?" they ask.

Why are they spending so much time on me? They probably just don't want to see me again next semester.

"No, but I could can braid it like challah."

"Oh, I love challah," Fatima coos, and I grin.

"I'll bring you some if I remember."

"Do you like to bake?" Mx. Rasmussen asks, and I just nod. "Ceramics and baking aren't all that different, you know. Both involve heat and chemical processes, both require attention to air, time to rest."

"Okay, but I will not eat Christopher even if you drizzle royal icing on him."

Fatima giggles again, and my instructor just lifts one eyebrow, then sighs. I think I'm exasperating them again. *Hillary, exasperating someone? No, couldn't be.* A young Black man comes up to them with a question, and they finally turn their attention to someone else. Now that they mention it, I do remember how to do the coil pot, and I show Fatima and the women at the table in front of us how to stack the coils on top of each other, spiraling upward.

That's all I have to do: keep stacking one piece of knowledge onto another until I've climbed my way out of this mess. I'm smart. I can do it. It would've been easier if I'd had the extra time over the summer, but I can do it. I will do it.

I think.

CHAPTER FOUR

THAT EVENING, AS I come through the front door of my childhood home, my brother greets me. "There she is. Finally. Class run late?"

"No. Just me running late." I drop my bag near the front door, so I'll hopefully remember it on the way out, and I hand him the bottle of wine I picked up on the way because I was supposed to bring a salad. What? Grapes grow in the dirt, just like vegetables.

Colby smirks but doesn't comment on my choice. "Lasagna's ready."

"Great, let me wash up." I duck into the downstairs bathroom, which is tucked under the stairs. My hair is wild and wavy, and I attempt to tame it with wet fingers, turning streaks of it a darker brown. It doesn't do much for the shape, either, and I sigh. I'm tempted to just have Janey cut it all off, pixie the crap out of it, but I don't think I'm petite enough to pull that off. Most of my makeup has worn off except for my mascara. At least my tunic sweater still looks cute with my leggings and boots. Although I don't know who I'm trying to impress; most of my brother's roommates are gay. And the rest are like brothers and would be weird to kiss, let alone bang. Just the thought sends a little shiver through me, like the disgust needed to remind me it would make my skin crawl.

"Hil?" Colby calls, and I rush to dry my hands.

"Coming!" I call back as I open the door. Everyone else is already at the table, and I smile at them. I love that we do family dinners; it's so adorable. Colby sits at the head of the table like the Godfather, and I plop down between his bestie Evan and Antonio, my sweet Latin hottie. Chance sits next to Colby bien sur, because that's how these dinners all got started; Colby wanted to let his guy get to know his boys more than just during the odd basketball game. I came for moral support. Then next Thursday, somebody asked if Chance and I were coming over again, since Chance would already be here for basketball, and text messages whizzed around or however text messages work, and the rest is history. Thursday night dinners were officially A Thing™. We all dig in without preamble, taking whatever's closest and passing it.

They're talking about their days: Tony works at Marble, the fancy-schmancy farm-to-table restaurant where Colby used to work, and some blonde lady with a big chest gave him her number, scribbled into the margin of the $100 bill she tipped him. We all agree that we respect the energy there, but not the execution...especially considering she was there with her husband.

I pass bread to Evan, and he rolls his eyes.

"It's the other way. Pass it to Tony."

"No, it's this way," I hiss, pushing it at him insistently, trying not to interrupt Darren's story about almost getting hit by a sports car as he was crossing Glisan. Evan puts one finger on the edge of the wicker basket and pushes it back toward Tony, who quickly accepts it. He passes it to Pat on the end. There's no salad, obvs, but someone made these lovely garlicky green beans, and I'm thinking about how they kept them so crisp and wondering if they used steam and if they roasted the garlic when my brain registers that someone is missing.

"Where's Leah?"

The noise around the table dies back to clinking utensils. I swear, I can hear the condensation forming on the water glasses. I turn to Evan.

"Uh, we broke up. Couple of weeks ago."

"Oh, I'm sorry." Being the queen of awkward, I scramble to come up with something else to say that isn't "why" and "when," which will just drive the hurt deeper. But I can't help my surprise—those two were attached at the hip for months. I kind of thought they were going to move in together. When we all went to a Timbers game together, Leah and I sat next to each other in the middle of the row, and I saw the way Evan kept glancing at her every time she shouted at the officials. There was love there. (For her, not the officials.)

"Yeah, well. It's for the best. Pass the wine, please?" Conversation stirs back to life as Chance passes Evan the bottle, and I try to get my brain to let go of the topic.

"How was your day, Col?"

He sips his water. "Not bad. How's your schedule this quarter? Your last one, right?"

"No, I do the whole year," I say through a bite of pasta. "And it's fine. Except for the pottery thing."

"What pottery thing?" Beautiful Tony asks. I know I'm harping on his looks, but I can't help it. For one thing, he has an eyebrow ring, which is just hot. But it's the amber color of his skin and his raven black hair, his close beard...it's everything.

I wipe my mouth with my napkin because I can pretend to be a lady sometimes. "I failed my pottery class, and my terrible instructor wouldn't let me take the summer class, so now I'm stuck in the same section. I was supposed to have a different instructor, but it turns out, they're baacckk." I throw down the napkin because it feels good. Yes, I'm aware it's irrational, but it would feel nice to be supported in my grudge. But that's not what happens.

"Glenn is not terrible," Chance says softly, scowling at me.

"Wait," Evan says, "Not Glenn Rasmussen?"

I nod. "Do you know them?"

"Yeah, they play double bass in the symphony with me. They're very talented."

I snort into my glass. "At the bass, maybe. Not at understanding their students."

"They're good at pottery, too," Colby adds. "They had a show or something. At that gallery. Tony, you know the one..."

"Union Labor Gallery."

He snaps his fingers. "That's the one. Union Labor. It was a big deal. And their stuff was so good."

"You can be good at *doing* something and not good at *teaching* something..."

"Like when you tried to teach me to drive stick?" Colby smirks.

"Ooh, I like this story," Evan says, apparently recovered from his earlier embarrassment courtesy of my impulsive brain. "It's a Cook family classic."

"Don't you dare," I growl, but they all ignore me.

"So here I am," Colby says, putting up his hands like he's steering a car, "about to turn onto MLK Jr., and I'm like 'Hillary, it's a one-way,' and she's like, 'no, it's not, just go,' and being an idiot, I listen to her." They're all chuckling, asking Colby about how I misled him. But I didn't *mean* to mislead him, and that seems to get lost in the story. I mean, nobody got into an accident. Yeah, that guy in the turban was super mad at us, but we survived. *I survived.* It's what I do.

I'm actually relieved that he's telling this story; it draws attention away from my apparently unpopular opinion about Mx. Rasmussen. I should've figured these guys would know them; they're artsy, all of them. The young artist community is apparently not as big as I thought. Not that Glenn looks all that young; they've got that bit of a gut that people over thirty often get, and there's a dusting of gray in their beard. I'd think it was hot if they weren't standing in the way of me graduating on time.

I always eat slower than everyone else, my mind drifting between food and conversations and a running internal commentary of its own, but they politely sit around until I'm done. I collect plates from Evan and Tony, then reach across for Chance's, but he shakes his head.

"I'll help," he says, standing up, and I shrug.

"Suit yourself, roomie." We gather the dishes and such and take them to the kitchen. I could never feel like a guest here; the kitchen is more or less how my mom left it when she and Dad moved to Thailand. There's a postcard on the fridge from them of a white sand beach, and I know her handwriting is on the back of it. I touch it out of habit, but I can't turn it over. I can barely stand to hear her voice on the phone, and I don't know why.

Chance notices me touch it. "Missing them?"

"Kind of, I guess." I'm close to my parents; we've always been close. But something broke inside me when they moved away. Because it didn't feel like they moved away. It felt like they left me. And maybe there's no difference, but it felt personal. It wasn't; I know it wasn't. It was a great opportunity for my dad's career, and Mom could finally go with him now that we're grown. I *know* that. But I can't *feel* it. They left me, and it shattered me. I'd sooner be able to put one of these plates back together if I dropped it in the sink, rough shards tearing at my fingertips, my eyes burning to see how it all fits together. Feels like I can't even find all the pieces of me their leaving broke. That's why I wash the dishes, so I don't have to look at the fridge and see the magnet we got in New Mexico at that crappy hotel with the statue of King Trident, and the one we got in Lincoln City when it was raining too hard to play on the beach, and the one I got in Seattle the first time I visited Nana overnight by myself. So I don't have to think about how petty this comes off when I say it out loud when it feels anything but.

I rinse plates and hand them to Chance. "I think most of these magnets are really mine. Should I take them home?"

Speaking of home, remember your bag. Don't forget your bag.

"Nah," Chance says. "How would they find their YMCA pool schedule?"

"I might like this recipe for roasted chicken," I reply, touching the recipe card.

"And what if they don't remember that trash day is on THURSDAYS, as this large garish flyer is informing them? Best to leave them. Magnets hold the world together."

I chuckle. "I do miss this house. Did you see the pictures of fourth-grade Colby?"

"I think he'd rather I didn't, but yes." Chance grins, sticking some stray cereal bowls into the dishwasher. Our family photos feature a gap-toothed Colby, his hair buzzed short. Little me, too, my hair saltwater washed and wild. In my senior pictures, I'm sitting against a weatherworn red barn outside of Gresham, my arms around one knee, wearing more makeup than I ever had in my life. And my mom's paintings...landscapes, mostly. Mom loves the ocean, and the one of Haystack Rock is my favorite. I should be glad they were posted in Thailand, since it has a beach...Colby keeps trying to nail down a visit, talking about Christmas. I do miss them, but I'm still so deeply hurt and angry about it all. As much as I don't mind escaping the rain for a bit in December...I don't think I'm ready to go see their new place, the fantastic house they have without me. Seeing it will just drive the painful reality that they're not coming back into my soul, and reality and I have a shaky relationship at best. I don't know what it would take to get me there.

When I'm ready to go, Patrick and Darren pause their video game to hug me goodbye. The other guys must be upstairs; I feel bad about what I said to Evan and want to apologize. I'll have to text him. Probably better that I don't bring it up again anyway. Colby's the last to hug me, and he rocks me from side to side like a goof. "Thanks for coming," he says into my hair, and I grin.

There's my bag. Gotta remember it.

"Wouldn't miss it. Thanks for having me." I step outside to allow him a more private goodbye with Chance, who, surprisingly, is actually coming home tonight. My breath clouds in front of me, ethereal in the porch light. I have the urge to tip back my head and pretend I'm a steam engine down the front walk. Chance's car is parked on the street, and I go lean against it, hands jammed deep in my pockets to protect them from the coldness of the damp air.

"Oh, am I giving you a ride home?" he asks as he digs out his keys.

"Yeah."

"That explains why I'm carrying your bag, then." He holds out my leather satchel. I accept it with a grin, even though resignation hits me like a lemon meringue pie to the face; I thought of it *twice,* and I still couldn't manage to get it.

"I would've been looking for that tomorrow."

"You would've been looking for it tonight, at our front door, when you're locked out."

I give him a little arm punch. "But that's why I have you. You'd let me in, wouldn't you?"

"Sometimes I think that's the only reason you *have* a roommate," he teases back, sliding into the front seat.

"False, sir! I am a social animal. I need a pack. You're my pack."

"Are we wolves, then? I don't think that embodies me. I'm not an apex predator."

"No," I say, "you're some sort of llama that skulks in the corner and hopes no one notices it."

"With a drink. Don't forget the drink."

I tap my chin. "I think llamas have packs. I'll be a llama with you."

"Gee, thanks, Hil."

As he pulls out into traffic, I remind him to look out for one-way streets.

CHAPTER FIVE

"I WANT TO GO OOUUTT."

It's Friday night of my first week of my last year of school. My brother and his partner are ignoring me, happily snuggling on our couch, sending each other funny things from Twitter, and snickering. It is extremely rude for two reasons:

1. I am bored.
2. Their love is adorable.
3. They are leaving me out.

"Please? I just need to see somewhere else."

"Why don't you go work on your pottery homework?" Chance asks without looking up.

"Are you trying to get the apartment to yourselves?"

"No, I'm trying to help you graduate on time."

He means it kindly, but the words sting a little. "I'm not going to flunk out. Even if I have to keep taking it, even if my terrible instructor won't accept any of the work I've already done, I will find a way."

Colby puts down his phone. "What do you mean, they won't accept the work you've already done? Glenn's the best. They wouldn't be unfair."

I glare at him. "Well, *Glenn* informed me I wouldn't be able to resubmit any of the projects I did last year."

"You told them you wanted to use your previous work? Slap them in the face, why don't you."

"How is that slapping them in the face?" Not that I'd mind trying it. They seem like they could use it. My

171

brain gently prompts me that they gave me another checklist on Thursday, which is still in my bag, that I should look at. I tell my brain that a few kind acts don't negate making me do unnecessary work and denying me entry into that summer class. I wish I could've made them understand how much easier that would've made my life; how my capacity to do what they're asking for would've been so much greater without a full course load.

"Glenn's a genuine artist. I mean, they really live and breathe that stuff. Some people play in the symphony because it's their job. But I'm pretty sure they see it as more of a calling. The same is probably true for ceramics."

"And not only that," I say, "they told me they expected better work than last time!"

"But that makes sense," Chance says, sitting up. "If you're really retaining what they're teaching you, you should be improving."

"Traitors. Both of you. I have plenty of *important* shit to do. I don't have time to play around with clay like a preschooler."

"Don't think of it like that," Colby says, pulling Chance back down to lie on his chest again. "Think of it as an adult learning to make art. There's value to your soul in it."

"That's deep," Chance says, tilting his head to look up at him.

"Yes," Colby says drily, "I am capable of deep thoughts occasionally."

Chance scowls. "You know that's not what I meant. Stop implying you're dumb. No one believes it."

"Maybe I believe it." He's just fucking with him now, and from experience, I can say that Colby fucking with Chance often turns into Chance fucking Colby with some variation on how quiet they're being.

"Fine," I say, standing up. "I'm going to go improve my soul, since you two McBoringPants boys just want to lie around here."

"Cool. Have fun," says Colby, going back to his phone.

"Key card," says Chance, doing the same.

"Right." I don't find the key card in my bag, purse, wallet, or slid inside any of my textbooks. On my way out, I swing by the laundry room on a hunch and find it on the bulletin board above the folding counter with a sticky note that says, "Hillary? Love, Janey." God bless that woman. I also take the number for a house sitter, because you never know. I will undoubtedly put it through the wash when I do laundry next, and then it will be lost forever. So I pull out my phone and take a picture. *Better.*

I'm halfway to campus when I remember I left Glenn's checklist on my desk. I text Chance, and he sends me a picture just as I'm swiping my way into the building.

"BEFORE TUESDAY"

[ ] Gather historical vessel examples.

[ ] Study them.

[ ] Come up with a design of your own that's symmetrical.

There are a ton of books in the studio, and even though I could probably look all that information up on the internet, sometimes a book is safer. For one thing, I know they'll be real historical examples and not some fifth grader's social studies project. For another, the internet can be a dangerous place for someone who's distractible. I open a tab to look up pottery, and somehow, I'm suddenly very invested in booking a trip to see Mayan ruins or doing a virtual tour up the Yangtze river, all because I started out looking at their artwork. Do I have money for such a trip? Don't make me laugh; my student loans are going to come crashing down on my head in a matter of months, so travel is out of the question. Unless it's to see my parents in Thailand, which I don't want to think about now. Or later.

I'm knee-deep in thought, absorbed in my phone, when I push open the door to the studio.

"Good evening."

I stop short at their voice. "Oh." I want to make a snide comment about their social life, but mine's clearly no better, and besides, they're my instructor. They're sitting at their desk, reading glasses perched on their nose, working on a thin, sleek laptop. "I'm sorry, I can come back later."

"No, please. Come in. I don't mind company."

I'm still not sure this is a good idea, mostly because they're on my shit list and I kind of hate them even if it's irrational, but I can't leave without being insulting.

"You must have gotten your key card, then." Glenn takes off their glasses and set them upside down on their keyboard, sitting back in a tan rolling chair that looks like it was manufactured in 1971. I can see their tattoos better today—they've covered both their arms in scrolling black ink. I notice as they cross their arms over their rounded belly.

"Yes, you put it on my special to-do list." It comes out more bitter than I mean it to, and I drop my stuff and head for the bookshelf.

"That was meant to support your learning. I didn't mean to offend—"

"You didn't," I say quickly. "It was...useful."

"Your ADHD must be a challenge."

In disbelief, I whip around to face them. They're staring at me levelly. "My what?"

"Your...ADHD? I should think that managing all the details of study and classwork even at the undergrad level with the intensity of your symptoms—"

"I do *not* have ADHD," I say through a laugh.

Their control slips, and I could swear it's anger that flickers across their face. "You've never been diagnosed with ADHD?"

"Nor any other learning disability," I say drily, turning back to the bookshelf. "I'm just scatterbrained."

Where were the ones on Greek stuff? That one had a lot of naked people. I like women's bodies. I bet I could paint one that doesn't look like a Barbie on a pot without sucking too much. Maybe I'll make it a chamberpot as a middle finger to my instructor. *Grade this, asshole.*

"Do you dream?"

Boy, they really will not leave me alone. I should've just walked out when I saw them; I'll check through the window next time. Still, it's rude not to answer.

"Like, do I have life aspirations, or do I see mind movies at night?"

"Mind movies."

I try to think. "No."

"But you sleep well?"

"I don't see how this relates to my performance in your class..." I don't, though. Sleep well, that is. I never have. I only get through the night thanks to my heavy blanket and a good white noise app. Chance introduced me to the blankets when he moved in, since they help his anxiety. And now the white noise helps me to not hear him fucking my brother through our thin walls. It's nice how things come full circle sometimes.

"You're a daydreamer, right? People say you're too sensitive? You take rejection personally?"

I roll my eyes. "Doesn't everyone?" Then I look up at the wall of windows in front of me and realize they could probably see that, given how dark it is outside. I turn to face them, resting my hips on the low bookcase. "Is this some kind of joke? You've seen me in your class."

"I'm going to take that as a yes. How many hobbies have you started this year?"

I huff. "I don't know." It's four. I was going to make a quilt, and then a rag rug, and then I repainted an old dresser for Chance in Colby's garage, and now I'm trying to cross-stitch a thing for my mom for Christmas that says 'But first, wine.' Sorry, I should clarify—it's for last

Christmas. And four is nothing—I've been busy with other things. Last year it was seven.

"Did you stick with any of them?"

"This has absolutely nothing to do with my academic career," I fume, storming back across the classroom. They're up out of their chair, and they get to the table before I do.

"Please. Wait. This is important." Their expression is intense, and I glare right back.

"No."

"With your level of impairment, it's incredible what you've accomplished, but it's astonishing and frankly somewhat maddening that no one's brought this up to you before."

My mouth drops open. "My *level of impairment*? I'm a fucking honors student; stop talking about me like I'm disabled."

"Those things aren't mutually exclusive. You're only hurting yourself by not looking this in the face."

"Better than you getting in my face," I shoot back, snatching up my stuff. "I'll do my pot research at home."

"Ms. Cook..."

"Have a good night."

"*Hillary*." Their hand grasps my arm, and I don't even think as I turn and push them away.

"Don't touch me." It was just a reflex; they didn't hurt me. I don't know why I did that.

"I apologize." Their hands are up, their face horrified. "I'm sorry. I shouldn't have touched you; I won't do it again." They press together their palms as if in prayer, as if to prove that they're trustworthy. "But please hear me out. I have five years of experience at the university, plus more teaching experience elsewhere and a brother who's diagnosed. I think the odds are very good that you do have ADHD. I would like you to look into it, for your own sake."

"Yeah, I figured that out, thanks. But if you wanted to help me, you would've let me into that summer class."

Their expression slowly turns dark, like those sped-up videos of roiling storm clouds forming. "Pardon me?"

"Oh, you don't like a truth bomb sent back in your direction, huh?"

Those big arms are crossed again, making their muscles stand out. They're not the kind made in a gym; they look like they swing hammers all summer, like some other teachers I know. Their skin has a nice tan, too, like they've spent a lot of time outside. And why I'm noticing this for the first time in the middle of an argument is unclear to me, too.

"I made a determination based on what I thought was best for a student of your ability. You would've been frustrated and discouraged in that class. And that's exactly the kind of rejection sensitivity I was talking about; I wasn't *rejecting* you, I was *protecting* you."

"That was *my* decision to make," I say, pointing at my chest. No, I don't say it; I shout it. I'm shouting at my professor. "You had no right to keep me out!"

"You're changing the subject," they say, still scowling. "I do want to help you."

"If I want your help, I'll ask for it." We're toe to toe now, and I can smell the mocha on their breath, and there's a nice jasmine scent around them like they just used lotion. And when I look into their stormy eyes, the strangest desire to kiss them bowls me over so hard, I almost do.

"Are you always this stubborn?"

"Are you always this invasive?"

"I don't consider making an observation about your learning disability to be invasive. I'm your teacher."

"Well, I wish you weren't. I'll be dropping this class as soon as I can get the paperwork together."

"So...never?"

It's a low blow, and my face heats on one side as if they just slapped me. They break our staring contest and step back, running a hand over their short brown hair.

"I...I'm sorry. I don't know why I said that. That was cruel."

"Yeah, it was," I agree quietly, gathering my stuff. "Goodbye." I'm out the door before they can say anything more, and my faint satisfaction at having the last word is muted by the realization that I've just yelled at one of my professors and promised to drop their class—only I don't know if I actually can.

Needing a distraction, I pull out my phone.

Hillary: You up?
Janey: Yeah. Just starting a movie with Giada.
You want to come down?
Hillary: It'll be coming up, but YES. I. DO.

ADHD. How ridiculous. How the fuck would I have gotten this far with ADHD?

Just...ridiculous.

CHAPTER SIX

SATURDAY NIGHT, I'M home alone. I make a three-layer chocolate cake, eat one piece, and take a piece upstairs to Mrs. Graham, who lives alone. We have a good talk about how much rain we're getting and why some people are bigots and whether taxes will go up this year. The talk is the point of going up; Mrs. Graham does not accept conversational charity, but she does accept excess sugar. I am therefore forced to bake.

I wander down to Janey's, but she's not home. I text Raina, but she says her house is "too messy to receive visitors." I think about inviting her to come here, but it looks like a bomb went off in my living room, books and shoes and mail and magazines all over the place. I clean it until I can mostly see the floor again—more like a small hand grenade than a bomb—but I think Raina would still wrinkle her nose, and it's probably not safe for her kid. But it should appease Chance for a while, anyway.

I make the mess bigger when I drag my bag over to the couch to study, stuff kind of falling out as I try to pull out the book I'm looking for. My computer is mostly dead, so I take notes on my phone. It's for Women in the Economy, not the most interesting class I've ever taken...this chapter is on nonmarket work, which I'm pretty sure is what I just did when I cleaned up. The book is drier than my mom's Thanksgiving turkey. Which reminds me that my parents still want me and Colby to come for Christmas. Ugh.

I try to force my brain back to the book, but I keep rereading the same page over and over. I try turning on the TV...which also does not help. Now I'm just watching TV with a book open. I shut it off. I hate it when my brain is like this. It's like I'm pacing inside my head. *Hate. It.* I get up and do twenty jumping jacks. Then some high knees, how I used to do when I played soccer as a kid, juggling the ball. I don't want to resort to push-ups—I'm not that desperate—so I eat more cake. I clean out the fridge because when I go for a glass of milk, I notice it's a bit funky-smelling. And when I say clean it out, I mean I pull out everything that's old and leave it next to the sink after I dump the first one. I'll probably do it later.

But I can still smell it when I sit back down, so I finish the dumping and take the trash down the hall to the chute, which I will never stop geeking out about, even though I'm sure I'm going to find a body in there someday. I really need to stop listening to so many true crime podcasts. The apartment smells mostly better once I do that, and I flop down again with my book, trying some music this time.

And that's better. Finally. I read about ten pages, taking good notes, before the song comes on. I had an on-again-off-again thing with this guy...what was his name? Dane? No, I would've remembered that. Tryon! That was it, Tryon like the creek. This one time, he drove us out to the middle of nowhere, and we made a fire, and...my body remembers what we did next while this song was playing. He was kind of a douche in the end, but wow, could he kiss. Seriously, if there was a kissing competition, Tryon would be crowned king, hands down.

It's been a long time since I had good sex. I haven't had even a fuck buddy in months. Truth be told, the last one left kind of an unpleasant taste in my mouth, and it had nothing to do with his come. He kept having to pull out because he was about to finish, and I wasn't even close. We'd both rubbed the crap out of my clit, I'd had plenty of foreplay, making out, stroking, touching. He was hot, and I was definitely attracted to him, it just wasn't...happening. So after the third time, he got off the bed, stood next to it, and pulled off the condom.

"Sorry, can you just finish me? I need to get home."

He wasn't unkind about it. We were just messing around. It was supposed to be fun, and we were both frustrated past the point of enjoyment. But I felt this awful blush from my face all the way down to my very naked toes. I mumbled an apology as I crawled over and sucked him off while he stroked my hair. Humiliation kink is definitely not my thing, and I haven't reached out to him again since...or anyone else.

But hearing this song has me...needy. Amped. Restless. I don't know who I could call. If it happens again...who's going to understand? I give myself a little rub over my leggings, and my body perks up and takes notice. All right—nothing wrong with a little jilling off on a Saturday night as a last resort.

I set my phone to repeat the song, hoping it'll encourage my body to cooperate. It's going to cooperate, right? I mean, why wouldn't it? There's no pressure here. My boys said they're going to Colby's tonight. It's just me, this music, and my fingers...

I don't bother going to my room. Despite being defiled by the boys, this couch is comfortable. *Maybe it's my turn to defile something.* I slip my hand into my pants, gathering wetness from my folds to spread over my clit. It's already swollen, and I'm more damp than usual. I close my eyes and let my fingers play over the parts that feel good, building up a rhythm because there's no point in dragging things out. I get a good buzz going...but my body wants more. I squeeze at my breasts, close my eyes, let my hips lift in rhythm with my stroking...but I've hit a wall. And the more frustrated I get, the farther away it feels. I try to bring up the memories of Tryon again, but it's not enough.

I grunt in annoyance, letting my hand still. I turn my head toward the dark TV, just staring at nothing, waiting for my horniness to subside. It does not.

"Fine," I mutter to no one, jumping off the couch. "I can solve this." After a little rummaging, I find my trusty pink vibrator. Since I'm already mad at my body, I just jam the silicone tip into my pants and stick a pillow between me and the bed. I pick the vibration pattern that feels like waves because why the hell not. But after a few minutes, I'm back to my plateau.

Time to kick things up a notch. I find the button and try one that's just a constant buzz meant to blast me into the stratosphere. It feels good. I'm warm and throbbing between my legs, and it's strong, and I'm close, and my hips are going, going, going against the toy and the pillow, and I need and I can't... I thrust harder, but my hips are already sore, and my clit is so oversensitive, it feels like I burned myself. I turn the vibrator off and push everything away in disgust.

I roll onto my back and cover my face with my hands. *I'm not going to cry; I'm not going to...* Oh, what the hell. There's no one here to see.

I let my hands fall to my belly and the quiet tears come, blurring the ceiling with its too-bright light and cracks and cobwebs in the corners. By the time I finish crying, my body has settled back down. I turn out the light and crawl under the covers, hoping I won't dream about Tryon or Can You Just Finish Me Jace or anyone else who might pointlessly turn me on.

CHAPTER SEVEN

FOR THE NEXT TWO WEEKS, I don't go to ceramics class at all. I use the time to work on my French literature translation project, as well as researching alternatives to ceramics for my arts credit...but the alternatives aren't looking great. There's an upper-level photography class that fits well in my schedule, but I'd have to convince the instructor to waive the prerequisites for me, and Giada said that professor is a stickler for the rules. I think I'd like photography, but the idea of getting the art department on my side sounds daunting. I mean, who knows what Mx. Rasmussen has told them about me? After I foolishly shouted in their face and accused them of trying to thwart my plans, I wouldn't blame them for making it known that I'm difficult.

I look through the rest of my options, but they're overlapping with my current classes, all of which are only offered this quarter. I guess I'll just have to fit an art class into next quarter's plans.

Only when I look, I can't do that, either. I end up in my advisor's office on Friday.

"I'm sorry, Hillary," she sighs. "I just don't see another way around it. You've put off your art credits until the last minute, and consequently, you'll need to complete this class if you want to graduate in the spring."

"What if I took another class online and transferred in the credit?"

But she's already shaking her head. "I mean, you could try. But there's no guarantee that the institution would process your grades in time for our registrar to confirm that you have indeed passed. It would put a lot of pressure on you—and on things you can't control—just in order to avoid this one class." She leans forward. "Is there a problem with Mx. Rasmussen? My impression was that they're a highly sought-after professor. But if you need a mediator or someone to speak to them..."

"No," I say quickly. "There's no problem. They've been..." *Invasive. Discouraging. Presumptuous.* "Fine." I swallow. "I had them last quarter. I just need to apply myself."

"Well, if you're not going to drop the class, you definitely need to start going to class again. You should probably speak to your instructor and see what you need to do to get caught up."

My heart sinks. That is the absolute last thing I want to do. I've been trying to erase our argument from my mind, but I just keep playing it over and over, feeling worse and worse about the things I said to them.

"Yes. I will." *Probably.* As I leave her office, I bump into Chance on the way out. "Hey, stranger. What are you doing here?"

"Oh, um..." Why does he look like I just caught him sneaking into my candy stash? "Nothing."

All I have to do is fold my arms, tilt my head, and give him my resting bitch face. He sighs hard, then rubs at his face.

"Okay, but you can't tell Colby..."

"OOH," I squeal, ignoring the dirty looks of people around us. "A secret! I love secrets."

"It's not a secret," he grumbles, dropping an envelope into someone's inbox. "It's just...I applied for this thing. It's a grant."

"Okay?" I'm genuinely puzzled now, because I know he applies for grants all the time. I actually suggested it as a name when he was trying to decide on a new one, pre-transition; that's how many grants he applies for. "Help a bitch out—where does the secret part come in?"

"It has a travel component. I'd go and study at their institute."

I lower my voice. "And you don't want Colby to know you like studying? I think it's too late for that."

Chance punches my arm gently, rolling his eyes. "No, it's just that...the institute is in England. At Oxford."

"Oh." Still super confused. I mean, if he comes back with a British accent, Colby would probably die of happiness. I know I would. "How long would you go for?"

"It's a really great program—one of the top AI research facilities in the world. And I'll have access to their algorithms, and we can let our AIs interact, creating different compositions... I'd get to work with scientists I've only dreamed of meeting."

"Chance. I'm distractible, but I'm not stupid. You're not answering my question."

"Six months." His hunched shoulders and the way he winces tells me what I need to know.

"And you think Colby's going to do, what? Break up with you?"

Chance shrugs after a long pause, like he's ashamed to even think it.

"Good news: you're my new favorite fool. It used to be Colby, but you just took the top spot. Kudos to you, sir. Really, well done."

His glower is brotherly, but genuinely distressed. "Hil, Colby isn't going to be happy if I have to leave." He shakes his head. "It's a long shot, anyway. Probably won't get it."

"You're right. Let's go get your application back. We can find someone with a parakeet and let them use it to line the bottom of their cage." I turn back toward the building, and Chance catches me before I can take a step.

"Knock it off. Anxiety, remember? I know it's not rational. I can't help it." We're blocking the sidewalk, so I tug him over to the grass before I put my arms around him. Chance sinks into my arms with a deep sigh, and I feel bad for how hard this has been weighing on him.

"Listen up, roomie. You're going to get it because you're amazing. And Colby's going to be happy for you, even if it means a short—"

"Six months is not short."

"A *short*," I continue, "separation. He's a big boy. He'll miss you like crazy and be totally intolerable, but maybe we can scrounge up the money and come visit you."

He pulls back to smile at me, a little wet-eyed, and I return the grin.

"Not at the same time, though," I clarify. "I don't want to be the third wheel while you guys bone for like three days straight."

"He can't go that hard. Being cisgender is a scam," Chance quips. "But there's always sexting."

"I don't want to know about this." I turn and weave my way back into the traffic on the walkway.

"We can create videos for each other..."

"Stop. I beg of you." I feel Chance at my elbow, and I shove him away. "Seriously, though. It would be fine. I'm glad you applied. I think you should try to stop worrying."

"Probably won't..." My harsh glare stops his disclaimer cold. "I'll try."

"Ms. Cook?" I know that voice. Irritation flows through me. If I stepped into a kiddie pool and tipped my head back, I could be a fountain of annoyance.

"Mx. Rasmussen."

"Hey, Glenn," Chance greets, sticking out a hand, and they shake it with a generous smile.

"Would you excuse us for just a moment?" they ask, and we step off the path for privacy's sake. That warm smile falls as they turn back to me. *Of course.*

"You haven't been in class, but you haven't dropped it yet. I'm concerned that you're going to fall behind if you don't start attending class or get it off your schedule."

"Yes, I have similar concerns. In fact, I have just come from meeting with my counselor, and she told me there's no way for me to drop the class and find a suitable alternative."

They watch me with a neutral expression. "You can come on Saturday, and I'll work with you to get caught up."

What? NO. The last time we were alone in that studio, it was disastrous. Yelling. Academic mess-making. I embarrassed myself. Not doing that again. But I pause too long, and they take a step closer.

"I'll be there anyway. You won't be inconveniencing me. I'm supervising the 510 class as they do their raku firing."

Even from a distance, Chance's gaze bounces between the two of us, and I try to ignore him. But his curiosity is obvious.

"Yes. All right. Thank you. I'll be there."

"What time?"

I cross my arms. "What? I don't know. Whenever I get up. It's *Saturday*, Professor." It feels strange to call them that, since I don't think they're really that much older than me.

They huff. "I just want to make sure I'm there when you arrive, so I don't waste your time. You can send me an email when you decide." They give Chance a cordial nod, then continue on their way. I glare at their back over my shoulder.

"You were rude to them, Hil." Chance is frowning at me, and I hate that.

"What? No, I wasn't. They're the one being unreasonable."

"No, they're the one offering to let you come in on Saturday so that you don't fail."

There it is again, The F-Word. My least favorite one. Except for maybe *fart*; it's too onomatopoetic.

"Glenn's a really nice person," Chance goes on. "I don't know them well, but...there's some kind of weird energy between you two."

I start walking again, and Chance hurries to keep up.

"Where are you going?" he asks.

"Home," I say without thinking about it. I want slippers and tea and a useless book and my room where no one wants anything from me.

"Thought you had Global Reproductive Rights tonight?"

"Chance!" I yell. "Stop knowing my life better than I do!" I attempt to storm off, but he keeps pace with me. *Darn these legs of average length!* "Maybe I'm not going! Maybe I don't feel like adulting today."

He mutters it under his breath, but I hear him: "Seems like that's true quite often lately."

"What else have I screwed up recently?" My head feels light. *Must've forgotten to eat again.*

"Nothing. You're doing great." I don't respond to the lie. Chance is too nice sometimes.

"You and I both know that's not true, so come on. What is it? The dishes in the sink? The mess in the bathroom? The food I left out?"

"All of those things happened, yes. It would be nice if you took care of them yourself, but I understand that you're under a lot of stress lately..."

"Fine. I will go home and deal with them now."

Chance hesitates, and I blurt, "What?"

"Global Reproductive Rights?"

I let out a loud string of curses. I just need a break, I need five minutes to pull myself together, and then I'll...I'll... Class. I'll go to class. And I need to eat something, I haven't eaten since this morning.

My head starts to spin. My feet feel heavy, and my knee doesn't lift like it should, and I know I'm going down. I reach out for the bench pointlessly, my fingers brushing the back of it, but it's not enough, I'm not enough, and the ground is coming up fast to meet me. I hear Chance call my name, a biting fear in his voice, and then everything goes black.

CHAPTER EIGHT

"HILLARY? WAKE UP, HIL. Come on."

A very concerned Chance is hovering over me, along with Giada and Janey. He's patting my cheeks, and I groggily push his hand away.

"Quit, dude. I'm awake."

"Did you hit your head? I tried to catch you, but I wasn't quick enough..."

"Don't make this about you. I'm the one who didn't eat."

"Do you have a snack or anything?" He looks between my two friends, both of whom look scared. *Crap.* Giada feels around in her oversized bag and comes up with a granola bar.

"All things considered, I'd rather have a blueberry muffin..." I say, trying to look up at my friends with wide, innocent eyes to drum up sympathy. It's mostly a joke, but I might as well use this situation to my advantage. Giada holds out the nasty bar more insistently, and I take it with a grimace.

"Did you call Colby?" Janey asks, putting a hand on Chance's shoulder.

"The answer to that better be 'no,'" I say through a mouthful of nuts, cranberries, and its one redeeming ingredient, chocolate.

He doesn't look even the tiniest bit sorry. "Yes, I called him." He turns to Janey. "He's on his way. He's going to help me get her home."

"Fuck, Chance." I sigh. "Why did he need to know?"

"Excuse you, you scared the shit out of me!" He is actually yelling now. I've rarely heard him raise his voice, unless he and Colby are arguing over Thai food. They both have surprisingly strong opinions on the matter. I don't have time to detail them for you now, sorry. "So forgive me if I called the man I love for support! Him being your brother was actually incidental at the moment!"

"Take it easy, Chance," I soothe, putting a hand on his arm. "I'm okay. I'm fine. See? I'm sitting up and everything, all in one piece." Truth be told, my shoulder hurts a little, but it doesn't seem like the time to mention it since I'm not sure if I've successfully wiggled my way out of going to see a doctor yet. I could cite the expense or the hassle, but the truth is I just don't wanna. I don't like them. I never have.

I hear my brother's voice before I see him.

"Yes. Yeah, Mom, I will. As soon as I know. Okay. Yeah."

There he is; green hat, medium build, light brown hair like mine. He's wearing the brown leather bomber jacket he got recently. I pointed it out to him at the thrift store. That find counts as mine. He doesn't look mad when he kneels where I'm sitting on the grass. At least I got off the path.

"You all right, Hil?" Colby's looking me up and down as I continue to eat.

I nod. "Fine. Just hungry, I think."

"Where's your wallet?"

"My wallet?" Is this a *Back to the Future* situation? Did someone take it while I was passed out? I don't see how they could've gotten past Chance the Wonder Roommate. "Why?"

"Because I'm taking you to urgent care, and we're gonna need your insurance card."

I'm already shaking my head before he can finish his sentence. "No, thank you. I would just like to go home."

"Well, I would like you to eat regularly, but here we are." He stands up and offers me his hand. "Also, did you know that when you go down hard, your smartwatch registers the fall and notifies your emergency contact? That should be me, by the way, not Mom, who is currently losing her shit in Thailand."

"Fuck. What did you tell her?"

"Oh, I'm not telling her anything. You're going to explain this yourself." He turns to his boyfriend then, taking Chance's face in his hands, leaving me to stew. "Are you okay?"

Chance nods, and I'll admit, he seems better now that Colby's here.

"Really okay, though?" he asks, nudging his hat up to bring their foreheads together. This time, Chance shakes his head. When he reaches out to touch Colby's elbow, Chance's hand shakes. *My heart.* I didn't mean to trigger his anxiety, and the guilt of being a burden is heavy. I didn't mean for any of this to happen, I never do.

"Okay," Colby says quietly, not letting go of Chance. "Here's what we're going to do. I'm going to get you both some food. We're going to take Chance home, and then we'll go to urgent care."

"Or," I say, picking up my bag and trying to brush the mud off it, "we might not need to go to urgent care. Once we have food in our hungry systems. Just saying."

Colby glares at me, and there's the anger I expected earlier. *Hillary, always screwing up other people's lives.* Giada and Janey both hug me and request updates tonight. Then Colby puts me on one side of him and Chance on the other and leads us away from campus.

"Where are we going?"

"I thought Dancing Earth. It's healthy. You both seem like you could use it."

"Is that a comment about my weight?" I snark, and Colby pulls me into a side hug with a sigh.

"No, Hil, it's a comment about you passing out cold on a campus sidewalk."

"I made it to the grass..."

"What I don't get," muses Chance, "is why you didn't grab for *me*. I think I could've caught you."

I blink. I have no idea why. The bench seemed solid; it seemed like the logical choice in the split second of consciousness I had to decide. Should I be concerned that my subconscious mind is reaching toward inanimate objects for help instead of people? I'm still tired. This walk is feeling farther than I should really go, but I don't want to argue with Colby. Also, their kale and almond chicken bowl is *chef's kiss.* Seriously.

Of course, they're out of kale when we get there, so I settle for an Asian chicken salad. Chance and I sit at the table while Colby pays and collects the food.

"I'm sorry," I say, reaching out for Chance's hand, and he meets my gaze.

"Hil, do you think you might have some kind of neurodiversity?"

I pull that hand right back. He said 'neurodiversity,' but I know he really meant 'disability.'

"No."

He leans forward, adjusting his glasses. "Seriously? You don't think your forgetfulness might be something else? Some kind of learning disability?"

"NO." This time I say it loud enough to draw the attention of others, and that is absolutely my intention because I do not want to talk about this. But Chance just cocks his head.

"Things like that sometimes present differently in women."

"Have you been talking to Glenn?"

When his gaze drops guiltily to the napkin dispenser on the table, I have my answer. My anger is a bonfire. It is a fucking furnace. It is one thing for them to express concerns to me as their student. It is a whole other thing for them to go to my roommate and probably my brother behind my back to pressure me into getting assessed.

"Whoa." Colby nears the table with a tray in each hand. "I feel like I missed something."

"Have they been talking to you, too?"

"Who?"

I stand up, totally prepared to blast out of there, but my head whirls, and I put my hand on the table to steady myself. "Glenn. Did Glenn talk to you about me and ADHD?"

Colby sits on the bench next to Chance. "Uh..."

"That's what I thought." I snatch my food and my bag, dragging everything over to another table. It's the only distance I can manage in this condition. But I am not eating with these traitors.

"Thought we were going to talk to her together..." Colby mutters as he passes Chance his salad.

"Yeah, we...were. We should've. Sorry." He glances over at me, but I'm focused on putting this food in my face, and then I am leaving. I pull out my phone so I have something to read and end up Venmoing money for the food to Colby. He makes an unhappy noise when he gets the notification.

"Seriously, Hil?"

I ignore him. I do not plan to acknowledge either of them. Maybe ever again. At least through tonight. Glenn's words about being sensitive to rejection float back to the top of my brain pool...and I quickly drown them.

When I finish, I stand up, separate my trash from my recycling because it's that kind of place and Oregon's environment needs saving, and then I head for the door. They scramble to follow me because they're busy chatting and laughing and being in love. One of them picks up my bag, and Colby shoulders it as they come up even with me on the sidewalk.

"You don't have to say anything, but I agree with Glenn. You should have this assessed."

I'm too angry to hold back anymore. "How would I have gotten through my undergrad with ADHD, Colby? How would I have gotten this far? It's impossible! The notion is completely ridiculous."

"I don't know. I've known you a long time, and yes, you've always been like this, but...I was doing some reading. We both were. A lot of this fits you. And Glenn really seems to think—"

"Ugh, I am sick to death of thinking about *Glenn.*"

Chance's voice is soft. "I thought you haven't been to their class in weeks?"

"I haven't."

Colby's voice is teasing. "Then why have you been thinking about them? Is it the tattoos? She loves tattoos."

"I do love tattoos, as you well know, but it is *not* the tattoos. I've been thinking about them because I feel terrible for the way I spoke to them on that Friday night." Both of them stare at me blankly.

"Why, what did you say?" Colby asks.

I huff. "I don't care to repeat it. It wasn't polite the first time. The point is, they just push my buttons. And I can't figure out why they care so much about this AD-HD thing. I'm just some random student to them."

"No, I don't think so. They take their students' success very personally," Colby puts in. "I mean, you already failed their class once. It doesn't surprise me they'd take steps to see that it doesn't happen again. Hence their Saturday invitation…"

"Which I am going to do. I just don't…get them. I'm not their problem."

"Maybe they don't see you as a problem. Maybe they just see the opportunity to help you."

Colby's phone rings, and he looks down. "It's Mom."

I sigh and hold out my hand. If I talk to her now, I won't have to later, and I can just try to sleep.

"Hi, Mom."

"Are you at urgent care? What did they say?"

"I did not go to urgent care."

There is a long silence on the other end of the phone, and I pull the screen away from my ear to make sure we're still connected. We are.

"Mom?"

"Sorry, I'm just…processing that information."

She's going to do it. I know she is. She's going to pull out her secret weapon, my kryptonite, the only thing that could make me go see a doctor tonight: Mom Tears.

"Hillary, I am very worried about you. You used to do this your senior year in high school, do you remember? You'd get so focused studying or reading or playing on the computer, you'd just sail right through mealtimes."

"That must have been a trick, sailing in northeast Portland so far from the Columbia."

There is no love for my joke. "You might have really hurt yourself. What if you'd been on the bus or crossing the street? What if Chance hadn't been right there?" We are audio only, but the tears are coming. I can hear them in the way her voice wobbles and how she tries to clear her throat.

"Those situations would've been worse," I admit. "But I can take steps. I'll set alarms on my phone if that will make you feel better." Uh oh. That was the magic phrase I meant to avoid. But it's too late.

"If you want to make me feel better, go see a doctor."

I close my eyes, which is probably dangerous because I'm still walking. But my boys will take care of me.

"Fine. A compromise: If I feel bad tomorrow, I will go to the campus clinic."

"Tonight, please."

"No, *tomorrow*. I am tired and want to sleep now that my stomach is full again. Passing out is surprisingly draining."

Another long pause. "All right, Hillary, but I expect a full update, or I'm getting on a plane."

"You'll get one," I mumble. "Love you."

"I love you, too," I hear her say as I pass the phone back to Colby. We're in the lobby now, waiting for the elevator. It cannot come fast enough. Colby plays the dutiful son and talks to Mom as we wait. We're all quiet as we enter the apartment. The space has never felt better to me. There's so much happening in my head. There's always so much happening in my head.

Colby sleeps over, and I'm pretty sure it's just to comfort Chance and not to make sure I go to the clinic in the morning. But when I hear their voices through the wall after midnight when I get up to pee, just talking to-gether, I feel alone.

Colby isn't the only one who'll be upset if Chance goes to England.

CHAPTER NINE

COFFEE IN HAND, I ARRIVE at the art building around nine. I do not text my brother back when he texts me to see how I'm feeling since I left the apartment and whether I've gone to the clinic. I did not wake him or my roommate when I departed. I do email my mom with an update and a selfie. Selfies seem to mollify her more than other forms of communication. I don't even sneer. I do not, however, email Glenn to let them know when I'm coming. I figure I'll just let it be a fun surprise.

But I don't even get inside because there are large cinderblock kilns with metal sheaths and propane tanks out in front of the building, and Glenn is there, wearing a big black apron and clear safety glasses. It's kind of hot, seeing them all decked out like some kind of black-smith. Their gray RCU hoodie looks soft and comfort-able. They're involved in a conversation with another student, which means I have to stand behind them. And they're wearing skinny jeans. I'm not trying to look at their ass, but it's *right there*, formed so perfectly by the denim it's wrapped in. They turn to me with a big smile, and I look up quickly...before they see where I was look-ing, I hope.

"You made it. Great! You can go up to the studio if you want to, or I brought some clay down for you in case you want to work outside. I'll be out here, so it might be easier if you're not too distracted."

I don't know why they're being so fucking friendly. They must not know my boys have outed their meddling...and I decide to keep it that way for now, even though the word *distracted* sets my blood boiling.

"I'll stay out here," I say with a smile that's so 100% fake, I probably look feral.

It's getting fallish, and this is my favorite time to be on campus. There's the fun of students just discovering college and getting used to their new environment. Add in the bustle and activity of the city, the changing leaves, and the nip in the air, and it's just...perfect.

"What are you going to work on first?" they ask.

I shrug. "I thought I'd just pull out some clay and see where it takes me."

"I know you want to get caught up, so let's add some focus to that. Please pick an assignment and bring me a sketch. Then you can have some clay." Then they turn and hurry back to where a student is about to pull their creation out of the fire, calling a reminder to use the gloves at their feet. Grumbling, I pull out my syllabus. *Create a symmetrical vessel that you have designed after studying historical examples. A contour drawing will serve as your "road map" in building this vessel. Target height: 12-14 in.* I find a blank notebook in my bag and pull out a pencil. I'll do the symmetrical one first; that seems easiest. I look around at the other students' work—this method of firing is called raku, which I actually remember from last quarter. I hate how little control they have over the final product: some are beautifully lined, with a wide variation of tones from the materials they put in the fire. And some look like I know mine would be: black. Boring. Not the gorgeous, metallic perfection these students are pulling out.

I get sketching. I want to press some leaves into the sides of it, since I'm out here anyway. I don't make it round. I don't know why I'm trying to make my own life difficult, but I choose a shape that's more pumpkin-like. I'm putting more detail into the shading along the ridges when a shadow falls over my paper.

"Looks great. You can go get some clay."

I haven't added the leaves to the side yet, and I want them to approve the whole thing. I can see it so clearly in my head, the muted orange undertones contrasting with the metallic vibrancy of the leaves, almost an oily look to them, like the Portland streets after not enough rain to wash everything away. I want the crackle in the leaves, I want spiraling down the side like the vine...

"Hillary." Their voice is quiet. "Did you hear me?"

"I'm almost done."

"It's good enough. I want you to get it made, so it can dry, and you can finish it next week."

I use my finger to smudge the edges of the pumpkin on the paper. "You can't rush art, Glenn. You should know that." They used my first name. I should be able to use theirs. That's only fair, right?

They sit next to me on the curb, close enough that I can feel their heat. "Do I need to take away your notepad?"

"You can try," I say, tipping my head to the side, trying to figure out if it's actually symmetrical. Even if it doesn't come out like I'm hoping, it'll still be okay, I think. As long as it doesn't come out white; this ain't no Ceramics Barn catalog.

When they don't respond, I look up. They're sitting with their black-smudged arms on their knees, clay-dusted hands clasped between them, watching their students work. I watch the students, too; it's fun to watch the fire flare up like it's trying to take their eyebrows off. My notebook leaves my hands with a whoosh.

"Hey!" I go to snatch it back, but they're too quick for me.

"Too easy. Now, go get your clay and start working." My stomach growls loudly. "But get something to eat first. Your brother told me about what happened." The crease between their thick eyebrows is deep, and I have the urge to lift my graphite-blackened finger and smooth away its implicit concern.

"My brother," I say, standing up and brushing off my backside, "needs to mind his own business and stop running his big mouth." I go over to the table they brought down. The big block of clay is wrapped in plastic to keep it damp, and I slice off a hunk with wire. Standing at the table feels nicer than sitting on the cold concrete, so I stay there. When I look up, Glenn's gone. Resting my hands on the cold, wet clay, I glance around. No, I don't *need* to know where they went; I just *want* to know where they went. I must monitor my enemies. Everyone knows this. I spend a few minutes watching the kiln again, watching the traffic along the park blocks, wandering off into thought.

"Here."

I straight-up jump when they appear behind me, sliding a sandwich onto the table.

"It's turkey. Hope you're not vegan."

"You thought about that, didn't you? You stood in line and tried to decide if I gave off a vegan vibe. How did you come down on 'no?'"

"Your shoes. Your bag doesn't look like pleather, either."

"Good call. I gladly accept your offering to support my artistic pursuits."

"Eat it now, before your hands get all messy..." Why does the word 'messy' make my heart thump harder like that? Why do I want to see them messy now, their hands covered in gray slip, their hair falling into their eyes, smudges on their cheeks for me to wipe away, their white spaghetti strap sliding down one broad shoulder...I shake myself a little. They're already gone, checking the temp on the kilns. I peek at the sandwich; it has sprouts. I do like sprouts. It reminds me of something Colby would do to a sandwich. I can smell cream cheese, too, and pickles as I unwrap it. But the clay is calling to me as I take a big bite. I wish I had more hands; eating is so inconvenient when I get into a project.

I stare down at the big wet lump. My fears start to creep in...*what if I can't make it symmetrical? What if it doesn't look like a pumpkin? What if the leaves don't look different enough?* I put the sandwich down and lick a little cream cheese off my thumb. *I'll just start a little bit, and then I'll come back to it.*

"Nope." From behind me, a large hand whisks away my clay before I can touch it. "I saw you eyeing it. Eat first." Where the hell did they come from? And who gave them permission to be bossy as fuck?

"Seriously, Glenn?"

"It's purely selfish. I don't want you causing a scene or hurting yourself if you pass out near the kilns. University could get sued. Can't have that."

"How perfectly logical," I grumble, picking the sandwich back up and taking another giant bite. Maybe I can eat faster. I pull out my phone and respond to a message from Janey, who wants to do dinner tonight (I'm in). I respond to a message from Raina, who wants to know if I can score her tickets to PDXtrings this weekend (maybe, let me ask Colby). I reach down again, but the sandwich is gone, I think because I ate it. Unless a dog came by that I didn't notice. Or an instructor.

"Now you can have your clay back. Put your phone away in class."

I'm biting my tongue so hard right now, I'm hoping I don't break the skin and start bleeding. If they weren't my instructor...let's put it this way: it will not be one of those post-class buddy situations. I have a few professors I've kept in touch with professionally or socially. Glenn will not be one of them. I want to tell them to get off my back. I want to tell them I'm twenty-eight, and I've been successfully managing my academic career up to this point. But I know the best thing I can do is show them I don't have ADHD and don't need their help passing this class.

Wiping my hands on my jeans, I pull the clay out from under the table where they stashed it. Forming it into a pumpkin shape proves more difficult than I imagined, and I end up molding it into a thick hemisphere, then carving the ridges into the side with a triangle-shaped tool that I vaguely remember Glenn demoing in class. I wish I'd taken video of how they did it. I wet my fingers and try to smooth out the odd streaks the tool is leaving behind. Someone behind me hands me a damp yellow sponge, and I take it. Glenn's gone again before I can even thank them. Not that I was going to.

An hour later, I have five ridges, and I'm searching for the right leaves to press into the sides. I decide the best thing to do is just find one and repeat it. But I haven't found the right one yet, and I'm still kicking leaves aside when Glenn finds me again.

"Lose your keys?" they ask, and the smirk in their voice is unmistakable.

"I happen to be working on my assignment."

"Your assignment is over there on the table, drying out..."

"You didn't look carefully at my sketch..." I sweep my toe through the thick carpet of leaves again. "Or you'd know what I'm doing."

"Oh, that was an imprint of the leaf? I thought you were just going to carve it into the side." They pause. "That's...an interesting idea. Might save you some time if you can press it deeply enough without affecting the symmetry." I spot a red maple leaf just the size and shape I'm looking for when Glenn walks through my search area and scatters it, and I glare at their back once they're far enough away.

"Still having issues with the professor, I see." I pivot to see Janey at my elbow.

"Hey, gorgeous." I give her a big hug. Janey is a snugglebug, especially when she's between partners. I can always count on her for a squeeze. Of course, she's dating my cousin Blake long-distance right now, so she's still short on physical affection. She pushes her horn-rim glasses up her nose, then pulls her hands inside the big sleeves of her taupe sweater and breathes on them, presumably to warm them up.

"Whatcha looking for?"

"A leaf."

She stares down at the hundreds at my feet. "I see."

I laugh. Only Janey would be so kind about my weirdness. "A special leaf. I'm going to make an impression of it on my pot."

"Ohhhh, I like that," she cries, far too excited over a simple pottery assignment. I find one I like again, and we go over to the table, chatting about weekend plans. It's simple enough, but I have to reinforce the inside with my other hand; I don't want any cracking. Even I know that's structurally unsound. But I think the walls are thick enough that it won't be a problem.

"It's pretty thick." Like a fucking ghost. I don't know how they keep sneaking up on me. I really don't. "We'll have to pre-bake it...might need extra time."

"Like a pie crust?"

Their smile catches me off guard. "Kind of like, yeah." Janey's draping herself over my shoulder, and from the way their smile turns quizzical and their gaze bounces between us, I wonder if they think we're...together. So, yes, I'm blatantly reinforcing that notion when I turn to her and say, "I'll see you tonight?" She grins and gives me a big ol' kiss on the cheek before she leaves.

"So, should I take this upstairs?"

"Did you bring your key card?"

"Uh..." It should be in my bag. I haul it up onto the table and paw through it, getting out my phone to illuminate the inside.

"Is that a bottle of hot sauce?"

"Yes," I say, not looking up because you wouldn't believe how often people ask me that. Do they not have a preferred brand of hot sauce? My mother is from Albuquerque. What am I supposed to do, pretend like all hot sauces are created equal? I don't think so.

Glenn wanders away sometime during my search. It's just as well. I don't have the contemptible key card. And I'm going to have to eat crow when they get back. My temper is swirling the way water does in the teapot, like it's just thinking about breaking apart. A shadow falls over me as I turn it over and shake everything out onto the table, lip gloss and lotion and a roll of stamps tumbling to the ground.

"No, huh?"

"I don't know yet," I mutter, sifting through receipts and theater ticket stubs.

"Just use mine." They're holding it out.

"Thank you, but I'll find mine. Or run home and get it." *Assuming it's at home...*which is a dangerous assumption, let's face it. My teakettle temper has those microscopic bubbles now, breaking away from my heart's hard surface to rise to where they might become words, nowhere near as innocuous as water.

"Don't be silly, I don't mind. As long as you don't lose it."

It's a joke; I know it is. And yet the heat of that little jab sends the bubbles hurling to the top.

"I wouldn't lose it," I snap. "But I don't need it, *thank you.*"

"Hillary..." Their voice is low, assuaging, but it's too late. I'm boiling.

"Don't," I grit out, and several students turn to look at us. *Mind your fucking business, undergrads. You're cute, but I will cut you.* I scrabble after my bag's contents, finally giving up and brushing it all back into the messenger bag with a wide sweep of my arm. I leave whatever fell. I'll get it later if it's still here. Slinging it over my shoulder, I stride away from the work area, making sure I have my house keys. It wouldn't do to storm off in a fit of pique just to be locked out of there as well.

There's something about being locked out. When we were kids, Colby locked me in the garage. That's what I'm thinking about as I cross the street to exit campus, breaking that invisible line between the city and the college. He was probably five or six, which means I was nine or ten, old enough not to be scared just because I was in the garage unsupervised. But it wasn't being unsupervised that scared me, I don't think. I just didn't feel safe out there, barred from my home. My brain has been superb at generating Worst-Case Scenarios™ my whole life.

By the time I get back, everything is cleaned up—and my pot is gone. I hesitate at the doors to the art building; I'm sure they took it upstairs for me. But what if they didn't? I worked too hard on that infernal thing to let it all go to waste. There are still students going in and out when I get to the doors of the studio, but I can see my pumpkin sitting on a table near the drying room. That's close enough.

I turn and leave, sticking my key back in my bag, zipping it shut as I start the walk back home.

CHAPTER TEN

ON SUNDAY, I GALLOP downstairs with M&M cookies in hand to Janey's. I do knock; she's basically my best friend, but that doesn't mean she wants me barging right in, or so Colby claims. I actually think she'd be fine with it. Giada opens the door with a smile.

"I could hear you coming down the hall," she says in her light accent that I love. "Like a horse."

"Yes, I'm very majestic and lanky, thank you."

"Lanky? What's lanky?"

I snort because I'm not lanky, so explaining this is going to be interesting. I let the task fall to Janey.

"It's like long and lean," she says, her brow furrowing. "I think."

I shove a cookie in my mouth. "Sure. Did you start without me?"

"When you don't come at the appointed time, you leave us no choice," Giada chides, and I grin again.

"What're we watching then?"

"*My Fair Lady.*" Janey hands me a napkin, which I apparently need?

I throw back my head and moan. "Not more musicals. Gals, I'm already surrounded by as many singing, dancing characters as a girl could ever want. More, even. My boys are on a huge musical kick right now."

"Come on time, then." Janey elbows me, and I elbow her back, then plop down on her futon. I haven't missed much; Audrey Hepburn is still singing in that grating

Cockney accent about how life would be better if she just had a warm place to sleep at night. Hard to disagree with on any level. I often feel sad when I see homeless people in Portland; we have lots of them because the weather's more temperate than elsewhere in the U.S.

My boys would probably have some kind of fun fact about this movie, like how it was the first film to use a wireless microphone and won an Academy Award for it. Actually, maybe they had told me that? It sounds familiar now. Something about Rex Harrison not being able to lip sync.

I stare at good old Rex; he's decently good-looking. Kind of like someone else I know...I shake thoughts of Glenn out of my head. But today I noticed they have an eyebrow ring, and that didn't help my attraction problem. I much prefer Glenn's style to Rex's, which is understandable given that it's a period piece. I try to imagine Glenn in a suit like that, and my nose wrinkles instinctively. They don't need stuffy clothes like that, even if the gray would bring out those nice silver highlights in their beard. *They're perfect just the way they are.*

"No."

Both Janey and Giada turn to look at me. Oops. Brain 0, Mouth 1.

"No what?" Janey asks, her head cocked adorably. "You don't think he's an ordinary man?"

"No!" Wait, those aren't the right pronouns; who's she talking about?

"The doctor is wrong. Hillary is right," Giada says, gesturing to the screen. "Women, we do not make things worse. Very much better."

"Yes," I say, swallowing my giggles, "that's what I meant. Rex definitely needs a lady. Or maybe a man; he seems really into his clothes and his books. Maybe he should branch out a little."

"It's not the gender that bothers him," Janey says, stirring her tea. "It's their meddling. Their families. You can get that from anyone."

"Boy, don't I know it," I mutter, but I escape their perplexed looks when I get up to get snacks to shove into my face to keep it from talking more about what's inside my brain. Those brain thoughts are doing me no favors right now.

"How's pottery class?" Janey asks.

"Horrible," I say, plopping back onto the couch. "I'm just not artsy."

"That's not true," Giada says, rubbing my arm. "You painted the dresser. You do the yarn. You bake things."

"Yeah, maybe you just need to use your actual skills to cozy up to the professor a little."

My cheeks go immediately hot. "I'm not interested in cozying up to them!"

I am, though, in a totally stress-release hate-fuck kind of way. I hate it here.

Janey rolls her eyes. "Not like *that*. Just, like, try to be nice. Maybe they'll be more willing to help you."

"They've already offered plenty of help. More than was needed."

"I can sense the drama," Giada says, her dark eyes glittering. I can't help but laugh.

"They think I have ADHD, and they won't shut up about it. They even talked to my boys about it."

Janey's head snaps back, and she and Giada share a concerned look.

"You...don't have ADHD?" Janey asks gently.

"No! At least I...don't think so." I stare at the two of them; they are suspiciously quiet. I expected sympathetic outrage, not these strange looks of collusion. I don't even know if I want to pose the question that bubbles to the top of my brain in the face of this weirdness.

"Did you think I had a *learning disability*?"

"Seemed like a fair assumption," Giada says. "You are often late, losing all the things..."

"And you've got that hyper-focus thing. Which is part of the not-eating thing, I think," Janey adds. And all I can do is stare at them. Because if *everyone* in my life thinks I have ADHD, then it's not just Glenn's weird suggestion. If *everyone* agrees with them...what's my responsibility to myself? Wouldn't it be foolish to just ignore all of them? They care about me; I know they do. But I don't want to have ADHD. There's a reason I weaseled my way out of going to urgent care: doctors are the worst. How do I even go about getting that diagnosed, anyway?

My heart is raging, prompting me to get up and just walk out. Go upstairs and be by myself. *Betrayal, betrayal, betrayal* it beats, thumping so loud I can hear it in my ears. *But it couldn't be. Not from all of them*, I whisper back.

"Hil?" Janey looks truly concerned now.

"Can we just watch the movie?" I mumble, sinking deeper into the couch, pillowing my head on my forearms, curling my knees in toward my belly. Giada rubs my leg a little, then lets her hand rest on my thigh, and I don't ask her to move it. Rex Harrison finishes his song about how he doesn't want a woman in his life, and I try to let it fill all the available space in my brain and push out these worries and fears.

Except one.

I think I owe Glenn an apology.

CHAPTER ELEVEN

MY PALMS ARE SWEATING as I approach the third-floor studio on Monday. It's not our usual class time; it's office hours. I'm hoping there's no one else there. I'm hoping I can just sneak in and out...but that hope dies a bloody death since I can hear voices through the door before I even touch it. I peek through the tiny window: there are five or six people standing near Glenn's desk in a blobby sort of order, chatting and laughing. They have to discuss grades in the drying room for privacy's sake, but I assume Glenn is sitting there in their ancient rolling chair, glasses perched on their nose, going over a paper or an exam with someone.

"How's the spying?" Glenn's voice in my ear is unexpected. When I rear back, they're leaning casually against the closed door.

"You scared me! What are you doing out here?"

"That's just what I was going to ask *you*." They smirk. "Office hours are usually held *in* the classroom."

"Yes, exactly," I fire back. "So you shouldn't be out here, either."

"I'm not allowed to use the restroom?" They're wearing short sleeves. I can see their tattoos up close. The flow of my thoughts is trying to divert from their question, bumping over the rocks of politeness as I stare.

"This is for you." I thrust the foil pan at them before I can embarrass myself any further. I turn to leave before they can react.

"Hey, wait. What's this?" They don't touch me, but they do lengthen their stride to get in front of me. They lift the corner of the lid, and I can smell the cinnamon wafting out.

"It's called bubble bread. Enjoy." I try to step around them, but they're too quick for me. Glenn's long fucking legs outpace mine to cut me off.

"And what's it for?"

I gesture to the pan. "Eating."

Glenn chuckles. "That's not what I meant, and I'm pretty sure you know that." They're not that close to me, but it still feels too close. They're wearing this soft-looking, thin pink v-neck shirt, and it matches their lips, bare today but still beautiful. Dangerously so.

"Fine, give it to a goat. I don't care." I start down the hall again, and this time, they let me go by. Relief reverberates in my head, making it almost buzz...until I hear them behind me.

"I don't know any goats. Can you recommend one who'd enjoy this?" *They really don't want it?* I can't pretend that doesn't hurt. I don't think I burned it or anything. Maybe they don't eat gluten? That'd just figure. I want to snatch it back from them, but I can't risk skin-to-skin contact right now, and if they don't let go, it'll just make me madder.

"No. Aren't all those students waiting for you?"

"The ones you were spying on? They'll keep."

I whirl to face them just before I get to the stairs. "I wasn't *spying*, for God's sake!"

"What were you doing, then?"

"I was just…I…" Having to make an apology feels super unfair right now, given that they're mildly harassing me. I was being *nice*. Why am I the one being interrogated? I huff. "It's a gift. Didn't your mother teach you how to say thank you?"

"She did, actually, but no one's ever just shoved baked goods at me before without an explanation. I feel like my questions are justified. I mean, it could be poison."

"An apology," I grit out. "It's an apology. For yelling at you the other day." *Like I want to yell right now.*

That cute little wrinkle between their eyebrows is back. "That wasn't entirely your fault. I should've brought up my concerns differently."

"Granted. Goodbye, professor." As I turn, I hear Glenn take a breath to say something, but the door at the end of the hall opens, and I hear someone call their name.

"Sorry, everybody. I'll be right there." But I'm already too far away to be caught, safe in the stairwell, taking the steps two at a time to scramble away from this confusing situation, not willing to be backed into a corner with them again.

I'm halfway home when my phone buzzes repeatedly.

> **Unknown**: Colby gave me your number. I hope that's okay.
>
> **Unknown**: Oh, this is Glenn. Sorry. Should've started with that.

They couldn't chase me physically, so my ridiculous brother gave them the means to chase me digitally? That's not right. I switch to my thread with Colby.

Hillary: You gave Glenn my phone number?

Colby: Did you not want me to? I mean, it seemed like a reasonable request since they could've looked it up in your records, anyway. They said it was urgent.

Hillary: It was not urgent! Not whatsoever! Not on any planet in our galaxy!

Hillary: Also, when I asked you for their number last summer, you said you couldn't give it out and I should go through proper channels!

Colby: oops

I wait for him to say more as the traffic light stays stubbornly red, but then I get tired of waiting for both. I jaywalk first as I decide what to say to my brother.

Hillary: Oops?!

I mean, I don't want to be savage, but I also want him to know I'm not happy. Meanwhile, Glenn apparently doesn't like waiting, either.

Glenn: Hillary?

Do I let them think they have the wrong number? When they find out they don't, they'll think I'm rude. Maybe they'll just drop it if I ignore them...

Glenn: You didn't have to bake me anything to apologize. We got off on the wrong foot a bit this quarter, and I feel I'm as much to blame as you are.

Hillary: If you don't want it, just say so.

Glenn: I didn't say that!

Hillary: you asked for GOAT RECOM-MENDATIONS

Glenn: It was a JOKE.

Glenn: And YOU STARTED IT.

Glenn: LOOK

Then there's a picture coming through—no, a video—and they're eating one of the small dough balls I rolled, the hard outside of it crunching as they take a bite, flecks of sugar and cinnamon catching in their beard as they fall. "It's good," they say through the bite, and it has the ring of sincerity. They stare into the phone as they pop the rest of it in their mouth. "*Really* good." When they lick their fingers one by one, I end the video with a bubbly feeling in my stomach.

Hillary: Good. Great. Fine.

Glenn: Is that all you wanted when you came by? To give me a delicious gift without explaining yourself?

Hillary: Yep. You and your students enjoy.

Glenn: Oh, I'm not sharing this with them. This is all for me.

Hillary: You're eating it right in front of them?

Glenn: Um. Yes?

Glenn: my classroom, my rules.

I have to laugh at that. At least they can't hear me. I'm sure it would go to their head.

CHAPTER TWELVE

THE NEXT DAY, I HAVE Feminist Theory, French, and of course, pottery. They all go fine, and Mx. Rasmussen hardly seems to pay any attention to me, which is a relief after I embarrassed myself with the baked goods the other day. They haven't texted me again, which is another relief. Not that I thought we'd be staying up until one in the morning becoming besties, but still. You never know. Some people don't show their true colors until they've got your number, and then it's too late.

On my way home, I stop at the library to look for a book I misplaced (it's still in my study area, thankfully), then stop by the grocery store and buy myself sushi for a treat. Say what you want about grocery store sushi, it's cheap and convenient, and I will love it until the day I die. Judge me if you will. I'm juggling my food and my bag and my keys and my phone (why? I don't know. I guess I forgot pockets exist? There's no excuse for me, really), when I hear an unexpected low voice through my door. Chance...has friends over? This is unusual. Not unheard of, but unlikely, especially on a work night. The man is very particular about his social schedule.

I finally get the door open, and three heads look up.

"What are *you* doing here?" I rasp.

Chance and Colby frown at me, but Glenn smiles politely.

"Your roommate wanted to learn how to crochet, and it just so happens I know how."

"Uh-huh. Also, how did you beat me here?"

"Fast walker. Long legs."

"I see." I cast them one more hard look, so they know they don't belong in my house. "Hello, boys. Good day?"

"Yeah," Chance says, scowling down at the navy blue yarn in his hands. "Did you eat? We're going to order from Thai Express."

I hold up my sushi package, but he doesn't see because he's still trying to untangle his mess. Colby nods, though...he has been unnecessarily tuned into my eating ever since The Incident™. I cannot pretend this is not very annoying.

"That's right, we're going to order from Thai Orchid."

Chance looks up then. "No, Thai *Express*. You promised."

Colby's rubbing at his chin the way he does when he's lying. "I don't think I recall any—"

"Yesterday, before work, you said, 'Is Glenn coming over?' and I said, 'Yes, they're going to teach me to crochet,' which was clearly a fucking mistake because it was supposed to help my anxiety, and instead, it's just pissing me off. And then you said, 'Great, we should all get Thai food,' and I said, 'I want Thai Express' and you said, 'Great.'"

My brother grins at his partner. "Yes, it's great that you want it. But we're getting Thai Orchid because it's far better."

Glenn leans over Chance's work. "You forgot to wrap it before you went into the next stitch."

"Oh, is that...okay. I think I..." Chance trails off as he scrutinizes his work. I eat my sushi in silence at the kitchen table instead of on the couch where I usually eat because it is full of adult people and not big enough for me. I could sit in the other overstuffed chair, but I am choosing to be ornery. I am pretending to read on my phone as I enjoy my dinner, but I'm really listening to their conversation.

"Down through both parts of the stitch...there you go. Try to relax your hand," Glenn coaches, and Chance sighs.

"What can we get for you, Glenn?" Colby asks. "Our treat."

"Oh, that's okay. I've got leftovers at home."

"And now you'll have more," Chance says firmly. "Dinner was part of the deal."

Chance despises charity of any kind. When he was saving money for his top surgery, I tried to get him to start one of those "Fund My Need" sites, but he wouldn't hear of it. When a few of our mutual friends slipped me some cash, I put it in his sock drawer, and he was none the wiser. I still wonder where he thought it came from.

"Well, okay. I guess I'll take a mango salad."

"Big mistake," I say, and they pivot to glance at me.

"Why's that?"

"Because everyone knows the best Thai food is pad Thai. It's got noodles, cilantro, veggies, tofu, peanuts, eggs...it is everything good and right in the world. A salad? With *fruit* in it? I don't think so."

Okay, so I'm not being as aloof as I'd like. Probably low blood sugar or something is making me ornery.

"Hillary's right," Colby says, still tapping his screen as he orders. "Pad Thai is the best. Babe, you want the pineapple curry?"

"Yes, please," Chance mutters, still concentrating on his yarn, and my heart glows. I still love seeing the two of them like this, so damn domestic and happy together. If I could bottle up what they've got, I could make a million. Heck, I'd drink a bottle myself. I go back to my California roll with a smile.

"Watch me for a sec," Glenn says, nudging Chance. "It's wrap, through, pull through two—not three. Always two."

"Oh..." Chance says. "Like this?"

"Col, get me a Thai iced tea," I call.

"Why?"

"Because I like them. And I didn't get a drink with my sushi because I was being cheap."

"So you'll just get me to pay for it?" He shakes his head, but I can see him ordering it.

"I mean, I can pay you for it, but if we're adding up food, then you owe me for like *years* of fridge mooching, so..." I lick some cream cheese off my thumb. "It's up to you."

Colby grumbles something under his breath, but I know he's getting it for me.

"Which one of you is older?" Glenn asks, and I wish I could see their face because *what kind of question is that? I'm clearly older.* Colby gestures toward me with his head.

"Why?" I ask, keeping my voice level.

"Just curious. Putting together the puzzle pieces of the Cook family."

"Well, we lost the box a long time ago, so don't expect a satisfying conclusion. Not that it's any of your business." I get up to throw away my trash, and Colby's glaring at me. Like, he looks *actually mad.*

What? I mouth behind Glenn's back, and my brother just shakes his head.

"That looks great, Chance," Glenn says. "You're getting the hang of it now. Keep the yarn loose."

"I'm gonna go take a bath," I say, shouldering my bag as I head down the hall. "Does anyone need the facilities before I monopolize them indefinitely like a bitch?"

"It's your house," Chance calls after me. "You're not a bitch."

"You haven't seen how long the bath is yet. Last opportunity?"

"Yeah, I'll just..." Glenn comes down the hall, and I turn so they can slip by. "Thanks."

"Whatever."

"Hillary!" Colby yells, and I hear Glenn chuckle as they close the door behind them.

"What?"

"Come in here for a sec." I'm not in the mood to be lectured, but I can tell that's what coming. *There's a reason I don't call Mom, dude...*

I drop my bag in my room as I shuffle into the living room. "What?"

"What do you mean, 'what?'" Colby whisper-yells. "You're being so rude!"

"Oh, forgive me if it wasn't a happy surprise to see my nemesis sitting on my couch when I get home at the end of a long day!" I whisper-yell back.

"Your nemesis?" Chance asks at a normal volume, and we both shush him. He's such a noob. Sometimes it's so obvious that he didn't have siblings. We're helping him, really.

"You can be polite for twenty minutes," Colby goes on quietly. "They're Chance's guest."

"Then why isn't Chance the one yelling at me?"

"Because unless you put a crop in his hand, he's too nice."

Chance's face looks the way I feel: horrified.

"What is wrong with you?" he breathes, glaring, and I am equally appalled.

"To quote the queen, EW, DAVID."

I hear the bathroom door open. Not eager to continue this conversation, I turn and hurry back down the hall. I meet Glenn in the middle, and they don't step aside. I fight with my face for a minute while I try not to grimace. I'm supposed to be *nice*? To *them*?

"I like your..." Hmm. This is tricky because usually, the thing I admire most about their fashion sense is their footwear, which they have left by the front door like a decent human being. "Sweater." And I do like it. It's intarsia, which I know from the two months I took up knitting five years ago, and it looks like someone just plucked them off a hillside in Europe where they were tending sheep. And they're wearing a corduroy skirt that shows off their legs. But I can't comment on that because it would be too close to an actual compliment about their body.

"Oh, yeah?" They cross their arms. "What do you like about it?"

"Well, it looks vintage, which means you're saving the planet by not buying new."

"It's not vintage."

I squint at it. "Okay, well, then get out of my way, Earth enemy."

"Hillary!" Colby hollers.

"Excuse me," I say, pushing past Glenn to get to the bathroom. I've already got the door locked and my shirt off when I hear them just outside the door.

"Nice to see you, Ms. Cook."

I try to figure out if there's anything I can say that won't get me yelled at by my brother again.

Can't say the same?

Stop pretending to be a nice person; it's confusing my silly brother?

Fuck off, jackass? No. But at least I'm pretty sure jackass is gender neutral.

If they weren't my professor, I'd just open the door and give them a piece of my mind— even in my underwear. I do actually need a passing grade in their class, though, so I settle for saying nothing.

I turn my back to the door and run the water, adding a little lavender and ylang ylang oil. The warm water disperses the fragrance throughout the room, and I take a deep breath. But their voice through the door is still stuck in my head. And I can hear them laughing in the living room, talking in that low timbre that hits me right in the gut. I've listened to hours of recordings of their voice, and it's never affected me quite this way.

I step into the water, hissing at the temperature and easing my stressed body under the surface while filling the tub to the brim. My hair's still up in a messy bun, and I leave it there, letting it cushion my head against the wall as I close my eyes. The stress is still leaking out of my muscles, and I release a big sigh.

The longer I sit there, the more my body starts to relax, the tension unwinding...but that voice. It's still coming through the thin door, and it's making me...annoyed. No, not annoyed. Horny. Maybe it isn't their voice at all, I tell myself. It's been a long time. The water feels good. *Your body's just doing what bodies do.*

With my eyes closed, in the dark, I can lie to myself. But that doesn't change the fact that when I move my fingers between my legs, it's all too easy to find my clit, practically begging for attention.

With my eyes closed, it's easy to just let my fingers do the work, and since 'easy' hasn't applied to this activity in quite some time, I'm not eager to examine things too closely. I toe at the drain and let some of the water out; it's going to splash over the edge otherwise. Because I'm going to town on my clit and making waves, and I've got no reason to stop.

"Hil? You want your tea?" My brother's voice is a bucket of cold water on my bath time fun.

"Can you put it in the fridge?" Yeah, even I'd be able to tell my voice is strained.

"Sure."

Now that there's less water, I'm eyeing that spout with extra interest. *This is shady,* my brain whispers. *Getting off to your professor's voice is weird.* My body tells it in no uncertain terms to shut the fuck up as I slide myself down to the spout. Giada told me once when she was very drunk that this was the only way she could get off when she was younger. You just slide under the spout, turn on the warm water, and let nature take its course... but I shouldn't. Not when it's Glenn's voice that's actually getting me off.

I keep saying that to myself as I adjust the water temp, spread my legs, and lie down on my back against the warm, wet porcelain. The position is somewhat awkward, my pelvis in the air and my body shoved into the small space. But oh fuck, Giada is wise, she's so smart, she's a fucking genius. My hips start going automatically, moving that fantastic stream with its perfect pressure against my clit, against my opening, and I'm trying to control my breathing, my fingers curled against the porcelain, nothing to hold on to. And then I hear Glenn laugh through the door.

It's a belly laugh, and my orgasm slams forward like it's just been waiting to hear that very thing. I cover my mouth with both hands as I come and come, legs shaking, pretty sure that if I open my eyes, I'm going to be able to shoot rainbows out of them because I am now made of sunshine and glory.

My chest still heaving, I take a minute to recover, but when I finally get the water shut off, I sit slumped in the tub for a minute, just taking in the heaviness of my limbs and the way my clit is still buzzy and sensitive. And God, what a fucking relief. Maybe it's wrong that it came to this...but I'll take whatever I can get.

I grab my robe from the back of the door and scurry down the hall to my room, since I forgot clothes. Safe in my room, a little laugh escapes my lips as I pull out my PJs. And then another. Suddenly, I can't stop, and I'm trying to muffle my embarrassed giggles against my terrycloth robe sleeve. I can't tell anyone about this. Along with how I broke my mother's favorite curling iron in sixth grade, I will take this secret to my grave.

I wander out in my unicorn pajama pants and RCU T-shirt, head held high, determined to chat in a civilized way and drink my iced tea without making eye contact with my professor...ever again.

CHAPTER THIRTEEN

YOU'D THINK, SINCE I am living with his partner, I'd see my brother all the time. Not so. Between him not being able to do Wednesday Watch Night anymore because of his church gig and me having a group study session on Thursday, I have had no meaningful contact with him for over a week. A week! Then on Friday night, Colby texts me.

Colby: I'm free tonight before work. Can I talk you into dinner out and a free symphony ticket?

Hillary: I'm sorry, sir, you have the wrong number.

Colby: this is your brother. Colby.

Hillary: I had a brother, but I haven't heard from him in a long time. I fear some nameless tragedy hath befallen him...

Colby: Look, I know I've been a little Chance-focused lately...

Hillary: a little? I came home the other day, and you two didn't even come up for air!

Colby: did you? That's funny.

Colby: I wonder if Chance heard you. I never did.

Hillary: this is my shocked face.

Colby: No, look, I really want to hang out with you.

Hillary: I ALREADY KNOW CHANCE IS AT A CONFERENCE ALL WEEK-END, JERKFACE.

Colby: I'll pay for dinner.

Hillary: Deal. When and where?

We end up going to Dancing Earth because it's close, I love their wraps, and it's far away enough and unfancy enough that most symphony-goers won't be competing with us for a table. I mean, it's almost anti-fancy because there's so much weed in the air. Not that symphony-goers can't smoke weed, just—never mind.

"How're your after-graduation plans going?" Colby asks through a bite of a pork verde burrito. I sigh.

"Okay, I guess. I've got that internship spring quarter with the American Association of University Women. After that, I don't know what I'm going to do."

"Mom and Dad talked to you about money at all?"

"Nope." Still not talking to them much at all. Probably should fix that.

"That's good. I'm sure they won't cut you off the minute you graduate."

"Right." My turkey cranberry wrap doesn't taste as good as it did a minute ago, and I set it down.

"What do you want to do?"

"I honestly don't know. I joked to Chance the other day about going for my PhD, partly because I've been in academia so long, it just seems like the next logical step."

"Do you want to teach? You might be good at that."

"I don't know. Little kids, maybe. Not adults. They're scary. But teaching little kids would mean more schooling, so...that's out. I need to start paying off my loans."

"Yeah."

"I mean, I could do social work, probably. I'd like to do something that helps people."

He nods, and I just know the next thing that comes out of his mouth is going to be sarcasm. "You could always write a book."

I burst out laughing. "I'm not qualified for that."

"Bullshit. You do all sorts of fancy kitchen shit. I'd help you with the salad section."

I stare at my brother, trying to figure out if he's serious. "You think I should write a cookbook?"

Colby grins. "I mean, you've got the name for it."

I throw a straw at him, and he dodges it, laughing. We clean up and head over to the Howitz. Going in the alley door with the musicians makes me feel sneaky and special.

"I've gotta hit the bathroom," I mutter because no one appreciates it when I exclaim it. He slips a visitor's badge around my neck. There's too much money (i.e., instruments) lying around to let just anyone back here.

"Okay, meet me up in the booth," he says, gesturing toward the hall.

I'm still thinking about our post-graduation conversation as I weave past people toward the bathrooms at the end. My parents have been super generous, helping support my monthly expenses with the understanding that I'd pay them back eventually. And then there's the school debt I have piled on top of that for my degree...which is going to start accruing interest the second I graduate. I'm sweating just thinking about it. My head is down, trained on my phone, when I come out of the restroom.

"Hillary?"

I forgot they were going to be here. Leave it to me to wander around backstage where my nemesis works. They trimmed their beard nicely, and they're carrying some kind of gigantic bow—the instrument kind, not the present kind.

"Glenn," I say politely, trying to shoulder past them. They turn and walk in step with me.

"What are you doing here?"

I should ignore the question. Just keep walking. Go find Colby. Find my seat.

"I took up the cello recently, and it turns out I'm a prodigy. I'm soloing tonight."

Glenn crosses their arms, but their face remains stoic. "In that case, you missed our rehearsals."

"I don't need them. Rehearsals are for normals."

"Interesting. And here I've spent all that time with my bass. What a fool I've been."

"Well," I sniff, "don't be too hard on yourself. We can't all be exceptional."

"Glenn, we're warming up," a passing man remarks, and they pat him on the shoulder in thanks. They look me up and down one more time, and something in their gaze makes my scalp tingle a little.

"It's nice to see you...prodigy." They smirk at me over their shoulder as they continue down the narrow white hallway. I watch them go, and there's something about them that's not quite right, but I can't place it. Seeing them out of our usual context has me all befuddled, and I go the wrong way before a helpful stagehand gets me going in the right direction, up the stairs toward the booth.

Colby's still tweaking the balance for the recording and livestream when I get up to the booth, and they're all finding a concert A, tuning to the same note. As much as I like the music, I like this part, too—the jumbled yarn ball of sound rolling around the empty concert hall, people warming up their fingers and their lips with scales and the tough bits of what comes later. I only ever played piano as a kid, so my musical experience wasn't group-oriented like this, and I think I would've liked it. There's a great swell of sound, and being in the middle of it would be...rapturous, I imagine.

The conductor, a Latino man in his upper forties, I'd guess, steps onto the podium, and the group collectively quiets. I can't hear what he says, but they all tuck violins under their arms and woodwinds across their laps momentarily as they shuffle papers to find what he wants to run. I don't mean to look for Glenn—I just happen to see them in the back corner. That must be why Chance thought they played the timpani; they're all in the back together, Evan included.

Glenn's adjusting a black stool, and I suddenly realize what's different about them: they're wearing straight-leg pants. I think I've only seen them in pants one other time, when they were raku firing outside in those delicious skinny jeans. I can't tell what color their nails are from here, and I kick myself for not looking in the hallway. Not that it matters. Why would it matter? It doesn't.

Colby's muttering about microphone placement, and he picks up a large black radio and speaks into it.

"Arnie, can you adjust the number six mic? It's not picking up all the woodwinds in the back..."

A redheaded man wearing all black hurries out onto the stage quietly and tilts the microphone down what seems like an insignificant amount to my eyes.

Colby radios again, "Perfect. That's great, bud. Thanks."

I make myself comfortable on a stool. The conductor raises his arms, and all eyes are on him. And I think in a flash that this is what my brain's missing: a conductor. Maybe that's what 'executive dysfunction' really means...

I've been reading about ADHD in women. It's...possible. But then Colby hands me a set of headphones so I can hear better, and the thought disappears.

"You don't have to come up here now, we can just run through it," the conductor says, his speech lightly accented. "Though, of course, you will for the performance, so perhaps if you prefer..."

"No." Glenn's voice surprises me. "Here is fine, since we're just warming up."

Oh, shit. I joked about being a soloist to *an actual soloist*. That figures.

"Just...when you do move up? Please make sure you're angled enough to be in my eyeline."

"Oh, for sure."

"And me in yours as well."

"Yeah. Of course." Glenn's smiling, but something about the way they're tapping the wood side of the bow against their leg makes me think they're nervous. They're never fidgety like that in class.

"Have they ever done a solo before?" I whisper to Colby.

"Uh, a few times. Not a regular thing." He's still fiddling with knobs, and his voice is vacant. "But they're amazing."

The musicians still. Then the violins lead off into a high, haunting melody. And I've heard this before; there's a recording of Itzhak Perlman, among others, playing this song. It's a show-off piece, written for a virtuoso—on the violin. Not the double bass. Which is what Glenn is holding between their legs.

"What's this piece called?"

"Zigeunerweisen. Sarasate." The first word he says like 'cig-ironer-vizen,' which sounds to me like someone had a terrible idea about smoking while doing their laundry. The second word is softer on his tongue and rhymes with latte. I don't know why it has two names, but they've started now, and I'm transfixed watching Glenn lean over their bass, reaching for the high notes *but not looking at their fingers.* They're staring off into the distance a few feet in front of them, casting these high ringing notes I had no idea a bass was capable of, their fingers not even over the black part where fingers are supposed to be anymore. And then they attack the low notes again, swaying. They're not as physically interesting to watch as most soloists, none of that head-shaking, swoony, eye-closing business. No, ma'am. Not with this player.

But what did I expect, really? I think as Glenn sits back, and the orchestra takes over the melody again. They seem so comfortable and steady, even now, in the spotlight, when given permission to absolutely show off...nope. No drama with this one. Which is why our thing...makes no sense.

But the piece is a love song now, sweeping and romantic, and my heart is beating harder. Their fingers race up and down but never lose the deep longing, the bass singing mournfully, Glenn sliding between notes instead of hitting them cleanly. I can almost see two lovers pulling each other away from the dance for a stolen moment in the garden at night, regretting that they can't always be together.

And I fucking hate the word lovers.

Colby touches my hand and I jump; I didn't even realize I'd closed my eyes. He's holding out a bottle of water, a question in his gaze. I snatch it and open it, chugging half of it. Which means I'm going to have to pee during the performance. *Crap.*

Now it's a dance again, and thank God, because I couldn't take another moment of watching Glenn playing to me like that. No, not *to* me. They're not playing to me, of course. They're still staring off into the distance at the stage in front of them, like even the empty seats would be too much to look at.

"He stole this part," Colby says, leaning over to slide something up a skosh.

"Who did?"

"Sarasate. He stripped it right out of Liszt's Hungarian Rhapsody #13, the melody. So it's extra ironic that he tried to attribute this to the Romani people." Colby shakes his head, chuckling, and I nod along like I have the faintest idea what he's talking about.

"I think all art is a little bit stolen," I say.

That has me thinking about my pumpkin. It should be ready soon. I shouldn't be this excited to see it, but I am. I'm still thinking about it when the piece ends. I applaud out of habit, then remember that I'm the only person who qualifies as audience, and several orchestra members shade their eyes against the lights to see who's being a weirdo. Which is me, of course.

"Excellent," the conductor says. "Just watch those high notes. Keep them clean, even at top speed. It's wonderful, Glenn. Really." Lots of people are smiling at them now, and they nod with a shy smile. I could swear they're hiding behind their instrument as they sit back and fiddle with something that absolutely does not need fiddling with.

And all I can think is, *I'm so glad I get to hear them do that again.*

CHAPTER FOURTEEN

SATURDAY MORNING, I get an email from my über-talented professor.

Greetings, all.

I will be firing your pots today, so if you want to come by and check them out, I'll be here until 8:00. Have a peaceful weekend.

Mx. Rasmussen

Peaceful is out of the question for me. First of all, I can't shake the image of them making music out of my head. The way they cradled their instrument against their body, the liquid way they slid between one note and the next...who knew I was trash for musicians? (I did, actually. I once dated every member of a band, and then the band stopped practicing. I think I was their Yoko Ono.)

Unsurprisingly, I am the only one there besides Glenn when I push open the studio door at 8:04. Social life? What? Apparently, neither of us knows what that is. I just want to see my pumpkin. I'm actually really excited to pick out the colors and stuff; I think it's going to look great on my kitchen counter. Or maybe I'll use it to keep track of my keys and stuff. Either way.

"Good evening," they say, getting up from their desk and taking off their thin glasses. "Here to see your pot?"

There's a joke on the tip of my tongue about being there to see them, but I hold it back. *Is it a joke?*

"Yup." I follow them into the drying room where the kiln is, admiring some of the other people's work. Some of it is better than others, but I really think my pumpkin will be good. I might even get an A. I fiddle anxiously with the tie of my red flannel shirt dress.

I hold my breath as Glenn opens the kiln, and I totally know I'm doing it. There's a tightness in my belly that feels like fear and hope are wrestling like two big dogs. But as the light penetrates the deep darkness of the furnace, hope rolls onto its back, and fear pins it down.

"Oh no," I murmur, dismay filling me. My beautiful pumpkin is no more. I didn't even get to use the colors on it. It looks like it literally exploded in the kiln—like a clay bomb went off, slivers and shards littering the inside of the kiln.

"Aw, looks like we didn't get it dried out enough," Glenn says sympathetically, and I turn away so they won't see the tears in my eyes.

It's silly. It's just a pot. Just a literal piece of earth that someone dug out of the ground for me and that I shaped and molded into something. *It doesn't mean anything.*

Right. Tell that to the tears now rolling down my cheeks.

Glenn hears me sniffling. "What's happening here?"

"Nothing." I storm over to the cabinet where the clay lives. "How late can I stay?" I won't be able to make it exactly the same because I'm not going outside to collect leaves in the dark, but maybe I can approximate it.

"You don't need to redo it. You did the work."

"It's fine. I don't mind." Great, now there's snot, too. *Good work, Cook.*

"Hillary, the kiln is unpredictable. I still blow things up all the time. I made a few extra pots if you want points for glazing it."

"No, thank you. Is this the right kind?" I peer at the gray hunk, wiping my tears with my shoulders, the soft flannel comforting me more than it should.

"You're not redoing it."

At their sharp, demanding words, I whirl. "Yes, I am. If I have to buy it with my own money or go dig clay up out of the ground with my own hands, I am redoing it."

They pace closer. "I am telling you, as your professor, that you don't need to. Your design was great. You did everything right. Solid B work."

"If I did everything right," I shout, "then why did I still fail?"

"You didn't fail," they shout back. "It's just...this is what clay does sometimes—which you'd know if you paid attention during my lectures!"

"I do pay attention! I listen to them repeatedly," I yell. Naturally, I leave out the part about how their sexy voice alone helped me find an orgasm. "Just let me make another one!"

"No. You did fine. You did enough."

If I didn't know what a teddy bear they are, this hulking person might intimidate me as they draw still closer, backing me toward the cupboard. I want to shut out their words as lies, but I'm not scared. If anything, their closeness is comforting, hovering near me without touching me—they haven't since that one day, the day they tried to diagnose me and caught my arm to keep me from storming out. But I know they want to. And I can't understand how they could look so unflappable last night and so shaken now.

"I don't want pity grades," I grit out. "Let me do it again. Let me do it right this time."

"I grade you the same as everyone else," Glenn growls. "Now pack up your stuff, and let's go home."

My heart is beating hard enough that I can feel it, and it's not helping me rein in my anger.

"You're right. This is pointless! I'm never going to pass! It won't matter how many pots I put in there," I cry, pointing to the kiln behind them, "they're *all* going to blow up! I'm never going to get the hang of this, no matter how many times I try! I'm just a fuck-up, and there's nothing anyone can–"

"Can I hug you?"

"What?"

Their eyes are ablaze, their face stern. "You heard me."

"I...I guess so?" There's more attitude in it than I mean for there to be, but when their warm, strong arms engulf me and press me against their chest, I can think of nothing else to say. I stand there with my arms out like a crane for a moment before I sink into the hug, tentatively wrapping my arms around their waist.

"What are you—"

"I don't want you to say that about yourself."

"You can't stop me."

"I just did."

Our volume is more intimate now, but make no mistake, we've lost none of the intensity. And when I pull back to look into their blue eyes, there's still fire there.

"You think you can shut me up?"

"Oh, I know I can." Their hand slides up to the side of my neck, their thumb caressing my cheek, and I know we both know what's happening here.

"Do it then," I breathe, and I don't even get my eyes closed before their lips are on mine, hungry, almost brutal in the way they're pressing into me, invading my mouth with their tongue, squeezing me like they can't get close enough. My face is already flushed, and I can't catch my breath. My heart is pounding like a jungle drum, and that feels about right because we are animals now, tearing into each other with absolutely no thought process beyond the consent I just gave.

I give as good as I get, nipping at their lip, tugging just hard enough that I'm sure I don't rip that piercing out. I rub over their broad shoulders, run my eager hands over their chest, and I can feel more piercings under there. *Fuck.*

Glenn's big hand is still on my neck, just holding me, and I want more. I pull up my flannel dress, yanking that hand to where I want it, on my breast. Their gaze is glued to mine as their thumb gently swipes the lace that covers my nipple, their calluses catching on the fabric. Then they lean forward and nose my collar away from my neck, latching on to suck a bruise onto my skin that I know is going to be visible tomorrow.

That has my brain snapping back into action. *Windows. People can see us.* Only with how the doors of the cabinet are, I don't think they actually can. But if anyone walked through the unlocked door, we'd barely have enough time to break apart, let alone try to right our clothes.

"Hillary." I nuzzle against their soft beard in response to their labored demand. "I want to make you come. Right here."

And for once, I'm so amped up, I think it might just be possible. Even with the distraction of maybe getting caught, I'm here for it. *Maybe because of it. Am I an exhibitionist?*

"Yeah," I choke out. "Do it."

Then those fingers are plunging into my leggings, dipping into my wetness, teasing me along my slit. The heat of them is so delicious, and they're not shy, stealing my breath with their brazen strokes.

"You're not a fuck-up. Say it." They growl into my ear, their fingers grazing my clit, and I suddenly have more empathy for the pot and its accidental explosion. Because, yeah. It me. But I still can't say it.

"I screwed it up."

"You didn't." Those wicked fingers aren't going nearly hard enough, and I whimper as my arousal starts to wane, my body distracted by where I am and the bright lights and the too-loud sound of us panting in the quiet classroom. "Say it, and I'll make you come."

"I can't be bribed, Rasmussen." I drop the Mx. because otherwise, I'll be forced to remember that this is my instructor, and I am in our classroom as their fingers caress my most private places.

"Not even with a mind-blowing orgasm?"

"The fucking gall of you..." They press two fingers inside me, and I gasp, my head falling back at how good it feels, my hips churning to get more friction. But they don't move.

"Say it, Cook. Say you're doing great."

"I'm fucking not!" I grab their wrist, trying to get the in-and-out movement that I need, but they won't budge. I either have to give up my pride or give up on this orgasm, and this is the closest I've been with someone else in forever. "Fine," I spit. "I'm doing *great*."

"Good." Their fingers hook and hit that sensitive spot on my inner wall, and I curse. "Now this time, drop the sarcasm."

"Oh, fuck you."

"No," they say, chuckling, "that's what I'm doing to *you*. Try again." They push their fingers in and out, long and languid, and that's just what I want, just what I need...only faster and harder.

"Glenn," I whimper. "Come on. Don't be an asshole."

"Say it," they whisper back, catching my earlobe between their teeth, and that teaspoon of pain makes me throw my pride out.

"I'm doing great. I'm not a fuck-up; I'm amazing."

"That's right," Glenn rumbles as their fingers pick up speed. They drop to their knees, and when they duck under my dress and tug my leggings further down, I grope around for something to hold on to. The cabinet behind me is already holding probably three hundred pounds of clay, and I hope it can take the additional weight of me hanging on for dear life as Glenn spears me with those thick fingers over and over and adds their tongue to the mix. I put one boot up onto the lower shelf, and they seem to appreciate the extra space because they pull me closer with their free hand, their fingers digging into my ass, and eat my pussy like I'm their favorite meal.

I'm going to come. I can feel it building like a sneeze (but nicer). It's going to happen no matter what I do. But I'm not a quiet girl when I come, and if I cry out like that in this classroom, someone is assuredly going to feel the need to check and see if I'm being murdered. So I do the only thing I can think of: I turn my head and bury my face in my shoulder to cover my own mouth. Just in time, too—when I break, it muffles the high sound...but it doesn't dampen the waves of pleasure crashing over me, making me feel scattered and lightheaded. I don't manage to pry my fingers away from the shelf until Glenn is already back on their feet, wiping their mouth with the sleeve of their sweater, leaving a large, dark slash.

I expect embarrassment or avoidance from Glenn; that's certainly what I'll be feeling later, even if the buzz of my orgasm hasn't worn off yet. But those gentle blue eyes are meeting my gaze just fine, even if the bravado is gone. I try to straighten my dress, but they've already reached out to do the same thing, and our hands meet. And when they tangle, I don't want to pull away.

I look down; their cock is tenting the soft jersey of their skirt, and it reminds me of a statue draped in a drop cloth before its unveiling. I'm not surprised exactly, but it wasn't quite so obvious with the cisgender cock-owners I've been with before. I don't know if it's okay for me to touch them; their body language isn't inviting that kind of contact, I don't think.

"Thanks," I say.

"For what?" Glenn asks, frowning.

"I don't know," I answer truthfully. There are several options: the encouragement, the comfort, the orgasm that made me feel like I dropped my brain into a blender but in a good way. But also in a confusing way. I pull my hands away from theirs slowly, and the loss makes my chest feel tight. "I'm gonna go home."

"Will you..." Their gaze is stormy now, and they've tangled their fingers in the soft folds of their skirt, their cock still pointing at me insistently.

"What?"

"Text me. When you get home. So I know you're safe."

"Sure." It's getting weirder the longer I stand here, so I brush by them quickly in pursuit of my bag.

"Huh."

I'm not going to turn around; I can still smell what we did hanging in the air, and it's definitely time to go. But I can't resist their cryptic noise.

"What?"

"Oh, I just expected a fight. But that must've been a good climax. It made you more agreeable."

I make sure they can see my extended middle finger as I push open the door to leave, and I hear them chuckle before it closes again.

CHAPTER FIFTEEN

WHEN I GET HOME, I change my clothes because they smell sexy. When putting them into the hamper, I notice that it's quite full, and the dress I want to wear on Monday is in there, so I grab my laundry basket and head down to the basement. When the elevator opens, Mrs. Graham is in there.

"Well, if it isn't the young lady in 7B! How are you?"

"Fine, thanks," I say with a smile. "How are you?"

"Oh, just headed out on a date."

"Well, that's perfectly obvious," I say. "Just look at that hat. That's a daring fashion statement if I've ever seen one. It's stunning." It's tan with fuzzy white earflaps that remind me of a lamb. Mrs. Graham giggles. "They're not going to know what hit them."

She leans closer, even though we're alone in the elevator. "He works for the postal service. They have good pensions."

"Get it, girl. Yes. Love that for you. Get. It."

Her shoulders shake as she laughs again, and she taps me with her cane. "You have a good evening, dear."

"Thank you, I plan to." When the doors open, I reach for my phone instinctively to fill the gap in stimulation. But it's not in my back pocket. I check the other one. Not there either. I mentally retrace my steps as I get off the elevator at the basement level. I think it's in my apartment. Probably. If not, someone's probably stolen it by now, and it's a moot point. I dump my laundry into the machine and borrow a laundry tab from Janey, who won't mind. But I don't have quarters...I sigh and put her tab back. I can grab mine when I go back up. I'm too tired to take the stairs, even though it's faster. I ride up, grab the quarter jar that's on top of the fridge (how'd it get up there?), and ride all the way back down before I remember the soap. So I re-borrow the soap from Janey, and I don't think about my phone again until I'm getting out my computer to watch a TV show in bed.

Teacher person: you didn't text me.

Teacher person: Hillary?

Teacher person: I bet you just forgot. But if I have to read about your untimely death in the paper tomorrow, I'm gonna be upset.

Hillary: do you read an actual paper, Earth enemy?

Teacher person: I happen to love the earth, thank you very much. I recycle.

Hillary: China's rejecting our recycling, actually, so you probably don't.

Teacher person: for real?

Hillary: I wouldn't joke about the toxic build-up of plastics, Glenn.

Teacher person: I'm glad you found your phone.

Hillary: You're welcome.

· · · ·

THAT WAS SATURDAY. I didn't set a reminder for my laundry once I found my phone because I was too busy flirting with my instructor, so I didn't run down to put it in the dryer until Sunday morning. Luckily, someone else had done it for me. I hope none of my undies went missing; that'd be creepy. Would I notice, though? Probably not.

And speaking of running, I went for a run in Forest Park. And I took MAX because I'm not an environment hater like Glenn. I took a selfie and informed them of this fact, thinking that I wouldn't hear anything back. Except I did.

Teacher person: you want to meet for coffee at the zoo when you're done?
Hillary: I'm sorry, coffee...at the zoo? when I'm all sweaty?
Teacher person: I thought that was pretty clear, yeah.
Hillary: Gross. No.
Teacher person: Gross me or gross sweat?
Hillary: Sweat.
Hillary: But also, we are not dating.

Teacher person: Why'd you come to my performance?

Hillary: my brother invited me. I didn't know you were soloing.

Teacher person: I think you're obsessed with me.

I scoffed and snorted several times before coming up with an acceptable retort, drawing some looks from the people around me.

Hillary: oh REALLY?

Hillary: I'd like to see you substantiate that.

Teacher person: Well, you keep showing up everywhere I am. Both my workplaces. My friend's home.

Hillary: which also happens to be MY home.

Teacher person: that's your side of the story.

Hillary: I am NOT obsessed with you. QUITE the opposite.

Teacher person: Interesting. What's the opposite of obsession, exactly?

Hillary: ignoringness. Which is exactly what I'm doing now.

Teacher person: yes, I can see that. Not texting me at 9 AM on a Sunday.

Teacher person: a sexy selfie no less.

The noise I make as I get off the train might give you the impression that I swallowed my gum. Only I wasn't chewing any. Most people are heading for the zoo, but I head the other way to the Wildwood Trail. It's foggy enough that I can't see the city, but the crowd has thinned out, and it's quiet for a weekend. I check my phone one more time before I put it away.

Teacher person: did you enjoy my performance?
Hillary: the one with your bass or the one in the studio?
Teacher person: OH ARE WE TALKING ABOUT THIS NOW?
Hillary: Nope, I'm at my destination, byyeee

I set my phone to Do Not Disturb and stick it in my sports bra so it doesn't bounce out on the trail where I will never find it again. I mean, I intend to talk to them about it. But not today. Tomorrow is also not looking good. Half past never, I will definitely talk to them about it. I break into a jog as I get a few yards down the trail, letting my muscles warm as I start downhill.

It's not like it was a mistake, I think as I carve my way down the damp trail, breathing in wet air that smells like moss and decomposing redwood—fresh and green.

I wanted it to happen. They obviously did, too. But it's the worst idea in the world for lots of other reasons.

1. They're my professor, so there's an imbalance of power.

2. They're older than me. I'm already pretty immature; I don't need someone who knows how to adult looking down on me all the time. Then again, maybe they like vacuuming? That'd be neat. My brain tries to add that lacking the organizational brain function to clean on a regular basis isn't the same as immaturity, but I tell it to hush.

3. They don't even like me. They're condescending and bossy and too talented for anyone's good. And yes, I know those sound like reasons *I* don't like *them*, but I assure you, they're not.

I pass another woman on the trail and we smile at each other. And I wonder if she's had sex with anyone who made her feel so confused lately. I mean, who just gets you off and sends you home with a pat on the head? Why didn't I get to touch them? Are they asexual? It's fine if they are, of course; I just want to know. My brain nudges me, as I avoid some big roots across the trail, that I could answer these questions if I just, you know, *talked to them*. But I've already scheduled that out. This is probably easier.

I'll just pretend like it didn't happen. Yes, that's the solution. Pretend it didn't happen, and don't let it happen again. No more late nights in the studio. No staying after class. I have no doubt in my mind that if I lay down a boundary, it'll be respected.

My brain calls up the memory of their fingers inside me, of coming so fucking hard I could barely stand, and I curse softly. I push myself harder. I choose the path that heads back up at basically forty-five degrees. I run until my lungs and my legs are both burning so hard, I can't think about anything else.

But when I check my phone, they've sent me a link to their next gig.

> **Teacher person:** I'll leave two tickets for you at the front desk.

Fuck.

CHAPTER SIXTEEN

I CARRY OUT MY PLAN to a T. Tuesday in class, I barely acknowledge them. I do my work. I don't even record their voice for fear that I'll misuse it. I do not make eye contact. It's not until after class that I get a text.

Teacher person: You looked really pretty today.

Teacher person: Did you get that sweater at Penny Collective? I think I saw it, but it was too small for me.

I don't know if someone told them about my very strong preference for informing people what a good deal I got on my favorite fashion pieces or if they're just that perceptive, but I can't resist.

Hillary: Yes. I. Did. And it was fifty percent off because it was Friday.
Hillary: Did you get your scarf there?

It was super cute, teal and sparkly like a mermaid, with nail polish to match.

What?

I said I didn't look into their eyes, not that I didn't check out their outfit. You can't blame me for looking; they're a style icon, frankly. There's nothing wrong with admiring that. Even if they're sometimes a jerk.

> **Teacher person:** No, Elephant Exchange. It's cute but scratchy.
> **Hillary:** Empathy.

Wait. I'm getting sucked into talking to them again; this was not the plan. I shove my phone deep into my bag, where I can't hear it buzz. I don't check it until after my next class. They'd texted me back right away after my empathy.

> **Teacher person:** I'm headed to Dancing Earth after this. You want to come?

> **Teacher person:** Like tagging along, not like my "performance" in the studio...

> **Teacher person:** which I would still like to discuss.

I ignore that. I had class, anyway. I didn't stand them up because we're not dating. I made that perfectly clear.

I bet they'd get something ridiculous at Dancing Earth, like some kind of tempeh bowl. What even is tempeh? Is it soy? And if so, why is it called something else? On the way home, I read an article about it, and I don't get hit by a big black SUV. But it does honk at me when I cross the street without looking.

On Thursday, I do an okay job with my plan. I need them to approve my design for my handbuild, which is due next week. It's a whale. I don't know why; I just like how they sing. Not that my pot will sing. Although, as I think about it, I could do a teapot that would sing…ooh, and the whistle could be on the top! Like a spout! It's a brainwave, but far beyond my skill, so I need their help with the details. But I don't watch the way their calloused fingers gently touch the paper where I drew lines along the whale's belly, and I don't notice the sparkle in their eye at all when I ask how I can support the bottom so it doesn't collapse. I definitely don't check out the tattoos on their forearm (a Nordic cross surrounded by tiny white flowers and a quote about fairy tales that I can't quite read) as they sketch a way to create removable supports. And I don't watch their pink lips as they talk about handle placement.

They hand my paper back to me. "It's a great concept, Ms. Cook."

"Thank you, Mx. Rasmussen," I say, tossing my hair over my shoulder.

"Are you free for dinner tonight?"

"No, I'm going to Colby's. Thursday night dinner is kind of a thing for those guys. And I missed the last two."

"Okay. I think you'd like this gig I've got on Friday. Jazz trio. Those tickets are still there if you want them."

I cross my arms. "How do you know I like jazz?"

"It's beautiful and improvises a lot. Just like you." With a grin, they turn to answer Marty's question, and I am left, mouth agape, to recover from that verbal riposte. But class ends before I can return their serve (yes, I know I'm mixing metaphors. I'm flustered, okay?) and deliver a zinger to put them in their place. I plan to hold on to it for later.

I drag myself to a grocery store and pick up ice cream. I can't remember what I was supposed to bring, but dessert can't hurt, right? They'd never give me the main course; they're too smart for that. The bus seems to take forever, and it's approaching drippy when I finally trudge up the front walk. I head straight to the kitchen and stick it into the freezer. A package of chicken thighs comes tumbling out and hits my foot, and in my anger, I kick it halfway across the linoleum. It crashes into someone's guitar case, knocking it over, and in the meantime, a pack of burgers has also fallen out of the freezer.

"What's going on in there?" Colby hollers from the living room, and I swear, he sounds exactly like our dad. Which is not what I need right now.

"I am being attacked by boy meat!" I holler back. "And it does not feel good!"

"Hang on," I hear Colby say to whoever he's talking to. "I'll be right back." He peeks uncertainly into the kitchen as if expecting something to jump out at him. "Hil?"

I'm sitting on the kitchen floor, rubbing my bruised arch and possibly broken toe.

"You okay?" My brother crouches next to me. He looks so genuinely confused. "Do you want an ice pack?"

"Frozen things got me into this situation. I don't think they're the solution." I'm rubbing my toe, but it *really hurts*, and my day has been long and tiring. "I think I'm just going to go home."

"Don't you want some food first? Here..." He jumps up and starts getting me a plate with some chicken on it, and I think they must have finally tried out that roasted chicken recipe that's been on the fridge for a while. And the real question is why I can remember that's there and not where I left any number of essential personal possessions, like my keys.

"Colby, stop policing my food intake. I hate it." Awkwardly, I get to my feet and start toward the front door.

"What is your problem lately?" He stalks past me to cut me off before I get to the front door, which isn't hard, given that I'm hobbling because of my toe.

I feel my eyebrows go sky high. "My *problem*?"

"Yeah, you've been in a perpetual bad mood for weeks. And you owe me an answer about Christmas. If we're going to Thailand, I want to book our—"

"I'm not going to Thailand." *Not now. Not ever.*

"Why not? It's supposed to be beautiful, and it would mean a lot to Mom, and they've got beaches..." I like how he tried to sandwich parental guilt between things I really like, but it isn't going to work. This part of me isn't responding to reason.

"I don't give a fuck about their beaches; I can drive to Seaside if I want that. And if they want to see me, they can come home." I start to push past him, but his voice is small and reminds me too much of the time he broke his arm on our friend Matt's trampoline. I hate the feeling that I've broken him now, too.

"Why can't you forgive them?"

I turn back to face him. "They didn't do anything wrong."

"I know they didn't. But that's not the way you're acting." He can't see the group of his housemates gathering behind him in a silent show of support, watching us with sympathy. "You act like they betrayed you. And I'm sick of it."

That makes my insides go all frosty. "Fine. I'll stay away, then."

"That's not what I'm—" Colby pulls off his hat and reseats it, and I recognize his frustration tic. "I want you around. But I also want them around. Can't you just bury the hatchet already?"

"I'm not the one who left." I pause. "Well, except for now. I am the one leaving now. You all have a nice dinner."

"No, look. Don't go. You need to eat. And your toe is clearly messed up. Let me at least tape it to the one next to it."

"No, thank you."

"Hillary, stop being stubborn for once in your life, and let me take care of you, please."

That comment pushes me right over the edge for reasons I can't begin to articulate.

"I'm a grown-ass adult, thank you very much, Colby Christopher Cook. I do not need my little brother fussing over me. And I do not need you to mediate for me, not with our parents and not with my instructor. I'm doing fine." I punctuate this by wrenching my foot into my boot, and I nearly sob from the pain radiating from my toe. "So quit trying to mend fences. It's not your business. I'm going to pass this pottery class and put this whole horrible quarter behind me. I'm going to start my internship, and I'm going to graduate, and I'm going to do it all without your help or anyone else's!" I take one step forward and cry out when I stub my toe against the threshold. It hurts so bad, I rock back, fighting tears, bracing myself against the door jamb, trying to breathe.

"Hillary..." Chance's gentle voice just moves me closer to a breakdown. "Do you want a ride?" I want to let him, but I can't, because he's maybe going to England, and he's going to leave me too. And then I'll be alone all the time instead of just when he sleeps over at Colby's. It didn't occur to me I was this sad about it until just now.

"No. Go eat ice cream."

Behind me, I hear Evan whisper, "Is that some kind of Gen Z insult?"

"No," I call, grabbing my bag and limping down the front steps. "There's literally ice cream in the freezer. You should eat it. Good night, gentlemen."

It takes me a long time to get to the bus stop, but I manage. By the time I get home, my toe is bruised, but I don't think it's broken. I tape it to the one next to it just in case and crawl into bed. That's when I see the group chat they created.

Evan: We missed you tonight, Hillary.

Tony: Definitely.

Chance: And not just because you didn't bring the rolls you were supposed to bring.

Darren: I'm not touching that ice cream until you come back and have it with us.

Colby: Agreed. #icecreampact

Evan: Me three.

Tony: Same.

Patrick: I'm in.

Chance: I guess it'll just get freezer burn.

Oh, that's it. He's openly baiting me now because he knows how tragic I think it is when ice cream goes bad. And that was not just any ice cream—that was Tillamook mint chocolate chip, the objectively best ice cream in the universe. Curse that roommate of mine!

Hillary: I guess I could come by tomorrow night.

Evan: I'll be here.

Tony: I'm working. Save me a scoop.

Hillary: No, we all have to be there. #icecreampact

Colby: How about Saturday after the symphony? I invited a few other people, too. It'll be fun.

Darren: That works for me.

Evan: and me.

Patrick: I'll be around.

Tony: Saturday works.

Chance: Party!

Chance's comment makes me literally giggle because I know he hates stuff like this, but he's trying to be positive for my sake, and I appreciate it.

Hillary: hugs to all of you. I love you. I will be there.

I plug in my phone and shove it in my drawer so I don't have to read all of them saying they love me, too.

CHAPTER SEVENTEEN

ON FRIDAY, MY GLENN plan starts to crumble. Because I went home early on Thursday and went to bed, I was up at a decent hour and got all my studying done before class even started. My cousin Blake is in town, and normally, we'd wrangle Colby into doing something fun with us, but this time he just wants to be with Janey, who he happens to be dating because I introduced them. But that means Janey's also busy tonight. That leaves Giada or Raina, who never seems to have a sitter. Having a baby sounds hard, and as I call Giada, I resolve once again not to have one anytime soon.

"Hey! How does jazz sound tonight?"

"Tonight?" Her voice is vacant like she's thinking. "Tonight...I cannot."

"Please? I don't want to go by myself. I've got a ticket for you."

"Oh, it is free?" Giada loves a deal, despite being a part-time model and fairly financially well-off.

"No, it's not free...well, I guess it is for us."

"What time?"

"8:30."

"Fine. But my date will not be happy."

"Oh? What date? Who date?"

"I cannot kiss and tell, Hillary. It is not polite."

I grin because I know several people who've kissed Giada, and they had plenty to say about it. Those big, pouty lips are not just for show.

"Okay, sorry. But you'll meet me?" I will totally press her for details later.

She sighs. "Send me the address."

When we meet out front a few hours later, Giada is still dressed to the nines in a form-fitting red dress with these beautiful smoky eyes and white stilettos, like she's not already a bombshell. I probably could've dressed up a little more, but I like to be comfortable.

"You look great," she exclaims, giving me an air kiss on the cheek. It's basic black with my black ankle boots, and my bare legs are freezing. I'm wearing my fancy white pea coat that I hardly ever get out because I'm...well, accident-prone. But I'm only going to drink light-colored things tonight. It's that kind of night.

They do have our tickets at the box office, and we head into The Hatbox. As the name suggests, it's small, and I like the way we have to go downstairs to get inside. It's got a real speakeasy vibe, including waitresses in flapper dresses. I order a sidecar with sugar on the rim because it feels in the spirit of the evening, and when I take a sip, my very red lipstick leaves a mark on the wide-mouthed glass. There's some kind of warm-up band still playing, but the place is packed; we finally find a two-person table near the back. The whole room has a warm feeling to it, like someone poured a room into a drink. From the red Persian rugs to the books lining the walls and the light diffused through antique chandeliers and Tiffany lamps, it feels like I've stepped back in time. I'm glad I went to the effort to curl my hair. *It's for me, not them.* I love going out. I love sitting at this tiny café table with Rhapsody in Blue playing, watching Glenn pluck away at their bass, standing this time. They're on now—did I mention that? I almost missed it myself; I was too busy vibing with the place, noticing all the little details of it, like freckles on a face. It's flawless.

"Who is your friend?" Giada asks, sipping her vodka martini with two olives.

"What?" No, I heard her. I did. It's not loud in here, despite the number of people. It's called deflection, and it's very effective unless your friend knows you quite well.

"The man who keeps looking over here." She points, and I slap her hand down.

"Stop that."

"Well, if you would not pretend you do not know of whom I am speaking..."

"They're non-binary."

"Oh." She squints harder at the stage. "I see." Their black T-shirt and jeans don't give much away, actually, but they do have nail polish on, bright yellow. They've finished Rhapsody in Blue now, and someone with a banjo is leading into the next song, The Ash Tray Blues. Probably more appropriate when you could actually smoke inside. Not that I'm complaining.

"You did not answer my question," Giada says, leaning closer to me over the fake flickering candle on the table between us.

"They're my professor."

Her eyes widen. "The pottery person?"

I give her a quick nod, and my eyes are drawn back to the stage. Glenn doesn't have much to do in this song, apparently, because they're just sitting back. Staring at me. I try to resist the urge to touch the big curls I put into my hair just before I left. I stare right back, and now it's a game, and they must know it because they get this big smile on their face. I'm fighting mine, but they can probably see my lips twitching even across the dim room, and it's so fucking annoying. Now they're going to think all they have to do if they want to see me is slide me tickets to this place. And they're so right. But maybe not because of the place. I almost spill my drink, trying to sip it without breaking our staring contest.

As the song ends, they step forward, holding the neck of their standing bass in one hand, and whisper something into the leader's ear. He turns to look at me, and I feel a blush cross my somewhat-less-covered-than-usual chest like someone blew a hot breath over me just for a moment.

He steps forward to the mic, adjusting his page boy cap. "This one goes out to the brunette in the back from our bass player." Everyone turns to smile at Giada, and she smiles back, but under the table, she pinches my leg. I want to stand up and yell at them for making cultural generalizations about beauty, but I'm just as happy for them to assume it's for her. Especially because I'm probably not the only RCU student here, and Glenn's probably not the only RCU staff member. It's a light, upbeat tune with a long lead-in, and they're looking at their music now. I wonder what's significant about the song until the band leader steps forward and starts to croon...

> *We're all alone, no chaperone can get our number.*
> *The world's in slumber, let's misbehave.*
> *There's something wild about you child that's so contagious.*
> *Let's be outrageous, let's misbehave.*

Outrageous is right. I may have stumbled across the staff-student relationships portion of the university policies handbook the other day in a weak moment, so it's not like it's unheard of...but they're basically propositioning me in front of the entire bar. Of course, the audience thinks they're propositioning Giada, and I sit back, enjoying her discomfort immensely.

When the band takes five, my phone buzzes.

Teacher person: You came.

Hillary: Don't get excited.

Teacher person: DON'T TELL ME WHAT TO DO.

Teacher person: I invited you, and you came, THAT'S EXCITING.

Hillary: Maybe I like free stuff.

Teacher person: Or maybe you like me.

Hillary: We don't get along.

Teacher person: we got along great the other night in the studio.

Teacher person: or are you still pretending that didn't happen?
Hillary: as best I can.
Teacher person: not itching for a repeat?
Hillary: of being badgered into admitting falsehoods about myself? No.
Teacher person: you are the most frustrating person on the planet.
Hillary: YOU'RE THE EXPERT.
Teacher person: meet me backstage.
Hillary: why?

I watch them lay down their bass and slip behind the maroon velvet curtains draping either side of the stage. As if my cooperation is a given. As if I'm just going to wander around the venue until I find them.

Hillary: I don't think I'm allowed back there.
Teacher person: I don't think you'll let that stop you.

They're right, damn them. I don't know what they want, but I came all the way down here. I might as well find out.

"I'm going to the bathroom," I murmur to Giada. "Will you watch my purse?"

She waves a hand dismissively.

"And don't go out and smoke. I know you." Giada scowls at me, and I laugh. She's so delightfully European, but smoking is terrible for you, and she's too pretty to die of lung cancer. "I'll be right back."

"Tell the person I say hello."

"What person?" I ask innocently before I head toward the side of the stage. And it's easy enough to pause near the edge, then step behind the curtain and into the shadow of the wings. Someone pulls my arm deeper into the dark, and I let out a little yelp before I smell their jasmine lotion.

"Hey. It's just me." They're caging me in against the wall, and even in the dim light, I see their eyes sparkling.

"What are we, sixteen?" And yet it makes me feel bubbly and giggly to be here with them, hiding from the audience.

"No, I was a stick in the mud when I was sixteen. All I did was play video games."

"Ones with the super disproportionate women, I assume?" I took a class on representations of women in popular media. I was not impressed.

"Those are them. Teenage hormones won out over realism, I'm afraid." They peer at me, head cocked. "You're prettier than they are, though."

I snort again. That noise comes up a lot with Glenn. "Right."

"You wanna fight about it?" *Why do they sound so happy about it?* "Because I can give you a handful of reasons why—"

I put a finger to their lips. "No, I'd rather you kiss me." It isn't boldness so much as simple impulsivity and a desire to make them stop complimenting me. Recklessness can look like boldness if you do it with enough panache.

They shuffle a little closer, and the gaze that was sparkling now feels like tinder and a match instead. "That so?"

I nod, and their voice lowers dangerously.

"Right here, in the dark? Where anyone might stumble upon us?"

I nod again, and my mouth is dry when I swallow. Then their soft lips are on mine, firm as they press me against the rough wall.

"I knew you'd be up to misbehave," they whisper, and I hear the smile in their voice before they kiss me again. Their tongue against my lips is slow, trying to tease me open, and I can't help but groan a little. I want them against me; I want their bulk and their muscle and their skin. I tug on their belt loops, pulling their hips to mine, and their hardness lines up nicely with my center. I lift my leg to give myself better access, and they hold it to their side like we're dancing, something Latin and sensual. Instead of me humping them in a dusty back room of a bar.

"Wanted to do this since you walked in," they murmur, moving their slow kisses to my neck.

"Just kiss me?" I whisper back, and when they pull back to gaze into my eyes, they shake their head slowly. I'm warm between my legs, and even though their jeans feel rough through my panties, it's majorly working for me. And the way they're working their hips in time with me feels like we were made for each other, made to be just like this, close and wanting in the dark.

"Ras? You back here?" It's the frontman, apparently looking for his bassist, and I smother a laugh against their shoulder.

"Yeah. I'll be right there," they call.

"Get back to work, *Ras*," I chide gently, pushing them back to a standing position, straightening my dress. I get one more quick kiss before they disappear through the curtains. I decide to wait a few moments, so it's not entirely obvious that I was just getting frisky backstage...and I spy a side door. So I slip out that way, pretending I really am on my way back from the bathroom, as I claimed. I sashay up to our table and plop myself back into my chair ungracefully.

Giada glances up from her phone, then her gaze seems to snag on something on my face. It's slightly alarming. Did they leave a mark? Does being Italian give her the ability to know when lips have been kissing other lips?

"Did you know someone is wearing your lipstick?"

I stall for time by rummaging through my purse. "They're wearing the same color?"

"I like the way you put that, yes. They are. Also," she reaches out and straightens the shoulder of my dress, "do not ever take a job which requires assignations."

"What does that mean?" I mutter, sipping my drink. And then I realize what it means—because there's no lip print on the drink this time. Because I have no lipstick left. Guess who does? My gaze flies to Glenn's. Yup, their face is rose red from my kisses. I whip out my phone.

Hillary: Wipe your face, you've got kiss evidence all over it.

I watch them pull out their phone, read my message, and then grin. Out of their case, they pull a rag that they not-so-subtly use to clean it off. I sigh.

"You couldn't remember the word *pickles* the other day, but you know the word *assignations*?" I grumble, but she's grinning like a kid whose test day became a snow day.

"You should not critique me. I watched your purse during your assignation. I did not smoke. I wanted to."

"I'm very proud," I say, patting her arm.

"You are using me."

"Yes. I thought that was clear."

"I can't believe I blew off..." She stops herself, then huffs as the music begins again. More Gershwin. Good choice.

"Yes?" I ask, batting my eyelashes at her. "Off whom did you blow?"

"It is *blow off*. Do not try to confuse me. I am not at liberty to say." She flips her straight, dark hair over her bare shoulder.

"Sounds like someone's having assignations of her own..." I muse quietly, and Giada opens her mouth to protest, then snaps it shut again, folding her arms grumpily over her belly.

"Let's see, it's probably someone I know..." I wheedle. "Probably a lady, because I know your type. Someone in fashion?"

She stares resolutely at the stage, lifting her chin a little.

"Fine, keep your secrets." I chuckle. That's when I notice Glenn's message.

> **Teacher person:** You want to get a piece of
> pie after? My treat.

My stomach drops. Pie is delicious, but I shouldn't. For one thing, it's not nice to ditch Giada again, especially after she apparently ditched someone for me. But for another, this wasn't a date. It wasn't even a hookup. It was something between, and the gray of it concerns me. I mean, what *is* this? Besides, you know, a lovely way to spend a Friday night.

> **Hillary:** not tonight

And when the band leader announces that it's their last song, Giada and I slip out before the first eight bars.

CHAPTER EIGHTEEN

IT'S NOTHING BUT GUYS at this party. I don't know why they invited me. I mean, it's my boys, so I came, and I had to considering the way I left a few days ago with the ice cream pact, but all things being equal, I'd rather have the apartment to myself and a bowl of vanilla ice cream with as many sprinkles as I want.

But I'll settle for ice cream and alcohol and dudes.

I'm finishing off my second glass of riesling because I'm a classy bitch, and this is Oregon, where we grow amazing grapes, when Glenn walks in. *Fuck.*

There's nothing but cheers from my brother and his roommates.

"Did you know they were coming?" I hiss at Chance, and his guilty face says yes.

"Colby wants you two to bury the hatchet. He thought this might help."

"Can I hide out in the guest house?" I ask, snagging half a bottle of vodka that's sitting on the counter because classy has just gone out the window, and I am now a desperate, opportunistic bitch.

"Of course. This is your house more than it's mine," Chance says, and I duck out through the kitchen to the back door. I'd go home, but I'm too buzzed to manage that, and I'd planned to just sleep on the couch here tonight. It's late, anyway. I'll just hole up in the guest house; this couch is as good as the one in the main house. I leave the lights off so Colby doesn't come looking for me out here...but Chance will tell him if he asks. Maybe he'll think I'm asleep.

Do I feel like a child for hiding out here? Yes. Is it how I'd envisioned spending a Saturday night? No. But what are my options? Go socialize with my...fuck buddy? I don't care if it would make Colby happy; I have to stick to the plan. Out here, I have my own bathroom. Heck, my own bed, my own TV. Is it a bit weird that it's my parents' bed? Yeah.

In fact, the whole place reminds me of them. It even smells a little like them. It reminds me of crawling into their bed after a nightmare as a kid. I clutch the bottle to my chest like a blanket, wandering through the small space, looking at the family pictures they hung up in here. Me and Colby making sandcastles at Cannon Beach, Haystack Rock in the background. Camping at Silver Falls, my dad helping me roast a marshmallow that's about to catch fire, if I remember correctly. My smooth-faced mother with large, fluffy hair, holding a baby in a blue blanket, looking just as beautiful as she is now. And I look like her; we're the same age in this picture. I stare and stare at her...she looks so happy, staring into the camera with absolutely no pretense in her expression. She really is as happy as she appears.

I sit on the bed and flop backward, but the ache only intensifies. I shouldn't have drunk so much; it's doing bad things to my body. I rub my belly with one hand, but it doesn't help. I have to get out of this memory palace; I don't care if that means talking to Glenn. I'll just ignore them. I'm still dragging my feet across the grass. Maybe I should just get a car home...but Colby would be upset.

I can hear him in the other room, telling a loud story about the time he tried to ride a motorcycle. I stay in the kitchen. There has to be junk food in here somewhere. Lord knows he's raided my kitchen often enough for me to return the favor. The problem is that my kitchen has a stepstool...but all these guys are tall, apparently. That riesling must be going to my head (never did open the vodka) because instead of getting a chair (like a grown-up), I just hike one knee up and climb up onto the small counter between the fridge and the pantry. I'd bet anything these guys are hiding their treats above the fridge. *Jackpot*. Oh, they've got those little circus animal cookies, and Oreos, and...are those tiny cinnamon rolls?! I grab all three...and that's when I realize I didn't think carefully enough about how I was going to get back down with my arms full of snacks.

There's no room to put them down, and if I throw them, all the cookies are going to break. I'm kneeling there, and I can't turn around in the small space and slide down on my butt. I'm distracted thinking about why this is where moms hide their booze (it's the highest point? are they trying to keep the kids out, or themselves?) when someone comes into the kitchen, and I might as well announce myself since they'll notice my bare feet sticking out soon enough.

"Um. Hello?"

"Hillary?" Oh, crap. Of course it's Glenn.

"Could you go get my brother? Or Chance. Any of those goobers, really."

"What do you need help with?"

I snort. "From you? Nothing."

They're crowding my space now, but there's literally nowhere I can go, and I feel heat rising on my chest.

"Is that so? Well, maybe I'll just leave you here, then." They step back, and I fling one hand backward and manage to grab them by the shirt. I end up sitting back on my heels, so we're closer together now. I twist as far as I can to see them; their shirt is black and collared with buttons up the front, and I am momentarily befuddled by this. Their clothes are always so much prettier than this...this...boymode crap.

"Don't you dare."

"Let me help you." Their voice is low and soothing.

"You can help me by going to get my brother or someone else I like."

"Only people you like can help you off the counter?"

"Yes!"

"You can hear how silly that is, can't you?"

"They're called principles. Trying getting some."

"Oh, I have plenty of principles. One of which is consent." They plant their hands on the counter on either side of my torso. "Another of which is economization of effort, which is sort of conflicting, honestly. But it's silly for me to walk into the living room to get your brother when I'm perfectly capable of helping you...but if you don't want my help, I won't touch you."

Their comment about touch makes me aware of the fact that I'm still holding onto them, and I let my fingers fall from their shirt, mostly because I'm hurting my shoulder, twisting like that. But also because I don't really think they're going to leave.

"Colby!" I shout. "I need help!" But there must be too much noise in the other room because no one appears. "Chance! Tony! Anybody?!" Evan has similar feelings about economization of effort, so I skip him, and I'd feel weird asking Patrick. He's so quiet. I feel around for my phone, but it's not in my back pocket where it belongs.

"Huh. Looks like no one's coming. Can I have a cookie?"

"No! These are mine. I rightfully stole them."

"Not even one? You won't let me help you off the counter; the least you can do is give me a snack."

"No!"

"You're a terrible hostess, to be honest."

I fluff my hand in their direction. "Back up." I'll just have to do this the hard way. I eat a frosted elephant first for strength and also increased sobriety. Sliding to the edge, I reach one leg back, trying to touch the floor with my toes...which is tricky because my toe is still sore from my last visit to this house when the meat attacked me. I think I'm still pretty far above the floor.

"Can I ask a question?"

"No."

"If you leaned to your right, couldn't you get turned around and get one leg out from under you?" They're right. If I rolled to my hip, I could probably turn around and jump forward, which would be far less frightening than trying to go backward with Glenn staring at my ass. I knock my elbow against the fridge and my head against the cupboards, but I do get turned around. I stick my tongue out at Glenn, whose arms are crossed over their chest, and they chuckle. My feet are still a good eighteen inches from the floor, and I slide down to the ground, arching my back to try to land gently. It still stings, but I look up at them triumphantly.

"Ha!" I cry. "Eat it, professor."

"I'd like to, but you wouldn't share."

Buzzing from my victory, I open the bag and pick out an animal. "Unicorn. Just like you." They don't break eye contact as they take the cookie from me, brushing their fingers across my open palm.

"How am I a unicorn?"

"I don't know," I say, ducking my head to paw through the bag. "You're good at everything. You have amazing style. The real question is why you're single." The riesling has officially gone to my head. I want to pull my brain out of my head and slap it in the face for saying such silly things. I've been thinking it, but I shouldn't *say* it.

"I want to kiss you."

I freeze, then slowly lift my head to meet their gaze. I could get really lost in those eyes, the sharp blue of them. There's no deceit there, but I still feel fooled, or maybe I just feel like a fool. Because I don't know what to say. They haven't eaten the cookie; they're just standing there, holding it in their fist. And I'm just standing there, too, my arms full of sugar, my hand still in the bag.

We've done it before, of course, but those times, we were...wild. Now it's just us—no, there is no 'us'—but I want that, too. Just thinking about their skin, of their lips on mine, has the blood rushing through me to get between my legs. And that pisses me off.

"Are you drunk?" It comes out harsh, and they flinch. Anger flares in that blue gaze.

"No. Why would I need to be drunk to want to kiss you?"

"You wouldn't *need* to be," I sputter, shouldering my way past them toward the table, where I unceremoniously dump the junk food. I am well on my way to embarrassing myself, and it'll be easier to flee if my arms are empty. "It just seemed possible. You're at a party. There's drinking happening. Also, we *hate* each other."

"You thought I *hated* you?" The cookie falls from their hand as they flex it open, rubbing it on their black pants, leaving pink trails along the way from the sprinkles still stuck to their skin. "Can I touch you?"

"Why?" My voice is quaking like those last few leaves on the farthest branch of a winter tree, the ones closest to the sky, that just won't let go.

"Because I need it. I think you do, too."

I'm backing away now, my head shaking, but they don't follow me. When my back hits the wall by the bathroom, they keep talking.

"I want you, Hillary. You frustrate the living hell out of me. You're beautiful, but you lack confidence. You know your shit, but you pretend you don't, and I just don't get it. You're smart but too stubborn." I can't listen to this; everything inside me rebels at their words, rejects their praise. I should've gone home.

"There's no such thing as too stubborn," I mutter, pushing off the wall like I'm going to leave, but they hold up a hand. And for some reason, I stop.

"And you're creative. No, you'll never be a world-renowned potter, but you have good artistic sensibilities. I enjoy your work immensely."

"Stop," I whisper, but they just shake their head.

"I never hated you or wanted your destruction. If I wanted to watch you burn, it was as a star, lighting up the night."

"Shit, you're a poet, too," I mumble, shuffling closer, ruffling my hair out of my face uncomfortably. *This is happening. They're going to touch you if you want them to, and it's going to change everything.*

"Not a poet. Just a lowly bass player, hanging out with friends."

"We're not friends." I peek past them, but there's no sign of my brother or anyone else.

"We should be." They stuff their hands in their pockets, still staring at me intently. I think they've initiated some sort of tractor beam with their gaze because I'm still coming closer, a moth to a flame, too curious to stop myself. *This is a different brand of mistake. They're your professor. You still have to work with them for a few more weeks.*

"You're my teacher." I lift my hand to touch their hair, then hesitate. I've never seen anyone stand still with so much energy...I'm afraid if I touch them, it'll start some sort of chemical reaction I can't stop.

"I'm allowed to have relationships with my students." Their eyes are begging me to just do it, to *do something*. I comb my fingers through their hair near their temple, and their eyes close as they lean into my touch. *They really do want me.* I didn't think they were joking or lying, but part of me just doesn't see how it's possible.

"I read a thing on the RCU website," I say. "According to the policy, if we're engaging in a relationship that is intimate, romantic, or sexual—"

"This would be all of the above."

The hard thinking I'm doing causes my fingers to pause momentarily, and their eyes open again.

"We'd have to talk to the administration."

"We would. On Monday."

I nod, resuming my slow caresses, and Glenn makes a low noise in the back of their throat.

"Hillary. Let me touch you. Let me find all your soft places, let me kiss you dizzy, let me make you come. I need you."

"No." I lift my other hand to their chest, rubbing the heel of my hand against their nipple, and it catches on something. "Do you have a nipple piercing?"

"I'll show you if you let me touch you. Show you more of my tattoos, too. I know you like them. I've seen you staring at them." They're not wrong, and I'm more than a little bit tempted. But this is too much fun.

"No." When my lips softly meet their neck at the edge of their beard, the noise they make is something between a snarl and a whimper, and I fucking love it. "How many other students have you dated?"

"What?" They sound spacey, not speaking with their usual calm, decisive timbre.

I punctuate each word with a soft kiss. "How many others?"

"None. I always considered it...unprofessional."

"Oh, you're not wrong. It was very naughty of you to stand up there, lusting after me."

"Fuck, Hillary, please. Don't be a sadist. Come on." They're shaking, and when I put my palm to their cheek, their soft, pink mouth opens as if I've stabbed them. "Let me. Please let me."

"Are you hard for me?"

"Hell yes. And you can touch it if you don't believe me, but it probably won't stay hard for long if you do."

"The thing about that relationship in the policy...it had to be consensual."

That shakes them. They spear me a hard look. "I'd never touch you without your permission. You know that."

"You grabbed my arm when I tried to leave. I didn't consent to that."

Their gaze drops guiltily. "Yes. I feel bad about that. But I promise I won't do it again. You can trust me."

"I do now." And when I lift their hand to my side along my ribs, that seems to be all the permission they need. They delve into my mouth, their tongue lapping mine, cupping my face in their hands, walking me backward until they get to a wooden kitchen chair. Glenn pulls me down onto their lap, kissing me, even as they try to scooch me closer to them.

"Where can we go? I want you now. Right now." They throw it out forcefully, as if I wasn't already on fire from their touch.

"Um. I don't know." My room became Antonio's room a long time ago, and I'm pretty sure he's not going to want me using it now. Definitely not interested in Colby's room...and the real question is how we'd get upstairs without getting caught.

"Think, star. Because I doubt you want me to make you come right here in the kitchen."

We've been together for about ten seconds, and they've already given me the most romantic nickname of my life.

"Might not be that easy," I say, leaning forward as their kisses move down my neck. "I have...problems."

"What kind of problems?" they ask, palming my breast, groaning into my neck. "Never mind—I don't care. I just want to be with you."

"Well, Mx. Patience, the only place I know of is my parents' room out back."

"Let's go." They're already moving to stand up, and I push their chest.

"No! Glenn, that's weird, even for us. I don't want to bang you in my parents' bed!"

"Where, then?" They're looking around, and the moment they spot the bathroom, they're up and moving. "Hang on." I lock my legs around their waist just in time, and then they're carrying me across the kitchen. Patrick appears in the kitchen doorway, and Glenn freezes.

"I saw nothing," Pat says, continuing on his way to the fridge.

"Great," Glenn replies, and a moment later, we're in the bathroom, and they're kicking the door shut. Glenn gently sets me on the edge of the white marbleized Formica, then locks the door and flips on the fan. I raise an eyebrow at them, and they grin.

"To drown out your noises," they mutter in my ear, bringing us close together again, and I don't know how someone I barely know can feel so right.

"That's assuming I'm going to make any noises," I whisper back.

"You'll make noises. Rasmussen guarantee."

"Fine, but I want my money back if I don't come."

"Deal. But I'm expensive."

I unbutton their black shirt and run my hands over their tattoos. I really do love them. One of these days, I'm going to catalogue all of them and make them tell me the stories that go with each one.

"This shirt isn't your style."

"No," they agree, kissing my cheeks, their short beard rough against the sensitive skin of my face. "Symphony says I have to wear boy clothes."

I pull back suddenly. "What the fuck?"

"I know." They lean forward as if to resume their kisses, but I slide down off the counter.

"Glenn! We have to talk to them about this!"

Their face folds into a look of utter perplexity. "Now?"

"Yes! Button up your shirt. Let's go." I turn toward the door. I am on a mission because that is the most sexist, transphobic, discriminatory thing I have ever heard, and someone needs to hear my complain about it right now. I have my hand on the door before they catch me.

"I appreciate the thought, but I'm sure they've all gone home by now." They pull me back against them, and I feel their hard cock against my ass. "And we were in the middle of something..."

Their powerful arms around me remind me that we were indeed in the middle of something, but it's not helping me feel less incensed.

"They should not do that to you."

"True." They're kissing my neck now, moving my hair out of the way to give themselves better access, and it's melting my brain a little.

"It is not right, Glenn. You have to stand up for yourself."

"Tried." Their hand wanders up to my breast, caressing.

"You're going to try harder," I say, turning in their arms and scowling at them. "For me."

"Why should I?"

"God, you're impossible." I shove against their chest. "We'll get you a lawyer. We'll send them a letter."

They shrug, moving those big hands down to my ass. "If you want. But I don't care that much. I can boymode sometimes. That's part of me, too."

"But *you* should get to choose!" I stab a finger into their chest and can't help but notice that it's firm. I push my hands into their open shirt, tracing their black tats with the tip of my fingers. Glenn's still holding me close by my ass, and their fingers are massaging into the flesh there as they smirk down at me.

"Does my body distract you?"

"Constantly." I pop another two buttons of their shirt free, and they let go of me long enough to finish un-buttoning and shed the black shirt, letting it drop to the floor. And then all that glorious skin, their gorgeous can-vas, is on display for me. I let out a shaky breath, trans-fixed, still running my hands over them.

"I love the way you look at my body." Their words jar me from my trance, and I stare up into those beautiful eyes. Their gaze is unmistakably affectionate, and I feel the need to move this back from the emotional cliff they're about to shove me off.

"Just your body. Not you. You're still annoying."

"Annoying, but you don't hate me."

I toss my hair. "You're all right." A shudder rolls through me when their chilly hands find the skin just above my waistband. "But this is just stress relief."

"No." They tug me closer by my waist until we're nose to nose. "I told you, this is a *relationship*. And if it's not, let me know right now, and I'll walk away."

No. I don't want them to go. But I'm angry that they saw through my bullshit and called me on it, and my temper makes me say careless things.

"Maybe you should go, then."

Their gaze narrows. "You don't mean that, do you? Because I don't want to play games."

"Why would I want a relationship with you? We don't get along at all! How would that even work? Can't you just appreciate the moment here?"

To punctuate my offer, I take off my shirt, and their eyes go hot. But they lace their words with frustration.

"Because I don't want a fucking moment. I've been taking moments where you offered them for months now, watching you look right through me when I thought you were magic. I know what I have to offer and what I'm worth. So forgive me if I want your full attention for a while."

That has my stomach clenching, and I turn my head to stare at a picture of Mt. Hood on the bathroom wall. "You don't know what you're asking for. My full attention is pretty tricky to keep."

They nuzzle the side of my head. "I think I'm up to the challenge."

I snort. "Of course you do."

A sharp knock on the bathroom door startles both of us, and I hear Evan's voice over the fan. "Are you two locked in the bathroom arguing?"

"No," I shout back. "We're having sex, obviously!"

That shuts him up, but Glenn chuckles. "You're exceptional, Ms. Cook."

"If you say so." I touch their beard tenderly. "So a relationship would mean, what? Dates? Flowers? Chocolate?"

"I like lilies. Nothing with nougat." They kiss me. "Don't worry, I'll write it down for you."

"Fuck. You. I'll remember."

"You sure? I don't mind."

I beckon them to follow me when I back toward the counter again, boosting myself up again, and they shuffle after me quite willingly. "When something's important to me, I find a way to remember."

"And someone?"

"Yes, someones, too." I pull them between my open legs, my heels propped on the edge of the counter. "But don't get your hopes up."

"Too late," they murmur. "I'm already touching you. That's farther than I ever thought I'd get." Their fingers aren't gentle on the back of my neck despite their sweet words. We kiss for a long time, long enough for me to lose track of where my own hands are. They devour my lips, and my skin heats everywhere they touch me...but they don't touch me between my legs. I grope around until I find their right hand, and then I attempt to pull it where I want it. But the devil resists me.

"Not yet," they murmur. "Soon."

"I think I'd know better than you," I pant, tugging again—again with no success. "Now get down there, Rasmussen."

"I definitely will. When I'm ready."

"I'm ready *now*."

"Patience, star. I want you to burn for me. I want to soak in your light." They bend to my chest, gently taking one cotton-covered nipple between their teeth and tugging. It feels like a bolt of lightning straight down to my clit, and I moan.

"See? Noises."

"Fuck you." I lean back on my hands, pushing my chest out more, and they chuckle. A thought occurs to me. "You present fluidly." My drunkish tongue catches on the word a little, but they understand.

"Yeah," they mutter, pulling down the cup of my bra, still lavishing my breasts with nips and kisses, flattening the broad warmth of their tongue against the nipple until my eyes roll back in my head.

"Would you like being inside me?"

"Depends on what you mean."

I pull their face up to mine, which is sad because the kisses stop. "I'm a little tipsy, and I can't word good. Before, in the studio, I didn't touch you back, because I didn't know. But I want to get you off, too, if you want me to. Tell me how."

Glenn's smile is surprisingly gentle. "I will. I promise."

Then finally, fucking finally, they work their way into my jeans and their fingers graze my clit, and I could weep with relief. When Glenn brings their fingers up to their lips to taste me, my mouth drops open. They hum with a deep sound. "I've been wanting to do that again for weeks."

I have so many questions. *Why didn't you? Why did you fuck me in the first place? You really wanted me all this time?* But then they're there, stripping off my jeans, pulling me off the counter while kissing me like I'm essential, like I'm air.

"I don't have condoms," they whisper. "You?"

"Right hand drawer."

"Really?"

"Fuck yeah. I'm not letting my guys get diseases. I stock them up once a month."

Glenn smirks as they tear one open. "In a variety of sizes and everything."

"Nothing but the best."

"So you can't remember to bring your laptop to class—"

"That was one time!"

"—but you can remember to stock a drawer in a house you don't live in with condoms."

"My brain is a marvel."

"It sure is." They're turning me now, putting my hands on the cold counter top, pressing our skin together at my back, pressing kisses to my neck and shoulders. The heat of them provides stunning counterpoint to the cold. "You ready?"

"I was ready about a hundred years ago, bud."

"Thought you said we weren't friends."

Then their cock is splitting me open, and I can't help but gasp a little. Condoms aren't my favorite sensory experience, but Glenn still feels good, hot and hard.

"We're not."

"This isn't friendly?" Their breathing is getting labored now, and frankly, I don't know how they're keeping cogent thoughts in their head. Watching them fuck me slowly in the mirror, their face flushed and tense, their reflected gaze on mine, has compacted all my words into adjectives: *beautiful, inked, muscled, blue.* They wrap a hand in my hair and pull back, and I suddenly know this is going to be unlike any sex I've had before.

"No," I moan. "Not friendly."

"You don't seem to mind..."

I can't find a single word inside my head. I'm just making imprints of this moment: the hot slide of them, the power of their hands on me, the cold of the counter...it all feels great, but...I'm afraid it's not going to be enough.

My gaze drops to the sink. It's plain white ceramic with a chrome faucet. Nothing special. The boys removed the pot-pourri my mom used to have in here; she made it herself, if I'm not mistaken. Rose petals from my dad's garden, cinnamon they bought at a Christmas market, some random other stuff. Pot-pourri is such a nineties thing, I—

Glenn slaps my ass, and I look up sharply.

"Hey!"

"Hey, what?" they grunt. "I'm doing great work back here, and you went somewhere else inside your head. Where'd you go?"

"Pot-pourri."

Glenn's mouth wobbles, and then a chuckle escapes. Their rhythm falters, and then they stop thrusting and pull me back against their chest, upright. They're covering up some of their tattoos this way, but I get a good look at my breasts and my belly and the way they look with their beautiful arms banded around me. The contrast is hot.

They just hold me, still inside me, staring at us in the mirror. "And why are you thinking about pot-pourri while we're fucking? Am I boring you, star?"

"No. This is just...how I am." But my arousal is coming back as I cling to their arm with both hands. Glenn angles over my shoulder to kiss me, and it's like a match lit in a room filled with natural gas. They start to move again, nudging at *that* spot inside me, the one that makes my legs shake.

"Tell me if your mind wanders again," they whisper against my lips, their hand moving to massage my breast. "I'm gonna figure this out. How to keep you here."

"Losing battle," I pant, rubbing against their bearded chin.

"Still gonna fight." Their other hand drops between my legs, and their slow circles have my eyes rolling back in my head. "Worth it." They pause to lift one of my legs so that my foot is on the counter. I'm just barely tall enough to make it work, but the angle...my God. The angle is amazing, and they're holding me up, and the hand on my breast tweaks my nipple hard before coming up to my mouth.

"Open."

I snag their gaze in the mirror again...and shake my head slowly. Their thrusts slow, too, and I love the game of it. That we're wrestling even though we're barely moving at all. A vision of wrestling with Glenn in my bed overwhelms my thoughts, and I struggle to keep my lips pressed together as I moan.

"Open, star. You'll like it."

I shake my head more vehemently, and they grin.

"A woman who knows what she wants."

"Or doesn't want," I mumble, leaning back into them harder, closing my eyes. I feel their big hand on the front of my neck, and I move to cover it instinctively.

"I'm not going to take your breath," they murmur in my ear, thrusting harder. "I'm just helping you stay here. I promise."

They're not wrong. While my attention is on that hand on my throat, I didn't even notice that their slow circles had become sharp little taps, and my body is about to come in a jumble of sensations, like I stumbled and fell into an orgasm. Fumbling, I move the hand on my neck to my mouth, and I come hard, squeaking into their calluses, my abs hurting from the sharp motion of my hips, sinking in their embrace. And I am Jello. I am a Jello person who cannot stand on her own, even when Glenn moves my leg back down to the ground.

"God, I love that," Glenn murmurs, turning me to face them, stroking my face gently. They kiss me deep, just a long communion of lips and breath, still holding me up. I'm stealing their warmth because dang, this bathroom is cold, but it's not like I'm going to put my clothes back on until Glenn comes.

This is the third time we've been together, and they still haven't so much as taken their pants all the way off. And that is not right. I may not be able to offer anything as fancy as the Rasmussen Noises Guarantee™, but I've got the Cook Fun Guarantee™, and that's worth something.

We're still kissing, and I tug a little on their nipple ring. Their sharp intake of breath tells me I've got their attention. I reach down and pull off the condom, dropping it into the trash rather than on the floor, where I will undoubtedly forget it. Their head falls back as I stroke them, and I manage to coax a quiet groan out of them.

"Help me out here, hon," I say, switching to a feather-light touch around the head. "What do you like? What do you want?"

"You." They're back to kissing me, brushing their fingers through my hair. But it's...less? Like we're done? And I don't want to be. There has to be something I can do to get them off. With both hands on their arms, I direct them over to the bathtub and sit them on the edge.

"Talk to me," I say, getting on my knees, rubbing my hands along their thighs, dusted lightly with beautiful brown hair. I take hold of their cock again, but they shake their head just a little, and I stop, sitting back on my heels. "Do you want my mouth?"

They nod, and I don't know why they've gone so quiet, but the fire is still there in their gaze. I bend and give it a lick. It's not a great taste because of the condom, but I'm in it to win it.

Their fingers start playing with my hair again as I kiss up and down their shaft, licking them like an ice cream cone. Their breathing is finally heavy again, and I think I'm doing okay...until I suck the head into my mouth.

Glenn shifts back and shakes their head. Okay, so mouth good, but sucking bad. *I can work with that.* I wrap my hand around the base and just hold it there, continuing my kiss attack. Their hands go to the side of the tub, and they brace themselves as they fuck up into my hand. I don't know if I've ever seen anything hotter.

I get distracted by the flex of their muscles, the beautiful tension in their face, the way their tattoos seem to stand out in greater relief. An idea comes to me, and I probably shouldn't mess with success because they seem like they're pretty close, but hey, this is a Cook Fun Guarantee™, not some piddly hand job. Letting go, I use both hands to press my breasts together, and then slot their cock in between them.

"Fuck, fuck, fuck," they chant softly. The sight of their cock poking up between my breasts is beautifully obscene. It's plenty slick from my mouth, and they don't last long after that, their legs shaking, staring down at me with something like wonder. When they come, it's a quiet huff, a gasp, a sigh. I wanted more drama, but I'll take it. I swipe the come from my chin and grin at them, wiping it on their leg.

"Hey." There's no ire in the word, but it makes me grin wider.

"I let you come on me; there's no rule that says I have to leave it there."

Smiling, they bend down and kiss me, licking the rest away. "There's no rule that says you have to give it back, either." They get to their feet, and I ignore their hand when they try to help me up. We put our clothes back on, and an awkward *what did I just do* feeling is setting in before the sweat is even dry. I think they must be able to tell, because they don't try to talk to me, but they're definitely watching me. I finish first, and I'm halfway to the door when they catch me in another hug from behind.

"I know today was a lot. You want to have another drink? Together?" I shake my head, suddenly mute. "That's fine. Monday. Administration offices. I'll bring the paperwork."

I nod. Since my lips are apparently on strike from talking, I go up on my toes and give them a light kiss. I'm going home. I don't care if Colby's mad about it, I've had a *weird* weekend. This is weird. Wanted, but weird.

I'm halfway to the front door when I remember what they said about dates and shit.

"Lillies, no nougat. Lillies, no nougat," I chant quietly, looking all over. "Where the fuck is my phone?" It's out in the guest house with the vodka I forgot about, and by the time I find it, it's already got a calendar request for Monday with multiple notifications added.

As if I'd forget.

CHAPTER NINETEEN

ON MONDAY, WE DO THE paperwork before class. On Tuesday, I work on my tiles with intense focus because they're due at the end of the week, and I'm behind. On Wednesday, I text with them but don't see them. On Thursday, I'm glazing again, and I think my tiles are coming out pretty good.

But on Friday night, I'm bored. Maybe it's the edges of my fraying mind, I don't know. But Janey is away on a trip to California, Giada is babysitting for Raina, and Raina is on a date with her hubby. Colby is working, so Chance is out with his nerds. So I lay in bed, laptop open, studying...refreshing my grades probably more than necessary. But I know Glenn, and they grade on Fridays. They are disgustingly self-disciplined that way.

So when my second project grade pops up, I get a little notification. I skim down until I find it, bending over the screen laid flat on my lap, scrolling with my finger. *B-*. I sit back. Okay, B- is okay. I don't have to impress anyone with my grades; I just have to pass the damn class.

My phone dings and vibrates, and I lunge for it because I'm tired of entertaining myself.

Teacher person: Did you see it?

Hillary: How did you know I was waiting for it?

Teacher person: The intranet tells me who's online for the chat...

Hillary: And yet you're texting me behind its back instead. Very interesting.

Teacher person: Maybe I didn't feel like being school-appropriate.

Hillary: Mx. Rasmussen, what are you suggesting?

Teacher person: I think you know.

Hillary: Excuse me, but I think you have me confused with someone else. I am a very innocent college student with no notion of impropriety.

I'm feeling a little weird about their name on my phone. Teacher person is accurate, but also inaccurate. So I tweak it.

Dating person: That's not what you told me when I was getting you off in your brother's bathroom.

Hillary: That was hot. You can't blame me for that. How am I supposed to resist your charms?

No, that's not right, either. A relationship, they said. So I bite the bullet and pick a relationship-y name. I can always change it later.

Enbyfriend: Many other students seem to manage it just fine.
Hillary: You've clearly never used the ladies' room.
Enbyfriend: Wait, what? There's stuff about me in the bathroom?

There's only one, but it feels like the kind of harmless exaggeration that would make them feel good.

Hillary: (insert eyebrow waggle)

Enbyfriend: and who put it there, you?

Hillary: No, not me, LOL. It said you were hot with two t's. HOTT. Had a little fire illustration and everything.

Enbyfriend: I'm sorry, but that absolutely sounds like something you'd say.

Hillary: Did I say I disagreed with it?

Enbyfriend: Still not convinced.

Hillary: Fine, I'll take a pic next time.

Enbyfriend: Don't touch your phone in the bathroom, that's gross.

Hillary: you're gross

Enbyfriend: yes, I see now. You're clearly a very mature college student. My mistake.

Hillary: Screw you, smartass.

Enbyfriend: I'd be up for that if you're offering.

Hillary: what, like text sex? is that a thing?

Enbyfriend: Or you could come over.

The invitation hangs in the air, my computer whirring loudly because I put it on the bed like Chance told me not to because the fan has to work too hard. I want to, partly. But going over to their house feels...fast. Which makes no sense because they've been to mine and to Colby's, which is also mine. But it has been kind of a long week, and part of me is happy to just...wait.

Hillary: Not tonight, hornypants.

Enbyfriend: Date tomorrow? I want to take you out properly.

Hillary: I don't do very many things properly, so we might have to do it skankily instead.

Enbyfriend: I think I can handle that.

Enbyfriend: I'm proud of you. You did good on your project. I liked the pattern you carved.

Hillary: And it didn't blow up!

Enbyfriend: I told you that wasn't your fault!

Hillary: And loudly.

Enbyfriend: So tomorrow? 7:00?

Hillary: Sounds good. Where should I meet you?

Enbyfriend: I'll pick you up.

Hillary: Oh, you have a car?

Enbyfriend: Yes. But I'll probably walk.

Hillary: ....::perplexed face::

Enbyfriend: what?

Hillary: What's the point in picking me up if you're not in your car?

Enbyfriend: So I can antagonize you on the way.

Hillary: While we walk through the city to dinner, you're going to antagonize me?

Enbyfriend: yeah

Enbyfriend: it's my favorite thing. Besides making you come.

Enbyfriend: Actually, you know what? I need more data to decide which is my favorite thing.

Hillary: Maybe you'll get it tomorrow.

Enbyfriend: ::wide eyes::

Hillary: WHEN YOU ANTAGONIZE ME, geez. How easy do you think I am?

Enbyfriend: you're the best kind of difficult, Hil.

I know. It doesn't even sound like a compliment, does it? And yet, I know I'm difficult, and I'm tired of people trying to tell me I'm not. Glenn doesn't deny it. And the fact that they just embrace it, embrace *me* and all my messiness...I'm fighting it. But I love it. I want to reach out and hug them right through the phone.

The front door slams and footsteps pound down the hallway. Chance appears in my doorway, face flushed and glasses askew.

"I got in."

I sit straight up, my heart similarly coming to attention. "To the grant thingy? In England?"

He nods, thrusting out his phone with an email on the screen. "Look."

"I don't need to look." I laugh, clambering off the bed and hurrying across the room to wrap him in the most enormous hug I can give. He hugs me back. "I knew you'd get it," I whisper, and I feel his cheeks puff when he smiles.

"Impossible," he mutters, but he squeezes me harder. I pull back.

"When are you going to tell Colby?" His smile dims, and he rubs his scruffy chin.

"Tomorrow, I guess. I want to do it in person."

"Makes sense." Excitement overtakes me again, and I attack him with another hug. "I can't believe I'm going to England!"

Chance laughs out loud. "I love that you're making this about you."

"Duh. You better find a place with a guest room, though. I know Colby won't need it, but I will."

He pushes my shoulder, his gaze dropping to his feet. "He's gonna understand, right?"

"Yes," I say, enunciating, so he knows I'm serious. "He's gonna be thrilled for you. Seriously, honey. I know he will."

Chance looks up at me, and he looks like he's on the verge of tears. So it's totally for his benefit, letting him save face, when I gather him in my arms again.

"And if he's not, I'll beat some sense into him."

"I don't want to lose him," Chance chokes out. "I can't. He's seriously the best thing that ever happened to me."

"What about me?" I say, pretending to be incensed, and he lets a laugh and a sob both roll out of him.

"You're pretty great, too," he says, giving my cheek a kiss as he pulls back, wiping his eyes with the heel of his hand. "Ugh. Sorry. I know I'm being ridiculous."

"You are. Luckily, I'm a big fan of ridiculous. And you." I rub his shoulder, and he manages a smile. "Say, 'Colby is going to be thrilled for me.'"

"Colby is going to be thrilled for me."

"Say, 'Colby wants me to be successful.'"

"Colby wants me to be successful because he loves me."

"There ya go," I cheer. "Say, 'Hillary is the best roommate ever.'"

"Hillary *is* the best roommate ever." His face is so genuine that I blush.

"Ha, that last one was a trick. You were supposed to deny it. Honestly, get with it, Nicholson."

Chance takes a breath, then his phone buzzes in his pocket. "It's Colby." He pauses. Then he thrusts the phone toward me. "I can't talk to him. I'll tell him. And I don't want to tell him that way."

"Don't look at me," I say, holding up my hands to clarify that there is no way I'm taking that machine.

"Please?" he asks. "Just talk to him."

"No, just let it ring, for god's sake!" I am already far too in the middle of their relationship.

"He'll think something is wrong," he says urgently. "Please?"

"No!"

"But I always answer, no matter what I'm doing..." Chance stares wistfully down at the phone screen.

"Really? Gross, dude, they're called boundaries."

"You'll get it someday." The phone stops buzzing, and he looks forlorn.

"You'll tell him tomorrow. Just go to bed. He'll take it better in person."

Chance glares at me. "I thought he was going to take it fine!"

"He is, muffin. Now to go sleep and dream about drinking tea and eating scones with me in London."

"Um, Oxford's not actually in London..." I turn him by his shoulders and push him down the hall to his room as I reassure my anxious friend. "And why am I 'muffin,' now?"

"Shh, muffin, shh. We'll take a train. Now go to bed. That's an order."

Chance rolls his eyes at me as he closes his door. And I stand in the hallway for a minute, thinking about Chance and how much I love him and how much I want him and my brother to work out permanent-style. Then I hear my own phone buzz, and I remember that Glenn and I were talking. I hustle back to my room, sliding on the wood floors in my socks to get there faster. Also because it's fun.

My screen is full of notifications.

Enbyfriend: That was meant as a compliment.

Enbyfriend: Seriously.

Enbyfriend: Did you get distracted or are you upset

Enbyfriend: Don't make me call you. You're too young to enjoy phone calls.

Enbyfriend: HIILLAARRYYY

Enbyfriend: I like you. And being with you.

Enbyfriend: Hil

Enbyfriend: Hil

Enbyfriend: Hil

Enbyfriend: I have enough focus for both of us, darling, I can do this all night.

Hillary: Hi, STOP. My roommate just had to share some good/distressing news with me and then there was bonding required.

Enbyfriend: Is Chance okay? What happened? Also hi, thank you for writing back.

Hillary: you're welcome, and he's fine. Everything's fine.

Enbyfriend: Well, not everything.

Hillary: oh? what happened while I was gone?

Enbyfriend: I forgot what you look like.

Hillary: if only there was some way to remedy that.

Enbyfriend: Sigh. If only.

I can't help my smile at their silliness, and it's obvious I'm laughing when I take the picture.
Enbyfriend: Still so beautiful.
Hillary: Shut up, you are.
Enbyfriend: Oh, you think so?
A picture comes through...shirtless Glenn in bed, their face bare except for their beard, surrounded by white pillows, naked except for a pair of heather gray cotton shorts, all those glorious tattoos on display. I send back a drooling emoji, and they text "LOL" like an old person. I have this happy, buzzy feeling inside me that wants to be love except it's too early. But my heart is definitely drippy and disgusting. An idea comes to me. I whip off my shirt, press my boobs together with my arms, and send one back.

Chance passes by my door, then does a double-take. "Shall I close this for you?"

I grin. "If you don't mind..."

He's gay. He doesn't care. And I'm wearing a bra, for heaven's sake.

Enbyfriend: YES

I snicker at Glenn as Chance closes the door, though the look he's giving me is decidedly curious. I haven't told him about Glenn. I'm definitely going to. Soon. But we haven't even had our first date yet. Yes, I'm just conveniently ignoring all the times we've had sex, okay? Those were hookups, not dates.

Enbyfriend: Do you want to switch to Quickchat?

I didn't even think about it. I'm usually careful about who's got my pictures...but with Glenn, I don't think there's a malicious bone in their body. But maybe it's for their protection, too.

Hillary: Sure.

It doesn't take me long to find them: ArtsyGlenn76. So adorable.

PasswordJunkie: You weren't born in '76, were you?

ArtsyGlenn76: You're not that bad at math, are you?

ArtsyGlenn76: And why are you a password junkie? Are you going to steal my identity?

PasswordJunkie: It's because I can never remember them. Your identity is safe.

ArtsyGlenn76: You really think I would put my birth year in my user name? Is this 1991?

PasswordJunkie: I don't know what you do.

ArtsyGlenn76: Well, at the moment, I'm doing this.

A few moments later, a video comes through, and I have to put my hand over my mouth to keep an embarrassing noise from escaping. That strong hand is stroking their cock through the cotton, giving it long, leisurely touches. My clit swells just watching them, and even though my head was turned on from the first picture, I'm surprised my body is so on board. I usually need more whole-body stimulation to get excited, which is why getting myself off is a pain. Too bad porn creeps me out; this is kinda working for me.

> **PasswordJunkie**: hot
> **ArtsyGlenn76**: yeah?
> **PasswordJunkie**: definitely

I let my fingers wander down under my pajama pants, and I figure maybe they'd like the reciprocation.

As usual, I don't know what I'm doing, but just vibing with what they're doing seems to be working fine?

> **ArtsyGlenn76**: Hil, you're killing me.
> **PasswordJunkie**: how do I put you out of your misery?

My fingers are slick inside my shorts, and it feels good to just...play, touching myself gently, rubbing my soft fingertips over my smooth folds. They're not going to know if I come or not. There's no absolutely no pressure. But there wasn't the other day, either, when I couldn't.

> **ArtsyGlenn76**: Just show me what you're up to. Show me whatever you want.

This time they've lost the shorts, and their cock is poking up obstinately out of these petal-pink panties, and I feel another rush of heat between my legs that has me arching my back a little. They're getting a little rougher now, rubbing this little spot below the head, which is looking brightly furious at being ignored. I can hear their soft moans under the noise of their fingers against their clothes and skin. Quickchat will only let me watch it twice, and I curse their annoying rules. Because something tells me this is tit for tat, like everything else we do.

I put down the phone and reach into my drawer for my wand: it's pretty to even look at, like a stream of water someone stopped in time, silver in a long, smooth curve with a small ball at one end and a big ball at the other.

I'm still just playing around, wanting them to send me more stuff, but my clit is begging for attention, and I hit record as I slide the small end over it.

"Fuck, that's cold," I mutter, but the sensory stimulation brings an extra dimension, and my brain goes a little fuzzy with the overwhelm. I send three videos because I just keep holding down the button. *Oops.* Something tells me they won't mind, and when I get the next video back, I smirk a little.

"Fuck yes, Hil. I'm going to put an ice cube around your poor little clit, and then I'll lick it warm again." I can't see their face, just their fingers, and the motion of them reminds me of the way they did vibrato on their bass, and now I'll never *not* be able to think about this when I see them play. The weight of the wand is just right, and I close my eyes as I move it faster, finding the spot that feels the best. I feel my nipples tightening inside my basic purple bra. I wish I'd worn lace for them. I think they'd like that. *Or maybe they'd like it if I just took it off.*

So I whip it off and make that my next video, cupping and squeezing with my cold hand. It's kind of chilly in the apartment, and it's making my nipples stand up even more. I play it back and grimace; I don't have sexy hands. My nails are short and stubby because I bite them, and I don't have polish on them like Glenn for the same reason. Maybe I shouldn't send it. But I don't know what else to do, and I know they're waiting, so...I hit send.

And then they're playing with their nipples, too, fingers caressing the nipple bar like I wish mine could. I'd have so much fun putting that thing in my mouth, feeling the metal warm. They're quieter now, but it makes me feel okay, actually...like we're not hurrying? I don't mind if they want to charge on toward an O, but the fact that they're sort of following my lead feels...nice? I catch a glimpse of their gaze, and the fire there tells me they're definitely into this. So I let them see my face, too, as I turn the wand around and sink the big end inside myself. It's warmer because I've been holding it, but it still feels so good going in, smooth and hard, and I let out a groan I hope Chance can't hear.

> **ArtsyGlenn76**: you want to come, star?

That fucking nickname. It melts me and haunts me at the same time.

> **PasswordJunkie**: dunno
> **ArtsyGlenn76**: Just enjoying yourself?
> **PasswordJunkie**: yeah
> **PasswordJunkie**: you?
> **ArtsyGlenn76**: yeah

I can't help but notice that they're back to texting.

> **PasswordJunkie**: you done?
> **ArtsyGlenn76**: not until you tell me you are.

The wand feels good, but I can feel my arousal slinking away with less attention on my clit...and I can't put down the phone. Frustration rises in place of my arousal, and I decide to fuck it.

I throw down the phone and grope in the drawer until I find my vibrator. It takes a little finesse because when the vibrator touches the wand, the extended vibration is unpleasant, but I angle to keep them apart, and then I'm coming, shaking, trying to keep my squawks inside, turning my face into the pillow. Relief and pleasure flood my insides from head to toe, and I turn to my side, the wand still inside, toys still in my hands and between my legs. But there's a face I want to look into and lips I want to kiss now that I'm done, and the joy ebbs away into a sideways kind of loneliness. Still breathing hard, I reach for the phone and start a video call. Glenn answers immediately.

"Hi." Their grin is lascivious, and yes, I am using that word right. Like they think they tricked me or something. Goober.

"Stop grinning like that."

Their grin just grows wider. "Like what?"

"Like you're satisfied with yourself. You shouldn't be. I did all the work."

Glenn snuggles deeper into their massive mountain of pillows. "I don't know; it sure seemed like my pictures were doing *something* for you."

"I can see how I gave you that impression, but–"

"And you said you're hard to get off. So I feel justified in counting this as a successful sexual encounter."

My insides go a little cold and stony, like biscuits left out overnight. "You shouldn't think of it like that. Seriously."

Glenn's face is openly concerned. "How should I think of it then?"

"I was having fun even before I came. That's enough for me."

"I had fun, too."

Their voice is slightly contrite, and I feel bad that I've brought down the mood, but I need them to know this about me. I've been broken up with for less.

"You sleepy?" they ask, and before I can answer, I yawn so hard that my eyes water.

"Almost always, afterward. I'm like a dude. Partners want pillow talk, and I'm already out."

"I'd hold you and whisper how wonderful you are. You could hear it in your dreams."

"Mmm." I toss the toys to the empty side of the bed and roll away from them, pulling the comforter up over my bare shoulder. "Sounds nice."

"I'm gonna let you go. I'll see you tomorrow. Sweet dreams, Hil."

"You too," I mumble, and I don't even get the phone on the charger before I'm out.

CHAPTER TWENTY

CHANCE GOES OUT EARLY the next morning, and I figure from the way he's fussing with his clothes that he's going to see Colby.

"Good luck."

"Thanks." He holds out his arms. "Do I look okay?"

"You look great." And he does. I'm sure it won't matter what he's wearing, actually. Colby's gonna freak no matter what. Looking more handsome isn't going to make the news easier to swallow. He still changes his clothes twice more before he leaves, grabbing a bagel as he goes because he ran out of time.

"That's my move," I call after him. "Be your own cliché." I do get a small smile as he closes the front door behind him.

I throw in some laundry in anticipation of a brotherly freak-out that might require sisterly consolation. So I'm dressed and drinking coffee when I get Colby's text.

> **Brother:** Can you meet me at that little coffee shop across from the Howitz?
> **Hillary:** who's buying
> **Hillary:** J/k, I'll be right there.

I think I might pass Chance on my way out, but I don't, just Janey. I stop to give her a hug, and we resolve to hang out. It probably won't happen, and we both know it, but it's okay. The resolution is the point.

When I find Colby, he's sitting with his head in his hands in the back, hat on the table. It's more serious than I thought.

"Hey."

He looks up sharply, then relaxes a small measure. "Hey, Hil." He pushes out a chair for me with his foot, and I sit down, unslinging my giant purse from its cross-body position.

"So he told you."

Colby nods miserably.

"Did you at least pretend to be excited for him?"

"I did," he says somberly. "I tried, anyway."

"I'm sorry, bud. But I think both of you are blowing this way out of proportion. It's only a few months. The internet is a thing. You can write emails and message each other. You can even send videos back and forth."

"Can't hold a video at night," Colby blurts out, and I cock my head sympathetically.

"True. Maybe we should get you a blow-up Chance doll."

Colby rolls his eyes, then puts his face in his hands, a picture of melancholy. I lean over and put my arm around his shoulders.

"This is a good thing, Col. You want Chance to shine. He'll go, have a great time, and bring you back some tea and imperialism."

His forehead wrinkles adorably. "Imperialism?"

"Well, yeah, I assume that's part of the England gift bag. If it's not, they really need to work on their branding."

Colby shakes his head and sighs. "I don't get half your jokes, but I think I get what you're saying. You think we're strong enough to weather the separation."

"Exactly. And you'll be even more sure you want to be together after this."

He shakes me off. "He's not sure he wants to be with me?"

"What? No, that's not what I'm—listen. You'll both be fine. Your relationship will continue to grow even when you're apart, maybe even in new and interesting ways. He's not going to leave you just because you're in different countries. And not just because it would be incredibly awkward when you come over on Wednesday nights...speaking of which, when are we starting that back up again?"

"Can't. I've got a church gig. Ongoing."

Well, that's annoying.

"Why do the religious need sound amplification if God is everywhere?"

"Hil, focus. I know you're probably right about Chance. I just...I keep picturing this scenario where some super-smart British dude with a classy accent sweeps him off his feet. I mean, I don't even know if I hold up to average American dudes. And that place is going to be full of nerds who can speak his language. People who can program the commercialized robot on the kitchen counter. I break out in hives just thinking about talking to it."

"All right, number one, as much as I tease you about it, your robot fears are entirely justified. When the AI uprising happens, we both know Chance is our only hope of survival."

"Damn straight." He sniffles.

"Number two, no British dude can hold a candle to my adorable little brother. Chance loves you because you're you, because you two get each other, not because of that other superficial shit. And it's gross that you're making me say this, but you're hot. Do you know how hard Chance has been freaking out that you will not be okay with this? Super hard. And I'd like it noted that I could've easily made one of a dozen sex jokes right there, but I didn't, out of respect for your pain and because I'm serious."

Now Colby just looks concerned, frowning at the mention of Chance's emotional state. "Was he okay, though? He didn't have a panic attack, did he?"

"I think he was close when you called last night. He wanted to answer, but he didn't want to give it away."

He rubs his scruffy chin. "I did think it was weird that he didn't answer. He always answers."

"Again, it's gross that you're both making me know these things. Please stop."

Colby stares down at the table for a long moment, then snatches up his hat and sits back.

"You know what? You're right. I should support him. We should celebrate this. Let's go to Thai Express tonight."

"Tonight?" *Oh, crap.* I could probably reschedule with Glenn, but I don't want them to think they're not important to me, and we scheduled our thing first. And frankly, I don't *want* to blow off our first date. "I've got plans tonight. I'm sorry. Sunday night?"

"No, I've got the symphony. What plans do you have tonight?"

"Nothing major, just...I can't bail on it, that's all."

Colby leans forward. "Hillary...are you trying to be secretive?"

Oh, dear. He knows I suck at secrets. "Me?" My voice sounds like one of the squeaky mice in Cinderella. "No?" I try to laugh, but it's just as high and weird. "What would I have to be secretive about?" I gather up my bag because it's believable that I'm going to get a drink, and it will allow this awkward conversation to dissipate.

And it's not a secret. The administration knows. I just want to go on this one date without anyone giving me crap about it, so I can decide if this is working for me. To see if it's just the sneaking around or if it's more. I think it's more. A lot more. I think if I throw myself off this cliff, I'm going to find a whole lot of things waiting for me with Glenn, but...I'm not great with pressure. I just want to give this thing a little room to breathe before all the guys know. I texted Janey and Giada last night to tell them, but that was a foregone conclusion.

Colby snags my sweatshirt sleeve as I stand up. "Wait, before you go..."

I don't like the way he hesitates. I suck at secrets; Colby sucks at conflict.

"Mom and Dad are coming for Thanksgiving. They said they tried to call you a few times to let you know, but they haven't been able to get a hold of you. They'd really like to see you."

"Oh." I sit back down. "Right."

Colby sips his drink, watching me carefully. "Thought we'd have it at my place because it's bigger."

"Sure. Yeah."

I don't want to do that. I don't want to see them. I've been nursing this grudge for so long, it's...comfortable? And seeing them is going to be...uncomfortable. Like, probably not *ruin the holiday* uncomfortable, but not fun either.

"Put me down for some side dishes," I say, just to say something. Just to get him to stop staring at me like he hopes I don't cry. "Nothing essential, mind you."

"Naturally." He chuckles, taking another sip of his probably cold coffee. The topic shifts to other things, and I sit and enjoy hanging out with my brother, just the two of us, for the first time in ages.

But I'm definitely still thinking about Thanksgiving and wondering how the fuck this is going to go.

CHAPTER TWENTY-ONE

GLENN INSISTS ON PICKING me up because "just because I'm not a gentleman doesn't mean I can't treat you politely." I insist back that I am fully capable of finding the restaurant myself, but when I hear a knock at 6:23, I know it's them. I rush to the door with one shoe still in my hand.

"What are you doing here?" I hiss, and they grin.

"Picking you up."

"Ugh. You're the worst. Come in, then." Thankfully, Chance isn't here; he's probably at Colby's, but I actually can't remember even though I'm sure he told me. Hands shoved in their pockets, Glenn takes in my apartment. This part is clean; my room is a disaster. I can't let them in there.

"Have a seat," I say firmly. Still grinning, they comply.

"You really don't want me here, do you?"

"It's not that," I say, and it's not a total lie; I'm just feeling frantic because I'm not ready to go. But I feel weird just leaving them here in my living room while I go back to the bathroom. "Come on."

I turn and hurry back down the hall to the mascara I abandoned earlier. I lean over the counter, trying to get closer to the mirror so I can see what I'm doing, trying not to care that I'm sticking my ass out right in front of them.

"Oh, mascara. My nemesis."

That wrangles a smile out of me. "Why? Did it foil your plans for world domination?"

"No, I just can't keep my hands steady enough to make it look good." They're leaning against the door frame with their hands still in their pockets. I can't see exactly what they're wearing because their peacoat is still buttoned, but just gazing at them in the mirror, I decide to take a chance.

"Come here."

Glenn shuffles into the bathroom, kicking aside the towel I left on the floor that I was definitely going to pick up before I left and also two outfits that I rejected because they made me feel chunky.

You're not supposed to share eye makeup because of parasites, I think, but it's just once, and their lashes are so pretty, I just can't resist.

"Look up and hold still."

I'm just reaching up toward their face with the brush when they mutter. "If you poke me in the eye, you pay for dinner."

My progress falters as I giggle. "Look, if you make me laugh, I'm *definitely* going to poke you. So this is on you."

"What if I like making you laugh?" they murmur, looking down at me with so much tenderness, my heart swoons.

"I think you can control yourself for thirty seconds," I say, taking their chin in my hand because it makes me more steady. Glenn dutifully throws their gaze back to the ceiling, and I gently brush upward against their lashes on one side, then the other, foregoing the bottom ones because I don't think I can do it cleanly. "There."

Glenn pivots and leans forward toward the mirror. "It looks good."

"Yeah, it does." I want to ask what they're wearing, but I don't want them to think it matters. I want to ask if they get dysphoric like Chance, but it feels too personal. I want to ask what they're expecting later, if they like having the door held for them, if they want me to pull out their chair, but I feel a strange weight given that they're still my instructor. Yes, we declared it to the administration, but there's still a power thing happening, and I never want them to think for a second that I'm here for a better grade or that school has anything at all to do with how I treat them.

"You're quiet. That usually means trouble." They've gone back to the doorway as I finish up my makeup, choosing a bold lip color. As a way of stalling, I hold it out to them, but they shake their head.

"Just thinking about us." I hesitate, holding their gaze in the mirror. "Does this feel a little weird to you?"

"Yeah," they say without hesitation. "It definitely does. But I'm willing to push through it."

I roll my eyes. "Oh, how generous of you."

"Isn't it?" they grin. "I'm a generous person."

When I turn to leave, I don't kiss them because they're blocking the doorway (although they are) or because their eyes are popping from that mascara (although they do). I kiss them because they are a generous person and because I'm glad I know them, and because

I'm glad we can talk about The Weird™ without having to suffer through pretense. And when I kiss them, some of The Weird™ melts away into that thing we have, the one that's growing more every day into a comfortable thing instead of an angry thing.

"Are you ready to go?"

"I think so. Oh, wait, no. We have to feed Janey's cat on the way out."

Their eyes widen so much, I think I can see all the way around their pupils. "Someone put you in charge of a living thing?"

I smack their chest with the back of my hand, and I let it sting a little bit because 1. RUDE and 2. Janey's already texted me three times to make sure I remember, and I hate that I needed that. I also set an alarm on my phone as backup. Mr. Fluffypants is healthy and would probably survive if I forgot, but he cannot die on my watch. I would never forgive myself.

They follow me down the hall, and when I put on my other flat, they are blatantly checking out my ass.

"Take a picture; it'll last longer."

"It's usually on a chair when you're in class. Gotta take my opportunities where I can get them. Hashtag no regrets."

"What have I gotten myself into?" I sigh as I claim my coat and my purse by the front door.

"It's gonna be an amazing night."

They wait in the hallway ("I wasn't invited to come inside by the apartment lessee"), and I can't find Mr. Fluffypants.

"Will you please help me look for this animal?" I plead, coming back to the front door. "Or at least come inside? I don't want to leave this open. With my luck, he'll make himself known by darting out the front door."

"Fine. But only because I'm not running after anything in these boots. They pinch my feet."

I laugh as I close the door behind them. "Then why did you wear them?"

"I was dressing to impress." Their tone is delightfully haughty, and I can't help but keep it going.

"Well, give me the full effect, then."

Glenn puts one hand to their coat zipper as if I might try to forcibly undress them. "At the restaurant."

"Come on," I wheedle, unabashedly pressing my breasts to their chest. "Don't be a tease. Show me what you put on for me, Mx. Rasmussen."

"No. Let's find this creature and go. We're gonna miss our reservation."

I bounce on my toes because I'm a child. "Where are we going?"

Glenn's smile is sweet as they lean forward to rest their forehead against mine. "Feed the cat, then you'll find out." At that moment, the skinny tortoiseshell rubs against my legs and meows. "*This* is the creature named Mr. Fluffypants? He's not fluffy at all."

"Quiet," I say, picking him up for a nuzzle. "He'll hear you. He's very sensitive about it."

I find the can of wet food that Janey left on the counter by the sink, open it, and plop half of the salmon into a small blue bifurcated dish. I give him a few pets as he digs in, wolfing down the food as if I haven't fed him in days rather than hours. Then I pull out my phone and take a picture.

Glenn smirks. "Your friend wanted proof of life, didn't she?"

"Maybe." I text Janey the photo, and she texts back a grinning emoji. "Ready, Freddy." When I look up, they're on their phone. "Everything okay?"

"Yeah, I'm just getting us a car. We're never going to make it walking."

"How far is this place?"

Glenn motions as if they're locking their lips, and I smile. I lock up, and we go downstairs. I debate sixty-six million times about whether to hold their hand, but I ultimately decide against it. And you might not think that's possible in such a small window of time, but that just shows you don't know how fast my brain can crank when it's motivated.

I see the unicycler from the back of the Honda Civic that picked us up, and I point him out to Glenn. They point out a bumper sticker that says "Make Portland Weirder," and we both agree that this is likely impossible, but we admire the spirit. And when we both point out the giant harvest moon that's peeking at us between the buildings, I reach over and put my hand over theirs, squeezing their fingers, and their smile is as bright as that moon.

And then the car stops in front of a familiar building, and my heart stops, too.

Because it's Marble. They chose the restaurant where my brother's roommates work.

CHAPTER TWENTY-TWO

"THIS PLACE IS SO GOOD," Glenn says as they slide out of the back seat. They turn back to offer me a hand, and I take it. "You're gonna love it."

There's no point in lying. "Yeah, I've been here. It's super good."

They haven't let go of my hand, which I only realize because they're towing me toward the maître d's desk, my body holding back like it knows the embarrassment I am about to experience. I scan the wait staff's faces rapidly as Glenn gets us checked in, but I don't see Antonio or Patrick, and I let out a relieved breath. They must be off tonight. I send a silent thank you to whatever deity saw fit to give me this space, this tiny bit of privacy, while I figure out this New Thing™ between me and Glenn.

They take off their coat when we get to our table, and their outfit makes me smile: a black and white striped dress with a cute denim jacket.

"You look great," I whisper as I pull out their chair for them, and the smile I get tells me I just earned myself some major brownie points. We chat about the decor (they are taking the farm-to-table thing very seriously, including black-and-white photographs of their cows on the wall, which is making both of us giggle). Someone pours us water, and we both thank them.

And then, someone else approaches the table, and I hear the last words I wanted to hear tonight.

"Good evening, welcome to Marble. My name is Antonio, and I'll be your...server."

That little pause? Yeah, he used that to give me this knowing smirk, this *OMG, you are so busted* look.

"Our specials tonight are mushroom-stuffed ravioli with crispy pork or roasted chicken with green tomato chutney."

"I'll have a steak," I say. "Medium. Turnip fries. Scrap the other veggies."

Tony's mouth quirks and I can tell he wants to comment about it being *farm-to-table, vegetables are part of the deal.* Instead, he pivots to Glenn.

"And for you, Mx.?" He must have put two and two together if he already knows their pronouns. My boys are going to be so ticked with me.

"I'll try that ravioli—that sounds good."

"Excellent. I'll just go put this in for you."

When he's gone, Glenn leans forward. "He looked familiar."

"He's my brother's roommate."

"Oh! But no, that's not it. I think I had him in a class."

I sip my water. "No, he doesn't go to RCU. Maybe you saw him in a play. He's also an actor."

"Yes!" they cry, as if that was going to bother them all night until they figured it out. "That's it. He played Mercutio. He was wonderful." They pause. "And hot."

"Mmm, bisexual, are we?"

Glenn shrugs. "I guess so. Can I ask about you?" It actually isn't something I've given much thought. My brother is bi. My roommate is gay. I've only dated one woman, but it was fun?

"Yeah, um...I guess pansexual? Though I prefer people with cocks." Glenn chokes a little on their water. The lady at the table next to us gives me a withering look meant to shame me, but I just smile at her. "I haven't given it a ton of thought, though."

"Neither have I, actually. I'd rather just find someone I enjoy being with."

"Yes, exactly."

Antonio reappears with a small white plate with what looks like deviled eggs.

"What's this?"

"Bacon-stuffed eggs with smoked roe."

I stared at him blankly. "That we did not order," I finish.

"On the house," he grins, and I roll my eyes. "No, I asked first. I didn't take my dinner because I'm trying to drop weight for my next role."

"Oh, really? Where are you performing?" Glenn asks, leaning forward to claim an egg.

"It's a small production," Tony demurs, and I jump in.

"It's Portland Perfunctory. He got the *lead*."

"It's not the lead," he mutters, glancing around at the other tables.

"Well, it's a speaking part, and that's what matters. You'll be an amazing Charon." I turn back to Glenn. "They're doing *The Invention of Love*."

They're usually so even-keel, the fact that they're literally squirming with excitement has me grinning.

"Oh, I adore Stoppard! I saw *Rosencrantz and Guildenstern are Dead* in high school, and I've been hooked ever since. And I *loved* you as Mercutio." They reach out and grab my hand as Antonio blushes. "Please let me know when opening night is, and we'll make a date of it."

"We will?" I ask softly.

"Unless you're busy?" Man, they are killing me with the long, vulnerable looks tonight.

"No, I'm probably not busy." *I just don't know how you're so sure we'll still be together then.* And I can tell our mushiness is showing through when Antonio starts to back away.

"I'll let you get back to your date..."

I pick up an egg and take a tenuous bite. The saltiness is perfect, and the roe gives it a freshness I didn't expect.

"So do you–"

"Hang on." My brain has snagged on what just happened here, and I need to wrap it up. I pull out my phone.

HILDAWG: So we don't need to mention to Colby and Chance why I blew off their thing, right?

TONY THE TIGER: Take it from someone with five siblings: that is a pathetic attempt at a bribe.

HILDAWG: Please? With whipped cream on top?

TONY THE TIGER: the talk of food is getting us closer...

"Everything okay?" Glenn asks, leaning over to see what I'm doing.

"Yes, nosy. I just blew off a thing my brother invited me to, and I don't want Antonio to tell him why."

"Oh." They reach for another egg and pop it in their mouth whole, but it feels like a "food will impede me from asking questions" maneuver instead of "I'm so unconcerned with my date's behavior that I'm going to stuff my face" behavior.

TONY THE TIGER: Is baking on the table?
HILDAWG: Yep.
TONY THE TIGER: I want those blonde brownies for the next family dinner.
HILDAWG: Done.

"Wait, why is it a secret? Are we a secret?"

Uh oh. Glenn's beautiful eyes, set off by my mascara, are dimming as if their thoughts are troubled.

"Uh, no," I say, putting the phone away. "Not a secret. I'm just..." I motorboat my lips. How do I explain this part? "I'm not ready for the teasing. We're new; we're still...forming what we are." The perfect metaphor comes to me, and I snap my fingers. "We're still in the lump stage of the pot, you know? Just getting our hands dirty, just getting the wheel spinning. I don't want them sticking their noses into things, throwing off my...balance."

They're staring at me, and I don't have a blessed clue what they're thinking, so I take another breath to fix it, to explain better. And of course, this is the moment Antonio comes back with our salads. I glare at him because *did I not say to ditch the vegetables?* I know I did. I swear, he's just bringing bonus food to eavesdrop.

He puts a little carousel of dressings on the table, and I'm willing him with all my brainpower to *go away*...

"Sorry, I didn't want to say in front of your friend..." Glenn glances toward Antonio's retreating back. "But that actually makes sense."

"And not just because of the pottery metaphors?"

"No." They chuckle. "I mean, it didn't hurt. But no. I'm okay with letting us be a work-in-progress."

"Okay, good," I say, trying to force more air into my lungs.

I've just stabbed my first bite of this unwanted vegetable garbage when they say, "As long as that's the only reason."

Something a bit breakable in their voice tells me to handle with care. I set my fork back down. "What does that mean?"

"Nothing." Their smile is so forced, it's painful to look at. "Never mind."

I say nothing. I do not pick up my fork again. I do not shift my weight. I just stare at Glenn until they sigh. I call it Stubborn Mode™, and I am very good at it.

"Okay, fine, look...some people..." They hesitate again, then sigh. "Some of my partners have not been so comfortable with the way I present myself. So they made excuses to stay home, and I didn't figure out why until I was already invested emotionally in the relationship, and I don't want to go through that again. So if we're hiding because—"

"No."

"Can I finish?"

I'm warring between Big Mad that their partners treated them that way and the desperate need to reassure them that that's not me.

"Yes. I'm sorry I interrupted. No, that's a lie—I'm not sorry. I wanted you to know that's not me."

Glenn smirks at me. "Okay, Ms. Impulsivity. If we're hiding because you're ashamed–"

"We're not."

"Hil!"

"I know. I'm sorry. I'll try." I slap both hands over my mouth. Maybe one of them will manage to stay there long enough for them to finish their sentence.

Glenn gives their head a little shake, but they're still smiling with one corner of their mouth. "If we're hiding because you're ashamed, then there's no future for us. But if you're just tentative because we're new, I get that. I know rejection and perceived rejection is hard for you. Has your brother shown any signs of not liking the idea of us?" Glenn systematically rolls the tomatoes to the side of their plate, away from the rest of the salad.

"No, not at all. If anything, I think he likes you too much. I just don't want him to raz me because I made such a big deal about hating you."

"That's understandable. I mean, I plan to give you a hard time about it for the rest of our lives, so..."

"Glenn," I whine, but they're undeterred.

"I know I'm fantastic, so I can't imagine what you were thinking."

I reach out and put a hand on their smooth forearm. "Hey. You *are* fantastic. It was about me, not you." Glenn smiles as they lean forward and kiss me. Their lips are soft and perfect. I lower my voice as we part. "And if you need more proof, I'm happy to climb into your lap and make out with you in the middle of this swanky restaurant."

Glenn waggles their head side to side, still close enough to kiss me again. "I don't want to make the cows uncomfortable."

"I thought they were called Karens."

Glenn's laugh comes out so hard, I kind of worry that they're going to hurt themselves. It's not loud. It's that almost-silent, laughing-so-hard-I-actually-can't-breathe kind.

"Not the Karens, the..." They point to the framed pictures on the wall. "The *cows*."

"Oh," I say, grinning. "*Those* cows."

"Hillary. My god, woman."

I shrug innocently, digging out a package of tissues from my bag to wipe the tears of laughter from their face. They've collected themselves by the time our entrees come. And we're still having such a good time when the dessert cart comes around that we hit that, too. In fact, we're so busy talking that I don't notice they're walking me home until we're in front of my building.

"I had a great time," I say, flashing them a smile as I dig around for my keys.

"Me too," they say, stuffing their hands in their pockets. "Let's do it again."

"I'm free tomorrow."

Glenn's smile widens. "I've got the symphony. I could come by after, but it'd be late."

"I should probably go to bed at a decent hour, since I have class..."

"Yeah. Right. That's fine." They seem completely genuine, but I still feel like I rejected them, and the idea of them leaving now seems terrible.

"You want to come up?"

CHAPTER TWENTY-THREE

"DO YOU WANT ME TO COME up?" Their voice is low and rumbling in the way that I like, and it reminds me of when a big truck is coming down the road, and the engine is a warning, and the ground trembles, and everyone looks around for a second before they relax. Only I don't think I can relax.

"Yeah, I'd like that." I reach out and touch the edge of their coat, pinching it between my fingers to tug at them, rubbing it up and down suggestively. "You want to come up?"

"Yeah." There's wonder in their voice, and they're giving me that soft look again. I'd rather it was the hot, branding one they gave me the other day in the studio, but I'll take this one, too. Because tonight has been about us in a different way. It was more about the dreams you think about on a rainy day, curled up by the window, than the daily minutia of getting minor tasks done, like pots and grading and class attendance.

"Come on, then."

They follow me inside, hands shoved in the pockets of their peacoat, and we wait for the elevators in silence. It seems like it's taking a long time, and I want to turn to them and ask if it seems like it's taking a long time, but then it comes. But the wound-tight feeling I had while waiting is still there, cranked harder by the silence.

Do they want this? Do they know I meant sex? Should I have just said sex? Do they think they're coming up for coffee, or something? What if they just want to watch some-thing? We could do that, I guess. That would be okay. Maybe I could still sneak in some making out.

We get to my front door, and I'm digging for my keys when I hear voices through the door. I can't hear what they're saying, but it's obviously Colby and Chance, and my heart deflates. As nervous as I was about this, I still wanted to try. And it took courage to ask them up, and now that energy is gone, in the wind, un-salvageable.

"Do you want to go to my place?" they ask when they notice I'm hesitating.

"No. That's okay." I unlock the door and push my way inside. They don't look up from their video game when I come in. "Hey, guys..."

"Hey, Hil."

"Did you have a good time?"

They're still not looking up, so I clear my throat soft-ly. "Yes, it was a good date."

Still nothing. *Dumbasses, I went on a DATE.* I def-initely should've texted one of them while I was still downstairs. *Lack of executive function, you will be the death of me.*

"*Really* good." I put my bag down and take off my coat, and Glenn does the same.

"Hey, guys." Their low voice has the boys' heads snapping toward the door, finally, and they both stand up.

"Oh, hey! We didn't see you there," Colby says, of-fering his hand and shooting me a glare. I smile because it's not my fault he's clueless. "Wait," he says, pivoting to me. "Your plans were with…"

"Yeah."

"We were just headed out," Chance says quickly, and I roll my eyes because he is the world's worst liar. And the fact that he's in his pajamas is not convincing evidence. "Sorry we can't stay and hang out."

Glenn looks truly perplexed, cocking his head to the side. "Pajama party?"

Chance looks down at himself, and I can tell Colby wants to facepalm over his boyfriend's silly antics.

"Oh." Chance laughs. "No. I'll just change real quick."

"Since we're already caught in your ruse, can I ask why we're leaving?" Colby gripes.

"No, you may not," Chance says primly, in total contradiction to the rather rough way he's pulling Colby after him into his bedroom. I turn to Glenn.

"Would you like a drink or something? I think I have some chocolate cake…"

"How can you eat more? I'm so stuffed." They put one hand on their belly and grimace with apparent regret.

"Maybe just a bubbly water, then," I tease, giving them a small smile, and they give me back a bigger one. Glenn leans in, angling me so my back is toward the counter, boxing me in. When they come in for a kiss, it's a quiet one, like they're shy about it, like they don't want to get caught. But we're kind of already caught. I rest my forearms on their shoulders, ruffling the back of their hair. It's getting a bit long in the back; the brown hairs are soft, but the grays are wiry between my fingers, and when I give it a tug, I finally get that hot look I've been wanting. They raise their hands and run them over me softly, almost petting me, their thumbs tracing along my ribs, over the swell of my hips. I want that soft touch between my legs, in my hair, over my lips. I want it everywhere.

"Sorry, we're finally off," Chance says, dragging Colby through the living room by one hand. My brother is smiling like a fool, and based on the way they're dressed, he's convinced Chance to go dancing with him. *Any excuse to wear leather pants and embarrass Chance.* Looks like we're both going to have a fun night. "We'll be out late."

"You really don't have to—" I don't entirely mean that, but I do feel bad that I've thrown a wrench in their evening plans.

"No, no, this was our plan," Chance lies. "Goodbye." The door slams behind them, and Glenn and I look at each other, smirking.

"Your roommate is a kind person."

"He is," I agree. He's going to be hard to replace when he and Colby finally move in together. One of their hands slides up to my neck, and when that calloused thumb caresses the front of my throat, I let out a little sound I don't think I've ever made before. Something between a whimper and a whine.

"I want you, Hillary," Glenn whispers, leaning forward to sweetly take my lips again.

"I want you, too."

"Can we talk about why it's taken us so long to get here?"

"You mean as opposed to studio smuttiness and bathroom hookups?" Glenn grimaces, and I laugh softly. "No judgment, professor. They were hot."

"Yeah." Their hands are still moving, but the rest of them is still. "Is it too much? For you?"

"I don't...maybe?" It's hard to explain, but their gaze is patient, unwavering. But it isn't making words come easier. "It's like...the danger banging and the angry sex is fun. But letting you into my bed..." I swallow. "Letting you into my real life is just different. But I want to try. I am trying."

"I see that. And I appreciate it. I know this is different for both of us. But based on what we've done so far, I may want to fight with you and fuck you and fondle you and find your keys until we're old and gray."

"You're already gray." They glare at me, and I can't help but keep going. "And old. Older than me, anyway."

Glenn mutters something about cheeky students, and I grin at them, cocking my head.

"I didn't know you were so good at alliteration. Guess it makes sense for a poet."

"Stop," they gripe. "Can you just respond to the emotions, please?"

See, that's the part I'm not good at, and I never have been. So I pull them close until we're chest to chest and I can whisper into their ear.

"I want that, too. I'm just scared. I'm complicated. I'm a mess."

"Stop." It isn't a complaint this time. It's a plea. "You're not. You're a wonder. You sparkle. You make my world lighter."

I let my chin drop to rest on their shoulder, which isn't easy on my tiptoes. "Doesn't feel that way."

"Trust me." They fumble for a moment before they find my hand, then they bring my fingers to their lips and kiss them like some kind of duke in a historical. It makes me want to call them "my lord." What's the gender-neutral of lord? Feminine would be lady, but that's not right...maybe if I combined them? Lody? Lard? *Not lard.*

"Hil. Come back." They're working their way down my arm, pressing gentle kisses to the inside of my wrist, right on my pulse.

"I didn't move."

"Your brain left. Come back. Show me where your bedroom is."

"So fucking bossy, Rasmussen..." I pull back to see their face, this face that makes me weak.

"I can carry you if you'd prefer."

My impulse is to back up, but they've already got me cornered against the counter. "You can't."

Their grin telegraphs their intention even before they hinge at the waist and throw me over their shoulder.

"Glenn!" I squeak. I am not a small person, and this display of strength is doing effective things to my libido. I do not hate it.

They give my ass a playful slap. "See? Now I've got your attention. First bedroom or second?"

"Second!" I grab on to the back of their shirt as they start to move across the living room. They're still wearing their boots, and I wonder if Janey can hear their heavy footfalls downstairs.

"Nice," they comment as they survey my mess. *Why didn't I clean? Why didn't I think we'd end up here?* Glenn tosses me onto my unmade bed, then gets to work undressing...they don't break eye contact as they take off their coat and denim jacket. They pivot and put one boot up on the footboard, undoing the laces slowly, flicking them open, putting their long legs on display.

Then they stop, and I realize they're staring at my hand, which has found its way under my dress. Yeah, that's how wrapped up I was in Confident Glenn's Striptease. I wasn't even aware.

"If you're gonna show off, I'm gonna take advantage," I say, putting my other hand behind my head.

"Did I complain?" they ask, going back to their task, sliding out of the black boot.

I shake my head, and I let my fingers wander over the silk under my dress. "Talk to me."

"About what?" they ask, and the mattress shakes as they put their other boot up on the end of the bed.

"Anything." I close my eyes to make the truth easier. "I like your voice. Sometimes when I'm having trouble getting off..."

"Yes?"

They must have hurried through the second boot now that I'm not watching, because their dress brushes my knees, and the mattress bends as they crawl over me.

"What naughty thing did you do?"

I swallow. "I listen to your lectures. The ones I recorded."

Their kisses against my cheeks are light, but my own touch against my clit is getting rough in response to their question.

"And you touch yourself?" I swear, if their voice gets any lower, I may spontaneously combust. That would be a heck of a mess for someone to clean up, right? All I can do is nod jerkily. My own touch is fire as I rub my poor swollen clit through the silk, wet now.

Glenn's lips move to my neck, and I can feel the heat of their skin hovering just above my arm, making no move to stop me. "Did you come?"

"Yeah," I sigh dreamily. Their voice is even better in person than on my recordings. I'm surprisingly close to coming now, so I hastily force my fingers away from myself. I run them through Glenn's hair, and they lean back a little to see me better.

"Why'd you stop?"

"Oh. Well, most of my partners want to be the one to make me come. So I guess I assumed—"

"I'm not like any of your other lovers, Hillary. I can promise you that." Their gaze is focused and intense, like they're memorizing all the little dots and lines of my face. I hope they don't draw my face. I'd die of embarrassment. But first, I'd frame it and keep it forever.

"Don't say lovers, old person. Lovers is gross."

"Be a good girl and put that hand right where you want it."

Their words send a shiver up my spine, and they smile a little like they know. Ugh, why is that hot? I'm only a few years younger than them; it's the *good* part, not the *girl* part, that just cuts right to the core of me. It sticks in my heart like an arrow. Because I don't feel good, I feel like a fuck-up all the time, and it's so hard to shake even when I know it's not true.

"Would you prefer my tongue to your fingers?" Their voice snaps me back to reality; they're pressing light kisses to my chest now. I enjoyed that time they got on their knees for me in the studio, and something tells me that a Glenn who has all the time they want to make me come would be twice as devastating.

"No." I move my hand back between my legs, less eagerly this time. Because I have more confessions to make. "I got off in the tub when you were here."

Glenn lifts their head from my chest. "You did?"

"Mmm-hmm."

They scooch higher. "The day we got Thai food? I was sitting out there with your roommate and your brother, and you were touching yourself?"

"Because I heard you laugh. That's when I came." I close my eyes so I can't see their reaction. "If you'd have known, what would you have done?"

"You mean if I'd come to the bathroom door and opened it? Seen you there with your fingers in your pussy, making yourself feel so good?"

I whimper, since that's still what my fingers are doing.

"I'd have called you my perfect girl." They're kissing my neck now, and they lower their body to mine. "I bet you looked hot doing it, too. Maybe you'll re-enact it for me sometime."

My brain is fuzzy from their praise and their touch, and I say the only thing that comes to mind. "Not with my boys here..."

Glenn chuckles. "No. We'll send those two on a date. Have the place to ourselves." They go back to kissing me. "Would you have wanted me to watch?"

"Yes..." I curse softly. "Glenn."

"Yes, star?"

"I need you."

"Good. Because I need you, too. I need your mouth open in rapture. I need your sweet noises and your soft skin."

"Hunh." Yeah. That's what I said. *Hunh*. And they weren't even done.

"I need to hear you pant like a perfect girl who's hot for me."

"*Glenn*." I'm almost too sensitive now, and I back my hand off. "Come on."

"Take what you want, star." I open my eyes and find them gazing at me with that fiery blue. And I don't know what I want.

No, I do know—I want to be together. I want to make each other smile and gasp and moan. But there are feelings in the way of the lightness I've always approached sex with, and I can't break it.

The moment in the bathroom at my parents' house comes back to me, when I had the sensation of wrestling with them, and I decide to make it a reality. Though it takes all my arm strength, I roll them off me and put them on their back. The air leaves their lungs with a whoosh, and they look like they're about to combust.

I kneel over them and lower my face close to theirs, making my voice stern. "You want to wrestle with me, Glennie?" Okay, so I think maybe the Glennie thing ruins it, but their face goes slack and they nod ardently, and deep down, I know we both get off on the struggle. I've known it all along. It's what I saw in their face that first night we fought in the studio. It's there now, too.

"Do you know how to tap out?" they ask.

I shake my head slowly, holding their gaze.

"You can slap the mattress or just say the word 'tap.'"

I sit up and pull my arm across my chest, giving it a good stretch. I do the same thing to the other, holding their gaze, and they break into a slow, sultry grin.

"You're taking this very seriously."

"Bien sur," I reply. "I can't let you win."

Their hands come up to my ass, stroking and massaging. "How are we defining winning in this situation?"

"Whoever holds off the longest. That's the only scenario where I can win."

"So if I make you come, I win? That seems fair." Without warning, they surge up and roll me onto my back, lifting me up so my knees don't bend weird.

"Oh shit, you're like a professional. This is not fair!" Their hands are on my shoulders, and I can barely reach them to fight back. I buck up underneath them, but it's useless as they plank away from me, chuckling.

"I haven't won yet. I haven't made you come." Which is a good point. In point of fact, both their hands are busy holding me down...so I bring my foot up to their cock, and there's something delicious about going under their skirt to find it.

"Hey, that's—you can't do that."

"Why not? You cheated. You started before we said 'go.'" They're breathing heavier now, shifting their grasp on me, and I love to see it.

"A start—" they break off, and their eyes flutter shut under the gentle ministrations of my arch. "A start time was not specified," they pant out.

"You. Cheated. Glennie. Admit it." They're not even touching me anywhere sexy, and I'm hot as heck. Playing with this one is my favorite. They're my favorite.

"Never."

I find that little spot they like, the one on the underside of their cock, and I slot it into the soft space between my toes. They squirm, but they can't get high enough to get away from me. Then a grin flashes on their face, and they lower themselves on top of me, forcing my leg out to the side. Their cock is against my clit, bumping it gently, and a surge of lust rips through me.

"Unbelievable." I rock my hips to get them off, finally getting my hands on their shoulders to try to flip them, but they're so much heavier than I am. Also, that hip rocking? Yeah, it's definitely making things worse—for me. They seem completely unaffected. A scheme creeps into my head, and I manage to keep a straight face as I deliver the line.

"Hey, we didn't figure out protection." Glenn stops their rubbing immediately and sits back.

"Oh, no. We should probably..." I shimmy out from under them before they can even get the sentence out, but I don't get very far. They tackle me from behind, crushing me to the bed on my side. "You're quicker than you look," I wheeze.

"Mmm-hmm," they agree, kissing the back of my neck as they pin my hands.

"We really should cover that cock, though..."

"Nice try," they whisper, "but I don't need to put this inside you to make you come." As their hips continue to pin me down on my side, I feel their fingers at my opening, dragging through my wetness. "Mm, very nice."

"It doesn't mean anything. Bodies just do that, and mine's broken." I didn't mean to say that last part. I thought it, but I wasn't going to say it. I can't deny that I believe it, though.

"Doesn't seem broken to me..." They're stroking my skin adoringly with their free hand.

I snort as they continue to kiss my neck, my arousal growing despite my protests. "Tell that to Jace."

Glenn pauses. "Jace who? Jace Gordon?"

Oops. Kinda forgot there was a chance they were going to know who I was talking about.

"No."

Their fingers resume their caress between my legs. I squirm to get away, but they've got me tightly in place. "You're a terrible liar. What did Jace Gordon do to you, star?"

"Nothing."

"Come on. I'm not gonna tell anyone about his sins."

I try to free my hands to whack them. No use. Their grip is firm, and it's fucking hot. I might actually lose.

"He didn't commit any sins."

"He doesn't seem like he'd know a clit from a cardboard box."

"He found it just fine. It just wouldn't...cooperate."

Their fingers are plunging in long, deep strokes now, and I moan, arching my back.

"And he made you feel bad about that? What an ass."

"Y-yeah," I stutter out, my voice breathy. Maybe it's just the incredible pressure growing between my legs, or maybe it's Glenn's calming weight on top of me, removing my choice by choice, but I suddenly can't remember why I thought the pain of that encounter was my fault. "Huge ass."

"Got it. I'll pass it on."

"No." I laugh, hiding my face in my pinned arms. "*Glenn.*"

"Hil, if he made you feel small, I'm allowed to dislike him." I can feel their cock rutting against my thigh, hear the little catches in their voice as they try to keep up this conversation, and it's pushing me higher. "I want you to feel amazing. Because you are."

"Stop," I whisper, and they nuzzle my ear, giving me a lick just beneath it.

"That's not the magic word…"

I lift my head to face them, but before I can say anything more, they capture my lips in a scorching kiss. I wasn't going to tap out anyway. My hips now have a mind of their own, and they're determined to rock Glenn's hand to a climax.

"That's my girl," they murmur. "Get what you want."

"Not yours," I murmur back, giving their bottom lip a gentle nip as punishment for their sentimental foolishness.

"Not yet. Working on it."

"Keep dreaming." I thrust harder as their fingers slow because they're a fucking tease.

They lean closer and rumble into my ear. "Oh, star. We haven't begun to act out the things I dream about…"

"Shut up." That voice. It's my undoing again.

"I want to get into the bath with you and wash your hair until you smell like flowers. I'd tease you for hours, running my hands over your warm, wet skin, painting you in bubbles and brushing soft touches over your whole body…"

That's it. That's all I can take. I close my eyes and cry out, writhing under them, the ringing in my ears almonst erasing the wet, obscene sounds of their fingers still in my pussy, wringing every bit of pleasure out of me until I'm spent. My eyes are still closed. I'm content to remain in the dark, feeling their fingers brush the hair away from my face. Then I feel their breath against the side of my face, and I brace myself for more tenderness when I'm already broken open, broken so differently now than before.

"I win."

I burst out laughing. I can't even try to be quiet. I laugh until tears gather in the corners of my eyes, and when I lift my hand to wipe them away, Glenn releases me. They're gone for a moment, and I hear the rip of the condom wrapper, then they're back. As they slip inside me with a groan, all I can think is that I want to keep them. We barely know each other, but I want to. I want to give them the good things they deserve. I don't know if I can, but I'm going to try.

I want to keep them.

CHAPTER TWENTY-FOUR

ON MONDAY, I MAKE AN appointment with a counselor. I couldn't tell you why, honestly. It makes as little sense as anything else I do. I clean the same way: when I find the intersection of incentive, annoyance, and emotional energy, I pick up my room. Otherwise, it stays dirty. And my mental room has been dirty for a very long time.

The receptionist seems nice. I can't remember where I heard this gal's name before, but someone said she'd been good for them. If I could remember who it was, that might be more helpful...if Giada said it, helpful. If Raina said it, perhaps not. But anyway, the name rang a bell when I did my thirty seconds of internet research, so now I have an appointment with Dr. Thacker on Thursday. Right after class. Monday, I forget about the appointment as soon as I've made it and set five alarms to make sure I actually get there. On Tuesday, I only think about it when I check my calendar to see if I'm free to have dinner with the boys. Wednesday, my 24-hours before reminder goes off while I'm cooking eggplant parmesan, and I think obliquely about what I'm going to wear before wiping my damp hands and swiping the notification away.

But Thursday? On Thursday, I think about it every moment from the first time my eyes flutter open until I'm standing in front of her office door. Afternoon appointments fuck me up; I can't help it. Class is okay because it's predictable. But random appointments you're waiting for all day? Nope. I get no studying done at the library, even though my playlist is on point and no one tries to bother me. I stare out the window and think about nothing until my alarm goes off for Glenn's class.

I'm still getting my computer out to record when they approach me.

"Hey."

I give them a small smile. "Hi." I continue navigating to the page I need. "What's up?"

"You want to get dinner tonight?" We've texted a few times during the week, and I saw them Tuesday night briefly after class to grab tacos before they had jazz practice. But mostly, our thing has been breakfast.

"Uh, I can't." I can't find my power cord, and this thing is going to die if I don't plug it in. But it has to be in here, unless I left it in the library, but I barely even used it in the library because I was stressed and–

"Hil."

"Hmm?" No, I know I didn't leave it in the library because when I went to find my wallet with my student ID in it, I brushed over the plug in my bag. Now, how come I can remember *that* and I can't remember—

"Did something bad happen today?"

"No, it's happening later; I'm just panicking pre-emptively." Gulp. That's more honest than I should probably be.

I glance up at them. Their arms are crossed over their chest, and their stance is wide. I recognize Threat Mode™. "What's happening later?"

I find the clock on the wall, and my suspicions are confirmed. "It's time for class."

"Like you care. Don't dodge my question."

Fatima's eyes widen.

"It's okay, we're dating. The administration knows," I say, patting her arm in a way I hope is soothing.

"Hillary."

"Mx. Rasmussen. We can talk about this later." I glance around pointedly at all the people now listening to our conversation, and of course, they quickly look away. Glenn is still scowling when I glance back at them, and I can tell they want to make a scene. I give them a little head shake to affirm my previous position on the matter, and their shoulders drop a little, their gaze still stormy. Then they turn and walk to the front of the classroom.

And I swear, it's like listening to an old car in cold weather, cranking without turning over. Glenn can't find their notes, and once they do, it's for the wrong class, and then they're reciting information, but it's like our instructor has been replaced by a badly-programmed robot version of them. They demo a throwing technique on the wheel, and it's the one thing that's gone right so far. Even so, they knock over a water bucket, have to try twice with the clay, and manage to slice their finger on one of the sculpting tools sitting nearby. When they set us free to work on our projects, I follow them over to the sink.

"Looks kinda deep," I say, peering at their finger.

"I'll live." They're *sulking,* scrubbing their hands with total focus, not so much as glancing at me, and it's hard not to laugh at them.

"Glennie, I'm going to counseling tonight. I'm going to get my weird brain diagnosed." I don't think that nickname's going to stick, but I wanted some way to show them I care.

They stop, then slowly raise their head, eyes burning with excitement. "You are?"

I nod.

"Can I pick you up and swing you around in elation?"

"No."

"A large, smacking, 'I'm proud of you' kiss on the cheek?"

"No, thank you."

"What if I painted a large sign that says 'My girlfriend is very brave and amazing?'"

"Stop," I hissed. "I'm going back to work." They catch my arm as I try to escape this intolerable praise.

"Hey." They touch my forehead with theirs, and I close my eyes. "Super impressed. I know it's hard."

"Okay." I swallow. "Thank you. Also, you're the worst."

I get a small peck on the forehead as I pull away, and that, I don't mind as much. Which makes no sense. And that's it for me—my focus is completely shot for class, so I sit and look at their face instead of studying, putting out my books again for show. It's still over too slowly, even with something nice to look at.

"Knock 'em dead," Glenn whispers as I pack up, and I eke out a smile.

I have to take the bus to get there. I think about nothing while I wait, which is not at all normal for me, and it's freaking me out. My brain should be buzzing, making up stories about other passengers on the bus, wondering where she got her purse and what book he's reading and when they started building that new bank. But instead, I'm staring at a low autumn sun, watching leaves move in the wind, letting my brain be empty.

When I get to the office, there's a sign that says to sit and wait, so I do. My knee is bouncing. I hold my phone. I don't look at it. My heart feels like a netted fish, thrashing for water. I can't remember the counselor's name, so I look it up: Dr. Thacker. A door opens down the hall, and a large, middle-aged white woman in a maroon sweater and a stretchy black skirt appears. "Hillary?"

"Yes," I say, trying to gather my stuff without forgetting anything. "You must be Dr. Thacker."

"Yes, it's nice to meet you. I'm this way." I follow her to the office. And suddenly, I do not want to do this. I can't remember why I did. I must have had a break with reality to make this appointment. And I mean, maybe that means I'm in the right place after all, but it doesn't feel right. It feels terrible.

"How are you?"

"Fine. How are you?"

"Oh, I'm fine." She smiles and parks herself in one of the overstuffed leather chairs and motions for me to do the same.

"I'm here for an ADHD diagnosis."

"Yes, I was going to ask–I don't think I got your intake paperwork."

Paperwork does sound like something I'd ignore or forget. I start to sweat.

"I'm sorry. Is that something I could do now, or...?"

"No, let's just get to know each other first. See if we're a good fit." She's making notes. I don't love that.

"What makes you think you have ADHD?"

"One of my instructors suggested it, and some parts of it made sense."

"Which parts?"

"I'm forgetful, like with the paperwork. I lose stuff a lot. I don't know." I should've written shit down. I can't think with her staring at me like this. I feel like a zoo animal in a habitat that's not quite right, that's basic in too many ways.

"Were they the first person to suggest that you have ADHD?"

I had to think about that. "No. My mom also suggested it once."

"Recently?"

"No, when I was in high school. So...about twelve years ago. Man, that makes me feel old."

Dr. Thacker smiles. "How did you react to Mom's suggestion?"

"I thought she was smoking something, and I wanted in on it." When she lifts one eyebrow, I blush. "Sorry. I don't use drugs. I don't know why I said that. Just nervous."

"Do you get along with your mom?"

Wait. What? She's clearly angling us away from the ADHD thing.

"Mostly. We're a lot alike."

"In what way?"

"We look similar, except she dyes her hair blonde. And we laugh the same." *About the same things.*

"Mmm. So you weren't open to Mom's suggestion at that time. What changed?"

I shift in the leather chair. "I...have a professor who suggested I look into it."

"Based on your school performance?"

Irritation stabs at me. "No, my academic performance is excellent. I've nearly earned my undergrad degree in liberal studies with a certificate in women's studies."

"So you passed this professor's class?"

I realize I'm turning my phone over and over in my hands, and I make myself stop. "No."

"I see." She's smiling. That ups my irritation like a splinter that you just drive deeper when you try to get it out.

"Why did you fail?"

My gaze is drawn to the window. It's nothing special, looking out on a parking lot with azaleas and rhodies, neither of which are blooming this time of year. Good, sturdy plants that don't need much special attention. I wish I was like them. I feel overgrown, out of season, dropping fruit no one wants, like a flowering plum.

"I didn't turn in enough assignments, and the ones I did turn in, I didn't do well enough on to pass."

"Do you struggle with organization?"

I snort-laugh as I turn back to her. "Definitely." We're back on level ground now, discussing my academic life, and I start to relax, start to make a few jokes, and she laughs. I tell her about the reading I've done about AD-HD, and she makes a lot of notes about the things I tell her. Before I know it, our time is almost up.

"All right, so here's the deal." She puts aside her journal. "I think it's possible you have ADHD. Unfortunately, there's no simple test I can give you to confirm that. If you want to come back and work with me, I can go through all the diagnostic criteria with you, send you to your doctor to get your thyroid tested, all that jazz. But it can take several months." She pauses, and I fight my way through a muck of disappointment that feels like quicksand, pulling me down, making it hard to listen. "So the question is whether your impairment is enough to make all that worth it. The other thing I'd like to suggest is that we come up with some ways to improve your relationship with your parents." And that comment is what sucks me all the way under. Dr. Thacker is still talking, something about bringing a family member with me to share how they've seen ADHD manifest in my life, blah blah blah. But I'm gone. The quicksand owns me now. My mind and heart have conspired against my body and left without it. They are walking down Interstate Avenue toward the New Seasons Market, intent on sushi, a bag of chocolate chips, and an artisanal jam that I will put on the scones I'm going to bake. There will be clotted cream, also. I'm shaking her hand now, promising to be in touch, but I'm not there. I'm looking at fancy salads and smiling at women my age and frowning at kids who mess with the end cap displays because I've worked at a grocery store, and it's not cool. I leave her office in a daze, do my shopping, and catch the bus running.

CHAPTER TWENTY-FIVE

WHEN I GET TO MY SEAT, I pull out my phone and see a text from Glenn.

Enbyfriend: How did it go?

I don't want to cry on the bus, but it's happening. I just wanted to go in there and get an answer, but instead, I came out with more questions.

Hillary: um
Enbyfriend: Are you okay?
Hillary: kind of?
Enbyfriend: What's with the question mark, you're scaring me.
Hillary: Can you come over?
Enbyfriend: I'll be right there.

Apparently, they were closer to my home than I was, because they're sitting in the lobby when I get there.

"Hey, what happened?" The moment I see their concerned face, I burst into tears again. I am blubbering incoherent nonsense, and they manage to get me into the elevator and upstairs to my floor. Chance has the door open before we even get there.

"What happened?"

I blubber at him in response, and he looks just as concerned as Glenn did. He looks at them.

"Did you get anything from that?"

"Not a word."

That makes me laugh. My tears are starting to dry, and I find a paper towel to blow my nose.

"There was facial tissue right…"

I glare at Chance.

"Never mind."

Chance is making me a chai tea, which he knows is my sadness drink, and I plop down on the couch and let out a shuddery sigh. Glenn sits next to me and offers their hand. I'm not ready for that. I spill the story–all of it. They are both being good listeners, nodding, not interrupting, giving me sympathetic shrugs and head tilts.

"You might not want to hear this," Glenn starts.

"Then maybe don't say it," I quip, wiping my nose with my paper towel again. They give me a Hard Teacher Look™, and I smile.

"But I think the fact that you didn't get a diagnosis today is actually a good thing. They're taking it seriously. If Dr. Thacker was willing to just whip out her prescription pad, you might end up on something you don't need."

They put a soothing hand on my leg, and I smack it. "No touchy."

They put up their hands like they're being arrested. "Sorry."

"S'fine," I mutter. "I'm just disappointed."

"That's understandable," says Chance. "Expectations can be hard to manage."

"You're both entirely too rational and sympathetic!" I cry. "Be irrational for once, would you?"

They both look conflicted. Finally, Chance says, "I don't think that's in my programming unless it's about my own fears."

"Same."

"It's just so frustrating. I finally got up the courage to go. I finally called someone. I got the appointment set up." My voice is crescendoing, rising in urgency. "I showed up on time. I didn't get the paperwork filled out, but I made it. I went. And now, I just..." I sigh, but it comes out shaky. "I want to break something."

Glenn's staring at me. I think I know what's going through their head: *She's too much. She's too loud, too wild, too emotional.* When they stand up, I know they're leaving.

But then they hold out their hand again, and they just wait.

"What?" I ask impatiently. They don't flinch.

"Let's go. I know the perfect place."

I slowly shred my paper towel; I can't even look at them. They bend down and put their hands on their knees so we're at eye level.

"The name is a pun."

I wipe my nose with the shreds. "What's the name?"

They shake their head slowly, not letting go of my gaze. "Nuh-huh. You wanna know, you get your shoes on and come with me. I'll get you food on the way." They straighten again and hold out their hand. And it isn't easy, honestly. I am incredibly curious where they want to take me, but I don't want to be touched. But I don't want them to feel rejected. But I'm tired. But I want to know.

I look up at them plaintively. "I don't want to hold hands."

They put their hands behind their back and shrug. "Okay. Can I get you your coat?"

"Yes."

They turn to my roommate. "Chance, my man, would you like to join us?"

I smile a little because Glenn affirms people so casually, and it's glow-inducing.

"No, Colby's coming by later. But thank you."

"Ugh, no sleep for Hillary," I quip, and Chance turns a dark shade of red that I have dubbed "Dom Rouge."

"That's not..." he sputters. "We're very...Hillary!"

That does make me laugh, even though it's phlegmy from the crying. "I love you, roomie." I put my arms into the coat Glenn is holding out for me like a gentleperson.

Chance just rolls his eyes at me. "Have fun."

"I'm sure we will," I say, strolling toward the front door.

"Shoes, Hil."

"Right. Foot protection."

"Wear something close-toed."

Oh, now I'm really curious. I dig my walking shoes out of the basket by the front door, and then we're off.

"Does it bother you that I don't want to hold your hand?" I blurt out once we're in the elevator.

Glenn seems to consider it. "Not really. I would enjoy the connection, but if you didn't, then that would ruin it."

I smile at them in the reflective door. And when we get tacos and walk up to a large, black building that says 'HAMMER TIME' in big letters, that smile returns, wider.

"Are you familiar with rage rooms?"

I may or may not be bouncing on my toes by this point.

"I have been wanting to do this since forever!"

"Okay. But maybe don't yell." Glenn chuckles as they lead the way inside.

"Who's yelling?!"

"You, star." They're still smiling, though, and the way they keep rocking forward onto their toes makes me think they want a kiss. Their gaze drops to my lips. I'm feeling better than I was, a little more touchable, but my body still says no. Maybe afterward.

I'm saved the trouble of telling them this when a young white woman with a streak of pink in her blond pixie cut comes up to us.

"Hey, welcome to Hammer Time. Do you have an appointment?"

"Uh...no. You must be Kari. Tom's my brother."

Wait, I'm about to meet their brother? I do some obligatory hair fluffing and clothes smoothing. It's weird, because that step kind of got skipped with Colby and Chance since they already knew each other.

"Oh! Right!" The woman brightens visibly. "You must be Bear."

Glenn smiles. "He's my twin. I'm Glenn, and I use they/them pronouns." They hold up their hand with cotton-candy pink polish on it and wiggle their fingers, as if to prove it.

"It's great to meet you, Glenn," she says, reaching out to shake their hand. "Did you want to see Tom?"

"No, that's okay. Don't bother him."

The employee looks confused now. "Are you sure?"

"Yeah. If he knows I'm here, he won't let me pay, and I don't want to interrupt whatever he's up to." They lean forward to peek at her clipboard. "Do you have any rooms available?"

"We sure do." She grins. "Come on back, and Tendai will get you set up with your safety gear."

"You have a brother *and* a twin?" I hiss as we head down the long hallway. "How long were you going to hide this from me?"

"Well, I was planning on introducing you when you weren't my student anymore, but the situation is out of my hands now. You need chaos. Tom sells reasonable chaos."

"Hey." I reach out and grab his elbow, knowing the woman will stop for us. "Thank you."

They cover my smaller hand with their big one. "You're welcome."

After a long moment, we keep going down the hall to an alcove.

"Hey, Tendai."

"Hey, Glenn. Haven't seen you around lately."

"You come here often?" I ask, not trying to lower my voice whatsoever.

"Uh..."

"Oh, yeah. For a while, they were here every Tuesday and Thursday like clockwork. Could set your watch by them."

"WAIT!" I spin to face them. "Were you burning off *sexual energy* in a rage room?"

Their cheeks are a very telling pink. "Um..."

"Glenn!" *Saved by the sibling.* A chestnut-haired white man who's skinnier and taller than Glenn appears from a door to our left. "You're here!" His gaze falls to me, and then bounces back to Glenn. "Who's your friend?"

"Tom, this is Hillary. She has a little angst to work off."

I'm glad they stop there; I know he's their brother, but I wouldn't mind if my problems stayed private for a while.

Their brother whacks them in the arm. "You didn't tell me you were dating someone!"

"And you knew we were dating because I have angst to work off? That tracks."

Glenn scowls. "No, her angst is about something else."

"I understand," Tom says with a smile, and when he shakes my hand, he covers it with the other one. "What a pleasure to meet you, Hillary."

"Nice to meet you, too. Of course, I didn't know you *existed* until about thirty seconds ago, but it's nice nonetheless."

He grins. "Oh, Mom's gonna love her."

I turn to Glenn, but I can't read their expression. "Sarcasm?"

"Oh, no. She will love you." Glenn herds me gently toward the safety equipment. "Let's get you suited up."

"Did they already pay?" Tom asks the pink-haired lady, and then glares at his sibling. "You did that on purpose!"

"It's a Thursday night. You're slow. You could use the income."

"Yeah, because you're rolling in it, Mx. College Professor. You can expect a refund."

"Whatever." There's no displeasure in the word. Glenn is so chill. "Can we have the window room?"

"You sure can. Have a great time."

"I'm sure we will." Glenn leans forward to give their brother a hug, and the word rattling in my brain is 'genuine'; they both seem to really enjoy each other. Warm queer families make me melty deep down inside where few other feelings can touch. My parents have always supported me and Colby in whoever we loved...well, maybe loved is a strong word. *Whoever I was with*, might be more accurate. Love is a word I throw around lightly, but I don't know if I mean it the way I should.

"Hil."

"Hmm?"

Glenn is smiling at me, amused. "Did you hear anything Tendai said?"

"No. I was thinking about love."

Glenn mutters something under their breath that sounds like *fucking adorable*, and they gather our safety gear. "Come on. This way." They open a door with a reinforced glass window that's labeled '4'. "Here's the rules, spacecase. Smash anything you want. Keep me behind you. Always wear your eye protection."

My eyes go wide. The room is full of random junk: computer monitors and ceramic plates and printers and toasters and glass bottles and...

"I'm not smashing the violin."

"Me either." They hand me a baseball bat. "Anything else is fair game."

"Thank you," I say quietly. Then I turn and put my wooden weapon through a plate glass window.

And it feels amazing.

CHAPTER TWENTY-SIX

WHEN I WAKE UP SATURDAY morning, there's a text from Glenn.

Enbyfriend: you wanna go shopping?

That's got my attention.

Hillary: Yes! yes! I want to buy you cute things! I'll get coffee on the way and be right there, where are we meeting?

Enbyfriend: um. GoodFood?

Hillary: whaaat

Hillary: hello, yes, I would like to report a crime.

Enbyfriend: Don't you think that's disrespectful to people who've actually suffered crimes?

Hillary: fine. How do I get a hold of the tragedy police, then?

Hillary: why would I want to buy apples and bread when I could buy shoes and sweaters

Enbyfriend: Because your partner is out of apples and bread.

Hillary: fine, but none of this granny smith crap. We're going to get you good apples.

Enbyfriend: and then you can make me a pie?

Hillary: did it ever occur to you I might have other Saturday plans?

Enbyfriend: Plans better than pie with me?

Hillary: Sadly, I think Chance is going to start poisoning my food if I don't do at least a little housework. So yes store, but no pie.

Enbyfriend: Should I meet you out front?

Hillary: yes, I'll be there in ten. No wait, twenty, I'm not dressed.

Enbyfriend: See you then.

They have coffee for me, and their pink Timbers beanie is adorable. They look cold, probably because it's been thirty minutes instead of twenty. At least they're wearing leggings under their denim skirt.

"I haven't told you about the Hillary Conversion Factor yet, have I?" I ask as I take the coffee they are holding out to me and give them a kiss in return.

"No, but it sounds like something I need. Lay it on me." We both grab carts because I might as well shop while I'm here instead of whatever night at 10 PM when

I go to make my lunch and have no bread. The carts even have a little cup holder. This grocery store is nice; it smells like roses, and its lighting isn't as harsh as the cheaper grocery store closer to my house.

"You take the time I told you I'd be there and you increase it by 50%."

Glenn nods seriously as they pick up a pear. "So you said twenty...but it was thirty. So that works. Does it work for all time periods? Like, if you say it's going to be an hour, will it really be ninety minutes?"

"It could be. There's also a distance factor they sometimes incorporate. Like, if I'm on campus, that's like a 1.1, but if I'm at Colby's, that's 1.4 at least. And if I'm eating, they compensate for that somehow, too. I guess I'm a fast eater."

"I've noticed that, actually. I watched you scarf down a donut once in class, which I assume was your breakfast..."

"Naturally."

"And you put that thing away in record time. It was one thing I liked about you, honestly. I like eating all kinds of food."

I stare down at their cart. "The high percentage of fruits and veggies in this cart is not reinforcing that statement."

"I'm making soup," they protest. "That takes a lot of weird veggies."

"Only if you're making weird soup. Glenn, are you making weird soup?"

"I want to go back to your time conversion..."

"The Hillary Conversion Factor. Yes. Go ahead." We're finally at the bakery section, which is good because my poor cart is looking sad with just baby carrots and pre-cut butternut squash. I know what I'm about—a whole butternut squash would be compost before I even thought about using it. Guaranteed.

"Does it work for very short times? Like, if you say you'll be there in one minute, is ninety seconds enough?"

"Undoubtedly not. Five-minute minimum for the HCF. The boys could tell you more about it; I'm not an expert."

"Just the subject."

"Exactly. It's their theory, I'm just disseminating the information."

"Well, if they ever publish, I hope they credit you."

"I feel like they'd have to," I say, sniffing some sourdough. That's coming home with me. I don't have the patience for the starter. It requires regular feeding, and as we've established, I can barely remember to feed myself. That poor sludge would have no chance.

"Are there any other theories I need to know about?"

"Hillary-related theories?"

Glenn nods, bumping my cart with theirs. I bump it back as we turn the corner into the dairy section.

"Mm, not that I can think of. Ooh, yogurt. I love yogurt."

"I saw you throw out like five of those the other day."

"Yeah. That was sad." I grab five more. All vanilla. Vanilla forever.

Glenn chuckles. "Okay then." They pick out a mixed berry, an apricot, and a strawberry of the same brand.

"Good work, dear. Bowel health is very important."

Their scowl is skeptical. "I just like creamy things."

"That's fine, too. It's better for you than ice cream."

"Also more acceptable for breakfast."

I stop my cart. "Glenn. You only live once. If you want ice cream for breakfast, eat ice cream."

"That's not healthy, Hil. That's so much sugar to wake up to." I hurry to catch up to them, but I don't have to go too fast because they're picking out breakfast cereal. Shredded something.

"Which is why it's perfect!"

They scrunch up their face, and I shake my head.

"Tell me, what is it you plan to do with your one wild and precious life?" I ask, and they turn to me slowly.

"You're going to quote Mary Oliver at me? For real?"

"You needed it. Anyone who won't eat ice cream for breakfast isn't taking their life seriously enough."

When they don't answer, I turn to them, and I'm surprised by a very ardent kiss. A two-handed kiss, my face cradled in their cold palms. I hum a little into their mouth, wrapping my arms around their big canvas coat. We're blocking the whole aisle in both directions. Some lady clears her throat. We ignore her. She turns around and leaves eventually, I assume. I wouldn't know. I'm being kissed in the peanut butter aisle by Glenn Rasmussen, and everything and everyone else is taking a back seat.

"GoodFood is not the place to tell you this," Glenn murmurs, kissing the tip of my nose. "But I think I might be a little bit in love with you."

I smile at them. "Just a little bit?"

"A skosh. Just a tad."

My grin widens, but I'm now aware once again that we're blocking the aisle, and it's probably kind of rude, so I get us going again.

No, I don't say it back. I'm aware of that. I'm not there yet. I just started accepting that I like Glenn; I don't think I'll get to love for another few stops on the bus. But they don't seem bothered by this. They grab instant mashed potatoes like we just had a normal interaction. I can't help but give them a hard time.

"Rasmussen. What is that?"

They hold up the box. "This? Instant deliciousness. I put chicken, broccoli, and BBQ sauce on top, and it's a meal."

"No, that is glue. That's not food."

"It is if you're just cooking for yourself."

"Well, you'll have to up your game if your girlfriend is coming over."

"Do you want to? I could make you something. I'd really like that." They look so excited, and it's so adorable.

I laugh. "If you wanted me to come over so bad, why didn't you just invite me over?"

"I don't know. I didn't want to pressure you. I thought maybe it was weird since I'm still your instructor."

"But you sleeping over at my apartment isn't?"

"I didn't sleep over. I left in the dead of night."

I laugh again. "Whatever you say, Mx. Rasmussen. Tell me what time, and I'll be there."

"Okay, great! Now I've gotta go back to the produce section to get stuff for fancy salad."

"Oh, that's fine. I usually do at least three full laps."

Glenn is staring at me like I just admitted to being a Republican. "Why?"

"I don't always see all the stuff I need on the first two passes. Gotta make sure I don't have to come back."

"And using a list would be..."

"For basics."

"Ah, yes. I see. And I assume you don't mean food staple type basics."

"Not at all."

"How's 7:00?" They pause. "Wait, how do I use the HCF on the time *I* told you to be there?"

"Well, let's see," I say, grabbing some almonds. "If it takes me half an hour to get to your house—wait, where's your house?"

"Maybe I should just pick you up..."

I snort. "Like that'll make me be on time. Do you not remember picking me up for dinner?"

"I do. It was delightful. I got to meet a cat."

"Just text me your address. I'll do my best."

"Do you maybe want to invite Chance and Colby, too?"

I consider this as we stroll along. "Yeah, I think that'd be fun."

"Maybe I'll just order food when you get there."

"No, you coward. Cook for us. Be domestic. You know you want to."

Glenn glares at me sidelong for a long moment, then sighs. "Okay."

"Oh, and I'm a vegan now."

"Like fuck you are."

I laugh like a maniac as Glenn shakes their head and turns the corner to go find some pasta.

CHAPTER TWENTY-SEVEN

I GIVE A LECTURE WHILE we're on our way to Glenn's the next night. When I say we, I mean me, Colby, and Chance, who apparently had nothing better to do than come with me to my enbyfriend's house. Actually, I suspect that they had plans already, because there was some surreptitious discussion after I texted Colby. I only know this because I was too lazy to get out of bed to ask them, and they didn't realize I was in my room.

"Aren't you curious to see them together?" That's my brother.

"Of course I am, but this exhibit is only in town for a limited time. And we already have tickets." That's my roommate.

"Come on. This will be worth it. I can get rid of those tickets on the internet no problem."

"That's the point. It's a *celebrated* event."

Colby's voice dropped then, apparently out of habit more than caution, but I did hear the words "celebrate your event," and a few seconds later, I got a text from Chance.

Roommate: We're in. What can we bring?

And the answer I gave—nothing—was unacceptable, so I got up and made an apple pie but only because it was funny based on my previous conversation with Glenn at the grocery store. It's on my lap now, cold and covered in foil, as Chance drives us into Goose Hollow, one of my absolute favorite parts of Portland, while I finish my lecture.

"Just be polite, and don't say anything weird about me as a kid."

Colby snickers. "Like that you used to watch TV upside down?"

"Aww, that's so cute," Chance says with a grin. "I want to hear about little Hillary."

"She was a weirdo," I deadpan, "and Glenn does not need to know about her yet."

"Can I tell him about the red cowboy hat you wouldn't relinquish?" Colby asks, leaning forward from the back seat to rest his arms on our seats.

"Hattie and I had a long and storied history. You wouldn't understand."

"She slept with it," he adds for Chance's benefit, and my roommate's face goes all soft and pouty.

"And it had a *name*? This is adorable! Why wouldn't you want your new person to hear these things?"

"I haven't...it's just complicated, all right?" I say, looking out the window. "Is that it?"

"Oh. Yup. Let me just find..." Chance mutters, looking up and down the street for a parking spot. With help from both of us, he parallels into a tight spot right in front of Glenn's house. I almost forget the pie because I am suddenly rethinking my outfit, and my hair is being weird and floofy because I didn't get it all the way dry because I wanted to stop for vanilla ice cream because everyone knows bringing pie but not ice cream is like having no turkey on Thanksgiving.

Colby nudges me as we go up the stairs. "You okay?"

"Of course. *You're* being weird. I'm normal."

Colby rolls his eyes at me. "Hil, it's just dinner. Chill."

"You chill."

"I am chill!"

"Oh, right, you're chill. That's why you took twenty minutes to pick a ten-dollar bottle of wine."

"There's a big difference in quality," he huffs.

"Why are we just standing on the porch?" I ask, and Chance clears his throat.

"I was waiting to knock until you two were done arguing."

"So, never?"

Suddenly, I hear a dog barking from inside—a small one, from the sound of things—and I hear Glenn's voice calling. The dog stops. Chance finally knocks, and Colby and I giggle. He turns around to glare at us just as the front door opens.

Glenn stands in the doorway wearing a pink, pin-striped apron, holding the most adorable gray French bulldog I've ever seen in my life.

"Sorry, I forgot to warn you about the dog. Is anyone allergic?" This little wiggly thing with giant ears is wagging its tail so hard, I'm impressed Glenn can hold onto her. We all shake our heads, and they smile. "Well, come on in, then. What can I get you to drink? Ooh, wine. Thanks, man," they say, taking the bottle Colby extends. "You didn't have to bring anything."

"Wrong as usual," I say. "Where do you want this pie?"

"Haven't you forgotten something?" they ask, one eyebrow cocked. My boys are staring with open curiosity, and I want to scatter them with a swift kick and a threatening hand gesture, but Glenn's still watching me, too, and my brain is in hyper-drive trying to figure out what I promised that I forgot so completely that even the moment I did it has been erased from my mind.

"Hey." They put down the dog, who immediately sniffs my shoes. "I just wanted a kiss hello. Ne panique pas." Their use of French breaks the feeling of looming disaster their nebulous demand cast over me, and I smile.

"Right. Of course." I start to lean forward, but I can see my boys grinning like fools out of the corner of my eye, and I turn to them. "Be about your business, gentlemen. To the kitchen with you." I hand Chance the pie and ice cream and they shuffle off because they're easily led, and I have to admit, I do love that about them.

"Not a fan of PDA, star?" they murmur, leaning closer, and I tip my head to the side as I think about it.

"I don't usually mind it, but this particular public was enjoying it too much."

"Oh, I see." They chuckle. Their kiss is shaped like a smile still, and they put a hand to my cheek. "I'm glad you're here."

"So am I." I turn to go into the living room but pause to kick off my boots. "Something smells good." Ironically, it smells like apples, and I hope they didn't bake a pie, too.

"Thank you. I hope it's my food."

Their house is an explosion of art. It should be chaos, the way the white wall to my left is covered in muted watercolor landscapes and charcoal drawings and acrylic abstracts in every shade imaginable. But it's mesmerizing instead. And on my right, clear shelves hold interesting clay pieces, wood carvings, even metalwork. I feel like I'm standing in front of a bookshelf, knowing that there are stories here. I'm peeking into Glenn's whole life, and frankly, it's rude of them to wear their heart on their walls like this. I feel like I'm invading their privacy just by standing in their living room.

Glenn's voice in my ear makes me jump. "Which one's your favorite?"

A quick glance at the boys tells me they're busy bonding with the gray furball, so I turn to them. "Look in a mirror, bud." I'm close enough to see them blush under their beard, and I lean over to kiss their sweet cheek.

"No, really, though. I want to know."

I cross my arms as I stare at each wall some more, and then I feel their hands on my hips. A soft kiss is pressed to the side of my neck.

"That's distracting," I murmur, trying to decide between a landscape of dome-topped, European-looking buildings and an abstract that reminds me of what surprise feels like.

"I don't mind."

"Well, you're going to get a sub-par answer, then," I say, leaning back into their body. Their arms come around me to hold me. They're warm and solid, and I could get used to this.

"I missed you yesterday," they murmur.

"You saw me yesterday," I murmur back.

"I missed you for the part that I didn't see you."

"So you just want me around all the time?"

"Now you're getting it." They kiss the top of my head. "I gotta go finish my salad."

"Make Colby help. He's a whiz at salads."

"Oh, he doesn't have to—"

"Colby, wash your hands. You're making a salad," I call, still staring at the wall as Glenn leaves because I can't decide. They're both so good. And I haven't even really looked at the other wall, the one that's full of three-dimensional things. I look around the rest of the room: black futon, light-colored wood floors, a few end tables...wait.

"Glennie, where's your TV?"

"I don't have one."

That's when my brain breaks. I love noise, and I know not everyone does. But no TV? What kind of person doesn't mindlessly consume content in the evening? Television is a significant part of my personality.

"I don't understand your words, darling. I see that you don't have one in here. What about your bedroom?"

"Nope."

"Your basement?"

"I don't have a basement." That's a surprise only because we kinda had to climb a hill to even get to their front door.

I stare at the surprise painting again, and it will now forever symbolize the way I felt when I found out Glenn doesn't have a television.

"The attic? The back porch? Don't tell me you're one of those 'books only' people. I have nothing against them, but there's simply no future for us."

They poke their head into the living room, licking something off their thumb. "I watch stuff on my laptop."

I put a hand to my chest. "Thank god."

They grin, then disappear again. I am therefore drawn into the kitchen. Chance is drinking a glass of wine while Colby grates Brussel sprouts and Glenn wraps bread in foil. I feel rather unnecessary until the dog comes and sits in front of me.

"Yes?"

It looks up at me silently with its cute, scrunchy face. Then it starts to pant, and it totally looks like it's smiling.

"She doesn't want to pet you, Lulu," Glenn says without turning around. The dog turns to look at them but ultimately ignores them, and I think we're going to get along fine. I kneel in front of the dog, and she puts a paw on my knee.

"It's very nice to meet you, Lulu," I say, picking up her paw to gently shake it. "You have much better manners than your owner."

Glenn snorts but doesn't turn around. "You clearly don't remember when we met."

"Why, what did I do?" I'm petting Lulu now. She's very soft, and it just seems like the thing to do.

"You complimented my outfit, then you asked about extra credit."

My boys laugh. "She was angling for a better grade from the first day?" Colby asks.

"Yup. And she was wearing a shirt that said 'spinster,' so I thought she was a TERF."

Colby is choking on his drink now, he's laughing so hard, while Chance and I just stare. "You thought I was a TERF? Why?" My heart is beating very hard, and I feel a little bit sick. I've always tried to be nothing but supportive of my trans friends, and I have no idea how Glenn got that idea. Whatever it was, I'm going to fix it immediately and possibly make amends to Chance.

They pivot so they can see me. "Spinster is the name of a large online echo chamber for radical feminists."

"Well, I'm gonna go home and throw out that T-shirt," I say, ruffling Lulu's ears as she keeps sitting in front of me contentedly. "Colby, did you know that was a TERF thing when you gave me that shirt?"

"Nah, I just thought it was funny."

Glenn sprinkles the last of the green onions on the salad. "I figured out I was wrong a few classes later when she interrupted a student who used my pronouns incorrectly." They take on a high falsetto. "Excuse me, Karen, is it? Oh, it's Sara? Well, as you can see, it doesn't feel nice when someone gets your details wrong."

I actually do remember that incident now.

Chance looks aghast. "Hil, you didn't."

"Fuck yes, I did. It was like the fourth time she'd done it that period. And she was doing it on purpose. Bitch got what she deserved."

Glenn pulls heavy, yellow plates out of the cupboard above their head. "I was going to talk to Sara about it after class. Hillary saved me the trouble. I even got an apology."

"She is still terrible. That redeems nothing."

I get up and wash my hands in the kitchen sink. They have this weird foam soap that smells like Meyer lemons. It's mid-November now, so I should see Meyer lemons in the store soon. I should make a tart or something amazing. I'm still subtly sniffing my hands and thinking about baking with citrus when they come up behind me.

"I fell a little bit in love with you that day," they say quietly as the boys take their seats, "and just kept falling."

Then they just grab the bread out of the oven like this is a perfectly normal thing to say to one's significant other and not at all personally devastating.

I watch them with my boys for a minute, just because they're being silly together and I like seeing them all get along. I suppose I have a little empathy for Colby now, even if he shouldn't have interfered in trying to make us get along. Can't argue with his results, though.

"All right," I say over the top of them. "Let's get this vegan feast started."

Turns out we're having pork, but my vegan joke segues into a conversation about Thanksgiving. My parents are coming, and Colby and I still need to iron out who's doing what.

"I can do the turkey." Colby sips his water. "I've been roasting chickens lately."

"Not at all the same," I inform him. "Not even close."

"They're both poultry," Chance points out. "So I think it's mostly the same."

"It's so sad when smart people say silly things. Like that thing you just said, for instance..."

"No," Colby says, pointing at me with his knife, "I really want to do the turkey. Seriously, Hil."

I sigh. "All right. I'll bring stuffing and rolls, then." There's a weird vibe in the room. I can't quite place it. Until I glance at Glenn. They're giving me this raised-eyebrow, meaningful look. "Oh, I'm sorry. What are you doing for Thanksgiving, Glenn? Do you have family in town?"

"Yeah, I'll be with my parents, I guess. And my brothers and their families." *I guess?* What's the *I guess* for? "I'd love it if you wanted to stop by and do pie with us or something."

"I should probably spend time with my parents, since I don't see them that much. Sorry."

Now Chance and Colby are giving me the look.

"Yes, since they're in town," Colby pipes up, "it might be a nice opportunity to show them what you've been up to for the last few months. You know, introduce them around or whatever."

Not happening. I know what they all want, but I have no idea how this is going to go with my mom, and inviting Glenn into that would just be cruel. So I pretend I don't know.

"I don't think they want to see my crappy pottery." I turn to Glenn. "Do your parents live in Portland?"

"Hood River."

"Oh, that's not too far. Hopefully, you'll have nice weather going out toward the Gorge."

Their response is quiet. "Yeah, I hope so. I'd love for you to meet them soon."

"Yes, we can figure that out. Tom said your mom would love me. I like being around people who love me."

That makes a half-smile reappear on Glenn's face, and they proceed to tell stories about their brothers that make us howl. But I know they're upset with me. It's an undercurrent. There will be a conversation later, I'm sure. But I have dodged it for now.

Barely.

CHAPTER TWENTY-EIGHT

I HAVE SURVIVED THE hors d'oeuvres. I have limited my alcohol intake as Dr. Thacker and I agreed in advance in order to prevent the Unplanned Sharing of Feelings™. I am eating my incredibly dry turkey (they didn't brine it; I told them to brine it) without complaint when my mom starts in.

"So I hear you're seeing someone, Hillary? Tell us about them." She's holding her wine glass in front of her casually, leaning back from the table. She's sitting between my dad and Tony.

"No, thank you." I reach for the stuffing. I don't have enough carbs for this conversation if alcohol is out.

"Come on," she wheedles. "I want to know something about them when we meet them."

"That's not a planned activity on your welcome home tour this time."

"Oh." Her disappointment literally fills the room. "I see." She's doing that murmuring thing I hate, and I feel itchy like my skin is yeast, proofing in the bowl, bubbling and feeding off my feelings to take on a life of its own.

"Hillary." My dad stands up. He sets his napkin beside his unfinished dinner. "May I speak with you in the kitchen?"

"Sure." I want to say no. I want to take off out the back door like I did when I was fifteen and a half. Instead, I follow him into the kitchen. And as if it wasn't uncomfortable enough, I haven't spent much time in here since Glenn and I banged here, and the memories are too fresh to be in the same room with my *dad*.

"Hillary." His arms are crossed over his chest. "What's going on with you?"

"Besides a full course load, fulfilling social activities, and general household maintenance, nothing."

"Bullshit."

I eye him. He's not mad, but he's unhappy. "Look..."

"No, you look. Your mother wants me to break my contract and come home early. And she says if I don't, she's coming home without me. That's how much you mean to her."

"Mom's going to leave you?"

He huffs. "No, not *leave me*, just come home early from our contract. Split time between here and there. Lots of couples in diplomatic service do it."

See, I know him, though. Without her, he falls apart. He's moody and he sulks and gets sad; the last time she went away with her girlfriends for a week, I found him eating mini ravioli out of a can in front of the TV at 3AM in his underwear, crying over a Lifetime movie. And that was Day Three. He's this great hulk of a man reduced to patheticness whenever she's away for any length of time.

"Daddy..." Yes, okay, I know I'm an adult. But sometimes it just still fits, like a T-shirt you've had since eighth grade and everyone thinks you're wearing it ironically but you're not. You slept overnight at Camp Mukiluk; it's part of you now.

I sigh. He opens his arms, and I step into them without thinking about it. His bear hug sinks down deep, and I sigh again, but it's shaded with contentment this time.

"I would like her to return to Thailand with me. Therefore, I would like you two to talk this out. And it's as much for you as for her. I don't think this detente is working for either of you, honestly." He rests his cheek against the top of my head. "Can you do that for me?"

"Fine."

"Thank you, sweetheart." He gives me a squeeze, then lets go. "I'm gonna go finish that cardboard masquerading as turkey."

"Right? It's *so* dry. This is the last year I trust those noobs to roast poultry. I didn't even know it could be that bad."

"It's even worse than Mom's. At least there's gravy. Utilize sauces to their fullest capacity."

"Thanks for the tip."

"You got it, kiddo."

The worst is not over, not even close. But I feel a pinch better just hearing that Mom's unhappy, too. I wasn't trying to hurt her, but hearing that it's two-sided helps. And knowing that my dad doesn't blame me entirely, even if that's probably fair.

We step back into the dining room and take our places again. My family members—okay, let's be honest, that's the whole room—are glancing at us while trying to look like they're not, which is pretty funny, and I only smirk a little. Dad raises an eyebrow at me, and that just makes it harder to hold in the giggles. There's more pleas-ant conversation and terrible turkey until everyone's done.

Evan suggests pie, and we all throw things at him be-cause I can't even think of eating anything else right now. It's agreed that we'll take a break for video games and clean up and such, then convene back in an hour or so.

"Want to go for a walk?" I ask Mom quietly, and she nods.

"Just let me get my coat." She's up from the table and across the room before I can even process her words. She does a lot of Pilates.

"Sure." I shoot Colby a look because I think I was supposed to clean up. "I'll do it when I get back."

"No, no. That's fine," he says quickly. "Take your time. We'll cover this."

"Yeah, I'll help, too," Chance says, giving me a squeeze around my shoulders. "Have a good walk."

"Unlikely," I mutter, but I slip on my flats and my puffy winter coat. I can see my breath, and it's a gray cold; all the pretty leaves are long gone. The dreariness is settling in like how dogs knead their beds, circling until they get it just right.

Thinking of dogs makes me think of Lulu, which makes me think of Glenn, and I shove both of them away in my head. Maybe I'll text them later.

My mom finally comes outside. "Sorry. Restroom."

"That's fine." I try for a smile, and I think I mostly get it, but I can feel the sadness in the corners of my mouth, tugging them back down.

"We used to do this a lot, didn't we?"

I nod. "Walking to the park for Colby's soccer games."

"Getting donuts at Pip's."

"Excellent, yes. More than once."

We're walking at a brisk pace now, and I'm admiring the houses that already have their holiday lights up. "Trudging up and down the street selling Girl Scout cookies."

My mom groans, her head flopping back. "I thought you were going to kill me. You were just determined to win that tiny safe."

"Colby kept getting into my stuff! I had to keep it safe somehow."

"And then," she says, laughing, "we had to repeat all that walking to deliver the boxes a few months later."

"We had the wagon," I say. "It wasn't that bad."

"No," she says, putting her arm around me. "It wasn't." She pauses. "Can I tell you about Thailand?"

"I guess so."

She tells me about visiting some ancient ruins and this floating market. She went to a full moon party, which apparently is a big beach bacchanal of some kind.

"Do you eat street food?"

"I do," she says, nodding slowly, "but I am picky about where we get it. I did have a bad experience once. I lived in the bathroom for a day or two."

"What's the best thing you've had?"

She looks up at the bare trees. "I had some fish cakes once that were to die for. They had this spicy dipping sauce..." She makes a kissing sound and brings her fingers up to her lips.

"That sounds amazing."

And that's when it hits me: I'm jealous. Someday, I would like to be able to process things slowly. I would like to sit with Dr. Thacker and muse and mull and come to conclusions after in-depth conversations. But instead, I get them like a revelatory whack upside the head every time. Am I not in touch with my feelings? Do I not spend enough time in reflection? I don't know. But I couldn't figure it out until exactly now.

I really thought it was just about feeling rejected by them. But it was about this odd jealousy, too. Dr. Thacker is encouraging me to process out loud, so I open my mouth and things start falling out.

"I want to see the world so badly, and it feels so far out of reach."

"Really?" She lets her arm drop. "Why?"

I shrug. "I've got so much debt. I owe you guys so much money...I just can't see it happening any time soon. And it was hard to see you going off and having adventures without me."

"Oh, Hil. I didn't know you felt that way."

"Neither did I, until now." I swallow hard and stare ahead, letting the rhythm of my feet act as a metronome for my thoughts, slowing them down. "I think I felt abandoned, which I know is silly because I'm 28, but it's partly that I was stuck here while you were free."

"No, that makes sense. We always intended for you to come see us."

"I know. And Dad wants to do his thing overseas, which I get." I look at her. "But I miss you."

She tugs me to a stop and gives me a huge, over-the-top hug right there on the sidewalk. My hands are still jammed in my coat pockets because I left my gloves somewhere, so I just lay my head on her shoulder and let her hold me. When a tear slips down my cheek, I let it.

"I love you, Hillary." She rubs my back a little. "We never meant to hurt you. I want to fix things between us."

"I love you, too," I mumble. "Maybe we could start video calling."

"That would be wonderful, sweetheart. We'd love that." She pauses, and it's one of those charged ones like football players have just before a field goal attempt when the wind is whipping in their faces, and if that's the best analogy I can come up with, I've been watching too much TV with Colby. "And we really would love to meet this new person in your life. Or at least hear about them."

I break the hug gently and try to get us walking again. "Their name is Glenn. They're pretty great."

"How did you meet?" Mom loves a good meet cute. That will not be happening today.

"They failed me in a pottery class and became my nemesis."

"Oh." She should really be used to things like this from me by now. I'm predictably strange. "So they were your professor?"

"Still are, technically. I had to retake the class."

"Hillary." My mother sounds shocked. I don't mind it. "You're actively dating your professor?"

"Honestly, it's more a passive, fell-into-it kind of..." She still looks alarmed, and my joke has officially failed. "Yes. But the administration knows, and they're fine with it."

"Well, that's..."

I think I stumped her, because her words just stop. She's probably envisioning some sort of predatory situation, so I try to put her at ease. "They're a very considerate, kind person, Mom. You'll like them. And they have amazing style, just like you. They're not that much older than I am. Only twenty years."

Her eyes go wide, and I start laughing so hard, there's no sound coming out. Her face goes flat, and she glares at me.

"Your face," I gasp. "Oh, that was classic. I wish Colby was here. Oh, god. I can't breathe."

"How old are they really?" Mom asks, elbowing me.

"31, I think."

"Oh, well, that's quite different."

"And I think I'm even going to pass the class this time! Not because we're dating, that's not relevant to me passing the class, I'm just putting more effort into it this time around."

"Are you still on track to graduate in the spring?"

I nod. "Should be. But I really have to pass this class."

"We can get you a tutor if you need one."

I wrinkle my nose. "I'm sure Glenn would help me if I needed it."

"All right. Just know that we want to support you."

We talk about ADHD. I tell her the sanitized versions of going to the rage room and Marble and the speakeasy. I tell her about my counselor, and she seems happy that I found one even though I've only been a few times.

I don't think I realized how stressed I was that my mom was unhappy because of me. I feel like skipping along instead of walking. I don't, but there's a definite bounce in my step by the time we get back to the house. I get another side hug as we come up the front walk.

"Thank you for being honest with me," Mom says quietly. "I missed you a lot. We're gonna have to make up for lost time."

"Works for me. But keep in mind I am also still a student and very forgetful."

"We'll figure it out."

My dad opens the front door for us like he's been waiting (see what I mean? We were gone maybe forty-five minutes, and the man's a wreck!).

"Good talk?" he asks my mom as she goes inside, and she nods, then gives him a long kiss on his cheek. His answering smile makes me smile, too. "Thanks, kiddo," he says as I pass him.

"You owe me stuff. Good stuff."

"You mean beyond paying for most of your living expenses for the last twenty-eight years?"

"Oh, right. No, we're even."

"Even?" he calls after me as I head into the kitchen. Those boys better not have eaten all the pumpkin pie.

My phone buzzes.

Enbyfriend: Happy Thanksgiving! I'm thankful for you.

Hillary: you're lucky I'm not lactose intolerant, because that was cheesy.

Enbyfriend: Can't help it if it's true.

Hillary: Did you have a good day with your family?

Enbyfriend: Yep. You? I know you were stressed about it.

Enbyfriend: Do we need to hit the rage room again? Tom's here, I bet I could grab the keys from him.

Hillary: No, I'm good.

Enbyfriend: are you sure I can't come by?

I pull my lips to the side as I consider this. Yes, things are better than I thought they would be, but that doesn't mean things are good. All I know is that a fragile peace has been re-established. Not sure I'm ready to test it yet by dumping this sweet person into the mix, especially since Mom did not seem thrilled about the *still my teacher* detail.

Hillary: yes
Enbyfriend: okay. Have a nice night.

I can't read the emotion of that response. It might be perfectly tepid, but...I kind of thought we were going to hang out later tonight. I'm like 90% sure that was the plan, which means they're blowing me off because I said no. But what if I'm remembering wrong? My faulty brain might just be trying to cause trouble. But it's not in my calendar, and I usually put things in my calendar. Maybe I didn't because there wasn't a solid start time? Because it was kind of a when we're both done with the families kind of thing?

Hillary: you too
Hillary: I'll miss you

I check my phone seven times over the next hour around the following events: using the bathroom, getting apple pie, getting more whipped cream, helping unload the dishwasher, getting beaten by my dad at chess, and breaking the wishbone with Colby because we are still kids at heart (he won. He probably wished that Chance wouldn't go to England. Poor kid.).

There is no answer.

CHAPTER TWENTY-NINE

I END UP STAYING UNTIL almost midnight at Colby's. My dad drives me home. I manage to get into my bed without falling down, which feels kind of like a miracle. Chance is staying over so he can hang out with my parents more; I'm fairly sure he is my mother's new favorite person. They're going to the Portland Art Museum, and then I'm going to meet them somewhere for lunch, I think…it's been such A Day™ that my head is too blurry to know. *Hopefully, someone will text me,* I think as I fall asleep.

I wake to someone knocking on my door. It's light out, but not very. I squint toward my bedroom door; I left it open since I was alone, and there's no one there. I flop back down. The knocking comes again. *Must be the front door.* I check my phone; no messages. It could be Mrs. Graham or Janey; maybe something bad happened.

I hurry to get out of bed, pulling a hand through my hair. I pull on a sweatshirt, yawning, and try to quickly pick my way through the dark living room as another knock comes.

"Yeah, just…I'm coming." I fumble with the locks and open the door because surely no one up this early intends to rob me. I open the door to find a thirty-something non-binary person with a beard in jeans and a cream, cable-knit sweater, looking very anxious, holding a thin, brown cardboard box. "Hi."

"Hi." Glenn steps forward and kisses me, but it's a short one. Like they're not sure. "Can I come in?"

"Uh...sure?" I step back to let them inside and close the door quietly.

"I hope I didn't wake up Chance."

I cross my arms over my stomach, aware of the fact that I'm not wearing a bra. "He's not here."

"Oh." They step forward and put the box on the counter. "I was pretty sure I was gonna wake you up, so I brought donuts."

"Okay." I'm not awake enough to be hungry. I probably won't be for a while. I waltz into the kitchen and pull out stuff to start coffee.

"You seem tired."

"Got to bed late," I say through a yawn, and somehow they understand it.

"Do you want to go back to bed?"

"Glennie, what do you want? Why are you here?"

They're still wearing their canvas jacket, hands shoved deep in the pockets, their shoulders hunched forward. "Sorry. I should let you go back to bed..."

The coffeemaker starts tapping out a rhythm into the pot, and it's annoying me.

"No. You should tell me what you want. You do this all the time, and I'm tired of it."

They straighten at that. "You're tired of me?"

"No, I'm just tired of you *not telling me what you want*. I'm not a mind reader, babe. If you wanted to come to my family Thanksgiving, you should've asked." Before-sunrise Hillary apparently has no filter because I barely register their gaping mouth and their sharp frown before going on. "And you did the same thing at Hammer Time. You wanted to pay, but you let him comp you. You wanted me to come over for dinner, but you waited until I suggested it. You make these little suggestions and drop these little hints, and I'm supposed to know what they mean. Just fucking ask for what you want!"

Their gaze is stormy, unhappy. "Fine. If I'd asked to come to your Thanksgiving, what would you have said?"

"I'd have said no. But it's not about you; my mom and I have had a very strained relationship the last year or so, and I was extremely stressed about seeing her. And I would've told you all that if you'd asked. But you didn't."

"I shouldn't have to. You should want me there. You should want to tell me things."

I throw out both my arms. "Even if it's gonna be messy and awkward, and there might be yelling and crying? Because I don't know about you, but that does not sound like a ticket to a good time."

They pace a step closer, their heavy boots clunking against the wood floor. "I don't care! I could've supported you. I could've distracted you or taken you home or bought you ice cream afterward."

"Well, I didn't want to put you through that, and honestly, it would've been stressful to have you there witnessing all my family garbage. It was an internal thing."

"An internal—wasn't Chance there? And all the roommates?"

"I couldn't avoid that!" I sputter. "What was I supposed to do, kick them out? Leave you at the dinner table with my father to make the smallest talk imaginable while my mom and I hashed things out?"

"Sure. Yes. If you want me to tell you what I want, that's what I wanted. I just wanted a fucking chance, Hillary. They're not coming back for months, and now I've missed out. And I'm pissed about it."

We're both breathing kind of hard, our chests like magnets drawn toward each other without the momentum to close the gap. And, of course, their honesty and their anger are turning me on. They have enough of a point that I have to consider it even though I'd make the same choice again, and I'm not happy about it, but I am happy that they finally came clean.

"Don't look at me like that," Glenn warns, and their tone sends a rush of heat like a whirlwind around my body.

"Like what?" I fire back. "How am I looking at you?"

"Like you want me to bend you over and fuck you."

"So you want me to lie?" My nipples are tight and pebbled under my shirt, and they're so sensitive, it's almost uncomfortable when I shift my weight.

"Don't, Hillary," they groan, but they shuffle close enough to put their palm to my cheek. "This is serious. I'm really mad."

"Yeah, I am too. Let's be mad horizontally."

Glenn curses softly, and then their lips are on mine, a mosh pit for two rather than a delicate pas de deux, a clash of teeth and tongue as they strip off their coat and toe off their shoes. Their cold hands move under my shirt, finding those hard nipples, and I gasp into their mouth as they give one a firm pinch.

"Couch," they mutter, pushing me backward.

"Bedroom," I parry, pushing on their chest, and they groan again, longer this time.

"Is there anything you won't fight about, star?"

"I like the way you make me come..."

"Good. Then sit down." They're already tugging down my loose, plaid pajama pants.

"Wait, I can't. Chance and Colby had sex on this couch." *And they'd both kill me if they knew I told you that.*

Glenn slides to their knees. "Then this is your revenge." Their mouth is warm against my needy bits, their breath hot and tantalizing. I let my hands slide through their hair, more for balance than anything. Their talented tongue is making my knees a bit weak. I glance back at that couch. I don't feel great doing the same thing to them as they did to me. Wherever Glenn and I go, sexwise, dampness tends to follow.

"No. Can't do it. Bedroom or nothing. We need condoms, anyway."

Their deep growl buzzes against me, their beard lighting up my nerve endings. "Not today."

Grabbing a handful of hair, I tip their head back and relish their messy mouth and glazed gaze. "Pardon you?"

"Not coming inside today. Not in the right...headspace."

Oh. While I'm a little disappointed, that's better than what I thought they meant at first. It doesn't seem like them to make unilateral decisions when it comes to protection. Then my mind drifts back to our conversation about fluidity...I wasn't saying it right, but this is what I meant.

"You wanna use a toy?" I ask, massaging their scalp because I feel bad for pulling on them like that a minute ago.

"Fuck yes." Their blatant enthusiasm makes a little shiver run through me. *This is gonna be good.*

"Top drawer next to my bed."

"Oh, you're going to make me go get them?" Glenn kisses my inner thigh, sucking lightly where my leg meets the rest of my body.

"Yeah."

"Power play, Ms. Cook," they say, getting to their feet. They smirk over their shoulder as they cross the living room, and I follow their gaze down—I've got my pajama pants around my knees, my damp panties hanging there limply, and suddenly, I don't feel as in control as I did before. Yanking my pants up, I trot after them and flop down on the bed, which is where I wanted to be anyway.

"Cheater," they accuse softly without looking up from the drawer. They're bent over, hands behind their back, inspecting my collection, a rather meager collection compared to some (*cough* Giada *cough*). But they pull out three dildos: a hot pink rigid one that vibrates, a softer tan one that's very anatomical, and a green, curvy, tentacle-like one that looks like you broke it off one of the aliens in those monsterfucker romances. "Choose."

I love screwing with them, so I point to the tentacle. *Good luck getting me off with that thing, Mx. Rasmussen.*

"Great." They pick that one up and toss it back in the drawer.

"Bastard."

Glenn picks up the pink one. "I didn't say what you were choosing. Learn to ask more questions, beautiful."

They lean over me, and I can smell the early morning still on them: the dampness of outside, the coffee they drank with a hint of caramel, and the unwashed scent of *them*, ready to get going without bothering to shower. They don't smell bad at all, just a little musky, like sleep. And I think that I would like to wake up next to them just to bury my nose into their scratchy neck.

"Besides," they go on, "I have to keep that beautiful brain of yours engaged, or it wanders off. Gotta keep you on your mental toes." The way they touch the hair at my temple is fighting its way into my heart, and it's getting harder every time to keep up the mental friction. I'm strangely soft for them. I touch them back gently, and they close their eyes. They offer trust like I deserve it, and I wish I felt like I did. But it means a lot that they do.

"Stand up," Glenn says.

I cross my arms and stare at them. "Not going back to the couch."

"Fine, I'll fuck you here, but I'm still going to bend you over. That's what your eyes said you wanted. Tell me I'm wrong."

"No."

"Because I'm wrong or because you're contrary?"

"Fuck off."

"Fuck you? I'm trying."

"I like you," I breathe, breaking the long kiss to peck at their face, and they smile.

"I'll see your like and raise you a love." There's that word again. They keep using it. It affects my soul a little more each time, like it's gathering energy in a battery, collecting up the light of them to say it back. Not today, I don't think. But I'm getting there.

I unfold my arms and pull Glenn to me, bringing their lips to mine. They brace themselves against the mattress on their elbows, probably trying not to crush me, still holding the other two toys. Even clothed, it feels so good to have them close to me, our soft cotton bodies rubbing and sliding together, teenage-style lust and lips colliding.

"Is there anything you won't fight about, professor?"

They shake their head as they dive back into our kisses. It's the quieter kind, compared to how this started. Maybe it's being in my warm bed, maybe it was my late night, but even their touch is slow when they dive back into my pajamas. I hum my pleasure.

"Good girl. Show me if you like it. Don't hold back." *Fucking praise kink.* They're still kissing me as they caress me between my legs, and having their hand down my pants just makes it feel dirtier. "Did you want to get into the bath?" they murmur against my lips.

I shake my head. I just want to be here. I bring my hands up to hold their face close to mine, and a buzzing between my legs makes me jump. Their smile is vindictive.

"I want to keep kissing you. That's the only reason you get to stay on your back."

"Gee, thanks." I barely get the snark out before they capture my mouth again in a scorching kiss. The vibrating head of the dildo between my legs is making me try to spread them more, but I'm stuck still in my pajamas, and I whine a little.

"Did you want more?"

I close my eyes; the truth is easier that way. "Yeah." A moment later, their weight shifts. Something soft touches my lips, and I open them automatically. The warm softness of the other dildo dives into my mouth, and I groan. Glenn chuckles again.

"Still not asking the right questions..." They slip the vibrating one inside me and start moving both dildos as they kiss my neck, hovering over me on their elbows. I can't get my bearings; I don't know where to focus. Their gaze goes hot as I start to actively suck off the toy, and they gesture toward the toy with their head. "Hold it."

Normally, I wouldn't be so compliant, but my brain is befuddled, and they flip up my sweatshirt and begin lavishing my breasts with kisses. "In and out, star. Just like I was doing." Fucking my own mouth with a toy is weirdly hot, and paired with the light vibration against my clit and the unintentional bondage of my pajamas, I'm boiling inside.

I let my other hand wander down to the front of their pants and fumble with the zipper; they're being too one-sided again. They pause when I get inside, then they gently start to rut against my hand. They press the vibrator into me harder, and then they're pushing my hand out of the way to take the dildo back again, and when I figure out that they're mimicking the motion of my hand on their cock with the toy...*oh fuck*. I'm not in control, not at all, and yet they're handing control back to me to make this exactly what I want, and if that's not enough to set me on fire, I don't know what ever will be.

I moan around the toy, my hips snapping forward for more pressure, and I'm close, I'm so close, but it's not...enough. I squeeze Glenn's shoulder with my free hand, and they pull out the toy.

"What do you need, love?"

"Your weight. On top of me."

They toss the toy that was in my mouth to the side and clamber up on top of me, reaching down to slide the pink one inside...pinned between us. Their happy groan tells me it's working for them, too.

"Good?" I pant, and they nod.

"But you worry about you."

"No." I wrap my legs around their still-clothed hips. "This is more fun."

"Oh, you want to see me screw up this outfit? Is that what you want?"

I smile. I would like that, yes, but it's their voice that's got my arousal spiking like a heatwave in July.

"Talk to me. Tell me." They wrench down their clothes as much as they can without taking them off.

"Tell you what, star? How good you feel under me? How much I love your throaty little moans? How I don't mind working hard if it makes you feel amazing? Because I don't. I can stay here and fuck you all day if that's what it takes, if that's what you want. I'll bang you like it's my job and I'm angling for a promotion."

A laugh spills out of me, but it soon turns into a groan. I want them inside. I want it so bad, I'm literally whimpering with frustration. But I know they don't want that today, so it's not fair to ask.

I manage to wedge my hand between us and get the toy inside me, and that vibration is suddenly against just the right spot inside me, and their weight feels so calming and sweet in the face of my frantic, muted thrusting under them. It's building now, it's coming, I just need...I need...

"I can't wait to hear you scream for me," Glenn murmurs, and that's it, that pushes me over the edge, and I do scream, just three sharp cries in time with my straining hips, and then I collapse onto the bed. I have no breath. I have no brain cells. There's just a toy buzzing in my oversensitive pussy and a big, strong enbyfriend on top of me, giving me a big smile for the first time since they entered my apartment today.

That's okay—I can remedy that. I pull out the pink vibrator, but I don't turn it off.

"On your back, you."

They must be befuddled, too, because they don't fight me. I'm all tapped out in terms of sexy feelings, but I still get a rush from seeing them on their back all spread out for me. I push their pretty sweater up, revealing the line of hair on their belly, and I can't help but give it a lick. I feel them tense under me.

"I'm not going to put you in my mouth," I murmur, kissing their soft belly, and incrementally, they relax, once again a mass of muscle and warmth under me. Until I touch the vibrator to the end of their cock.

Glenn curses, and I snicker. Then I slide down to kneel on the floor, kissing along that hard line beneath their balls as they squirm under the vibration still on their cock.

"Hil...oh...fuck...*yes*." They come quietly again, and I think it must just be their thing...though I wouldn't mind hearing them roar someday. They lift their head blearily, and I grin at them as they let it flop back against the bed, as though even sitting up is too much work. I kiss their hip as I stand up to go grab them a washcloth from the bathroom. Once they're cleaned up, we crawl under the covers.

"I'm sorry I didn't say I'd miss you too last night," they say, caressing my face. "That's what I came here to say."

"Well, thank you. That did hurt my feelings. Probably could've waited to hear it *not* at the butt crack of dawn on a vacation day, but I appreciate the thought." I pause. I want to invite them to lunch with my parents, but I don't want anyone to feel ambushed. I'm pretty sure it would make my mom super happy, though. Glenn, too.

"I made up for it. I brought sugar. And orgasms." They kiss my forehead. "I'm also going out of town next week. The symphony is traveling." Lunch is suddenly gone from my head.

I jerk back, suddenly thrust back into student mode, an uncomfortable kind of thrusting compared to what we were doing earlier. "What about class?"

"Ms. Ketchum is going to open the studio and be there to answer questions."

"The lady who abandoned me? I don't think so." I shake their shoulder a little. "I need *you*. You know my...quirks and shit." I should just say "neurodiversity" or "learning disability" or "ADHD," but I don't have an official diagnosis yet, and I feel awkward about claiming it without a doctor to sanction my decision. "Quirks and shit" works for now.

Glenn smiles gently. "You'll be in good hands. You'll be fine." I scowl at them, and their smile just grows. "Oh, dear. My star is displeased."

"I am sure as shit displeased."

"It's for a good cause. It's to benefit Doernbecher. We're playing with the Central Oregon Symphony."

I say nothing because it's impossibly selfish to wish that they didn't care about kids with cancer so they can stay here with me. And yet...

"How long will you be gone?"

"Just a few nights."

"I see. Unrelated: do you want to come to lunch with my parents today?"

Their face pinches. "I can't. I've got rehearsal. I'm sorry."

I wave a hand. "It's fine. Maybe they'll come back for Christmas. I wouldn't be surprised. Do you need me to watch Lulu?"

They smile. "No, my neighbor's going to do that. But thank you."

"I would send proof of life," I say, scooting closer. "Does she do that?"

"No. But she already knows where everything is and her routines and stuff. She's right there. It's fine, really."

"Mmm." I don't like it.

I don't like it at all.

CHAPTER THIRTY

IT WOULD BE A WEIRD week even if Glenn wasn't gone. But it is definitely made weirder by their absence. The substitute is fine. She brought her cute baby, so that was nice. I love to see a mama who feels free to bring her kiddo to work. That's how women have gotten shit done for thousands of years; I don't know why business-es suddenly decided women were bad at multitasking. I've been in child-inclusive work environments, and they are the most gracious, fun places to be. This baby blows spit bubbles at me from their linen sling as their mama helps me pick out glazes.

But it was weird before Tuesday. I'm too used to Glenn now. On Wednesday, I try to tell myself that I'm a strong, independent person as I eat my breakfast alone instead of meeting them at the café on campus. But Chance is gone, and everything is too quiet, even when I turn on the TV. Also, the TV wanted to play news, and it was very depressing. I'm doing my part by walking places and taking public transportation and using reusable bags. Why can't we get with it and save the earth?

Morning classes are fine; we're starting to wrap things up for the quarter. This is our last week of regular classes before finals. I'm slightly concerned about my Global Reproductive Rights final project...but at least with Glenn gone, I have more time to work on it. I eat a healthy lunch because they've programmed me to go to

Dancing Earth now, so I just go automatically, and now I'm sad that they're not here with me. I'm *sad*.

Hillary: how's your trip going? do you have to share a room?

Glenn: no, I get my own room.

Hillary: did you sleep on both beds? I'd sleep on both beds.

Glenn: I know you would, chaos girl.

Hillary: ONE MIGHT BE BETTER THAN THE OTHER, GLENNIE

Glenn: can't argue with that logic.

Hillary: I'm at Dancing Earth, and you're not here.

Glenn: it's true.

Glenn: wait, do you miss me?

Hillary: of course I fucking miss you, you doofus.

Glenn: Huh.

Hillary: You are the doofiest doofus who ever doofused.

Glenn: ::smiles::

Hillary: STOP ENJOYING MY PAIN

Glenn: Can't. Sorry.

Glenn: Gotta go, rehearsal. Talk later?

Hillary: Can I come over tonight?

Glenn: I won't be home until really late. Tomorrow? After class?

Hillary: Counseling.

Glenn: so Friday?

Hillary: yeah, Friday, I guess.
Glenn: Okay.

They send a kiss emoji with it, but it doesn't feel a thing like their real kisses, all warm and prickly and sweet. I'm so morose, I've just been letting my wrap sit there while we text, and now that we're done, my appetite is completely gone. Before I put my phone away, I text my dad.

> **Hillary:** now I know why you get so pathetic
> when Mom is gone
> **Dad:** it's called being in love, kid.

I respect that he doesn't even deny it. I stare at my turkey bacon avocado wrap as I let that sink in. I should've picked something else. I'm still tired of turkey from Thanksgiving.

> **Hillary:** I don't know if I'm in love.

> **Dad:** Sure sounds like it.

> **Hillary:** but how do I KNOW

> **Dad:** How do you know anything, kid? Experience. Outside confirmation from people you trust. Your gut feeling.

> **Dad:** Is this the person you want changing your diapers when you're ninety?

Hillary: gross.

Dad: Is this the person you want to have kids with? See the world with?

Hillary: 98% yes.

Dad: What do you need for another two percent?

Hillary: I don't know. Intangible.

Dad: You'll figure it out, Hil. You're smart.

Hillary: you have to say that, you're my dad.

Dad: Doesn't make it not true.

Hillary: I guess.

Dad: What's your rush? Are they going off to war?

Hillary: Dad.

Dad: Are they headed to the international space station?

Hillary: I WOULDN'T BE SURPRISED

Hillary: DADDY, THEY ARE ANNOY-INGLY CAPABLE

Dad: Good. They'll take good care of you when I'm dead.

Hillary: I don't want to love them just because they love me.

Dad: That's valid.

Dad: They're not pressuring you to say it back, are they?

Hillary: Nope. We haven't even talked about it.

Dad: Better not be.

Hillary: Are you gonna go all Dad-Mode on their ass?

Dad: No, I know you're capable of setting boundaries and enforcing them.

Dad: but if you need me, just say the word.

Hillary: you got it. Love you, Daddy.

Dad: Not as much as I love you, kiddo.

My wrap is still staring at me judgmentally. I ask the kid behind the counter for a box and stuff it in my bag to take home and ignore. My walk home is very long, despite being the same length it always is. I do not get hit by a car due to distraction, but my head feels light and funny when I unlock my front door, so I go for some almond milk (that's got protein, right?). But it's not until I close the fridge that I hear the music.

It's coming from Chance's room. That's not so unusual—he often works with music on. He usually uses headphones, though, and this is loud. And then it stops.

"Hang on," I hear Colby say, and then someone's tuning a guitar, and now I'm confused. Because I know for a fact that the last time Colby played for another person was his instructor in order to pass his required music classes at community college. He plays the piano at my parents' house sometimes, but this is different. This is him and his boyfriend in their room, having a moment, and I'm totally intruding on it.

I creep closer to hear better, getting as close to the open doorway as I can without being seen.

He starts playing again. *And then he starts to sing.* I'm so shocked, my hand flies to my mouth. And the song he picked is gorgeous and sentimental, but it's the chorus that makes tears spring to my eyes.

> *I'd pick you, all over again*
> *A million times, start over and then*
> *I'd pick you, all over again*

And I can tell he's starting to step into his confidence as the song goes on. I peek into the room; he's on the bed, one leg tucked under him, playing with his eyes closed, singing to his beloved about how it's them against the world and how they're gonna have grandkids, and that's when it hits me.

Love is when you don't just want to be with the other person, you want to sing about it. You want to express it, because it's too big and too utterly incomprehensible to keep inside. You have no pride left when it comes to them. You have to let it out.

Colby finishes his song, and I can hear Chance sniffling. "Couldn't just pick Aerosmith or Stairway to Heaven," he mumbles. "No, you had to wreck me. And don't say you didn't fucking know, because I know you did."

Colby chuckles, and I hear him set the guitar aside and climb off the bed. The wheels of Chance's desk chair creak as he wraps his arms around him. There are kissing sounds next; that's my cue to either show myself or leave. Lucky for them, I've got somewhere to be. But the floor creaks in the middle of the living room.

"Hil?" Chance calls, trying to force the frogginess out of his voice.

"Yeah, just forgot a book. I'm headed out again. Bye!" I grab a quilt off the back of the couch and my bag. I'll buy more snacks if I need them.

I just walk to Glenn's because it's not dark yet, and I feel weird getting on the bus with a big quilt in my arms. It's a nice night—cloudy, but what else is new? But I don't need stars. I am the star. But I do need one thing; I make a quick trip to the grocery store, where the other customers are definitely wondering about the quilt, and then I'm on my way.

CHAPTER THIRTY-ONE

I MAKE MYSELF COMFORTABLE on their porch swing and settle in with my turkey wrap and my laptop to wait. Lulu sees me out the front window, but she doesn't bark. She just sits down like she expects me to open the window and pet her through the opening.

"Sorry, Lulu," I say softly. "We've both gotta wait for them to get home."

They weren't kidding when they said it would be late. Headlights wake me up, my laptop about to topple onto the wooden front porch, and I just catch it as I'm stretching. I hear someone sigh as they come up the front steps.

"Hey."

Glenn freezes, then a hand flies to their chest. "Shit! You scared me half to death."

"Sorry."

I push off the quilt, and they seem to consider the circumstances for the first time. "What's wrong? Did you and Chance have a falling out?"

"No. I'm pretty sure Chance is gonna become my brother-in-law sometime next year." I stand up and stretch again, then scoop up the flowers. "These are for you. Welcome home."

"Lilies. You remembered." Their smile is goofy and embarrassed and perfect, and I do want to sing about it even though I can't sing. "Thanks. You want to come in?"

"No, I want to take the bus home in the dark," I say, sarcasm dripping from every syllable. They shush me, moving in to press a finger to my lips, and then to kiss me, and then they're setting down their black duffel bag and the flowers to hold me. And the kisses are good, the long kind that I like and missed. I sigh into their mouth. "I love you, Glenn."

"Do you?" They sound surprised, and it makes me giggle.

"Mmm-hmm."

"I thought you just missed me."

"I did. Because I love you."

"Mmm. I love you, too." Their voice is cracked, and there's exhaustion written in the lines around their eyes. I don't know what they're expecting now, but I'm tired, too.

"Can we please go to bed?"

"Yeah. I gotta let Lulu out first and bring in my bass, but you can go on up."

The little dog is just as overjoyed to see us as she is every time. She licks Glenn's face ardently and repeatedly when they pick her up, and I giggle. She is irrepressibly adorable.

"I'm not competing with a dog for your affection. You better wipe off that slobber before you come to bed." The words sound so damn domestic coming out of my mouth, I can hardly stand it. But I want to wake up next to them. I'm ready for that.

"Why, what's gonna happen when I come to bed?" they quip as they head through the dark house to the sliding door that leads to the backyard. I drag all my stuff into the entryway and dump it by the door. I did not think this through. I don't have pajamas. Or a toothbrush. Or clothes for tomorrow. I guess I'll go home in the morning before class...it's on the way to campus. Maybe they'd drop me.

I head up the stairs, realizing when I get to the landing that I actually don't know which bedroom is theirs. The whole house is theirs, and I'm assuming there's no forbidden west wing with a magic rose under glass that I'm not supposed to touch...but still. Maybe I'll just wait.

Maybe this was dumb. Maybe I should go home. I pause, halfway up and halfway down, unsure which way to push. I said what I came to say; there's no reason why I can't go home. But I haven't seen them in days, haven't felt their skin or held them in my arms. That's reason enough to push past this weird feeling. It's just late. I'm just thinking too hard.

"Star." Glenn's coming up the stairs, Lulu under their arm again. "Bedtime."

I nod, then I move to let them pass and lead the way...but they grab my hand as they go by, and we go up together. Now it feels right.

Glenn opens a white door, then lets out a big sigh as they put down the dog. She hurries over to a small, white dog bed at the foot of Glenn's queen-size bed and turns around a few times before flopping down happily.

"There really is no place like home."

I spy another door leading to an adjacent bathroom, and I quickly duck inside to go pee and finger-brush my teeth before bed. I can hear them in the bedroom, unpacking and opening drawers, the shuffle of clothing. I peek at them. They're pulling a pair of oversize T-shirt-type pajamas over their head, and I'm sad they're covering up their tattoos. At least it's a V-neck. I'll get a peek before I fall asleep.

"How was your trip?" I ask as I come back into the room. They brought up the stargazers, now in a vase, and their scent is filling the room.

"It was fine. We did the Ravel and the Schumann tonight."

"Not your amazing solo?"

They smile as they pull back the covers of their neatly-made bed. "Nope."

"Their loss." I pull my shirt off over my head and reach back to pop my bra off. That's when I notice they're propped up on one elbow, head in their hand, watching me with undisguised interest. "Thought you were tired," I taunt as I hook my thumbs into my waistband and shove my pants down, leaving my black underwear on.

"Not feeling so tired at the moment," they murmur, as I slide under the covers. "Beautiful naked people do that to me."

"All naked people? Like, if you think about nude beaches, it keeps you awake?"

They pillow their hands under their head, facing me. "Have you ever been to a nude beach?" When I shake my head no, they smile. "They had them in Italy. Lots of saggy old people. Still beautiful, of course...but not arousing. At least not to me." They reach out to play with an errant lock of my hair. "You, however, make me want to stay up all night..."

"We should sleep. It's after one." I fake a yawn. "We both have stuff tomorrow."

"So I washed the slobber out of my beard for nothing?"

"I didn't know you'd been to Italy."

I think their yawn is real. "Yeah. I did an apprenticeship there for ceramics. Went in thinking I knew a lot. Came out realizing I didn't. Just scratched the surface, really." Their hands settle into my hair at the back of my neck, and they brush their thumb against my cheek. I scoot my hips closer to theirs to let our legs tangle. But we're going to sleep. Really.

"I can't imagine you cocky."

"Because coming on to my student isn't cocky?"

"It was clear it was done with trepidation. There was no cockiness involved." I pause. "I still can't believe you got me off in the studio like that."

"I know, right? I lived off that high for days."

"That is *not* what I meant. Do you know how mortifying it would've been if anyone had caught us?"

"I guess that would've been bad. I was just so happy to be touching you. It totally clouded my judgment. Probably still does from time to time." They bring our faces just a breath apart. "Considering I wanted to get you off in the rage room."

"Um. Cameras?"

"I'd delete it later. Or maybe send myself a copy. Either way, Tom would never have to know."

"You're a wicked one."

"Love, you have no idea…" They seal the idea with a kiss, and I can't deny that I'm tempted. Maybe I do have a public sex thing.

"Tell me more about Italy. Did you see the Sistine Chapel?"

"Mm-hmm."

"Did you see the David?"

"I did. But Moses meant more to me."

I'm struck by this. "Michelangelo sculpted Moses, too? All we ever hear about is David."

"If that's true, it's a tragedy. I don't know how to describe it, Hil. But it was one of the seeds that led me toward authenticity in my life. Moses is sitting there, and you know it's a statue, but he just looks so pissed, like he's holding back. And he's tucked these tablets under his arm, but he's also got his fingers tangled in his beard like a security blanket, like he doesn't know what to do. And I'd been thinking a lot about gender while I was there, and seeing those strong fingers in that stone beard that looked so real…I realized I wanted to keep my beard. Some of the stuff I'd been doing like the tattoos and the piercings, they were meant to mask my softer side. But I loved my beard."

"I love it, too," I say, petting their face gently, and they press a kiss to my palm. "I'm glad I'm not the only one who gets revelations at odd moments. So which tattoos are post-coming out? Did you change your name?"

"Nope, I was always Glenn. I still liked it." They hold out their left arm. "This one's new."

I tilt their arm so I can see the quote better. 'The way to read a fairy tale is to throw yourself in.' I gaze at them, trying to suss out its meaning in the dim light.

"Have you read any W.H. Auden?"

I shake my head.

"He's a queer poet from the 1930's. British guy. Anyway, he's not so important to the quote..." They clear their throat. "It was just one of the seeds that planted the thought in my mind that I could express myself the way I am, that I could throw out whatever society expected that wasn't Glenn. That I could be the princess in my story if I wanted to. So I wrote it on my arm so I wouldn't forget."

"And these?" I ask softly, running my fingers over the raised lines under the ink. "What were you trying to remember with these?" I've seen them before: horizontal scars across the inside of their forearm.

"Those were when I was trying to forget." Their voice is husky, and I feel tears pressing at me, a tight, scared feeling in my chest. When I look over at them, the tears spill out, and I let them roll down my cheeks unhindered.

"I'm sorry, honey."

"What for, star?"

"I'm sorry someone made you feel that way. I'm sorry you felt that was the only way to cope."

"So am I." They kiss my forehead. "But it's not your fault."

"If I make you feel that way," I say, my voice still thick with tears, "you have to tell me. If you're tempted to do that again, please, please let me help you."

"Oh, Bear would kill me if I ruined his artwork. Plus, I laid down a small fortune for..." They notice that I'm not amused. I can't be. I just want to squeeze them until they promise to never hurt themself again. "Hil. That's my past. I don't cover it up because I don't want to forget what trying to hide cost me. But I'm also not in that place anymore. I've got lots of love and support now for who I am." They tip my chin up, even though it's wobbling with more tears. "And I've got someone I want to spend my life with."

"You shouldn't say that," I whisper, swiping at the tears.

"Why? It's true."

"You don't know me that well yet, and I just got to 'I love you.' You don't want to tie yourself to this forever. Trust me."

"I love you, Hillary. I'm not ready to get married today, but I'm going to stick around, and I get to decide who I want to bond myself to. All relationships are messy. You know that."

I try to hide my face in their neck. "I just want to be what you need. And I don't know if I can."

"Did I not get lilies today?" They gesture insistently at the vase on the bedside table. "Did I not get clear communication about what's going on with you? I'm a simple creature, Hil. That's all I really need. Oh, and sex. I need sex."

"Simple might be overstating it." I sniffle, but my smile shows through. "But I'll try to take your word for it."

"I mean, calla lilies would've been better, but stargazers are acceptable..."

I punch their shoulder gently, and they take this as a signal that it's time to play, smothering me with kisses to my hair, squishing me under their bulk.

"Ugh, get off, doofus! We're supposed to be sleeping!"

"Unconsciousness is for basics, as the kids say," they purr. "We can have way more fun than that. Do you need me to show you?"

"You can try." I sniff, turning my face away—which only gives them better access to my neck, damn it. And when I spread my legs and they kiss their way down to where I'm wet, it's tender and unhurried and thorough, and I come with my clit pressed against their pulsing cock, pulling them closer. We talk and we touch, a tide washing back and forth between us, a rhythm in its own right, crashing over us to leave us breathless before receding to a gentle lap.

I fall asleep much, much later, their chest my pillow and their heartbeat my lullaby.

CHAPTER THIRTY-TWO

IT'S OUR LAST CLASS...and I still have my vase to throw. If I don't throw something decent, I cannot pass this class.

I avoided this last quarter for a reason; it's hard. Like, really hard. There's the coordination of keeping the heavy kickplate spinning to turn the table—I mean, god forbid the university spring for electric pottery wheels. And even when I keep that spinning, I can't seem to make the clay do what I want it to. It has a mind of its own, I swear.

There's a white index card on my desk, just like the ones they've been giving me all quarter. *It's just a vase. You can do it. I know you can. —G*

It's unspeakably sweet and very annoying at the same time. They don't *know* I can do it because *I* don't even know. I have tried before. Janey called it a disaster if that gives you an idea of what we were working with here. *Janey*, queen of kind, ambassador of encouragement.

Janey's own vase had reminded me of spring in Washington D.C. She painted these delicate cherry blossoms on the side with such movement, you almost wanted to reach out and try to touch them, to see if you could catch them before they fell. I didn't even get a vessel with a hole in the top, forget firing. I'm sure Glenn did grade my first attempt, but I'm also sure it was a big part of the reason why I failed.

It's just a vase. I stick the card in my back pocket, ignoring the platitudes on the rest of it. *Focus on the truth—it's just a vase. Just make something serviceable and you can walk out of here with your head held high.*

Fatima's at the wheel, too, and I smile at her as I go grab a hunk of cold clay. Am I supposed to soften it up first? I think so. I do that for a while, slamming it against the table.

"Are you going to get your vase done tonight?" Fatima asks. "You left it until late."

"You're not wrong," I sigh. "What are you working on?"

"Bonus project. Mx. Rasmussen said I could make a set of plates."

"Nice." I stand there, watching her. She sinks her hands into the clay, and it just seems to give way to her. It's the same feeling I had when I watched Glenn at the symphony, like the instrument knew what they wanted, like it was an extension of them.

Speak of the devil...I can smell the light jasmine perfume of their lotion before I see them out of the corner of my eye, and I go back to softening my clay as they pass by.

"Hey." My tablemate leans over, showing me her phone. "Did you see this?" It's a funny video that someone made on campus, just outside this building, some kind of parkour parody. I watch with her until my conscience nags at me to get back to work.

I run down a mental checklist: I've eaten. I know the steps I need to take. I just need to do it. But the minutes are ticking by, and I'm just watching everyone work around me.

"Everything okay?" Their voice is low. I don't turn around.

"Yes. Of course. I'm fine." I heft the clay into my arms and head over to the wheel. I slam it down onto the table so it'll stay attached, but I can still feel them watching me. Someone comes over to say goodbye and shake their hand, thank them for a good class, and I'm relieved that it's just me and Fatima again. She already made her plates...and now she appears to be making another vase?

I sit there and watch her, trying to figure out how she keeps it so even and symmetrical all the way down. More people are packing up and leaving, their arms weighed down with large paper bags Glenn provided to take things home in. They're very considerate, and here I am, just sitting here, staring at this contemptible gray lump I'm supposed to turn into a work of art in...fifteen minutes? Yeah, not going to happen.

There's no classes after ours. Maybe they'll let me stay. I hope they'd trust me by now. I pull out my phone and text Chance that I'm not going to be home on time, and he and Col should go ahead and eat and whatever without me. It turns into a conversation about our weird plumbing situation...contemptible old building. Contemptible brain. Contemptible clay.

Glenn clears their throat behind me. They're looking at a clipboard, but I know they're there for me. I dip one hand in the water near the wheel, still suspiciously clean for how long I've been sitting here. Fatima doesn't even wire her vase off at the bottom of the clay; she's throwing it off the hump. I thought that was supposed to be an advanced technique. I wish I could ask her to do it again so I could watch. I guess that's what YouTube is for.

I get the wheel spinning and just stare at it, mesmerized. The scrape of a chair breaks the spell. Glenn pulls it up next to me, then sits down with their computer. Glenn's glasses are perched daintily on the ridge of their once-broken nose as they peer down at the laptop.

"What are you doing?"

"Grading."

"So go grade at your desk." I glance around, feeling self-conscious, but there aren't that many people left, and no one seems to find it strange that our professor has just taken up residence on a stool next to me.

They don't even look up. "I like it here."

"Why?"

"Well," they said, taking off their glasses, "I've been doing an experiment. When I leave, you stop working. You talk to Fatima; you look at the clock and your phone and out the window. You wander around in spirit even though your butt stays here. But if I sit here, you stay here."

"You're not supposed to help me." It's childish—I know it is. And there's hurt in the words that I wish wasn't, but I can't help it. The helplessness is drowning me, making me small, making me fight just to stay in this classroom.

"I can't put my hands in the clay, no," they murmur softly. "But I can make sure yours stay there." Then they put their glasses back on, more like a proper, one-room schoolhouse teacher on the prairie than the bad bitch they apparently are, tattoos and all. And they start typing again.

I stare down at the wheel. I don't know how to do this. My fear of failure feels like a fog in my head, making perspective impossible; success could be metaphorically one foot away or one mile away, and I'd never know. But I'll really never know unless I try. And it feels so fucking ridiculous that my whole academic career has come down to this one project in this one class...

And then it hits me. I'm not afraid of failing at all. I'm afraid of success.

Because once I finish this, I've done the hardest part. I'm good at school, I know I am. But once I'm done, I have to go out into the real world and succeed, and that's going to be a million times worse than this ugly vase.

Tears roll down my cheeks, and I don't wipe them away. My cheeks are hot, and I feel sticky and sweaty under my arms.

"You can do this," Glenn mutters under their breath. "Inhale. Exhale. Hands in the clay."

I push my shoulders back and stare down at the wheel again. *Fuck yes, I can do this. I can do all of it. I will graduate. I will leave the safe, comfortable academic space and go get a real fucking job.* I mean, not a *fucking* job, probably; no judgment, but I don't think sex work is for me. *But I will make this vase, and then I will wash my hands and go buy myself dinner and update my resume.*

Because I am Hillary Fucking Cook, fucking not included unless your name is Glenn Rasmussen.

The clay is still there, mocking me with its nasty silence, but I put my thumbs in the center and push down, just getting comfortable with the feeling of the resistance. Yes, life is full of resistance, but so. am. I.

"Good. Keep going."

I glance over. Glenn's body language says they're still ignoring me, and for the sake of my focus, that's probably for the best. I can't even touch them because my hands are covered in gray slip. I want to lean over and kiss their shoulder through their T-shirt. I want to thank them for loving me.

I start working the kickplate, and the blob spins under my fingers, my indentation growing into something kind of like a small goblet. I support the side with one hand, but I can feel it wobbling.

"Slow down. Bring it back in." They're still not watching; how do they know what I'm doing wrong? By the sound?

"I don't know how." I pull back, and it wobbles out of control, folding over on itself. I stare at the spinning mess, then sit back hard into my chair. I wipe the sweat from my forehead. "Do I need a new lump?"

"Just re-form this one."

"Bye, Professor. Thanks," calls a young Black man from the doorway.

"Colin, I really enjoyed having you in class," Glenn calls back. "I hope you'll continue with your ceramics work. You did some beautiful pieces."

He smiles bashfully under their praise. "Yeah, I'd like to. See you next quarter." Then he pushes open the door, and he's gone.

Everyone's gone now. Class is over.

My lower lip trembling a little, I turn to Glenn, ready for them to kick me out. Or just leave me here.

They shut their laptop, apparently willing to give up their grading ruse. "You like to dance."

It's not a question; they know I do. But I nod.

"Ever fallen over?"

That makes me smile a little. "Yeah. Once or twice."

"Why do you think that was?"

"My center of balance shifted when I..." Wait. I remember something about that.

Despite my dirty hands, I go digging into my notebook until I find the page about throwing on the wheel. *Centering.* That's right—I'm supposed to center it first. Maybe I didn't center it enough. Glenn opens their laptop again, and a moment later, there's music playing, low-key guitar and piano with a guy singing. I'm not really listening because I've found the wire and taken off that part that fell over, and I'm making it round again. I slam it into the middle again. And this time, I take my time centering it, forming a dome with my wet hands, letting my finger drag to make a spiral in the top so I'm sure I've found the middle.

I still need my notes, but I hear Glenn hum approvingly. My brain is still buzzing, but now it's buzzing about *this*, and I gently push my thumbs into the middle.

Then I search until I find that needle thing to measure that I have enough of a base...I think it's enough.

I don't glance at them. More water.

This is the part that's hard for me, pulling out gently enough to keep it even. It's not even pulling, it's like *angling* your fingers outward just a little, and the clay springs back. It's such dichotomy of motion with clay...you have to slam into onto the wheel and fight to get it centered, but then, these tiny touches change its shape so easily, like breathing.

Kind of like the two of us...we slammed into each other, and now we're shaping our relationship like water shapes a landscape, carving into the rock and river of us. But I'm getting distracted again.

I take a deep breath, then move my thumbs out from the center until I've got a wider diameter to the opening, and I even remember to support the outside edges with my other fingers.

"More water," Glenn mumbles.

Right. Water. That's not cheating, they're constantly being annoying about water to everyone. And I really don't want this thing to crack.

I'm starting to get excited, actually. I think I might actually pull this off. Now I just have to make it taller...one hand inside, one outside. Gentle, gentle pinching, rising up like smoke...but I think I pinch it too much at the top. I think I was supposed to leave a lip on it. It's probably too thin now.

"Breathe into the bottom of your lungs."

I do. It makes me sit up straighter and push my shoulders back. I do it again. A thin lip isn't the end of the world. I will have something gradeable. I will have a finished vase, even if it's not fired. Even if it's not glazed, I think I can get a C. I did well on the other stuff. It just has to be passable.

"I can do this," I say forcefully into the quiet room.

"You can," Glenn agrees.

I'm getting tired, though. Waging a mental battle is surprisingly exhausting. You'd think that fighting yourself, the energy would come back to you somehow. Not the case.

It's definitely wobbling at the top. *Ignore it.* What is it Dr. Thacker says? *Perfection is the enemy of good enough?* Maybe that's what I'm really fighting.

"Almost done, Hil," I tell myself. Taking the battle to physical space seems to help, somehow. Getting outside of my head. I pick up the rubber rib to flatten out the surface. I remember that much. I don't remember everything I have to do to get it off, though. And if I can't get it to the drying room, they're not going to grade it, I don't think.

When I hesitate, Glenn's voice brings me back to the present. "You're doing great. Almost there."

Skip it like a rock, don't push. Don't dig. That's what they said last time when they showed this part. *Let your inside fingers guide it toward the tool. Just skim the surface; we're just getting the slip off.*

I think this is the part I messed up before; I think I was so anxious to get it off, my hands were still wet, and it stuck to them. So this time, I make sure it's dry—all of it. The pot, me, everything. Wire off at the bottom, stay away from the rim, carry it from the base like a candle. Carefully, carefully, I take my gray cylinder, which is the most boring shape imaginable, into the drying room and set it on the shelf with my name on it. My whale is still here, and I give its head a pat. And when I exit the drying room, Glenn scoops me up immediately.

"You did it." Wild kisses pepper my nose and cheeks. "Hillary, you did it! You did it!"

"You helped," I protest.

"I did not!" they bellow, and nervous laughter pours of me, and maybe a few more tears.

"I did it," I whisper, hardly believing it. "I made a vase."

"Fuck yes, you did. An amazing vase."

"A basic vase," I correct, wiping at my eyes, their arms still around me.

"It's fucking amazing if I say it is. Who's the expert here?" They're still being uncharacteristically loud, and it's making me laugh.

"Apologies, Professor. I'm sure you're right."

"Fuck yes, I am. And class was over an hour ago, so I'm just Glenn now. Which is why I can do this." They walk me backward until my back hits the taupe wall, kissing the living daylights out of me, murmuring pride and praise. I try to keep my hands away—they're dry, but not clean...but eventually, I give in, wrapping my arms around their neck and putting my fingers into their hair.

Something tells me I'll have the opportunity to shower them off later if I want it.

"Dinner. Let's celebrate," they murmur between kisses. "My treat."

"Yeah. Just let me clean up first..."

"Hmm, never heard you say that before."

I whack their shoulder gently. "My hands, doofus. Not your room. You can handle that."

"Oh, I see. That does make more sense."

We get Italian delivered to their house. And when we have sex against their bedroom door, we're not *making* love—we don't need any more. We've got all we need.

CHAPTER THIRTY-THREE

WHEN ANXIOUS INTROVERTS leave the country, it turns out they don't much want a giant send-off. But when they're my roommate, they get one anyway. It's not giant, actually; Chance only invited three friends from work plus the roommates at Colby's. Which is only fair since we had the party at their house.

Chance has been a good sport all evening, shaking people's hands and nodding along and accepting their gifts of random guidebooks and money and those funky converter plugs you have to use because English power is weird, I guess. But I'm slowly encouraging people to say goodbye because I know he's bad at it and I love him. I love my roommate. I want the world for him. I'm not even jealous that he's got this opportunity, just genuinely happy for him.

But as I round the corner to take out the trash, I almost bump into him and Colby having a moment. Chance has to leave at like 3 AM, and I heard him telling my brother a few days ago that he thought it would be too hard to say goodbye like that. So apparently, they're doing it now.

"It'll be fine," Colby's telling him, but I can hear the tears in his voice. "We'll talk every day. I promise."

"How? The time difference is significant. I'm *eight hours* ahead of you. By the time I get off work, you'll be at rehearsal."

"You'll call me on your lunch break. It's fine."

"That's 4 AM! You really want to talk to me at four in the morning?"

"Chance, I need to talk to you every day."

"I can't do this." I can hear the rising panic, and I feel itchy to round the corner and console him, but I cement my feet in place. "I can't leave you, Col. I'll call and tell them I'm not coming."

"No, you won't." Colby's voice is muffled like they're holding each other. "It's fine. I promise. You're going to kill it over there, and I'm going to come visit you. The minute you figure out when you can get time off, I'll book my ticket. I want you to go. And you're coming back for that conference here in just a few weeks, right? We can spend our six-month back-together anniversary together. And when you're done in England, I'll be here waiting for you."

"You better fucking be. This isn't worth losing you over."

"Won't happen, babe."

There's a long silence, and then Chance speaks up. "Will you come home with me?"

"Are you sure? I thought you wanted a good night's rest before you—"

"It's a twenty-hour flight; I'll sleep on the plane. I want you more."

Colby chuckles, and I can't hear what he says next, but it makes Chance laugh, giving a snotty sniffle.

I poke my head through the doorway. "Does this mean you don't need a ride from me?"

Colby curses. "Hillary, it's called privacy. Seriously. Why are you constantly skulking around when we're...ugh." I think he just doesn't want me to see him all teary. As if this could somehow dampen my opinion of him when I'm so proud of how he's handling this. My sweet baby brother.

"No, Colby can take me. You can sleep in, Hil."

"As if. I've gotta get a hug goodbye, too, you know."

"Okay." His smile is watery, and if I stand here any longer, they're going to get me going, too, and then it'll never stop.

"I'll wait for you in the living room."

Chance gives me a thumbs up, and I unpoke my head to give them some privacy. As if that's a real thing. I pull out my phone.

Hillary: Tell me something funny.

Glennie: Dolphins use puffer fish to get high. They antagonize them until they release their toxins, and then they swim around in it and get buzzed.

Hillary: I thought dolphins were so pure. Poor puffer fish.

Glennie: Nah, they're assholes just like the rest of us.

Glennie: why am I sending you funny things?

Hillary: Chance leaves tomorrow, and I need distraction from the sadness.

Glennie: oh, that's right, I forgot. Do you want me to come over?

Hillary: No, I only have one set of noise-cancelling headphones. You'd have to listen to their marathon goodbye sex.

Glenn: you wanna come here?

That's tempting. Then they could have the apartment to themselves...that mythical privacy.

Hillary: I wouldn't be very good company.

Glennie: Hil, I didn't ask you so you could entertain me. I thought you might need support snuggles.

I do. I super do need them. As much as I did want to see Chance off tomorrow, I could say my goodbyes tonight, especially since Colby's giving him a ride. And then I could let Glenn take care of me tonight.

Hillary: Okay. Come get me? I'm at Colby's.
Glennie: I'm on my way, babe.
Hillary: thanks

I text Chance to let him know I need to say goodbye now without interrupting them again in person, and a few moments later, he appears in the living room. I take his shoulders in my hands and level my gaze at him.

"Don't fall in love with any other roommates over there, muffin."

Chance laughs softly. "Like anyone could compare to you."

"Damn straight. And I know you're there for the robots, but don't forget to go see random shit like Shakespeare's grave and Buckingham Palace and the London Bridge."

"That's in Arizona now." He sniffles, wiping his nose on a tissue he pulls from his pocket.

"I don't think so. Anyway, be good. I promise not to completely trash the place while you're gone. Or not your room, anyway."

"Okay," he says, chuckling. He reaches out and pulls me into a tight hug, so tight he forces the tears right out of me, the ridiculous man.

"You're gonna do great. I just know it. But don't forget your meds, okay?"

"I won't." He drops his voice. "Look after Col for me, will you? He's acting tough, but I know he's breaking." And by the way his voice cracks, Colby's not the only one.

"Yeah, I will."

"Don't forget."

"I won't. I promise." Glenn's headlights shine into the living room for a moment, and I release Chance. "I'll see you in a few weeks."

"You know, using the Hillary Conversion Factor, you're probably not far off..." He walks me to the front door.

"Oh! Right, also, I need you to explain the HCF to Glennie. They're confused about how to use it for shorter time frames."

"I'll send them an email from the plane tomorrow."

"Check." I can't handle another hug, so I just give him finger guns with both hands as I back through the front door. "Love you."

"Love you too."

Aww, geez, I'm crying again. This should not be wrecking me like this. He's only going to be gone for six months. And since I'm backing up, I don't see Glenn standing behind me, and I stumble into them as I hit the bottom of the stairs. When I whip around, I can't keep myself from launching into their arms.

"I'm so glad you're here." I don't know how they can even understand me with how muffled my voice is against their shoulder.

They stroke my hair. "Me too. Do you need consolation dessert?"

"Consolation sex would be fine."

"If you insist." They squeeze me tight, then take my hand and lead me to the car. I get a text from Colby before we're even out of the driveway.

Colby: I'm sorry I got upset with you. You don't have to leave for the night.

Hillary: I don't mind. Really. Love you both. Enjoy your "privacy."

Colby: Thanks, Hil. I really appreciate it.

Colby: Also, I'm gonna propose to Chance in England. Will you help me plan it?

I send him a gif of a baby freaking out with joy at a hockey game with the word "YESSSSS" at the bottom. I'm still sad, but this makes up for it a little bit. And frankly, the fact that I was able to hear his concern without getting bent out of shape feels like...progress? Still don't know where my keys are, but I know where my head is, and that's a start.

And when I look over at Glenn, I'm really glad to be in their dumpy little car, heading home with them. And not only because sleeping with noise-canceling headphones isn't comfortable at all.

CHAPTER THIRTY-FOUR

IT'S MAY, GRADUATION day, and I'm not distracted by the tassels. We're outside, miraculously, but there's heavy clouds threatening above our heads, and the wind is blowing the tassels on our flat black hats. But I'm not afraid I'm going to miss my turn. ADHD meds sometimes get a bad rap, but I fucking love them.

"Benjamin Irving Clark." The MC says each name distinctly, as if to distinguish them between some other Benjamin Clark who's hanging around, planning to sneak up on stage. I'm waiting behind Fiona Cloverdale (who, in a school this size, I have, of course, never met before today, my last day of college). She's a mom of three, and she's been doing classes online for the last two years to get here. Her kids are out there somewhere in the giant sea of audience before us, as are my parents and my brother and Chance. But not my enbyfriend. No, they're up on stage already, sitting with the rest of the faculty, subtly texting with me.

> **Glenn:** You're the cutest in that cap and gown.

> **Hillary:** Not exactly high fashion.

> **Glenn:** Granted, but it's tradition. And I love what it signifies.

> **Hillary:** and what is that exactly

Glenn: someone who doesn't give up. Someone who got a B- in her Ceramics class.

Hillary: And passed lots of other classes...

Glenn: but those ones didn't lead you to the love of your life, so they don't matter so much.

Hillary: it's true.

Glenn: which part?

Hillary: all of it.

"Fiona Evelyn Cloverdale." She pivots to grin at me, shrugs, then walks across the stage, beaming. I'm up next, so I put away my phone and get ready to walk across. I chose flats so I wouldn't worry about falling (unlikely), I have tissues in case I start crying (likely), and I left my purse with my mom, so my keys are safe. Let's face it: this is the most put-together I'm ever going to be. I'm ready to walk into this chapter of my life.

"Hillary Danielle Cook." To my right, a shrill whistle sounds, and I see the other faculty cringe, but Glenn doesn't seem to notice. They're giving me a standing ovation all by themself, and I motion for them to sit down already. They ignore me, of course.

"Congratulations, young lady," says the smiling older gentleman who hands me my empty diploma. The real one will come in the mail in a few weeks.

"Thanks," I say, shaking his hand. Then I follow the flow of graduates across the stage and down the other side, back to our seats.

This part is fine, but my real graduation is later today with the rest of my liberal studies people, including Giada. They made us each write up a little blurb about what we're up to next, and I think mine came out okay.

Hillary is transitioning from an internship to full-time employment with the League of Concerned Women, a group dedicated to empowering unhoused women in Portland to find steady employment and become homeowners through education, microloans, and career counseling. She and her partner Glenn plan to live in Portland for the foreseeable future.

I live with Glenn now. It's weird. I like it a lot. And I can still walk to the LCW offices, which has been great; they're making me their liaison for women who've been incarcerated, and I love it. Lulu is mine now; we spend a lot of cozy evenings together watching stuff on our new TV while Glennie's off playing their bass like a badass (don't look at me like that. You know I had to do it.). Lulu may change her mind about me when we leave her next month to take our first trip together. We're going to France for two weeks. I've got so many tours set up, Glenn's sure we're not even going to have time to sleep. But I've been waiting for this.

"You did it!" As usual, I don't hear Glenn come up behind me, but their bear hug is not unexpected. I wish Colby's roommates and Glenn's family could've come, too, but tickets were limited. I grab onto their arms, still crushed around me.

"Yes, I walked across a stage. Go me."

"Not when I meant, star, and you know it." They lower their voice as they lean closer to my ear. "I love watching you sparkle."

I say nothing, but I lean into them. I spot my parents; Chance and Colby are right behind them. I try to wave, but I'm still impeded.

"Do you think you could let go sometime soon? My parents are going to get lost..."

They lift their arm to wave, and since they're tall, my parents spot Glenn right away.

"Problem solved." I can hear the grin in their voice. I turn to face them.

"Did you ever imagine the woman in the spinster shirt would end up making such a mark on your life?"

"Never. But Hil, watching you figure out your melody has been the greatest gift. I'm just happy to sing the harmony."

I tip my head back to give them a quizzical look. "Have you not heard me in the shower?"

"Metaphorical melody."

"That does make more sense. And we found our metaphorical harmony, too, instead of fighting all the time."

"We're amazing."

"No argument here."

I just have time for a short kiss before my family arrives, and then it's hugs all around. My mom's hug is extra long. From here, we're going to the beach together for the weekend, just us. There are tacos, beach walks, thrift shopping, and a pedicure in my future, and I'm thrilled about it. But I'm not thrilled about leaving Glenn.

"You'll be okay while I'm gone?"

Glenn nods. "I'm not your dad."

"Gross. Also, give Lulu the shredded chicken and rice food. We don't like the salmon."

"Hil, you're spoiling her," Glenn complains.

"Oh, gee, Hillary and Glenn are arguing," Colby says drily. "Write down this day in history. Just like every other day."

"It's not an argument; it's a difference of opinion. That salmon food made her gassy," I say, leading them toward the exit.

"Why doesn't she just give it to a goat?" Glenn quips, and when I throw my head back and laugh, the rest of the family smiles at us.

"Let's get out of here before it starts raining."

"That we can agree on." Glenn grins, and hand in hand, we head into our next chapter.

FACE THE MUSIC

CHAPTER ONE

"YOU'RE DOING IT AGAIN." I look up from the piano, but don't stop playing. My best friend stands by the front door of the house we share, hands jammed into the pockets of his green canvas utility jacket. It's the house he grew up in, still full of his mom's knickknacks and school pictures, even though his mom lives elsewhere.

"Doing what?" I ask, even though I already know.

"Playing jazz standards that sound happy, even though the lyrics are melancholy."

"What's wrong with 'Don't Get Around Much Anymore'?" I ask. "It's a classic."

"Nothing," Colby says, shaking his head slowly, "but in combination with 'You Don't Know What Love Is' and 'Cry Me a River,' it's got me a little concerned."

I shift my gaze back to the worn black and white keys, but say nothing.

"Sure you don't want to come out with us?"

I smirk. "So I can watch Darren hit on straight dudes, ladies hit on Tony, and you and Patrick drink in silence?"

"I don't always drink in silence," Colby mutters. "We could play pool. We could dance."

"Chance doesn't mind that?" At the mention of his absent boyfriend's name, Colby's shoulders fall, and I wish I hadn't brought him up.

"No, he doesn't mind," he mumbles, but the way he kicks at the Oriental rug tells me that maybe Colby minds; that even though he has permission, he'd still miss his guy.

"You seem droopy. I'll pass."

Colby sighs. "You can't sugarcoat it at all? Not even a little?"

Uh...that *was* sugarcoating. At least in my mind. I want to tell him if he quit acting like a kicked puppy just because Chance is away for a while, I'd think about it, but I don't want to make him sadder. But some of us have lost our favorite person permanently instead of temporarily, and since the constant comparison is making me a little bitter, it's probably better if I pass on tonight. I reach the end of the song, so I start in on an old song by Peggy March.

"What's that one?"

"It's called 'Leave Me Alone.'"

Colby rolls his eyes, then shuffles to the bottom of the stairs. "Hey! Are we going or what?"

A duet of low voices calls back, and by the time I've finished my song, Darren, Patrick and Colby have noisily trundled out the front door, slamming it behind them, and I'm left with the quiet. Just how I like it. Or, at least, just how I'm used to it these days.

They aren't back yet when the knock comes. I'm just tidying up the kitchen when I hear it. Yes, I'm the kind of man who tidies; I hate coming down to cereal bowls in the morning, stuck with cornflakes and whatever 'heat and eat' food my roommates scrounged up in the night. It's one reason I stay up so late. The other is that I just can't sleep. The knock is tentative, uneven in tempo. You notice that kind of thing when you're a percussionist. Call me a drummer, and you'll be out on your ass, even in the pouring rain, like it is now.

In fact, it's so rainy and windy, even when it comes the second time, I think it's nothing more than the bushes out front tapping on the bay windows. Colby keeps meaning to cut them back, but he's been moping since Chance went to England for six months. I can't blame him; I lost the love of my life three months ago, and I'm still not over it.

But the third knock is desperate, loud, knuckle-bruising, and I take six big steps to the front door and throw it open, ready to run off whatever drunk person has the wrong address.

But the person standing in front of me could not possibly have the wrong address, because he's been here before. He's cooked dinner with us. He's played Risk and watched soccer. He's celebrated birthdays and holidays.

He's slept in my bed.

"What are you doing here?" I ask, but without waiting for an answer, I pull him inside by his canvas jacket sleeve—it's soaked through, and he's dripping on the hardwood floors.

"I didn't know where else to go..." That's when I notice the duffle bag over his shoulder, and my heart goes feral.

"What's going on? Are you okay?"

"Keep it down," he hisses. "You're, like, yelling."

"You're damn right I'm yelling," I fire back. "You can't just show up here in the middle of the night and expect me not to have questions!"

"Don't be melodramatic, it's only 12:30." The way he mumbles does not inspire confidence that everything is okay—and he hasn't even bothered *claiming* that everything is okay, now that I think about it. "You don't even go to bed until 1:00."

"That is *not* the point." I shut the front door, finally, and the quiet house now makes him feel too close and not close enough. *Give him space. Don't make him want to leave.* Whatever's driving him here has to be serious, and I have to force myself to be still instead of pacing.

"Where's Colby?" he asks, looking toward the stairs.

I cross my arms. "Out. Along with everyone else." I can't emphasize enough how terrible he looks: brown eyes rimmed red, dark circles under them. Black hair buzzed short, choppy, like he did it himself without a mirror. Fingernails with chipped blue paint. His clothes look brand new, but they don't fit him right, like he didn't try them on first. And yet, this sopping mess of a person is the one I've been playing songs about, and I couldn't be happier to see him.

"I was hoping I could stay for a few nights," he says, still dripping.

"Of course you can," I say quickly, scowling. "But would you please tell me what's going on?"

"Can I have a towel?"

"You're not answering my question..."

He nods slowly, staring at the rug. "And I don't plan to. So, if that's contingent on me staying here..."

"Still using those big, fancy words," I mutter, but I motion for him to follow me as I start up the front stairs. I pull out my phone and call Colby.

"Change your mind?" he asks over the noise. "We're at The Hatbox." That is more tempting than their original plan, because the music is good there, but there's no way I'd leave him here. Also, I have just realized that I don't know how to explain this situation without using his old name, and I don't know the new one. And now *I'm* missing Chance, because he's trans—maybe he'd have an idea for me. "Ev? You there?"

"Yeah, just a sec." I am totally stalling as we arrive at the bathroom and I pull a towel out of the cupboard. "Sorry. Our favorite Timbers fan will be spending the night tonight." It's the only way I can think of to describe him that Colby will definitely know. And when I glance at him, a grace note of a smile crosses his face before it's hidden under the towel.

"Oh, reeeeaallyyy?" If my cringe isn't outward, I don't know how.

"Stop being a gay cliche," I say, my voice low, stepping into the hall and closing the door before Colby can do any more damage. "It's not like that."

"I am *bisexual*!" Colby yells. "No erasure!"

"Okay, whatever you're drinking, it's stronger than you think it is, so I'm gonna ask you to switch to water for a bit. Who's driving?"

"We did a ride share. Best. Choice. Ever."

"Good, I didn't want to come get you. Have fun, and I'll text you the details for when you sober up."

"Coolio. Love you, man."

"I love you too."

"No, I really mean it, though. I love you. Like, love you love you."

"Me too, bud. Be safe." When I hang up and turn around, he's right behind me.

"What did he say? Can I stay?"

"I already said you could!"

When he rolls his eyes, I can see the whites of them. "It's not your house, Ev."

"Friends stay over all the time, L–" I stop before his birth name pops out. "I actually don't know what to call you."

He frowns for a moment. "We're friends, aren't we? I thought we ended things amicably."

"Yes, shit. I'm fucking this up. I meant your new first name, if you picked one."

"Oh." His expression clears, and he gives a shrug. "I've been leaning toward Andrew."

He must have taken off that soaked jacket and hung it in the bathroom, because I can hear it dripping on the tile. The air up here is warm, but it smells like the rain he brought inside. The only light is coming from behind him, and he's shifting his weight nervously, his hips swaying, just like they were when I first met him in a club with a pathetic name like Germ. That's the five seconds I got to decide if I like that name on the person I love.

"Andrew is good. It's nice. Not too...you know, out there." Mentally, I rehearse his family now: Nick, Roselani, Grace, Mark, James, Luke, and Andrew. It really does sound nice. It fits.

"Well, with a last name like Kahananui, I thought I'd make it easy on people."

"You don't have to. Make it easy on them. It's about you and what fits. And if you change your mind, just tell me, and Andrew is out." I point down the empty hallway. "And if any of those assholes give you a hard time, just let me know, and I'll take care of it. You–"

"Ev. Chill. You're not my protector anymore, remember?"

He's staring at me, and all I can do is stare back, my heart a melted glut of regrets and wants and needs, like some kind of sculpture that didn't quite work out, now solidified, immoveable. I'm just going to be stuck this way forever, aren't I? Hopeless and in love? Because I'm sorry, but I will be his protector forever.

"Right. Sorry. I..." I start down the hall the wrong way, then double back. "Tony's out of town. I guess I can put you in his room?"

"The couch is fine..."

I cross my arms. "You really want to sleep in the basement?"

Andrew glares at me, because I already know the answer. Plenty of people sleep down there, since it's a futon. But it aggravated his asthma the last time he did...the time we fell asleep down there, just talking. We'd talked all night. These things happen when you meet the most interesting person in the universe.

"I don't want anyone going to any hassle for me."

"Therefore, you'll refuse to sleep in an open bed, forcing people to tiptoe around in the morning. Yeah, that makes sense."

He's still glaring.

"Well, I'm tired. So I'm gonna change the sheets on Tony's bed, then I'm gonna go to sleep. Feel free to sleep there. Or in the bathtub. Or in the creepy basement. Totally your call."

Grumbling under his breath, he follows me down the hall. "You're the absolute worst."

His face has a poked bear quality, so I decide to put down my proverbial stick and just let him be. He's obviously been through something tonight. I desperately wish I knew what it was. The pang in my chest gets stronger when he sinks into the high-backed wooden chair in the corner like he can't stand up anymore. He's silent as I change the sheets, opting for some light blue ones. Tony's not the kind to get mad that we used his room; once upon a time, he needed to crash here himself. He'll understand, but I still text him in case he comes home early.

"I can't put you in Susan and Chris's room without talking to them first. But maybe Colby can call them tomorrow. I think they might be planning a trip soon..." When he says nothing, I turn to look—and he's asleep. He's bent his arm, resting it on the back of the chair, and laid his head on it like a pillow. It looks spectacularly uncomfortable, and I want to reach out and touch the fawn velvet of his face, count each dot of the light spray of freckles across his big nose. They come from his grandpa Barry—I've seen pictures, but never met him before we broke up. They spend the cold part of the year in Hawaii, in the same town they grew up in. My gut still churning with a weird concoction of emotions, I kneel and carefully untie his soaked Converse, tugging them off with his white tube socks. His jeans are still wet, too, where his coat didn't cover...but I obviously can't take those off. Even I know I can't undress my ex without permission. I stand up, contemplating whether I can successfully carry him to the bed when he stirs.

"What?"

"You fell asleep."

He rubs at his face blearily, and I pull back the covers, gesturing to suggest he get into the bed. He stumbles during the few steps it takes to get there, mumbling something incoherent, then falls face first into the pillow. Andrew's asleep again before I can even get him all the way in, his legs trailing behind him. I lift his legs to help him the rest of the way, then cover him up. On my way out, I turn out the light and close the door, taking one last peek at him, but he's out cold.

And I am officially worried.

CHAPTER TWO

IT IS MORNING, I THINK. I don't know. At some point, when you've been lying awake all night, time blurs, like a drumroll fading out. There was no reason for him to come to my door, but I still sat up all night every time the floor creaked outside my room. And since my room is right next to the bathroom, that's often. I sat up at 12:45 when he went in there and brushed his teeth with the spare toothbrush I put out for him. I sat up at 1:10 when my roommates came home, mildly inebriated, stumbling down the hall. And whoever had the audacity to take a shower at 1:34 is gonna hear about it from me in the morning. Normally, it wouldn't be a big deal; I sleep like the dead. I mean, I used to. Before. I could never fall asleep without music, but once I was out, it was until morning. But with my door open, it doesn't seem like a good idea.

I think I must doze for a while until 6:30, when Pat's door closes quietly. I sit up again, and our gazes meet as he passes my open door, pausing quizzically as he puts in his wireless headphones.

"Why's your door open?"

I shrug, slumping back down into bed. "Wanted fresh air, I guess."

"Really." It's not a question. If anything, it's an indictment of how badly my brain works after tossing and turning for hours. And it shows on his face as his gaze now narrows to slits.

"Yep." I stretch and yawn, trying to act casual.

"Tony back? Door's closed."

"No. Not him. There's someone else in there. For a while."

Patrick is known for many things, but patience is not one of them, and apparently, he's fed up with me, because he stares at me for a moment, then continues down the hall without a word. I cover my head with my down comforter, and suddenly, I am confronted with how bad I smell; stress does that to me. *Gee, why would I be stressed? Just because the person I'm still in love with is sleeping down the hall, after coming here out of desperation he wouldn't share with me?* I decide to get up and shower in case we run into each other at breakfast. No, that's too weird. He'll know that's not normal. Besides, I should go running, and then I'd be showering twice. My only choice is to reek. I sniff myself again, then remove the comforter in disgust. *No, my only choice is to shower, or I risk offending everyone in this house.*

The hot water revives me a little, even though it should probably be cold with where my mind is going. *He'll be using this shower in a few hours. Naked. Wet. Touching his skin, luxuriating in this hot water...* Speaking of touching, my hand has somehow found its way to my stiff cock. I lean against the shower wall, my feet braced against the tub. This wouldn't be my first choice for getting off, but if I'm going to continue the charade of keeping my door open...I close my eyes, letting the water hit my back so my hand stays soapy, and I think about the last time we were together.

*Long, dark hair tickling my chest, clever fingers play-
ing around my ribs, urging me to sit up. Sinking down
on my cock, forcing me to hold that beautiful brown gaze,
bossy fingers on my chin, hungry kisses keeping me in the
moment as I caress chest and ass and thighs...*I come hard
a minute later, but it's marbled with guilt, because I'm
still getting off to the old him. That's what got me into
this mess. My cock is barely satisfied; it's been like this
for months. It's like my cock knows he's right down the
hall.

It's only 7:00 by the time I get out, but I'm too
freaked out to sleep again. It's time to do a little digging.
Finally closing my door all the way, I give myself a little
eye roll before I turn on my laptop. Sitting at the desk
feels like a *task*, so I curl up in bed on my side with it.
To my surprise, his Tracebook page still shows him with
long, dark hair and his birth name. Huh. We broke up
three months ago, and my impression was that he intended to transition right away. But he really only kept a
social media account so he could spy on people he went
to high school with, so maybe this is an outlier. I believe
that right up until his Tweeter account loads, and it's the
same, only this time, he's drinking beer from a plastic
cup, hair pulled back under his pristine Timbers baseball
cap, and he looks a shade more like he does now, except
for the makeup.

I touch the picture without thinking, and it gets bigger. Those eyes. They wrecked me from the moment I
met him, noticed him across the room at the concert. He
grabbed me and shook me with it, holding my gaze even

when it was obvious I was checking him out. He flaunt-ed his curves back then, his skin-tight tank top low over the chest and high around the middle. I read it as con-fidence instead of what it was—compensation. A mask. A disguise. The highest heels, the darkest eye makeup, all of it. He was trying so desperately to be something he wasn't. And when he decided to stop trying, he trust-ed me enough to be honest with me, and I pushed him away.

Gently. I told him I was proud of him, which sounds so hollow now, knowing I withheld the support he really needed. I told him it seemed like it fit him, and that wasn't a lie. But when he pressed me to predict what this would do to our relationship, I...choked. Up until that moment, I don't think I actually knew we were in a Relationship with a capital R—I was just spending all my time with someone I really liked. He said he'd give me space. We didn't talk for a few days. That turned in-to a week. Then two. And then—rightfully so—he was done waiting. Once he was gone and I realized what I'd done...no words could make it right. I wrote a dozen emails I deleted, trying to apologize, trying to explain myself. Even now, I don't know what to say. Because I had no clue he was thinking about gender before he dropped that bomb.

My phone pings. It's his big sister.

Grace: (Andrew) didn't come home last night, do you know where (he) is.
Evan: Nope

Because she didn't say Andrew, she said the old name, the one he had when I met him. Nobody by that name here. And even if there was, there's no way in hell that I'm outing his location until I know more about the situation. My heart is beating faster now, saying *fix it, fix it, fix it*, like there's any way I could. But I won't make it worse, either.

> **Grace**: If you see (him), will you let me know?

> **Evan**: Did something happen?

> **Grace**: I wasn't here, but Zara and Hannah had some kind of blowup with (him). Not sure what it was about, no one's talking.

If he came home with that *G.I. Jane* haircut and came out to them and it went badly...that might do it. I'm pacing now without meaning to, and I pull out coffee and pop a pod in the machine to help me focus. Grace might be using his dead name in good faith, then. Maybe she really doesn't know. That eases my irritation a little, but it also puts me in an awkward spot. Because I can't write back without using names or pronouns.

Okay, he's here. Oh, you didn't know he's a he? Oops.

Yes, Andrew came by last night, distraught. Who's Andrew? Oh.

"Yikes," I mutter aloud, still staring at the screen.

"You all right?" Colby's voice makes me jump, and I quickly stuff my phone into the back pocket of my jeans.

"You're up early."

"I've got a—" He lets out an immense yawn. "A wedding this morning. Around ten."

I shook my head. "People are hiring a sound guy for their weddings now?"

"Oh, yeah. Gotta make sure they can hear the audio on the video." He waves a hand as he steals my coffee. "It's a whole thing."

"Hey. That was *mine*."

He smirks as he takes a sip. "I need it more."

"You know, for my best friend, you're kind of a jerk."

"That hurts," Col says, putting a hand on his bare, mostly hairless chest over his heart. "That cuts me to the quick. First you won't come out with us, now name calling. And in my wounded state."

I cough out a laugh. "Because Chance is gone? Is that the wound?"

"Obviously." He takes another sip of the coffee, which seems to animate him in front of my eyes. "As my friend, you should want to support me in this difficult time."

"Mm-hmm," I hum, opening the cupboard to get out another coffee pod. "Well, I'll try to be more consid—" I scream. I'm not proud of it, but I did. Because instead of a coffee pod, my hand touched something fuzzy with legs. Now, let me assure you that it was a perfectly average scream, even if it was uneven and came to kind of a strange crescendo. Colby, having spit out his coffee into the thankfully nearby sink rather than choke on it, is now wiping tears of laughter off his face. Because once again, I have fallen prey to their ridiculous game. I pick up the rubber spider and throw it at Colby.

"I fucking hate that thing!" He's still laughing. Still. That's when Andrew shuffles into the kitchen; apparently, my shout has not roused the rest of them.

"Hey."

He's wearing the same clothes as last night, and my heart sags. Does he not have any other clothes? What's in that duffle bag, anyway? *Fix it, fix it, fix it,* my heart pounds louder. He used to tell me *everything.*

"Hey," Colby says, immediately putting down his mug and approaching him with his arms out. But when Andrew visibly stiffens, Colby's smart enough to stop. He lets his arms drop awkwardly to his side, then gestures toward the stove. "Do you want some breakfast? We were just..."

"Yeah. Sure." Andrew's gaze shifts to me, and just like across that fucking club, it ignites, like heat lightning across a desert sky. Then I blink, and he's looking at Colby again. "Can I talk to you for a minute? In private?"

Don't shut me out. Please say no. Please be an actual jerk and make him tell me what's going on here in the kitchen. You can still trust me. Please...

"Sure. Of course." Colby gestures toward the back door, and they both shuffle off that way. Colby gives me a *chill* look over his shoulder, and it just makes me more anxious. I turn back to my coffee attempt and jam another pod into the machine. It works serenely, and it just makes me madder. I throw myself into cooking breakfast, cracking eggs and digging bacon out of the freezer that probably belongs to someone else, but I'll figure out who and pay him back later. Andrew likes bacon. That's all I can think about right now. I'm adding cheese and chives to them, like they do at Marble, even though it is flagrantly over the top for someone who's crashing with us. Except this someone isn't just anyone.

What could they be talking about for so long? Does he need money? He's just finishing up school to be a history teacher, but I never got the sense that it was that important to him, just something to do. To fill time. And it made his parents happy, even though teachers get paid like shit. *Did someone hurt him? If so, I will be forced to do something about it.* What? I don't know yet, but it depends on who it was and what they did. I can help. I can do *something.*

I survey the kitchen. I've made way too much food, but I make him a cup of hot chocolate anyway in the machine. It's just finishing as they come back inside. Andrew looks like he's been crying, and he heads directly up the back staircase.

"What the fuck is going on?" I whisper-yell at my best friend, who's already holding up his hands. He shouldn't worry; I can't kill him until I hear about their conversation.

"You should ask him. I know it's complicated...ooh, is that bacon?"

I slap his hand away from the platter. "That's for Andrew."

His eyes widen. "All of it?"

"As much as he wants," I snap back. "But he's got first crack at it." I'm grabbing the platter and cocoa to take with me before I can think about it, and I stalk through the hall to the back stairs, vaulting myself up it two at a time. *Stop and think,* my brain pleads, but I ignore it. There's not enough coffee or calories in my system yet for it to be fully online, so I'm running the Pure Instinct™ back-up program. My hands are too full to knock effectively when I reach his closed door, but I try with one knuckle, sloshing hot liquid on my hand. *That's gonna hurt when I practice this afternoon.*

"Go away, Evan." His voice is thick, but firm, and I want to hold him so badly. I know my physical comfort is unwanted, so I'm not going to try; if he needs to be here, then I won't make it harder. But I'm desperate to make it easier, and this is all I can think of.

"Should I leave the hot chocolate and bacon or take them with me?"

There's a pause, during which my heart fills in the silence with its kick drum impression, but it's rushing the tempo. Then I hear his footsteps, and I force my feet to stay where they are when he opens the door.

"There's eggs, too, downstairs," I say, afraid he's going to tell me to leave to my face. His eyes look haunted, wary, and it's killing me. "I can bring you up some."

"Not hungry." He already looks like he's lost weight, but maybe his clothes are just hanging differently now with the binder on. I didn't notice it last night with his coat on.

"So...take them back?" I ask, gesturing back down the hall, and his lips form a flat line.

"This isn't going to work."

"What isn't?" I ask with an innocence I don't entirely feel. At least he's talking to me now.

"You. Baiting me to come out." He crosses his arms, making his chest stand out more, and leans against the door frame. I'm just relieved he didn't say "me staying here."

"Who's baiting? Breakfast is the most important meal of the day. I like breakfast. I remember you liking breakfast." I try and fail not to think about the time we took our breakfast upstairs and fed each other in bed like the lovesick fools we were. He bites his lip, and oh God, it's such a good thing my hands are full so I don't already have both palms on his cheeks, my soft lips pressed against his chapped ones, giving the bottom one a little nip myself, walking him back toward Tony's rumpled bed behind him, drinking him in the whole way. His dark gaze narrows on my face, and he wordlessly takes the platter and the mug, then toes the door shut again.

"You're welcome," I call, trying to recover my lost dignity. When I turn, Patrick is staring at me again. "What?"

Shaking his head, he goes into the bathroom. I go back downstairs to eat cold eggs with my roommates, who are probably grumpy that they can smell bacon but didn't get any.

CHAPTER THREE

ANDREW SPENDS MOST of the day in Tony's room, and I can't blame him. I knock again around lunchtime, but there's no answer. So after I finish my concert run through, playing video games with Colby until my curtain call is a good distraction.

"Your dads weren't married, right?" It's a weird question to ask during Call of Duty, but hey, he's my best friend.

"Not when I was little, no." He already knows my dads conceived me with the help of my Aunt Cathie, who was blessedly willing to carry the weird baby their friends had made through IVF. They went to all this trouble to mix their sperm and find an egg donor, and I came out looking exactly like Nico, so I guess we know whose stuff was stronger. Greg was never gonna win that fight against his "Italian stallion." His words. They're both gross.

"Were you ever...worried about it?"

"Um." I take out a sniper. "Not...really? It wasn't even legal until I was fourteen."

"Oh. Right."

He throws a grenade to get the doors open, and we both head inside.

"But they had legal power-of-attorney documents and stuff. They showed them to me once. I'm fairly sure it was because they'd been arguing a lot. That was the year my best friend's parents got divorced, and I think I asked too many questions about it and made them nervous."

"Huh." He's quiet for too long, and I know he's thinking. "Just—like, maybe I don't even need to propose to Chance."

"That's what you're worried about? Dude, he's gonna say yes!" I knew he was thinking about it—he's going to visit him for the first time next month.

"But maybe we're beyond that as a society, you know? Maybe marriage is archaic. And by not getting married, it's actually, you know, better."

"Better for who?" I'm not paying attention and get shot. Damn it.

"You know," he waves one hand distractedly. "Everyone. Society. The world."

"You know what I think?"

"Tell me."

"This is the same problem you had before you were dating. Colby doesn't want to put himself out there. He just wants to have fun and not think about the future."

"That's not it at all." He calmly takes out three enemy soldiers. "Seriously. I am thinking about the future. A lot." He sighs. "I don't want to lose him."

"And how is telling him you want to be together until you die going to make you lose him?"

"Maybe it would scare him off. It's kind of a serious thing, right? I mean, it's more than just being together. Marriage is like financial crap and maybe parenting and...taxes."

"But Chance would probably love doing your taxes."

He pauses the game and rubs his chin. "He did, actually. He already did them for me."

"Are you guys thinking about kids?" I sincerely hope so. As an only child, he's my only chance at nieces and nephews. Except for Sadie, Patrick's niece, but she's sort of a niece by proxy.

"A little," he admits, and now he's rubbing the back of his neck, his face pink. "Not any time soon, just...yeah. A little."

"Col, if he's talking about kids with you, he's ready to get married. It's legal now. You can't use my dads as an excuse. If they could've gotten married, I think they would have."

When he doesn't say anything, I keep going.

"And you know what? Screw society. If you want to lock it down and Chance is up for it, give in to that possessive caveman feeling and put a ring on it. Frankly, I think you'd both sleep better at night."

He restarts the game, but his words are quiet. "Yeah, I think we would, too."

"And then, next time he goes somewhere fancy, you can go with him."

Colby laughs. "How much money do you think academics make?"

I wave away his question. "You're a sound wizard. Wizards can find work wherever."

"I'll keep that in mind." When it seems like the conversation is over, I respawn my character.

"Did you..." Colby's doing that goofy, one lifted shoulder thing he does when he wants to ask a question, but he's not sure if he should. "Never mind."

Now I'm curious, though. "No. Ask me."

"Did you want to marry Andrew? You know, before?" The question hits me in the gut.

"I..." My voice falters, even as my fingers deftly weave my character in and out of the corridors, looking for the enemy. I'm looking around the house, too, but he's still upstairs as far as I know. "I don't know. Maybe."

"You didn't talk about it?"

The memory hits me like a real grenade. Because I didn't realize what he was trying to say at the time...

"Can't you ever see yourself putting on the white dress for somebody?" I asked, licking the hot sauce off my fingers. We were sitting in the backyard in slouchy lawn chairs in an attempt to get some privacy from the rest of them, watching summer shiver into fall.

"No." (He) reached for the last wing. "It wouldn't suit me."

"Marriage or the dress?"

"Can I have a wipe, please?" (He) waited until I passed (him) one, then cleaned (his) fingers in a more polite way. But there was an intensity to it I didn't understand.

"Did I say something wrong?"

"No," (he) muttered. "Just...if I ever do get married, I want to be myself, you know?"

"Being someone else is an option?" I laughed. Because I am a tone-deaf asshole and a completely incompetent partner.

(He) stood up, brushing off his backside. "I'm gonna head home."

"Wait, what?" I'm not going to lie—I was hurt. We'd planned to hang out all night. (He) was going to sleep over. And all I could see in that moment was my chance to get laid slipping away. "Are you mad? Seriously, what did I say?"

"Nothing." (He) fucking smiled at me. "Don't think those wings are settling right, that's all. My stomach hurts."

But it's my stomach that hurts now—maybe my heart, too—thinking about all the hints he was trying to drop that I probably missed. Openings for conversations I didn't know he wanted to start. There was so fucking much I didn't know.

I recount the story for Colby, and he whistles, low. "He must have known then."

"Yeah, when he told me, he said he'd been thinking about it for a long time."

"Chance did, too. Ever since he was a kid."

"I don't think it was that long, but I'm not sure."

"You didn't ask?"

"No, I was kind of...in shock." I pause, feeling myself sink back into that moment, holding him in bed, letting the warmth of his body against mine ground me when he started speaking words that did not make sense at first. "Not that it's about me."

"I mean, it's a little bit about you. It affected your relationship a lot."

"No, it's about Andrew and what he needs. He was right to leave me." I spent those two weeks after he told me doing a lot of reading. Long threads on Tweeter that all had the same gist: "no time for cis tears." But there were things I loved about him that I was going to miss. I couldn't find a way around that, and therefore, I couldn't find a way forward.

"But how are people supposed to stay together if they're not allowed to *process* the change?" Colby says, irritated. "You're supposed to just jump on board immediately?"

"I wish I had. I wouldn't have lost him." I haven't ever said that out loud, and I don't feel any better now that I have. I keep one eye on the front door in case someone comes through it so I can shut up quick.

"But it wouldn't have been honest. Your relationship wouldn't have made it. You both had complicated feelings about it, I'm sure. You both needed to be able to work things out. If Chance hadn't already transitioned, I would've needed some time to get used to the idea."

"If I'd just met Andrew two years from now, maybe we'd have had a shot. Sometimes I'm jealous that you got Chance fully formed."

Colby smirks at that. "And yet, he's still a work in progress. It was really hard for him to leave because of his anxiety. He's working through that. So I don't think I've actually met someone who's fully formed."

I hadn't thought of it that way. This conversation has been...a lot. Enlightening, but a lot. My character dies again because I'm not really paying attention, so I stand up. "You want anything?"

"Fizzy water."

"What kind?"

"Any kind. My throat's dry from imparting all that wisdom to you."

"Oh, is that what it was?"

"Yes," he says solemnly. "It only *sounded* like I was making shit up."

Seems like he's ready to move on, but I'm not. "You gonna ask him, then?"

He stares at the screen for a minute, then a smile breaks over his face. "Yeah, I am."

CHAPTER FOUR

IT DOESN'T OCCUR TO me to invite Andrew to the basketball game until I see him standing there, arms crossed over this chest, listening to the other guys shoot the shit. It's their standard thing, standing around trash talking until everyone arrives. But Drew (Drew? Yeah, Drew feels like a good nickname. He's sure as hell not an Andy.) isn't saying a word.

Come on. You can dish it out with the best of them. I know you can. He used to tease me mercilessly, and I loved it. *Just open your sweet mouth and let them have it.*

But he doesn't. Why can't he hear my silent encouragement? Aren't we telepathically connected after all this time? We should be. He could tease me all day without ever saying a word, and I'd love it.

I bump his shoulder like it's an accident as I walk up to the group. He glares at me, dark eyes flashing, and I grin. *There you are. Found you.*

And like he hears me this time, his shoulders drop.

"Did we already choose up sides? I call the new guy."

"Funny," Colby says, checking me the ball, "before you got here, he said, 'Don't pair me up with that loser.'"

"Ouch," I say, clinging to my chest with my free hand. "I'm wounded. That hurts."

"I didn't say that," he mutters, looking away. "Are we going to play or what?"

"Same teams as last time," Colby calls, "except you get Andrew since you're down Chance." I'm not sure it's really a fair trade: Chance plays like he has something to prove, and he's scrappy. Drew looks nervous AF, like he's trying not to make waves. I know he played soccer as a kid; classic, if I'm not mistaken. That's the kind where they let you slide tackle and you have to travel more for games. That's the fire I'd like to see him bring to this game...and there's only one way I know to bring it out of him: trash talk.

"Tony's gone, too, though," I say. "So he should be yours."

"What, you don't want me?" Drew snarks, and the others laugh.

"I mean, I *have* seen you play, so..." Now they're *oooh*-ing, and Drew's gaze is narrowed when I check. *Oh, game on.* The first time he throws an elbow in my direction, it doesn't seem personal—we were both going for the rebound, after all. But when he blatantly goes for my balls with his knee, I catch it before he makes contact.

"This is a low-contact sport, in case you forgot," I hiss, and he smiles. And why does that make me feel like I just won the solo and ensemble competition in high school again? Somehow, I keep ending up guarding him...I could swear my annoying-ass roommates are guarding other people on purpose, but maybe I'm imagining things. They're not below that, though. If they try to tell you they are, don't believe it. But to my everlasting relief, they're not treating him with kid gloves. They're treating him like a guy, patting his butt when he nails a three-pointer (how did I not know he could do that?), shoving him when he's crowding them...wait. I don't think I like that after all.

When Patrick checks him too hard, the ball hits him in the chest. His wince is obvious; being bound like that, his chest must already hurt like a mother.

"Hey!" I bark, and everyone turns to look at me. Only I can't embarrass him. And he made it clear I'm not his protector. So I cover. "Is that a hawk?" I ask, pointing up at the sky, and Colby, to his credit, is the only one who doesn't look, deciding to smirk at me instead.

"Why are you pointing out birds?" Patrick asks, eyebrows drawn in confusion. "Is this a pastime you've recently taken up? I wasn't aware you were interested in avian life. You can come to the Audubon society with Sadie and me. We–"

"No, I'm good, thanks. Are we going to play or what?"

"You're the one who—" The others cut Patrick off, because we know how long this can go on. I'll explain it to him later, I guess. Half an hour in, we take a water break. I'm sweating and winded, but not as bad as Drew, who looks like he is going to die.

"Doing okay there, sport?"

"Do *not* call me *sport* like I'm some twelve-year-old in your Webelos pack. I am a grown-ass man." I do not take the bait to look at his ass. I am not that knuckle-headed. I want to, but I don't.

"Of course you are," I coo. "That's why you're here, getting trounced by me."

"Ten points down is not *trounced*." He's not drinking. Then I realize why—he didn't bring a bottle. It's not hot out, being in the middle of January, but I still can't help thinking about how thirsty he must be...

"Here, let me give you every advantage to beat me. Not that you will." I hold up the bottle at an angle, the squirting part poised to do just that into his mouth. He has a thing about mouth germs; he rarely shared food with me when we were together, even though I put my mouth basically everywhere on his body. Come to think of it, maybe that's why he didn't. He looks confused for a moment, and I think I've made a mistake, and he's about to reject me here in the park, where I will have to relive this moment every Thursday. And every time we bring Patrick's niece Sadie down here to play. And every time I run with Patrick. My brain is so busy accumulating tiny traumas that I don't notice right away that he's tipped his head back, his distracting, pink, lush mouth open. So when I squeeze, my aim is...off.

"Bastard!" He splutters with a laugh. "I should've known." Without thinking, I lift the edge of my shirt and move to wipe his face, but he shoves me away.

"I didn't mean to, I swear." The way I can hardly get the words out through my laughter is not convincing. "I'm sorry."

"Oh, right. Sure. I'm sure you didn't."

"I really didn't!" I say, still chuckling. I hold out the bottle. "Do you need payback?"

Drew eyes the bottle like this is still some kind of trick, so I lift it higher insistently.

"No, but I would take an actual drink…"

I toss him the bottle. "It's all yours."

"Hey," Colby says, walking over to Drew. "Tony's coming back soon, so I wanted to talk to you about sleeping arrangements."

Not your business. Walk away, my brain prompts, but it is a very silly brain, because there's no way in hell I'm doing that.

"There's no reason for you to leave," Colby goes on, "but the futon in the basement is the best we can offer you right now, I'm afraid. Normally, I'd move you to the guest house, but my parents are coming in soon."

"No, it's fine," he says quickly. "The futon is great. And I also wanted to talk to you about…"

No, it's not, my brain screams, having apparently forgotten that it tried to extricate us from this conversation. *He has asthma. It's musty and gross down there. He should sleep upstairs with me.* Wait. Update: what I thought was my brain might actually be another body part. Instead of saying things out loud, I am simply staring daggers at Drew, and I think our psychic connection is still good, because he draws Colby away from me so they can finish their talk without me. Is he leaving? Staying? Both sound intolerable, to be honest.

Who's the bastard now?

CHAPTER FIVE

IT'S A TYPICAL JANUARY day when several of us sit down with Colby. If it was a planned meeting to help him plan his proposal, I missed the memo, but it is the kind of day that just lends itself to introspection: overcast, sprinkling on and off, and cold enough that I'm wearing wool socks against the chill of the hardwood floors.

"So," I say, clapping my hands together, "what have you got so far?"

Colby flips through a notebook that appears to have lyrics and the start of a melody and lots of notes about England.

"Not much."

I peer over to see better. "But you're writing him a song?"

"I don't know, maybe?" Colby sighs. "I'm going to screw this up. I just know it. Maybe I'm rushing things. Maybe I should wait until he gets back."

"Dude," Darren says, leaning forward, letting his beer drop between his knees. "No. Proposing in England is romantic. He'll like it. You gotta lock it down while they're missing you the most."

"Wow, that's incredibly cynical," I say, sipping my beer. I'm not sure how our Friday night hangout has turned into helping Colby plan his proposal, but they all seem willing to help. "But I agree you should go for it. You guys are disgustingly perfect for each other."

"How long until you fly out?" Andrew asks, his voice quiet. This is the first time he's come out of his room today, and I'm trying to ignore him so I don't scare him away. Or annoy him away? Is that a thing? I'm sure I could make it a thing.

"Three weeks," Colby says, rubbing his forehead, and he leaves a smudge of graphite on it from his pencil. "I was supposed to go in December, but it didn't work out."

"And he was the saddest little muffin on Christmas," I add, earning me a smack. "I don't know why you didn't go to Thailand."

"Hillary wanted to spend it with Glenn and their family, and I didn't want to go by myself. That's a long flight. And I'm not good at shit like Customs." I don't point out that he'll still have to do both those things, because it's probably more palatable with the promise of sex on the other side.

"Are you going to take him somewhere?" Darren asks, shifting back to the original conversation. Someone put music on—Patrick, I think—and it's a vibe; the percussion is so crisp and clean. I didn't notice it before now. But music is always nicer than TV. That's just a fact. That's why I fall asleep to music.

"There's an art museum that's got a little restaurant on the roof. I thought that might be nice..." Colby groans. "If I wait long enough, maybe he'll just ask me."

"Anxiety Guy? Not too likely..." I say, pulling the notebook out of his hands, but he snatches it back before I can see anything. "I'm just trying to help!"

"There's also some kind of castle nearby his university," Tony said, squinting at his phone. "I think you could walk there. Where does he live?"

Everyone's pulling out their phones then, except for me and Andrew. With everyone distracted, I can't help but stare. He's got dark circles under his eyes; he's never slept well, but this seems like more than usual. His shoulders are rolled forward; he's practically hiding in those giant clothes. Is he borrowing them from someone? Did he buy them? I wouldn't have thought flannel was his style...my Hawaiian guy never thought dressing to the weather was all that important.

"What do you think?" Colby asks, turning to me.

"About the castle?"

"No, about the cocktail cruise up the river. Come on, Ev. Focus."

"I am focused," I say, finally dropping my gaze from Andrew's face. "Do you have a ring?"

Colby flips through his notebook pages. "That...was not on my list. How am I supposed to pick a ring? Wait, why do I need a ring if we're just getting engaged? Isn't that for our wedding day?"

"Some guys wear them on their right hand before they get married, then switch 'em," Darren offers, and Colby mutters something under his breath about not being in the budget.

"I'll go with you tomorrow if you want. Help you pick something out."

My friend's shoulders drop. "Yeah?"

"Of course. I'll even buy lunch."

Patrick stands up, glares at me, then stalks into the kitchen.

"What's his deal?"

"He's mad you stole his bacon last week," Tony says through a bite of cereal, which is apparently his dinner. "And we didn't even get any."

Andrew's eyes widen comically. "You didn't share *any* with them?"

I wave a careless hand. "I'll replace it. I just haven't been to the store yet." I tap out a syncopated beat on my thighs...nervous habit.

"You'd better!" he shouts from the kitchen. "I mean it, Rhodes!"

"Pat, I'm so sorry," Andrew says when he reappears. "I had no idea."

"Oh, I'm not blaming *you*," he says, his voice growly. I roll my eyes. After four years, I've learned that he's more bark than bite. And more than that, he's a huge romantic at heart. I know he gets why I needed it.

"I said I'd replace it!"

"Should've asked first. That's the rule," Colby says, but his voice is vacant, and when I glance over, he's still looking at his notebook. He erases something and writes something else, and I think he's playing around with the lyrics again. Chance better not break his heart, that's all I can say. There's some serious softness to my best friend deep down, and I don't want to see that get squished.

"Oh, and speaking of things we should all know—Andrew's staying for a while, so the basement is officially occupied. If you were planning to use it and you've got people coming, just let me know and we'll figure something out."

There's lots of friendly nods and fist bumps and welcoming smiles from the rest of them, but all I can do is sit there, cold. Because if he's not moving back in with his roommates, things must be really bad. It's not just a want—I *need* details. I *need* to know what's happening here or I can't help him fix things. Because as much as I'm glad he's safe here, it's also a unique form of torture—for both of us, I'm sure. He probably wouldn't be here unless he literally had nowhere else to go, and that kills me.

I stare at him, challenging him to meet my gaze, but he's focused on everyone else but me.

"How long do you think you'll be here?" I blurt out, and the rest of them fall quiet.

"Ev..." Colby warns, but I don't care. I need to know how long this is going to go on. I need to set expectations for my poor heart. I have important moping to get back to, after all.

Andrew finally looks at me, and his eyebrows snap together. "If you don't want me here, I can—"

"I didn't say that. I just asked how long. A week? A month?"

"As long as he needs to be," Colby says, and there's a bite to the words. As if *I'm* the one being ridiculous, not my ex, who wants to come *live with me.*

"I'm looking for a job now. I'll know more once I find one."

He finally meets my gaze when I nod. *Lost.* He has none of the bravado and sheer moxie he used to wear around like a crown. Which, as it turns out, was all a lie. Him pretending. But he's not pretending now, and my heart fucking breaks at the meekness, the shame in his gaze.

"Sorry, I..." I don't know what I'm apologizing for, but I do. I feel so damn sorry. I can't even say how much—the feeling overwhelms, burning all the words out of my brain. "Stay as long as you want, of course."

He gives me half a smirk. "The free welcome bacon does give me a reason."

"That's a one-time thing," I say, and Patrick stomps out again. "And I said I'm sorry!" Grumpy bastard.

But the real question isn't how long he's staying. It's how I'm going to live with him indefinitely without losing my heart to him all over again.

MY WEEKEND IS FULL of performances (two evening and a matinee), so I don't see him again for a few days. I thought he'd go to church, but he's still around on Sunday morning when I leave. I'm still jumpy, but I manage to sleep a little more than usual, probably just because I'm still wiped from that first night, plus work. On Monday, Tony takes him to work at Marble; they're always short-handed. And they always seem to have free food around at the restaurant, so that's a plus for his budget. Why am I thinking about his budget? Great question. I am thinking about it because I can't get him off my mind. I can't keep avoiding him if he's going to live here for a while, but he's got a cough, and it does make it easier to know where he is in the house.

On Tuesday, he's on the couch, scrolling on his phone as I leave for symphony practice, and I pause.

"Got plans for today?"

"No, Mom."

Okay, so *not* ready for me to check in with him. Got it. I turn and head for the front door silently.

"Sorry, that was...bitchy."

"A little," I say, turning back slowly with half a smile pulling at my mouth. I anchor my hands to the strap across my chest, holding my bag to my back, wedging my fingers under the weight of it. "Didn't think I was allowed to use that word for you anymore."

Drew cocks his head a little. "Which word?"

"Bitchy. That doesn't fit your gender expression."

"Well, if the attitude fits. I obviously couldn't think of a better one, either."

"It doesn't make you dysphoric?"

"Not today," he says, pulling his knees up and giving them a hug. Basically, I put the poor man in the fetal position just by saying "dysphoric." I wish Chance was here for the tenth time this week, because I am clearly failing at basic conversation with the man. And more than that, I wish Drew's body language matched his words. I hate that he's lying to me.

"Well, good. You can always let me know if I cross a line. I don't want—I mean, I want you to feel comfortable here."

Andrew snorts, but his shoulders drop a bit, even as he squeezes his fingers tighter against his shins. It's on the tip of my tongue to ask about school, but that didn't go over great a minute ago, so I bite it back. And I'm aware that I'm going to be late if I don't get going.

"Have a good day, whatever secret thing you're up to."

He mumbles something I don't hear, but I open the front door and leave anyway. It's a cloudy, cold day, and I'd rather have my hands in my pockets, but I can't do that and call Chance. He answers right away.

"Hey."

"Hey, am I interrupting?"

"No, I just got done for the day. What's up? What's—your video's not working."

"Video is the worst. You can have my voice."

Chance chuckled, his voice low. "Very well. Good to know you're still contrary."

"Am not," I say, fully aware of the irony. "I can't talk long, but I wanted to pick your brain about Andrew." I hesitate. "Is there any way I can...help him? Like...when you were first transitioning, how did you..." I falter. "Sorry, I don't really know what I'm asking."

"No, that's okay. It's hard for cisgender people to put yourselves in our shoes. I get it."

He's too nice. He's perfect for Colby, who is also too nice.

"It's tricky." I sigh. "Because I don't think he wants my help, but he's here, and I don't have many details on why, but he's obviously hurting, but I can't lean too hard on Colby to tell me why, so..."

"I'm not going to tell you anything, either."

"That's not what I meant," I say quickly. "I'm not trying to pry. Just wanted your insight into your experience, if you don't mind sharing."

"It's different for everyone, but I remember being pretty depressed when I first came out."

I blink, sure I heard him wrong over the traffic noise. "Depressed?"

"Yeah. Some of my friends didn't take it too well. Plus, once I had a taste of gender affirmation, sometimes it made dysphoria worse. I just wanted it all fixed right now."

The way he curled up into a ball...was he trying to hide his chest? It's on the large size for his overall build, and even though he's got a binder, it's probably bother-ing him. *Fuck.*

"Do you mind me asking how much your top surgery cost?"

"About ten grand, all told."

Double fuck. He doesn't have that kind of money. He's already gone into debt for his history degree and his teaching certificate. If he had money, I can't imagine he wouldn't just live by himself. Then again, he's fairly so-cial, like me. Well, like me when I'm not depressed and heartbroken. Maybe him, too.

"Is there anything I can do to help with dysphoria? Like, things I should say or shouldn't?"

Chance made a thinking noise. "In my experience, brains and bodies do what they want. You can try to be affirming about other things, but it doesn't necessarily reduce the parts that bother him. I guess it helped to talk to Hillary and other friends. Just being there is good." He paused. "Do you know if he's seeing a counselor?"

"No, I don't...not sure he'd be happy if I asked him that."

"You're kind of in a tough spot, Ev. I'm sorry."

I run a hand through my hair and find it damp—it's misting, and I hadn't noticed. "Well, thanks for the ad-vice."

"No problem. How's Col?"

"Seems to be okay. He went out a few nights ago. I didn't go, but they seemed to have fun." I heard Colby mention he wanted help with finding a ring yesterday, so I make a mental note to make time for that.

"Good, that's good. He should go do things. I don't just want him sitting at home." He sounds downright morose about it, and I want to slap them both.

"He's miserable without you, though. I think they had to bribe him to go."

"A few more weeks. Then we'll see each other."

"Yeah, it'll be good. I know he's really looking forward to it." I'm at the performer's door now, so I need to wrap this up.

"Can you keep a secret?"

Oh, no. I am many things: entertaining, forthright, even encouraging at times...but I am not a secret keeper. Worse still, I think I know where this is going. Dismay troubles my belly, and I cringe. "Sure."

"I'm going to propose to him. Hillary's been helping me work on it." I hold back a groan; I'm pretty sure she's helping both of them, then. I wonder who'll get to it first.

"That's fantastic, man! I'm happy for you guys." I wave at Glenn and Daria, who wave back. Daria's trans too, but she's a woman, so she probably couldn't help Evan much. She's a violinist, but she's down-to-earth, not a prima donna. Not that we don't have plenty of those in other sections...

"You think he'll say yes?"

"Hmm?" People are already warming up, and the noise is making it hard to think.

"Colby," he says impatiently. "Do you think he'll agree?"

"Oh, definitely. The guy's head over heels for you, man."

Chance lets out a shaky breath, and I grin. This is going to be entertaining. "When are you planning to do it?"

"As soon as he gets here. At the airport. Then we can celebrate the entire weekend."

"Or if he says no, you don't have to run him back there. Win-win."

His voice is high and panicked. "You said he was going to say yes!"

"He will," I soothe. "He definitely will. It's a joke, bud."

"Okay. Okay."

"I gotta go. Try to relax, okay? It'll be fine. You'll just get down on one knee at the romantic baggage claim, hold out that ring, and he'll say yes."

"Wait–ring?"

"Gotta go," I chuckle, then hang up. So apparently, I've stressed both of them out about the ring thing now; I'll make it up to them later. Do I think Chance will chicken out and not ask Colby at the airport? Yes. Do I think he'll work up the courage before Colby's planned dinner? Maybe. At any rate, I quickly start a group chat to place bets on who will propose first with a ten-dollar buy-in as our conductor waves his arms for our attention.

It's sectional day, so after a brief meeting, Carlos splits us up into our various instrumental categories, and soon, we're the only ones left on stage. The percussionists, that is. Me, Mara, Walter, and our section leader, Lindy. Why is Lindy our section leader? I'm so glad you asked. Lindy's been here the longest. That's it. We haven't discussed it explicitly, but I'm pretty sure all three of us are waiting for her to retire.

"Let's run the Rimsky-Korsakov and find any trouble spots, then we can do the end of the Holst and figure out the timing for the switch between—" I raise my hand, and Lindy pauses. "What?"

"I'd like to take the lead on the marimba next time." Why did I challenge her today of all days? God knows. My compatriots turn and give me a dirty look, but hey, some of us are better at waiting than others. If she's here forever, maybe I can at least get the parts I want in the meantime.

She scoffs, the rude noise harsh in the back of her throat. "I'm sure you would. But I assign the parts as I see fit, so you'll take what I give you." Her speech turns patronizingly slow. "Now please get out your sheet music so you can take notes."

I know my part. I know it backwards and forwards. She still finds fault with a note she says should be a flat, but she's just trying to catch me slacking. Not going to happen. But apparently, neither is getting a good part. And it looks like there's fuck-all I can do about it...there's a lot of that going around lately.

CHAPTER SEVEN

PATRICK IS CROSSING his arms over his chest again, glaring at us as we all sit on the couches in the living room. It's like he doesn't even understand that we're doing him a favor. It's Thursday night, and we're about to go live on his YouTube channel, doing some kind of speed build in Minecraft. I'm not as skilled as the rest of them, but I can mine stuff and fight off mobs. And it's kind of fun being a little famous–he's got almost 450,000 followers. Maybe it's even more now–I haven't checked in a while.

"What are the rules?" he asks, and when no one pipes up, he gestures toward me with his head. "You, loudmouth. What are the rules?"

"No cursing, no adult topics of conversation, no innuendo."

"That's right," he says with a curt nod. "Sadie is going to not only see this, she'll be here in a few minutes to help us. My sister will kick my ass if I teach her any shitty words." I love Sadie; she taught me how to set screen time limits on my phone. The kid's going places. Sadie's dad passed away a few years ago, so we're kind of like bonus uncles.

Colby raises his hand. "Isn't she like, thirteen? Does she think she doesn't hear those words at school?"

"She's *ten*, and she better not be hearing those words, or I'm going down to that school myself to straighten them out on their role in her education."

"She's tall for ten," Tony comments, but he goes quiet when Patrick directs the glare at him.

"What's that supposed to mean?"

He holds his hands out in innocence. "Just that I can see how Colby thought that. That's all."

"Anyway," I say loudly, "I think we all know what to do on your channel. We've done this before."

"I haven't," Drew says. "What's the objective of this game?"

"It's kind of like a big sandbox," Darren offers from beside him, and I curse myself for being slow to get to the living room; both the seats next to him were taken. He's played shooter games, mostly, and this is more of an imagination game. "We'll be playing creative mode, right?"

"No, it's survival, so there will be mobs."

"That's monsters in laymen's terms," I add, and Drew lifts an eyebrow.

"I do know something about the game, thanks. It's a kid's game, right?"

Patrick sighs. He has deep feelings about Minecraft and its potential as a source of entertainment for adults, so I quickly speak before he can climb onto his soapbox.

"It's fun for all ages. You'll see. There's magic and shit."

"Language!" Patrick barks, and I see he's regretting inviting us to play with him already.

"Sorry, sorry."

He glares at me harder, then says, "Tonight, we'll be attempting the all-achievements speed run in under forty-five minutes. I've assigned each of you a role." He pulls some notecards from his back pocket. I take the one he offers me.

"Seriously? Just building beds? Tipping cows?"

"You're good at it. It's a compliment," Patrick deadpans, and I crane my neck to see what Colby got.

"He's building iron armor and killing the Wither and I'm over here crafting beds? Oh, come on, at least let me kill *something*."

"No. You can eat a pork chop."

"How is that even an achievement?" Tony asks, pulling his computer out of his bag.

"I think it's because you have to kill the pig first," Colby says, putting on his headset. He looks like a giant nerd, and it makes me feel a little better. Also, the reason I'm not as good at this is that I'd rather be out with lights and music and people.

"See, Rhodes? You can't say I never let you kill anything."

The front door opens, and Sadie flounces inside, rushing over to Patrick. She stops short in front of him, glancing at us. "Is it okay if they see?"

Patrick nods. "If they tell anyone, I'll ruin them." With that, they shake hands, melding it into some kind of elaborate flourish, complete with a nose pinch, a sprinkler-like move, and a snap at the end.

"I swear, you two, the secret handshake gets longer every time you see each other," Kennedy says with a smile, closing the door behind her as she comes inside. We all give her a wave, since we can't get a word in over

Sadie's chatter about the stream. Kennedy's got a large purple duffle bag over her shoulder, which she sets by the stairs; Sadie must be staying the night on Patrick's floor on an air mattress tonight. She thinks the basement is creepy...which it kind of is.

"Okay, be good for Uncle Pat," Kennedy says, giving her daughter a kiss on the head, and Sadie pauses long enough to give her mom a hug goodbye.

"I'm always good," Sadie chides, and Patrick just shakes his head.

"Thanks as always," Kennedy says, giving him a one-armed hug, and he gives her arm a squeeze without taking his eyes off the screen. "Love you."

"Yeah. Okay, let's get started..." If it bothers Kennedy, she doesn't show it, and she quietly lets herself out as the rest of us get on the server and the stream starts. And Patrick becomes a whole different version of himself.

"Hey everybody, it's Captain Mooshroom here—"

"And the Sprout," Sadie chimes in, and he gives her a nod.

"And today, we're attempting something we've never tried before: an all-achievements speed run. And we've got all hands on deck with my roommates."

We all give a hello at once through our headsets, and the fun begins. I'm on a tablet, so I kick back in my chair, sitting sideways with my legs over the arm. Queer people can't sit normally on a chair, I don't think. Science has yet to agree. But it's giving me an acceptable excuse to stare at Drew while I work.

And when I say work, I mean chopping down square trees and collecting pork chops from passing pigs. The rest of them are finishing their tasks at lightning speed, and I'm still working on the bed. Drew's brows are furrowed intensely...I don't think he's doing any better than I am. And then a message pops up on screen from another app, directed at me.

> **Drew:** is there some trick to this bread thing?
> **Drew:** I don't think my wheat is growing

I smirk; at least he knows that everyone can see his comments when we're streaming, so he hasn't outed himself as a newbie right away.

> **Evan:** I think you have to plant it near water.

> **Drew:** Thanks. Really should've done some kind of research before I agreed to this...

> **Evan:** where's the fun in that?

He flashes a lightning smile at the screen when my message comes in, but goes back to work immediately on his bread baking. What he doesn't know is how many tries it took us to break a record Patrick was aiming for the last time...we blew right past Sadie's 9:00 bedtime and didn't finish to his satisfaction until 10:30. It's the only time I've ever seen Patrick break a rule, besides the hacking, which he considers a public service.

We work for a few minutes, but we're nowhere close to done when the timer goes off, and we all groan.

"What happens now?" Tony asks, and Patrick stands up from the dining room table.

"I don't think you're all pulling your weight. Based on what was left undone, we need to redistribute. Evan, I'm pairing you with Colby to keep you focused; you looked like you were flirting with someone at one point. Andrew, come sit next to Sadie; she can help you with the more advanced tasks." I guess that foils his plan of asking me for help without anyone noticing...but I'm sure Sadie will be kind. Also, I should've known better than to assume that Patrick wouldn't be able to read my body language. Andrew moves the computer over to the table next to Sadie, and Darren scoots down the couch so I can sit by Colby.

"Oh, damn. You only got three things done?" she says. "You really do need my help."

"Sadie Abigail, none of that language in my house," Patrick barks, and she giggles ruefully.

"I was muted!"

"Irrelevant. It's not a word you can say," he says sternly, and she nods. "All right, let's get going."

I don't get the chat window closed fast enough, and Colby sees it as I sit down. I glance at him, but he stays focused on his own screen, getting logged back into the server again. I do the same, but I quickly decide that I hate this new setup. For one thing, I can't see Drew anymore, but I can hear him chatting with Sadie, laughing at her jibberjabber, enduring her gentle teasing at his lack of knowledge of the game. Sadie's so knowledgeable, she whips around like it's nothing. Meanwhile, Colby elbows me.

"Start the iron ingot so you can make the cake."

"Right." I've been so busy listening to his voice over my shoulder, I haven't done a damn thing. Or a darn thing, since we're playing with Sadie. I look down at my list. "Wait, I got riding the pig? Doesn't that mean I have to walk off a cliff? Are you trying to get rid of me?" Death jokes are on the list. Captain Mooshroom really tries to keep the trigger warnings down. It's so sweet, really.

"Not if you build a trapdoor," Patrick calls. "Get to work."

I grumble under my breath about his bossiness, but try to buckle down and make it happen. Then I realize I can still see Drew—on the screen. Seeing his avatar is not the same, obviously, but at least I can keep tabs on what he's accomplishing. And he's doing better this time. Too bad I can't say the same.

"And time!" Pat calls. "Rhodes, you're killing me, man. Give your task card to Andrew—even he's more productive than you are."

"Hang on now—I want another chance! I didn't know about that trap door thing, I'll get it done this time, I swear." *I'll push Andrew out of my head somehow. Really.*

"This is your last chance, then you're out."

"What's that teaching the children, Captain? Where's the grace?" I'm surprised to hear Andrew's voice...it's the first time he hasn't mumbled all evening. And more than that, I'm surprised he's defending my shitty playing. Is he trying to repay me for my help with the wheat? Patrick must be surprised, too, because he doesn't say anything for a moment.

"You know what? You're right. What tasks would you prefer?"

I rattle off a list of ten things I know how to do in my sleep, only three of which are on my index card. From behind me, Patrick calls out.

"All right, you all hear that? If you've got that on your list, cross it off. That's for Rhodes now. Come pick something else from his list." Tony gets up to look at my card, and he, Darren, and Colby briefly confer to decide who's going to craft the enchantment table and kill a ghast with a fireball and create a full beacon and all the rest of my list. Who knew these things were even possible in this game? Apparently, they did. But at least I didn't get my ass kicked out of the game. And I have Drew to thank for that.

We still don't quite make it in the next round, but we're closer. Patrick decides we should take a break, and while he and Sadie are debating about how many cookies she's allowed to have so close to bedtime, I grab a cup of lemonade from the table.

"Hey."

Drew looks up from the screen slowly, like he's still trying to learn how to do something. "Yeah?"

"Thanks."

"No problem." He goes back to the game, and I only feel a little slighted. It's not until we finish the next round that I get another message from him.

Drew: is Patrick always such a despot?

I do know the word despot, but his choice of words still makes me laugh. He's such a brainiac sometimes. We're between tries, so it's safe for me to answer.

Evan: He takes Minecraft very seriously. So, yes.

Drew: Why do you play with him?

Evan: I don't know. He needed help. Trying to be nice.

Drew: When can I go to bed?

Evan: well, he's putting out more sugar, so I'm guessing he expects us to keep going for a while...

Drew: Duck

Evan: ?

Drew: Sadie was watching over my shoulder. I didn't want to get in trouble.

Evan: HA

Evan: Afraid of the ducking despot?

Drew: Exactly.

There's a bunch of things I want to ask next: why are you sleeping so badly? Do you want to sleep in my room, with or without me? I'd crash on that crappy futon if that's what he needed. If it would make things better. It's not like I sleep much, anyway. But I'm pretty sure it would make it weird to offer that now. This is the most pleasant interaction we've had since he moved in, so I don't want to do anything to tarnish it.

But when Patrick finally lets us give up for the night, watching him shuffle down the stairs feels slightly less painful than it did yesterday.

CHAPTER EIGHT

I AM NOT REALLY AWAKE the next morning when I get out of bed to turn off my alarm. It's across the room for a reason; too easy to hit the snooze button and let my morning slip away. Already, I'm almost too late to go running with Pat. I give my scruffy face a rub and then a slap as I shuffle down the hall...I need to pee before we take off. My hand is on the bathroom door before I hear the shower running and a voice over it. Which normally would mean nothing, because no one in this house cares about someone using the toilet or sink if they're in the shower, but it's Andrew singing. He must figure it's too early for anyone to hear him; his voice is high and light. Pressing my ear to the door, I can just make out the lyrics over the white noise of the water—it's "Cover Me Up," letting a little twang into his voice. And it's wistful and sad, and I press my forehead against the old door, eyes closed, just listening. The doorknob feels like smooth, cold temptation under my fingers, and the lyrics are getting to me...about wanting to fix things, but not knowing how. About making mistakes, which I definitely have. And I'm about to make another one when I hear Patrick's voice behind me.

"Are you going in or what?"

I spin to face him. "No, I'm not going in. He needs privacy," I say, completely ignoring the fact that I was, in fact, about to go in.

Pat smirks. "Does he? It's not like I'm gonna peek."

"Go downstairs. There's a toilet there, too."

"What's wrong with this one? No one in this house is shy."

"He might be. You don't know. Have you asked him?"

Pat crosses his arms. "Have you?"

"I don't need to," I say, crossing mine, too. We're so busy in our stand-off, I don't even notice the water stopped. The door behind me opens, and Andrew's head pokes out.

"Evan, stop being an overprotective asshole. You're gonna wake up the whole house. Pat, you're welcome to use whatever."

He's wearing a blue and green plaid robe that looks new, and I'm simultaneously annoyed that I can't see more of him and relieved that Patrick can't, either. They switch places as I stand there like a fish with my mouth working silently open and closed, trying to figure out what to say. Andrew stops next to me as the door closes behind him. "I can advocate for my own needs."

"He's being inconsiderate," I mumble, and I wish like hell he'd change body wash because we used this one together once, his pretty hand stroking my cock in the shower, the scent of honey and tropical flowers filling my senses as he teased my lips with sleepy kisses.

"If I wanted to lock the door, I would," he says, glancing toward his room.

"So you wouldn't care if I came into the bathroom while you were in the shower?"

He shrugs, but I know it's a lie. There's no outward sign, but *I know him*. That's what they're all forgetting: I know him better than anyone alive. And all it proves is what a fool I am for ever letting him go. Because he's different, but the core of him is the same. And I don't know why I thought that would change.

"Okay," I warn. "I'm gonna do it then. You'll be all soaped up in the shower, warm and wet, smelling like honey, and I'll be just on the other side of the curtain, in my boxers..." I drop my voice. "Brushing my teeth...real slow."

"Fine," he says, but I see a shiver pass through his shoulders. "Good."

"Great," I say, grinning. "Super."

"Shut up," he says, giving my shoulder a half-hearted shove before he turns and quietly goes back to his room. And I stare after him like a lovesick fool, because he touched me, and I really want to goad him into that again.

"Ready to run?" Patrick's voice startles me, and I scoot past him into the bathroom.

"Just let me pee real quick..."

"Oversharing. I'll be downstairs." True to his word, Patrick is stretching with his foot braced against the wooden front steps when I exit. "Which way?"

"I'm barely awake, so...just don't get us lost."

Pat snorts, then he leads the way down Thompson Street at an easy pace.

"You have no idea what you're doing with him, do you?" Okay, so apparently we're only warming up our bodies; we're just gonna take off at full speed conversationally.

"What makes you say that?"

He ticks each one off on his fingers. "Taunting. Sexual imagery too early in the morning. Inappropriate boundaries."

"Okay, yeah, that's enough, thanks."

"No, wait, I had more. Assuming things. Being an asshole."

"What's your expert advice, then? Come on, let's hear it."

He turns us into the park, and we start around the outside. "You need to woo his heart. That's where you wounded him."

"Damn it, Pat—it's too early for your bullshit."

"Fine. Have it your way. Make him horny in the hallway and let him slip through your fingers. Maybe I'll take a stab."

My head snaps sideways, and I think I pull a muscle in my neck. "Are you fucking serious?"

Patrick shrugs, and he's still annoyingly in control of his breathing, whereas I am already bordering on winded. That may not be entirely due to the exercise. "Why shouldn't I? I like his eyes. He's funny. Not too bubbly. We could watch sports together. I like some sports."

Speaking of bubbling, my feelings are doing an excellent impression of a pot left unwatched. "You hate sports, but beyond that, you cannot date Andrew! And you especially cannot date him in the house where I live!"

"Okay. Maybe when he moves out, I'll go with him. Earn his trust by being a good roommate first, then slowly win him over..."

If we were at home, I'd have him in a headlock by now, forcing him to recant the awful images he just put into my head. But we're in public, so I try to keep my voice down and my feet moving.

"You *cannot* date Andrew. Do you hear me? I mean it, Pat. Hands fucking *off*."

"Why? Because he's yours?"

"Yes!" I try to catch the word before it leaves my mouth, but it's too late. "No. I mean...I know he's not, anymore."

Patrick laughs. It's quiet, but heartfelt. "I knew it. You have no idea what you're doing."

"Like you'd do better."

"I'd have never let him go." I cannot see it, but I'd swear he just stuck a knife in my chest. Now I really can't breathe, and the path in front of me is getting blurrier by the second.

"It wasn't that simple. And you're actually being hurtful now, so maybe drop it." I can hear the frown in his voice, even though I don't dare turn my head to look at him. I love him to death, but sometimes, he doesn't see what he's doing.

"That wasn't my intention. My intention was to help."

"I know."

"You either love him or you don't, right?"

"I asked you to drop it, remember?"

Pat makes a harrumphing noise that tells me he's not happy. We run past the splash pad where the kids play in the water, cold, silent and full of leaves at this time of year.

"Fine, you want the truth? I was afraid I'd miss the person he used to be, and I didn't want to put us through that. I thought someone else could love him better than I could. And frankly, I just waited too long to come to any kind of conclusion, because I didn't know what the fuck I was doing, and it was a secret, so I couldn't ask for help."

He's quiet as we turn out of the park again, and we slow down a bit, which is nice, because after that monologue, I'm really out of breath.

"That's incredibly dense."

"Gee, thanks for the support."

"He really told you it had to be a secret?"

I nod. "He did. He wasn't sure what he wanted to do physically. Obviously, he's decided now."

"Obviously." Patrick doesn't say anything for a block, and I think maybe this painful conversation is over. But of course, it's not. "I won't ask him out, then."

"Thank you."

"As long as you do."

"You can't blackmail me into dating someone, bud. I will not make life in the house awkward as hell."

"Well, I still think you should. You obviously still adore him."

"It's like I said. Love might not be enough. Not this time."

"How do you know he doesn't want you anymore?"

"Besides breaking up with me?"

"But he came back. When he was hurting, he came to you for refuge."

"Where else was he going to go?"

Pat shrugged. "A hotel. A friend's house. His parents. Homeless shelter. There were other options."

"Yes, but..." I actually couldn't argue with that. It was the one thing I couldn't explain in this whole mess. "Beyond not wanting to be around his roommates and his sister—which I can understand, because it sounds like they all reacted poorly—it's not like he doesn't have other friends. Classmates at RCU. People he's known since high school. Why come here?"

"Because of you."

I huffed. It was hard to tell, because of the subsequent puffing, but I did. "*Not* because of me. He thinks I rejected him. That's why he ended it."

"That doesn't mean he doesn't want you. Just that he thought you didn't want him."

"But also that I'd want to help."

"Yes."

On the one hand, it's incredibly cathartic to talk all this out with someone so logical, especially when I'm not worried about Drew hearing me. But also, I'm not sure we're coming to the right conclusions.

"You think there's a way to find out without asking him?"

Pat seems to ponder this. "Does he keep a diary?"

"I don't think so..."

"Does he lock his phone?"

"Definitely."

"I mean...ethically?" Pat says. "No. There's no way."

"What about unethically?"

"Still no. I only use my hacking skills for good. Like ruining shitty exes. And righting wrongs."

"That's fair."

"So you're going to ask him?" He urges.

"Hell no." When I look up, we're back in front of the house and Pat waves toward the front door.

"Bye. Thanks for coming."

"Where are you going?"

"I'm going to do the same loop at my normal speed, so I get an actual workout."

Rolling my eyes, I drag myself up the front walk and back into the house. So much for a run to forget my troubles.

CHAPTER NINE

"WE'LL START WITH THE Ravel," Carlos says, flipping pages like he's looking for it, too. "Then the Saint-Saën, then the Purcell." I rifle through my own music until it's in the right order, the corners bent appropriately in the places where it's a quick change.

"I'm sick of Ravel," Mara mutters, and I flash her a smile.

"Probably means we've practiced it enough." I'm sick of it, too, though. Not that I'd admit that to anyone...I'm supposed to love this job, and I mostly do. But after a week of Ravel, sometimes I need some Ramones to even it out. The timpani is a little out of tune; I think someone moved it this weekend. I really wish I could take my instruments home like every other musician. At least my piano is safely at home, out of range...not that it's never subjected to shenanigans. My roommates decided it would be funny to put Post-it notes over every hammer to deaden the sound, and it took me a day to figure out what was wrong with it. They remain unforgiven. But mostly, no one touches my piano but me. I bet you didn't know the piano was a percussion instrument, did you? Well, now you do.

We run the Ravel, *Pavane for a Dead Princess*, which is slow and haunting and appropriately regal. The flutes carry this one, and our principal flautist definitely does it justice. Mara is still talking. Why does she have to talk during rehearsal? I like her, I do, but...no.

There's a lot of counting when you're a percussionist, and she's putting me off my game. I pretend I don't hear her, and she seems to get the message. But as soon as the piece is over, she's at it again.

"Ugh, just as depressing as always. It's like he's conspiring to bore people."

I glance at our conductor, and I see him cock an eyebrow in our direction. I try to hold still and shuffle through my music in a way that says, "Yes, I heard her too, and I have no opinion about it."

My friend Glenn also turns, and they've got their teacher voice on when they respond.

"It's a classic for a reason."

"Boorriinngg," Mara whispers, and I didn't know it was possible to put so much attitude behind your words without even using your vocal cords.

"Ms. Frost, were you trying to ask something?" Acoustics. They'll kill you every time.

"No," she says, only somewhat chastened. I hope she quits. She stays mostly quiet through the rest of rehearsal, but I can tell she's struggling with the xylophone runs in the Rimsky-Korsakov. What she needs to do is come in and run it five hundred times until she could do it in her sleep. But I already know she won't. She doesn't want to be a professional. But wanting our group to be an excellent one obligates me to offer my help. When the piece ends, I lean over.

"That's a tricky run. You want to come in and run it together?"

"No, thanks. I've got it."

"Okay."

She's quiet for a beat while everyone shuffles to the next piece. "Also, I have a boyfriend."

Well, that's not at all how I thought she was going to take that. I scowl.

"I didn't mean it like that."

"Okay," she says, but her body language sings with tension; she's practically leaning over like she wishes she could get away from me. Did I really come off that creepy? Sometimes I hate how society sees men. I should be able to help her, one professional to another, without her worrying that I'd make it weird, but her experience has clearly been otherwise. I leave her alone, and she bolts as soon as rehearsal is over. Glenn turns to me casually, loosening the horsehair of their bow.

"Did I make that weird?"

"When? With Mara?"

They frown when I nod. "I don't think so, but I'm not usually intimidated by men."

I stare pointedly at how they're taller than I am and poke at their bulging biceps as they lift their bass into its case. "I can't imagine why."

"Don't let my stature fool you. Emotional intimidation has nothing to do with size."

It's a fair point. "I wasn't trying to be creepy. I was trying to help. And I didn't even want to."

Glenn grins at me. "No good deed goes unpunished, I guess."

I wasn't looking at her that way. I haven't looked at anyone that way in a very long time. That's the thing with a broken heart; it takes more than a spunky personality or a pleasant face to heal that. I'm not sure what it's going to take, honestly. I've been waiting for it to heal on its own, and it just...isn't. My guys keep asking me if I'm okay. But I feel like I can't even see okay. Okay is on the far side of the moon. And it isn't helped by seeing couples like Hillary and Glenn, so happy and goopy together. They're coming to Thursday night dinners now. I can tell Colby is suffering, too, even though he's happy for his sister. I didn't tell any of them, but I'd thought about asking for Chance's old room in Hillary's apartment...but now, I wouldn't be escaping the romance. I'd be swimming in it. That'd be no good.

Speaking of escaping the romance, I have a job to do now that rehearsal is over. I pack up my music and duck backstage to find Sammy. He's scowling at a clipboard as usual, and he holds up a finger to say "just a minute" as he finishes his phone call.

"No, we can't wait until Monday. Because our performance is on Sunday, that's why, and right now, I've got two lights out. Unless they want to memorize their music, that's not an option." There was a long pause, then he says, "I'll wait." He covers the mic of the phone. "What do you need?"

"Remember when we played poker at Friendsgiving?"

His expression turns pinched. "I said I'd pay you back, and I will."

I hold up a hand. "I'll wipe out the debt right now for a favor."

Sammy's mouth pulls into a straight line, and he cocks one pierced eyebrow upward. "What kind of favor?"

"I want you to hire my housemate. He's kind of going through a thing and he needs a job."

"Tony?" I swear, the man has literal stars in his eyes, and I hold back a snort and file that information away for later. They're both Latino, both fairly quiet...that could work. But it isn't my job to help people find love. If I couldn't hold on to it myself, what makes me think I can help anyone else? Not that Andrew and I were in love, I don't think...

"No, he's new...do you remember meeting my partner?"

"Yeah." He turns back to the phone. "Yes, I'm here." He pauses to listen. "No, I don't have time to drive to Tacoma, just overnight it." He sighs again. "Yes, I'll hold."

"He's trans, He/him. Goes by Andrew now," I whisper, and Sammy gives me a contemplative nod.

"What can he do?"

"Anything. He's good at everything, absorbs facts like they're going out of style. And he *loves* music."

"Good with kids?"

"Uh..." He did well with Sadie the other night, but kids are more difficult in groups sometimes. I can't remember seeing him around many kids, now that I think about it. Except that one time at the Timbers game when he covered the ears of a little boy in front of him before he cursed a blue streak at the ref. But he's studying to be a teacher—how bad could he be? "Maybe?"

"He can usher. And give school tours on a trial basis."

A sideways grief washes over me, marbled with relief, because a job means he'll probably move out. But maybe it's not such a great job that he can afford to move, just feed himself. I have no idea what the ushers get paid. And maybe it'll mean less time at Marble. It bothers me that it bothers me, but I can't seem to quit. Both feelings are annoying.

"Thank you," I whisper, my palms pressed together, as Sammy turns back to the phone.

"Yes, I'm here. No, I'm not driving to Boise either...do you know how far apart these cities are, man? Where do you live, New York?"

It's something. I make myself walk to the HR office and pick up an application, because that seems like something that should be required. I make myself walk home, forcing my feet into a steady rhythm, which should be easy considering my vocation. It *should* be, but I'm jogging by the time I hit Thompson Street, and running by the time I arrive at our front door. I didn't think about how weird it was going to look, showing up all out of breath, so I stand on the doorstep for a minute, hands on my knees, trying to slow things down. It does not really work.

When I get inside, I'm still clutching the now-damp paperwork in my hand, because I'm a sweaty dork.

"Here," I say, feeling very smug as I thrust it toward him. He stares at the paper like it's a snake.

"What's this?" he asks, muting the TV.

"Got you a job."

Drew blinks at me, then his gaze shifts down to the paperwork. "Doing what?" He's not taking it. Why isn't he taking it? I'm feeling like a weirdo, and my brain rolls its eyes at my behavior and tells me to *go with the feeling.*

"Ushering. And giving tours, I think, I couldn't ask too many questions. Sammy was on the phone with someone who doesn't know west coast geography."

Then, slowly, he reaches out and takes the papers from my hand. "Is it raining outside?"

"No, I'm a weirdo. It's fine. What do you think?" *I could keep an eye on you there,* I don't say. *I could make sure no one fucks with you.* I don't beg him to take it. "I think it'd be great. Don't you think? You love the Howitzer. I know you do." He does. The first time I took him there, you would've thought I'd taken him to Disneyland. It's this gaudy art déco beast, but he fell silent like he was in church. Fucking adorable.

"And I could catch a ride with you. Maybe."

"Sure."

He was staring down at the paperwork. "Or Glenn or Colby."

"Yeah." *No. I'll give you a ride.* My fragile heart is still beating out of my chest, tinny as a steel drum in my ears, holding onto hope that my peace offering is enough. I would make peace offerings to him the rest of my life if given the chance, but I'm not fool enough to think that's possible. But friends. He said we're friends.

"Why?" His gaze is so earnest—this is why I want to build a fence around him, an electric one that keeps assholes and transphobes away. It's too much, so I start toward the stairs, but I still feel like I have to answer.

"Didn't you need one?"

"Well...yeah."

"Then that's why," I say, continuing up the stairs to my room. I'm going to practice until I've drilled his stunned expression out of my head, because he should never have to wonder why I'd help him. I only wish I was brave enough to say it out loud.

CHAPTER TEN

"ALL RIGHT, IT'S ROOMMATE Meeting time." My best friend has this almost manic look on his face, and I roll my eyes. I love the Roommate Meeting, because the Roommate Meeting brings order to chaos. The Roommate Meeting means I can have the TV when I need it. It forestalls arguments over who's cooking or using the laundry machines in the basement. It is essential. But what's not essential is Colby's dorky clipboard and doing it in the middle of the basketball game I'm watching.

"Can't you just take notes on your phone like a normal person?" I ask, but he ignores me, scribbling down something at the top of the page.

"Let's do the calendar first—I leave in four weeks on the 4th."

"And I'm taking you," I confirm.

"Provided you can fit all his bags into your car." Darren smirks.

"Hey, do not knock the Porsche. My baby is amazing. She goes from zero to sixty faster than a Ferrari. It—"

Their groans drown me out, and Colby raps on his clipboard with his pencil like a judge. "This is about my airport ride, thank you very much. I want to leave at 3:00."

"In the morning?" I clarify, and Colby nods.

"3:00 in the morning. Sharp."

"What kind of luggage does he even need? Do we think Chance will let him wear clothes?" I joke, and even Patrick laughs at that.

"I will be wearing clothes when I propose *like a gentleman*," Colby announces loudly over their chatter. "And while I am gone, Evan's in charge." This sparks another round of complaints, which makes me grin. I glance over at Drew, who's sitting on the floor by the TV. Why didn't he get a seat on the couch? He's a guest, for god's sake. Under their bitching as Patrick gripes about how I'm "an agent of chaos" and Tony whines that they'll never get me out of the bathroom now, I motion to my seat, but Drew gives his head a tiny shake. He holds my gaze, though, and I don't let go as I announce, "Don't worry, everyone—my reign will be one of peace, by any means necessary."

"Seriously, though, why him?" Patrick asks, throwing out an arm in frustration. "I'm ten times more responsible than he is."

"Because my parents know him and he's got their contact info and all the information on the house if anything goes wrong."

I get a weird feeling down my spine when he says that last part. Houses know when their owners are leaving. They resist it. My childhood home always threw a tantrum when my house-knowledgeable dad went away on business, choosing that moment to saddle my other dad with some fresh crisis involving an expensive appliance or broken water pipe. At some point, I'm pretty sure they decided it didn't make sense financially for

Greg to leave...or maybe they just decided it didn't make sense for Nico to fix things "as a surprise" while he was away. Either way, I suddenly have a bad feeling about this.

"Chris and Susan know who the best man for the job is," I say so the house can hear me, and Patrick just glowers at me.

"Any other travel or car needs?"

There's a brief silence as people check their phones.

"I've got a job interview at Marble at 2:00 tomorrow if someone doesn't mind giving me a ride..." Drew trails off, then clears his throat. "Don't want to show up sweaty."

"I'll do it." I don't think I even really think the words, I just propel them straight out of the center of me. Probably my heart. Don't worry about it.

"Uh, don't you have rehearsal?" Tony asks quietly, because the man doesn't know how to project unless he's on stage.

But yes, I do. Fuck. And doesn't he want the job I got him? Was I overstepping? Looking back, maybe that was inappropriate.

"I can skip it if it's important." I really can't. Carlos has been very clear about this, and I'm extremely lucky to have this job and I can't ditch just because I want to. But whenever he needs something, I just...bubble inside. I *need* to help him. It's not optional. But neither is having a job, so...

"I can take you." Oh. Great. Send Patrick, King of the Grumps, with him when Drew's already nervous.

That'll work out fine. And he's intentionally avoiding my glare, I can tell. He's not just looking at Drew because he's waiting for a response, he's *ignoring* my response. Bastard.

"Thanks, Patrick, that'd be great." Now Drew is ignoring me, too? Fine, then. I see how it is.

"Great, moving on to food..."

"I replaced the bacon. It's in the freezer."

Patrick smirks, and now I'm ignoring him.

"Okay. And the dinner schedule I sent out last night works for everyone?"

"Why am I always on Mondays?" Darren complains. "It's like the hardest night to cook. Evan has Fridays, which is obviously pizza. Patrick has Tuesday, which is obviously tacos. Colby cooks Thursday and he's got Glenn and Chance to help bring stuff..." The obvious yet subtle dig at Hillary (who rarely remembers to bring anything) makes me laugh. "Tony has Sunday, which ends up being leftovers from when people go out on Saturday..."

"I'll trade with you," Tony says, because he's a peacemaker. Growing up with a lot of siblings will do that to you, I hear. Not that I'd know.

"Would you rather have Wednesday?" Colby asks, frowning.

"No. Wednesday is just as bad. I want a good day. I want an easy day."

"Very well," I sigh. "I'll take Monday. But not because you're being a whiner."

"Or I could take it," Drew says casually, as if he didn't just announce he was planning to stay for a while. You don't sign up for a night to cook if you're just crashing here, right? Tell me I'm not misreading this. And the worst part is that my heart goes lightheaded, dizzy, so happy I could jump to my feet and burst into song like a damn Disney prince. 'Look,' I try to tell it. 'He's not ours anymore. We fucked it up. He doesn't want us.' But just like everyone else tonight, it's ignoring me. *He's staying. He's staying.* And it gives me the tiniest sliver of hope that he doesn't hate me after all.

"Good, that's settled. Darren will take Fridays, Drew will take Mondays, so Evan, that leaves Wednesdays for you. Moving on to the cleaning schedule..."

I stop listening there, because I do more than my fair share of cleaning. Because he's staying. How long doesn't matter—he's staying.

CHAPTER ELEVEN

ON FRIDAY, IT'S RAINING again, so I decide to drive to work instead of walking. Only I'm just about to pull away when Andrew comes running out of the house. So naturally, being obsessed with my ex, I roll down my window and stop.

"Can I catch a ride?" he asks breathlessly. "I'll pay gas money."

I unlock the doors and gesture for him to get in, which he better not be interpreting as an acceptance of his insulting offer to pay me when we're probably going to the same place.

"Where you headed?"

He gracefully slides into the front seat. "The Howitz. We've got some school tours coming today."

"I know. I'm playing for them." So, he did take my job. Maybe it just didn't pay enough; it probably makes sense for him to work at Marble, too.

"Oh. Right." He's staring straight out the windshield, seemingly transfixed by the wipers. "I wasn't sure if it was everybody or..."

I give a nod. "Right. I mean, some people teach lessons or have other jobs, so not everyone can come to the school performances, but we do the best we can with a small ensemble, if that's how it ends up." Secretly, I love these performances, because Lindy often can't make it, which means it's just me doing everything. I don't have to fight for decent parts. I don't have to dance around someone else. I'm not saying I wish she'd just retire already or get hit by a bus, but...oh, who am I kidding? A bus couldn't kill Lindy. If it was that easy, someone else would've knocked her off ages ago. She's steel.

"One kid asked how many people do this full time on my last tour, and I wasn't sure."

"I mean, we really only get paid for about twenty hours of work. So almost everyone. Maybe not my section leader."

"Lindy, right?"

Sometimes I forget he knows me so well...he's the same person, but also, not? And I'm not sure I'm the same person as I was before I lost him? And sometimes that feels more significant than his transition.

"Yep. Lindy. But as you know, we all practice a lot, too."

"Yes, I remember. Unfortunately." He was sensitive to the drum set early in the morning, even though it's electric and I wore headphones.

"Hey, if I wanna be top-notch, it's 24/24."

He rolls his eyes. "Be an American and say '24/7' like everyone else."

"Not everyone!" I insist forcefully. "Not Nico! And not smart people in France!"

"You're just being antithetical."

"I'm not going to charge you gas money," I say, leaning in to make my point, "but I am going to charge you for all these big words. You are *ridiculous*." And more than that, it makes me all the more frustrated that he's not going to school anymore. And I've got plenty to be frustrated about anyway when it comes to him...as evidenced by how even fighting with him is making my cock wake up. *No, no, go back to sleep. Not now.*

"You can't charge me money for being educated."

"You're not, dropout."

He chuckles at that, letting his arms fall to his lap. "Articulate, then. Not that not graduating and being educated are mutually exclusive. Speaking of Nico, how are your dads?"

I'm surprised he's asking. He hopped on the call with us a few times, but they haven't ever met in person...

"They're good. Still just as goofy as ever."

"Are they still thinking about getting a dog?"

"I don't think so. They haven't talked about it in a while. They want to travel to see their friends and come see me and go up to the cabin and stuff. Greg thinks it'll be too expensive to board it all the time. But I think Nico's just biding his time before he asks again."

"It's so weird how you call your parents by their first names. That is some next level modern shit. My parents would freak if I called them Nick and Roselani."

"They didn't mind when I called them that," I said smugly. "How are they all doing?"

"Grace is getting married." He sounds baffled.

"No shit?"

"Swear to God. She met this guy on one of those perfect-match-type sites, and it turns out they went to summer camp together years ago and knew each other already. He's a chemist."

"What do you think of him?"

Drew shrugs. "Kai seems nice enough. He bought me a beer at the Timbers game and knew enough about soccer to curse when we got a red card. A completely un-merited red card, I might add."

"Aren't they all?"

"Fuck yes." He paused. "And he makes Grace laugh."

"That's not that easy to do."

"I know, right? She never thought *you* were funny."

"That's true," I say with a laugh, and when I glance at him, he's smirking at me. I don't know if it was getting him the job that helped break down whatever was keeping this kind of conversation from happening, but I'm kind of in awe that we're...friends again? Just like that?

"Where's she getting married?"

"At the church." The church he hasn't been to lately, I've noticed. He's some kind of Christian...not sure what flavor. Also not sure how to start that conversation, so I let it die. I park in the Salmon Street parking garage on the top level where I won't have to endure other people scratching my baby, and we take the stairs down to the street in silence. It's not hard to cross against the mid-morning traffic, but I still give a white SUV my death stare when it gets too close to Drew. I don't think that woman was paying a bit of attention.

"Hey..." He gently pulls his sleeve from my grasp, where I have apparently trapped it without realizing it, to my embarrassment. "So, what pieces are you playing?"

"Usually, it's 'Carnival of the Animals'..."

"Naturally."

"'Peter and the Wolf,' if we have an oboe..."

"Classic."

"'Ride of the Valkyries' and 'The Typewriter.'"

After a moment of fumbling with the keys, he opens the door for me. "I'm not familiar with that last one."

"Leroy Anderson's the composer; it's more modern."

"Like your dad-naming protocols. I see."

Despite my nervousness at *what is happening here*, I chuckle. "The problem is that none of the kids know what a typewriter is anymore. It's a cute song, but..."

"I brought one to show them today!" Carlos' distinctive voice floats out into the hallway, and I pause. When he appears, he's hauling the gigantic thing out into the hallway to show us. "You see? Now they will know. It's about how art imitates life. They will understand, because children know this instinctively. They must be able to draw inspiration from their world, Mr. Rhodes." When I smile, embarrassed that I was caught sounding critical, he goes on. "Who is your friend?"

"Oh, I'm sorry; this is our new school tour guide, Andrew Kahananui."

"Yes, I was slated to meet you today, I believe."

Drew offers a hand, and Carlos tries to shift the machine to his hip to accept it, but it's slipping. We catch it together just before it hits the ground. Can't have the antique prop getting broken... Carlos sets it on the floor.

"Very nice to meet you, Andrew. You are new to Portland?"

"No, I've lived here all my life."

"He's a history major at Rose City," I offer, and he glares at me.

"I was, yeah."

"Well, we are glad you're here. Maybe you can demonstrate the typewriter for me?" The two of them chat, and it seems like the perfect time for me to slip away. I go about my business getting ready for the concert, tuning my timpani, uncovering the piano. I think that needs to be tuned also, but of course, there isn't time today. I'll have to talk to Sammy about that. I run my fingers over the keys out of habit; this really is a wonderful instrument. It makes the one I've got at home look like a piece of junk. It responds to the lightest touch, but the keys are just the right weight (unlike electric keyboards, which I cannot handle no matter how convenient they are). I wish the practice room ones were this nice. I wish all pianos were this nice.

"Just saying good morning?" Daria asks, and I can tell she's smiling before I look up.

"More like coveting."

"Fair. It's a marvellous instrument."

I nod. I should really go get everything else set up.

"That's a heck of a haircut your partner got..."

My stomach drops. "He's not my partner anymore."

"Oh." Daria tucks her violin under one arm, perhaps freeing the other for a hug, so I turn and start checking the xylophone immediately to prevent sympathy contact. "I didn't know he'd transitioned."

"It's pretty new."

"Not being your partner. Is that pretty new, too?" There's an edge to her voice, and I can't tell if she's angry or sad.

"No, actually. But he's living with us now. It's...complicated."

"I'm sorry to hear that." Whatever the feeling was before, it's drained off and been replaced by sincerity. "Please consider me and Charlotte available to help if you need it. We've been through that, the complicated parts of transition. It's hard." She reaches out to squeeze my shoulder, and I let her. I don't know why she's telling *me* this, when I just told her we're not together, until I look up to see Drew staring at me. He walks away quickly, and I can't continue the conversation due to the noise of everyone tuning and warming up. Even with a smaller ensemble, it's quite the cacophony. Inside, I've got one, too. Daria's assumptions about me aren't wrong, but I still hate them.

I warm up, too, practicing some runs and quick transitions between instruments, and when the little kids file in behind Drew, bouncing their way toward their seats, changing order to sit next to their friends, their teachers trying to separate the troublemakers, I'm ready.

He and Carlos must have talked after I left, because Drew's got more information about each song now. He's mostly reading off his phone, but he still has a nice, natural way with them. When a kid puts his feet up on the seat, he wanders in his direction and quietly signals him to put them down. And the kid does. Shit. Kids just ignore me most of the time. What kind of super teacher magic is this? Best of all, Carlos beams approvingly when he tells them about the typewriter. Carnival of the Animals is fine, The Typewriter is fine. As expected, we can't do Peter and the Wolf because Leonard isn't here. It's too bad, because my part is dramatic and the whole piece has a great atmosphere. I check the time...it's going to come out pretty significantly short. Carlos must do the same math, because after Typewriter, he turns to all of us.

"Does anyone have a solo they'd like to share since we have some extra time?" I look around. No one moves. Someone should. And maybe, it dawns on me, this is a chance for me to shine a little, given that Lindy's gone...I want her job someday, and I'd love more time at the piano. I can show Carlos I've got more.

I raise my hand.

"Wonderful. What piece?"

"Uh, the Warsaw Concerto?"

The orchestra makes an "ooo" noise which makes me smile. "They don't have to accompany me..."

"No, no, let's give it the full effect. It should be on the iPads..." He turns to Daria. "Do you have it?"

She nods, and everyone settles as they find it. I wish I could. See, I have made one substantial miscalculation: Drew is watching me with great interest. It's not like he's never heard me play before, but...not like this, exactly? Not as a soloist. I'm sweating before I even start pushing the piano to the front of the stage. Glenn jumps up to help, and so do Felipe and Kelsie. And no, in case you're wondering, they don't need to practice it first. That's how talented these people are. And I'm just the guy working my tail off to be good enough to keep up with them. It's a good thing the opening chords are bruising and dramatic, because my heart is pounding hard, and it doesn't slow down until I get to the first tender section. The runs up and down feel like my breath traipsing over my ribs–a little jerky, but it's getting the job done. And while it's not as polished as I'd like, I get rousing applause when I finish, and I stand to give the kids a bow. That's when he catches my eye–Drew's clapping too, and he puts his fingers in mouth and whistles loudly. Even though it'd be more appropriate in the stands at Providence Park after a goal, I still feel a rush of pleasure at his enthusiasm. The concert's over, so there's no need to rush back to my other percussion instruments, but it still feels safer to return to the back of the stage.

"Mr. Rhodes." When I turn, Carlos is offering his hand. "Thank you for that offering; it was very moving. I don't think I've heard you solo before–is that right?"

Although I can't say for sure what he's heard, I shake my head. "No, sir. I've never soloed with the symphony before."

"We should change that." His gaze is appraising, his baton still tucked under his arm. "Would you like to add the Warsaw Concerto to our regular school concert repertoire?"

"Absolutely."

"Wonderful. It'll take a little more polish, but I know you're up for it."

"I am, sir. Thank you, I appreciate this."

He gives my shoulder a squeeze, then turns to someone who's waiting to talk to him. And you know who I want to call? Drew. But that's probably not appropriate, so I call Colby.

"Hey, guess who just got a solo with the symphony for kiddie concerts?"

"Daria?"

"No!"

"Frieda?"

"Who the fuck is Frieda?" I'm still on stage, putting things away, so I should really watch my language.

"You know, Frieda. She plays trombone. She's new."

"Is she?" I subtly look over my shoulder, and sure enough, a dark-haired woman I don't know is talking to the other horns. "Oh, yeah. Look at that."

"But it's you, isn't it?"

"It is me, thank you very much."

"Congrats, man. Love that for you."

"Thanks. We still on for ring shopping?"

He sighs, and it reminds me of the way my dad sighed when I broke his car window with a stray golf ball four years ago. It was a "this is gonna be expensive" sigh. "Yeah. Where should we meet?"

We end up going to a place downtown, and they're polite, even though they assume he's got a woman at home instead of a guy.

"They're all so...basic?" Colby mutters once the salesperson is out of range, leaning over the glass case. "Like something my dad would wear."

"I think that's the idea." I lean over to scrutinize them, too. He's right; they're pretty plain. "But the internet's a big place. We could probably find something younger."

"It just doesn't say...Chance? You know? I want to show him that I know him."

"Makes sense. You wanna hit a pawnshop?"

He straightens up, and his chin drops. "I can't buy someone's *heirloom*."

"Why not? They're the ones who needed the money. They knew it might not be there when they came back."

"That doesn't mean it's not important to them!"

I lift my hands in surrender. "Fine, fine. What do you suggest, then?"

"I don't know. Are titanium rings a thing? He's pretty hard on his shit."

"Good idea." I pull out my phone to search, aware peripherally that the salesman has returned. "You know what? Let's go to lunch. We can always come back."

We grab sandwiches down the street, both searching for rings on our phones as we eat.

"What about this one?" he asks, turning the screen.

"I think that's a mood ring."

"Oh."

"This?" I turn for him to see.

"That's BB-8!"

"What? He likes Star Wars, doesn't he?"

"Not that much..."

"I just searched for a robot ring..."

Colby frowns. "The internet says titanium is a no go. EMT's can't cut it off you in an emergency and you could lose a finger."

"Holy shit."

"Yeah." He puts down the phone and picks up his sandwich with both hands. "Maybe I don't need a ring."

"No, no—come on. Don't give up. We'll find something great."

"In my meagre price range? Before I leave? How much was that mood ring? Maybe I should consider that harder. I'd never have to wonder if he's mad at me."

"Thought he was the one who wondered about you."

"He is. Maybe I'll get a matching one."

"Yeah, that won't be weird at all..." We look at each, then laugh. But I haven't given up.

"Oh, look at this one." I show him, and his eyes go bright. It's got these tiny cogs embedded in the metal with a polished wooden band around the top. It's kind of wide, but it's so Chance. He loves mechanical stuff; he's constantly tinkering.

"Oh, shit. I love that."

"Yeah?" I feel relieved since this was my foolish suggestion. "It's not too much?"

He squints at the price. "I think my dad would loan me part of it. He mentioned something the other day."

"They'll be here soon, yeah?"

"Yep. Coming end of next week, staying for a month."

"Yay for Susan cooking one day a week!" I cheer, and he chuckles.

"It doesn't hurt the budget, does it?"

"No, because she makes three times as much as she needs to. She still thinks we eat like teenagers."

"No complaint here."

CHAPTER TWELVE

A FEW DAYS LATER, I'M sitting at the piano at home when I hear Drew curse for the first time. I'm right in the middle of "All the Things You Are," not singing the words, just humming a little, but it must be loud if I can hear it. His voice is high, tight, stressed, and I lower my volume, but don't stop playing. He's coughing, too, but that's just his asthma, which, as predicted, has been terrible since he's been downstairs. I can't rush in there every time he's in distress, right? I mean, it's not like he yelled out, "Evan, I need you! Get your ass in here!" But I'm listening as I keep going...and that's when I hear him curse again.

I pause. "Everything okay in there?"

"Uh. Kind of no?"

I slide off the bench, shuffling my bare feet over the hardwood floors as I peek into the kitchen through the swinging door.

"Do you want help?"

"No," he snarks, "I'd rather crash and burn my first time cooking dinner for our roommates. I'd rather be known as the person who messed up Mondays, the person they regret putting in charge of sustenance of any kind!"

"Okay, take it easy. No need to bust out the ten-dollar words."

He pauses, stirring a boiling pot of sauce. "Which one was overpriced? Never mind—can you preheat the oven?"

"Sure..."

"And get out a big pot and fill it with water?"

"Yep." Being bossed around is not my favorite thing, but he's clearly in distress...and I don't know exactly why, but I don't want him to look bad, either. We work in silence for a minute, him turning down the sauce so it won't spatter him (which I think was the source of the cursing before based on the little red dots on his arm), me doing what he asked and then turning to get out the pasta.

"No, I want fettucini."

"What are we making? Also, you're welcome."

"Pasta pomodoro."

"Sounds great." There's a slight lag as I search for the fettucini...it's kind of big and round, right? I think it's big and round and you stuff them with cheese. But I don't see anything like that.

"You don't know what fettucini is, do you?" Drew asks, amusement in his tone.

"Hey, I am offended. I definitely don't know what it is."

When he reaches past me to pull it out, his cologne wafts into my space, and it throws me for a second when my brain still expects perfume, but he doesn't seem to notice. He turns away to cough before he hands it to me. "Can you put in the garlic bread, too?"

"How were you going to do this by yourself?" I ask with a laugh. "You've got, what, thirty minutes until dinner?"

His mouth is a flat line. "Yeah, we'll need to hurry."

"We? I beg your pardon? I haven't heard so much as a 'thank you' since I came into the kitchen."

"You won't leave," he says, but when he glances at me, his gaze isn't so sure. With faux grumpiness, I hip-check him gently out of the way so I can put the bread in the oven. It seems the safest way to touch him without losing my tenuous grip on reality. He blinks at me, clearly surprised.

"What?"

"You could just *ask* me to move, weirdo." *Lean in,* my body prompts. *Get closer. He wants you to. He used to love playing with you like this.* But that's not what he's saying, is it?

"Sorry," I mutter instead, shoving those thoughts away hard. "You want a salad?"

"Sure." His voice is quiet, and the tension in the kitchen thickens like the sauce, the steam of whatever moment almost was evaporating. Because for a split second, I saw what my body saw: his wide eyes, the brush-stroke of pink on his cheek, the way he angled his face toward mine a little more squarely, like he was lining himself up...

I set up the cutting board on the other side of the fridge, and he probably thinks it's because there's more counter space...but I'm hiding. I lean over the food, focusing on the carrot I'm slicing, mostly because I'm not very good at chopping.

"Hey." His chilly hand on my elbow makes me jump, and I turn. His gaze is confused, searching, and I hate that I made him feel that way. "You know I was just kidding, right?" His hand is still on my arm, and I want to cover it with my own, to keep it there. But I can't. He says something else, but I can't hear him over the noise of that touch, even though it's not making a sound.

"Sorry, what?"

He squeezes my arm as he gives me a small smile. "I said I appreciate your help. I'm sorry if I was being an ass."

"No, you're fine. It's fine. I'm happy to help you. Any time."

He's looking at me like he's trying to read me, searching my gaze so earnestly that I feel my emotions wash up on the beach for a moment when Darren walks in.

"Whoa. The vibe in here is...intense." Drew's hand disappears as Darren angles his way into the fridge that he's blocking. "Is dinner almost ready?"

"Yup," Drew says quietly, "thanks to Evan, it'll be done soon."

Darren stands up out of the fridge, munching on a carrot stick. "So you guys switched?"

Drew's watching me, so I answer.

"No, we're just...collaborating."

Drew holds out his hand, palm up. "Ten dollars, please."

"Fuck off." I chuckle as I turn back to the salad.

"It's no worse than sustenance!"

"It's ten times worse than sustenance, thank you very much."

Then I feel his fingertips on my ribs, lightly, and I jerk. "Hey, I'm using a knife here! You know how fucking ticklish I am. How is it going to help dinner get done if I lose a finger?"

"Not to mention continue your music career," Darren says, now pouring himself a glass of milk. Drew's just grinning, and in spite of myself, I grin back. Over dinner, everyone compliments his cooking, even the garlic bread we burned a little. And I swear, every time he steals a glance at me from under those dark lashes, I pat myself on the back for sticking my nose where it didn't belong.

CHAPTER THIRTEEN

I CAN HEAR HIM COUGHING from the kitchen. He's all the way downstairs, where the futon is, and I'm sitting here listening to him, barking like a seal, while I drink my coffee. And I can't do anything about it. Colby's dad is sitting with me at the table in silence, scrolling on his phone.

"What's that sound?"

"Andrew. He's got asthma."

I'm trying not to be miserable and resentful, but I am mostly failing. I try harder when I heard his footsteps on the creaky wooden stairs.

"Morning," I greet him, and he gives us both a nod. When he turns sideways to pour himself a bowl of cereal, I can tell he's wearing his binder. He better not be wearing it to bed. That's not healthy—his skin needs to breathe, and it's not good for the tissue to be compressed. *And it's not healthy to obsess over someone you're not dating or be controlling about their body...* Point taken, brain.

"What're you doing this afternoon?"

Is he asking me? He's looking at me, so I think he must be. My heart cautiously peeks out of its cave of suffering, opening one eye as if it's a bear whose hibernation has been disturbed. "No plans after rehearsal. Why?"

"I was thinking..." He nudges a chunk of banana with his spoon. "If you're not busy, maybe you'd like to..."

I wait. And I am very patient about it. I don't tap my foot or sigh or anything. I just stare at the man I love and wait for him to ask me to do something very repulsive that I will probably say yes to, even if I don't want to. I would take him to the airport at 3 AM on a Monday morning. I'd help him paint a house. I'd pick him up after dental surgery, anything. Whatever he needs. And whatever my face looks like must convey that, because he takes a deep breath and lifts his gaze to mine before he finally—*finally*—makes his request.

"I'm going to get a tattoo, and I thought you might want to come with me." It comes out in a long string of words without pause. Now that he's said it, he's totally hiding behind his hands, putting his palms over his cheeks as he sits at the table.

My gut impulse is *no. No,* you can't defile your amazing skin with something so permanent when you're in such a fragile state. *No,* you can't walk into some skanky place that's not sterilizing the needles and ask them to ink something on your skin, which gives you an infection that kills you. Or worse, spells something ironically wrong, which is then permanent. *No!* my brain is still throwing a tantrum, tossing the word around like a child with blocks when asked to take a bath. *No, no, no!* And I know it's not really about the tattoo, it's about all the change he's been through already. All the ways he's changed without me. But at least he's including me this time.

"Sure, I can do that." He's decided to do this; the determined look on his face tells me that there's no way

I'll stop him. At least if I go with him, I can make sure it's sterile. That's the lie I'm telling myself, anyway. And this'll be good practice for me in letting go of control.

"You don't have to if you don't want to..."

"No, I want to! I do want to." I am making this awkward so fast, it's mindboggling, but he smiles anyway. "What were you thinking of getting?"

He shrugs with one shoulder. "Pride flag or something, probably."

"Huh." I make eye contact with Chris as he stands up to leave, and he smirks at me.

Drew rolls his eyes so hard, I'm amazed they stay in his sockets. "What's wrong with a pride flag?"

"Nothing! Nothing. It just doesn't feel like...you." I take a sip of my coffee. "You seem more like a *chainsaw, punk rock, Jesus still on the cross* kind of a guy."

"Not an orca?" he asks, straight-faced, and it takes me a moment to realize this is an oblique reference to the Timbers' rival's mascot, in keeping with my chainsaw comment.

"No. Though I'm sure your blowhole is amazing."

The way he chokes on his cereal is extremely satisfying. "Which part of me is my blowhole, exactly?"

"If you don't know, I'm not telling," I say, wanting to push at his shoulder, squeeze his hand, anything to get that contact between us. But all he gives me is a skeptical, amused stare.

"Jesus still on the cross? You know that's a Catholic thing, right?"

Of course I didn't. "Of course I do. I'm just saying. Something religious might make more sense for you than a flag that's only been part of your life for a short time. You can be more than your sexuality."

"I *am* more than my sexuality, asshole." Drew stands up fiercely, and I go with him instinctively, afraid he's mentally tearing up the invitation he just issued. I don't want him going through that alone. And more than that, I'm expecting too much. I've seen plenty of guys go through this stage—having been in the closet so long, they just want to shout about this facet of themselves. They buy all the T-shirts and hang their flags in the windows and get bumper stickers that say "Keep Portland Queer." It's just that the dam breaks, and they need some way to finally express that they're here, that they've waited long enough, and that they're part of the group they've been watching from the sidelines, hurting, benched, bottled. So, of course he wants a pride flag. How could I be so dense?

"I'm sorry," I say quickly, reaching out to touch his shoulder, but he steps back before I can make contact. "You should get whatever you want. It's your body. I have no right to an opinion."

"Damn straight." The fire is fading a little from his gaze, but he still looks pissed.

"I don't think you can use that expression anymore."

He crosses his arms, but his mouth quirks. "How do you know I'm not into girls?"

"Are you?" I try to picture him having sex with a woman, and it just makes jealousy pang in my belly. *Hopeless heart, always thinking he's still yours.*

"I'm not sure, but I don't think so." He sits back down, so I do, too. "Might give girl sex a try if I thought I wouldn't be a tremendous disappointment to my partner." It's a risk, talking to him like this. I'm revealing too much, giving myself away. But I can't keep the endearment or the sentiment inside.

"Sweetheart, having experienced the full Andrew, I feel confident that no one's ever left your bed unsatisfied."

He snorts, shoveling his now-mushy cereal into his mouth. "That's a ringing endorsement. Maybe that's what I should get tattooed on my body."

"Just make sure you credit me." My stomach is twisting as I watch him eat; he doesn't seem as mad as he did, but I'm not sure I'm out of the doghouse yet for my ill-considered comment. "Am I still allowed to tag along?"

Drew sighs deeply. "I guess so. But only because I don't want a hack job, and I think you can help me find a good place."

"Of course I can. Who do you think goes with Colby?" His bowl is now empty, and I reach for it slowly, asking with my eyes if I can take it. Drew leans back, wiping his mouth with a napkin, and gives me a nod that seems reluctantly grateful. Standing up, I swallow hard, and I can only ask my next question while I'm facing the sink and giving him my back. "How's the new job going?"

"Pretty good. The money isn't as good as Marble, but the hours are better."

"Well, if anyone fucks with you, just let me know."

He's loading his mug into the dishwasher, and he bumps against my side a little, but I'm not sure he meant to. "What is that supposed to mean, Ev?"

"Just that not all musicians are nice. If they're giving you shit, you can let me or Sammy know, and we'll take care of it."

"Because suddenly, I'm not capable of taking care of myself? Is that it? You never tried to coddle me like this when I was presenting as a woman. I just don't get it."

You didn't seem as broken then. But even I have to admit that some of the brokenness is smoothing out, sanded down as he settles in here. My roommates are doing a good job of making him feel welcome...unlike me. I still wish he'd go back to school.

"So, what time are we taking off?"

"Whenever you're ready."

I pause by the living room door. "But what time is your appointment?"

He blinks. "Appointment?" It's such an innocent face, and it wants kisses, I can tell.

"Yeah, appointment. You didn't think you could just walk into a nice tattoo parlor and get this done, did you?"

"Well...yeah. I guess I did."

"Come 'ere," I say, gesturing with my head towards the living room, and cautiously, he follows me.

"What we doing?"

"Using Picstagram for the one thing it's good for," I say, opening up the app. We spend the new few minutes looking at the artwork of some local artists, trying to get a feel for what style he's looking for. And coincidentally enough, the one he chooses is someone I know: Glenn's brother, Bear. So, I call him on speakerphone. "Hey, it's Evan."

"Hey!" His voice sounds exactly like Glenn's and it kind of weirds me out. Twins are kinda creepy. "What's going on?"

"Got a friend who wants a tattoo. Do you have any appointments before he loses his nerve?" I get the smack I deserve, and Bear chuckles.

"He gonna jump around under the needle and ruin my work like a certain sibling of mine?"

Glenn's tattoos are gorgeous, so this is total bullshit, but I respect the energy. It reminds me of the way I love Colby; it's there whenever I come back for it, no matter how much we hang out or don't. It's steady. It's predictable, but somehow, not boring? It's like making a really great pancake recipe—you know how you want it to taste, and the fact that it always does couldn't possibly bother you, because that's the reason you make it. No one's trying to reinvent pancakes, and if they are, they should fucking stop, because pancakes are perfect just the way they are. Also, I thought about banging Colby for about ten seconds before it was obvious he'd make a better friend. That shit is irreplaceable...strangely, as irreplaceable as what I feel for Drew. I'm feeling bad that Colby and I haven't spent much time together lately, but we've both been too busy moping about our men. Not that I'm going to invite him along to this. But I do resolve to find something for us to do together. I could stand to get out of the house now that I'm not doing my hibernating bear impression, complete with roaring at anyone who dared approach the mouth of my proverbial den.

"Nah, he's got nerves of steel. Or he can fake it to impress us."

"You are the absolute worst," he growls, but he sounds like a wolf pup trying to convince the big dogs that he's fierce, nipping at their ears and paws because that's what he can reach. I hold up a finger to my lips chidingly.

"Please. I'm on the phone."

Bear chuckles again. "Yeah, I've got a spot in two weeks—somebody cancelled. Saturday at 2:00 or you can get on the waitlist. It's four months long."

I glance at Drew, and I think I can see a thin sheen of sweat on his forehead at his hairline, but he gulps and nods. *Brave.* He always was.

"We'll take it. Thanks, Bear." As soon as I hang up, he's holding out his hand for my phone.

"Can I see those pictures again?"

"Let's do one better." On the website for Bear's shop, Spiked, there's a whole portfolio of his work, so I pull it up on my laptop and pass it over to him. I expect him to just dive into it himself, but as usual, he surprises me.

"What hurts more, just the black outline or the color?" he asks.

I lift an eyebrow, settling down into the old couch with him, and it creaks beneath my weight. "What's more important, how much it hurts right now or what it looks like for the next ninety years of your life?"

Now it's his turn to be skeptical. "I'm going to live to be 115? Kinda doubt it."

"Why, you taking up skydiving?"

"I think skydiving is statistically pretty safe," he says, but his voice is a little more vacant, betraying the fact that his brain is taking in the crosses, roses, lion heads, and scrolled names on the website. My favorites of Bear's are the ones that are more abstract—no, that's not the right word. A little more metaphorical? He did one with someone getting picked up by an umbrella, propelled upward by rain falling in the wrong direction, and every few months, I think about it. I watch Drew's face, placid but interested, leaning closer to see the art better. "I think I've seen this one before."

"It's Glenn's, Hillary's partner."

"Oh!" He squints at it again. Does he need glasses? He'd look hot in something straight and black, square, metal, sitting on the bridge of his freckle-sprinkled nose. I shake my head to dispel the thought.

"You don't think my skin's going to be a problem, do you?"

It takes me a second to figure out what he means, since his skin is perfect and supple and divine. "Oh, no. I'm sure he can work with your tone. You don't have to be pasty white like Colby to be used as a canvas."

"I heard that!" Colby yells from the kitchen, and I grin.

"What about it? You're like a piece of paper!"

"I am not!"

Drew goes back to Instagram, ignoring our antics, and I wish I could touch him. His skin color is one of the things that first drew me to him physically...it's this sepia tone that I can't quite describe. Kind of a golden brown, fawnlike, but fairly light. He basically looks like a lot of Californians, only their pigmentation was purchased at a tanning place. He comes by his naturally, since his parents are from Hawaii.

"Still gonna get a pride flag?"

Drew shrugs, still looking at the screen. "Maybe he'll have a good suggestion."

"You should make your mom happy and just tattoo some of those smelly flowers on you."

His lips quirk, amused. "Do you mean plumeria?"

"Probably. I guess that's maybe too girly. Ooh, or just do an outline of the big island or something?"

"I think I'm good."

"Maybe you could find some quote about history or some—" My voice stops working abruptly when he puts his hand on my leg.

"Dude. I'm fine. I'll figure it out." I stare at the hand, his amber hand against my skin, a beautiful study in contrasts. And yet, inside, we're mostly the same. I've always felt that.

"Right. Of course." I leave him to look in peace, hoping he doesn't change his mind between now and two weeks from now...if only so we can spend time together.

CHAPTER FOURTEEN

THAT NIGHT, WE ALL make dinner to welcome Chris and Susan officially. "Boys, this looks wonderful," Colby's mom gushes as we all sit down at the dining room table. She doesn't need to know how many piles of mail and sheet music and laundry we cleared off this table yesterday. If she notices the stray pair of Darren's gym shorts under her chair, she's too polite to mention it. "Doesn't it look wonderful, Chris?"

"Yeah, looks good," he agrees. "Not even ordered in like last time."

"Hey," Colby says, and Chris smirks.

"Something to say, son?"

"It was still good food."

"It was. I don't get much Mexican in Thailand. Not decent Mexican, anyway."

"What's Thailand like?" Tony asks.

"Pretty interesting. Cheap to live," Chris says as he starts the potatoes. We roasted two chickens over them, so they're fatty and beautiful. I just hope there's enough.

I don't mean to, but I keep glancing toward the front door. Drew was supposed to be home five minutes ago. It's only five minutes, but...

"I have an announcement before the night gets away from us," Hillary says. "Well, *we* have an announcement."

"Are you pregnant?" Colby asks, and Chris's expression turns serious...and possibly a little bit pale.

"Wait, are you?" Susan asks, leaning forward.

"No way," Patrick says. "She doesn't look tired enough."

"I think that comes later," I say. "Maybe she's just a pregnant lady who still drinks caffeine. Are you giving your baby caffeine?"

"Family, this is not twenty questions!" Hillary huffs. "No, I am not pregnant! We're moving in together!"

"I thought you'd already done that," Chris says, but Susan elbows him.

"That's great news. We're so happy for you both." She gets up to hug them, and that seems to be closer to the response Hillary was hoping for. When she sits back down, she's glowing.

Glenn seems as laid back as usual, sitting back in their chair, arm casually slung over the back of Hillary's chair, fingers playing in her hair. The motion mellows her somewhat, and she snuggles into their side.

"Feel better?" they ask, and she smiles at them. And now I'm really staring at the front door, because the food's disappearing. It's not because their warm, clingy demeanor is making me want things I can't have. But if it was, it's easier to focus on green beans and oatmeal rolls and making sure he gets a thigh because he doesn't like white meat.

Everyone's catching Chris and Susan up on their recent accomplishments: Tony landing the part of Pepe in *West Side Story*, Patrick's YouTube channel breaking 500,000 subscribers, Darren's invitation to speak at a conference on adoption. I think I've gotten out of my turn when I slip into the kitchen to get some aluminum foil to put over Drew's food to keep it warm, but when I return, all eyes are on me.

"And what's new with you, Rhodes?" Chris asks as I sit back down. He always calls me Rhodes. He's such a guy. I wonder if he'll call Drew Kahananui or if he'll wimp out because of the pronunciation—he has lived overseas enough that he might not. I give it fifty/fifty.

"Nothing much," I say, hoping the conversation will move on. "There's dessert, right?"

"Yes, I made a maple apple torte," Hillary says excitedly. "I know it's more of a fall thing, but I couldn't help myself, I—"

"Hang on a second, Hil," Susan says, patting her arm. "Nothing at all?"

They're watching me patiently.

"Nope."

Colby scowls. "You're performing the Warsaw Concerto for the symphony. I wouldn't call that nothing."

"It's just for the kid concerts."

"Still. I think that's wonderful. And sometimes our dreams take stepping stones. And as Carlos sees that you're reliable, you'll be in line for bigger and better. This is great." Susan's smile is so warm and genuine, I know she believes everything she's saying. And in my head, I do too, so I smile back. But my soul is fucking tired of waiting. My soul thinks the line is outdated, that it shouldn't be based on who got there first; it should be based on who's the most talented. Maybe I'm genuinely not better than Lindy. But I want the chance to prove I am. This *is* a good opportunity, and I should be thankful for it. But right now, it feels like the smallest concession to my long list of discontents.

"Thanks, Mom," I say, but she ignores my slight sarcasm and gives me a hug anyway.

The front door opens, and I hear Colby say, "There you are. We were starting to get worried."

I break the hug, and my heart pounds harder when I see him. Every time, it's like someone's injected me with adrenaline, just seeing him in my house. Knowing he's here. Close by. It just...feels right. Like finding out there were more keys on your instrument, to notes you've never heard before, yet knowing just what you want to play with them.

"Saved you a plate," I say, because I'm selfish and want him to know it was me. He gives me a nod that's a little stiff as he puts down his stuff.

Susan is bubbling in the background, fussing over him, talking about how Chris might have some winter clothes he could have if he needs them. Her pace doesn't match her words, and she almost looks like she's stalking him, getting closer and closer to the hug I know she wants with every sentence. It's honestly adorable to watch.

And because she has Mom Magic™, Drew seems almost hypnotized by her, like he didn't know she was asking for a hug until it was upon him, but he'd somehow also opened his arms. Then he puts his head on her shoulder and something wells up inside me that wants to come out as tears. This family. They're gonna kill me. I don't think I thought about how much he must be missing his family until right now. They're close—I mean, my dads and I are close, too, but they're physically close. They'd do family game night and shit on a regular basis, too. I want to give that back to him. As much as I want to be all he needs, I think I just realized I can't be.

CHAPTER FIFTEEN

WHEN I WAKE UP, I'M out of bed before I'm fully awake, even though my alarm hasn't gone off yet. Yes, I set an alarm on a Saturday. Because it is tattoo day, and I can't risk him leaving without me. Wait—I'm driving. How would he leave without me? He could ask someone else to drive him. That's not okay, either. I want to be the one there with him, easing his fears, teasing him until he forgets the pain. I can do this for him.

I scrub away the sleep in the shower, and I'm downstairs making omelets when he stumbles into the kitchen. He's got his binder on under his PJ's and I bite back a comment about it.

"No pancakes?"

"No, this'll be better for your recovery. High protein. I did potatoes and mushrooms on the side, if you want them. Eat up."

He's just staring at me, looking still a little unstable on his feet. "What time is it?"

"Uh..." I check my watch. "6:15."

Drew swears softly. "You're this wound up, and we're not leaving for four hours?" He takes the plate I'm offering, and I smile.

"Three hours and forty minutes. Might hit traffic. Eat up while it's hot. Come on."

He groans, but he slumps into the kitchen chair. "I'm gonna make you run laps around the house or something."

I bounce a little in place, unable to contain myself. "Cool. I'm up for it. Put me in, coach."

Shaking his head, Drew carefully cuts himself a bite of the omelet with the side of his fork.

"Did you say mushrooms?"

I bring over the platter with a smile. "Here you are, sir. Anything else I can get you?"

The corner of his mouth quirks like he's trying not to smile. "Cup of coffee?"

"I'm sorry, sir, coffee is contraindicated. It'll dehydrate the hell out of you. We want that skin nice and supple to drink that ink. I'll get you some water." I hustle over to the cupboard and get him a big glass, filling it to the brim from the fridge—he likes it cold. I give Darren and Tony a nod as they shuffle into the kitchen.

"Ev. Seriously. You gotta chill."

"Caaann'tt," I moan, sitting down next to him. "Do you have the design all worked out? Do you have the appropriate lotions for after care? Do you want to go anywhere to celebrate afterwards, or do you think you'll be tired? Do you—"

Andrew's warm hand covers my mouth before I can say any more, and I grin beneath it.

"I'm gonna leave you here and take the bus if you don't chill." Even though I'm loving the contact, I pull his hand away by his wrist.

"Won't do any good. I know where you're going. I can just meet you there. No worries."

"Oh, it's tattoo day? What are you getting?" Tony asks, sticking a mug in the coffeemaker.

"I'm not showing anyone until it's done," he mutters, stealing a glance at me. "That way, no one can talk me out of it."

"Are you getting the lyrics to Hamilton?" I ask, and he gives me a critical glare. "Mickey Mouse? One of those 'I'm zipping open your spine' tattoos? Ooh, I hope not, those creep me out. Snoopy? Roses with the word 'Mom?'"

"If I am getting a creepy spine tattoo, when would you ever get to see it?" Drew asks, and I can't tell if he's joking. I'd get to see it, right? He wouldn't keep it from me forever?

"You don't have to tell anyone what you're getting," Tony assures him, but I shake my head.

"You have to tell your artist," I say, "but it sounds like you've already done that."

"Did I hear Glenn is meeting you there?" Darren asks, and Andrew nods.

"They were thrilled to hear that I was getting my first one, and wanted to come and support me." In the back of my mind, I'm now wondering if he really wants me to go after all. Maybe our group is just doing what our group does and coming around him in support. But maybe he was worried I would bail on him. Maybe he wanted backup. I've already shown my hand and how much I want to go. I can't exactly back out now gracefully. And it's not like I want to...but if he doesn't want me there, maybe that's the right thing to do. *Would he tell me if he changed his mind?*

"Hopefully Hillary doesn't come too," Andrew grumps. "I don't think I can handle two people bouncing off the walls right now." *Right. So apparently, my enthusiasm was too much.*

I get up from the kitchen table under the guise of making space for one of my roommates, but really, I just don't want anyone looking at my face right now.

"Where are you going?" Andrew calls, and I answer without turning around.

"Just going to take that run you recommended," I say. "Be back soon."

I head out the back door, curling around the side of the house towards the front. This really isn't how I pictured this morning going. I thought... I don't know what I thought. The walk is doing way more good than I thought it would, though. *This isn't about me. I'm just being too sensitive. I'm glad they're just doing what good friends do and showing up to help.* The next time I storm out in a jealous huff, however, I'm going to bring a jacket. One trip around the block is all it really takes for me to calm down and talk some sense into myself *(If he didn't want you to come, he'd say that)*, and I come back in through the front door. What I don't expect is Drew. He stands up quickly from the piano bench, but not quickly enough to hide the fact that he was sitting sideways, facing the door, not the keys...

"You really left? What's wrong?"

I shoot him a skeptical look to protect myself. "Nothing..."

"You're so full of shit." He stuffs his hands in his pajama pants pockets, then looks down in wonder. "Even guy *pajamas* have pockets? Clothes made for women are so overrated." Before I can make fun of him, he looks up again. "You're still coming, right?"

"Thought you were taking the bus..." I quip.

"I've had my breakfast now, and I'd like to reconsider."

I nod somberly. "We all make poor decisions sometimes under the influence of low blood sugar."

"And nervousness."

I can't shove my hands in *my* pockets, because they're too tight, so I fold them behind my back in a move I hope looks natural. That is, I hope it doesn't look like I'm trying to hold myself back.

"You'll be okay. I'll be there with you. Nothing bad will happen."

He rolls his eyes. "And if that was something you could actually promise, that might mean more..."

"I don't think you were this cynical when we were dating."

He chuckles. "I was, actually. I just had my body pressed up against yours when I rolled my eyes, so you were too twitterpated to notice."

I hold out my hand, face up. "Ten dollars."

He laughs. "Fuck off."

"No, I mean it. Pay up. That's a ten-dollar word if I've ever heard one," I insist, pacing forward, just because I fucking love to hear him laugh. And he does, twisting away from me like I've got cooties.

"Fuck off, I said."

"Twitterpated? You expect me to let *twitterpated* go? I don't think so, boy genius."

He turns and starts up the stairs—going where? No idea. But I'm gonna find out.

"I need all my money for the tattoo," he calls over his shoulder, and now I'm just chasing him on principle.

"I'll pay for the tattoo. Now fork it over."

He's laughing even harder now, vaulting himself up the wooden steps by the railing. "What's the point in that, you weirdo? That's a pyrrhic victory. You like dropping $250 on nothing?"

You mean on you? Hell yes.

"A prick victory? Are we talking about my dick now? Why, what's he going to get?" I catch him at the top around his waist and pin him against the wall with my shoulder. But he's laughing so hard, I don't think I even need to hold him. "Oh, man. I can't wait. My prick's been plenty lonely lately." As he catches his breath (which seems to be rougher than I think it should be after just going upstairs), his face is already close to mine, but he pushes it closer defiantly.

"Why, you forget how to flirt?"

"A master never forgets. Now cough up my money."

"Funny you should bring up the word 'master'...Haven't seen you bringing anyone home lately."

I can't believe he's asking about this, and paired with his proximity, it's got me a little flustered, so I back up without thinking. "How would you know, basement boy?"

He coughs, like the very mention of the place is irritating his lungs, and I cringe. But it doesn't deter him. "You used to keep me up all night, and now you're sending them home in the middle of the night? Your skills must have really atrophied..."

"Twenty dollars!" I holler, holding out my hand and pointing to my open palm. "That's *two* words! Now it's twenty!"

"Seriously, though," he says, stepping toward me, "when's the last time you got laid? It can't have been *that* long."

The truth is that I tried—I really did. I intended to bring lots of people home, just like I used to. In dark clubs, we kissed and groped, and it was terrible. I hated it. And gender made no difference—no one was doing it for me. I ended up going home before anything really happened. So, the last time I got laid? That'd be the day we broke up. But if I admit that, he's going to know how broken I was. Still kinda am. My silence has stretched on too long while I figure out whether to lie to him, and his face is turning stormy, his eyebrows pulled together.

"No one?" he whispers, crossing his arms over his chest.

I don't know what to say, so I just look down the stairs. I need a joke. I should celebrate his tattoo day. I just chased him up here to make him laugh, not make him sad.

"Don't worry about me," I say, finding a grin. "I always land on my feet." I'm ten steps away from my room, where I could be safe from this intrusive line of questioning. It's too tempting.

"Ev..."

"I'm gonna go change. Drink some more water. You gotta stay hydrated. It's super important."

He reaches out to stop me, but I step back, and he reads my gentle rebuff correctly—his pity is the last thing I want or need. But he doesn't look happy to see me going.

"Twenty dollars," I say, as I close the door, "and I'll bring my wallet for the tattoo."

I sit down behind my drum set, because it's the one way I know to keep people away from my door. They assume I can't hear them with the headphones on. But they're underestimating my ability to ignore things that I simply don't want to think about. This isn't the day to think about my doomed love life, so I'm not. I just slip on the headphones...and I don't.

CHAPTER SIXTEEN

THREE HOURS AND THIRTY minutes later, there's a knock at my door.

"Ev? You ready to go?"

I fling the door open. "Ready, Freddy."

Drew rolls his eyes, then stops. "I thought you were going to change."

I look down at my clothes; they're perfect. My gray hoodie that's already got paint on the sleeve, so I don't care if there's a blood or ink incident. My stonewashed jeans. My red Converse. I'm not changing.

"Oh, I did. Then I changed back. You know me. Fickle." He gives me a weird look, but turns and heads down the hall toward the back stairs. I follow him downstairs to get shoes on, and my phone buzzes with a text.

Glenn: Heard you're going with Andrew for his tattoo?

Evan: That's the plan.

Glenn: I'm not needed, then. Bear lives up to his name when the studio gets too crowded. Meet you guys after though, if you want? My treat.

Evan: Sounds like fun if he's up to it.

Glenn: Great. Good luck!

Evan: Thanks.

I wonder how they heard that...Drew's face is suspiciously neutral as we get into the car. He has this way of putting on an air of innocence even when he's guilty of sneakiness; when he threw me a birthday party, I had no idea until I walked into the house. That's the way I feel now: blindsided in a nice way. I hope Glenn's feelings weren't hurt; unlike Drew, Glenn wears their heart on their sleeve most of the time, so I feel like I'd know. I'll make it up to them.

Spiked smells like disinfectant and pastrami...Bear's just finishing up with the previous client, and someone else is getting lunch delivered. *They better eat that in the back.* But I should relax, because the person in question—a cute blonde with pink streaks and a lot of piercings—heads to the back immediately. *I should relax.* Bear's great. He'll do a good job. He's thinner than Glenn, with hair long enough to pull back and white skin untouched by the tattoo gun in the sparse places where I can see it. He also seems to favor flannel, however, and he gives us a beardy smile when we walk in.

"Hey, Andrew. I'll be right with you. Hey, Evan."

I give him a wave, then nudge Drew over to the seating area. The buzz of the gun is a baseline to the music of the place; there's no loud music over the top, which surprises me a little. Every other time I've been in here, it's been Metal City. It's got an ambiance, you know? But not today, I guess. The woman Bear's been working on sits up, and he gives her a mirror to look at it; it's a sleeve, and I'd guess he's already been at it for at least four sessions. It's going to be incredible when it's done, but right now, it's mostly outlines and some shading. It strikes me that that's a little like Drew right now...I know the outline of him, but not all the colors. I've got the shape, but not the full picture. Not yet. Like a good tattoo, these things take time.

She moves off to the side, and the front desk gal, who's back from eating her sandwich, is chatting with her as she eats a snack before she goes.

"Andrew?" Bear says, and they shake hands. "Great to meet you, man."

"Yeah, same." I think he's trying to make his voice lower. That's gonna take some practice. "Thanks for squeezing me in."

"Oh, it's my pleasure. I love breaking a tattoo virgin. And your design was an honor to work on."

I almost forgot that I hadn't seen the actual picture yet. Bear goes to work, getting fresh supplies and cleaning Drew's shoulder...the binder is posing a problem, however.

"If it's in the way now," Bear explains, "it's going to slow down your healing unless you want to go without it. And I know that's a very personal choice."

Drew's looking down at the tray, clearly disappointed, but I put a hand on his sleeve. "Where else were you thinking of getting it?"

"My wrist."

Bear nods. "That's a good spot, too. Not painful like ribs or feet. Though it would look gorgeous on your foot."

I'd swear Drew's blushing a little. See? I knew he wasn't into girls. He didn't give that cute receptionist a second glance when we came in.

"Maybe the next one down there. The wrist is good."

"Great," Bear says with a smile. "Okay, so here's the final artwork." He slides a white paper with a geometric drawing of a lizard on it over to Drew, and his face lights with interest. "I know it's not exactly what we discussed, but I didn't feel comfortable using actual Hawaiian designs, since those have cultural significance in terms of materials and practice."

"No, it's great. Really great. And we can do the whole thing today?"

Bear smiles again, like he's adorable. Which he is, so...fair. "Yes, I can have you out of here in about an hour since it's just the one color and not too big."

"Fantastic." Drew settles back into the chair, and I sit on his right side. And everything's fine—he's chatting with Bear, with me, looking around the place...until the work starts.

"Holy—" Drew bites his lip. "That fucking *hurts*."

Glenn's mouth twists. "Some people are more sensitive to it than others. Try to take your mind off it. We can take breaks if you need to."

Drew turns to me. "Talk to me."

"Uh, okay. About what?"

"Anything. California history. Something."

I scratch my head. "California history? Like...the gold rush?"

He rolls his eyes, and when the gun touches him again, he jumps a little. "Just—anything. Distract me."

"Most of what I remember about California history comes from the Oregon Trail game. My computer mom always died of dysentery."

Drew mumbles something that sounds like *hopeless*, and I grin at him. But my grin fades when he reaches down and grabs my hand with his free arm, twisting our fingers together. His hand is warm, and his skin is soft, and the sweetness of it makes my eyes flutter shut for just a second, trying to keep it together. Tearing up in the tattoo parlor was not on my to-do list for today, but we've both always been needy when it comes to physical touch.

"Keep talking." It's not a request, but my brain's feeling pretty stuck on *we're holding hands. He brought me here so he could hold my hand when he's in pain.* He's sweating, and I wish I could wipe it away for him, but that would probably cross the friend line.

"I think you should talk. Tell me about the tattoo. What does it mean?"

"A few things," he says, his voice strained. "We have lots of lizards in Hawaii, obviously. The geometric design is evocative of Hawaiian artwork, and the word is significant."

"Word?" I ask, peering at the paper. "What word?"

"Māhū," he says, and as soon as he says it, I can see it, hidden in the lines like it's been written in a spider's web.

"Whoa." The word comes out quiet, and Bear chuckles.

"Did I blow your mind, bud?"

"A little bit," I say, looking closer at it. It's like an optical illusion, like Escher's stairs, and I'm just staring. "What does it mean?"

"It's kind of like two-spirit in Hawaiian. An idea that's been around for a long time."

"So you heard about māhū growing up?"

Drew snorts. "No. But I was reading about Hawaiian history, and I came across it. It's one thing I was thinking about studying in grad school. You know, before..."

"That'd be amazing," I say, and I mean it. I give his hand a tiny squeeze, and he squeezes mine back harder.

"You want a break?" Bear asks, but Drew shakes his head, his gaze resting on our joined hands.

"I'm good."

"Is there more to the lizard?"

He nods slowly, trying not to jostle his arm, I think. "There's a Bible verse about them. They're one of the wise creatures. 'The lizard you may grasp with the hands, / Yet it is in kings' palaces.' And in Hawaiian culture, lizards are resilient, because they can lose their tails and just keep going."

I lean forward and lower my voice. "Forgive me, but this is so much better than a pride flag."

Drew chuckles a little. "I think so, too."

"That's so weird that you never heard about māhū before."

"I mean...I guess I did. But it was more like an insult. It didn't used to be. They used to be respected as leaders in the community, spiritual leaders. Some people are trying to bring that meaning back."

"Like you."

"I guess so." He's quiet for a moment, and his thumb swipes along mine. "It's weird, because it was Christianity that kind of fucked things up."

"So you're part of the problem and part of the solution, huh?"

"Yeah. It's an odd balance, to be honest. Christians have done so much damage to indigenous cultures all over the world that I can't ignore that part of it. But I also wasn't directly at fault for that, so taking the blame feels strange. Especially when I've also been hurt by it."

I'm nodding slowly, but that's a pretty deep conversation for the tattoo parlor, and I don't know what to say, so I settle on, "That sounds complicated."

"What can I say? I'm an enigma."

"Thirty dollars."

"Dream on."

"Look, I was being nice—I let you get away with 'evocative' earlier as a freebie because you were in pain, but 'enigma'? No. No, sir. Not on my watch. Super smart boys with big vocabularies must pay the tax so that less intelligent boys like me can buy beer."

"That makes zero sense."

I shrug. "That's the rule, dude."

"It's a ridiculous rule, and I defy it."

"Forty dollars."

"For what?! 'Defy'?"

"For the delay in paying the original tax. You now owe interest."

Bear chuckles. "You guys are funny. How long have you been dating?"

We look at each other, and I don't think either of us knows what to say. So I go with the truth.

"We're not, actually. Just here to support my friend."

"Uh-huh." The word is polite, but skeptical. Bear wipes away the blood, and I crane my neck to see it better.

"How's it look?" Drew asks. He hasn't looked over there once...is he squeamish about blood? I had no idea.

"Really good. I love it." *And you,* I say with my gaze, but he just keeps staring at me, like he's trying to memorize my face. "Tell me more about Hawaiian history."

He does, and I hold his hand until Bear bandages him up. Glenn's offer sticks in my throat when I try to bring it up afterward...for the first time since he moved in, we shared an actual physical connection. And call me selfish, but I just want to keep my resilient, defiant, brave guy all to myself today.

CHAPTER SEVENTEEN

ON SUNDAY MORNING, I get up early to make sure he was still doing okay. I've never gotten a tattoo, but I've gone with Colby before to get them, and I know they can hurt like a mother the next day. He'll need to hydrate. He'll need...

A quiet knock at the front door startles me. Almost everyone else is still in bed...maybe everyone. I rise from the couch where I was noodling around on my phone in my boxers, coffee still in hand, and unlock the front door. But when I open it, the dark-haired woman before me makes me freeze. It's like my muscles are locked in place. Because even though Andrew and his sister don't have the same coloring, they do have the same face—the same dimple, the wide ears, the cute nose. Grace hides hers with hair—the ears, that is—but they are so alike. Even her voice when she says, "Hi, Evan."

"Hey," I croak, and take a sip of my coffee. "What's up?"

"Can I come in?"

I glance down at my boxers meaningfully. "It's not a great time..."

Her hands tighten around her giant purse. "Just...are you sure you haven't seen (Andrew)? We're all so worried about (him). And I know (he) cares about you, trusts you."

I frown. "We broke up months ago, you know..."

"(He) still kept a picture of you two by (his) bed. I guess I thought maybe it was one of those 'on again, off again' things..." That's an interesting new piece of information, and it has my heart beating faster, remembering yesterday.

Tangled fingers, mingled sweat, his steady gaze as the tattoo gun approached. I sip my coffee again.

"Just an *'off'* thing, no *'again.'* Sorry."

Her lower lip trembles and a sob escapes. "I'm getting married, and (he's) supposed to be a bridesmaid..." Her eyes meet mine, and I know she knows. Drew must have told her, and she reacted even worse than I did. "I think that's part of what set all this off. I think (he) couldn't imagine..."

"Imagine what?" I say, even though it's a dick move. I want to hear her say it. I want to hear her say that she rejected him.

For what it's worth, I didn't mean to reject him. I needed time. I thought it was going to be weird, and honestly, it kind of is, but it's also glorious and wild and tender and sweeping in a way I couldn't have imagined. And that's the point, right? I couldn't imagine him like this, so I didn't know. Just like Grace doesn't know. And that isn't her fault, either. But she's still not saying anything, and it boosts my respect for her that she's not willing to out him to me.

"Tell you what," I say slowly, "if I see the person we're talking about..." Her eyes flare with hope. "...I will let that person know that you'd like to talk."

She's tempted now, I can tell, to use the right pro-nouns, but she doesn't. She swipes at her face in annoy-ance; at least her tears have mostly dried.

"Would you give...the person a message?"

I cross my arms, but nod, mostly because it's too cold to be standing at the front door in my underwear hav-ing this conversation. "Tell the person that I'm so sorry for what I said. That the more I think about it, this fits. That it makes sense. I was just caught off guard, and I..." She trails off, examining the azaleas near the front porch, dormant now. "I just needed time to adjust. But I'm ready now. And I can't imagine getting married without this person at my side."

"I'll try to remember all that," I say dryly, and she laughs a little. "If I see that person, who is safe and with people who care about them." And here I pause, because the whole Mara thing has made me leery. But what the hell? "Would you like a hug?" It's not in my nature, I'll be honest, but she seems like she needs one, and I know what that feels like. Also, I wouldn't mind if she was my sister-in-law someday, and that visit to the tattoo parlor's got me thinking that might be back on the table...some-day.

She eyes my bare chest. "No, I think I'm okay. But thank you for the offer."

"Oh, and if you happened to stick that person's in-haler in the mailbox, that'd be very helpful."

"Oh. Yes, of course." She gives a little wave as she turns to go, and I give one back. But as soon as I close the door, Drew comes tearing down the stairs.

"Was that my sister? What did she say? Did you tell her I'm here? What did you—"

I grab him by the shoulders before he can tackle me. "Dude, take a breath."

He takes several heaving gulps of air before I go on, but his gaze is still panicked.

"Yes, that was your sister. She asked again if I'd seen you. She was very concerned. I did not tell her you were here, but I told her you were safe and with people who cared about you. She expressed a strong desire to talk to you, especially about her wedding."

His hands have come up to my arms just above my wrists, and he's rubbing the hair on them idly, still staring out the front window. I had no idea my forearms were an erogenous zone, but I am attempting to ignore the casual contact and focus on him. Because he's trembling.

"Do you wanna tell me what happened between you and Grace?"

He shakes his head violently.

"Okay," I say gently. "You're safe here. I'm not going to tell anyone where you are...but she did ask me to tell you that she's sorry, and she gets it now and she's ready to talk."

"I can't be in her wedding," he blurts out. "I can't stand up in front of all those people with my roommates like nothing happened." The way his face pinches around his eyes, the way he's fairly *wincing* now has my ire up.

"Did they threaten you? Hurt you?"

Drew seems to snap out of it. "No, of course not."

"Because you could tell me if they did. I would very calmly get Patrick to hack them and ruin their credit."

He laughs a little. It's probably good that he thinks I'm joking. We definitely didn't do that to Darren's shitty ex. As far as the police know, none of us were involved.

"No, they just..." He's still rubbing my arms, and holy shit, my body does not understand that this is not *that kind of moment*. In fact, this is about to get rather embarrassing, given that I've started tenting my boxers. But I physically cannot pull away when he's so vulnerable, not right when he's starting to open up. "They just didn't understand. They thought it was a joke. I don't think I exactly went about it the right way. I was just tired of being alone in it, and I cut off my hair and showed up in different clothes at home without warning and it didn't...didn't go great. I know I don't owe them anything, but...I think if I'd explained myself better first, they'd have had more time to collect themselves."

"I'm sorry you were alone in it," I murmur. "That's my fault."

"In part. Not in whole. I should've been more patient with you, too." There's more there, in his gaze, more words about what happened between us. More wants and needs, and it is not helping my dick problem *at all*.

"I'm sorry I wasn't faster in coming around," I say, sliding my hands up to his neck, and he shudders. "If I'd been able to picture you like this, I think I would have been." I stroke my thumb along the column of his neck, smooth and soft.

"What, a fucking wreck at the sight of my sister on the front porch?"

"No," I say, my voice low and sincere, "an incredibly brave man who's going after what he wants, no matter the cost."

I'm not moving closer. I'm going to let him come to me. But seeing as he's basically panting, I don't think it'll take all that long before he leans forward and —

"Everything okay?" Colby's voice, which I usually like just fine, is very unwelcome in this conversation that I forgot was not private.

"Yeah," Drew says, his voice strained and high until he clears his throat. "Just fine. My sister came by looking for me, but Evan took care of it." I swear, the way my chest puffs out at being painted as his hero is completely involuntary. He retreats a little, and for the first time, he notices my small problem...which is growing by the second. The grin he gives me is wicked—I swear, the guy *likes* to see me suffer—but he claps me on the shoulder as he goes by. "Thanks, man."

"You're welcome," I croak, still keeping my back to my best friend to preserve what's left of my dignity.

"I'm gonna make waffles. Colby, can you show me where you keep the iron?"

"Uh, sure..." Colby follows him into the kitchen like a puppy, and I sigh with relief. It was nice of Andrew to cover for me, but he didn't have to be so fucking amused over it. I grab the throw on the back of the couch on my way up the stairs in case I see anyone else, resolving to wear pajamas from now on. Loose ones.

CHAPTER EIGHTEEN

ANDREW PICKS UP AN extra shift serving at a wedding where half the staff got sick, so I don't see him the rest of the day. My practice time, reliably, is shit. I'm still thinking about those little touches, the way his eyes burned into mine, just for a moment. Despite the heat of it, it's a moment frozen in time, encased in amber, a piece of history right in front of me. It took me right back there, to when he loved me. But it doesn't sting like it used to. In fact, it feels a little more like...possibility. I don't want to think that—it's the danger zone, for sure. But he's giving me these little clues that I want to put together into something more...solving the mystery of us.

Like I said, the practice was shit. Good thing I'm using headphones so no one can hear but me. After dinner, I change and head to the Howitz. Lindy's still annoyed about the Warsaw Concerto, apparently, because she hardly says two words to me the whole evening. I'm no fan of hers, either, but I wouldn't begrudge her any success, so the whole thing irks me almost to the point of distraction. Not like my Andrew distraction, but still. So, when Glenn and Daria invite me out for a drink, I decide to go, even though I'm kind of beat.

"Your partners don't need you at home?" I ask with only slight bitterness.

"My beloved is getting ready for her parents to come to dinner and being a little intolerable about it, to be honest," Glenn says, stroking their beard, watching me as

I cover the timpani. "They're still gonna love her even if we have mystery food in the back of the fridge."

"It's true. I love Chris and Susan." I never missed having a mom as a kid, but having people in my life like Susan is nice.

Daria tucks her straight, blonde hair behind one ear. "Charlotte's working on a big case. She told me not to expect her until brunch tomorrow morning, so I'm free as a bird." She shifts her violin to her other hand. "But let's face it, I'll probably poop out about midnight."

Glenn and I laugh. "We better get going then," they say, offering her their arm. She tucks her violin into her locker on our way out, and I wish my piano was that easy to transport.

"Where shall we go?" she asks, and given that I'm shit company right now, I feel like I should make up for it by taking her somewhere fancy.

"How about the Blue Bunny?"

"Ooh, that sounds nice," Daria coos. "They do...fusion or something?"

"Yeah, small plates and stuff. It'll be fun." And it's close by, so we don't have to move our cars. The two of them lead the way down the sidewalk, looking glamorous in their black and white concert wear. I don't know how they do it; I always end up looking like a waiter. It's probably just because I'm young, but I'd bet ten bucks someone asks me to refill their Auntie Leopard while I'm on my way to the bathroom.

Lucky for me, those two are chatty, and they don't seem to notice that I'm mostly smiling and nodding.

Once we get a table, the discussion turns to orchestra stories.

"I played with a percussionist one time who fell asleep during the 1812 Overture," Glenn says, sipping their Moss Back.

"He did not," Daria says with a laugh.

"He did, I swear. He hated the conductor, and the feeling was mutual. But he set a vibrating alarm and came in on time, so he couldn't fire him because he never missed a note."

"Did he actually sleep or just pretend?" I ask.

"I could've sworn I heard him snore," Glenn says with a shrug. "But it's not like I could turn around and look."

"That's right," I say, lifting my whiskey. "Because no matter what happens, musicians play on."

"Hear, hear," Glenn says, raising their glass. "To playing on!" They're getting louder, and I think it's time to move them toward home before they can't drive. But the conversation persists as we walk down the sidewalk, and Daria bumps me with her shoulder.

"I think sometimes that 'play on' mentality gets us into trouble. We think there's no other choice. But sometimes it's healthy to just set your instrument down, so to speak..."

"I think Daria's trying to get me canned," I say, and Glenn chuckles. "Also, how exactly do I set down a drum set or a piano?"

"You could set down drum *sticks*," she points out, and I have to concede the point.

"I think life's easier if I just keep moving," I say. "Less time for pointless navel gazing." I'm starting to feel my fatigue through the alcohol, like it's hiding under a blanket, waiting to pounce on me as soon as I lie down. But it's not lying down time yet. I have to drive home first…I fumble for my keys.

"You all right?" Glenn asks quietly, and I nod.

"Just tired. Really." Like I'd risk my baby on a drunk drive home? I don't think so.

"Okay." They pat me on the back. "Drive safe, Ev."

"See you Thursday for dinner."

"We gonna jam?" We haven't in a long time. Colby hasn't been as interested since Chance left. But it sounds like a lot of fun to me.

"Yeah, let's do it."

"Nice. I'll bring my flute."

"Or you could bring something cool," I say as I get into my car.

"That's uncalled for," they shout, their booming voice echoing through the garage as they walk Daria to her car. I should've thought of that. I'm a shitty friend to women, I think. I should work on it. I roll down the windows and let the cold air keep me awake as I cruise home. I hit all the traffic lights, and I think I should go buy a lottery ticket, because how often does *that* happen? But it turns out I'm too tired to do anything but park and stumble upstairs, shedding my concert dress as I go. Bowtie, stiff white shirt, cummerbund, all that shit. I dump it on my drum set so I'll remember to wash it tomorrow, and it clacks a little. Then I hear fabric moving.

I flick on the flashlight on my phone, and that's when I realize there's someone in my bed, their sleeping form nothing more than a lump under my comforter.

"Hey," I mumble. "You can't be in here." It feels like a valid thing to say, no matter who it is. I touch their feet, and they roll over—it's Drew. Thankfully, I have not woken him with my ill-considered attempt at eviction. He's out hard, drooling on my pillow. He probably stumbled home exhausted from his double shift and forgot where he was supposed to be sleeping; he used to sleep here often enough. Muscle memory is stronger than our brains sometimes. I find pajamas, because I have learned something from the last few days, and slide into bed next to him.

And as I drop off, I think that maybe I didn't need that lottery ticket after all.

606   LONDON PRICE

CHAPTER NINETEEN

DREW IS ASLEEP ON MY chest. His back rises and falls softly, and his legs are tangled with mine; apparently, he gave up shaving some time ago, because his hair is soft. Even the light is muted–gray, but happy, like the sun is about to break through. There are things I should do: practice, laundry, exercise. But basically, I have no desire to move. According to my phone, it's almost 10:30, and even though I went to bed late, I don't think I've slept this well in months. Drew twitches in his sleep, and instinctively, I put a hand on his fuzzy head. The way his body melts back into mine is...perfect.

My phone pings with a text.

> **Colby:** Hey, have you seen Andrew? He's not in the basement.

Um. I answer with one hand.

> **Evan:** yeah, he's up here.
> **Colby:** oh, he's in the shower?
> **Colby:** weird. Didn't even see him go by.

"Hey," I whisper, scratching his back. "If you don't want people to think we were banging, you should go get in the shower."

"Five minutes," he mumbles vacantly. Drew snuggles in deeper, sighing. My heart is lobbying hard to leave the man alone and let him rest here, breathing in time with me, but I don't want people jumping to the wrong conclusion.

"You should probably go," I try again, rubbing him harder, the way Nico says gets your blood moving. "Drew."

That does it. He snaps upright when I use his name, flinging himself out of my arms, panic etched on his face. "Oh shit. I don't—I didn't mean to—"

"Of course you didn't. It was late, you were tired."

His eyes are wide and somehow still wary. "Why didn't you kick me out?"

"I was exhausted, too, I guess. It's not a big deal."

"The fuck it's not!" He still has the sense to keep his voice down. "It's a huge fucking deal!"

I reach for him, my heart cracking, but he shies away, getting off the bed. He seems to compose himself a little, because his volume drops.

"Evan, I respect that you don't want to be with me anymore. I'm not trying to push you."

"That's not fucking true." I don't just sound angry—I am angry. Of course I want to be with him; I've given him enough clues that he should get it by now. I told him I made a mistake. I told him I wished I'd been there for him. What else does he need?

He throws up his hands. "Well, I didn't have anywhere else to go!"

His meaning snaps into clarity, but I can't quite force the right words out of my mouth.

"That's not what I meant. I just meant that I don't feel disrespected. In fact, I think you should sleep up here from now on. You haven't coughed once since I've been awake."

When he says nothing, I blunder on. "If you don't want me here, I can go down to the futon. I really don't mind." It's such a lie. It's creepy and cold down there, and I hate spiders. When his gaze narrows, I think he's seen through me.

Drew puts his hands on his hips. "You wouldn't care if we shared a bed?"

I shrug as nonchalantly as I can while propped up on one elbow. "We've done it lots of times." I tug on the covers to bunch them up over my crotch so my considerable erection is less noticeable. He probably felt it before, but...

"But not as friends."

I gaze at him steadily. "I think we can handle it. Especially if it means you feel better."

He's swaying now, looking anywhere but at me, his gaze swinging around the room like he's watching a monkey on a vine. "I think you should take the couch."

That's not what I expected, and it throws me for a second. But I swallow down my disappointment and take comfort because he's accepted my offer.

"Then I will. I'll change the sheets while you're in the shower and—"

"I can do it," he interjects. "And thank you."

"No problem."

He starts toward the door, then stops, clutching his chest, and I figure out what he's missing. I'm holding out the binder that was still twisted in the sheets when he turns back.

"Thanks."

"Sure. I'll just give you some space..." I start, then stop. Because yeah, that boner is still doing its thing, and now it's extra excited at the prospect of seeing him unclothed. I guess if it's his dignity or mine, I'll sacrifice...maybe I can get it to calm the fuck down in the shower. I grab my phone and exit the bed with my back turned to him, sliding toward the door. I close it behind me quietly despite the late hour of the morning, only to turn and be confronted by a confused Colby.

"I thought Andrew was in the shower."

"Oh. Yes. No. But he's getting in the shower. In a minute. We were having a...conversation."

He looks down at me pointedly. "What kind of conversation?"

I give him a half-hearted shove. "It wouldn't look like that if it was a good kind of conversation, now would it?" Although now that I think about it, it actually *was* a good conversation. Or at least, a good outcome to a situation that could've been awkward.

Colby chuckles. "Okay, I'm sorry."

"You're nosy. And a nuisance."

"I just want to know what's going on!"

"He's going to sleep in my room..." His eyes light up. "And I'm going to take the futon."

"Oh."

"Yes. Now if you'll excuse me..." I slip into the bathroom, even though Colby's presence has mostly taken care of my problem. Which, much like the conversation, really isn't a problem at all.

. . . .

THAT NIGHT, I DUTIFULLY head down to the basement, and it is just as terrible as I imagined. More actually, because I think something is dripping in this basement. I look behind the washing machine around 12:30, but that isn't it. I'm still awake an hour later, staring at the television that's turned off. It still has this kind of dim glow, and I think about getting up to unplug it, but I don't. Instead, I roll over to face the back of the couch, pulling the thin quilt up over me higher. I left my down comforter upstairs for him, of course. I didn't bother making the futon into a bed, because I know it's always full of crumbs when we open it up, and I don't feel like vacuuming. I've got my music on, because that's a given, but it's not inspiring sleep tonight. I palm my dick, but he's not interested; it's unfortunate, because I always pass out after sex. I wonder what we have in the house...somebody's gotta have NightQuil, right? Allergy medication? Something? I bet Darren has some homeopathic shit that would put me out.

Am I desperate enough to try tea? Warm milk? I check my watch; it's 1:45. But I also missed a message. From Drew.

Drew: you up?

Should I text him back? That was half an hour ago. He's probably asleep now. I roll over again. Then I go for my phone, because I'm weak.

Me: yeah

I stare at it for a minute, then put it down. But three dots pop up.

Drew: get up here
Evan: ?

My first thought: he feels guilty and wants to switch back (um, no). My second thought: I am getting a booty call and this is the best day of my life. But it is neither of those things.

Drew: you were right. We can handle it. We're both adults.
Evan: you sure? Because I'm fine down here.

I have already scooped up my pillow and bedding. I am jogging up the stairs as I type, dragging the quilt behind me up the creaky wooden steps. *Goodbye, creepy basement. Hello, warm bed with the one I'm not allowed to love.* I don't know exactly why he changed his mind, but I can't help but be glad.

Drew: I'm sure
Drew: hurry up, I'm exhausted

I open the door just as his texts come through, and we both laugh.

"Get off my side," I say, wishing I could push him over instead and cop a feel while I'm at it. I don't dare. Not here. Shoving in the kitchen is one thing, shoving in my bedroom is *something very else*.

"This is my side now," he says, snuggling down deeper under my comforter.

"I don't think I heard you right," I drawl. "You think you're going to invade my bed—"

"I was invited!"

"Kick me out…"

He points at me, his arm shaking as he laughs. "You left voluntarily."

"And now steal my side? I don't think so."

"Snooze, you lose."

"Yes, that's what I'm trying to do—snooze." It's on the tip of my tongue to call him a princess, but I can't risk him taking it the wrong way. What's the masculine form of diva? Divo? I'll ask my dad later.

"Cool, your side's that way." He points to the other side of the queen-size mattress. I take off my shirt, because it's gonna be warm in there…but I think I made it weird, because his eyes go a little…hot.

"Can you get the light?" I ask, giving him a reason to roll away. But I hope he rolls back in the night. I hope we wake up tangled again, twined like ivy around each other. I hope I get to hear his soft sighs and mumbled dreams.

I hope.

CHAPTER TWENTY

THE FIRST FEW NIGHTS go fine; we go to sleep about the same time without a lot of talking, and during the day, it's not too awkward. We give each other space to change or change in the bathroom, and it's working well. There is no more snuggling. One time I ask him to turn his phone brightness down, but it works out. It's all good. And his lungs sound better, and everything is good, except...

I want him.

Here's right here, breathing next to me in the dark, and my body is tired of the distance. In fact, it's throwing a fucking tantrum about it, and there doesn't seem to be any relief in sight. I roll over, facing my desk, trying to let the dry books inspire me toward more wholesome thoughts. My rock-hard dick has other plans, and it's still filling my head with memories of Drew in all sorts of compromising positions in this bed. I feel the heat of him behind me, not touching, but creating that little bubble of warmth between us under the sheet.

Then he says something I don't hear.

"What?"

"Come on, don't make me repeat it."

"I really didn't hear you."

He turns. "I said maybe we just need to do it one more time. Get it out of our systems."

My dick is appalled that my ears didn't pick up this information the first time and immediately sue them for divorce.

"I don't think that's a good idea," I say, even though in the history of all the things I've ever said, it is the most difficult thing I have ever forced out of my mouth.

Then his fingers trail down my arm, and I can't suppress the shudder. Hormones flow into me like someone released a dam somewhere.

"Evan." Fuck, I can't stand it when he says my name like that. A little bit vulnerable, a little bit higher than he's been aiming for lately.

I roll onto my back. "One time?"

He nods, his fingers now on my chest, playing around my right nipple. Fuck, fuck, fuck. I should not be doing this. One time won't be nearly enough. I should not be doing this, because I'm going to have to get over him all over again, only there won't be anywhere to hide. He's going to see me cry and mope and be pathetic because we fucking live together.

I turn my head to tell him no. No, really, I was going to say no. 'I'm sorry, but' was already forming on my lips.

But then I look into his eyes, and the *want* there could've knocked me on my ass if I wasn't already lying down.

"Andrew," I say, but I sound uncertain. Probably because I am. Probably because I want this so fucking bad and he's so close, and I really don't know if I can force the right words out of my mouth.

"I love the way you say my name," he whispers, and now he's touching my face, and fuck, now I'm kissing him, and I don't know who started that, him or me, but it feels so good and so right even though I know I'm going to regret this so much in the morning. It feels like Christmas and coming home after a long trip and those really tight hugs people give you when they missed you a lot.

"One time?" I rasp out between kisses, pressing myself against him, and he nods somewhat frantically, then shoves his hand down my pants. "Just once?" I need to hear it. That he's not going to play with me, string me along.

"Once."

Well, that's decided. I yank his hand out of my pajamas.

"Then I'm gonna need to make this last."

And it should be easy from there on out...kiss, bang, boom. And the kissing is great–don't get me wrong. It's amazing. He's already pretty amped up, and his little moans and gasps are taking me there, too. But there's too much history trying to get out. Too many pet names that don't work now, too many parts I want to touch that I don't know if he'd like now. He's still wearing his binder–what else is off limits? *Beautiful. Sexy girl. Put those pretty lips on my cock.* I can't say any of that shit, and it's got my heart stuttering. This is a lot, his hands wandering freely while mine hesitate. And I'm trying to force past it all because I can't let him think I don't want him—I do. I definitely do. But it was a mistake like this. I need to slow things down, but I don't know how. Daria's advice about not just playing through whispers in the back of my brain, and that's what breaks me. Pulling back, I pull the pillow over my head. I feel Andrew's hand on my back, rubbing hesitantly. Then it stops.

"Everything okay in there?"

"No!" I yell into the cotton. "I can't do this." My heart is pounding my chest like taiko drums, these huge Japanese timpani, and I can feel the reverberations in the same way, vibrating through me. "I'm going to fuck it up."

The bed sinks and bounces as he lies down next to me, his head on my back. "You were doing fine..."

"No!" I yell again. "I'm going to say the wrong name, I'm going to say the wrong thing, I'm going to touch you somewhere you don't want to be touched and then it'll be weird and you'll move out and I can't bear that." It is hot under this pillow that smells like him and I almost can't breathe, but the feeling of his heavy head against my skin is grounding me, and I force air into my lungs.

"Ev..." His voice is quiet, hard to hear, and I want to take the pillow off, but I really don't know if I can. Maybe if I just hide here, he'll leave. My embarrassment can remain cloistered in cotton and never have to see the light of day...such as it is. He tugs at the pillow, but I hold it tight.

"I'm sorry. You can go if you want."

"Dude, I wouldn't leave you like this, no matter what we were doing. I can put my clothes back on, but I'm not leaving until I know you're all right. So you can just forget about that."

Hot tears are running down my nose, and when I sniffle, I give myself away.

"Come on," he coaxes. "Talk to me. What's going on? You can keep the pillow, just lift it a little so I can hear you better."

I lift it just enough to peek at him with one eye. "There's nothing to say."

"Bullshit. There's a lot to say." He pulls at the pillow again, but I grip it so tight my knuckles hurt.

"I *am* going to keep the fucking pillow, thank you very much."

The bed bounces again, and he slides to his belly, and the next thing I know, he's eye to eye with me, pressing his way under the pillow with me, forehead to forehead.

"Nice place you've got here," he says, and I want to kiss him for being so ridiculous. Then again, he always was.

"You're the same, but not," I blurt out. "And I care about you, but I don't know you. I don't know Drew."

He nods, and I hear his smooth face rub against the fuzzy flannel sheets. "Do you want to?"

Those four words break the fragile grip I had on my heart, and it shatters. "Yes, of course I do. I do, very much."

He nods again. "Well, I have good news and bad. Which do you want first?"

"Bad. Always bad first."

Drew scoots somehow closer and gently rolls me to my side, all the while letting this awful pillow, this protection that I desperately need, stay resting on our faces. Facing him feels okay; even here in the dark of my own making, his eyes are that calming deep brown, like the shade in Forest Park off the trail, where the sun can't penetrate past the maples and cedars and firs. I know that doesn't sound sexy, but god, it is. I promise it is. Those eyes are alive with possibility and understanding right now, and it just makes me cry harder.

"The bad news is that there's no way to get used to this without making mistakes. You're going to misgender me sometimes, probably. And maybe use my birth name. And even if you're careful, you will not be able to avoid making me feel dysphoric sometimes. That's my reality right now. Even I don't know all my triggers yet." His hand comes up to my cheek, and he's wiping my tears away with his thumb.

"What's the good news?" I ask, my voice shaking.

His smile is brilliant, and it lights the darkest corner of my secret, safe space. "That I care about you, too. And I know you're trying. I know you're doing your best, and your best is enough. I just want you." I'm crying hard now, my tears unstoppable. I pull him toward me and unleash the sob that's been itching inside my chest, pressing my face into his neck, knocking the pillow off. I'm being loud, and I don't know how he can stand it, but he's just petting my hair, shushing me in a way not meant to silence me. Just a white noise, an ocean wave breaking, and he rolls us so I'm on top of him. His arms are tight around me, and I'm fighting for breath against the cage of him, trying to get under control again. I slide off and slot myself next to him, still touching him everywhere, still clinging to him by his neck.

He doesn't say a word, and eventually, my breathing slows and the tears become a trickle rather than a torrent, until we're just lying there, me in his arms, exhausted, him calm and still.

"Evan?"

"Yeah?" I wipe my wet face as a reflex, but it's hard. I'm still so close to him.

"Can I kiss you?"

"*You still want to?*" My outrage is obvious, and again, loud. Drew laughs.

"Yeah, I still want to. A lot. Now more than ever."

I tilt my head up, and he puts a tender hand to my still-red cheek, warm from the darkness and being pressed to him. He kisses me deeply; apparently, my warm-up phase has already happened. Because this is not holding back, not at all. My arousal roars back to life, and we are a clash of teeth and tongues, me still sniffling and pathetic and teary.

"Close your eyes," he murmurs, a little breathless, and I do. He rolls me to my back, and I can feel his legs straddling me, his wiry inner thighs pressing against my sides. He gets in close to me, our cheeks pressed together. "Do I smell like me?"

"Mostly." It's subtle, but it's there, hidden under a musky body wash.

"And my voice? Do I sound like me?" I nod. It's the bottom of his natural register, one I usually only heard when he was at Timbers games, bellowing at the officials over a red card. But I'd know it whispered or screamed or anywhere in between.

"What about my skin?" I'm afraid to put my hands on him...but he picks up my right hand and does it for me.

"You have more muscles now."

That voice in my ear is stern. "Don't lie, Evan. It's not nice."

"I'm not," I choke out. "I swear. You're still soft, you're still...you feel good. But you do feel a little different." Tentatively, I move my hand against his back, tracing some of those muscles in his deltoids, and he lets all his weight come down on me. Maybe the muscles are mostly the same, but I want him to feel like he's changing. It'd be important to me if I were him. The soft hair between his legs is caressing my stiffening cock, and I know he's letting them slide together on purpose. In retaliation, I slide my hand up toward his neck, but I stop.

"Can I touch your head?"

"Yeah," he whispers, and slowly, I let my hand continue its path upward into the short hair of his head.

"Is it okay that I miss your long, pretty hair?"

"Sometimes I miss it, too," he admits, and then I feel his hot lips against my neck as I ruffle his dark hair, my eyes still closed, just taking in the feeling of it. "But this is much easier to maintain and less confusing for people. Maybe I'll grow it out again when I've been on hormones for a while...some kind of undercut thing."

Dread fills my chest, and I try to push him back so he can see my face. "I-I'm not trying to pressure you," I stammer, but he soothes me again.

"I know. It's okay to be honest with me. You'll get used to it."

"Yeah," I say, letting out a long breath. "I'm sure I will." That silky hair is still against my cock, and then he notches me into the gap. All that soft, wet heat cradles my cock, and I curse. Andrew chuckles, nuzzling at my neck, and it hits me how much I want to hear him come, want to compare that. Now that I know it's okay. I put the soles of my feet down onto the sheets and start rocking him onto me, pushing at that nub I know he needs me to touch.

"Ev..." His voice is strained. "Fuck."

"Good?" I grunt, and he nods a little frantically into my neck. I wrap him in my arms, loving the feel of him, if only because he is so precious to me, so deep inside my heart already. "Want to hear you come."

"Yeah." He's squirming and panting now, caught in my arms. His hands find their way into my hair and *grab*. I'm trash for a little pain with my pleasure, and he's doing it just right, the way someone who's fucked you hundreds of times can do, the thing I've never tried to find with anyone else. I didn't mean to find it with him, either. But I'm desperate for it now.

I feel him shuddering against me before he plants his knees onto the bed and snaps his hips forward a few times before he comes, cursing, pressing himself against me so hard, it hurts. But I don't care, because I know this. It's not like it was, but it's not foreign. And the face he's making is all too familiar. I fucking love his O face; it's like it surprises him every time. The cords of his neck strain as he throws back his head, gasping, and I let myself trace the lines of them with my nose as he keeps coming and coming. When he comes back to me, he's smiling from ear to ear, pressing quiet kisses to my face.

"Ev. Missed you." The mumbled affection helps me scoop up the shattered heart pieces from a few minutes ago...and it doesn't hurt that I really, really want to come. But I need this more. I need to hear his real voice with this kind of lust traveling through my veins, imprinting it onto me. Sealing us together.

After a second, he rolls off onto his left side, letting his right hand drift up to my cock. It's sticky and wet with him, and he wastes no time in giving me his hand. He holds it in an O just above the head of my cock, and I do the same thing I was doing a minute ago—fucking up into him, already wet with him.

"Yeah. Yes. Fuck. Come on." That last one's frustration, because it's good, but I don't know if it's going to get me all the way there. He must figure out what I mean, because his hand disappears for a minute between his legs, and when he grasps me again, he's slick as anything. I moan, turning toward him, gripping his shoulder as he works up and down my length with a perfectly firm grip.

"Yeah." I'm the one writhing now, completely lost to the pleasure of his touch. "Don't stop, don't...."

"I'm not going to stop." He kisses me hard, and I take his face in my hands and bring him in, drinking in his mouth.

I'm so close. And his old name, it's taunting me, on the tip of my tongue, and I'm too fried because of his fingers and his lips and his whole body to think straight enough to force out the new one.

"Cover my mouth," I beg, and he does immediately. *And don't listen to a thing that comes out of it,* I wish I'd added. It muffles my cries enough when I finally come that I know it doesn't matter what I said. My chest is heaving, and so is his, and we just stare at each other as he slowly pulls his hand away, like he's not sure if it's okay, even though I'm clearly done.

"Fuck," he says in awe, and an unexpected laugh bubbles out of me.

"Yeah. That was intense." I lift my head and look at the mess on my belly, then let my head fall back to the bed. I keep my face covered with one hand. And this time, he lets me, snuggling up next to me. He lets out this big sigh that brushes over my skin and gives me the tingles all over. We lie quietly together like that for a minute until I start to feel the mess drying on my skin.

"I need...."

"Yeah." Without letting go, he turns and reaches into a drawer. Drew pulls out a package of wet wipes.

When I lift an eyebrow in question, he grins sheepishly. "Testosterone is the best, but also the worst. Easier to just wipe my hands when I'm done than fight for bathroom time." He pulls out a wipe and starts cleaning me up carefully as I stare.

"So you've been rubbing one out...in my bed when I'm not here?"

He shrugs. "No other place I wanted to be."

Hang on—I think my heart just went supernova. Words are not forthcoming. Then a thought surfaces.

"Weren't you afraid you'd get caught?"

He leans back with his hands behind his head. "Nah. Your schedule is pretty predictable. And when you play the piano, it makes it easy to know where you are." My new goal? To catch him.

"Well, I'm glad I could provide entertainment for your wanking," I say, and he pushes at my face gently.

"Shut up and go to sleep."

I think about obeying him, but there's a lot of questions and feelings still rolling around inside me, and it's got me rolling in the bed to put my head on his chest.

"Why Andrew?" I ask, but I doubt the question before it's even done leaving my mouth. "Sorry. I shouldn't..."

"No, I'm glad you asked. Andrew was one of the disciples. He's not one of the brash, popular ones that you hear about...he kind of lurks in the background. And that felt appropriate, given that I don't know exactly where I stand with my faith right now. So it's kind of a reminder of who I want to be, even if I'm on the fringes. But it doesn't hurt that it also means 'manly.'"

I can't help it: I laugh. "That's fucking fantastic."

"Right? I couldn't resist the irony."

"There's no irony," I say, giving his arm a squeeze. "You're Andrew. You're a guy. And your faith is important to you. It's great that you found a name that communicates all that." I pause, thinking. "Fuck, I have no idea what 'Evan' even means."

"It means asshole," he deadpans, and I kiss him, laughing.

"Probably."

"Now sleep," he says, and I'm already sliding into that half dream-state as he strokes my hair, so warm and soft and familiar.

"Drew?"

"Mmm?"

"You gonna be here when I wake up?" My brain isn't thinking about how we said this was a one-time thing. My brain (and let's be honest, my dick) is just thinking about how to keep him here forever. But despite my best intentions, the wave of sleep crashes over me before I hear his answer.

CHAPTER TWENTY-ONE

ON WEDNESDAY, I'M PLAYING the piano at home, and I'm actually getting tired of it. I've played my trouble spots in the "Warsaw Concerto" about six hundred times, so I've moved on to classics. Chopin, Mozart, a Sibelius etude that I haven't played in a long time. But I'm not quitting for today. Because Drew hasn't walked in yet. I don't know where he is, but I can't exactly text him and ask. *Clingy much?* my brain taunts, but let's face it, I was feeling clingy long before our "let's bang out our feelings" night a few days ago.

Colby stops next to the piano and leans on the top.

"In a classical mood?"

I shrug. "Guess so. How's your song coming? Can I hear it yet?"

He drums his fingers on the old wood. "Not yet."

"All right. I respect the creative process." I haven't mentioned the bang to anyone. I'm not exactly proud of it. Not that I think I took advantage of him, just...well, it's not exactly helping me get over him, is it? Which isn't exactly fair to the people who have to live with me. *It was just one time...* The problem is that I want another time. Let's face, I want a lot of times. I don't know about a lifetime, but...yeah. A lot would be good. And I think he might be open to a little wooing, which is why I'm still sitting here. I played "Cold, Cold Man" on Monday and "Swallowed in the Sea" on Tuesday. But today, I'm tired of being subtle.

"You want company?" Colby asks, gesturing toward the guitar in the corner.

"Not right now."

"Why not?"

"I'm kinda...in the middle of something." That's when the front door opens, only I can't see who it is.

"Hey," Darren greets us without taking off his head-phones.

"Hey," we greet back. Then I look at Colby. "Can you scooch?"

"Scooch?"

"Yeah, you know," I lift one hand and gesture side-ways. "Scooch."

"You want to see the door?"

"Yeah."

"What did you say you were doing again?"

"Practicing," I say with a grin, but Colby steps so he's against the wall by the kitchen door instead of blocking my view. And just in the nick of time, too. When Drew walks in, I stop what I'm playing abruptly and switch to a country power ballad I know he'll recognize, singing along in my head. *If you could see that I'm the one who understands you / Been here all along / So why can't you see? / You belong with me.* He pauses in the doorway to the kitchen, peering at me around Colby, and I give him a big smile.

"Welcome home, roommate. How was your day?"

"Fine...and yours?"

"Oh, just fine, thanks." I keep playing the song, be-cause he's going to notice. I know he is. I ignore Colby's curious glance between us, because he doesn't know this song...but my guy is a T-Swift fan for *life,* and no transition to going to change that. "Are you watching the Timbers game tonight?"

"If the TV's free..."

"I reserved it. You can watch with me. If you want to."

"That's what you *want* to watch?"

"Yeah, I mean..." I stop playing. "I like soccer."

"Right." His wariness is amusing me for some reason, like he's trying to figure out what my ulterior motive is. He narrows his gaze, as if to say, *That was a one-time thing. You're not getting back into my pants.* And I smile as if to say, *I know. I'm just being nice.* Drew turns slowly toward the kitchen.

"I'm...going in here now. To cook dinner."

"You want help?"

"...sure?" All his sentences sound like they have question marks at the end of them, but none more than this one. Which is silly, because I've been helping him on his night for weeks. And he helps me on mine. But Drew leaves, glaring at me like I'm up to something.

"I'll be right there."

Drew gives me a stiff nod, then the door swings shut, and Colby leans over to get in my face.

"What song was that?"

"I don't know what you're—" I wrinkle my nose. "Dude, your breath smells terrible."

"It does not. What song was that? That song had meaning. What was it? Tell me." I push him away from me so I can slide off the bench.

"It does. You have total coffee breath."

"It's not my fault Chance's in such an inconvenient time zone! I have to stay awake! Wait, no—tell me what song that was."

"Excuse me, I promised to help my roommate with dinner."

"Ev!" He protests as I push the door open. Told you he wouldn't know what it was. When I come into the kitchen, though, Drew's got his head in his hand, staring at his phone with wide eyes.

"What's wrong?" I crane my neck to see what's on his phone and catch a glimpse of Grace's name.

"Nothing." He puts it away too quickly. "Let's make fried rice."

"With pineapple?"

"Of course, with pineapple. But they only had canned."

"That's too bad. What did Grace want?"

He hands me green onions and a carrot with a sigh, like he knew I'd seen but was trying to pretend he didn't.

"We're having a video call tonight. About her wedding."

"Oh." I think about this as I find a knife and a cutting board. "Are we...excited about this?"

"Kind of? I don't know."

"What time is that?"

"Halftime." So he *was* planning to watch the game. Ha! I am a flirting genius.

"You gonna go upstairs?"

"Yeah." He's defrosting the chicken, but he punches in the numbers wrong and has to start over.

"You want me to come with you? I don't have to say anything."

"No, I'm okay." Patrick comes into the kitchen, and the conversation ends when he sits down at the table with his laptop.

"I need advice."

"Do we have broccoli?" I ask, and Drew nods and tosses me a head. "Thanks."

"I need advice," Patrick says louder, and I pivot to look at him.

"Sorry, were you talking to me?"

"Both of you. A fan reached out to me, and I don't know what to say."

"What did they want?" Drew asks, still watching the microwave spin. He subtly tugs at his binder, and I wonder if it's bothering him. I doubt he'd take it off with Patrick here.

"His daughter is trans, and they just moved to Portland. He knows we live here and that Sadie has other trans friends and wondered if the two of them could meet for a playdate."

"Oh, wow. Is that normal? Just, like, emailing strangers to help your kid make friends?"

Drew turns and leans against the counter, bracing his arms behind him. "Probably depends on how desperate you are to help your kid."

"How old is she?"

"Nine. Third grade."

"And Sadie's ten."

"Yes. But Sadie isn't my daughter, so I feel strange about it."

"What was the proposition, exactly?"

"He thought they could meet at Grant Park. And that made me nervous, because maybe he only suggested that because he knows where we live and that it's close by? I don't think I ever mentioned the park in our streams. I'm careful about that shit."

And Patrick's probably also aware that hacking to find out a person's address is the kind of thing he'd do, if he wasn't an ethical person.

"Or maybe they just live in our neighborhood?" I suggest, sweeping the little white ends into the trash can. "It might mean nothing."

"I don't believe in coincidence." He steeples his hands in front of him like a villain.

"Then don't write back. Surely you get messages from fans all the time that you ignore."

"I only ignore the dick pics. And the requests for dick pics."

"Really?" Drew seems moved by this. "You respond to everyone else?"

"Lots of kids write to me. This is one of the few adults with good intentions who has contacted us. Assuming he has good intentions."

"You don't have any proof that he doesn't," I say. "Maybe you could offer to meet him without the kids first. Kind of vet him in case he's a creeper."

Pat sits up straighter, then closes his laptop. "I have a better idea."

"You're going to hack him, aren't you?"

"I'll learn far more that way and get better data. It's only logical. Then I can tell Sadie about the opportunity only if it's valid. Thank you for your counsel, gentlemen." He gets up and heads toward the back stairs.

"So what are you going to say?" I call after him.

"That depends on what I find," he calls back. "I'll shoot you a draft."

Drew meets my gaze as the microwave goes off. "I fear to read that email if he's unhappy with what he finds."

"As you should," I say. "Done with veggies. What now, boss?"

"You wanna make dessert?"

With you. Hell yes, I do.

"Sure."

I make chocolate chip cookies because we don't have stuff for anything else. I only realize they're Patrick's chocolate chips when I'm throwing out the bag, and we groan.

"He's not going to be understanding about this," I say. "Not after Bacongate."

"We could run to the store right now." He checks his watch. "We've got time before the game."

"Let's go." We book it there and back in my baby, laughing the whole way. And I forget about Drew's stressful phone call with Grace until halftime when he quietly goes upstairs. I can't focus while he's gone, and I eat a lot of cookies. But he's back before they kick off the second half, and even better, he plops down in the same seat right beside me, our shoulders touching.

I glance at him, trying to read his expression, but it gives away nothing. Damn him, why is *this* the moment he develops a poker face? A few minutes later, I pull out my phone.

Me: Talk go okay?

He sends me back a shrugging emoji. What does *that* mean? Maybe I can tickle it out of him tonight in bed. Yeah, it sounds weird to me, too. But I like it. I like it a lot.

CHAPTER TWENTY-TWO

I'M NOT AVOIDING HIM. Staying up until two in the morning is just...normal. No, I don't usually wait for Tony to get home from his after-party to lock up. (And yes, he gave me a funny look when he came in the front door.) And yes, it's weird to run the dishwasher at 11:00 and then unload it immediately without waiting for morning (only burned my fingers a little. That's gonna hurt on the keys tomorrow). But I'm not avoiding him.

I thought he'd be asleep when I went upstairs, but he was watching something on his phone. He's still a social media junkie, which is why it surprised me so much that he hadn't changed over any of his accounts to his new name and picture. He's still wearing a shirt, but it looks like he finally took the binder off. If we wake up intertwined again, I hope don't grope him.

I turn my back to him as I put on my pajamas (because I learned from that Grace moment), and then I ruffle my hair as I slide into bed.

"You get everything done?"

"Yeah."

"Good." The room's dark except for his phone. "You want to listen to something?"

I don't say anything, mostly because I am trying to swallow down the emotion of how well he knows me.

"We don't have to," he says quickly, shutting off the phone.

"No, I mean…I usually do."

"But you haven't been since I've been sleeping here, so I wasn't sure…"

"No, I still do." *I just didn't want to make it seem like I thought it was old times. And I didn't want you to know the sad songs I've been using.* It's too much. It's all too much. Him here in my bed, knowing it's temporary. Here in my house, knowing he won't stay forever. Even at my work. Why the *fuck* did I get him a job where I *work?* I don't mind being able to keep an eye on him, but *fuck,* how big of a masochist can I be? I am still contemplating this, even though I know I would've done it all the same again, when Drew starts the music.

It's "Used to Be" by Matt Nathanson, and for a second, I freeze. Maybe I'm not the only one who's been listening to breakup songs. *Write how I made you shiver, the ground underneath us shook…*

"Oh, uh—" He sputters. "I just put it on shuffle. Sorry. That's not—"

"It's nice. You can let it play."

I mean that. It is nice, lying here in parallel, just breathing together, listening to a plaintive (albeit horny) song about wanting his partner to come back. But it is making me feel things, too. About all the times I lay awake in this bed and wanted him here. And now he is…but he's too far away to reach.

"What was that Grace thing about?"

"I was supposed to be a bridesmaid."

"Oh. Well, that's obviously not happening."

"Right. But she still wants me in the wedding party. She thinks I should stand on Kai's side of the wedding party with the other guys."

"But that's for his friends, right?"

"Yeah. That's what I said. I want to wear a suit on her side." He kicks his feet a little, like the sheets are wrapped around him. "Well, I actually don't—standing up in front of all our family and friends at this point in my transition is very unappetizing."

"Unappetizing is a ten-dollar word."

"Add it to my tab."

I pause; I shouldn't have joked. I should have listened—he's sharing something real. "No, but I get it. You might feel extra scrutinized."

"Yeah. I mean, I'll do it for Grace, but it's not high on my list of want-to's."

"What is?"

"High on my list? I don't know. Burning my old clothes?"

I laugh. "Love it."

I make myself lie still, but he's shifting around like he's trying to get comfortable. It's really dark in here. Which is better, really—if I could see things, then I'd be able to watch his chest as it rises and falls, take in the curved line of his hip, his rounded belly. From there, it wouldn't be hard to imagine kissing those wonderful lips, pulling his hips into mine, spreading his legs and plunging between his legs...*Not going to happen. That first time was just...* I don't really know what. But I know I can't ask for that.

"Ready for sleep?" My voice is rough, but I can't help it. I want to pull him close and spoon his sweet ass. I want to nuzzle his neck with my nose and relish the scent of him. My heart needs the connection, to say the things I can't say. *I want him.*

"No." The mattress moves and the covers shift, but the music keeps playing. I only realize he's not reaching to turn it off when the light goes on, momentarily blinding me. When he turns back, I feel his hand gently on my cheek, turning my face toward him. "How about you?"

"Not really, no." It's late. I should be tired. But I feel electrified, like it would take hours to come down off the high of him touching me. If anyone else touched me, they'd get a leftover static shock, bits of white lightning connecting us for a moment.

"Okay, honesty time: I'm not going to be able to sleep until I get off, because right now, I'm so turned on, I can barely see straight." He swallows hard, and his next breath is shaky against my skin. "I know we said just once. I do. But I don't want to go into the bathroom and put my hand to good use when you're right here..." He's gazing into my eyes, and even in the low light, there's a deep vulnerability there, prodding at me, urging me toward action. It's a siren call without words, and I don't think I'm strong enough to resist it.

I've got him on his back before I even realize what I'm doing, and his eyes go wide, deep brown pools of hope and greed. I want him so bad, it's like fire in my veins, like my heart is pumping need and longing instead of blood. But I need something else first. "Why me? There's three other single men in this house."

When he finally blinks, there's frustration there, his manicured brows crowding each other. "You know why."

"No, I really don't," I say, planking to keep my weight off him, still caging him in with my knees, the covers falling off me, even though I all want to do is kiss him and crush him and help him and love him. "We broke up. I took too long. I fucked up." I don't register of the burning behind my eyes until I feel the tear run down my cheek. I can't stop it; it falls onto his face with a tiny splash, like a raindrop. "So why? Why me? Because you know it's more than helping for me."

"That's why," he says gently, wiping the wet track from my cheek, his soft fingers lighting up the nerve endings there. "And I should've said that before. This just seemed...simpler."

"Nothing about this is simple, b—" I was going to use an old nickname. It doesn't work for a guy...but it's right there. It's what's in my heart, that he is *beautiful* in every way, and my mouth and my mind are about ready to slap it. I really don't want him to walk out right now and go back to that musty basement.

"Sorry. I'm not exactly thinking straight..." He lets his hand rest on the back of my neck, the skin there drinking in his warmth against the coolness of the room. "I'd just rather be with someone who cares about me. And I think you still do."

"Of course I do," I say, lowering my forehead to his, and I hope he feels all the affection I mean with it. "But what's the plan here?"

"Thought we'd start by getting naked..." he says, kissing across my jaw, making me shudder. "Need your skin, babe. Need you against me in all the right places." Between us, unseen, his fingertips brush against my still-clothed half-erection, and I tilt my hips forward, chasing his touch as my hormones surge through me. I feel like a teenager again myself; has someone been slipping his T into my orange juice? I shake my head, trying to clear the lust from my thoughts.

"I mean after that..." I say slowly, and he smiles.

"You wanna make me an omelet?"

"Andrew," I say sternly. "I mean it."

He sighs roughly. "I don't know. Would you really rather I go down the hall? Knock on Patrick's door?"

"Not him," I mutter, thinking about our conversation on that run, trying to ignore how good Drew's lips feel against my chest. "Maybe Tony. Wait, what the fuck am I saying?" I pull the covers over both our heads, and he giggles. Something about the dark makes me honest about what I really want to hear. "Do you ever think about me when you're taking care of business?"

He huffs a laugh against my neck. "I'm not telling you that."

"Then go rub one out in the bathroom. I suggest you light a candle for ambiance." It's a bolder suggestion than I really feel, and he moans as I kiss him hard. If he walks out now, it'll crush me like a dropped pretzel in a crowded nightclub. But he owes me this if he wants my help.

Andrew gropes for me in the dark until his hands find my face. "Let me start over: Evan, I need you. I want *you*. Yes, I want to get off so badly I think I might actually die if I don't, but getting off with anyone else seems to have momentarily..." I bite the inside of my cheek so I don't fill in the words for him. "Lost its appeal. You know?"

"It's not momentary for me," I whisper. "You're *everything*, D. You're everything to me." I feel his stomach tense against my cock, but I force the words out, my arms shaking. "You have to know that. If you still want me now, great. But if not...then that one time should be the only time. I don't need a ten-point plan, just..." I let out a grunt in frustration. "Sorry, it's late, and I'm not—"

"I hear you," he whispers back. "I do. I don't know where we go next, but can we just...see? Try a little?"

My gulp is audible. "It's gonna be messy."

"Sweetheart, I quit school, I'm avoiding my family, and I'm technically homeless. My whole life is a mess. At least this mess will be worth it."

I go back to kissing him, and I resolve to make that true with every touch of our lips. Because this? It feels like forgiveness, even richer and sweeter than getting to touch him again like this, like my soul can breathe again. He's trying to pull me down against him, but I'm stronger than he is, and he whimpers like he can't take it anymore.

"Ev..."

"Shhh," I say, running a hand over his short, soft hair the wrong way. "I got you." I give in to his tugging and press our bodies together, his skin like velvet beneath me. He changed his body wash, and I don't know if it's because I mentioned it the other day. This one reminds me of a high school locker room...I can't quite put my finger on the scent, but it's sort of...ocean-y? Then it hits me: *Hatchet body spray.* I do not laugh, but I find it adorable that my guy is gravitating toward the same products that younger men going through puberty are also attracted to.

Our legs tangle together, rolling under the covers, until I can't take the stuffiness anymore and shove the sheet down a little.

"What do you need, D? What do you want? Tell me what you've been imagining, staring at my chest at the kitchen table over breakfast."

"You noticed that, huh?" he asks, chuckling ruefully.

"It would be hard not to. The drool was very distracting."

"Not my fault you walk around half naked..."

"We're getting off-topic here," I murmur, kissing him again, "when the topic is supposed to be getting you off. Tell me how to make you sing, make you scream." Drew moans, arching up against me, the suggestion making him dig his nails desperately into my arms.

"You know how. I can't think for wanting you. I barely know my own name right now."

I lean forward, blowing gently over the damp shell of his ear. "I know it. It's Drew."

In answer, he hooks his legs around my hips, sheathing me inside him in one swift motion. Stunned, all I can do is stare down at him as he rides me from below, all sloppy, desperate heat and unabashed pleasure contorting his face. And he feels so perfect wrapped around my cock, his knees squeezing my hips for leverage to take me deeper, that I almost miss why it feels so good...

"Condom," I gasp out. "We forgot."

"You stop now and you're a dead man," he says, his voice as shaky as his legs, and I know he's close. I grit my teeth as I reach down between us and thumb his clit, hoping he can get there even if I'm not moving. Because I'm telling you, it is taking every shred of my self-control to watch him fall apart in my arms without coming. But then he plants his feet on the mattress, snapping his hips up into me, driving me inside over and over, brokenly whispering, "Evan, oh fuck. Oh, please. Evan...Fuck me, Evan. Evan..." I don't even recognize the low keening sound I'm making, but I do what he tells me and start moving. It sends him the rest of the way, and he gasps, his movements lengthening, deepening, just for a moment before he slows to a stop. And then he says the one thing I somehow don't expect: "Again."

Slowly, I pull out, giving myself a squeeze, even as I start working him back up again, pressing my face into his neck. Thankfully, I don't have to tell him what I need; he's rummaging blindly in the drawer for a condom before I can even ask. His hands deftly get me squared away as I kiss softly back up toward his sweet mouth.

Kicking off the covers, I roll us until he's on top now...that's the only way I can see lasting long enough to get him a second one, assuming he wants it on my cock. And let's face it: I adore watching him ride me. In fact, I find my phone and click on the flashlight, putting it face up on the bed, just to see him better.

"I thought about this at the breakfast table," he says, bringing my hands to his hips.

"Hush," I say, still on edge. As usual, he ignores me.

"Thought about looking down at my tall, dark-haired, handsome boyfriend again, watching him smolder up at me just like this..." He runs his hands up my arms. "Thought about these shoulders...the way your hands look when you make music. I love listening to you play."

"You're such a dick." Even now, I'm groping for something—anything—to distract me. I swear, before him, I could fuck for hours...but he's getting to me. I'm too close already.

He bends at the waist, and I can feel his chest through his shirt, his nipples stiff. "I'll take that as a compliment, since dicks are great. I'm riding a fantastic one right now. I thought you wanted to hear this?"

I squeeze his ample curves even as I squeeze my eyes shut to try to regain control. "No. Shut up. I'm trying to do something here."

Chuckling, he pulls my hands from his hips and puts them over my head, pressing them down into the mattress, leaning close to my ear. "Me too."

"Bad. Bad man," I pant. "I'm sending you to the naughty corner when we're done."

"Normally, I'd play the teacher in these scenarios, but I'm up for some role reversal. My ego could stand to get an A. Unless you're all talk, Mr. Rhodes."

All talk? No, I am all feeling right now, most of those being centralized in my very needy cock, which is about to go off before he's done, but also in my heart, which missed him, missed this so fucking desperately. "Shit. I can't..." And then he *slows down*, arching his back, planting one hand on my chest to grasp my chest hair, which only proves my previous comments correct. "Drew, come on. Please, I'm trying to—"

"But more than anything, I wanted to play with you. I fucking love playing with you. And I'll do it anywhere you want to, baby."

"Tell me you're close," I groan, but he shakes his head. "Then come up here." He climbs his way up my body until his thighs are bracketing my head, and I grab his ass with both hands, licking my lips, eager for the taste of his juices. Then I pause. "Wait—do you...still like this?"

He smiles down at me. "Only one way to find out."

I pull him forward and give him a long, slow lick, dipping my tongue inside him, then glance up to check. When I find his eyes closed, I smile and resume my meal. I love this part of sex; it's messy and weird and fantastic. I love the little noises he's making, the way he's grinding against my face a little, but trying not to smash me. Then he sits back onto my chest.

"Hey, um—is it...bigger?"

"Huh?" I wipe my mouth. "Is what bigger?" Then I realize what he means. "Your clit?"

"Yeah, my...arousal." It feels like a funny moment to be examining him a little more clinically, but I get why he's asking. It's probably tough to tell for him. I cock my head as I examine him.

"I mean...I've seen it this big before, but only when you were really into it. You don't seem like that's where you're at now. You're still..." I gesture vaguely. "Talking."

I don't think that's what he wanted to hear, because he just pushes back against my mouth, and I take the hint. Was I supposed to lie? Fuck, it would be hard to be in that place, wishing you had a cock, waiting for it to grow, wondering when it's going to. I put my lips around it and suck at it harder, more like a nipple, trying to see if I can stimulate him a little more. Then I pull back again.

"You know, I think it is a little." I suck it again, lapping at it with my tongue. "Yeah. Wow. That's hot."

He runs careless fingers through my hair, fluffing it up. "Don't lie."

"I'm not! I'm really not." I mean...I sort of am. But it's the nice kind. "And it's just going to keep growing, right?"

"That's the hope." His voice is quiet, and I think maybe I screwed up, so I just focus on making him come. I can't make him feel better, but maybe I can still make him feel good. Feel desirable, even though he doesn't look the way he wants to. And it doesn't take too long, because I'm talented in this department. So talented, in fact, that my dick hasn't taken the opportunity to cool it whatsoever. But when he comes, I don't really care. I got him what he needed. And I did it without embarrassing myself. Gold star for Evan.

But then he slides down, sheathing me inside him again like it's the most natural thing in the world.

"Again?" I ask, baffled, because I'll be honest, I'm getting a little tired. Drew just nods into my neck, sighing happily.

"Just one more. I'm sorry. I'm so horny all the time…"

"Hey, don't apologize. I remember puberty. If my cock had been willing to go three times, I would've never made it to school on time."

"I bet you never did anyway," he says, smiling, finding my lips for a long, deep kiss. I grope for the covers, because even though he's wearing a shirt, I'm sure he's cold. He rides me gently, staying up at the top to reach my lips, and if I come too soon, it'll be because of the way he's kissing me more than fucking me. He's seducing me with tongue and teeth, caressing me, all the while giving me those little thrusts under the sheet. It's the way I imagine someone would kiss if they were dying, like they needed to wring all the pleasure out of life before it's extinguished. Like what we have is a candle about to flicker out.

"Drew," I pant between kisses, "you gotta hurry, handsome. I can't keep this up."

He grunts in acknowledgment, and all the words in my head vanish, trying to hold it together for him, but lost, so lost in the feeling of him on top of me, fucking me in earnest now. He's got a hand between us, rubbing his arousal hard, and when he comes, I go over the edge with him, a little dizzy from how long he's been edging me. He melts on top of me, letting his entire weight crush me, and despite that, I'm already halfway to sleep.

"Love you." I don't think I heard him right. It can't be. It's a sharp right turn from "hey, let's fuck and maybe see where this goes" to "I love you." It's a good thing I'm pinned down, or I'd probably run. I can't go through this again. I can't.

I won't.

CHAPTER TWENTY-THREE

THAT NIGHT, I CAN'T sleep. Drew doesn't seem to have the same problem; he's asleep before I turn off the music. But I'm staring at the ceiling again like it's his first night in the house, however long ago. And when he rolls over in his sleep and put his head on my chest, all I can do is put my arms around him. I savor holding him like it's a meal at a Michelin star restaurant—this tiny thing that's so small, but so, so delicious that it's worth the cost. Make no mistake; it is costing me something to lie here in the dark, holding the person I love, wondering if he meant what he said the way I want him to. Wondering if this is going to end in disaster again and crush my heart permanently. He sighs when I brush a hand over his stiff hair, snuggling deeper into me, throwing one leg over me. But my heart is settling deeper, too, into our strange arrangement. And for the first time since he got here, I think maybe I need a little space. I know, I hear the irony, trust me—all I've wanted was to get closer to him again since he arrived, but now I'm...still not close enough. Not in the ways I need to be. That part of me is a little hard to feel right now, with his body curled against mine, warm and trusting in how he presses our skin together. But it's still there. It's too dark to see the ceiling, but I feel like it's coming closer, closing in on me. I can't give myself away unless I know it's for good. And I don't know what this is, but I'm afraid to ask again. I'm afraid it'll disappear forever if I do. I creep out of bed and shuffle down the hall to go downstairs, but something catches my eye.

Through his open door, I can see Colby sitting on his bed. He's staring at his phone—not scrolling, mind you, like an average human being—just staring. And from the look of it, he's looking at a selfie of him and Chance. I was really just stopping by to tell him I'd be away for a few days, but his expression when he looks up makes me change my mind unexpectedly.

"Bet you could use a change of pace."

Colby shakes his head, not appearing to mind that I caught him being sad. "I'm headed out soon to England. Can't afford to take any more time off."

"I was thinking about heading up to the cabin..."

"In Zigzag?" Yes, in case you are wondering, Zigzag is an actual place. And the road leading up to it has given me carsickness more times than I can count. It's better when I'm driving, though. And it's my favorite place to be melancholy. In some ways, it feels more like home than my house in California, like the warm memories have melted into the walls. We used to drive up and spend time here with my aunts and uncles and grandparents. My cousins and I would run around in the woods together, playing pretend games about superheroes, throwing things at the chipmunks, who were thankfully much too fast for us to actually injure. And I guess I'm still headed there to throw things, only this time, it's a pity party for my sad heart.

"Yes," I confirm, "in Zigzag." Even though he's my best friend, he's never been up there, and now seems like the perfect time to introduce him. He seems like he could use a break.

"You don't have to stay the whole time. I know you're busy."

He lifts one eyebrow. "Aren't *you* busy, too?"

I shrug one shoulder. "I'm blowing off rehearsal. Think I'm coming down with something." I give an anemic cough into my fist, and Colby smiles.

"Yeah, I'm game. As long as you're willing to run me back down on Thursday, I've got a gig."

"Sure."

Right now, it seems like a small price to pay to put a smile on his face and not be alone.

．．．．

I KNOW FROM THE TIME I took off on tattoo day that he doesn't like it when I disappear, and I know we're not really together. But at the risk of being too relation-shippy, I decide to leave Drew a note. Well, actually, I'm too chicken for that, since it's him I'm running from, so I send a message to the roommate group chat.

Hey all—Colby and I are headed to Zigzag for a few days. Cell service is spotty so use the internet if you need us. See you in a few.

And since I'm a really truly certified Grade A no hormones organic chicken, I wait to hit send until I'm getting into the car.

Which means I'm sitting in the car, fighting traffic to get on I-84 with everyone going toward the Gorge to windsurf and hike when his text comes in.

Drew: Uh. Why didn't you mention you were going out of town?

Colby glances at me when it pops up over the GPS. "Gee," he says, his voice suspiciously flat, "why would one of our roommates want more information about your comings and goings than the others? How strange."

"Okay, fine. We might be seeing each other again."

"Seeing each other or banging each other?"

"You'd know the difference," I retort. "How'd you and Chance meet again?"

"Not relevant," he says with a sniff, and I laugh. "But to my point—"

"We're banging. It's just stress relief. Or hormone re-lief, or something."

"Uh-huh. And your heart isn't in this at all?"

"Well, I wouldn't say 'at all'..."

"Meaning you're completely invested in getting him back."

"Uh..." There's no point in lying to him. I've spent too long giving him straight talk about our love lives to expect anything less from him. "Yeah, basically. Yes, I'm totally invested. I'm fucked, aren't I?"

"Not necessarily. Are you sure he won't take you back?"

"How can I even ask him that? There's no way—"

"Who initiated the sex?"

"Well, he did."

"And now he's sleeping in your bed?"

"Yeah. I mean, we started out because he climbed into the wrong bed one night..."

"But then he never went back to the basement."

"Yeah. Basically. But because it was helping his lungs, not because of the sex."

"Interesting. And you just...didn't question this?"

"I mean...I did. Sort of." I rub at my temple, which is surprisingly sweaty for the time of year. "We said we were just going to do it once, to get it out of our systems."

Colby laughs. "That obviously didn't work. How many times will it take to get it out of your systems?"

"I'll let you know when I find out," I mutter, and he laughs again, which is fucking galling. "You're really enjoying this, aren't you?"

"I don't mind telling you that I am. I really am. It's nice to see the shoe on the other foot since you gave me such a hard time about Chance."

"That was just the truth."

"So's this: I think you two are good for each other. We all think he's great. And before he came out, you guys seemed...happy."

"I was." A thought occurs to me, and I blurt it out. "Until I felt like I was being asked to commit to something I didn't know was coming."

"What do you mean?"

"It's like...I was happy, just existing together. But when he came out, it was like—I didn't want him to think that if we broke up, it was because of that."

"But wasn't it?" he presses, playing with a quarter he found in the drink holder.

"No, it was just a lack of imagination on my part. And not realizing how much I loved him. But I didn't want him blaming himself. It would've been my fault if we didn't stay together, I'm sure."

He nods slowly as we creep along. "Have you told him all that?"

"No." I drag a hand through my hair. "I doubt he wants to hear my knuckleheaded-ness rehashed."

"Or maybe that's exactly what he needs to hear. Maybe you need to dredge up the past a little in order to move on."

"Move on? To where? He'd never take me back."

"I wouldn't be so sure..." he says, nodding toward my phone, which is now blowing up with texts.

Drew: Please call me when you get there. We need to talk.

"But I left to avoid the talking..." I whine, and Colby just laughs. "Actually, that's not true. I need to get my head straight, you know? Breathe a little."

"The woods are a good place to do that. Is there a piano there?"

I nod.

"Good. I still need to finish my song."

"I thought it was a guitar thing."

"Oh, it is. But I didn't want to drag my guitar all the way to Oxford. So I'm adapting it. I'll record the parts and put it together. I'd be too nervous in the moment."

"Adorable."

Colby whacks me with the back of his hand, and I jump.

"Hey, do not assault the driver, please! I want to get there in one piece!" We talk and laugh and listen to music all the way up the mountain until we pull into the driveway. The red A-frame is simple, but it's cozy. The wood stove will keep us warm, and it's got indoor plumbing. The log furniture is cheesy, but it's part of its charm. I'm trying not to dread talking to Drew, but I kind of am. I wait until the car is all unpacked to step outside with my phone. He picks up on the first ring.

"Hello?"

"Hey." There's a long pause, and I look at my phone to see if I lost the signal. Nope. "You there?"

"Yeah, I'm just...is everything okay?"

"Sure. Why?"

"Seemed like you kind of took off suddenly."

"Just needed a change of pace."

"Uh-huh. But we're okay?"

"Is there a 'we?'" I ask, my voice gravelly and sincere. And when he doesn't say anything, I feel my own cowardice so acutely, it's like someone just held up a mirror to my soul. Because I really should've asked this question to his face instead of driving an hour just to have this conversation over the phone.

"I don't know," he says quietly. "I thought maybe."

"I thought maybe, too. And it scared the shit out of me. I can't—" I stop to try to clear my throat of the emotions thickening my voice. "I can't go through losing you again. So let's just both take a step back and think about what we want, okay?"

"Okay...but we'll talk when you get back?"

"Yeah. I promise."

"See you then." He hangs up without saying good-bye, and for the first time since we arrived, I take a deep breath. The fresh smell of pine hits me, and I can hear the creek running nearby, high with snow runoff. I close my eyes, and the emotions slowly recede. The back door opens, and I hear Colby shuffle out.

"You okay?"

"Yeah. You turn the oven on?"

"Couldn't figure out how..." he says ruefully, and I gesture toward the kitchen.

"I'll show you. It's not hard when you know how."

CHAPTER TWENTY-FOUR

NO SOONER DO I HANG up with Andrew than my phone rings again—it's a video call from Nico.

"Hello, son. I'm doing the thing—all by myself! Are you proud of your old man?"

"Very proud," I assure him with a grin. Greg sits down next to him—they're outside, as it is still delightfully warm in California. "You helped him, didn't you?"

"Just a little!" Nico protests, pouting. Greg pats him on the shoulder.

"It's all right. You'll get it."

"You're really too young to have such problems with technology," I tease, and his scowl deepens.

"That's ageist, and it's his fault! This new phone isn't set up like my old one. I could do everything—*everything*—on that one. I miss it so much."

"They upgraded the network," Greg explains, chagrined. "Otherwise, he would've been buried with that thing."

"I'm very busy. I don't have time for this ridiculous device..."

"Did you just call to complain about your new phone or was there a purpose to this?"

"Just wanted to make sure the house was behaving itself," Greg says. A timer goes off in the background, and he gets up and leaves the screen.

"You know what? Thank you for saying that, because I tried to tell him that Colby's house was going to know I

was an interloper, and they all thought I was off my rock-
er."

"Oh, no—the curse. It is real. You were right to warn
him. Which roommate was this?"

"Andrew." I hold my breath, but he just smiles.

"It sounds like you are friendly again."

"Yeah, you could say that..." Was what he did to me
yesterday morning friendly? I'm sure it was by some
standard.

"Friends, even?"

"Yeah." And saying it out loud breaks something in
me, because as much as I'm relieved that he came to me
when he needed a place to live, as much as I'm delighted that he wants me to touch him and make him come,
as much as I'm grateful that we can joke around and be
comfortable together...I don't want to be his friend. Or
rather, I don't want to be just his friend. How far do I
take that? I'm not sure yet. But probably as far as he'll let
me.

"And where is the cheese?" Nico asks. "Ah! There he
is. I'm glad you're not all alone up there. The cheese will
be a good companion." He's talking about Colby, who
just waved in the background.

"Hi, Mr. Arosio. And Mr. Rhodes."

"Colby, please—I tell you many times to call me
Nico."

"Where'd Dad go?"

Nico peers over his shoulder. "He is baking something complicated, I believe. We don't mean to intrude,
go and have your fun. Just call if the water turns brown."

"Thanks, I—wait, what? What's wrong with the water?"

"The pipes, they are old. You see what happens when men and houses age is..."

"Okay, okay, enough, thanks. I don't need to hear about your broken pipe."

"You should know about these things, son. Someday, you'll be married. It will matter."

I massage my temples, even though they don't hurt. "I don't even know where to start with that statement. My junk doesn't matter unless I'm in a relationship? Also, you really think I'm the marrying type?"

He cocks his head. "Why wouldn't you be? Your dad, he has made me so happy. We have you. We have a good life because we are together."

"Amen," Greg says, sitting back down. "Sorry I disappeared. What'd I miss?"

"It is all right, amore mio. I am just teaching the boy about the joys of marriage." Greg blushes, as he always does when Nico uses that nickname, and takes a sip of water to cover it.

"I hope you're not oversharing..." Greg says.

"Not this time," I say with a smile. "Also, don't know if you noticed, Dad—not exactly a boy anymore."

"Ah—and this brings us back to the point. First of all, you will always be my boy. That is nonnegotiable." The word gets lost in his thick accent, and that's why I'm blinking back tears. Not because I needed someone to tell me they love me when I feel like such an asshole lately.

"And secondly, yes, I believe you will marry. Your papas have set you a good example. For you to find the right person who can convince you completely will not be easy. But I believe you will make that choice."

"What about you?" I say to Dad. "Do you see me getting married in your crystal ball?"

"Maybe," he says, tipping his head the exact same way Nico did a minute ago, and it makes me need a hug. "I think Nico's right about needing the right person. Honestly, I kind of thought you and Andrew could go the distance. You seemed very..."

"Twitterpated?"

They both laugh. "Yes, exactly," Greg says. "Haven't heard that word for a long time."

"That's what happens when you talk to history majors," I mutter, but I don't think they hear me. "And I can have a lifelong relationship without getting married. You did."

"It is true," Nico admits, "but for me, I needed the...the...what is the word, caro?"

"The formality."

"Yes, grazie—the formality. Not only because I grew up religious, but because it would've made my mama proud." He shrugs. "These things, we cannot explain them. But they also matter."

"And you wouldn't have cared if I married a trans guy?" It was a ridiculous fear, I admit that.

They both blink at me.

"Of course not!" Greg says, and I think I've stunned Nico into silence. I never asked them, because I was afraid of the answer and we weren't that serious. I don't know if we are now—or if we're even really together—but it helps to know. "Why would you even ask that?"

I shrug. "Some LGB people aren't into the T."

Nico's found his voice, apparently, and it's tinged with anger. "Those people, they do not know what trans women did for us—for all of us—at the Stonewall Riots. Marsha P. Johnson and Sylvia Rivera, they fought back against injustice and sparked something new. Do you think we would be married, your dad and I, without that thing? No. How can you ask me this? How can you think—"

"I'm sorry," I say over his protests, and after a moment of shoulder patting from Dad, he calms down. "I just never asked you before."

"It should not be a question. I do not understand why some would exclude, as if we do not know the taste of it."

"Agreed," says Greg, "and well put. We'd have happily welcomed Andrew into the family."

"Still could," Nico says with a grin, and Greg elbows him subtly.

"We're happy you're friends again, kiddo."

"Might be more than friends..." I admit, and Nico claps his hands.

"Did I not tell you, amore mio? He is suffused with light in his face, I knew there was love there still. Did I not say?"

Wait, *suffused*? Am I dating my *dad*? Oh, shit.

"Yes, you're very smart," Greg says placatingly, "but let's not put too much pressure on these two…"

"Who's putting pressure? I'm not putting pressure. I just want to see them happy and in love, like us."

Greg switches to Italian, and I'm pretty sure he says something like, "Leave them alone, for God's sake, let them breathe," which just makes Nico huffier.

I'm pretty sure I could hang up now, and they wouldn't notice. They're not even looking at the screen. It's just as well; I'm all jumbled inside, and words are just getting in the way of what I want to say. I don't know how it's possible, but it's true.

"Fathers, I'm out. I'll call you if the water turns brown."

They pause their argument.

"We love you," Greg says, waving.

"Ciao, piccolo ribelle, siamo fiere di te." I don't speak a lot of Italian, but these words I know: "Goodbye, little rebel, we're proud of you."

CHAPTER TWENTY-FIVE

WE SPEND THE NEXT 24 hours just...chilling. I read. Colby writes. We jam. We play video games. I stay off the internet as much as I can, but the temptation is too much at one point. I hold out my phone to Colby, despite his focus on his notebook.

"A present? For me? Aww, you shouldn't have."

"I just need you to keep it away from me so I don't text him, smartass."

He gives me a sad, pouty face. "What's it going to hurt? I bet he misses you..."

"Can you just take it, please?"

"Just text him. What's the harm?"

I jam it in my pocket discontentedly. "I told him we'd talk in a few days. We're giving each other space. But I'm probably just convenient; he's super horny."

"Yeah, Chance has told me stories about those early hormone days. Not fun." He puts his guitar aside. "You really don't think it's more than that?"

"How could it be? If someone had made me feel shitty when I came out to them, I'd have ghosted them without a second thought."

"He's a better person than you are."

"Undoubtedly. But some things are unforgiveable."

Colby cocks an eyebrow, then picks the guitar back up, strumming idly. "Pretty sure he'd disagree with you, and not just because of the church thing. It wasn't a sin to need time to think about it. It would've taken some serious getting used to."

I pace to the front of the house to look out the big windows. It must've caught a little signal, because my phone vibrates rapidly.

> **Tony:** Has anyone seen Andrew? He didn't show up for his shift.

> **Darren:** Last I knew, he was upstairs.

> **Patrick:** No, I saw him leave.

> **Tony:** When was that?

> **Patrick:** About an hour ago. I offered him some dinner, but he said he was going to eat at work.

I sit down on the window seat because my knees are doing their cabasa impression...I'm sure Colby can hear them shaking from across the room.

"Everything okay?"

"Andrew didn't arrive at work."

Colby comes over to peer at the phone, then pulls out his own when he sees how many messages there are. "And he didn't call in? That's unusual."

"I mean, he took off on his previous roommates, including his sister, and didn't tell them where he was. Do you think he moved out?"

"That feels like you're jumping to conclusions..."

"None of this is worth it if he's not safe. What if he left because of me?" I hold up the phone, trying to get a better signal, but it's still mocking me with its miniscule bars in the corner of the screen. "I mean, if it comes down to it, I'd rather move out than him leave. I have other places I can go. Hell, I'd live in a cardboard box if it meant he was safe. You don't think someone did something to him, do you?"

Colby frowns. "Like what?"

"I don't know! Why isn't he answering? What if he just happened to walk by the wrong transphobe who decided to fuck him up?"

My best friend puts a heavy hand on my shoulder. "Dude, take a deep breath. He's probably fine. I'm sure there's a good explanation."

In my head, I know he's right. But my heart does not want to hear it. It will not be comforted right now by anything but hearing from Drew. I snatch my coat from the coat rack by the front door and shove my feet into my shoes without tying them. "I'm going to walk down by the creek to try to get a better signal."

Colby straightens. "Now?"

"No," I deadpan, "I'm just gonna wait for sunrise on the front porch. Yes, now!"

"Aren't you worried about bears?"

"If I was carrying a raw steak or a bag of marshmallows, I sure would be." I slam the door behind me and tromp away from the house. It's cold, but there's no clouds overhead, and I look up at the puzzle piece sky. The stars are brilliant out here, even more so the farther

I get from the house. There used to be a spot up the road in this direction...

Something snaps in the forest ahead of me, and I flick on the flashlight on my phone. A squirrel stares at me, momentarily stunned into stillness, then it tears off under a wild azalea. I check the signal again: it's a little better.

Darren: And you tried texting him?

Tony: Yeah. No answer.

Patrick: Interesting.

Tony: He seemed upset earlier. Does anyone know who he was talking to when he answered that call?

Patrick: I've got a guess...

Patrick: Give me an hour and I can hack his phone.

Darren: Let's call that Plan B.

Patrick: Spoilsport.

Tony: Guys, focus.

Andrew: I'm okay. Bus broke down, so I had to run. Not the easiest thing to do with a piece of nylon suffocating me.

Darren: Glad you're okay, man.

Patrick: For future reference, I would've picked you up.

Andrew: And ruin my reputation by showing up in that junker? I don't think so.

Tony: we can't all own Evan's fancy ride.

Patrick: "fancy"

I turn off the flashlight and slide the phone back into my coat. Hands in my pockets, I stare up at the stars again. I felt like I was suffocating, too, when I didn't know if he was okay. I really wanted to jump in the car and race back down the mountain to try to find him, but I didn't. That's progress, but the wanting is still there. I don't know how to turn off that protective, quasi-alpha male thing I feel about him. Is that love? Maybe in part. But more than that, I want to fall asleep holding him, listening to The Lumineers. I want to sit shoulder to shoulder on the couch, him on the end, so I'm the one touching him. I want to listen to him talk about Hawaiian history. I want to tell him to calm down when we watch football, and I want to bump into him while cooking dinner. I want to get him off hard and be the silent show of support for family shit. And if I could do all that without getting my heart crushed again, I'd be in. All in. Call it whatever you want: marriage, relationship, trust, faith. But he's got mine.

I breathe a little longer, slowing my racing heart before I go back inside and tell Colby the good news.

CHAPTER TWENTY-SIX

COLBY AND I STRATEGIZE most of that night, both on his song and on my plan to win Andrew back permanently. Our opinion is this: there's three parts necessary. One: apologize for running off, because it was knuckleheaded. Two: Have an honest discussion about what we want (and don't want). Three: Start showing my support everywhere he wants to be. Even if that includes going to his sister's wedding, which is going to be awkward AF.

I think he must have been waiting by the front window, because I don't even see him before he slams into me. I assume it's him; most of my roommates don't engulf me in a gigantic hug when I walk through the door after being away for a few days. When I turn my head, his face is temptingly close, but the drawn lines of his face are transmitting annoyance, not delight.

"You left."

"I did. I'm sorry."

"I missed you."

I hear Colby coming in behind me, chuckling. "Where's my hug?" he asks, but Drew just ignores him.

"I missed you, too," I say, dropping my bags to hug him back, and we just stand like that, awkwardly, with the front door still open. Finally, I break it. "Who's home?"

"Everyone." And as if on cue, I hear them all cracking up in the kitchen.

"Uh-huh. I see. You want to go for a walk?"

"I'll get my coat." He darts away, and I chuckle. Yeah, I'm wishing we had a little more privacy, too, but that's not gonna happen, unless we just blatantly go upstairs, and that feels like a little much for this time in the morning. He's back with a cute gray beanie, a puffy black coat, and running shoes in a few moments. "Let's go."

I take his hand as we descend the front steps, and he smiles at me.

"You're back."

"Dude. I went to the cabin, not to war."

He sobers at that a little, like he just remembered he was mad at me. "I would've gone with you. I would've left you alone so you could think."

"That...wouldn't have worked, I don't think." It's raining a little, so I put up my hood, but it makes it harder to see him. I push it back down. These kind of walks are nicer when the trees aren't so skeletal.

"But it worked with Colby?"

I glance at him, my eyebrows making a deep V. "You're not jealous, are you? Because you've gotta know Colby and I are just friends."

"I know that..." He sighs. "In my head."

"He's very taken. He's gonna ask Chance to marry him in a few days, remember?"

"Yeah, I know."

"So..." I nudge him with my elbow. "What's that about?"

"I don't want to be the one who stresses you out. I want to be the one you can relax with."

"And you are," I insist. "I just...needed to figure out what I wanted."

"And?"

"I want...you. In all the ways you'll let me have you. But I think we need better communication going forward. In both directions."

He squeezes my hand, and I'm so glad I put that pointless hood down so that I could see this radiant smile. I'm gonna get wet anyway, right? "That seems fair."

"What do you want?" I press.

"I want to be together, like we were. I think I didn't give you enough time before...I'm sorry I was impatient."

"No. It wasn't your fault. I owed you more of my process. I owed you...details." I swallow hard. "And speaking of details..."

"Yeah?"

"I'd like to know why you dropped out of school."

He looks down the street, and even though I'm nervous, it helps to be moving. "I don't know."

"Drew..."

"No, it's not bullshit. I just..." His breath clouds in front of him. "Okay. So I had this little thought in the back of my head that maybe people wouldn't want a trans guy teaching their kids. That I wouldn't be able to find work. So there was no point in finishing. And it just got louder and louder the closer I got to really going full guy mode. But more than that, I think I didn't want to go around correcting people all the time on my name and my pronouns. It was easier to just...leave."

"But if you have a degree, there's so many more options available to you."

He tips his head to the side. "True. But I just...couldn't. I think I could now." He squeezes my hand again. "I don't know. I'm going to look into what it would take to finish. They don't always offer those classes every semester. I might have to wait until next year."

"Okay." This next question is even harder. "Are you ever going back to church?"

Drew nods slowly. "I've been going online. Mostly at night."

"I didn't know that."

"It seemed like a safer way to try out some different places."

My brow furrows. "Safer?"

"Yeah, you know. I don't want to find out they're transphobic when I walk into the sanctuary for the first time and someone yells, 'Sinner!'"

I tug him closer on instinct, but I can't keep the horror out of my voice. "Would that happen?"

Drew laughs. "Probably not. They might think it in their heads, but they wouldn't shout and point. Probably." He side-eyes me. "Would you ever want to come with me?"

"Oh. Uh." I never did before, but I can see why he wouldn't want to go alone. But I also have zero desire to do that. "Can I think about it?"

"Sure. I think you'd like the music, though."

"Is that what you like about it?" I've never really asked him. It was just a thing he did, sliding out of bed on Sundays, leaving with me a kiss on the forehead, the way I did to him when I went running.

"That's part of it." He's quiet for a minute, and I can't tell what he's thinking. "You know when you're in the symphony and the music is just... everything? And your heartbeat syncs and you're breathing with everyone else. And you know it's not everything–you know there's more things–bad things–outside those walls, but inside the walls, there's no room for that shit. That's how I feel when I worship God. Like I'm enough, because They're so big. They're everything, but I'm not pushed out, I'm part of the everything. And I can feel my soul."

Huh. Well, that doesn't sound like something he should give up. "Okay."

"Okay to what I said, or okay you'll come?"

"Okay, I'll come with you. If you want. I'm not going to pretend it would mean as much to me as it does to you, but yeah. I'd go."

"We wouldn't go back to my old church; I'm gonna find a new place. But that's where Grace's wedding is."

"And I'm allowed to punch anyone who looks at you the wrong way, right?"

"Wrong."

"A little punch. A love tap, really. Aren't they supposed to be all about love? They'll understand."

"I don't think so, sweetheart."

"Damn."

We walk through the quiet of parked cars and bundled-up kids and an Oregon winter, just walking. Thinking. Touching. And it's so, so nice. When he gets cold,

I buy him a hot chocolate. And then I take him home, holding his hand the whole way, pulling him straight up the stairs past all our roommates, to warm him up right.

CHAPTER TWENTY-SEVEN

AT 2:40 AM, I ROLL out of bed and put on pants.

"Where you going?" Drew mutters, stretching.

"Airport run, remember? Go back to sleep." The speed with which he complies is almost comical, sinking back into the bed and going still like he's a robot I'd just powered down. I jog quietly down the front staircase, only to meet with a surprise. Colby is on the couch, back straight, hands folded, one leg giggling rapidly.

"Have you been there all night?" His nervous motion makes it hard to tell if he's nodding, but I think he does. "You should've knocked. I would've kept you company."

"Thought you might be...busy with Andrew."

"Nope. Just sleeping." But I may have been busy with him in the middle of the night. A man has needs. Especially when he's just gotten back together with his favorite person. And god, there's nothing like quiet, middle-of-the-night fucking when everything just...gels. He didn't say anything; I didn't say anything. We just knew.

Colby rubs his face. "I hope I can crash out on the plane. The flight attendants wake you up when you land, right? I just didn't want to sleep through my alarm."

"Yes. Right. I definitely wouldn't have dragged you out of bed."

"Ev..."

"I would've let you miss the most important moment of your life thus far. That would've happened for sure."

"Coffee, smartass."

"Yes, sir." I throw him a salute as I head for the kitchen to make my own cup. "Wait, isn't your mom still here? Why am I driving you?"

He runs a hand through his already-mussed hair. "My mom was making me more nervous. I told her you wanted to do it."

"Yes, it's an honor." I lean back against the counter with a yawn. "Seriously, though. It's gonna be fine."

"I know."

"Do you, though?"

"No, not at all." Colby chuckles. "It'll be fine?"

"I think I just said that. Chance loves you. And I happen to know he misses you like peanut butter misses jelly."

He grins a little at that. "How exactly do you know this?"

"He's been emailing with Drew. I happened to see over his shoulder."

"What do they email about?"

"Transition stuff. Dating hot cisgender bisexual guys. You know."

"Makes sense. I'm glad they can do that."

"Yeah, I am, too."

We're quiet on the drive to the airport; the closer we get, the more Colby's leg bounces. So I call an audible and park to walk him inside instead of dropping him at the curb. He lifts an eyebrow as I turn off toward the garage.

"More likely to get scratched here."

"It's true. But right now, if you don't settle down, they're gonna think you have a bomb, so I'm just gonna see you through security in case you get arrested."

Colby laughs. "Oh god, can you imagine? I'd have to use my one phone call to propose to Chance. 'Baby, I love you—ooh, sorry, we only have thirty seconds left. Yes or no? Quick!'" That gets me chuckling, too.

"Do they let you call internationally?" We both laugh harder. But it's not lost on me that this is going to change things. Colby's getting married...is Colby's going to move out? Or will we all be able to stay in the house? His parents are pretty great, but Chance and Colby might want privacy. I hadn't thought of it before, and it's a little troubling. At least wherever I end up, I know Drew will be with me. I think the other guys could figure something out with us...wait, do Drew and I want privacy, too? This is a lot to think about at 3:30 in the morning. I decide to table this mental conversation for later. But I still give Colby the biggest hug before he gets in line to do the metal detector, and it seems to help him calm down at least a little. Let's put it this way: he did not get arrested. At least, not here.

· · · ·

WHEN I GET BACK, IT'S still dark, so I undress and crawl back into bed to snuggle with my guy. I must drop off, because when I wake up, there's a pair of hot lips on the bit of my cock that's poking out of my boxers. Drew's on his belly, his dark hair soaking up the morning sun as his head bobs over me, and I put a hand on him. He glances up.

"This okay?"

I nod, but I prop my pillow up on the headboard so I can watch him better, and he slides off my plaid boxers smoothly. He's still wearing that soft cotton shirt he went to bed in, but I can see his chest hanging down. I want to see them, even if I can't touch them, but he's already showing trust in me by taking off the binder at night. It's a conundrum.

His mouth is back, and I shiver with relief. His tongue dances and slides over me, his shoulders pinning down my hips so I can't buck up into him, and it's a sweet torture. He plays with the slit at the top, and I groan, trying to take control, but he shifts out of my reach, kissing down one leg, lingering at the back of my knee.

"Get up here," I say gruffly, wanting his wetness on my fingers so badly, it's like an ache. Wanting to stroke those slick folds, to touch his...what did he call it? Arousal? I can't think when he's doing that to my cock, and it brings back that old fear, the one that had me cowering under my pillow. How am I supposed to tell him what I want when I can't even remember what it's called?

"Come. Here," I growl, and he grins, wiping his mouth with the back of his hand. I run a finger over the hem of the loose white shirt he's wearing. "Will you take this off for me today?"

Drew throws me a glare, and I just grin. "Why do you love them so much?"

"Can't help it," I say, leaning in to fondle his ribs over the fabric a little, kissing along the ridge of his shoulder. "They feel good in my hands. On my lips. And I like the noises you used to make when I played with them. I enjoy making you hot."

"Well, I wish I didn't have them." His voice is husky and a little strained, and I feel bad for asking. "So no. The shirt stays on." He throws his leg toward the edge like he's thinking about leaving, and I grab him around the ribs, pulling him back into me backwards.

"All right. I'm sorry."

"You're not," he says coldly, and I chuckle.

"I am, though. I'm sorry I made you feel bad. Not my intention."

"What was your intention, then?" he asks, and his voice is soft, fragile again.

I nuzzle his neck. "To enjoy you. In all the ways that you are."

His arms cover mine, giving them a hard squeeze, and I take a deep breath, relieved that he's given in.

"I hate being like this. I just want to skip ahead to the part where I'm ripped and my chest is flat and I can grow a beard and my voice isn't cracking and I'm not horny every minute of the day." His voice crescendos at the end, and I shush him, chuckling again.

"I've never been able to grow a good beard."

"You're hotter without one," he says dismissively, and I give him a squeeze.

"How do you know you won't be, too?"

"I don't know. That's the whole point. I just want to get out of this weird..."

"No-man's land?" I tease, but he nods.

"Yes. Exactly. I'm caught in this awful gender desert between where I am and where I want to be. You shouldn't like it. It's traitorous."

"Okay, first—your ten-dollar words have really been affected by watching that pirate show, and it's gotta stop."

"Never. Ed and Stede are everything."

"But seriously, I..." I breathe in the sleep-saturated scent of him, then press a kiss to his shoulder. "I'm sure it's frustrating right now, not seeing the results you want. Not looking on the outside the way you feel on the inside. But don't be mad at me for loving you in the in-between like I should have all along."

He pivots in my arms until he can see my face. "You don't mind being with a guy with curves?"

I shake my head slowly, holding his gaze. "Guys come in all shapes, you know."

"You don't mind that I don't have a big cock to play with?"

"Those are purchasable. Just ask Chance."

"Maybe I will," he says, leaning in for a kiss. "Maybe I'll buy a pretty glass cock and fuck you with it." He kisses me again a little longer, and holy shit, is it just me, or is it hot in here? I feel like nearly feverish at the idea, my skin heating everywhere he touches me. "Would you like that?"

I try to be cool and sound indifferent. "I'd give it a try."

"I bet you'd like it." He's teasing me with his fingers now, tracing the muscles in my shoulder. "And you'd look amazing on all fours, ass up for me. I'd love taking you like that. It'd be so affirming."

My mouth is dry. I lick my lips, and Drew's gaze drops to them, thick with want. Without thinking, I blurt out. "You can do it now."

His eyes flash, but he cocks his head. "You don't have any dildos."

Why is it so hard to swallow? Am I getting sick? "I didn't when we broke up. I do now."

He shifts so that he's straddling in my lap, and his caresses are getting more aggressive—when he pinches my nipple, I gasp. "Are you serious? You'd let me?"

I have seen this man in all sorts of situations in bed, but never this outwardly excited. How can I say no? I mean, if it was anyone else, I would—it's not my jam, I don't think. But Drew looks like I felt when my dads gave me my Porsche.

"But I don't have a harness."

"Do you have a pair of tighty whities?"

Uh, what? I nod. "Top drawer. But I don't want to be gagged with them."

Drew chuckles as he goes to retrieve them. "Anything else you don't want?"

"Uh...getting injured?"

"Yes, I do know that about you." He's sliding them on now, and when he fits the slim silicone dildo through the pee flap, I shiver. They're tight enough on him that this might just...work?

"Oh."

"Bend over, gorgeous." I move my feet to the cold floor and hinge at the waist, putting my elbows on the mattress, even as I look over my shoulder. He's lubing up the toy, running his fingers languidly over the smooth purple surface, which is probably premature, but fuck if it doesn't look hot. My own hand drifts to my cock, enjoying the sight of him.

"I'm gonna get you one that's got a little curve in it to hit your prostate better. You're gonna lose your mind," he purrs as he lines up behind me.

"Wait a sec," I cough out, going up on my toes because it's cold. "You gotta make room for it first."

"Oh."

I relax back down when he retreats. "Eager beaver."

"No beavers involved," he shoots back. "It's all cocks here." Then I feel his fingers probing me up and down my crack. My hand on my dick speeds up a little, because his slick fumbling actually feels great. And when he finds the hole, his finger is sweetly invasive.

"Do you want me to play with you like this, too?" I ask, my voice rumbling. "Turn you around and bend you over?

"Maybe. But I already have a hole."

"It wouldn't feel the same, babe..."

"I know, just...I don't know."

"That's okay," I say gently. He's trying to get the end in without success, and I hold back a laugh. "Sir, are you in some sort of hurry? It's 'one, two, three, me,' thank you very much."

"How should I know that?" he asks, slapping my ass, and it makes the laugh break free. "You're a dick. We can't all be sex toy experts."

"You're a quick study, smart guy. I have no doubt you'll—ohh." One finger to three is quite the adjustment, and I take a second to gather myself. I clear my throat. "More lube, please. You can't use too much."

"Check." He curls his fingers when he puts them back, and I'm up on my toes again as my prostate lights up.

"Hnnn..." He works me for another minute, then the blunt end of the dildo is back. And this time, he's still struggling to get it in.

"Are you clenching or something?"

I muffle my chuckle against my free arm. "Nope." I can tell he's getting frustrated, so I stand up and turn around. I kiss him deeply, gathering him into my arms, but he pulls back, a wrinkle between his eyebrows.

"Are you giving up?"

"No, baby. Just resetting..." I guide the two of us onto the bed and put him in the position I occupied a few minutes ago, sitting against the headboard. "Maybe this'll be easier." His gaze goes back to inferno mode as I push down onto the head, slowly breaching myself. It's pressing into his arousal, I'm sure, but his gaze is on where the toy is slowly entering me.

"Fuck, that's hot." He's touching my chest now, scratching through my chest hair. Then, he sits up so quickly, we almost collide. Because he's taking off his shirt.

"Hands on the bedframe."

I groan, riding him faster. "This is unfair. Cruelty."

"At least you get to look at them," he smirks. "Take what you can get."

"I plan to," I say, dipping my head to kiss his mouth. Then I take his hand and put it around my cock before I return my hands to the bedframe. He picks up quickly on what I want: he's moving opposite me, stroking up as I go down, down as I move up. And paired with the action at my backdoor, it means there's always something for me to feel, something changing, lighting me up.

"You look incredible," he breathes, and his expression is almost awe. "Truly, Ev."

I might be flexing more than strictly necessary—keep it between us, please. I spiral my hips a little, grinding down on the base of the toy, and his head falls back in pleasure.

"Yeah, do that. Ride my cock." Even though I want it harder and faster, there'll be time for that—I keep it slow, and soon he's panting, scratching at my chest, scrambling for something to hold on to.

"Love your cock," I whisper. "I could ride it all day." He moans, thick with emotion, then comes hard. He's so spent, his hand slips off my cock, and I take it up myself, finishing myself off fast, letting it hit his chest. It takes both of us a minute to let our breathing return to normal, and then we survey the mess.

"Boy, what I wouldn't give to have Colby's en suite bathroom right now..." I mutter, and Drew laughs.

"You wanna wipe them off, since you made them dirty?"

"With pleasure," I say, lunging for the wipes.

CHAPTER TWENTY-EIGHT

"HOW LONG DOES IT TAKE to fly to England, anyway?" Patrick is pacing in front of the TV again, using his fidget spinner. The spinner is quiet, but I can't see the game, and I feel Drew squirming, too. Because he's sitting right next to me, pressed into my side, as he should be.

"Normally, about nine hours," I answer, "but he took a cheap flight, so it's more like fifteen. Dude, you gotta pace behind the couch."

Patrick glares at me, but he changes his route. "Shouldn't we have heard from him by now? Wasn't he going to do it at the airport?"

"I don't think so...He's got that song and everything," Darren says. "I don't see how he can do the song at the airport."

"I think he made a recording of the accompaniment," I say. "Because he didn't want to drag his guitar along."

"So when does he land?"

"9:30 our time."

Patrick checks his watch, because yes, he wears an actual watch. It's very expensive and powered by the sun. Nerd. "It's 9:45 now!"

"Dude, chill! He's probably just going through security and customs and stuff. He's never done this before. It takes a minute."

All our phones buzz, chirp or ding, and we pull them out.

Colby: through security

"See?" I say to Patrick. "He didn't crash."

"Good." He flops down onto the couch across from me and Drew. Everyone seems to be giving us space, and they haven't teased us nearly as much as I anticipated. It's concerning. I don't know how to account for it. Unless...they're planning something big to tease us? Nah, that's not likely.

> **Colby:** and I'm going to ask him now. As soon as I see him.

The room explodes into cheers, and I hold up my hands. "All right, people. Get out your money."

Drew looks alarmed. "What's happening?"

"Oh, yeah—" I turned to look at him. "You hadn't been here long enough to be in on this. I set it up right after you moved in. We made bets."

His jaw drops, and I noticed he actually has a little scruff on it. *Freaking adorable.* "Excuse me, what? You're betting on your best friend's proposal?"

"Wait," Tony says, holding out a hand. "Was it whether he proposes or whether Chance says yes?"

"Neither," Patrick and I say together, then I go on. "That would be a terrible thing to bet on. No, it was who proposes *first*. And Colby just upped the ante—Chance said he's proposing at the airport, too."

They're uncontainable now.

"Wait, when did you know this? Before you all made the bet?" Drew asks, and I put my finger to my lips to stop him...but Darren hears him.

"Whoa, whoa, whoa. Prior knowledge is unacceptable, Rhodes. You cheated. Forfeit your winnings now." He taps his finger on the coffee table meaningfully.

"So it's my fault you all assumed I wouldn't have inside knowledge as Colby's best friend? Nice try."

A chorus of complaints, including Drew's at being excluded, is silenced by another group message.

> **Colby:** I'm at the baggage claim.
> **Evan**: You got this, dude. Go for it.

I shove Drew out of the way, just as my roommates pile on, trying to get my phone away from me. But to my surprise, he's in here, too, taking the opportunity to flick my ear, which he knows I hate.

"Hey! Ow! There were no ground rules about influencing the outcome, you punks!"

I am being called a lot of names, none of them nice. But I know my best friend; he's got this. Chance is totally going to hesitate. I don't blame him, he's got anxiety—but still. Colby's going to win this. Someone is sitting on my chest, and they finally wrest my phone away from me.

"Oop." Around Darren's giant butt, I steal a peek at Drew, because that was a very telling noise.

"What? What was that, babe? Everyone shut up!"

Drew points to his phone. "Someone's live-streaming it for Chance on his Tracebook."

The room erupts in noise again, most of them pointing at the TV and shouting for Drew to cast it. He does, and suddenly, the screen is full of Chance, waiting at the baggage claim. He's watching the crowds flowing out of the escalators, searching for Colby...who's already there.

"Turn around, damn it!" Patrick yells, and then I see Colby, on the other side of the carousel, making his way quickly to Chance. He drops his bag and breaks into a run.

"Don't drop your bag at Heathrow, you're gonna get arrested," Darren bellows at the screen, and everyone shushes him. He gets in front of Chance and engulfs him in his arms, but I can see that he's making a fist with one hand.

"He's got the ring in his hand—that counts! I win!"

"No, he's gotta say the words first," Patrick objects.

"Maybe you could all shut up so we can hear," Drew yells, and we all stare at him. "What? I want to know what's happening!"

I grin at him, and he gives me a glare before he turns back to the screen. *Divo.*

Then the kissing starts, and I can tell they're both crying, and it's so adorable. Even my grinchy heart has to admit that I'm thrilled we got to see this. Then we all watch in horror as they both step back and get on one knee at exactly the same time. Laughing, wiping tears, they both show each other the rings they got. I'm not sure they even actually asked each other. Chance's friend turns the camera around and says in a posh British accent, "I guess that's a yes, then?"

"Damn it!" I throw a pillow. "Who won, then?"

"Everyone," Drew says. And you know what? He's exactly right.

CHAPTER TWENTY-NINE

COLBY'S BEEN GONE FOR days, and we've heard almost nothing from him except for a few pictures of them in touristy places. We are all quite positive that the rest of their time is rated X and cannot be shared, as it should be. But Drew and I are getting ready for our own event...it's Friday, and Grace's rehearsal dinner is tonight.

"Can you help me with my tie?" Drew looks truly flustered, flapping the ends of the polyester fabric like they're his arms and he's drowning.

My smirk is gentle. "I wouldn't mind being dressed first." When he came bursting into the bathroom without knocking, I'd just turned off the water, and even now, I'm still toweling off. "What time are we leaving?"

"In less than an hour." He flaps the ends again at me insistently, and I chuckle as I step over the tub, still drying my hair.

"But less than an hour by like...a minute, right?"

"Technically yes," he concedes, and I force solemnity into my face because I know he's stressed. I turn him by his shoulders until we're both facing the mirror, because I won't be able to do this in front of him.

"You want a Windsor knot, handsome?"

"Uh...sure?"

I press a kiss to his neck to try to reassure him as I pull his collar up to thread the tie underneath. "I like this color on you." Our eyes meet in the mirror, and all I can see is the stark dread in his dark gaze and the rigid set of his jaw. "It's going to be okay."

"What if it's not?" he whispers, leaning back into me, and I release the tie in order to wrap my arms around him.

"It will be. I'll be with you. If it's bad, we can leave."

He sighs. "You don't know what it's like growing up in church. I couldn't even question these things because it was just understood that if God made you one way, that's how you were meant to be." He's right. I don't get it. My dads taught me to ask too many questions.

"I think that can still be true. Maybe He made you trans."

He snorts at that, and it's a little watery, so I squeeze him tighter.

"Stop. You're gonna squeeze the tears right out."

"No mascara to run. Let it out," I whisper, nuzzling his cheek with my nose, and he chuckles a little, coughing it out like he resents I could make him laugh when he's so stressed. But it's something about how forced his smiles looks, even as the lines in his face draw downward, that convinces me he's going to cry after all.

"I love the way you're made." We're rocking a little now side to side, a rhythm of comfort, and I hope no one intrudes on this moment, because it feels as strangely holy as he described singing in church to be. "I love your body and your brain." I hold his gaze in the mirror, and silently, a tear slips down his cheek. But he's still holding onto me, his hands hooked over my forearms like I'm a lifeline. "I love that you're a fighter. I love your big words and your undying loyalties, even when they encroach on my Sundays. I love that you've embraced a new life, but still have room in your heart to forgive me. I love that I get to watch your transformation as you become the man you're meant to be. And more than all that, I love you." Is it a little weird to be having this conversation when I'm only wearing a towel around my waist? Yeah. But maybe it's appropriate that I'm baring my soul in this state. Based on the vulnerable light in his welling eyes, he's feeling stripped down in plenty of other ways. "And no, they might not understand right away, but they're not assholes. They love you, too. Love can hold a surprising number of disparate things together, in my experience."

He uses the back of his hand to wipe his eyes then, sniffling. "Yeah?"

"Yeah." I kiss his cheek. "Plus, they *have* to accept you. It's cultural, right, māhū?"

His laugh is a cynical trumpet blast. "If only it were that easy."

"I feel like I could make a case. Let's send them some articles."

"Sure," he says, rolling his reddened eyes. "I'll do that from the car on the way there."

"And then text them to read them," I say, flipping the wide end of the tie over the narrow one. "Some people don't check their email compulsively. No judgment."

Drew stills my hands, searching out my gaze again in the mirror. "Thank you."

"Of course." Silly man. He really does not realize how unable I am to refuse him anything he needs. Even his whims are my obligation to fulfill.

"And next time, you can teach me how to do it myself."

"That costs extra," I deadpan, and he grins. As it fades, he sucks in a long breath, then lets it out slowly, like a bellow.

"Did you know my tutu's name is Leah?"

My heart sinks. "No," I say quietly. "But that's rough."

"What if she sees it as rejection? Like I didn't want to be named after her?"

"Then she's missing the point," I say firmly, even though I think Tutu will get it. "It's not about her. And you could always leave it as a middle name or some diminutive like Lee."

He doesn't even ask me for ten dollars. That's how stressed he is.

"It'll be okay," Andrew says to himself in the mirror, but I affirm the cliché anyway.

"It will," I say, kissing his shoulder. "Now I'm gonna go find some pants."

"Okay. I'm gonna do my hair. Pray for me."

"That's not my department," I say over my shoulder as I leave.

"Do it anyway!" he calls after me.

· · · ·

HE'S STILL NERVOUS as we walk into the hotel fifty minutes later. I grab his hand as we search for the right room, but when we find it, he pulls it free.

"They couldn't even spell our name right?" he asks, shaking his head, and when I look closer at the sign, he's right. "Kahanaui Wedding Party" it screams in a slanted, calligraphy script. But there's a pen sitting on the windowsill. With a smile, I grab it.

"What are you doing?"

"Fixing it."

"No, Evan—don't. I—"

I point to the sign. "Is this your name?"

He puts his hands on his hips. He really does look good in this color, even if the angles of the clothing aren't as flattering as he wants them to be. And the skinny tie was a good choice.

"No."

"And aren't they paying a lot to have this event here?"

He nods.

"So, you deserve to see your name spelled right." Before he can argue any more, I put in a little arrow and add the missing 'n.' "There. All better."

"If only changing my first name was that easy..." he mutters, and I give him a squeeze and a soft kiss on his mouth.

"Let's go find out," I whisper, glancing toward the door. It's rumbling with the sound of many people talking, even from out here, and I can hear his dad's booming laugh. But I still hear Andrew take a deep breath as he opens the door.

I guess I watch too many movies, because I expected the conversation to stop and all eyes to be on us, the dead silence in the room making everyone uncomfortable until Andrew says something. But that's not what happens. Everyone keeps talking, sitting around the long table, picking at appetizers. Nick, his dad, notices him first, lingering near the door. He stands up and motions him over with two hands, arms out for a hug. That's when the tears start—mine, anyway. I can't see Drew's expression—he's currently being smothered in a bear hug, his face in Nick's neck...but he's definitely hugging him back, the muscles of his back standing out even through his shirt. It's that kind of embrace. And then they just kind of pass him down the line: his mom Rose is next, a petite woman with wavy, black hair—so he leans over to hold her better. But Rose's hug is just as fierce, and she's whispering something to him, and he's nodding, wiping his face. Then it's Grace's turn, and hers is less intense—she squeals with delight, stomping her feet, and Andrew gives a sniffly laugh.

"Evan?" I stiffen; Nick sounds surprised to see me. I push past the feeling and hold out a hand, and I'm met with a firm handshake.

"Yes, sir."

"Didn't expect to see you with us again–how are you, young man?"

"I'm well, thank you, sir." We're side by side, watching Andrew run his gauntlet of hugs.

"No need to be so formal," he says. "Grace tells me Andrew's been crashing with you."

"That's right." My brain spins with possibilities: he's mad we're sleeping together again without being married, he's mad that I wouldn't tell Grace he was there, he's mad I didn't bring him to their doorstep...

He pivots so he can look me in the eye. "Thank you for taking care of my son when I couldn't."

Oh, shit. Now I'm really crying. My lower lip is trembling, but I manage the word clearly. "Always."

"Can I ask you a question?"

I swipe at the unwanted tears on both sides, trying to sniffle them down. "Sure?"

"Do you know why my son named himself after a hurricane?"

A laugh bubbles out of me. "I think it was supposed to be for an apostle or something?"

"Oh." He turns back to look at Andrew, nodding. "That does make more sense."

"Though he can be a bit of a hurricane when he wants to be."

"Some things don't change, right?"

"Exactly, sir." Sorry—the 'sir' just feels right. I respect the hell out of this guy. I don't know if he gets the trans thing yet, but he's saying all the right things so far, and that means a lot. "A lot of things haven't changed...is what I'm finding. Now that we're together again."

His eyes widen as he faces me. "Together as in..."

"Yes, sir."

"Oh." He looks back at Andrew, and then at me. "I didn't know you were interested in men."

"Always have been."

"Huh." He crosses his arms over his chest as he considers his son again. "Well, at least he didn't pick Iniki."

CHAPTER THIRTY

THE REST OF THE NIGHT goes smoothly; as soon as they release him from all the introductions, they start in on me, and he stays by my side the whole time. I do the same for him; we even go to the bathroom together. Nothing happens, okay? Not even that night, when we collapse exhausted into my bed, safe in our space again. The morning is another rush of stress and hurry, but at least we know the family is all accepting, even if they're not affirming yet.

His burgundy suit looks great as we hurry back into the church, late. Everyone's gathered around Grace and Drew's grandmother...Leah. The one he was named after. She wasn't there last night; she got in too late from her flight from Hawaii. I could swear he's hiding behind me as we approach the group...but then he steps forward, curious. And I am, too. Because she's giving out leis.

"Mom?" Rose's eyes are wide, horrified. "Where did you get those?"

Tutu ignores her. "This one is for the groom. Tuberose and ti leaf. Beautiful."

"Mom, you cannot smuggle flowers out of Hawaii! That is *illegal!*"

"And of course," Leah goes on, "lei po'o for the bride..." She pulls out a gorgeous crown of big white flowers, and I have no idea how she got those here without being caught or them getting crushed in her suitcase. They smell amazing, but strong.

Rose is still fuming. "You're lucky they didn't stop you at the airport. You'd be spending the wedding in jail."

Tutu sighs impatiently. "I explained it to the man. He too had a granddaughter who could not do the ceremony in Hawaii. He understood we had to bring her culture to her. We had to bless them." She turns to scan the room, and her gaze falls on Andrew. "And for my grandson—kukui."

Drew doesn't move, and I nudge him. As if he just woke up, he steps forward and accepts the string of shiny black nuts with some greenery woven in, looking stunned.

Leah puts a gentle hand on my arm. "The kukui nut was worn by royalty, you see. But more importantly, it gave us the light. Just like this one. He helps us to see, to know. An educator. Our māhū. He guides us." I don't know exactly what she's talking about, but I glance at him as I nod, and he's definitely tearing up. He puts the lei around his neck carefully, wiping a tear away as he moves to give his grandmother a hug without crushing it. "Also," Leah says, "this lei will last a long time, so I won't have to bring another when you marry Evan."

Immediately, I cover my mouth, nodding, so my perplexed facial expression will be less obvious, even though I am *freaking out a little.*

"Breathe, Ev," Drew says quietly, pulling back, wiping one more tear.

"I am breathing," I hiccup. "Water. Does anyone have some water?"

Drew reaches under the padded pew and grabs a water bottle, handing it to me.

"Is it hot in here?" I mutter, and Drew just shakes his head. That lei looks good on him; it suits him. Tutu is still handing out leis, and I'm pretty sure Rose is going to lose her shit if the Department of Agriculture shows up. But given the circumstances, it doesn't seem too likely.

As soon as Leah's done, Drew is swept up into the getting ready of it all, and I'm left to stand around and look at things. The stained glass is nice, if a little basic. More unfortunately, the musicians are warming up, and that bassist really needs to invest in a good digital tuner. He's what, seventeen years old? He must be a relative or something, which is even more unfortunate, because I have no one to complain to about him and his very, very flat tuning. This is Grace's wedding, and I haven't been invited to play, but I still can't help myself.

"Did you need an A?" I ask, hopping up onto the stage to find one on the piano. The kid takes the hint and checks it again my tone, frowning.

"Oh."

Yeah, kid. OH. That is *not right*, is it, bud? So, what I'm saying is that I used my time well while I was waiting for everyone to come back and people would thank me if they knew how I'd saved the music part of this wedding. Nick makes me sit with the family in the front rows, and I'm only fidgeting a little when Drew comes down the aisle, escorting one of the bridesmaids, who I think is a cousin. Then he takes his place next to her. *He got to be on her side.* I can hear people whispering behind me, but I tune it out. They don't matter. He matters, and he's gazing down at me from the altar, so I shoot him a wink, and he grins. Then we're all standing up for Grace, who truly looks amazing, and the service rolls on with lots of religious talk that I'm not sure I really understand, but I can't text Drew because everyone will see him answer. After the ceremony, we're shuttled into a different part of the same building; I had assumed the reception would be somewhere else, but I guess not? It's a big room—some kind of multi-purpose room—and they've tried to hide the basketball hoops by draping flower wreaths over them. There is dancing, thank God, because otherwise it's just us, standing around, drinking sparkling cider, waiting for cake. After a little while, Drew pulls me aside.

"I think I need to go talk to them..." He moves his head toward two women I recognized as Zara and Hannah, his old roommates.

"Sure, go. I'm fine here."

He grins and gives me a peck on the cheek, which feels far too chaste, but we're still getting a few looks from the people around us. One woman's gaze follows Drew as he crosses the room, and...I don't like it. I don't like it at all. But it's not my conversation, and I said I'd stay over here. I'm half-listening to his brothers talk about the stock market when I see the woman break off from her group and start toward him. Drew's oblivious, focused solely on his former roommates.

I don't have a clue what to do. He's told me over and over again that he doesn't need me to protect him...but

I love him. The pastor said it himself in the sermon: "Love always protects." I'm just supposed to stand here and watch Drew get taken down a notch by a TERF?

But yeah. That's exactly what I'm going to do. Because that's what he *asked* me to do, and love also means listening. Trusting. Being a partner the way he needs me to. I excuse myself from the group and move closer to him under the guise of getting more cider. But I'm listening. I catch his eye as I go by so he'll know where I am if he needs me, and he gives me a wink. I give him half a smile, even though I'm stressed. Based on the hugs happening, it was a needed conversation with the roommates, and I'm glad they could make up. The woman's waiting to talk to him, shifting her weight...just how slowly do we think I can pour this drink so I have a reason to stand here? I stare at the woman as I take a sip, and to my surprise, she gives me a shy wave. I feel like I've fallen down some kind of rabbit hole here; I don't know the rules. But a wave seems innocuous. So...I wave back.

Damn Drew and his ten-dollar words, infecting me with his smartness. He turns to the woman, and I can tell he's nervous by the way his shoulders are up by his ears. But her body posture is open, her hands out, and she's not raising her voice. Drew glances around the room as she talks, but he's nodding, rubbing at his smooth chin. Then he's talking, and she's listening, nodding, too. Then they're both pulling out phones, and I think they just made an appointment of some sort. And then, I can't believe my eyes—the woman offers him a one-armed hug, and he takes it. A little stiffly, but he does. As soon as they're done, though, he turns and makes a beeline for me.

"Oh my god," he mouths.

"What was that?" I whisper, and he grabs me by my elbow and drags me with him toward the hallway.

"That was the pastor's daughter. We used to be in a youth group together that then went defunct, but she and I kind of kept in touch on socials, and it turns out she's a lesbian. She said the church wants to do a panel about queer Christians and what they could do differently to support us. She wants me to participate."

"And the pastor's on board with this?"

Drew nods. "He's the one pushing for it—she said he's come a long way toward understanding since she came out. But they're not sure the elders will approve, so it would help to have people from our actual congrega—what are you doing?"

My face must look weird. "Oh, I was just picturing this group of old men with gray beards sitting around in robes in a drippy cave being homophobic. Continue."

Drew laughs and kisses my cheek. "I think they usually meet at the coffee shop around the corner, and most of them are in their fifties."

"Men, though, right?"

"Yes, they're all men."

"Bearded, any of them?"

"Not sure. Keith might have one. But it's brown."

"Damn." I look up at the ceiling. "Sorry, God." Drew shoves me lightly, and I laugh. "So are you going to do it?"

He shrugs. "Not sure yet. But at least if I wanted to come back here, I'd have an ally."

"Two, counting the pastor," I say, snagging him around the neck so I can plant a kiss on his cheek. "Three, if you count me."

Drew's gaze is warm. "You always count."

And that's how I end up making out with my boyfriend in the coat closet of his church while the rest of his family cuts the cake.

DREW

"Dearly beloved, we are gathered here..." My boyfriend raises his beer. "To burn Drew's clothes."

I lift mine in acknowledgment as our housemates and friends all whoop and clap as best they can with drinks in their hands. The campfire crackles along in agreement, its orange flames sending sparks up toward the trees overhead. We're using the fire pit at Evan's house in Zigzag...I didn't want to do this at a campground and disturb some random family with kids. But I also don't want to start a forest fire. That's not how I imagined my name change celebration going.

"Would anyone like to say a few words?"

Evan, you turd. He knew I didn't want him to do this. I can feel a blush creeping up my neck as Chance raises his hand.

"I didn't get to be around for your arrival, but I'm glad these guys gave you a proper reception. Welcome to the club." More cheering. My blush has overtaken my cheeks now, but I give him a grateful nod. His emails meant more than he knows...assuring me that my dysphoria will get better, that my looks will adapt, that I'll find my own sense of style and demeanor as a guy. He was a lifeline. Evan must be able to sense my discomfort, because he moves to hang off my shoulder, and he bumps me with his hip. *Damn you for reading me so well.* Because it does help, actually.

"When you first came back," Colby pipes up, "I wasn't sure we were going to be able to keep Evan alive in your presence." I think I laugh the loudest of anyone at that, because yeah. Hard same. "You two have been through a lot, but I think I speak for all of us when I say we're glad you're together. When you're not fighting or fucking, anyway."

"When is that?" Darren calls from the back, and everyone laughs.

"I also would like to say something," Nico pipes up, and the young people part to allow him to be better seen. He puts a hand to his chest. "You are very precious to us, Andrew. Very precious. And we are honored to be here to witness this destruction of your wardrobe. Grazie."

Wow. Tears don't come so easily now that I've been on T for a while, but I'm feeling that hot feeling behind my eyes at the moment. I gesture him over, and the hug I get is perfect. Greg follows it up with his own. I didn't tell Evan that I'd invited them up from California, and it was a good surprise.

"Can we burn my miniskirts now?" I complain, swiping at one tear that escaped, and light laughter bubbles around me. I'm gonna take that as a yes. I pick up the first piece—I mostly chose cotton stuff, only because I don't think I'd like the way rayon or polyester would smell when it burns. But Hillary and Glenn's faces both light up.

"That's such a pretty top. Are you *sure* you want to burn it?" Hillary wheedles, and I roll my eyes as I toss it to her.

"Just come over here and take your pick."

"It won't be weird for you?" Glenn asks, already starting over, and I shake my head.

"Have at it. Someone might as well enjoy it."

But I am definitely burning a miniskirt. I didn't like them when I *wore* them, let alone now. It's too bad I can't burn the platform shoes, too—it would be a decent retribution for my pinched toes. I look down at the shoes I'm wearing now—thick-soled boots in beautiful brown suede—and smile.

Evan bumps me again.

"Stop being an attention whore," I mutter, and he smiles, too.

"Who, me?"

"Yeah, you. This is my day."

"I know it is," he says, and his satisfaction is so clear in his gaze. Gosh, he's handsome. I still can't believe I got him back sometimes. He thinks it was the other way around—he thinks he won me back. But I was always his. I never stopped loving this asshole, and I don't plan to.

Once all the clothes are gone, someone pulls out a guitar, and then there's another one. Evan's improvising with a bucket. Seriously, Glenn? A flute? These people are ridiculous, and I love them. I've patched things up with Zara and Hannah, too—they're across the circle flirting with Tony, who looks like he would like to escape. I listen to all of them talk and laugh and sing under the trees, watching the sparks fly up, until the full moon is smiling down at me. Greg and Nico said goodnight hours ago.

But Evan's been quiet. He's sitting right next to me, still shoulder to shoulder, just how I need him. But I think I hurt his feelings when I called him an attention whore. Not that it's not true, just...something's off. Usually, he'd just laugh. We don't let shit like that go now; he should tell me if I screwed up.

"You okay?" I murmur, and he nods, but he's avoiding my gaze. "You want another beer?"

He shakes his head. Again with the non-verbals. What is going on with this man? This is a night to celebrate; I don't want him sad. We've both spent enough time in that state during our separation. He's bouncing the bench we're sitting on, his leg jiggling nonstop, so I put my hand on the still one and give it a firm rub. Evan leans over and puts his head on my shoulder with a sigh, and the other leg stops.

"What's wrong, baby?"

"I'll tell you later." I look around the circle; these are our closest friends. I can't imagine what he doesn't want them to hear. I drop my voice lower.

"Nothing I did?"

"No! God, no. Sorry I'm being a downer."

Now he's rubbing my leg, and I give his a squeeze back. Our lazy petting continues for a while until he tips his head up, and I feel his lips against my stubbled jaw line. I say 'stubble' because I am nowhere near a beard yet, but I do get a little growth during the day. Now his fingers are rubbing dangerously high on my leg...drifting his fingertips along the seam of my jeans, and my answering shiver has nothing to do with the cool night air.

"How drunk are you, exactly?" I ask, and his low laugh tells me everything I need to know.

"Not all the way drunk. Just love you," he says between kisses. "Sorry."

To be honest, I don't mind him getting a little frisky in public—no one's really paying attention to us, probably out of politeness. But we might as well go to bed if that's what he wants. It's been a good night, but I'm wiped. I think I did what I needed to do to put Leah's life behind me. Whenever I regret that I didn't do this sooner, I think about Evan. Would I have him with me? I'm honestly not sure. But I do. I dragged him along into Andrew's life; I fucking *fought* for him. And it wasn't easy, but we're here. Can't help but feel grateful for that, despite the lost time.

"Bed time?" I ask quietly, and he stands up, offering me his hand. But after he helps me to my feet, he kisses me again, longer this time, and I flush with the heat of the fire next to us and his closeness, his naked want. Maybe I've drunk more than I realized, too, or maybe I'm just high on the happiness of this day, but I wrap my arms around his neck and pull him in harder. We don't part until someone clears their throat.

"Bed time," Evan repeats, and I nod, smiling. Then he takes my hand and basically drags me across the yard to the house.

"Good night," I call over my shoulder. "Thank you for coming, see you in the morning." Lots of them wave in acknowledgement. Some of them are sleeping out in the woods in tents, because we didn't have enough space in the house. Can't say that's a scenario I anticipated when I started thinking about transition—"too many friends." Quite the opposite.

I'm already in my pajamas by the time I realize Evan's not getting undressed. I smirk at him.

"You going to bed fully clothed?

"Look," he says, shuffling his feet a little, crossing the small room to me. "I have a confession to make. I know you just changed your name, and it was a pain in the ass, but…" He gathers me into his arms, rubbing my back.

"What are you trying to say?" I murmur, putting my hands on his chest.

"How do you feel about Andrew Lee Kahananui-Rhodes?"

"I feel like that's a mouthful," I say honestly, and he laughs. I still can't believe he's doing this…yeah, we've talked about it. But I thought that was years off.

"I was going to propose tonight in front of everyone, but then you called me an attention whore, and I realized you were right. I couldn't steal your spotlight—it wasn't right after everything you've been through. So I had to wait, only I'm absolute shit at waiting, so this was the best I could do, and I'm so sorry, because I had a much better speech planned, but I think maybe I am a little bit drunk, because it's not coming to me now. I should've written it on notecards or something. Why didn't I write it on notecards?" He takes a deep breath, which is good, because I kind of thought he was going to run out of air. "I know you're not happy with your gender presentation yet, so it doesn't have to be any time soon, we can totally wait. After your top surgery if you want, once that's scheduled. But I need you to be mine." He reaches up and touches my temple, trailing his fingers down the side of my face. "I need you, and I need you to know that I need you. And I love you. I couldn't wait for that part anymore."

My heart is burning at his clumsy, rambling speech; he's right that I'm not ready yet, for a lot of reasons. But I love that he's asking. I love that he cares so much. A revelation hits me, and I shove my hands in his front pockets. "Where is it?"

"Where's what?"

"My ring! If you were going to propose, you had a ring, right?" I move to the back pockets and find a small stack of paper—probably the proposal that Not Drunk Evan prepared for himself. I throw those away, but he grabs my wrists before I can get to the last pocket.

"You can't have it, I didn't do this right. You have to wait for the romance."

"Don't want it." I try to twist out of his grip, but he's stronger than I am. But I have the advantage of being sober and having gone to the gym with Chance a lot lately, who came back from England very into tae kwon do for some reason. I spin us and sweep his leg, putting him on his ass on the bed before he can blink.

"Hey! That's fucking cheating, D."

"You should've known better. Now give me my ring." I go directly to that last pocket, the smallest one inside his other pocket, but he covers it with both hands.

"No! You have to hear the proposal first. I have to get on one knee and shit."

"Let's say you already did. Lifelong love and devotion, blah blah blah. Now gimme."

"Oh, I fucked this up," he groans as I put one knee between his legs and continue to attempt to pry his fingers away from the pocket that has my ring in it. "I'm never gonna live this down." That does give me pause. I'm not one of those superstitious people who thinks that how you start a marriage has any bearing on its quality, but I don't want him to have regrets. I bring my hands to his shoulders and climb on top of him to straddle him, waiting to speak until his gaze meets mine.

"Okay. I'm listening."

His eyes brighten in the moonlight. "You are? Really?"

I nod, running my fingers through his hair. "I am. Give it your best shot, baby."

"I still don't have notecards..." He says with a sigh.

"It's okay," I say, stroking him gently. "The big thing, the airport proposal with songs and live-streaming? Writing it on a billboard or a scoreboard? I never needed that. That's why we work, Ev. That's why you're fucking *perfect* for me. The only romance I want is Timbers tickets on my birthday, someone to go to church with me on Easter, and lighting stuff on fire together for the Fourth of July."

His brow furrows, even as he leans into my touch. "We did all that."

"That's what I'm trying to tell you," I whisper, bringing our foreheads together.

"So...our life is my proposal?"

I kiss him, because he's silly and I adore him with my whole heart.

"And that's a yes? You're saying yes?" he asks, but his voice wobbles a little this time.

"Can I have my ring now?" I ask, climbing off him and pulling him to his feet. Then I draw him into another kiss, because he's mine and I'm his, unromantics that we are.

My mom's going to flip out, but Tutu, we're gonna need another lei.

ONLY WANT TO BE WITH YOU

CHAPTER ONE

GREG

January 1995

"I can do this," I mutter, palming the letter in the long white envelope as I climb the steep stairs. They creak like they agree with every step, and I nod, giving myself yet another internal pep talk.

You can do this. You saw him kissing that guy outside a few weeks ago, but then they broke up. It's okay to ask him out. It's okay to put yourself out there and ...

The walk up the apartment stairs was too short for my pep talk, and too soon, I'm standing on the landing of the third floor, staring down the worn, burgundy-carpeted hallway toward 307. The chime of the streetcar outside reminds me that time is passing, but my palms are getting sweaty, so I shift to hold the letter with two fingers, letting it dangle as I try the pep talk again.

It's just coffee. It's not like you asked him to spank you. And where on earth did *that* thought come from? The very idea of asking the tall, blond guy with the dimple in his cheek to do *anything* to me is making the sweat situation worse, and I startle when I hear heavy footsteps starting up the stairs below.

Oh, no. What if it's him? What if he sees me leaving the letter? What if he makes me stand there while he reads it? Oh God, I can't—

Before I can tell who's coming, I bolt across the landing to the next flight, then straight up to 401. I slam the door behind me, breathing hard, then look through the peephole. There's no one there. My shoulders relax for the first time since I entered the building.

Cathie looks up from her books. "You do it?"

I let my shoulders slump and lean against the closed door. "No."

She cackles. "Again? What was your excuse this time?"

"I heard someone coming up the stairs. It might have been him!"

My roommate takes off her glasses and sets them on her books, and I know I'm about to get a lecture. "Greg. Why did you come to San Francisco?"

"To meet a guy," I mumble, playing with the zipper on my raincoat.

"You've been here since September, and how many dates have you been on?"

"Hey," I say, sounding defensive, "I asked that waiter, but he was married! He's allergic to metals, so he can't wear a ring."

Cathie pinches the bridge of her nose. "My point is, if you were just going to hang around staring at guys, you could've done that in Kansas City." She points meaningfully at the door. "Go back down and do it now."

I throw down my stuff by the door, then wince. Downstairs neighbors might not appreciate that, whoever they are. "No, I can't now. I've gotta practice."

"Greg!"

"No, seriously, Cath, I gotta practice. I'm falling way behind."

She grabs for me playfully as I cross the apartment to my bedroom, but I manage to pull my arm away before she can trap me.

"That New Year's resolution isn't going to make itself come true!" she calls as I shut my door. I stand there for a moment, holding it shut in case she comes after me again. The trouble is that her words follow me anyway, and my gaze falls to the bulletin board above my tiny desk where I tacked those resolutions three weeks ago.

1. Eat one vegetable a day.

Back in Missouri, I ate them all the time, but my mother isn't here to set them in front of me now and I don't seem to have developed the habit of getting them myself. I miss her. Also, my body is mad at me.

2. Practice my horn four hours a day.

It should probably be more. I wasn't kidding when I told Cathie I'm falling behind at the conservatory. Talent got me by in the youth symphony in KC, but not here. Everything is so much more competitive than I was prepared for, from the practice room times to the solos to who gets to be first chair. The black, bell-shaped case by my twin bed is taunting me even now, and I motorboat my lips reflexively.

3. Spend less time on the computer.

This was undoubtedly linked to the previous resolution not happening, because every time I get home, I just want to sit down and mess around with my game. It's just a basic thing, but I'm coding it in Python for the first time, this new language that just came out, and it's leagues better than BASIC, which deserves its name.

I'm pretty good at HyperCard, and I'm curious about R too, but that's really new, and my uncle didn't know a lot about it when I asked. It's just so addictive, you know? I keep daydreaming about it when I should be doing something productive, and that's gotta stop.

4. Get a boyfriend.

I daydream about that too. I'm twenty years old, and I've never even been kissed. But no more hiding my Madonna tapes under my bed. Cathie convinced me to come here because she said it was different, and she's right—men walk down the street hand in hand here. It's basically a gay hot spot, and I still can't get anyone to notice me. Is it my clothes? Is there some gay symbol I'm supposed to be wearing around my neck? I've had that damn letter in my backpack for two weeks now, and I still can't deliver it to the handsome guy downstairs. What is wrong with me?

It appears I'm safe from Cathie for now, so I move away from the door and toward my window. I love watching the street here; people are moving past night and day, on foot and on bikes and public transportation and in cars. It's endless. I wasn't brave enough to live by myself in the Castro District; maybe that's my boyfriend problem. But I like our little apartment in North Beach, even though the beach isn't included, apparently. There's lots of clubs nearby with great music, even some gay bars, and we're not far from Chinatown or Little Italy. Takes me about half an hour to get to school on the bus, but I don't mind. And I think my parents would have worried if I was living here alone; living with Cath is working out well, infernal pestering aside.

"Thought you were going to practice!"

Case in point.

CHAPTER TWO

It's Tuesday afternoon, and I'm scraping years of built-up dirt off a carburetor.

I sort through the nuts and washers in the old tuna can until I find one I think will fit. The sunlight filters through the dirty window onto the newspapers covering my cheap kitchen table. It's filthy like only a city can dirty things, that window. Exhaust and smoke, not just dust.

I covered this wobbly POS table with yesterday's newspaper like Mama would have made me do at home in Maranello. I try to read it a little as I scrape, but much of the English is too advanced for me. Actually, I wasn't allowed to bring car parts into the house; the only times I remember my mother cursing at my father was when he'd try to sneak his little projects inside. I chuckle at the memory, even though my heart aches.

It's worth it. It's all worth it. To care for my family, my sister, my nieces and nephews.

I haven't hung up their pictures yet, but I should. It hurts too much, in this all-white place, like a skeleton. Bare walls. Bare windows. I look around again and sigh. I keep meaning to do something about it. But I meant to do something about it weeks ago, and still it stands as empty as a football stadium on Christmas. Football like in Italia, played with feet, not here, where they play with hands.

Scrape, scrape, scrape goes the sandpaper against the metal, an ugly sound, and I blow on the carburetor to get rid of the filings, scowling when most of it falls to the floor. It's not silent here, but the noise is so mechanical. Cars going by. The hum of the fridge, the hiss of the radiator.

No nephews playing nascondino under the workbench in the shop—no nieces rolling marbles on the smooth concrete floor and losing them in the pit.

God, I miss them so much.

My new boss, Giacomo, his son comes to the garage after school sometimes, but all he wants to do is play on the computer. Giacomo seems not to mind only because the boy is practicing his arithmetic, making the little character jump on the correct answer. He's pushing only letter keys, but the character jumps on the number, so I don't know how that works. I tried to ask the boy, but he doesn't speak much Italian. His mother, she's American, and Giacomo works too much to teach his son. Someday, I promise myself, my son will speak Italian.

Not that it will be easy for me to have a son since my dick does not like women, but I'll find a way. There are many children who need homes, and I would be a good papa.

My thoughts finally quiet as I finish up the carburetor and put it back into the box I snuck it home in. Giacomo doesn't want to give me too much to do at first; he says I should be acclimating, learning English. I frown at the newspaper again, trying harder, but it's too much. He must not remember what an empty place this full city can be. I need to work; I have nothing else. Nothing else that feels as right as a warm engine roaring to race down the road. I don't even have a driver's license here yet.

I hear the full noise of a French horn above me, and a smile floats onto my face, just like the notes coming through the floor. The musician is home. I think it's the man; I sometimes hear the higher voice while the musician is playing, and I have seen the two of them together, coming and going. He has a nice smile: very white, straight teeth, like a movie star. Nice hair, also—gold, like Adonis. The skin of many men here is pale, and he is no exception, but I can hardly blame him with all the fog surrounding us. The locals, they even give it a name: Carl. Some days, it does not break until evening, even though this is not what I was told about California.

But that music? It is my sunshine. The warm sound of it wraps around me as I put my work away, packing parts and rags carefully into the old fruit box before I put on the lid, and then I sit, eyes closed, enjoying the lilt and the way the music wanders; the melody reminds me of an old dog with big ears sniffing around the yard for any dropped food.

I'm still imagining that when I hear footsteps in the hall outside my door and a *whoosh* as something slides under it. I open my eyes; it's a white envelope. It doesn't look like another ad for the disgusting "pizza" down the street, all grease and tiny, thick circles of meat pretending to be pepperoni.

I look down at my hands; they're greasy too, black with carbon and dirt. I stare at the envelope. It looks like a ... letter? But it has no name on the front? I can't imagine who in the building I have so offended that they would write to me this way. Could it be from the management of the building, thinking I am not at home? But there was no knock. I stare at it again. I wish I could open it with my feet so I don't have to take the time to wash these dirty mitts with the harsh soap required to get them clean enough to touch something white.

My horn player is doing scales now. He is so dedicated. He leaves his favorites for the end, opting instead to do the work first. I imagine, as I scrub away at the blackness under my fingernails, that as a boy, he never snuck a cookie from the kitchen. That's right, he was that kind, I think as the whorls and lines of my fingertips become visible again. A good boy. He always takes his trash out too, not leaving it by the door like some do until the flies come. Finally, my skin is red, but spotless, and I wipe my hands on a clean part of my coveralls as I go back to the door. I break the seal on the letter and pull out the crisp, lined paper to read.

You probably don't know who I am, but I live up on the fourth floor, and I've been wanting to introduce myself for weeks now.

I stop to get my Italian/English dictionary, looking up "probably," "fourth," and "introduce." My high school English teacher mostly focused on kitchen vocabulary for some reason, which has not helped me here except to express some angry thoughts about that "pizza." I did some practical tapes and practiced with my father before I left, but even that has only gotten me so far. Someone has noticed me here? It hasn't seemed that way to me; I feel like a ghost, floating by the other tenants with barely a nod, afraid they'll start a conversation where I can't hold up on my end, sputtering like a faulty transmission. But maybe I have not been as alone as I thought. My eyes skip to the end: *Sincerely, Greg.*

Not only noticed, but *by a man*?

This is serious now.

I'm new in San Francisco and I was wondering if you wanted to get coffee or go listen to some music or something. I'm up in 401 and I'm home most evenings. Just let me know if you're interested.

After a little rummaging, I find some paper and a pencil to compose a message to my shy neighbor, hope swelling for the first time that my stay in America will be more than long days passed working by dirty windows in too much quiet.

CHAPTER THREE

GREG

After two hours of practice, I decide to take a snack break. I did some scales and practiced the Mozart Concerto No. 1, my jury piece, then worked on the trouble spots. Nothing that interesting. That's the thing about music: playing with the symphonic groups, be it band or orchestra, is an immersive experience. You feel in the midst of greatness, all the instruments and musicians working literally in concert, the melodies and harmonies flowing around you, the call and response. You're part of something big. It sets my hair on end sometimes, the electricity of it sending shivers down my back.

But practice? Well, it's just me, sitting on the edge of my bed, music propped up on the white windowsill, playing one part of what should be a greater noise. In case it was unclear, it's boring.

When I open my bedroom door, Cathie jumps a little. She's still studying, but it doesn't look like she's made it very far in the time I've been gone.

"Everything okay?" I ask, raising an eyebrow as I cross the living room to our tiny kitchen, and she just nods, lips pursed. The microwave popcorn is calling to me, and even though I'll have to clean my hands thoroughly in order to not get grease on my horn, I don't fight the urge. I unwrap and sling the bag into the microwave and hit the button. But when I turn back to Cathie, her pale face is drawn. Is she ... crying?

"You sure you're okay?"

She throws down her book as the words come out in a rush. "Okay, so I think I did a bad thing, and I don't want you to be upset, because I was just trying to help, but now that I think about it, I was probably kind of overstepping, and—"

"Whoa." I hold up my hands. "Back up a little. What happened?"

She's shaking her head, her dark waves softly swaying, covering her face now with both hands, her chipped yellow nail polish on full display. Leaving my popcorn, I cross to our funky brown plaid couch and sit next to her.

"Cath? It can't be that bad … "

"It is," she says, her voice muffled, and I put an arm around her shoulders, pulling her into my side.

"What'd you do, give away my bike?" I joke.

"Worse."

"You ate all my yogurt raisins," I accuse playfully, and her wet laughter says I couldn't be more wrong. I'm becoming quite concerned, but I can't imagine what she could've done as I look around the apartment for anything that's different. Our little TV is still sitting against the wall, my computer is by the window, the dishes are stacked neatly in the sink, my backpack is still by the front door, my—

Just as the popcorn chimes its finish, it hits me, and the sound of the popping kernels slowly stopping matches the way my heart feels. Something *is* missing.

"Cath … " I say, trying to keep my voice steady. "Where's my letter?"

My roommate pulls her hands away from her face then, and while she's not crying, she looks chagrined. "I delivered it."

I pause, my mind turning over this information, frantically trying to make it mean something other than what I know it means.

"You slid it under the door of 307?"

I have never seen the blood drain out of someone's face that fast. Not even when they told my mom I got that concussion my senior year when I got beaned with a baseball, and there wasn't even an open wound. Cath goes so pale, she reminds me of her costume at Halloween, when she dressed up as a "sexy ghost," even though I discouraged her as hard as I could. Surprisingly, she went home with a girl dressed as a hot vampire. Maybe it's not that surprising, now that I think about it.

"Cath. Say those words. Say, 'I slid it under the door of 307.'"

"I can't."

"Why?"

"Because."

"Because why?"

"301," she whispers, and in the microwave, the last kernel gives a weak pop. "It was 301."

I get to my feet and pace. "Shit. Shit, shit, shit." I try putting my arms over my head, because that's always what my mom said to do when you can't breathe, and I'm much closer to hyperventilating than I'd like. "Do you think we could get it back? Do you know who lives there?"

"I'm sorry," Cathie moans, hiding her face again. "You were just having so much trouble delivering it, and I felt bad for you, so I thought it would be a good surprise, but clearly, I did not think this through, and I especially didn't think about what was going to happen if I put it under the wrong apartment door ... "

"What if it's not even a guy? What if I have to pretend to like a woman? That's why I left Kansas City, Cath!" My volume is rising, and I attempt to control it as I continue. "Why, why, *why* did you do this?"

"I told you," she says, hands out beseechingly. "I was trying to help."

I look at my best friend's face for a long moment, my chest still heaving, my hands still on my head, and that's when it clicks. I don't have to do anything. It wasn't for them; I can just explain the mistake if anyone comes to the door. We'll have a good chuckle about it. I lower my hands to my hips, still glaring at Cathie, who gives me a grimace that looks like a smile that gave up.

"I'm so sorry."

I stalk to the microwave and throw it open, claiming my bag of popcorn by one piping-hot corner before heading back to the couch. I open it carefully, waiting for the steam to escape as I wait for my anger to dissipate, then tip the bag toward Cathie. Hesitant, she watches me as she takes a handful.

"There's no way you could poison this between here and the microwave, is there?"

I shake my head slowly, then grab my own handful with a sigh. "I guess it could be worse," I mutter as I cram it into my mouth.

"How so?"

"I mean, you could've delivered it to the right apartment, and then I'd be mortified in front of the person I actually wanted to talk to."

"You were never going to deliver it?"

"I was," I protest, but even I know it's not true. "But it doesn't matter now."

"You won't write another one?"

"After this?" I snort. "I don't think so. I'll just go back to trying to pick up guys in clubs."

"Sweetie, that only works for guys who have game," Cath says, tipping her head to rest it on my shoulder as she grabs another handful of popcorn.

And that's when I hear it. A smooth, sliding sound. I look over at the door, but it doesn't look like an ad for my favorite pizza place down the block. It looks like a sheet of yellow legal paper, folded neatly in half. Cathie and I look at each other.

"Um ... " she says. "Looks like it might matter after all."

We both lunge for it, tumbling off the couch, falling over each other to get to the letter, and I'm halfway to it, pulling her back by the hood of her hoodie, when I realize that I don't know who this letter is from, but it's not from my crush. Whatever. It's for me, and she's the one who got me into this mess. She doesn't get to read it first. From the floor, I use my superior height to reach and grab it, popping back up to my feet immediately.

"I want credit when you move in together and adopt a thousand cute babies," Cathie says with a grin, and I just shoot her a quelling look. But when I open the letter, it's not at all what I expected.

Hello, dear Greg!

I am Nico, your neighbor down the stairs.

It's not just the intimacy of the words that surprises me: the handwriting is sharp, angular, like someone with a lot of confidence, but "neighbor" looks like it was erased and rewritten. Also, why say "down the stairs" instead of just "downstairs"?

"What does it say?" Cathie clamors, tugging on my arm so I'll let her see. I shush her and move away.

I also have seen you. You are looking good.

Heat gathers in my chest and rises up my neck into my face. Cath chuckles.

"It must be good if it's giving you the whole body blush."

"Shut up."

I feel a momentary pang of guilt that I don't have any idea what he looks like, when we've apparently passed each other at some point.

Let us arrange a time to meet and get to know one another. I also like coffee and music.

A date. I've got a date. The knowledge pulses through my veins, and the heavy failure I've been living with since I moved here suddenly lifts off my shoulders. My brain is still skeptical: Nico's letter seems unusual, and there may be something else happening here that I haven't anticipated. I'm pretty sure my Midwestern parents are still praying I'll change my mind and come home. But I want to give this a try. What do I have to lose?

I must warn you, my English is not so good sometimes, but I will try very hard. I look to the front for it.

Regards,

Nico

This last line has more erasures and smudges under the letters, and I wonder what he wrote originally. I wonder if he's from another country or just speaks another language at home. And is it "NICK-oh" or "NEE-co"? And what does he mean by "look to the front"—does he mean "looking forward to it"? I'm still standing there wondering when Cathie finally explodes.

"Dude, *what. does. it. say?*"

"He wants to go out for coffee," I say, smiling despite myself, "and his name's Nico."

"And you're going to go?" Her initial excitement seems to have tempered.

I shrug with one shoulder. "I'd like to. But is that unethical, since I didn't intend the letter for him?"

She pushes up her glasses and crosses her arms, looking serious now. "What did you say in it?"

"Just that I'd been wanting to get to know him and wondered if he wanted to go out sometime." I pause, frowning, then skim the letter again. "Which is technically not true."

Cathie groans. "Don't you dare overthink this. A potentially hot guy wants to go have coffee with you. You're going." She gives me a squeeze. "Besides, it sounds like he wants to practice his English. You'll be doing him a favor."

"That's true," I concede as she wanders back toward the couch.

"And who knows what else he wants to practice?" Cathie adds, batting her eyelashes, which earns her a handful of popcorn to the face.

CHAPTER FOUR

NICO

It takes a few days, writing notes back and forth—he never seems to be home when I am—but we finally find a time to meet. I like his handwriting, very flowing and nice. He lets me pick the place, and I chuckle—I am likely as new as he is, so I guess we are both just stumbling in the dark about what's good. I pick a little Italian bistro down the street. There are lots of Italians here, in this part of San Francisco, and it helps a little to hear my language spoken at the garage, at the café, even if their dialect is different. I met also my boss's wife, Wanda, and the next day, she sent Parmigiana di melanzane, a whole tray of it for only me, and I nearly cry. I have been savoring it for every supper, freezing half to make it last longer. Giacomo said his mother taught her to make it when she visited, and the jealousy hits me like a prizefighter. I wish my family could be here, even for a little while. But the point of me being here is to send money back, so I know it is an impossibility.

My heart craves it still, more than Parmigiana, more than crostata, more than anything.

But today, I will meet my shy neighbor, Greg! The coffee here will be good; the macchiato feels like the right thing for a Saturday morning, though it is not too early. I smooth down my shirt. It has a bold print, and I hope it will express the excitement I feel better than my halting speech can. I have also the body language, I remind myself. You can say a lot with that. I do not want him to gain the wrong impression about me—in my language, I am funny, you know? I like to talk with all the people and laugh and tell them stories, some of which are true. But in his language? I am so dull. I cannot make his shining smile come out from behind the clouds.

But no. I will not be thinking this way. I am Nicodemus Arosio; I know who I am. In time, if he is patient, he also will know. That is good enough. I laugh at myself for thinking so much of one coffee date. It is too early for such thoughts, and shy neighbor Greg will also take some time to know, I am sure.

At that moment, he walks into the shop. I take him in—his cotton polo shirt in the same blue of his eyes tucked into his nicely pressed pants, his light raincoat in a dark green. His gaze passes over me, but he doesn't seem to see. Has he forgotten my face? Did he not say in the letter how he knew the look of me? Strange. But when his gaze passes again, I give him a wave, and he breaks into a smile. *That smile.* He looks to me like the smartest kid in the class, always sitting in the front, always raising his hand to show that he knows. I bet he is a good student in all the ways, and I tell my prick to cool off as it imagines. No, it is too early to think of fevered kisses and untucking his careful clothes. We must woo his heart first.

"Nico?" he says, still so shy. "Or is it Nick-o?" He holds out his hand to shake it, but oh no, we do not start a date that way. We save handshakes for business meetings and meeting his father if he agrees to marry me. Ignoring his hand, I pull him in for a quick hug, letting my rough cheek brush his smooth one, but after a little gasp, his arms close around me too. He smells only of soap and dandruff shampoo, so pure and innocent, and the rightness of it, the goodness, it overflows inside me. Not only for him, but for what can be here, far from my small village where the way I am is not accepted.

"You say right first time," I tell him quietly. "Nico."

"Oh, okay," he says, also quietly, and I hope he does not faint. I pull back to see him.

"Come. Sit." I roll my eyes inside at the way I sound, like I am commanding a dog, but I can't really help it.

"I'm just going to get a drink first," he says, edging toward the line.

"Me also," I say, following him.

"Do you know what's good here?" He sticks his hands in his pockets like he does not know what to do with them. Adorable.

"Here? No. But is Italian coffee. Is good."

He smiles, but I don't think he's laughing at my speech. "What's your favorite?"

"Favorite?" I echo, not knowing the word.

"Uh, best of all," says Greg, watching my face. "One you like the most."

"Oh, favorito," I say, feeling embarrassed. Such a close cognate, and still I did not understand. I push away the feeling that this is doomed and remind myself again who I am. "Uh, macchiato."

"Macchiato," he repeats, rolling the word around in his mouth, and I smile to hear my language from his gorgeous lips.

"You know it?"

"No, I'm from a small town in Missouri. We just drink whatever Folgers makes."

I laugh, because I do know this word—it is on the red can of disgusting instant coffee at the garage. I chided them for owning such a thing; they have forgotten their heritage so quickly.

"You are funny," I cry, delighted. "Where is small town? Where Missouri?"

"Uh, Missouri? Do you know Kansas?"

"No. I know ... California."

He laughs. "Well, it's in the middle." He puts his hands out then brings them together in front of his handsome face.

"Okay, I see. In the middle," I echo with a smile. Then it's our turn to order.

"Ciao, fratè," I say, using the southern expression. Lots of Italians here from southern Italy, and it's strange to me, but I am learning their ways. The boy greets me warmly, glancing at Greg, clearly curious what our association is. He reminds me of my cousin Benicio, about seventeen, lanky and lean, the way boys get when their height goes shooting up. I give him my order, then we both turn to Greg.

"Uh ... " He's looking at the menu, but in the end, he still spits out the word I gave him. "A macchiato?"

I want to tease him for phrasing it like a question, but I can't find the right words, so I just grin.

When he chooses a small, I hope it's because of money and not because he wants this to be over soon.

I'm just getting started.

CHAPTER FIVE

GREG

I don't recognize him at all when I walk in. Foolishly, I thought something would click when I saw his face, some time he'd passed me in the hall or on the stairs coming back to mind. Nope. Zippo. Zilch. And I don't know how that could be, because he's good-looking—very good-looking. He looks like an extra in *The Godfather*—no, he looks like a *lead* in *The Godfather*. Thick dark hair, deep brown eyes, high cheekbones, a strong jaw, and a build my grandfather would call "strapping." The only reason I'm not completely intimidated is the language barrier. It's keeping me on my toes in a good way, weirdly enough. I'm so busy thinking about what he's saying and what I'm saying and trying to talk around the vocabulary he doesn't know that I've kind of forgotten to be nervous. Which is a first for me.

"Where you work?" Nico asks, taking a sip of his coffee. He wasn't wrong; it's very good. I'd say it's bad for my budget that this place is along my route to the conservatory, but I didn't really look at how much it cost, and Nico paid before I could even get my wallet out. That made me blush; I don't know the payment protocol on a date. But do I mind that this big, strong guy wants to take care of me? No, I do not. Not at all.

"Oh, I'm still in school, actually."

"You study the computers?"

My mouth falls open for a moment, then I glare at him. "Because I wear glasses?" I ask, tapping my thick frames. "Are you saying I'm a nerd?"

"No, no," he says loudly, laughing, waving his arms between us. "You look smart. Computers are smart. This is all."

"Uh-huh," I say skeptically, sipping my delicious coffee with faux annoyance.

"Oh no," Nico says, face palming, and I can't help but grin. "I give you the offense!"

"No, no," I assure him, reaching out to grab his flailing arms, and we both still at the contact. I try to pull back quickly, my face hot, but Nico catches my hand and holds it across the table with both hands, a twinkle in his eye.

"Study what, then?"

"Guess," I say. The sensual way his thumb is rubbing circles on the back of my hand is giving me butterflies in my stomach, even as I glance around to see who cares. Right now? No one. They don't even seem to notice ... except maybe the cashier.

"No fair," he complains, but I just laugh, leaning forward. "Okay, okay. Mathematics?"

I shake my head.

"You build the bridges?"

I cock my head slightly ... I'm feeling a little distracted by his touch, the warmth of his hands seeping into mine. I want to sink into the feeling of it: this strong, veiny hand holding mine.

"Oh, engineering? Nope, guess again."

"You make the money?"

"Economics?" I'm strangely enjoying this game, circumlocuting our way around the words he doesn't know. "I'm good with money, but no."

"You are cheap?"

My mouth falls open again. "No! Just careful."

"Ah yes, careful," he repeats, saying it more like "carefool," grinning. He murmurs something in Italian, and I nearly swoon. He's all bravado, this one.

"Give up?"

"Huh?"

"Do you want to guess more?" I clarify, and he shakes his head.

"You tell."

"I'm a musician."

Nico's face brightens. "Music?" He lets go of my hand to pantomime a violin, and I shake my head, pantomiming my horn instead, tracing the spiral shape of it with my index finger.

"Ah, yes! I know! I hear you." He points to the ceiling. It takes me a minute to figure out how he can hear the hand signs I'm making, then I realize.

"Oh, at the apartment? I didn't think anyone was home." My face is hot again. "I'm sorry for the noise."

"No!" His voice is too loud for an indoor space to my ears, but he's reaching for me across the table again, and I give him my hands. "No apology!" He looks downright agitated, and I give his hands a squeeze. He's got calluses, and it reminds me I haven't asked what he does. He's stammering, and I can't understand him, until he finally lets loose a string of enthusiastic Italian, gesticulating into the space above his head.

"He says your music is like angels singing," the cashier says. "He says it's the best part of his day."

"Oh." I want to crawl under the table now. Not because I mind him saying it, but because I wish we didn't need someone else to hear it. "Um, thank you."

That's the moment. That's the moment I decide to go to the library on campus and see if it has any books on Italian. Or if not that library, the public library. If he can sit here and try so hard to communicate with me, the least I can do is to try back. This assumes, of course, that he wants a second date at all, but the way he's looking so deeply and earnestly into my eyes, I can't imagine that he's done with me. Something tells me this is just beginning.

"And you? Where do you work?" I ask, clearing my throat.

"Ah. Uh, I fix the Ferrari. Gallo Motors."

"Oh!" I say, delighted. "I know where that is! Those are some nice cars!"

His grin is lopsided this time. "Yes, very nice. Very ... " He enlists the help of the cashier again, now that he's proven himself willing, and gives him a word in Italian.

"Expensive," the boy calls back.

"Sí, expensive," Nico echoes. "I come from Maranello; the Ferrari come also from there. My father work there, and he learn me also."

"Taught you also," I correct automatically, then wince. "Sorry."

"No, no, no sorry! You help." Nico looks exhausted. It can't be easy, talking with me like this.

"I love those cars," I say. "Will you show me some of them next time? Take me for a drive?"

He holds out his hands sheepishly. "Here, no license."

"Oh, right. Well, we can take my car. Maybe I can help you study for it." Nico frowns, and I think for the first time in my life, maybe I've been too forward with another guy. Nico turns to the cashier, who volunteers a translation.

"Is no problem for you? You not too busy?" He's frowning like he's torn—I can tell he wants to agree, but he also seems concerned about my schedule.

"Not at all. How's tomorrow? I'll pick up a manual on my way home."

I don't think he caught all of that, but he breaks into a grin anyway. "Grazie. Uh, thank you." I want to keep chatting, but I can tell he's tired.

"Ten o'clock tomorrow? My apartment?"

Nico stands when I do, then holds out his arms for another hug, and I go gladly. It's just as intimate as the first one, even though he says nothing. That rough voice in my ear before? I thought it was going to be the death of me, firing my blood embarrassingly quickly. But something about Nico's arms around me, holding me tight, feels like ... home. I can't explain it. It's not like a family hug, which makes you feel loved, but not like this. This hug makes me feel ... wanted. Like I belong in his arms. Like he never wants me to leave. I'm the one who finally pulls back, and even though it was long by my standards, he still seems disappointed. *Just wait until you get me into bed—then you'll really be disappointed*, I think. As we walk home, we decide to go see the cars first, then study.

It turns out the DMV is nowhere near my apartment, but I don't even care. I had my first real date with a real man, and I didn't fuck it up. Maybe 1995 is going to be my year after all.

CHAPTER SIX

NICO

Sunday is the worst day, I think as I lie in bed. No tinkering with an old car, just for fun. No Nonna rolling fresh pasta, no Mama simmering sauce or soup while we're at church, no Papa and my cousins arguing about whether Bologna's or Parma's football team was better. Just food that comes from the microwave and pointless American football.

I get out of bed and wander into the kitchen, then pick up the phone with a sigh. I call my family collect, but we hang up before the charges hit. I just say my name, and they say no, so that my mother knows I am alive, but it depresses the hell out of me to be so close, to hear her voice only a little, but hear no news. I tell her before I leave to send the electronic mail, but I don't think she trusts it not to get lost somewhere between California and Maranello.

Unless it's an engine, they don't think much of technology, and they have to go to the library to check the email; it doesn't happen much. So I write them letters. A little like the letters I wrote with my neighbor.

I blink awake a little more as we hang up, rubbing at my skin to wake me up, and then I remember with a jolt—I got the key from Giacomo. I'm showing my nerd friend Greg the garage today.

Energy hits me like I just had an espresso, and I hurry to the shower. It's fairly early, but I'm 100 percent awake now. We are friends now, I think. We had coffee together; that's friendly, no? And he *is* shy, a little bit, but he teased me in the café, tried to communicate with me. But I don't care what he says; he is a big nerd. Cutest nerd. Wonderful nerd.

The nerd of your dreams? my mind prompts, but I ignore that question for now. Too soon.

But there was a strange connection between us like I have never felt before. Not just when I hug him, but also in the way I felt I knew him already, like in a lifetime gone by. I shake my head at myself as I strip and start the water, but I can't shake the feeling. I have been with other men—I try with women, but it just doesn't work. Was useless, my dick. He just lies there, doing nothing. I try to encourage him, but he doesn't listen. So once I accept this, I go out with a few men. Nothing serious, just young people having fun. I don't bring them home. Not that kind of thing. But I liked them, and they liked me, and they could keep things quiet for those who should not know.

I wonder how many people Greg has been with.

I wonder who his first love was, when he knew he liked men only. Perhaps he does not—that's okay too.

I wonder if he wanted to touch me when he first saw me. I felt it so strongly, even then; my dick perks up between my legs as I give it a thorough wash, but it wasn't even that kind of wanting. I wanted to brush the hair off his forehead and give it a kiss. I wanted to hold him, rub my cheek against his. I finish up and get out before my dick can get any more ideas; I've got places to be.

I throw on clothes and go in search of food. But when I open the fridge, I'm disappointed—I was so busy thinking about Greg after our date yesterday, I forgot to go shopping. Entenmann's to the rescue—they make cakes. It says coffee cake, but it is so light, I do not think there could be coffee inside. Maybe to eat *with* the coffee? Either way, it is food, and I wolf it down as I get ready quickly. It gives me an idea.

I am out of breath when I rush back up the stairs to meet Greg at his apartment; we are going to walk to the garage together, but I had to get my surprise.

"Ta-da!" I say, holding out my gift when he opens the door, and he smiles so big.

"You got me a coffee?" he asks shyly, then takes it. "Another macchiato?"

He's been practicing that word, I can tell, and it makes my heart swell.

"Sí," I say, so happy I forget to speak English. He likes gifts. I tuck that information away in my mind. He's still smiling as we get to the stairs, and he motions for me to go first.

"How was your night?"

"Good, good," I say. "And you?"

"Pretty good." I hear him take a sip of the coffee, and he hums. "Cathie made me go to this open mic thing with her." I glance at him, confused, and he goes on. "It's like, for artists. They can stand up, read their work. She's kind of an amateur poet."

"Cathie?" I ask as we come out onto the street. It's a beautiful day; kind of cold, even though we both have jackets, and the sun is shining down on us like it's glad we are together. I'm glad too. In the crystal-blue sky above us, seagulls whirl, looking for scraps.

"Oh, my roommate. Well, she's more like a friend. We grew up together; she convinced—uh, talked me into—moving here."

"Oh," I say, the light dawning. "When first I see you, I think you are … " I make a slightly rude gesture with my hands, and my message must be received because his face contorts.

"Me and Cathie? Ugh, no. First of all, she's a lesbian—she likes women. But also, I know her too well. She's like a sister."

"Mm," I respond casually, even though I am so happy to hear this news. The less competition for my sweet friend, the better. "And you do not like the women?"

Greg shrugs. "I like them fine, just … not to date."

"Can like both," I tease, poking my elbow into his ribs a little.

"Oh, I know." Greg blushes. "I just … don't." I think I could make him blush like that so easily with just a little dirty talk, and now I have an assignment for my English learning time with the dictionary.

"Me, I like men. Only men."

"How do you know?" he asks quietly, and I glance at him. He looks a little vulnerable, a little unsure, and I desperately wish I had the perfect words to tell him my story. But I will try.

"With women, I am ... cold. No ... " What was that word they used when the engine wouldn't turn over last week? "No spark."

Greg nods slowly, but I see the mischievous gleam in his eye. "I get that." He pauses, pursing his lips like he's keeping in a question. I nudge him again, enjoying the teasing between us.

"What? What you say?"

He huffs, and the cold breeze catches his straight blond hair, sending it standing on end in the front. "Just that I feel ... a spark with you." My sweet friend—no, more than a friend now—swallows hard like it was difficult to say, and I reward him with a grin.

"I also am sparking."

Greg chuckles, cheeks coloring again, and I have never wanted to kiss anyone more. Why is he so attractive? We can barely speak to one another! But I know when the attraction is hot, and this is on fire.

"Good to know." His hand is in his jacket pocket because of the cold, but I can't resist: I hold my palm up in invitation, my gaze firmly on his. I want that warm hand clasping mine, driving away the January chill. I want contact with him, to let him know for sure that he is not alone in this feeling. I wish him to know my skin, my body, even in this small way.

Greg glances around, as if nervous, but I don't reassure him. I just wait. And after a moment, he puts his hand in mine, threading our fingers together, his smile warm and genuine, even though he's still checking to see who notices. This feeling, I know it too. But people here seem very used to men like us.

We get them wrapped the wrong way at first, and laughing, I readjust us, beaming at him. Based on the softness of his face and the way his gaze keeps going to my lips, I'm not the only one who wants a kiss. *Patience, caro.* I'm still startled by how the endearment for someone I met yesterday rolls out of my brain when Greg pulls us to a stop.

Is he going to kiss me?

"This is it, right?" He gestures with his head to the shiny showroom, all glass and steel, of Gallo Motors, where I work.

"Yes. Right." I have not forgotten the kiss, but it is fermenting, I decide, in the way of wine. I pull him toward the side door so we can go directly to the garage, but I haven't been planning out enough what I will say. The other guys, they use a lot of English, so maybe I have been picking it up, and I will be more okay than I think.

It's dark inside, but I flip on some lights awkwardly with my other hand, reaching across Greg but still holding on to him. The fluorescents warm up, flickering and blinking on dimly, and he sucks in a breath. So adorable.

"Is that the 328?" He doesn't drop my hand either, hauling me over to have a better look at the car, shielding the light so he can see inside the window with his other hand. "I love this paint job. God, what a color."

"308 Quattrovalvole," I correct, glad I understood what he asked and had an answer. He's not wrong: instead of a classic red, this car is a deep teal that reminds me of mermaids.

"So it's got the Bosch K-Jetronic fuel-injection system? No carburetor?"

I'm thankful his eyes are still on the car, because I stare at him, slack-jawed, for a moment before I answer. *He was not kidding. He really loves cars.*

Some people, they say to me, "oh yes, I like the cars," but it is something silly like Volkswagen or Toyota. They do not know the Ferrari; they do not breathe, eat, and sleep it like we do in Maranello, painting our town red, raising the logo in honor everywhere you look, following every race in the Formula 1. But Greg, he understands.

I nod, delight welling up in me and stealing my words, so I mutely pop the hood. I have to let go of his hand, but something even more important connects us now: love. For these cars, I mean.

We spend the next hour lurching our way through conversation about the vehicles in the shop, and I show him some things I think he'll enjoy—and he does. But his eyes go wide when I open the door to the showroom.

"Should we be in here?" he whispers, and I chuckle.

"You will steal?"

Greg pokes me in retaliation, and the contact zings through me. "No," he whispers again. "But I don't want to get you in trouble." Feeling bold, I reach out and gently turn his face toward me by his chin.

"I like trouble." I think it's the first perfectly correct sentence I've said to him, and it seems to have the effect I meant it to when he shivers a little. That need to kiss him comes back strong, but I just rub my thumb over his smooth jawline a little before I let my hand drop, opting to grab his hand again instead so I can drag him farther into this paradise. I can tell he's still nervous, but I make him sit in the driver's seat of the 250GT, and the awe on his face is well worth the effort.

He likes the 288GTO also, I can tell, but I can't convince him even to touch it. Such a good boy, Greg. We argue in stilted terms about the 365GTB4 Daytona—it is so ugly! But he likes the seats—until he checks his watch.

"Wow, it's late." We've talked right through lunch; it's nearly two o'clock. "Come on," he says with a grin. "I know a great place you'll love."

Then he's seeking out my hand again, pulling me back out the way we came. I barely remember to stop and lock up; I'd follow him anywhere. Anywhere ... except the absolutely atrocious pizza place he stops in front of.

"Oh, no," I say before I can stop the words, and Greg's brow wrinkles in confusion.

"Have you tried it? It's so good!"

"No, caro. Not good," I say, taking his sweet face in both hands this time, patting his cheek. "Garbage."

"What?" Greg looks aghast. "This is, like, the best pizza I've ever had! Cathie and I get it at least once a week. We love it."

"I will cry. We eat here? Crying." I mime crying my eyes out, and he shoves my shoulder.

"Come on, you'll hurt their feelings. Don't do that." He's laughing softly though. We're still out on the sidewalk, but it's clouded over and it's getting colder now. His face felt freezing in my hands; I want to get him inside somewhere, but I cannot subject my stomach to this slop.

"Fine," he says with a sigh, throwing his hands in the air. "Let's get sandwiches and go to my place. We can study there."

I cock my head, trying to understand. Greg also looks confused again, and his shyness is coming back.

"You wanted to study for your driver's license, right?"

"Oh, yes!" A wave of fatigue hits me that feels at odds with the excitement I feel to see Greg's apartment, like when the wake of two boats crosses in the bay, making all the water choppy. I want to talk more, be together in his space, but I am tired ... and my empty fridge still needs to be filled. "I would like, but my head is not ... uh ... " I swear, it's like the past four hours of interacting has drained all the words out, and when I try to finish the sentence, my brain just shrugs at me. I look at him helplessly, and Greg nods, understanding.

"Let's just get some food and call it a day, then. You should rest before you have to work tomorrow. We could always meet up on Tuesday."

Tuesday? What's wrong with Monday? My disappointment must show on my face, because amusement lights in his eyes.

"I have a class that goes until eight o'clock on Mondays, and then I still have to take the bus home."

"No car?"

He takes my hand again, towing me down to the crosswalk. Americans. They love their traffic laws, except for stopping, but I think maybe this is Californians only. They roll right through the big, red stop signs.

"It's Cathie's car, but she lets me use it. We can use that when you take your test."

I smile. "No test in 250GT?"

Greg cracks up laughing, and I have to admit, it's a funny picture: me, pulling up in the little old race car to practice the signaling and parallel parking and whatever else may be, the examiner shoehorned into the front seat. Two men pass us, and they smile at us meaningfully, and that's when I know—we look like a couple. We look like we're in love.

CHAPTER SEVEN

GREG

Sunday afternoon, I call my parents at my grandmother's house. They like to pass around the cordless phone, so I get to talk to everyone, and they always have dinner at my Nana's on Sunday. I miss that, but this is a suitable substitute, and since my uncle is a computer genius, he insisted I get a good machine and a voice over IP number to save on long-distance calls before I left.

"You sound happy," my mother observes, and across the room, Cathie snorts. I give her the "knock it off or else" sign, but reply, "Yeah, I had a great week. I made a new friend."

"Ohhh, how wonderful," she coos, "and what's this man's name?" Then she sobers. "You're not getting diseases, are you?"

Cathie's covering her mouth with both hands now, trying not to let the laughter out.

"Not from holding hands, no," I respond drily.

"You guys held hands?" Cathie's done pretending not to be part of the conversation now and comes over to sit next to me. I'd put the computer in the living room so we could both have access to it, but I'm coming to regret that decision.

"His name is Nico, and yes, we've held hands." It felt so big just walking in the sunshine on a beautiful morning, holding hands with a man I really like out where everyone could see me. I kept looking around, expecting something bad to happen, and that's not to say that it won't someday, but it didn't then. Nothing happened. We were just ... people. Living. Enjoying being together.

"Nico ... is that short for something? Nicolas?"

"Uh, I'm not sure. He's from Italy."

"Tall, dark, and handsome, am I right, Mrs. Rhodes?" Cathie says, and holds up her hand to me for a high five, which I ignore until it makes me too uncomfortable, and I slap her palm even as I roll my eyes.

"We'd love to see a picture of your guy," Mom says, her voice warm. "Maybe of the two of you together? Oop, your father wants to say something."

"Looked like your account was a little low this week, so I topped it off. Let me know if you need more; I didn't account for dates." That's as close to "I love you" as Dad usually gets, but he cares, and the comment stuns me for a minute.

"Thanks, Dad. He paid, actually," and this garners more ooh's and ahh's from Cathie and Mom—she must have jumped on the extension. I've had enough of that, so I end things soon afterward and hang up. But I can't hang up on my nosy roommate.

"Whatcha reading?" Cathie asks when I settle on the couch with my Italian book, and I hold it up so she can see. She laughs. "Really? His English is that bad?"

"No," I say, scowling. "But why should he be the one putting in all the work?" Also, I want to see his face when I start speaking some Italian. I bet he'll glow like a firefly.

"Aw, you got a children's dictionary?" Cathie's eyes are big and her voice is all sappy again; I suppress an eye roll.

"Yes, people who are learning a language often begin like a child. There's nothing weird about it."

"Nothing weird. It's just freaking adorable," she says, paging through it. "The library had this?"

I shift uncomfortably. "I'll donate it when I'm done."

"You *bought* this?" Now I think she might melt. Good Lord.

"It's not a big deal," I say, snatching it back from her and snapping it shut. "I just want to talk to him better."

"You should get one of those tape programs. Listen to it on the bus," she says, popping more trumpet-shaped corn chips in her mouth.

"Don't chew in my ear," I say, giving her a gentle shove.

She tsks. "You're such a picky gay."

"What does being gay have to do with manners?"

It's not a bad idea, though, the tapes. I bet I could get them at the library. God, I love libraries. And it's weird how much I enjoy hearing those words about me being gay come out of her mouth; she's not really being critical, just playful. And speaking of playful ...

"Do you think 'caro' begins with a C or a K?" I ask, thumbing through the thick paperback dictionary with thin, yellowing paper.

Cath crunches thoughtfully, her mouth still open. "It's a romance language, so I'm going to guess C."

I squint at the small text. "Let's see … oh, here! Caro. He called me that yesterday."

She leans closer to see, reading aloud. "Dear or expensive." Her lips form a little pout, like she might cry. "This is the cutest thing ever. I love this for you."

"Don't get excited," I say. "It probably just means 'friend.'" But I'm tamping down my own reaction, not wanting to read too much into it, but *so wanting to read too much into it.*

"Look up 'friend,'" she commands, and as usual, I go along with it. I skim down the F's until I find it. "Amico," I read flatly. "But there could be more than one! Languages are tricky."

Cathie's just grinning at me now, and she punches my shoulder a little too hard. "Told you!" I'm not sorry when she wanders away to refill her bowl because it gives me time to think.

I still think it could be a coincidence … but I also look up "boyfriend" ("ragazzo"), and making sure she's safely across the room, I also look up "lover" ("amante" if sexual; "innamorato" if romantic). I've never thought to separate my romantic and sexual feelings, and I still don't think I can.

I don't know why it makes me feel a little disappointed that "caro" is so benign, and it's not that I think I'll need to use the other two any time soon. *That's silly,* I chide myself. *It's two dates.*

But I commit those words to memory as I dig into the children's picture dictionary, flipping directly to the section about transportation … that would be the most help to him if we're trying to study, right? It also might not hurt if we're taking a drive somewhere, maybe to a romantic overlook, a place where he'd put his arm around me while we watch the city twinkle ... San Francisco has a lot of hills, right?

Chiding myself again, I root around in my bag for the driver's manual I picked up for him. On my notepad, I make two columns: one for English, one for Italian, noting any words I think he might not know.

This would be easier in a spreadsheet ... I'm already moving toward my computer when I'm hit with the thought that I could take this even further with HyperCard ... In fact, with a little work, I think I could even make him a basic practice test, linking my spreadsheet as a database using hyperlinks so he could click on the words he doesn't know. I can see myself grinning in the dark screen's reflection as I boot up my computer. I check my watch: it's only two o'clock. I'll practice my horn later. Plenty of time.

CHAPTER EIGHT

"Why does this damn thing never do what I want it to do?" My boss, Giacomo, is muttering under his breath again, glaring at his computer like it licked his cannoli.

"What's it doing?" I call in Italian, wiping my hands on my coveralls as I come over to see.

"The screen, it's black again," he complains, "but the little light is on. I go away for a few minutes just to get a coffee, and boom, this again!"

"Move the pointer," I say, motioning to the mouse, but careful that I don't touch anything with dirty hands. "The mouse. That will wake it up."

His face crinkles in confusion. "Computers sleep?"

"Yes, to save electricity."

Giacomo looks skeptical, but he nudges the white mouse, and the screen lights up again.

"This is why I keep young people around," he says, triumphant at having beaten the machine. I laugh. Little does he know, I'm generally terrible with technology.

"Are you studying English?" he asks, switching languages, and I mutter a curse under my breath.

"A little." I show him a few centimeters between my fingers. "My friend is helping me. Neighbor who lives in my building." I feel slightly guilty, referring to Greg like that, but nothing more has been promised to me ... yet. "We're going to study tonight."

"In English," he prompts, and I wince.

"Uh, my friend study with me today."

"I'll study with my friend tonight," he corrects, but he seems pleased that I'm making the effort, and I relax a little. "You almost finished with that 365GTB4 for Mr. Howard?"

"Already done. Moved on to the other one. I'll have it done tomorrow ... unless I can stay?"

"No," Giacomo says sternly, then goes on in Italian. "Study. Learn how to ask for roma tomatoes in the grocery store. Learn how to tell a policeman you didn't mean to speed. These things are important too."

I want to tell him it doesn't matter, that I'm going back to Italia as soon as we have more money ... but in truth, I don't know when that will be. It is as depressing a thought as I've ever had. And yet, I am making a friend. It helps, having him. And some of the meccania have asked me out for a beer, but I always said no because ... because I want to go home. Because I don't want this place, not really. And this is hitting me between the eyes as my boss goes back to his computer, jiggling the mouse again to wake it up. It's not the only one.

I go back to the shop, and Elio looks up, still singing with Hootie and the Blowfish. "But there's nothing I can dooooo," he caterwauls, "I only wanna be with youuuu." The radio never plays anything good, but at least I can learn from the words. I wish they'd find a station with some Madonna.

"Buy me a drink first," I joke in Italian, and he rolls his eyes. They know I like men. It's not a big deal, to my surprise. And then, since the opening is there, I keep going. "But if you're going out this weekend, I want in."

Elio's eyebrows go up. "All right, sure. But you buy your own."

"But what if some very cute man wants to buy it for me?"

Elio just shakes his head and goes back to singing. This song is okay, I guess. I hum along, then straighten.

"Elio?"

"Hmm?"

"What means 'dolphin'?"

He frowns, then calls across the garage. "Ehi, Massimo!"

"Sì?"

He asks my question, only in Italian.

"Ah, delfino," Massimo calls back, rolling out from under the car. "Come mai?"

"It's in the song," I call back. "He says it makes him cry."

We stare at each other for a moment, baffled, then laugh.

"Americans," Elio mutters, going back to his work.

"Song says Italy," Massimo calls, and as I listen, he's right. Maybe it's more than okay.

I FEEL ANTSY WHEN I knock on Greg's door at seven o'clock; I kept peeking out the window all weekend for a glimpse of him coming up the walk, but no. Nothing. I don't even hear him practice his music on Sunday or Monday; he must be very busy with something. But not too busy to help me study—I hope.

He must be eager to see me too, because I hear his steps approach quickly and he opens the door almost theatrically, his face bright and flushed, and I want to kiss him already.

"Buongiorno, Nico!" he enunciates carefully, clearly so proud of himself, and I can't completely smother my smirk that he's wishing me a good morning when it's after dinnertime.

"Ciao, Greg," I return, grinning. "Come stai oggi? Cosa hai fatto? Mi è mancato il tuo viso dolce anche se sono passati solo due giorni." I'm teasing him, of course, but that last part surprises me with its truth. I did miss him. A lot.

"Mascalzone." Greg whacks me with the back of his hand as I come inside. I cackle with laughter then, surprised yet pleased that he would look up "rascal" in anticipation of my response, pulling him into a hug around his neck, even as he complains. "You were supposed to be impressed!"

"Oh, yes! Good job, Gregory. Good work, sì. I am in press." I don't know what it means, but he wanted it, and it's becoming more and more difficult not to just give him whatever he wants, hoping we want the same thing.

"Can I get you something to drink?" He gestures toward the fridge, but I wave a hand. College is expensive, I know. He can keep his money. But I seat myself in the middle of his big couch so he'll have to sit next to me, wherever he sits. His raised eyebrow says he knows what I'm doing, and I grin as we get comfortable. Greg opens up a small book.

"Okay, here's the manual," he says, speaking slowly, but not patronizingly, which I appreciate. "This first page is just a letter that reminds you that people die when they don't drive safely, which I think you know."

"Yes."

"This page is how to make an appointment for your test, which I can help you with."

"Okay." This one-word business is getting old already, and we've only just started. *You are Nico, funny, good with cars, with a good brain in your head. You can do this.*

"Uh, paperwork requirements, citizenship, driving schools, blah blah blah," he says, flipping rapidly through, and I watch his face as he skims, so serious. His glasses make him look smart, but I still want to take

them off carefully ... before I give him some serious kisses.

"Okay, here's something. Red light means ... "

"Stop." I bring my hands together in a "that's all" motion, thankful to know one answer.

"Correct. And when can you turn right on red?"

"Easy. You cannot." Greg pushes his glasses up his
nose as he considers me, and I swoon a little.

"Yes, you can. Unless there's a sign."

"What?" My voice is loud, because I am outraged.
"What if someone come?"

"Well, that's the exception," Greg says, still serene,
crossing his ankle over his knee. "You have to look for
people walking, pedestrians, as well as cars coming from
the left. Or if there's a sign that says you can't. But if you
stop first, you can turn right when the light is red."

"How you not hit everyone like this?" I say, throwing up my hands, and Greg chuckles.

"I don't know. We just make it work. We're careful."

"Yeah, careful, careful," I say, rolling my eyes. "*You*
are careful. Other people, maybe not."

He's gazing at me, my Greg, and I gently tap the
book to focus him again.

"Right. Solid red arrow means ... " He shows me a
picture, covering up the words so I can't cheat—as if I'd
be able to read them.

"Turn right?"

"No, it means stop. Only stop. You can go when it
turns green."

"Why they have a arrow, then?"

"To say that you can turn later. When it's green."

"Caro, this no make sense."

"What does that mean, 'caro'?" He's blushing a little. "I tried to look it up, but … "

For a moment, I think he is calling me caro, and my heart trembles. But it settles again when I realize what he meant.

"Caro? Is like friend. But good friend," I clarify when his face falls. "What is word … close friend." I don't say intimate—it sounds like the word we use, but I think it means something else here.

"But not 'ragazzo'?"

"Well," I sputter, "I cannot say 'mio ragazzo' until more time pass, sí? You and me is only … new."

"Of course," he says quickly, going back to the book, but I think I have made a mistake. I let him go on so he can become comfortable again, but I inch closer until our legs are pressed together. He glances down but doesn't comment, and we keep practicing, talking about four-way stops (so complicated) and roundabouts (this I know) and how much space to leave between cars.

"Why is this question?" I scoff. "You leave just enough not to … " I smash my hands together and his eyes grow wide.

"No, you need more than that. Especially on the freeway. The faster you go, the more space you need."

I shake my head and laugh. "Why so much?"

"Three, four car lengths," he insists.

"No!" I laugh harder. "Is too much. You never get anywhere. Just—" I hunch my shoulders and pantomime driving down the road slowly, squinting to see the car ahead of me.

"I don't know if we should give you a license," Greg says, his doubts clear.

"Who, me?" I say, innocently. "No accident! Very good driver."

"Uh-huh," he says, but with obvious skepticism. "Maybe we'll rent a car instead of using Cathie's."

"Okay, okay," I say, still chuckling. "I leave space." Then, to drive home my point, I lean in toward his ear and hear his breath catch. "Between cars."

If he turns his head, we'll be nearly kissing. I know he can feel my breath caressing his neck, and he reaches over to twine our hands together, as if centering himself.

The apartment is warm—my heat coming up through the floor, I'm sure—but here, next to Greg, it feels almost too much. I don't know why I want to wait for him to turn toward me, want to see if he will, my shy guy. But when he does, those blue eyes flashing behind his glasses, his fingers squeezing mine, it is worth the wait to see the want and fear marbled in his beautiful eyes.

He's just leaning toward me, so slowly, his gaze skipping around my face as if asking if this is all right, when we hear the key in the lock. Before I can blink, he's up off the couch and across the room.

"You said you wanted a drink, right? Let me get you something—we've got soda, water, milk ... "

His roommate comes in the door, glancing at us with a knowing smile. Greg's cheeks are so flushed, he looks like he just came from a hot bath, and I decide to make it a little easier on him.

"Ciao," I say, rising from the couch with my hand extended. "I am Nico. I live down the stairs."

"It's very nice to meet you," she says, shaking my hand firmly, her smile only growing. "I'm Cathie. I live here."

Greg is still making himself busy over there, his back to us now, probably trying to hide his face. "You want some food, Cath? Did you have dinner?"

"Oh, I grabbed something on my way home," she says, heading across the room to what must be her bedroom. "I don't want to ... interrupt." Oh, she likes mischief, this one. I am trying so hard to be good, but the smirk on my lips is irrepressible, and she and I share another look of understanding before the door closes.

"We're not doing anything. We're just studying," Greg calls, but then his shoulders slump and he leans against the counter on his palms. I cross the room to him and put a stabilizing hand on his back, rubbing his shoulders with the other one. Just fucking adorable.

"Do you think she knows?" he whispers urgently, and I am very good and do not laugh at him.

"Yes," I say, my voice serious. "So kiss me."

When his head lifts, he looks like he's torn between laughter and mortification. "How will that help?" he asks, slightly desperate. "Won't we just be doing what she thought we were doing?"

I shrug. "Yes." Then I take his face in my hands like I did on the street, turning him so his back is against the counter. I take a moment to appreciate his face; I wonder if he can even grow a beard. His skin feels like a razor's never touched it. We're nearly the same height, but I am a little taller, even without my shoes.

"I wanted to," he whispers, lifting his hand to brush my afternoon stubble with the back of his fingers, and the contact thrills me. I pull him forward a little, watching his eyes for any resistance, but there is none. They flutter shut as our lips meet, but I keep it sweet, just pressing our lips together gently. I think he lacks some experience, and if I am his first kiss, I must make it romantic. You only get one first.

Honest to God, that is the intention of my heart until his tongue sweeps against my lips a little, and then my mouth falls open like it has a mind of its own, and he's inside. Okay—so my shy guy is not so shy with kissing. I swear, he's going for it like someone is grading him, like a judge will come out from behind the curtain when we finish and hold up the scorecard. I slow him down a little, and he follows my lead so beautifully, it sends a little shiver down my spine. Handsome *and* a fast learner.

We're explorers now, our hands joining the fun, but never straying too far beyond what I think he would mind Cathie seeing if she came out. But his mouth—my God. The long, drugging kisses of him, the way he's playing with the back of my neck, pressing his hips and his growing hardness into mine shamelessly, and we've barely gotten started. I want to move him back to the couch, stretch him out and show him how to take our time, make him warm and squirming with desire. Well, I *want* to move him to the bed, but it's too soon for that. For him, anyway.

To my surprise, he pulls back first. "Wait, I want to show you something."

I hope it's something in his bedroom.

He's pressing our foreheads together, like he doesn't want to lose contact, and I smile. "Show me," I prompt gently, pushing on his hips, and he grabs my hand and leads me across the room to ... a computer?

"I wrote something for you. Well, *made* something is more accurate." The machine is already on, and when he moves the mouse to wake it, I see a program is loaded. "Here, sit down." He offers me the chair, and I do ... but not without some fears creeping in.

"Not good at computer," I warn him, but he just shakes his head.

"No, this is easy. It's a study program. Here, look." He highlights the first part. "See, these are the questions based on our studying, and if a word is blue, you can click on it and see the Italian translation."

It's jarring, going from making out against the kitchen counter to trying to call all my blood back to my brain instead of my dick, but he seems excited about this. He's talking too fast for me to understand, touching his glasses a lot, pushing them up his nose, and he drags a chair from the breakfast table over to sit next to me. I read the first question under my breath, clicking on the blue word like he said, and what do you know—it says "roundabout" means rotatoria. I think I could have figured that out, but the smile on his face when I try out the feature is bright, and it becomes incandescent when I answer correctly.

"You make this?" I'm astounded. Truly. This looks almost professional to me. Greg shrugs, and the shyness is back.

"It wasn't that hard."

"For you, maybe not. For me? Impossibile."

"Oh, hey, that's almost like us. We say 'impossible.'" He reaches over me to advance to the next question, and all I can do is stare, amazed. He really thinks this is nothing, even though it means everything to me. "Will you teach me some Italian?"

I wish my brain was not so tired after this long day. I wish I could tell him the big things in my heart, how much I appreciate his devotion, the way he's taking care of me. Instead, I kiss him again, tenderly, sweetly.

"Sì, of course," I murmur. "We start soon."

CHAPTER NINE

GREG

I wasn't sure I'd ever come down from the high of Tuesday night, but I get myself to class on Wednesday morning. The dynamics are in Italian in my music—forte, pianissimo, crescendo—

and it's distracting. I wonder what he'll teach me first? Family words? Greetings? I'm already learning a lot from making the practice tests. My mind is only sort of on my part as my brass quartet practices, but I make it through, even though I haven't practiced since last week. I'm packing up my horn when our instructor, Mr. Claire, puts a hand on my shoulder.

"Can you hang back a minute, Greg?"

"Of course," I say, a sinking feeling in my stomach. As I suspected, he waits until everyone else has left the practice room before he turns a concerned gaze on me.

"How much time are you putting into practice?" The directness of the question rattles me, and I swallow hard.

"Not as much as I could be," I admit.

"I know it's your first semester, and it can be a big adjustment. We want to be patient, but I've conferred with some of your other instructors, and they agree you need to focus more. Your tone is just not there, and you're not blending with the others in your ensembles." He crosses his arms as he leans against the open door.

"I'm sorry," I blurt out. "I'll practice more. I'll do better."

"We just want to see you do well here. I know you have a passion for music, but it takes more than that to succeed in this line of work." His expression seems almost apologetic, and my chagrin makes me grimace.

"Thank you, sir. I won't let you down."

NICO COMES OVER TO study that evening and Thursday evening too—but I make sure I practice before he arrives. He kisses me hello when he comes in the front door, but then he holds off on more until we've worked for a while. On Friday, he brings groceries and cooks dinner: pasta pomodoro. He says it's not as good as his mom's, but I still have high hopes. Far better than the jar of Ragu I try to hide when he goes looking for real Parmesan cheese. Nico hums a little while he cooks, throwing my dish towel over his shoulder, chopping garlic and looking perfectly at home here in my apartment.

"Why haven't I been to your place yet?" I ask, dutifully spreading butter on the bread like he showed me.

"My place is … " He pauses, stirring while he thinks. "Nothing. Here is good." He's quiet again for a minute, then adds with a grin, "Also, the bed only for kissing." It takes me a second to figure out what he means.

"You don't have a couch?" I ask, frowning.

He shakes his head, still humming a little. "No couch, no TV, no computer."

"God. What do you *do* at night?"

Nico's dark eyebrows bounce, and I roll my eyes.

"Listen to radio. I sing along, learn English."

"That's a good idea. But we could look on this new website for a used couch. It's called Craigslist; people all around San Francisco can post stuff for sale." I start toward the computer, but he stops me with a gentle hand on my arm.

"No money for couch. All is for send home."

"Oh, I see." I'm not giving up that easily. There's gotta be a way to get one without bugs in it for cheap. Maybe a thrift store or something. "Will you tell me about your family?"

"My nonne are Lauretana and Adelasia, my nonni are Cristofaro and Luigi. My mama is Immaculata, my papa is Canzio. Married—" He spreads his hands wide. "Long time. They meet in school."

"Aww." It gives me warm fuzzies. I hardly know any gay people who were high school sweethearts … at least, people who didn't have to keep it a secret. It's not even legal for us to get married. "Brothers? Sisters?"

"Four sisters. I am biggest, then Maria, Gloriana, Petra, and Elisabetta. My mama, she give to us Bible names."

"Except for yours," I say before tasting the bite of sauce he offers me from the wooden spoon. The fresh basil and oregano give it a burst of flavor on my tongue, and I hum my approval.

Nico laughs. "No, me also. Nicodemus."

"No!" I gasp, a big smile spreading across my face. "For real?"

"Is true." He chuckles, taking his own taste of the sauce. "Good?"

"Yeah, it's very good. Are they married?"

"Yes," he says, serving up the pasta on three plates. "Maria marry Vittorio, but he leave. Four kids."

"That sucks," I say, and he looks at me quizzically. "Oh, it means, I'm sorry. I feel bad for her." She must have been pretty young if he's the oldest and she's already divorced.

"Me also. But she is a good mama, and my mama help her. They are Bernardo, Julio, Marco and Geronimo. Petra marry also, to Orlando, then comes Bella, Antonia, Susanna, and Virginia."

"Four boys and four girls," I comment, and he smiles.

"Yes. Is many people when we ... " He mimes convergence by bringing his hands together. "But family is everything."

There's a soft look in his eyes as he reaches over me for the cheese, but he blinks it away quickly. He'd be a good partner ... especially if he doesn't mind cooking.

Probably a good dad too, from how he's talking about his nieces and nephews now. I can tell he misses them a lot. An idea starts to percolate, bubbling up like the sauce.

"Do you talk to them much?"

"Sunday I call, hang up, so Mama know I am living." His shoulders are down, and he's staring at his empty plate. My heart goes out to him.

"All moms are such worriers," I say. "I call mine every week too."

"Is expensive," he says with a sigh.

"That's too bad—I call on the computer for free." As soon as I say it, I realize a factor I didn't consider: will it work internationally?

Nico's mouth falls open. "Free? No money? How it's called, this?"

"Yeah. It's great. It's called voice over IP. It's kind of new."

"How you do this?"

I wipe my mouth with my napkin and push back from the table to show him. "Come on." I'm already sitting at the computer when I realize I can't show him, because our phone line will be tied up by the internet. "What's your phone number?"

He fishes his wallet out of his back pocket and pulls out an index card. "510-555-6017."

I dial it, then point to the floor. "Listen."

Distantly, I can hear a phone ring beneath us. I've never noticed it before, which probably means that no one's ever called him when I'm home. The thought troubles me. But Nico is too busy being delighted.

"We can call now?"

I pause. "Well, we can, but isn't it, like, really early there?"

He says something under his breath in Italian that sounds like a curse.

"Yes, too early. Sunday?"

"Sunday," I confirm, then seal it with a kiss, just because I can. I adore kissing him—and not just because I've dreamed of having a stubbly face to rub against mine. It's Nico. I don't know if I can even picture kissing anyone else now. I know it's fast to feel that way, but I can't help it. It feels like our thing, even though I know it's not.

"Tomorrow, I will take you outside to drink."

"Oh? Won't that take away from money you could send home?"

He shrugs. "Is okay. The meccanica will go out also."

"Great, I'd love to meet your friends."

Nico looks like he's doubting himself—a look I have never seen once from him thus far.

"They is ... not like us."

"They're straight? Not gay?" I clarify, and he nods. I laugh. "Most people are, you know. It's not like I don't know how to get along with straight people."

"Can be very ... " He flexes his biceps like he's preening, and I laugh.

"Yeah, I know. It's okay. I don't mind." It's not like I want to take him to a gay bar; someone would probably steal him from me in about five seconds. "It's a date."

CHAPTER TEN

NICO

Greg is quiet on the walk to the bar the next night, and I steal a lot of glances at him before I finally break the silence.

"Okay, mio ragazzo?" That prompts a smile.

"Just thinking."

"Thinking for school?"

His eyebrows go up. "How did you know that?"

I shrug. My intuition is strong when it comes to him, but I don't know how to say that. "Tell to me."

Greg lets out a big sigh, like it comes from the depths of his soul. "I just don't know if I'm in the right program. Like, I love music, but ... "

"But?" I prompt, resisting the urge to tell him again how much I love his playing. I want to hear him, not sway him in one direction or another.

"But I don't know if I really want to make it my job. It *feels* like work. But when I'm coding or making that HyperCard program for you, it feels ... exciting?" I don't get all of what he says, but I think I'm getting the gist of it.

"You like computer, not horn?"

"I like both," he says, shrugging, his hands still stuffed into his pockets. "But I don't know if I like music enough to make all the work worth it."

"Mm."

"How did you know you wanted to be a mechanic?" he asks, then tentatively tries, "un meccanico?" I smile.

"Is like 'Nico' at the end, sí? Since I am small, is all I wanted. Papa show me, I learn like ..." I snap my fingers.

He nods like he understands. We're at the doors of the bar now, but I tug him away from the entrance by his sleeve. With mild embarrassment, I lay a hand over his heart.

"You will feel it, here."

He puts a warm hand over mine, and his gaze is soft, even as his heartbeat picks up speed. "Yeah. Thanks. That helps."

I'm hoping I didn't pressure him as I open the door for him—it sounds like a tough decision, and I can't give a lot of advice, since my path has always been laid out pretty clearly for me. But I saw the way his face lit up when he showed me his program. It's not like that when he talks about music. He plays beautifully and I always enjoy my ceiling concerts, but he doesn't have that same ... joy? I make a mental note to look up some of those words.

I spot Elio first, and he waves. We weave our way through the darkened room to where they've set up at the bar in front of the TV with the basketball game on. I introduce Greg around to Elio, Massimo, Pasqual, and Gianluca, and they all shake hands like this is some kind of a business meeting. I put Greg between me and Elio, so he's not on the end by himself, but this leaves me straining to hear.

The Golden State Warriors are likely heading to the playoffs, it seems, and I try to absorb all their rapid English about Rick Adelman (the coach?) and their latest draft picks. They talk faster with each other than they do with me, and I'm surprised how much Greg knows about the sport. Is it something he likes? I could probably learn something about it; we have the LBA in Italy, but I never paid it much attention. Who wants to watch skinny, sweaty men chase each other up and down the court when you could watch Formula 1?

"Hey," I call to Elio, "when's the first Formula 1 race? March?"

"In Brazil, end of the month," he replies, then switches back to English to ask Greg about his work. I find it somewhat frustrating ... but I brought my boyfriend here to meet my coworkers.

The music is shitty again: more songs about crying Americans, this time by The Pretenders. At least the words are pretty easy to understand. I hum until they hit the chorus, then add in the words about how they'll stand by their love and not let them get hurt. The line about talking about problems affects me, given that I just tried to help Greg outside.

He turns to smile at me when he hears my low voice. "I wish they'd play some Madonna," he says, leaning close so only I can hear him.

"Yes, thank you! This is what I say!" I agree loudly, and the meccanica all turn to look at us, their faces amused.

"What'd you say?" Massimo asks.

"You wouldn't understand," I tell him in Italian. "Gay guy stuff."

At this, they roll their eyes, cursing at me good-naturedly, then go back to their beers.

Greg leans into me again, and I want him to stay close. He smells good tonight, musky and clean. I want to bury my nose in his neck and not come up for air for hours. "What did you say?"

"I say is not for them."

"Good call," he says, chuckling. "They probably don't like Madonna as much as we do."

Looking into his bright face, glowing in the neon lights over the bar, I want to kiss him, but I don't know how the meccanica would feel about that. It's one thing to know that a man is gay—it's another to see it in front of your face. Plus, most of them are single; I don't want to flaunt my relationship when they only have their left hand for company.

We're having fun, talking up and down the line. I get up to hear them better, standing between Elio and Greg. But then he starts yawning. I can tell he doesn't mean to; it's not his fault. It's the end of a workday, and we've been here for several hours by this point. When I hear his jaw crack with the force of his yawn, I make a decision.

"Time to go," I say firmly, sliding his coat off the back of his stool and holding it out so he can put his arms in.

"Oh ho, I guess we know who wears the pants in this relationship," Pasqual calls in Italian, and I flip him off.

"We both do. That's what makes it gay," I retort, and they all laugh. Greg smiles awkwardly, saying it was nice to meet them as I herd him outside.

"Why are we leaving?" he asks as I take his hand. The night is cold but clear, and I look up at the nearly starless sky.

"You not tired?"

"I could've stayed—" He has to pause to yawn again, and I just smile and squeeze his hand.

"Also, we not yet study tonight."

"Oh!" He perks up. "You still wanted to study?"

I manage to keep a straight face. "Of course." We chat in stilted terms about other things the rest of the way home ... the cars I'm working on, Greg's classmates, Cathie's dating adventures. But once we get inside, I spring my trap.

"Did you want to work from the book or use the computer?" Greg asks, taking off his coat.

"Mmm, something else," I say, like I'm musing. I walk him backward until his legs meet the couch, then gently push him down onto it. "Body words."

"B-B-Body words?" Greg stammers. "Th-That's not on the test."

"Could be," I disagree, and his eyes narrow as I position myself over him, my knees on either side of his hips, not quite touching. "If signal no work, could need to ... " I sit up and mimic the biking hand signals he showed me for right and left turn.

"Uh-huh," he says, clearly holding back a smile, which breaks when I bring myself close to him again, rubbing his chest with one hand.

"I will kiss, you tell to me what is called."

Greg's eyes widen adorably as his gaze shifts to the front door, but he swallows hard and nods. I have my doubts about how long he'll last at this game, but he looks like he's determined to give it a go. *My sweet nerd.* I start him off easy, trailing my lips under his ear.

"Uh, neck."

"Mm, neck of Greg."

"Greg's neck," he corrects, clearly amused, and his arms slide around my neck, sending tingles across my skin.

I kiss the lump under his chin.

"Adam's apple." His voice is already cracking a bit, and I'm just getting started.

"Adamo like Bible? He no—" I swallow hard in demonstration and Greg laughs.

"No, I guess Adam didn't swallow," he says, his voice a little breathy, and I can tell from his pupils that he's thinking about other kinds of swallowing. Is this the night he's going to invite me into his bed? I'm more than ready, but he hasn't brought it up yet, and I don't know if he's ready for me to do the inviting. I bring my body down to align with his and run my fingers through his hair, tipping his head back as I give his neck more atten-tion with my lips and teeth.

"That's still my neck, and my hair," he says, his voice strained, and I chuckle, moving up. "That's my ear." I give it a little nip and he sighs, melting more into me, and I feel his hips tip up toward me a little. *Yes, that's it.* I meant to seduce my boyfriend, of course, but I'm still relishing every little catch in his breathing, the way his fingers tighten in the hair at my nape, how his body is growing more loose and languid the longer I kiss him.

When I pop one of his shirt buttons open at the top, he starts breathing harder.

"This part?" I ask, giving his pale skin a peck, trying to draw him back into the game.

"My chest."

I hum my approval, even as I pop another button, revealing a dusting of the same golden hair as his head. As much as I like this, it's going too slow. I pull up his shirt to show his belly, loving the way his muscles contract.

"My stomach." When I lick a line up the highway of hair leading into his pants, Greg shudders, and I know the game is done. Now we can—

"You guys just get back?" Cathie's yawning voice startles us both, and Greg goes from a happy puddle of kisses to nervous again in an instant. He pushes on my shoulders and I sit up with a sigh. "Also, you know you have a bedroom, right?" she adds.

"Yeah, thanks, Cath," Greg says, reddening as he looks at me. "It's late. We should probably go to sleep. What time should we call your family tomorrow?"

"They are eight hours after," I say, rubbing at my head. I'm tired too, truthfully. Not that I'd have turned down an invitation to stay ... "Nine o'clock too early?"

"I'm heading to the library around then," Cathie adds, pouring herself a glass of water and drinking it all in one go. "So you'll have the place to yourself."

She is not subtle, Cathie. But I appreciate her candor.

"Until tomorrow, mio ragazzo," I murmur, kissing him goodnight.

CHAPTER ELEVEN

GREG

"More coffee? You're spoiling me," I say, accepting the paper cup.

"Espresso," he says. "To wake you."

I spent a long time last night staring at the ceiling, wishing I'd asked him to stay the night. Even if we didn't fuck, it would've been nice to let him wake me instead of the coffee. I do get a hello kiss, but then he makes a bee-line for the computer, pulling up two chairs eagerly.

"The boy at the cash ... " He mimes the motion of the register, and I nod. "He was wear a rainbow. He is like us?"

"Could be," I say with a shrug. "What's his name?"

"Enzo. His family run the shop." I can tell he doesn't really want to talk about Enzo, even if it made him happy to see another young gay person, especially one who speaks Italian. I experience a brief pang of jealousy that Enzo can speak freely with Nico, then focus on dialing in the long number. Nico's leg bounces under the keyboard tray as it rings.

"Mama? Non riattaccare; ho un nuovo modo per chiamarti. È gratis."

I can tell he's trying to keep it out of his voice, but I can see what they can't: the tears streaming down his face faster than he can wipe them away. I go into the kitchen and get him a paper towel, because I don't think a tissue is going to do the job, and he accepts it gratefully, still chattering away loudly with them.

I snag a few words out of the deluge of Italian: "love," "family," "food" ... and "boyfriend." He's using my name sometimes, and every time he does, he reaches out to squeeze my leg, even though they can't see me, like he's trying to make sure I don't leave. But I won't. I don't want to. I'm just watching this amazing man connect with his people, wishing I could talk to them too. He doesn't need privacy, because I can't understand anything, but even if he were speaking English, I don't think I could leave him like this, so emotional. I feel connected, as if we're tied together by an invisible string.

They pass him around: his grandparents, his sisters, his father, his mother, even some of his nieces and nephews, though they seem confused. Nico turns to me, covering the receiver.

"They think is expensive. They won't talk long."

"You told them it's free, right?"

"Sì, I tell them." He shrugs, wiping his face again.

"That's okay. We can call them again next week. We'll try to explain it again in a letter."

He nods emphatically, then goes back to talking to them, laughing despite the tears. I put an arm around his shoulders, and he moves closer, shifting until our sides are touching and his arm rests on my knee permanently.

I shouldn't distract him, but I'm drawn to that dark hair, and when I card my fingers through it gently, I feel the tension dissipate from his shoulders and he closes his eyes. He curls into me, resting his head in the gap between my neck and shoulder, and I keep playing with his hair, twirling the straight strands around my finger, tugging on it a little.

Then he's saying goodbye, and there's a crackly chorus of admonitions and adoration before he puts down the receiver, letting out a big, shuddery sigh as he sits up. Nico tries to wipe his face again; his eyes are red and swollen, but he never looked better to me.

"Fuck."

"Oh, that word you know?" I tease, wrapping both arms around him and pressing a kiss to his temple.

"Meccania say it. A lot." The tears seem to be slowing, but he still seems embarrassed as he wipes them with the paper towel again. "Is happy crying, you know?"

"Unlike when I tried to take you to that pizza place."

Nico chuckles a little, then pivots so he's holding me too, his warm, firm embrace around me.

"Thank you," he whispers, voice still choked up. "Thank you. My family, they are everything."

"I know." I put a hand on the back of his head, hoping to comfort him, but feeling wholly inadequate. "What do you need now? What can I do?"

He barks out a laugh. "More?"

"Of course, more. Whatever you need." I pull back to see into his eyes, but he won't let me go entirely, his hands sliding down my arms until we're intertwined again. "Do you want to eat? Take a nap? Watch a movie? What sounds good?"

There's something in Nico's gaze I can't place exactly, but it's tender and exasperated and intense all at once.

Then he's standing and he's pulling me with him toward my bedroom. I'm not surprised he's tired; that seemed like a lot, even if it was in Italian. But when we get there, he kicks the door shut and pins me against it.

"Catty is where?" he asks softly as his big, soft lips find my neck, and we're chest to chest, his hands on my hips, even as he presses into me everywhere.

"Uh ... " My heart has never quite beat this rhythm before, like it's fighting its way out of my chest by punching through my ribs, and it takes me a minute to answer. "She wasn't sure how long we'd talk, so she went to the library at UCSF."

"Mmm," Nico hums, and I can feel his lips curving into a smile as he kisses down my neck, making my dick sit up and take notice, as if being pinned by a handsome man in my bedroom wasn't enough. I finally wrap my arms around him, and my head falls back against the door with a thump when he takes that talented tongue and licks a long line up my neck.

"What are you doing?" I gasp out, not sure why I'm out of breath.

"You ask what I want? I want this. I want you."

"How is your English *better* when you're horny?" I gripe, and Nico laughs low, but the sound makes me shiver, because there's plans in that laugh. He steps back a pace, and he's unbuttoning his shirt, kicking off his shoes, still giving me that intense look from before. But not having him pressed against me causes my brain to stop giving a 404 error and come back online, and with each button that comes open, my nervousness increases. Nico can tell, of course.

"Is easy, amore. Don't think."

"Easy for you to say," I shoot back. "You've done this before." But when he takes off both his shirts, the sight of his broad chest, thick with hair, helps me shove away some of the nerves. It's even better when he presses himself against me again, taking my lips in a slow kiss, one rough hand cradling my head, the other undoing my buttons. Also, amore? That's new. That's got fireworks going off in my chest, because it means I'm not alone in this falling-fast feeling.

"English never easy for me to say," he returns, but my brain is busy, cataloging all the ways he's touching me, especially the hips pressed into me where something is growing rapidly. "But this? This is just us. Just together. Don't think. I am the boss." He steps back so I can take off my shirt, and my glasses come off too, but he catches them before they hit the ground.

Perfect. Wonderful. Kind. Hilarious. Persistent. Brave. My heart is beating out all the adjectives I love about him, and it's distracting me from his words. He's pulling me toward the bed, shoving down the covers, when his words land.

"You're the boss, huh?"

"Sí. I am the boss," he confirms, pulling me on top of him. "Now no talk." I'm still nervous, but Nico just starts kissing me again, our bodies pressed together, and when he pulls the covers up over us even though we've still got pants on, I feel some of the tension melt out of me. I know this. Know him. I don't know how. We've been together less than three weeks, but it's like I've always known him. We stay like that for a long time, just him caressing my back, my sides while we kiss, me scratching lightly at his chest, running my fingertips along his neck and jaw.

I don't realize how hard I'm breathing until he rolls us so that he's on top, and need flares in my belly like I've never felt before. Nico sits up for a second, breathing just as hard, and his strong hands wrench his belt open. I shove my nervousness back and sit up a little because I want to see this, even without my glasses. I want it so bad. I've been dreaming about it, my mouth basically watering in anticipation, and the crooked smile on Nico's face says he knows that.

"Shut up," I say, laughing, and give him a small shove.

"What? What I say? I say nothing!" He might protest, but the way he drops his zipper and pulls himself out says he doesn't mind. His gaze is so intense; I don't think I could look away if I wanted to. I'm trapped here with him, under him, pulled into his orbit and his power like a planet ... and I don't mind either. And when he grabs my hand and pulls it to his cock, so warm I swear it nearly burns me, I choke out an incoherent sound.

Timidly, I grab ahold of it, but that feels wrong. I turn my hand so the backs of my fingers stroke his reddened skin, and that's when it starts. The Italian. It's like he's been holding it back before, and now it all comes flooding out. Even though his cock is magnificent, just because it's him, I find my gaze drawn to his face, and the swell of pride I feel that I've reduced my boyfriend to an eyes-squeezed-shut, shaky mess is new.

Wait. Shaking?

"Are you okay?" I ask low, still playing with him, this time with the uncut skin near the head.

As if in answer, Nico opens his eyes, that scorching, dark gaze now let loose on me, and I feel a little shaky myself. Reaching behind him, he grabs the sheets, pulling them up as he covers me with his body, and holy hell, how did I not know that this would be my favorite thing?

My hips buck automatically, trying to get closer to him. But my nerves resurface because my pants feel very in the way, and I don't want my belt to scratch his tender flesh. I push on his hips, urging him up again, and the heat in his eyes when my hands go to my buckle is unbearable.

"Um, can you … " I put one hand over my eyes, pantomiming what I want him to do, but then I feel his knuckles against my belly, working open my pants himself, and this is ten times worse, but also a thousand times better. "Uh," I croak out. "I can't … are you … red light?"

The fingers stop moving, and I mourn the loss of them. Nico slides back down, his weight solid and comforting. An anchor.

"I forget you are shy," he whispers, kissing my neck. "Tell me, amore."

"I—" His lips are making me momentarily forget what I was so afraid of as they caress my neck, but then it comes back to me. "I-I don't want you to look at it."

Nico shrugs. "Okay." He covers me more fully, and the feel of his hard cock against my hip has me losing my mind a little. "You are the boss."

My heart turns to Jell-O, wibble-wobbling around in my chest like it's drunk on the sentiment. I didn't mind him taking the reins earlier, but giving them back to me is somehow even more of a turn-on.

I angle my head to kiss him, but I still don't know how to ask for what I want. Slipping my hand down between us, I grasp his cock again to try to protect him, but he lets out a groan that shoots straight down my spine. He's mumbling something against my neck and I think it's Italian again until my brain sorts it out.

"Touch you, amore. Need to touch you. Make it good. No look. No look, amore. Please." He says it like a prayer, reverent and repetitious, sounding so genuine and so desperate that the combination fortifies me. It gives me enough courage to do what he did just moments ago: grab his hand and shove it down my halfway open pants.

We both moan, and I'm relieved that I don't have to think about being quiet with his apartment empty below us and Cathie out. My brain is being swamped in sensations anyway—his hot cock in my hand, his hand wrapped around me, the weight of him pressing against my side, his soft lips on my neck. He's jacking me painfully slowly; I'm leaking, and he's using it to ease his path, and that's so hot I can hardly stand it. The pressure and slide of his big, rough hand is making my eyes roll back in my head, and suddenly, I can hear my own breathing, loud and fast in the small room.

"Nico ... " I've forgotten to move my hand too, but he's got it pinned against my side, rocking into me, and he doesn't seem unhappy about it. He's moved to kissing my chest, sucking on my nipples, and it has my blood feeling like lava, my head spinning, curse words coming into my head that never, ever do, and—

"I put us together, amore," he murmurs, a tinge of desperation in his voice. "Okay?"

"Yes." I get flashbacks to me saying yes to Cath's various manipulations, but this yes, this is different. I don't need to know exactly what he means, because I trust him. If he wants to spread my legs, I'll let him. My heart is in this, and even though I never meant for it not to be, it scares me a little how much.

But true to his word, he's not looking at my dick when he eases my pants down further, and he looks so silly staring up at the ceiling that I can't help but let a snicker escape.

"Hey, you say no look!" He sounds indignant.

"Yes," I say, still trying to hide my smile, and I tug the sheets back up over us as he comes back down on top of me, the warmth covering us again like a wave, and I lose a little more of my heart when Nico smiles.

"My shy guy," he says tenderly, brushing his fingertips against my face, and I wrap my arms around his neck, wanting to lose myself in him and this love that's growing between us. Love? Yeah, love. That's what it is. Then Nico starts to move slowly.

"Oh God," I gasp out, finally registering what he's doing. Our cocks slide together as he holds them in one hand, the head of his rubbing against the head of mine, and the ecstasy has me throwing back my head. "Oh, fuck."

"Is good, amore?"

"Sì," I manage, and his chuckle rumbles his chest like an earthquake, but then we're too busy for talking—kissing and thrusting and stroking and letting it all come to a fever pitch, his hand working us fast as I curl myself around him and hold on for dear life. I come first, letting out a sharp cry, but I haven't even opened my eyes yet when I hear him make a desperate, keening noise, and he follows me over. Despite my post-"doing it" haze, I look up to watch his face, and the way his mouth falls open, the way his eyebrows lift and his eyes flutter shut, the slack joy of it all. Nico rolls to his side instead of collapsing on top of me, which seems prudent given the mess. We breathe hard together, and I'm smiling, but his gaze is searching.

"Good, amore? All good?"

I kiss him in answer, feeling shimmery inside, full of glitter like those gay clubs where I never found anyone half as special as Nico, floating on the buzz of falling hard and fast in love.

CHAPTER TWELVE

NICO

Once we get cleaned up, I convince Greg to just order food for lunch (I pay), and we get pizza—from a *good* restaurant where we can get margherita. We're still snuggling on the couch, watching football, when Cathie comes home. She shakes out her black umbrella by the front door, launching a spray of water droplets that don't reach us.

"Is it raining that hard?" Greg asks, turning toward the front windows. I hadn't noticed either; I'm all wrapped up in Greg, inside and out. I think I went into this looking for a friend or a fling, but I somehow got a lot more. Not that I'm complaining. I put my hand on his knee, and he gives me a fantastic smile.

"Cats and dogs," Cathie says, and I have no idea what that has to do with the weather. She grabs herself a piece of pizza, then grins at us. "Look at you two. Who would've thought that you'd end up here, given how it all started?" Under my hand, Greg's leg tenses, and my mind snaps to attention out of my comfortable Sunday post-sex fog.

"What that means?" I ask. Greg sits up, turning toward me with his hands up, but before he can speak, Cathie goes on.

"You know," she says, taking a bite, "the wrong apartment thing."

I can feel my heart begin to frost over, and I shake my head slowly, wishing that I didn't understand what she was saying for once, wishing I could gloss over it as another bit of English that slipped away from me like so many do. "What thing?" I turn to Greg. "What thing?"

"Listen," he says, then pauses, like he's trying to figure out what to say. I fold my arms and stare at him, recounting the contents of that letter in my mind, the one I pored over so many times, trying to understand it. *I've been wanting to introduce myself for weeks now.*

"Who it was for?"

"I don't even know his name," Greg says weakly. All the color's gone out of his bright face, like he's been unplugged. "Please, Nico. When she delivered you my letter and you seemed so interested in meeting me, I just thought I'd see how it went before I told you. Just thought I'd see if we had a ... connection."

I am so upset I can't move. Can't speak. When he said he'd seen me in the hall, it was someone else. That's why he didn't recognize me at the café. He wrote that sweet, shy letter for *someone else*—he was too shy even to deliver it, which makes it both charming and completely heartbreaking at the same time. I finally find some words.

"But you never tell," I say, my voice low. "You not say."

"No," he admits, dropping his gaze to his lap. "I didn't. I didn't think it mattered—we just get along so well, and ... " His face reddens. "Honestly, I just forgot."

"Which is: didn't matter or forgot? Not the same," I say, getting to my feet. My shoes are still in his room, so I storm across the apartment.

"Nico, wait. Just stop. Please." His voice is tinged with increasing desperation with each word. "I don't even know that guy, but I know you." He's followed me into the bedroom, and now he's blocking my path to exit as I tie my shoes. And there's nothing shy about him—chest heaving, stance wide, gaze stern, like he doesn't believe I'd knock him over to leave, but he's not taking any chances.

"I know you," Greg says, his voice strong. "No, we don't always communicate well, but I know your heart. I can feel it when you look at me, and I can see it in your eyes when you talk about your family and your work. I hear it in the way you talk and joke and tease. You like this. You want it just as much as I do."

"Then why hide?" I shout. "Why not tell?"

"Because I didn't want you to think it was a mistake!" He's shouting too.

"It *was* mistake!"

"No, this is fucking fate," he shoots back, pointing at me. "This is destiny; we just—we just needed a little help to get there." I'm too ramped up to think and I don't know all those words, so I can't reply, but then he puts his hands on his chest, over his heart.

"Give me another chance. Amore, please. I've never lied to you about anything."

The hardest part is that I believe that, but right now, my mind is spinning in Italian—accusations and hurt and anger, and it's actually a blessing that I can't let any of it out. I push past him, intent on nothing but the front door, but he follows me again.

"Nico!"

I've got the door already open when I stop, my heart still revving like an engine at the start line, needing to *go, go, go*, but my feet unwilling to just walk out on him when he's so upset.

"I think on it. Give to me time."

His voice is small, but relieved. "Okay."

I manage to close the door without slamming it, but I don't start breathing again until I get inside my apartment. I lock the door and put my back to it, sliding down until I hit the floor. I can't hear everything that's happening up there, but I hear their quiet voices—Cathie apologizing, Greg saying no, it was his fault. I sit there for a long time, thinking about that letter. Thinking about our first date, when the connection was so strong, it overwhelmed me. I think about showing him the Ferraris, the spark of us that other couple saw, the way we were in his bed. But the idea that it wasn't me he wanted hurts my pride, as evidenced by the tear I wipe away.

I hear the TV shut off upstairs and the front door slam. I tense, waiting for him to come down, waiting for a knock or another letter shoved under my door. But nothing comes. I get up quickly and cross to the front windows, looking down, and there he is, working his way up the sidewalk. He's wiping his face too, jacketless despite the deluge drenching him ... my sunshine, out in the rain. My dictionary is still on the table, next to the radio where I was looking up song lyrics. I flip it open.

Fate: The will or principle or determining cause by which things in general are believed to come to be as they are or events to happen as they do.

That isn't very helpful, but I realize as I'm searching for the other word that I already know it: destino. And could he mean fato for the other? I huff out a laugh as I toss the book back onto the scratched table. Ridiculous. We've known each other only a few weeks.

I mean, it couldn't be, right?

CHAPTER THIRTEEN

GREG

Space? How am I supposed to give him space? I spend about thirty seconds feeling sorry for myself before I start making a plan to get him back. Maybe Nico can't see a future for us, but I can. I don't know if or when it ends—maybe it doesn't. But I know it doesn't end like this. I know it as sure as I know I need to quit the conservatory.

Cathie comes timidly out of her room. "I'm so sorry—"

I hold up a hand. "My fault. I didn't realize it would hurt him. I should've."

"So it's over?"

"Not if I have anything to say about it." I'm full of nervous energy, but not like when I couldn't deliver the letter in the first place. It's paired with that deep resolve again, in my gut. I don't think I've ever had to fight for anything like this before, but I'll be damned if I'm going to let something so silly come between us.

She crosses to me and lays an arm around my shoulders. "You know, this isn't really how people hook up. Shit happens, you can't—"

"It is when you're hooking up with your soulmate." Her eyes widen as I brush her off, then grab my wallet and keys as I head for the door.

"Where are you going? I thought he wanted space."

"He does. I'm going for a walk."

"In this?" Cathie asks, gesturing to the downpour out the front windows.

"Yeah."

"When will you be back?" Her arms are crossed, and she looks genuinely concerned.

"Before dark." I don't know exactly where I'm going, but I know I need to move to think, and I can't do that here. It's out there, whatever I need to make this happen. I shove my feet into my shoes and I'm down the stairs in record time, even though I can't keep myself from looking toward his door. I never even got to see his place.

The rain feels good on my skin—the stinging drops feel like they're washing away the parts of me I don't need anymore, bringing something new. The cold wakes me up, bringing my mind into focus: how do I give someone space but also communicate how much I love him?

I don't have much at my disposal there. My Italian dictionary will definitely be put to good use, crafting an apology letter. But other than that, I'm not sure what my method will be. Could I make something on the computer? I don't know how I'd get it to him, and I don't think he wants to come back up to my place. I pass the crappy pizza place, a dry cleaner, a used bookstore ... and then a music store. I don't think I've noticed it before. I pause, chuckling at my wet cat appearance before I push the door open. Because it's not a record store—it's a music store.

Instruments line the walls, and in the middle, there's milk crates full of sheet music, scores for symphonies alongside solo and ensemble parts. There must be a thousand of them. Every music store I've ever been in is a kind of organized chaos, things tucked into corners and nooks where I'd never think to store things. It's a little strange that I feel pulled into this place so soon after deciding to quit, but I can still play my horn. I don't have to give it up completely just because I don't want it as a career.

I head to the register toward the back with squelching steps, but the college-aged woman seems unfazed. I guess this is San Francisco; she probably sees some weird stuff working here.

"Hey," I greet her. "Do you have any solo music for brass?"

"Of course," she says, pointing to the right. "The classical's over here, and the pop stuff is on the far side."

"The pop stuff?" That piques my interest. "Like, Madonna?"

She tilts her head. "Might be. Let's go see."

Forty-five minutes later, I have five purchases and a plan.

TODAY SEEMS TOO SOON to start—I'm exhausted and hit the hay right after dinner. On Monday, I have my late class. I stop by the Italian café on my way to school, hoping Nico will be there, getting a coffee, but no such luck. I console myself with the idea that I can enact my plan tomorrow.

The timing is the tricky thing, because I don't know exactly when he gets home. I end up practicing for a little while, then sitting on my bed, watching out the window until I see a tall, dark, and handsome someone coming up the front steps. Then it's showtime.

Truth be told, it doesn't sound much like Hootie and the Blowfish, but I know he knows this song; we've discussed the dolphin line. I wait until I hear his footsteps in his bedroom when he goes to change his clothes so he's got the best chance of hearing me, even though I'm pretty sure he can hear me everywhere in his apartment.

I sing along the lyrics in my head as I play, enjoying the mention of how we come from different worlds. I hold back a chuckle at the extra portion of irony for me never wanting to look at them. But the chorus is what I'm hoping he'll take to heart: *Well, there's nothing I can do / I only wanna be with you.*

I play it through twice, then put my horn away. I don't expect any response this time—he's probably still mad. So I just work on my letter while I eat the leftover pasta pomodoro from the other night. Was that only a few days ago? Feels more like a lifetime. But having something he made me, something we shared, is a comfort. A little piece of his home and his heart. I get some sauce on the table and on the paper, but that's okay—I'll probably need more than one draft anyway.

Then I get on the computer and spend the rest of the evening looking at computer programming majors in the area. I don't want to move, but … I may have to. I don't think UCSF has the program I'm looking for, but I don't have the confidence to just try to teach myself everything I need to know from books. The rain's gone today, so I open my window and go to sleep with the sounds of the city for company, just to feel less alone.

Wednesday night, I serenade him with *I'll Stand by You* by the Pretenders, which he was singing along with at the bar, so I think he knows this one too. I'm out of pasta, so I take myself out for dinner, even though I'm nervous that he'll come up while I'm out. He probably won't. I'm going to keep trying, though, until he tells me to stop. Until he tells me we're done. He may be out of reach, but my heart's aching for him, and I know he's missing me too when I see a shadow on his window as I cross the street in front of our building. That's something, anyway.

I get a sandwich at the Italian café, greeting Enzo warmly—he is indeed proudly wearing a rainbow pin on his tan apron, and when I compliment him on it, he grins.

"Where's your boyfriend?" he asks, giving me my change.

"Oh, we had a little falling out, but I think he'll be back soon." He seems concerned, which is sweet, but I just give him a reassuring wink as I go find a table.

I think my letter is almost done—it's just missing a big finish. Writing in another language is really hard—even with the books and the tapes, I feel like a toddler who's been given a pot of language paste and is just making a mess for the hell of it. It gives me more empathy for how difficult it must have been for him, trying to communicate at work and with me all day long. I'm tired after just an hour.

Thursday night, I pull out the big guns: Madonna. I thought about saving her for Friday to cap off the week, but I can't wait anymore. I know he loves her, and I do too. Again, I can't help but sing along the words in my head about how he'll feel it when we kiss, that everything is new with him. The pounding knock on my front door startles me so badly that I nearly drop my horn.

I open my bedroom door and peek out, not sure what I'll find. Cathie is doing the same.

"I think it's for you," she whispers.

The pounding comes again. I must have pissed someone off with my playing; I don't usually play at this time of day, but I wanted to be sure he'd be home from work

...

"Amore! Open this door!" Nico's voice booms out in the hall, and I rush to comply. When I fling open the door, he's standing there in a black sweatshirt and blue jeans, his hair damp, thick arms crossed over his chest.

"Shoes," he growls, and I get the impression that we're going somewhere.

I snatch a jacket off the rack as I toe into my Nikes, and to my surprise, he holds out his hand. Let me be clear: he still looks *ticked,* but I put my hand in his and he pulls me down the hall to the stairs. To my surprise, we don't stop at his floor, but he keeps going down, down, down and out the front doors of our building. It's a cool evening, but it's clear except for a few high, wispy clouds, moving fast. Nico's hand is warm in mine as he basically drags me down the street, but I can't help but grin.

"Where are we going?" I ask, but he ignores me. I don't care. I'm happy. But I admit, I'm a little perplexed when he veers suddenly into the café where we first met.

"Ciao, Flora. Enzo è qui?" he asks the dark-haired woman behind the counter, and she points upstairs. They have a short conversation in Italian, and she seems a little baffled, but he's still holding my hand, so I'm good. Apparently, we've been granted permission to use the back office, because he pulls me down a narrow hall-way and points to a chair by a desk piled high with pa-pers and books.

"Grazie, Flora," I call to the older woman as she re-treats, and I sit down, still grinning, but I try to tone it down when he glares at me fiercely. Enzo appears a mo-ment later in a white T-shirt and khakis, like he hadn't changed yet after work, and Nico asks him something in Italian, which prompts wary agreement from Enzo. The kid turns to me.

"Nico would like me to translate so you can have a real conversation without the language barrier. Do you agree?"

I have a feeling Nico's about to lay into me, but I nod anyway; Enzo likely plays for our team, so hopefully, it won't be too awkward. I rub my hands over my thighs nervously as Nico starts. Enzo asks some kind of clarifying question and Nico answers shortly. But he's staring at me. He's talking to me.

"Do you think you can just charm your way out of this? What's with the music?" Enzo's tone isn't half as agitated as Nico's was. I look at Nico and speak to him, not sure if Enzo's going to translate for me too.

"I'm not trying to charm you, it's just the way I feel. You can ask Cathie—I have no game."

Enzo snorts, and Nico asks him a brief question, to which Enzo nods curtly in reply, and Nico lets loose another volley in Italian.

"Do you think playing me love songs through the ceiling is going to make what you did okay?" Enzo translates.

"No, I don't think that," I say in a rush, my stomach churning. "I just missed you. I never meant to hide anything from you. The first letter was an accident, but I wrote one special for you this time ... " I pull the folded paper out of my pocket and hold it out to Nico. His expression softens when he unfolds it and sees the Italian written there. I must have done something right, because when Enzo peeks over his shoulder, he breaks into a grin.

He mumbles something to Nico, and I think I hear the word "adorabile," which feels like a good sign.

"Um," I say, the back of my neck heating, "maybe don't let Enzo read the last paragraph. It's a little bit R-rated." I still never gave it the big romantic finish I wanted, and Nico's still frowning a little, but I think he's weakening, because he folds the paper carefully and puts it in his pocket.

"You still lie to me," Nico says in English, and I nod.

"I know. I didn't mean to. I never will again."

He puts his hands on his hips, staring down at the thin brown carpet. "You scare me," Nico says quietly. I'm not sure I heard him right, so I lean forward.

"I what?"

With a huff, he goes back to Italian, and Enzo translates.

"You scared the shit out of me, Greg. All I could think about these past few days was, 'what if someone else had gotten this letter? Would he have this connection with them?'" I'm shaking my head already, but he goes on talking. "What if someone else was his first kiss? His first boyfriend? His first ... " Enzo trails off, and I can only assume Nico did the same, knowing I'd understand. Nico's still not looking at me, so I get to my feet and shuffle closer to him.

"If someone else had gotten that letter, and they'd been fool enough to say yes, I probably would've gone to coffee with them and had a fine time, then we would've gone our separate ways." I glance at Enzo, who dutifully translates for me. "Then, one day, in the hallway, I'd have finally noticed this tall, handsome Italian guy with big hands and laughing brown eyes."

I lift a palm to his cheek and he turns into it, like he needed the contact. "And he'd have asked *me* out, since we both know I'm chickenshit, and I'd have said yes, and we'd still be right here. Because me without you? That's impossibile."

I pause while Enzo translates, looking around the office, my gaze landing on the "Best of the Bay Area" award from a few years ago that's on the wall. "Well, not *here* here. You know what I mean."

Nico chuckles finally, and then he's wrapping me in his arms.

"Does this mean you forgive me?" I murmur, and he nods, pressing his face into my neck and placing a tender kiss on my skin. I kiss him back, because I can't help it, and Nico grunts.

"Grazie, Enzo," he says, fishing around in his pocket for a second before he pulls out a twenty and holds it out to the kid.

"You're mine," I whisper as he pushes the office door shut on his friend's grinning face and pops the lock. "Ti amo, Nicodemus."

"I love you too," he echoes in English, turning to pin me against the door as he takes my lips in a searing kiss that conveys perfectly how very much he missed me. All I can do is give in and hope that Flora doesn't need a calculator any time soon.

CHAPTER FOURTEEN

NICO

"Buon San Valentino, amore," I say, lifting my glass. We're in my apartment this time, because Cathie had her own date for the holiday. It's strange how much the place has changed, just having Greg in it. True, I took the time apart to settle in more, putting up pictures of the family, getting a tablecloth, buying some dishes that require washing. But he's the one who's making it feel like home. Sitting cross-legged on the hardwood across from me, face glowing in the candlelight, Greg's giving me that shy smile again, and he clinks my glass in a toast.

"Happy Valentine's Day. This was a good solution," he says, nodding to the Chinese food in front of us. "A compromise."

"Un compromesso," I agree, because he's practicing his Italian now—far more than he ever practiced his French horn. We spent a few hours earlier doing a campus tour at San Francisco State University, even though he's going to finish out the year at the conservatory. The glow on his face the whole time was unbearably precious. "Wait—I get you something."

"We said no presents!" Greg protests as I get up and go into the bedroom, and I just chuckle. He should know this about me by now—I could never let the holiday go by without marking it with a gift. I hand him the newspaper-wrapped book, and with a playfully condemnatory look, he eagerly rips off the covering.

"Oh, *yes*," he says gleefully, opening the thick book immediately.

"You ignore me now all night?" I tease, and he grins, but keeps his eyes on the page.

"Maybe," he teases back. "Oh, this is great. I've been wanting to learn more about R—and I'm impressed that you found this! Where did you get it?"

"Un segreto," I say, deadpan. "I also have secrets."

"Grazie, amore," Greg says, putting the book down to lean across the food and kiss me deeply. "I love it. But I feel bad that I didn't get you anything."

"Mmm," I pretend to muse. "Have an idea."

"Oh?" he says, picking up one of the takeout containers to dump some lo mein onto his bright yellow plate. "Dimmi."

I put my hand over his to still his movements. "Is better before we eat." Greg gets that slightly glazed look that he often gets right before we have sex, and a slow smile spreads across my face.

"Won't the food get cold?" he says, even as he gets to his feet, and I just point to the microwave we got at the thrift store as I follow him into the bedroom. Greg strips off his shirt, and I do too, taking in the beauty of him all over again—his strong back, his lean form, his cute ass and his golden hair, still my sunshine in the San Francisco chill. I grab him before he can get to his pants, pulling him against my bare chest from behind. I rub a hand over his nipple, making it stand up.

"I can look today?"

"Still no," he says with a sniff, and I chuckle as I press my hips into him, banding my other arms around his waist for leverage.

"Must show sometime," I say.

"Says who?" His breathing is getting heavier already, and I enjoy the feeling of him responding to me like this. My shy love; my sweet, sexy nerd. Mine. All mine.

"Mm," I say. "Fine. No show." Without warning, I move my hands down and grope around a little until I locate his belt, pulling the end through the buckle, and he groans. I find his growing prick and give him a little squeeze, caressing the velvety skin. Greg lets his head fall back onto my shoulder; I love it when he gives me his trust like this, knowing I am strong enough to support him, knowing I have his back.

"But I forget to punish you."

He goes still at that, then his voice comes out breathy. "Pardon?"

"You were a very bad boy to lie to me. I punish you now."

Tugging him by one arm over to the bed, I sit down on the edge, but I keep my eyes on his face, as promised. His eyes are wide, but they say to me *yes, yes, please yes.* I pull him to his knees to avoid the temptation to peek and kiss him for a long time, bringing him back to that soft place where I need him.

"If you no like, you say red light as before, sí, amore?"

"Sí," he agrees readily, and I chuckle. Then I lean back and pat my legs. "Lie down." It took some time with the dictionary, but I think I know all the commands

I'll need to "punish" my boyfriend. Playing with him is worth any cost I can think of, certainly my study time.

His nose crinkles. "On my back?"

Oh, now I'm picturing that, me curved over him, taking his cock (without looking) in my mouth as he moans and writhes with nothing to hold on to, his head dropped back in ecstasy ...

"No, the stomach," I clarify. "See? You say I no need body words, but look."

Greg smirks as he gets to his feet and drapes himself beautifully across my knees. "No, I said you wouldn't need them for the *driving test*. And you didn't."

It's true; he did a wonderful job preparing me, and I am now a fully licensed driver in California. Now I just need to save up for a car. I massage his strong back a little before I reach under my pillow for the oil, then add some to my hands as I continue.

"Mmm," he sighs contentedly, pillowing his head on his folded arms. "This doesn't feel like a punishment."

"It not start yet. Be patient."

Greg pinches my leg behind the knee, and I lay a stinging slap on his still-covered ass in retaliation, just to test the waters. I watch closely as his mouth drops open, and a small "oh" comes out.

"Good, amore?" I can't help it; I know I'm not a good boy like him, but I want his reassurance, his buy-in, before we go further.

"Yeah, good," he says, and I urge him up so I can work his pants down a little. But not all the way ... he'll feel the game more if I leave them on. I work a little oil onto his prick so it doesn't chafe against my leg, and he groans.

"Can't I ... " He already sounds a little spacey, and he seems to lose his words as I spank him on his bare skin this time.

"Can't you what, amore? What does a wicked boy ask for?"

"I ... "

I deliver a smack to the other cheek—not too hard, but it's a little red now. Greg moans and hides his face as I go back and forth, delivering blows with slightly more force than before. The way he's bucking against my leg has my own dick feeling needy, and I'm half tempted to have him turn his head and put his mouth to good use ... but I don't know if he wants that. I pause to rub his rosy flesh; he's had about enough, I think. But he lifts his head and gazes at me through glassy eyes.

"Why'd you stop?"

"You no want sit down tomorrow?" I run my fingers through his hair, and he closes his eyes at the tender contact.

"Just a little more," he pleads. "I'm almost there." He swallows hard. "And I've been terrible."

"Oh?" I say, popping him again. "Tell to me your sins."

"I didn't tell you about the letter," he says, planting his feet to rut against me harder.

"Bad boy," I agree. "And?"

"I got a parking ticket driving Cathie's car and I forgot to pay it."

God, even his sins are adorable. "Naughty one."

Greg makes a low, desperate noise in the back of his throat, and it makes all my studying worth it. My blood is on fire, desperate to press him into the bed behind us and make him feel so good he cries out.

"I'm quitting the conservatory."

That one brings me out of my need for a moment. I watch his face as I massage his ass, adding more oil. "Amore, this is corragio, not sins."

He ducks his head and mumbles into his arms. "Feels like failure, though."

"You no fail," I tell him firmly. "You just ... turn on a new road. New highway. Use the signal; no problem." That's when I realize his laugh is caught up in a sob. "Oh, amore. Come here."

I give him a hand up, then tuck us into bed like I did that first time and kiss him again, wiping his tears, enveloping him in my arms, whispering that he is good, that he is my love, that everything will be fine. That he is brave and strong to change his life, that I am so proud of him. Some of this I must whisper in Italian, but he seems to know. Greg rests his head on my shoulder with a shuddery sigh.

"Sorry, I don't know where that came from."

"From your heart. More body parts. See? Very useful."

Greg laughs, then kisses me again. I thought the sex was over, but then Greg works a hand between us, tugging gently at me, and when I groan, he disappears under the covers, out of sight. From the lump under my covers,

I can see that he's on his knees, ass in the air, probably chafing against the sheet from the way we played, and I throw my arm over my eyes as he takes me in his mouth. He's not great at it—not yet, anyway—but he's clearly giving it his best effort.

"That's right. Suck me. Lick me. Show me what a dirty boy does." When Greg moans around my cock, it just gets harder from the vibration, and I gasp.

Maybe by the summer, I'll convince him to lie naked with me where I can appreciate all of him, but today, this is good ... and I no longer have any doubt that we'll still be together in the summer. I want five hundred summers with him—warm California days and clear Italian nights and wherever he wants to be. As long as it's with me.

A new urge surges to the forefront of my mind: I want to fuck him, but my words are failing me. I pull on his shoulders until he lets go of his new toy, his blond head emerging from the dark.

"Yes?"

"On your belly."

I feel him shudder where we touch and his gaze goes hot. "More punishment?"

Yeah, I can do both. I nod and we trade places. It's no burden for me to rub and smack that beautiful ass as I open him up. We haven't done this before, and I make sure I spend plenty of time and oil on the prep. I'm not sure he even knows the goal I have in mind until he starts pushing back against my fingers, meeting my gentle thrusts. He hardly sounds like himself when he starts to beg.

"Fuck me, Nico. Please. I need you. I want you on top of me." For once we're on the same page, language barrier be damned. And when I roll on a condom and slowly sink into his heat, squeezing the lightly reddened flesh of his ass, the sounds he makes are everything.

"Those are bad words," I chastise him sternly. "Not for nice boys."

Greg bucks against me, trying to get me to move in and out, and I oblige, being so careful to go slow, but loving watching my cock disappear and reappear, admiring my own handprint on his ass.

"More," he growls, trying to reach back for me, and I respond by pulling his hips up higher and picking up speed, even as I take his flailing hand and let him cling to me. The new angle is hitting his prostate, and he starts to pant unevenly. But even the scorching sight of my bent-over boyfriend doesn't compare to the sweetness of holding his hand while I give him exactly what he needs.

I feel his muscles start to contract just before he comes, but I don't let go, riding him through as he climaxes. It only takes a few more snaps of my hips for me to follow him into the stratosphere, above the fog, into the stars. I know what awaits us: silly conversation and cold Chinese, doing the dishes together, maybe a walk, hand in hand. But for now, I just hold him. I just hold the best thing I nearly didn't get if not for meddling roommates, the best thing I almost let slip through my fingers because of my pride. And I'm not letting go.

EPILOGUE

"Cufflinks?"

"Check."

"Pocket square?"

"Check."

"Bouton—bouton—what's it called, amore?"

"Boutonniere," my husband says, straightening my black, skinny tie. "And I think they're still in the fridge."

"We need them!" I say, probably too emphatically. "It is almost time! We must get to our seats APSA!"

Greg smirks at me. "Rilassati, tesoro. Andrà tutto bene."

"Relax? How can I relax when our son is getting married today? We must check on Andrew; we must make sure he has everything he needs."

His face crinkles in confusion. Though to be fair, after almost thirty years together, his face is always more crinkled than it was when I met my shy neighbor. I love it regardless. "Check on Andrew? But not Evan, our son?"

"Evan will be fine. He is like me," I say, straightening his clothes too, even though he doesn't need it. I feel better when I touch him; he's so handsome in his black suit. "But Andrew? He is so nervous, I can tell. He would rather get married during the commercial break at the Timbers game than this hullaballoo."

"Hulla—" Greg breaks off, bending over, laughing so hard that no sound comes out.

"Amore! This is no time for laughing!" I clap my hands at him, but he gives no response. "We must go! I will not ruin this most important day for these boys!"

"Where did you even learn that word?" my husband asks, straightening, as he wipes a tear from his eye.

"From you, amore! Obviously from you! Come now, we must go find those flowers ... "

"Wait," Greg says, grabbing my arm to haul me back against him as I make for the door. "You're really not going to let me look at your speech?"

I recoil. "No! You don't trust me?"

"No, no, no, I do. I just ... know that giving speeches can be ... nerve-racking."

"For you, maybe," I say, giving him a kiss, but he doesn't let me go.

"Can I just check it for minor mistakes? For idioms?"

"I am not an idiot," I say, my temper getting the better of me.

"No, I said *idiom*. I didn't—ugh, I'm sorry. You're right," he says, taking off his glasses to rub at his face. "You should give the speech you want to give. And if there's a little mistake, it doesn't matter. The sentiment will be there."

Okay, he's making even me a little nervous now, but I practiced a lot. I can't change it now. When he puts his glasses back on, I take a moment to look at him, then pull him into a hug.

"Remember when we got married?" I put my hand on the back of his head and feel his shoulders drop a little. "Was not perfect."

He chuckles, squeezing me tighter. "Given that our son had the stomach flu and your family got stuck in immigration at the airport? No, not perfect."

"But at the end, we are married. And we can tell the story now. It will be the same for Evan and Drew. They are starting their life, and we are here. That is what matters."

His tears now are not from laughter. "I knew you were going to do this to me today."

"Dads?" The church wedding coordinator—I can't remember her name—is motioning us out into the hallway. "Let's get you flowered up."

"Thanks, Donna," Greg says, giving her a watery smile, swiping at his face. "We'll be there ASAP."

Oh, right. I still get those mixed up.

The next few minutes are a rush of activity: the boutonnieres, lining up the groomsmen, finding Drew's grandmother, escorting Drew's grandmother down the aisle, then watching as my beautiful son comes in from one side of the stage of the church, and his amore comes in from the other, meeting in the middle. I wasn't wrong: Andrew looks nervous ... until Evan captures his gaze, and then he seems to forget about the crowd. He doesn't give us a second look.

"Well, this is a momentous occasion," the pastor says, a tall, bulky white man with thinning hair. "Our first wedding as an independent church, and I can't think of a better couple to commemorate the decision to leave our denomination. These two men have been the definition of love and devotion, and I have enjoyed getting to know them better in the past few months."

I look up at the cross and think how happy his nona would be to see her grandson getting married in a church. Greg squeezes my hand like he knows, and I smile at him. They keep it short and sweet, and soon, Evan is reading his vows. Greg helped him with them, I know.

"I vow to have your back, through every season of life and whatever changes the future will bring." He pauses, and I know he's fighting for composure, not wanting to cry in front of all the people.

Those words, they mean something to this man, who loved Andrew before his gender transition and loves him still. They mean something to me also—it was not easy when Greg changed his major and his life for me, just as it was not easy for me to stay in San Francisco. But we made it.

When Drew silently hands my son a white handkerchief, Evan takes it gratefully, dabbing at his face. But then he seems to decide to just let them flow, tears running down his cheeks through the rest of his vows, and based on all the sniffles behind me, we all decide to join him. His Uncle Enzo, who always gave him good advice; his Auntie Cathie, who carried him for us; his biological aunts and uncles and cousins from Italia; Greg's parents. Everyone.

"We did good with him," I murmur to Greg, and he just nods, clearly feeling emotional too.

After the ceremony, we get in the car and drive to another venue for the reception, because the church wouldn't serve alcohol. Marrying gay people? Sure. Leaving their denomination to do it? They said yes. But still no wine afterward, even though Jesus makes it in the Bible *for a wedding*? I do not understand this, but Evan says I am not to bring it up again, so I zip my lips.

Until it is my turn to give my speech.

"Thank you all for coming tonight, and to the Kahananui family for hosting this wonderful wedding." I practiced their name so much, and I nail it. It gives me confidence to do the rest of it too. "When I was twenty-three, I moved to San Francisco from my village in Italia for work, and Evan's father, Greg, also moved there from Kansas City, Missouri. We were neighbors for some months, but we did not know each other. Then Greg decided to have un'avventura—when we start an affair in Italia, we don't call it that. 'Affair' is a word for business; we call it 'an adventure.'"

There is some giggling in the crowd, and I glance down at Greg. His face is as red as the rose in the boutonniere. *Oops*. I rush on.

"It was not easy—we did not speak the same language; we did not always understand each other. We made mistakes. But even though it was not so smooth at first, I am glad he chose me to have his adventure with, and even more glad that he chooses me still." I glance at him again, and he's smiling at me now, love shining through the embarrassment.

"Evan has made a good choice also in Drew, and I wish you as much happiness as we have had." I lift my glass. "May your marriage be un'avventura, today and always." Everyone is still clapping when I sit down, and Evan is laughing, pressing his face into Drew's neck, but Drew gives me a thumbs-up with a shit-eating grin.

"See, amore? Everything is fine," I say, giving his still-red cheek a kiss, and Greg just laughs.

"Yeah, an adventure is right," he murmurs, kissing me back. "And I don't regret a minute of it."

Would you leave a review?

REVIEWS ARE WORTH MORE than you know! It's the best gift you can give to an indie author like me (besides enjoying my books, of course). Would you consider leaving a short, honest review wherever you bought the book? It allows me to build my business and create more books! Queer creators like me are under attack by restrictive new policies, and your recommendation is more important than ever.

Connect with London!

I LOVE CONNECTING WITH fans! Write to me and tell me your favorite parts and we can delight over these characters together! You can find me in the following ways:

- Bluesky: londonpriceauthor.bsky.social
- Email: authorlondonprice@gmail.com

Need more stories?

WE GOT MORE STORIES! When you sign up for my bi-monthly newsletter, you get access to *Playing by Ear*, a bonus story from Chance's perspective, *Inspiration*, a sexy Glenn and Hillary studio story, and whatever else I've cooked up between now and then. Find a screen and sign up here: https://www.subscribepage.com/here-comestreble

www.ingramcontent.com/pod-product-compliance
Lightning Source LLC
Chambersburg PA
CBHW031640200726
48289CB00004BA/961